EDWARD LOUIS HENRY

Backbone
of the World

A personal account of the
American Rocky Mountain
fur trade 1822-1824

Christopher
Matthews
Publishing

www.christophermatthewspublish.com
BOZEMAN, MONTANA

Praise for *Backbone of the World*

"The plot and dialog have the ring of authenticity and from the outset the novel is an irresistible page-turner. Temple Buck has the spunk appropriate to a virile young adventurer. If you have enjoyed the fiction of Win Blevins and Terry Johnston, you will find a worthy continuation of the genre inBackbone of the World."

Eric Bye, Editor
Muzzle Blast Magazine

"...Henry has produced a meticulously detailed saga of the Rocky Mountain fur trade... through the eyes of his heroic adventure-seeking protagonist, Temple Buck... Henry has a ribald sense of humor, an accurate ear for dialect, and a genuine gift for sparkling characterization...These books belong on the shelf of any fur trade buff; for pleasure reading and reference"

Roundup Magazine

"... This is a novel,yes, but it is so absorbing that you'll completely forget that it isn't absolute fact....I recommend Backbone of the World very highly. I haven't enjoyed a novel about the fur trade as much as this one in quite a while."

Mike Nesbitt, *Muzzleloader*Magazine

"History at its best. Great reference for people involved in living history."
C. Juday

Also by Edward Louis Henry
Poredevil's Beaver Tales
Free Men
Shinin' Times!
Glory Days Gone Under

Backbone of the World

At the specific preference of the author, the publisher allowed this work to remain exactly as the author intended, verbatim, without editorial input.

Cover Design: Armen Kojoyian
Cover Photo: Lee Potter

ISBN: 978-0-9833164-3-5

Published by

CHRISTOPHER MATTHEWS PUBLISHING

www.christophermatthewspub.com

Bozeman, Montana

Printed in the United States of America

DEDICATION

For Gloria, without whom nothing would have happened, who never faltered in her faith and loving support; for Kelly, who always believed; and for all the saddle tramps and buckskinners with whom I've been privileged to share a cookfire, swapping lies and trading friendship, throughout my life.

Backbone
of the World

by

Temple Buck, Trapper

Euphemius Hobbes, Editor

Editor's Preface

I am not altogether sure, even as I pen these lines, that I wish to have my name and reputation attached to this book. The author, Mr. Temple Buck, has been a most obdurate client since he first contracted my professional services to edit his manuscript.

The sole reason for my continued association with this project, aside from a legal contract and the designated fee specified therein, has been my interest in the author's description of the remarkable personages and events which Mr. Buck has observed and experienced during the several years that he was engaged in the fur trade conducted in the Rocky Mountains of the North American Continent.

My reluctance to have my name connected with this work is based in part upon the author's stubborn refusal to heed my advice regarding content and description, as well as his reluctance to permit me, as his editor and literary advisor, to insert the customary adornments, embellishments, and literary refinements into his homespun recounting of his exploits, experiences, and impressions. He appears not to be aware of, nor to be at all concerned with, current literary taste and custom among his potential North American and European readers.

Although Mr. Buck does, in fact, possess a remarkable facility in capturing the *nuances* of common speech and an extraordinary gift of mimicry in reproducing that language for the printed page, it is necessary for me to declare here that I unequivocally deplore his employment of such gifts in a serious literary endeavor. Language in all of its uses, but especially in literary and epistolary applications, should be the ultimate adornment of a refined and genteel personality, but I have failed utterly in each of the frequent attempts that I have made to convince Mr. Buck of the importance of expressing himself in terms calculated to soothe his readers, to encourage their acceptance of his views and the veracity of his testimony, and to assure each one of them that nothing in his writing could possibly offend the tender sensibilities of even the youngest and most refined among his female readers.

Instead, Mr. Buck has insisted upon, in his words, "telling it like it was and is in the Mountains," which, as you will doubtless observe and agree, is obviously a profound breach of literary etiquette and good taste. Polite society dictates that such matters be left to the imagination, if indeed they are considered at all. It is sufficient cause for alarm to realize that if histories of the nature of Mr. Buck's *memoirs* of the years he spent in the Rocky Mountains are permitted to persist and proliferate, indeed to flourish, that the entire civilization and high cultural standards of the United States could be called in question and ultimately suffer dire peril at the hands of such reckless amateur writers. Our European brethren are ever quick to criticize whatever flaws they claim to discover in the American national character and cultural fabric; and it is the duty of each one of us who claim membership in our national *literati* to defend our pride in our Men of Letters and to prevent, by whatever means at our disposal, the creation of any vulnerability in the cultural visage that we, as Americans, present to the world at large. Works such as this present one, written solely by Mr. Temple Buck and not in the least by this editor, constitute a serious threat to our national prestige and our acceptance and approval among the civilized peoples of the world.

In all fairness I must state here that I have been well-paid by Mr. Buck for my efforts on his behalf in preparing his manuscript for publication. My chief complaint in this regard is that he has steadfastly refused to allow me to improve the content of his manuscript, either by addition or deletion; and he has stubbornly insisted on confining my professional efforts to matters of orthography, punctuation, and, in rare instances, to the organization and presentation of the material. I, as his editor, assume absolutely no responsibility for the author's use of colloquial and occasional coarse language, sometimes impossible digressions, descriptions of actions and events that a refined reader must most assuredly abhor, and his personal reflections upon the significance and moral implication of the experiences related in the following pages.

I have, in a single instance, prevailed over the author's objections; that is, in convincing him that he should confine the content of this volume to his experiences during his first two years in the Rocky Mountains. The account of his entire four years, 1822 to 1826, in the fur trade, if published in a single volume, would have resulted in an extremely bulky tome. Mr. Buck remained obdurate in his refusal to halving his manuscript until I mentioned that a book which contained his entire account would hardly fit into a saddlebag, at which comment his resistance melted and he conceded. Mr. Buck's history of the years 1824 through 1826 are contained in his second book, entitled *Free Men.*

It is with considerable trepidation that I submit this preface to the printer, lest I be accused of fostering a pernicious and deleterious trend in American Letters. Please, Gentle Reader, be assured that I have merely fulfilled the obligations of my legal contract, as an honorable man should do.

Euphemius Hobbes, Editor
Chillicothe, Ohio, 1828

Author's Foreword

Greed it was, I reckon, that carried the most of us out to the Shining Mountains. Not all, but most. There were other reasons, naturally — like my own — but the most common other reason was men who were but a half a step ahead of the Law. Then there was some few who came out because of their taste for adventure, the most of which appetite got pretty much used up before they traveled very far up the Missouri or across the prairie, where it was often no problem at all to get a bellyful of adventure in just a forenoon.

But it was beaver mainly that took us out to the Mountains to ply the trapper's trade, chasing down furry critters for their pelts — plews, we call them — in every nook and cranny of the Rockies and along all the rivers, cricks, and streams to the south and west. You could ask why would a bunch of otherwise sane men devote their life to harvesting a passel of flat-tailed rats. Well, perhaps you fail to recall that no proper gentleman anywhere in the world — in America or across the water in Europe and even some Chinamen, they tell me — reckons he is gussied up properly unless he is wearing a top hat made of felt fashioned from beaver fur atop his head. So it takes a powerful plenitude of beaver plews to keep the hatters in New York and Danville and London and Paris supplied and happy and doing business.

Which is where we come in. I mean us mountaineers, the sorry fools who go chasing off to the Shining Mountains to make a fortune, which hardly any common trapper ever does, but who find — besides a deal of hardship, like winter snows and summer heat and starving and thirsting and danger in the way of hostile Indians and bears and snakes and painters and suchlike critters — a freedom that no man in all of history has ever known before, an absolute freedom that no man will ever know elsewhere. Yes, it was greed that carried the most of us to the mountains, but what keeps us there is freedom.

There is no Law in the mountains and what a man might have been back home doesn't signify at all. It's handsome-is-as-handsome-does and hoss-what-can-you-do? Nothing else matters much and a man soon learns that lesson or he dies early on.

No man ever learned the Rocky Mountain trapper's trade without being there, for nowhere else is like that country and hardly anything you have ever seen or done is like what you are apt to find out there.

I reckon I ought to thank Mr. Euphemius Hobbes, my editor, for all of his help in putting this history together. It is only fair to mention here that we had our share of skirmishes over what was going to be mentioned in this book and how it was going to be said, but it is my book and I had my way, for the most part. We tried it his way, but Hobbes had me talking like a book. Well, I am not a book, I'm a man, a common man, and I mean to tell you this history like a common man would tell it, not some book. So we went back and told it pretty much the way I wrote it down in the first place. I do thank Mr. Hobbes for all his help in getting the spelling right and for using the punctuation marks in a proper manner, and here and there in deciding which part comes after what.

Mr. Hobbes also pointed out to me that the entire history of my four years in the Rockies was too much for just one book, so I agreed to cut it in half. The second half, 1824 to 1826, is in the book entitled *Free Men*. The two books concern my life and what I have seen and done in the mountains and elsewhere and I take full responsibility for everything that is told in this history, which should relieve the mind of Mr. Hobbes more than somewhat.

After I decided to publish my memories of the fur trade it appeared to me to be only right and proper that I tell you who and what I was before that time and how I came to go out to the

Mountains, so I wrote the forepart of this book to explain the early formation of one fur-trapping man.

Read on, if you have a mind to, and learn what life in the Shining Mountains is all about.

Temple Buck
Whynot Township, Ohio, 1828

Table of Contents

Chapter I
Ohio

The sun was always shining in Whynot. Leastaways it always appears that way to me when I think about that place and the time of my growing-up. Naturally the sun didn't always shine. It just seems that way in memory, most likely because of Ma. Wherever Ma went, no matter what she might be doing, sunshine just naturally seemed to follow her and it warmed every living thing around her –- or so it seems to me now.

No, we had rain, and snow aplenty, too. Too much rain come springtime and hardly ever enough in summer, when the corn shriveled in the field and we could hardly ever get the hogs out from under the cabin. They would crawl under there for the shade and no matter how much you cussed them or poked at them with a stick, it made no nevermind to those hogs until they were good and ready to come out from under there on their own account around the cool of sundown.

Pap never paid no nevermind to the hogs or where they shaded up. Pap said he reckoned those hogs were eating copperheads under there and since he couldn't abide copperheads nohow, let them stay put wherever they took a mind to be.

Thinking back on it, Pap never paid a great deal of attention to much of anything that didn't have to do with himself. He surely didn't care much about our hard-scrabble farm that got poorer every year, what with the good farming soil washing out of the fields in the springtime rains and into the crick and carrying all the way down to the Ohio River, like as not. Just so long as he got enough of a corn crop to keep on stilling whiskey to sell to the neighbors, he was content — leastaways as content as he ever allowed himself to be.

Pap reckoned he was one of the last of the great patriots of the War of Independence, although he never fought in it, nor the War of the British Return either, for that matter. No, it was the Whiskey Rebellion that caught Pap's fancy and he stood foursquare behind that particular fracas, insisting that the farmer who grew the corn had a God-given right to do as he pleased with his crop, including and especially making whiskey out of it, without paying a tax to the Government, which didn't know or want to know anything about folks like us, anyhow, living so far off in the wilderness as we did. He would say, for all the politicians cared, we could have been a bunch of heathen Chinamen.

Pap always said it was the principle of the thing and anybody in Whynot would testify that he sure was strong on his principles, just so long as the principle agreed with whatever Pap considered fitting. If it didn't, Pap would get to yelling that such and such a principle, like paying the whiskey tax, was a Tool of Satan and it was his bounden Christian Duty to have nothing to do with it.

Pap was a powerful yeller. Everybody said so. Which was likely how he came to be a preacher on Sabbath Days, sometimes in the woodlot down below our cornfield when the weather was fair or in Jacob Staples's store in Whynot, when wind or rain or snow made it too ugly to be out of doors. In summer on the Sabbath there would be folks sitting on stumps in our clearing and others perched on the high seats of their farm wagons, the horses snuffling and rustling and jingling harness when they shifted stance, whilst Pap hollered folks along the path to Eternal Salvation. I don't recall that he ever had much to say about Christian Charity or that he even mentioned God much at all, except perhaps as a weapon. No, Pap dealt mostly in threats. He preferred to scare folks with hellfire and sulfur and brimstone, whatever that is, and devils and demons and imps and Satan. Whenever he mentioned Heaven or Paradise as a final reward, he was always fairly vague about it, like the pleasant side of religion had ought to be some other parson's territory.

I was born in 1803, the same year Ohio became a state. Pap was against it, Ohio getting to be a state, that is to say. I have never been altogether sure just how he felt about my being born. But no matter how much Pap hollered against Ohio joining the Union, the whole county voted for statehood and Ma went ahead and had me anyhow.

Folks who knew them back then say that Pap wanted to name me Laddy, so he could call me Laddy Buck — Buck being the family name — or maybe something out of the Good Book, like Jehoshaphat, perhaps, but Ma put her foot down and said that he would do no such thing and that I would be called Temple, her family name. So Temple Buck it was and is and likely always will be, unless I get myself into some kind of serious trouble with the Law and then I would naturally have to change it.

They say Pap grumbled somewhat for a time but then he let it go, saying that anyway I didn't look like him nohow, what with my dark hair and eyes, which showed I took after Ma's side, and that he could wait until the next child came along and then he would be the one to do the naming.

But there never was another child, boy or girl, and I did my early growing up pretty much on my own, except for Ma and Pap. By time I was old enough to notice, Pap and Ma hardly ever spoke to each other, talking just enough to get the chores done.

For all his yelling and hollering, Pap wasn't a very big man and as I got some size myself I realized that he was halfway short and downright scrawny. The fire-red hair I remembered as a child had commenced to flick away and here and there threads of silver showed in what was left. His pale blue eyes, hard as iron buttons, still popped and snapped like always, but now they stared out of blue-veined pouches sunk into his whiskered cheeks.

Pap loved talking, just so long as he was doing the most of it, like down at Staples's store when we would drive the team into Whynot on market day, Pap to sell his whiskey, Ma to sell or swap her eggs and butter and garden truck in season. When I was little I would loiter somewheres out of Pap's sight in Staples's and listen to him talking politics and religion, usually both, with the other men in town. None of them had nearly as much to say as Pap did, but they would sit there nodding and spitting on the stove now and then, generally agreeing with whatever Pap had to say at that particular time. I recall they would spit on that stove no matter if it was winter or summer and I noticed, too, that Pap didn't always say the same things about the same subject, that he would change sides on himself from one time to the next, but that didn't appear to bother the other men. They just sprawled on their benches and whittled and nodded and spat on the stove and, for all anybody could tell, they pretty much went along with whatever Pap might be saying.

Ma never listened much to Pap. Sometimes it was like as if he wasn't even there, for all the attention she ever paid to his goings-on about politics and religion and Indians and foreigners ruining the country. If Pap made you think of a magpie or maybe a redheaded woodpecker — and he surely did — Ma brought to mind an oyster, silent and serene, secure and sure of herself and solid, like she knew she carried a precious pearl inside herself.

Ma was tall, taller than Pap, and slender and strong for a woman, her skin like fine old ivory, no matter how much time she spent hoeing out in the sun in her garden patch. She had long dark hair and blue eyes so dark they sometimes looked almost purple, eyes that could look deep down inside of you, but that you didn't mind if she did.

As I grew up enough to notice such matters, I commenced to realize that Ma was downright pretty, just about beautiful, but she never let on that she knew such a thing.

I wasn't the only one who thought Ma was pretty. Sometimes when she would take me with her into Whynot on market day I could see some of the men looking sidewise at her and see their fat, sunburned wives pulling at their husbands' sleeves and hurrying them on, but Ma paid them no nevermind at all and just went on about her business. I never knew if Pap thought Ma was pretty, but I reckon he did. Most of the time he was too busy talking to do much in the way of thinking anyway.

Pap wasn't much to look at as he got older, but he sure had a way with womenfolk, except for Ma. I never knew him to sleep in her bedchamber, even once. Perhaps it was because he was a preacher and the other women reckoned they ought to pay him some mind and heed what he said because of that. I remember once when I was about twelve that Pap and I paid a visit to the lady who lived on the next farm over when her husband was away on some errand or other and wasn't expected home for a spell. She was a timid, mousey little woman, sort of like a scared rabbit but halfway pretty, and when Pap thought I wasn't around I heard him sweet-talking her, leaning in close as paint and using that voice he usually kept for Sabbath sermons, only softer, and what he was telling her was, "Repent an' be saved! It's in the Book! It's the only road we got to Eternal Salvation! Ye got to repent! But if ye ain't done nothin' to repent, like ye tell me ye ain't, then it's nothin' but pure Christian Kindness and my God-ordained Duty as the Leader of My Flock to provide ye with the wherewithal so's yew kin have somethin' to repent and thereby guarantee yer Eternal Salvation!"

I have never been sure if that lady took him up on his offer to provide that wherewithal, but Pap was always a powerful persuader. Everybody said so.

ᕄ ᕄ ᕄ

Like I said, Pap and Ma never argued much, mainly because they hardly ever spoke to each other except for common matters dealing with chores and farming and the stock and such that needed speaking to, but as I was growing up I started noticing that more and more they were both using me to get their arguing done.

For one example, there would come a time when Pap would be hollering at me that Indians were nothing but filthy varmints who weren't fit to live anywhere near where God-fearing Christian white folks did, that they were all a parcel of dirty, thieving Redskins bent on murder and fire and destruction and taking the scalps of honest, hardworking white folks like himself. And even at that age I used to wonder what kind of Indian would ever get desperate enough to go to all that bother for a scalp like Pap's, which was getting to be pretty slim pickings indeed. And then the next thing I knew, when Pap was out somewhere, Ma would be telling me about Indians, without ever mentioning Pap or what he had said, and how there was good and bad amongst them, just like whites, and that all the land in America used to belong to them and now that we were here, taking up farms on land they used to hunt on, there was bound to be trouble, but that didn't make all Indians all bad nor all white people all good. And as for being dirty, all the Indians she had ever seen, and that was quite a number, she said, bathed themselves a sight more often than most of the white folks who lived around Whynot.

I never told Pap what Ma said to me about such matters. It wouldn't have done any good and it likely would have just set him off to hollering again. And he didn't need any help with that.

⁞   ⁞   ⁞

Ma was a schoolmarm back in Virginia before she came west to settle in Ohio with Pap. She never talked about that or much of anything else about the time in her life before she married Pap. For all she let on about herself, it seemed that everything about her had happened right there in Ohio, but I knew that wasn't so.

Fact is, for all his talking, Pap never had much to say about himself before he came to Ohio, either. Here and there, whilst I was growing up, I pieced together some sort of history about how Pap had somehow got hold of a land patent that had been granted to some old soldier from the War of Independence who didn't hanker after pulling up stakes in Virginia or some other place in the East and traipsing out west to live amongst the Indians and break new ground for farming. So one way or another Pap got the old soldier's patent and came west with Ma to settle just north of the Ohio River.

I likely would never have learned even that much if Pap hadn't been fond of telling the story of how the town of Whynot got its name. Most folks thought it was some sort of Indian word, like most of the towns thereabouts, but according to Pap, it appears like he and Ma had been traveling for weeks in their wagon, searching out their particular grant of land, and late one day when they and the horses were all tuckered, Pap whoaed the team near a pretty piece of land nigh a crick. As Pap always told it, Ma said, "Let's just stop and settle here." And Pap said, "Why not?" and it has been Whynot ever since.

Ma never said aye, yes, or no about the truth of Pap's story, so I can't testify to the truth of it, but it could have happened just the way he said, although Pap did love telling a good story better than he ever did the simple truth, even if he was a preacher on Sabbath Days.

∂∞ ∂∞ ∂∞

Ma commenced teaching me to read and had me trying to draw the alphabet on a slate and to cipher almost by time I was just learning to talk. Oftimes, after morning chores, she would sit me down on the stoop and read to me out of one of her books. Sometimes they were just stories and other times she would read to me about great men and women, critters I have never seen, and other places in the world and the people who lived there, how they looked and how they dressed and what they ate and the way they did common things different from the way we did. And when I would ask why they did like they did, Ma would just say that circumstances alter cases, which I didn't understand at the time, but I reckon I do now.

Then at night, when Pap was out somewheres or after he had gone to bed, Ma would sing to me or tell me stories, leaning back in her cane rocker with her eyes closed, her voice going sort of dreamy-like, the candle flickering and fluttering and guttering on the table, making puddles of tallow that later we would scrape up and melt again, come candle-making time.

She would tell me wonderful tales in that dreamy voice of hers about noble Irish kings and cruel English barons who stole their land and the battles they fought, of long-ago Virginia settlers and the Indians, some of them good and some of them bad on both sides, Simon Kenton and Simon Girty, pirates and bandits and good-hearted highwaymen, and tales of true-love which I didn't much understand but what I took her word for, King Arthur and his knights and a big round table where they met to tell where the dragons were, and Scottish patriots — she never said Scotch, like everybody else did — fighting as long as they could swing a sword to save Scotland from the evil English armies. Ma never cottoned to the English and it rubbed off onto her stories and naturally on me. And then she would tell of Chinese emperors and Persian princes and crusaders and Spaniards fighting the Saracens and Moors, whoever they were, and after awhile I would catch myself snatching myself back from the edge of sleep, my head in her lap and my eyes drooping nearly closed.

About then she would pick me up and put me on the ladder and steady me as I climbed up to the loft, where I would fall asleep dreaming of knights and ladies and dragons breathing fire on my corn-husk bed.

~ ~ ~

From just about the time I could walk a straight line, Pap put me to work, fetching water and splitting kindling for the still, then later working in the cornfield and milking the cows and helping around the still, when I wasn't helping Ma churn butter or weeding her truck patch or redding up the dooryard. Before long he started passing along so many of his own chores that there was hardly any time left for Ma to teach me my schooling.

It was about that time that Ma told him that she was going to start a proper school of her own and that I was going to be a scholar in it. No matter how much or how loud he spoke against it, Ma stood firm and let it be known in Whynot that come fall, after crops were in, she would be teaching a school of grammar and manners out at our place. Pap grumbled and carried on about how he needed my help, but in the fall, when he saw that Ma was making cash money with her teaching, he changed his tune somewhat and left off his nagging. Naturally I had my chores to do, but now Ma refused to let Pap haul me off to help him with his own work just whenever he had a mind to.

That first year, from just after harvest until spring planting commenced, we had about eight children in Ma's school, which she taught out on the stoop or under the shade trees in the dooryard when the weather was fine and inside the cabin when it turned cold. I say *about* eight children because a couple-three who came at first just stopped coming, but then a couple more families heard about Ma's school and started sending their kids to learn reading and writing and ciphering, skills that weren't too common around Whynot at that time.   All of them weren't there all the time, because when there was work to be done at home, schooling just naturally had to wait.

I was just coming twelve when Ma started her school and naturally I had a head start on most of her other pupils, which didn't set too well with some of the older boys, especially the ones from the German families that had moved west from Pennsylvania. I remember them being big and halfway clumsy, but strong and more than somewhat inclined to play the bully with anyone smaller or younger than themselves. Most of them didn't speak English too well, either, which slowed up their learning lessons and made them act hard against those of us who could.

After I had my nose bloodied a time or two and learned how bad a black eye can hurt, I learned to stay out of the way of those big German kids, more or less, and how to fight back when I couldn't. But I never liked the fighting. My heart wasn't in it, like it is with some boys who appear almost to enjoy getting their nose squashed and their eyes blacked and their ears pounded out of shape, just so long as they can get a chance to punish the other fellow with their fists and feet. About the only way that I could ever win one of those schoolboy fights was to lose all control of myself, when a red haze would film over my eyes and my ears would be ringing so loud I couldn't hear and I would be swinging my fists and kicking and then somebody would be dragging me off some boy who was lying on the ground and crying or just not saying or doing much at all.

I believe it was about that time that I commenced to realize that I was most likely a coward at heart and that I couldn't abide bullies any more than Pap could tolerate copperheads.

Even so, having other kids around the place was better than just being by myself there, with just Ma and Pap and the critters and visits sometimes from the neighbors and Pap's half-brother Ben and his pretty wife Penny, the only kinfolk we had in Ohio, leastaways that I ever knew about. What I liked most was the girls.

Aside from being prettier than boys, they were generally smarter and they could say out loud what they were thinking, especially Sarah Rutledge. She was three years younger than I was and smart as a whip, with long dark hair and the biggest deep blue eyes you ever saw on a little girl her size, eyes that made you think of Ma's, but not nearly so wise and knowing.

At first I would help her with her lessons, like I did some of the other kids, but it wasn't too long before she was helping me help the others and before I knew it I started thinking of Sarah Rutledge as being just about as grown-up as I was getting to be. Sometimes after lessons we would walk down to the clearing in the woodlot and I would tell her some of Ma's stories about Brian Boru or some other Irishman or fairy tales or histories of Wallace and the Englishmen, until Pap shooed us off, yelling that there might be Indians about and how they loved to snatch little children off their farms and take them home and eat them. Sarah and I didn't place much stock in what Pap said, but we would run back up to the cabin and then Sarah would start walking home and I would stand in the dooryard and watch her walking up the trace until she was out of sight.

Speaking of Indians, the War of the British Return, which folks nowadays are calling the War of 1812, was going on about the time when Ma commenced teaching her school. Nothing much happened around Whynot, except that Pap did a lot of hollering about how the British would burn our farms and turn the whole country back to King Georgie and the Indians. A lot of men thereabouts left farm chores undone and joined the militia, spending afternoons marching like soldiers on the bowling green, trying to look important. Pap never did join up, but he talked a lot about it.

Most all the Indians in our neighborhood were Shawnees and when Tecumseh threw in with the British, most of the younger ones followed their chief Powatawa up north to fight against the Americans. After Tecumseh went and got himself killed, howsomever, they didn't see much profit in loitering around up there, so Powatawa brought his band back down to their village and went back to what they had always done, which was a little farming but mainly hunting and trading. Mostly thieving and begging, Pap said. But we never lost anything to them.

Ma never had but a single vice, as far as I ever knew, which was she liked to smoke tobacco, but not in a corncob pipe like most of the other farm women did. Instead, she preferred to roll the tobacco leaves into little thin cigars and smoke it that way. She never would buy the rough-cut shag tobacco they sold down at Staples's. She got her tobacco leaves from the Shawnees who came around our place to trade.

Pap couldn't abide Indians any more than he could copperheads, so the Indians learned to sneak around behind the cabin and trade with Ma through the back window when Pap was off in the field or down at the still. Ma would barter bread and sometimes some cloth or beads and such with them for the broad golden-brown leaves, which, after the Indians had gone, she would store in the oaken chest that she had brought with her all the way from Virginia.

When I was little I used to sit on Ma's bed and stare through the window at the big, half-naked savages laughing and waving their arms and making signs with their fingers while Ma was swapping with them, fearful that they would snatch her through the window and make off with her. But they never did.

There was one Indian about that time that I noticed in particular. He was taller than most of the others, lean, and almost always laughing, except when he looked at me. Then his smile would fade away and his black eyes would just about bore holes in me. It wasn't a mean look, just thoughtful, and his face looked almost soft, for an Indian. After they went on their way, I asked Ma about him and she said that he was Powatawa, their leader. But she never did say anything else about him.

❧   ❧   ❧

The year I was ready to turn thirteen my Uncle Benjamin Buck came over to our place and did a most unusual thing, for him. He fetched me from the cabin and took me down to the still, where Pap was cooking mash, as he usually was. We had a good corn harvest that year and Pap was as busy as I had ever seen him be. When Pap looked up, Ben cleared his throat and said, "Lorenzo, it's past time your boy learns huntin'."

"Who's goin' to learn him?" Pap asked, and Ben said, "Me, fer I don't reckon you're ever goin' to git 'round to it."

Pap scratched his ear and mopped his face with an old rag he kept tucked under his belt and said, "So be it."

Ben just grunted and led me off, his rifle on his shoulder and powder horn swinging under his arm, the two of us heading down through the woodlot and into the trees beyond.

My Uncle Benjamin Buck was a curious sort. He was quiet, too quiet, some folks said, for his wife, my Aunt Penny, a sprightly lady from Tennessee, and they wondered what she ever saw in him. But she never appeared to mind his long silences or when he would be gone, sometimes for days at a time, roaming the forest, trapping or hunting or maybe just gathering mushrooms and such truck. She always said that she talked enough for the both of them or she would say that still waters run deep and that her Ben would do just fine.

Ben wasn't much of a farmer, but he was a crack shot and he knew all the critters and their ways. His table was never bare, for they always had plenty of meat and he traded what they didn't need for all the things he never could find time to grow for himself. He was always bringing over a haunch of deer or ducks or geese that he had shot, and sometimes a sackful of pigeons or fish, or maybe a possum or a coon, and now and then some mushrooms, walnuts, or wild plums. Ma would insist on swapping him truck from her garden patch and sending it home with him, for Penny, as she would say. They never kept track, but knowing Ma, I daresay they stayed pretty even.

Uncle Ben was Pap's younger half-brother, born of a different mother after Pap's ma died. He was taller than Pap and stouter, too, strong enough to trot through the woods half a day when he picked up some deer sign and to carry a big buck all the way home without stopping to rest. I reckon he came as close to being happy as he ever was when he was out in the woods, with just his rifle and maybe sometimes a dog.

Ben taught me a lot about hunting and living off the land. He never talked much, but I already had the habit of learning from Ma, so he didn't often have to say the same thing twice. Mostly he just showed me what was to be done and I learned the use of muskets, rifles, and fowling-pieces and how to keep them clean and in good repair, how to knap flints and cast rifle and musket balls and what was the best powder and shot to trade for at Staples's. Trotting along behind him I came to know deer sign and how to stay downwind from whatever we were tracking, how to catch movement out of my eye-corners and to sit quiet as a tree nigh a deer trail. Kids mostly ran barefoot in the fine weather, but Ben taught me how to make moccasins and how to make buckskin clothes as well. For a quiet man, Ben was a good teacher.

Aunt Penny and Ben never had any children of their own and I reckon that having me around sometimes was his way of making up for it. He taught me oceans more than Pap ever did and he had a sight more patience, too. As the years went by I came to think of him more as a father than I ever did Pap.

I commenced to spend less time around the cabin and Ma's school. She understood that I enjoyed my time with Ben and never let on that she minded when I was off with him, hunting or fishing or setting traps and snares for muskrat, coons, and skunks or dressing out their pelts to trade for store-bought wares down at Staples's. Sometimes I'd bring her yard goods or ribbons for a dress and Pap would start in complaining that I never brought him anything, but I reckoned that considering he sold his whiskey he likely didn't need help from me.

Naturally I had my chores to do whenever I wasn't out with my uncle, helping Ma and doing what I had to for Pap and then at harvest and hog-killing time pitching in with the neighbors to help get their chores done before cold weather set in, but the times that pleasured me most was when I could be in the woods, alone or with Uncle Ben.

æ   æ   æ

I reckon I was about sixteen when I noticed that Sarah Rutledge was just about the prettiest thing I had ever seen. She was thirteen-coming-fourteen at the time and it came to me that she wasn't a little girl anymore, that she was coming on to be a woman, and a beauty at that. Looking back on it now, I reckon I fell in love with her right then and there.

Sarah was helping out at Ma's school more and more and she was less of a scholar than she was a teacher herself. They had nearly a score of kids now, some of them older than Sarah and a few who were nearly as old as I was. Reading and writing was getting to be downright common around Whynot, except for some of the old German families who reckoned that such frivolities made a person lazy, but you could never reason with those people.

About that time, when I was sixteen, Ma said she reckoned she had taught me just about everything she could, so I wouldn't need to come to classes anymore. Naturally she and I would talk, sometimes late into the night, and she would give me books to read, mostly histories and ones about the lives of great men, and then we would talk about them after I finished reading them. I would have to say that Ma and I got to be what you might call real good friends during that time.

Pap, on the other hand, got to be downright unfriendly. Sometimes he would sneer at me and say that I was coming to look like a wild Indian. That hurt me and I didn't think that he had any right to say such things. Looking back on it, I reckon it was true that I had grown to where I was already nearly a head taller than Pap and there wasn't much extra meat on my bones, except for muscle, and roaming out in the sun in search of game and trapping and going fishing had darkened my hide considerably, but still he had no call to liken me to an Indian, considering how he felt about Indians. Ma never said by-your-leave about it to Pap nor to me, but about that time she stopped cutting my hair like she always had, which I reckon was her quiet way of getting back at Pap.

By then I knew the country around Whynot about as well as it was possible to learn it and I commenced to spread farther out in my tramping, sometimes hunting and other times just wandering, getting so far out at times that it was too far to come back home at night, so I would find a hollow tree or sometimes a big hollow log or maybe a little cave somewhere and then I would curl up and sleep there until daybreak. Those were good times for me, feeling strong and like a grown-up man, listening to the birds chirping and warbling and the squirrels chattering, watching the sunshine finding its way through the heavy overhang of the trees, and knowing that I could find or shoot the makings of my own breakfast, just like a proper hunter would do.

My roaming took me all the way south to the Ohio River, following to either side of our crick until I came upon it, stretching out like a giant lake or an ocean, with Kentucky, that some folks still called the Dark and Bloody Ground, on the other side, just a dim line of trees through the mist, the first morning that I saw it. I just stood there and wondered at such a river, watching the gray-brown waves turning white on top and lapping at the pebbles on the banks, and thinking what it might be like to build a raft or a boat and follow that river to wherever it went. But I never did.

I had just turned seventeen when I made the first real man friend I ever had who wasn't kin to me. The way it happened was that I was out tracking a deer, a big buck by the look of its tracks, when I heard a snuffling and a rough, gruff, coughing sort of noise somewheres behind me. I swung myself around and there about twenty yards away was a big sow bear cuffing a cub in close to her and raising up on her hocks, hollering something awful, and then she dropped down onto all fours and started coming at me, grunting and slobbering and once in awhile making an awful racket with her screechy kind of roar.

Now I had never shot a bear, but a couple times I had been standing close by when Uncle Ben did. He told me never to shoot until they roared and then to shoot straight into their mouth when it was wide open. I don't mind admitting that I was scared bloodless, but I tried to do like I remembered he said. Even a coward knows that when running won't succeed, it's best to stand fast and do whatever you can.

I cocked my musket and tipped the frizzen down and put the stock up to my shoulder, but by time she roared again she was almost upon me. I aimed straight into her mouth as best I could and squeezed the trigger, but just before the charge went off I heard that fearsome hiss that means a hang-fire. The ball just raked her jaw and clipped off her ear and then she was on me, grunting and slobbering and batting at me with her paws. I felt her rip at my shirt and then my arm went numb. I knew right then that I was sure to die.

I was burrowed in against her shaggy hide, trying, I reckon, to get away from those awful claws, when I felt that sow sort of straighten up and heard her scream — and then she just toppled backwards and I rolled free, trying to crawl away from her. I didn't get very far before I just curled up in a ball with my eyes closed and lay there shuddering. It didn't occur to me to pray or anything. I was just too scared, I reckon.

The first thing I saw when I dared to open my eyes was a pair of beaded moccasins, not the plain sort that Uncle Ben made, and then some deerskin leggin's and the edge of a britchclout, and I knew for sure it wasn't Uncle Ben.

I rolled over onto my back and looked up and there standing over me was an Indian, looking like a giant from where I was, standing calm, neither smiling nor frowning, holding a bow with an arrow nocked to the string. I scooted around on the ground and saw the bear lying on her back with an arrow sticking out of her eye, not moving at all. And then I reckon I just fainted.

     ❧   ❧   ❧

When you suffer a bad wound it doesn't hurt at first, but by time I woke up my left arm was paining something fierce and I was halfway propped against a tree. The Indian was nowhere to be seen, but then I heard some rustling in the bushes and saw him coming towards me, holding something in his hand.

He ripped away what was left of my shirt and laid a handful of spider web onto the gashes in my arm. Then he bound it in place with some fringes that he tore off his leggin's.

The Indian stood up then and I looked up and saw that it was Powatawa, the Shawnee chief who used to trade tobacco and sometimes some of what folks call Shawnee silver with Ma and most likely still did.

When I was able to pull myself together enough to stand up, he got himself under my bad arm and started me walking out of the clearing, me dragging my musket along behind me with my good arm.

I don't recollect a great deal about that journey. I kept coming in and going out, like walking into a lighted room and then going out into the dark. Whenever I was able to know myself I recall struggling to put one foot in front of the other and smelling the sweat on Powatawa and feeling his arm dragging me along.

ﰀﰀ ﰀﰀ ﰀﰀ

I have no idea how long I was absent from the world, but when I did return I felt a pulling and a tugging on my hair and when I slitted my eyes halfway open I saw a pair of hands and a clamshell comb and then the face of an Indian girl and she was smiling down at me.

She turned her head and called out something I couldn't understand. Soon there was a passel of Indian faces gathered around me, just about all of them looking solemn and not precisely friendly, but the girl kept on smiling, which made me feel somewhat better about it all.

I just lay there trying to get my bearings and taking stock of my situation, which wasn't at all reassuring. I felt weak as a caught possum and my mouth was dry as last year's corn shucks and as I came into myself I felt my bad arm throbbing and hotter than it ought to be. I was lying on a pallet of deerskins and they had my head propped up on what felt like a roll of hides and when I turned my head away from those hard black eyes staring down at me, I saw my musket lying by my side and next to it my powder horn and my belt with my knife on it and all my possibles. I didn't know anything about Indians at the time, but I reckoned if they had left me my musket they weren't feeling altogether unfriendly towards me, no matter how fearsome they appeared.

About then there was a stir somewhere behind me and the Indians who were gathered around me moved aside. Next thing I saw was Powatawa crouching down beside me and sort of half-smiling, which could have meant almost anything, but his eyes were soft, so I quit worrying. Fretting wouldn't have done any good anyway and I found myself getting halfway curious about where I was and what might be going to happen next, trying my best, mind you, to keep thinking strictly of good things happening and shunning thoughts of all the unpleasant things that folks who never met an Indian in their whole life said Indians delighted to do when they got hold of a white man.

Looking up and ahead of me I saw that I was in some sort of a halfway long hut made of woven saplings and branches and thatch. I could smell smoke from a fire that was somewheres behind me, most likely near a door where Powatawa had come in. He continued to sit there beside me with that half-smile on his face, so I reckoned it was only good manners to tell him thank you for all that he had done for me, but when I tried to talk my tongue felt like a dry twig and I just sort of grunted.

He said a couple of words I didn't understand and next thing I knew the young girl was propping up my head and putting a gourd to my lips. The water was fresh and cold and I gulped like a catfish flung onto a riverbank. When I had drunk my fill, I lay back and looked up at Powatawa and said, "I thank ye, sir." I wanted to say a lot more, but I wasn't sure if he would understand me anyway. Besides, I'd heard that Indians didn't talk much, leastaways around whites.

He just grunted something way down in his throat, but he smiled a proper smile. Then he stood up and said something to the girl and perhaps to the other Indians standing around my pallet, for they moved off and followed Powatawa out of the hut.

The girl moved away, too, but it wasn't too long before she came back with a big gourd full of water and a smaller dipper gourd to drink out of. After I had another drink, she went to work on my arm, stripping away the poultice of leaves and herbs they had tied there and washing the gashes that looked like they went clear to the bone. Then she put on a new batch of greenery and tied it in place with a soft buckskin thong.

It was about that time, whilst the young Indian girl was tending to my arm, that I realized all of a sudden that I was completely naked under the deerskin coverlet they had laid over me. I recalled how my shirt was in tatters after the bear clawed me. Now my britches were gone, too! Do consider that

I was just seventeen years old and I had no experience of girls or women. Ma had raised me to be proper and this wasn't proper nohow, even if I was amongst Indians, and especially not with one that was as pretty as this one was commencing to look to me.

She must have guessed what was going through my mind, because she started to giggle. Or maybe it was because she saw me grab my private parts with my good hand to protect them from her seeing them. I'm not sure, but I yanked my hand away and pulled the coverlet up to my chin and just glared at her.

About that time she burst out laughing for fair and got to her feet and ran outdoors.

Before long a young Indian about my age came in and handed me a wide strip of soft-tanned deerskin and a narrow thong which I took to be a kind of belt. I reckoned it was a britchclout and I had seen how Indians wore theirs, so I snatched it out of his hand and shoved it under the coverlet, where I struggled to get it all put together. Tying the belt knot one-handed was more than I could manage, howsomever, and after he watched me fiddle with it for a spell, he threw off the coverlet and tied the knot in place, not once ever cracking a smile. Then he rolled back onto his heels, stood

up, and went out, the while putting on as if I was hardly even there
— or if so, not worthy of his notice.

The girl came back about then with a bowl of broth and when I
finished that off, she handed me another bowl of some kind of
Indian corn porridge. Both were tasty and I thanked her in
English, which was naturally all the language I knew how to use,
but she smiled and nodded her head anyway and took the bowls
away. Then, with my belly full, I leaned back and before I knew it,
I fell into a deep dreamless sleep.

∾   ∾   ∾

I won't go into any detail about how I woke up later that night with
an urgent need to get out of doors, but I will always be grateful to
that young man who never smiled, who showed me where to go
and what those Indians did when they got there.

∾   ∾   ∾

When I woke up next morning I was feeling a whole lot better than
I had the day before. The throbbing was just about gone from my
arm and it was starting to prickle somewhat, which told me that
the healing had commenced. I rolled off my pallet and struggled
onto my feet and headed for the place where I had been the night
before.   There were several men and boys there, but nobody
seemed to pay me much attention, so after I conducted my affairs I
headed back to the hut.

Whilst I am on that subject, I might as well say one thing about
those Shawnees. After they did their business they always took
care to wash themselves, which is something I have seen very few
white men bother to do.

Soon after I got back and lay down on my pallet I heard the
sound of drumming coming nearer and before long an old Indian
came into the hut carrying a little stone bowl with some sort of
grass in it and a turkey feather fan. He squatted down next to me
and struck some sparks with his flint and steel and started the
grass smoldering with just a little bit of flame to it. It was mostly

smoke, which he kept waving over me with that turkey feather fan, mostly towards my bad arm, all the while chanting and muttering some Shawnee words that naturally I didn't understand. He wasn't too pretty to look at, what with his wrinkled face and his mostly-naked body all painted in curious designs in what appeared like forty different colors. Besides, the smoke was making me sleepy, so I closed my eyes and before I knew it, I was off in a dream somewheres, but I never could recollect what it was, except for a bear that was running away.

When I woke up there were fresh leaves and herbs bound onto my arm and Powatawa was squatting beside me. He pointed to a couple of nearly brimming-over gourd bowls sitting there, steaming in the morning sunshine that found its way into the hut. I took one bowl and he picked up the other. I drank deep of the best broth I ever tasted. Bits of meat and greens were floating in it and I finished it off in half a dozen swallows. When I looked up, Powatawa had finished his as well. He raised his arm and snapped his fingers and the young girl from the day before hurried in with two more steaming bowls in her hands.

When we each laid our bowls aside, Powatawa stood up and waved me towards the doorway. I rolled off my pallet and noticed that the pain was just about gone from my arm. I followed him out, wondering where he was leading me and why. It was late morning by then and everything looked golden in the soft springtime sunshine. I could see women bustling about their chores, pounding corn or working deer hides or hanging jerk meat over a cord to dry in the sun, a few old men making arrow shafts or knapping flints, and here and there clusters of men sitting or standing together, but it was like Powatawa and I weren't even there. Nobody looked at us or spoke a single word.

Powatawa led me out of the village to a little clearing nearby and waved me to a seat on a fallen tree. He sat down next to me and looked at me in a careful sort of way that almost made me feel naked, which I pretty nearly was, considering that all I was wearing was a britchclout. Then he spoke to me for the first time ever.

"I am Powatawa. You are Temple Buck. You are welcome here, always, Temple Buck."

I was surprised enough to just about swallow my tongue. He could speak English about as well as I could, maybe better. His voice had that sort of hollow sound to it, like he was talking back somewhere behind his nose, like most Indians thereabouts did, but the words were clear, a little stiff, but they were all in the right places. Right then I reckoned it was only right that I thank him properly for what he had done for me.

When I finally got them jarred loose, my words came out in a rush. "What you did for me, back there with the bear, why, you saved my life and I owe you. I don't reckon I'll ever be able to...."

He held up his hand and allowed a slow smile to creep over his face before he said, "No need for too much thanking. I was there. You needed somebody plenty quick. I was standing near. I believe you would do it, too, like that, like I did, with the mother bear, Temple Buck."

His words sounded rusty, like he hadn't used them in quite a spell and was just now sorting through them to get his thoughts out to where I could know what he meant. "Well, sure," I said, "but if it hadn't been for you I'd be a bear turd somewheres in the woods by now, I reckon."

Powatawa squinted a little as he tried to unravel what I had said and when he did, his grin spread all over his face. "You talk like a Shawnee, Temple Buck. Your talk makes a picture."

Right then I was sorry I had said it the way I did. After all, he was a chief and he had saved my life and I had ought to show him some respect, but what I had said didn't appear to bother him. He must have read in my face what I was thinking, but he just kept on grinning, and then he said, "You will remain with us until you are mended."

For the first time I thought of Ma and how she might be worried, not knowing where I was or what had happened to me, already gone for I didn't even know how many days. Trying not to sound like I was ungrateful for his hospitality, I said, "I sure do thank you and all your folks for everythin' you've been doin' for me, but I'd best be gettin' on home now. My Ma will be frettin' about me." And then I added, "You recall my Ma, don't you, Chief Powatawa? You and she have been swappin' tobacco for bread an' such for years now, I reckon."

Powatawa's face became stern for a moment and he said, "Do not call me chief, just say my name — Powatawa." Then he smiled before he went on to say, "Yes, I know your mother well. She is an honored friend, to me and all Shawnee people. She has no worry. In the dark hours of the first night that you came here she was told of you and all things happening before and that you will soon be with her. She knows that you are well."

That made me feel somewhat better, knowing Ma was at peace in her mind about me. Despite my uncertainty as to how the other Shawnees might be feeling about me, I had a powerful urge to find out more about them and how they lived and what their thinking might be like. It's a wonder how white folks have whole books about people like the Chinese and those in Europe and Russia, but living nearly right amongst these Indians, almost as close to our farm as the folks we saw around Whynot, maybe closer, I realized that I knew hardly anything at all about them.

They say that curiosity killed the cat and that may be so, but ever since I was little Ma had always pushed me to find out the next thing about just about everything and it had become a habit with me, one that I still possess. I might as well mention right here, too, that the way people talk has always held a curious fascination for me, like a pastime. Although I haven't been around but a few educated folks in my life, I have read just about every book I could lay my hand to. Then, too, the kind of life I have led has provided me with a lot of time alone for thinking and chewing over what I have read and recalling the people I have known and what they said and how they said it and even to wonder why they said what they did the way they did.

But that is neither here nor there. There is a history to be told and I had best return to it.

Powatawa stood up, as if the matter had been settled, although I hadn't said anything, one way or another. Knowing that Ma was peaceful in her mind about me clinched it, so I said, "All right, sir, I'll rest here amongst ye for a spell, thank ye kindly."

Powatawa gave me sort of a funny look when I said that, but then he shrugged and turned and started back towards the village. I got up off the tree trunk and started after him, but as soon as I got to my feet I felt giddy and I realized that my bear-clawed arm hadn't mended nearly as fast nor as well as I had supposed. Powatawa just kept walking on ahead, but I somehow knew that he was still keeping an eye on me and I tried with all my might to walk proper, like a man ought to do.

By time I got back to the hut I was just about staggering, but I made it to my pallet and threw myself down on it. I was most likely asleep before my head hit the pillow roll.

≈   ≈   ≈

Daylight still filtered in when I opened my eyes, but nobody but me was in the hut. Outside I could hear children playing and now and then a woman's voice raised in what I took to be a scolding tone. Somebody had left a water gourd next to my pallet and I drank greedily, letting the cool water trickle down my throat and then splashing some of it over my head and face.

I heard something rustle behind me. I turned and saw it was the young girl from the morning, carrying a bowl and strips of cooked meat laid out on a bark platter. I thanked her as best I could and I believe she understood what I meant, for she bobbed her head and allowed herself a shy sort of smile before she turned and skipped out of the hut.

When I reached for the bowl I saw that somebody had replaced the poultice on my arm with a fresh one and I almost said a prayer of thanks for the kind treatment I was receiving from those heathen savages. Leastaways, that is what Pap always called them. The bowl was filled with a succotash and there was a bone spoon resting in it. I scooted around and got my knife from my belt to cut the meat as I ate it. It was deer meat, tender as butter and flavored somehow with herbs and the faint taste of wild garlic and onions. What with that and the succotash and recollecting the broth and all, I found that I was getting to be downright fond of Shawnee vittles.

I was just shoving the bowl and the platter off to one side when I heard a drumming and before long the old man came in again, this time dragging a bear hide with him and holding his little stone bowl and turkey feather fan in his other hand. The bowl was already smoking and he put it down on the ground beside the fan. Then he signed for me to lie down and threw the bear hide over me. It was soft and clean-smelling and the hair was black and shiny, but the sight and feel of it made me stiffen up and shudder. The old man shot me a hard look that was enough to make me lie quiet. Then he picked up his little bowl and commenced singing in a high, hollow voice, all the while brushing me with his fan and sweeping smoke over me. Before long I started feeling sleepy and I noticed that I didn't mind the bear hide anymore. After a time I didn't mind much of anything at all. I could see myself slipping into a dark forest and a giant bear was running off through the trees ahead of me. And then there was nothing.

When I woke up the sun was shining in my face and making pretty patterns on my deerskin coverlet as golden rays filtered through the boughs and branches of the hut. The old man and his bear hide and all his odds and ends were gone, but that didn't surprise me. Nothing much could have done that, after all that I had been through. I was halfway through the doorway before it came to me that my bear-clawed arm wasn't paining me, even when I raised my hand over my head. I lifted the poultice and peeked at the gashes. They were still there, ugly and swollen, but they didn't hurt. Right then I allowed that the old man, they called him Willoway, and his smoke and feathers surely knew what they were about.

When I got back to the hut from the men's place Powatawa was sitting cross-legged on a deerskin and there were two bowls of steaming porridge in front of him. He waved me over to sit beside him and when I did, he looked at me closely and smiled.

"You are improved, Temple Buck." He didn't ask. He just said it as a fact and he was right.

I told him I surely was feeling a whole lot better and he smiled again and motioned towards the bowls. We each picked up a bowl and fished out a bone spoon and set about breaking our fast.

When we finished, Powatawa rose to his feet like water flowing upwards, with no effort at all. I scrambled to stand upright and followed him outdoors. He started through the village towards the clearing where we had been the day before and I walked right behind him. This time, though, I noticed as we went through the village that people were smiling and one or two spoke to Powatawa as we passed and I could have sworn that I saw one of the men nod at me, but I could have been mistaken.

We were sitting on the fallen tree when Powatawa said, "You need not remain in the medicine lodge, Temple Buck. You are healing well. It is safe for you to come to my wegiwa and stay for a time as one of my family."

I told him my thanks, feeling mighty good about not having to stay all alone in that hut anymore. After all, I was just a boy then and I was used to being around people, for the most part. Besides, I reckoned that as long as I was amongst Indians I might as well get to know some of them and see how they lived.

Powatawa made a sound in his throat and then he said, "When you and I spoke last I told you not to call me chief and you did not know why I spoke so. It is good that you know this thing. I will tell you now."

Without waiting for me to reply, he went on. "Tecumseh is called a chief in your language. Tecumseh was the greatest chief of all Shawnees, of all Indian people, forever. I am nothing beside him. I lead only a little band and I am not worthy even to do that."

When Powatawa spoke of Tecumseh, his face glowed. I nodded and said nothing. Powatawa continued. "Tecumseh tried to give us back our land, but we failed him. He called all Indian people to his side to fight the Americans, but they would not come. Delaware, Cherokee, Creek, and the others, even some Shawnee, would not come. They would not put aside old hatreds. They sat in council and smoked and talked like women, but they would not fight. Because they would not fight, all is lost to all of us, to all

Indian people. There will never be a chief to walk in the moccasins of Tecumseh! It is too late!"

Powatawa fell silent, looking like he was wrapped up in his thinking. I thought it best not to say anything right then, but I kept my eyes on his face. Then he said, "Some of us came to his side when he called. Some of us went to the North to fight against the Americans when the Englishmen returned. We were too few. Most of us fought bravely, but we failed. Tecumseh fell at the river white men call the Thames. We have no leader now. We have no chief. We will never have another."

Powatawa went quiet now and I saw that Indians really could cry, in spite of what folks in Whynot said about them. A tear trickled down his cheek and he wiped it away with an angry flick of his hand. He turned and looked me full in the face for almost a full minute before he said in a ragged voice, "The Shawnee are still proud, but our power is broken. We will soon leave this land where our grandfathers hunted. I am happy to know you, Temple Buck, before that day."

I wasn't at all sure where I fitted in, but I was surely glad that I knew him, even aside from the bear and all. I was rustling around in my mind, trying to come up with something to say that would sound right, when Powatawa slid onto his feet and said, "Come. It is time we go to my wegiwa."

He started towards the village and I swung off the log and trotted after him out of the clearing.

When we got to the village Powatawa walked right on past the medicine hut and on to a big long sort of a cabin made out of poles and covered with bark that I took to be the wegiwa that he had talked about earlier. White folks, the few who dared to come close to the Shawnees, called such dwellings wigwams. Powatawa ducked through the doorway but I tarried out front, waiting for him to inVite me inside. Whilst I was standing there, I noticed that Powatawa's wegiwa, big as it was, wasn't the biggest one in the village, even though I knew him to be the leader of that band. A moment later he stuck his head out of the doorway and motioned for me to come in.

I dodged through the low door and found myself in a long room, halfway dark after the bright sunshine outdoors and cool. A couple of small fires flickered in the space down the middle, the smoke curling upwards through some holes in the high roof. There were several little walls here and there that reached about as tall as a man's head, some of them draped with blankets and what looked to be soft-tanned hides, all of them festooned with bright copper pots and suchlike cooking gear and all manner of weapons — well-oiled rifles and muskets, pistols and fowling- pieces and powder horns, tomahawks and knives and bows and quivers of arrows and stone clubs and a power of quilled and beaded bags for carrying their possibles. It was a pretty sight and I recollect noticing that everything was clean and neat and proper. And as long as I stayed there, they kept it that way.

As my eyes got used to the gloom I could see several men sitting at the far end, where a little fire burned in front of another door. They looked to be young men, but as Powatawa led me nearer I saw that some of them were older, as old as Powatawa and a few even older than that, with scars on their arms and chests and here and there on their faces. I reckoned they were Shawnee warriors and I recalled stories that Ma had told me and some I had heard when some of the old men in Whynot told about Shawnee war parties and how folks feared them. Looking at those unsmiling faces I could easily understand why.

One of the men stood up as we drew near the group and I saw that it was the young man who had brought me the britchclout. He stood unsmiling, with his head bowed slightly when Powatawa spoke. "This is my son Chiksika, Temple Buck. Think of him as your brother." Powatawa said something in Shawnee and the young man held out both hands but he still didn't smile. Then Powatawa turned to me and said, "Take his hands in yours, Temple Buck. You will come to be friends."

I did as I was told but without a great deal of enthusiasm. Chiksika's hands were hard as horn, tougher than my own, which were considerably calloused from doing hard work all my life.

We looked into each other's eyes then and what I saw in his made me wonder if he and I could ever be friendly, let alone friends. Then I saw Powatawa look beyond me. I turned and saw the young girl who had been caring for my bear-clawed arm and fetching me food, looking just as pretty as she always did.

She stood back a respectful distance from us until Powatawa beckoned her forward. Then he said, "This one is my daughter Methotasa, Temple Buck, and you must think of her as your sister." I thought I heard an extra little bit of advice in the way he said sister and I knew right then and there that I had better stop thinking how pretty she was. I never had a sister, as you know, but I knew that what I had been thinking about would never do for a sister.

Powatawa never did ask me to clasp hands with his daughter. He said something to his son and Chiksika beckoned to me to follow him, which I did. He led me back about halfway through the wegiwa and then he stepped behind one of the little walls. I followed and saw my deerhide pallet spread out and my musket and what other plunder I owned lying on top of it. I noticed right off that the musket had been cleaned and oiled, and later, when I sorted through my possibles, I saw that nothing had been taken or tampered with.

Besides my own plunder I saw some clothes on the pallet, too, a deerhide shirt and some leggin's and a britchclout and a handsome pair of moccasins, all of it decorated with fancy quillwork. I looked at Chiksika and he just put his two hands out in front of him with the palms up and sort of pushed at me, which I took to be a sign that the clothes were to be mine, which proved to be correct. He still didn't smile, though.

I had never owned such fancy clothes before. About all I had ever worn, except for the common buckskins I made with Uncle Ben, were linsey-woolsey shirts and hickory britches and hardly ever any shoes, except in winter.

I reckoned right then that the evening chill would soon be upon us, or leastaways sooner or later, so I scrooched up against the little wall and shucked out of my britchclout, naturally taking care to turn my back to Chiksika, and pulled on the leggin's, then the new britchclout, and finally I slipped the hide shirt over my head.

All of it felt butter-soft and warm on my skin and I started feeling about as happy as I ever had been.

When I went to put on the moccasins I found a shell comb in one of them. The moccasins fit like they had been made for me, which I reckon they had been. My hair had grown quite long since Ma had quit cutting it and after I combed it out I felt that I looked like a proper Shawnee Indian, which most likely I didn't, but it made me feel good to think so at the time.

                          ه   ه   ه

The three weeks or so that I passed with Powatawa's band that first time were the happiest I could ever remember.

Next morning I was awake before Chiksika got up and when he did I followed him out of the wegiwa to the men's place and back again afterwards. I could tell that he had his orders from Powatawa and he would abide by them, but that didn't cause him to feel particularly kindly towards me. But as time went on, whilst he showed me around the village and out in the groves where they kept their horses, and later, when my arm healed up enough so that I could join in on some of the young men's games, he started to warm up considerably. He even commenced to call me by name, but he couldn't quite manage to say Temple. It came out more like Tempo, but it was close enough and quite a step forward, to my way of thinking.

Most of the games the young Shawnees played had to do with war, which made sense, because they had always done so much of it, with the white people lately, but before that, against other Indians of different tribes or persuasions. Chiksika showed me the use of the bow and how to use a knife and a tomahawk and even how to throw them, but he pointed out that once you threw them at an enemy, you didn't have the use of them anymore, although now your enemy did. I was a better shot than he was, but that was just about the only skill I could best him in.

What I liked most was when he taught me how to ride a horse. Like any boy who lived on a farm I had often climbed up on top of one or another of our plough horses to get from here to there and

Uncle Ben had given me some riding lessons, but mostly he and I hiked wherever we went. I really couldn't ride, not like those Shawnees, who appeared to melt right into their horses and become a part of them. All of them, even the girls, had ridden horseback all their lives. I wondered if I would ever catch up with them. Perhaps I never did, but they taught me a lot.

Sometimes when Chiksika and I rode out to a good hunting spot, Methotasa would ride along with us and I marveled at how easy and graceful she was on a horse. Howsomever, I was careful to keep my marveling to myself, recollecting the look in Powatawa's eyes the day he told me her name.

Days flowed into weeks. I pretty much lost track of time, but I knew that soon I would need to be getting on home.

The other young men and even some of the older ones had commenced to warm up to me. They often waved me over to join in some of their games, even times when Chiksika wasn't around. The women, too, especially Powatawa's two wives, quit being so stand-offish and when we were eating they would push more food onto me, just like they did with their own boys. I am sure that none of them thought of me as a Shawnee, but they weren't treating me exactly like they would a white-eyes either.

Then one day it was time to go. My arm had healed to where it was just about like before, except for the scars I will carry to my grave. I was feeling as strong as I ever had in my life. I hated to leave but I knew it was time to be getting home to Ma and the farm — and Powatawa did, too.

Indians generally aren't much on saying goodbyes, but the day I left for home it looked like most of the village turned out. I was togged out that morning in my Sunday Best outfit, carrying my musket and a roll of extra clothes they had made for me, ready to commence hiking homeward, when Chiksika rode up leading the prettiest solid bay gelding you ever saw, a young, fine-looking horse with a small head and wide-apart kind eyes, a short back, gaskins nigh as thick as my thighs, his chest as wide and deep as a village well. I was lost in admiring that horse when Powatawa reached over and took the bridle reins and handed them to me.

"You must not walk to your home, Temple Buck." His voice was husky and I could have sworn his eyes were halfway wet. "No. You must ride like a proud Shawnee. This is your horse."

I just stood there gawking, a lump in my throat as big as a gourd, not able to say anything, but I reckon he knew what I was feeling.

"This horse is called Kumskaka," he went on. "That name means in your tongue Cat-that-flies-through-the-air. He will serve you well."

I felt my eyes welling up with tears and I surely didn't want those other Shawnees to see that, so I just sort of lurched forward and laid my head on his chest. I felt him grip my arms really hard. Then I spun myself around and swung up onto Kumskaka's back and loped out of the village, never looking back.

I was out of sight of the village and fumbling with the stirrups on my hair-pad saddle when I heard a horse coming. It was Chiksika and when he pulled up in a flurry of dust I saw that he was wearing one of his rare smiles. It wasn't a happy smile, but it was friendly. He and I hadn't but a half-dozen spoken words between us up until then, so he made a sign that I took to mean friendship. Then he sat back and looked at me.

There wasn't anything that I knew to say, not even a sign, so I reached around and took out my knife and handed it to him. It was a good knife that Uncle Ben had made and I knew Chiksika admired it. I wanted him to have it. He took it and then he slipped his own knife off his belt and gave it to me. We both just sat there for a minute, looking at each other. Then he smiled once more, wheeled his horse about, and galloped off.

I remained there on the trail for minute or two, staring after him, feeling like I knew what it was like to lose a brother, if I had ever had one, that is. Then I shifted my musket on my arm, picked up the reins, and trotted home.

❧   ❧   ❧

Naturally Ma was glad to see me when I rode up to the cabin looking healthy and strong. She hugged me tight and even cried a little, which wasn't at all like her, and then she stepped back and looked me up and down. I was brown as a raisin from running around most of the time in just a britchclout, but she didn't appear to find any fault with that. She just stood there looking at me and smiling and dabbing at her eyes with the corner of her apron from time to time and not saying much of anything. It was good to be home.

Of course Pap pitched in to funning me as soon as he saw my Indian clothes, but I had long since learned not to pay him any mind when he did that. I saw right off that he had his eye on my horse, but there was no way in the world that he was ever going to get his hands on that animal. Kumskaka and my musket were just about the only two things of worth that I owned and I was determined to keep them both.

After I brushed down my horse and turned him loose in the hayfield, I heard Ma calling from inside the cabin, so I went in and sat down to supper. It felt odd to be sitting in a chair and using a fork and I missed the flavors of Shawnee cooking, but I never said anything about that. After I finished eating I climbed up the ladder and I daresay before long I was dreaming of the wegiwa and maybe seeing Sarah Rutledge once again.

ও   ও   ও

The next year or so went by pretty fast. I had my chores to do at home and at times I would hire out to the neighbors and naturally I passed a lot of time with Uncle Ben, hunting and fishing and running a trapline for muskrats and skunks and an occasional mink or otter. Beaver were just about gone from that Ohio country by time I came along, long since trapped out.

Sometimes I would saddle up my Kumskaka horse and ride over to the Shawnee village and after a time they got so used to my comings and goings that my showing up caused hardly a stir amongst them. I began to feel as much at home in Powatawa's wegiwa as I did at home and Chiksika and I got to acting almost like brothers. We would go hunting together and we started trying to teach each other our own languages. He improved much faster than I did because he had Powatawa to help him when I wasn't around, but I did manage to pick up a fair smattering of Shawnee, which helped more than somewhat in getting some of those old warriors to smile back when I showed up. Howsomever, Chiksika still called me Tempo.

~   ~   ~

It is only fair to say here that matters were getting to be thick as winter sorghum between Sarah Rutledge and me, but there didn't seem to be any future in it. I wanted her every which way and especially for a wife, but I had no prospects. I didn't own any land and besides I surely didn't want to be a farmer nohow. I wasn't what folks call shiftless, for I worked hard at home and for the neighbors and I traded game meat and furs for cash and kind at Staples's, but I could never get far enough ahead to make a start. And besides, I never could make up my mind what I wanted to do with my life, outside of marrying Sarah Rutledge.

I remember lying out on a river bank one time, my back propped up against a tree, looking at Sarah and wondering how just one woman could own that much beauty all by herself. I was just coming nineteen and she had just turned sixteen. She was already a woman, with her deep blue eyes and her hair almost black in the shade but glinting with little red lights in the sunshine, full red lips and a buttery skin like rich dairy cream. Her figure had filled out, too, and my hands fairly itched whenever she was near. But both of us had been brought up properly and we knew that it wouldn't do to do more than kiss and embrace when we were out somewhere alone. For my part, I reckoned that it was easier for girls to wait than it was for boys. Leastaways it sure did appear to be that way.

As I said, we were out by the crick, fishing lines out in the water and the poles propped up on forked sticks, but we weren't really fishing. It was just that, the way we were raised, a person had to be doing something useful and not just enjoying his pleasure, so we were fishing. I was looking at her sitting there across from me, quiet and smiling and looking out across the water, when something exploded inside of me like a charge of gunpowder and I knew that I had loved Sarah since I first saw her as a little girl. I scrambled over to her and took her hands in both of mine and I recollect that I almost shouted, meaning it more than anything I had ever said before in my life, "Sarah Rutledge, I don't know just when nor precisely how I will get it done, but I am going to make you my wife and I am going to love you as long as there is breath in my body!"

She looked at me with the softest eyes there ever were and she said, "I know you will, Temple. And I love you. But please don't fret yourself. I can wait and it will happen."

But like I said, waiting must have been a sight easier for her than it was for me."

❧   ❧   ❧

The village of Whynot was fairly boiling with excitement right about that time. A land speculator had come into the county, trying to buy up farmland and any land patents from the War of Independence that people had never claimed on and might still be lying around loose. He was offering hard cash, too, a commodity that was always in short supply in those parts. But even so, most folks hung onto their land.

Then one day I came riding into the yard and the speculator was there, talking with Pap. He was a big, beefy man wearing a plug hat and a bright blue broadcloth coat, with a fancy lacy stock knotted under at least three of his chins.

After I put up my horse, I sidled near and heard him telling Pap how it was a sin and a crying shame that good cropland was being held by a pack of dirty red savages just to hunt on when there were patriotic white Christian Americans starving in the cities because they had no place to go to farm for themselves and their poor, hungry wives and children. Pap was slopping up that kind of talk like a hog snouting into a trough, nodding his head and agreeing with every word that man let fall.

I didn't say anything and I don't think they even noticed that I was there. I just shook my head and walked up to the cabin, but it seemed to me like a shadow fell across everything thereabouts just before I stepped inside.

≈ ≈ ≈

Sure enough, next Sabbath morning Pap was perched up on a stump down in the woodlot, yelling at his congregation that it was the Will of God that every inch of this country ought to belong to White Folks because we had won it fair and square with the help of God Almighty and the Heathen Redskin must be driven out. From what I could understand from where I was standing, it appeared like God had told Pap all this personally. I never heard any other voices besides Pap's hollering around our place, but perhaps the two of them did their palavering down at the still.

Pap didn't let it rest just at his Sunday sermons, either. He commenced to spend a heap more time in Whynot than he usually did, preaching to his cronies in Staples's that it was their Patriotic Duty and God's Holy Will that they get together and petition the Federal Government to send Army troops out our way to rid our fertile land of every pesky redskin they found lurking in the territory, all of them just waiting to pounce on honest, hard-working, God-fearing farmers and murder and scalp them in cold blood and to commit unspeakable acts on innocent women and defenseless babes. Fact is, Pap wasn't at all shy about speaking about those unspeakable acts. It appeared to me that he took considerable satisfaction out of describing them in vivid detail.

I commenced to notice that for a change the men down at Staples's appeared to pay somewhat more than their usual indifferent attention to what Pap was saying. I also noticed that Pap was carrying a lot more pocket money than was customary.

I reckoned I knew what was going on, once I heard the talk about the Government sending Army troops and all, so I rode out to warn Powatawa. He already knew. I don't recall that I saw him smile even once that day.

≈ ≈ ≈

Matters kept heating up all over the county and particularly in Whynot, where Pap was fanning the flames against the Indians for all he was worth. He was in his glory, gadding all over the territory with his preaching and his hollering and getting folks to sign his petitions to the Government to send Army soldiers to drive out the Indians. He didn't have much trouble getting folks to sign up, either, for nothing seems to make some men feel more like they are worth something than when they can convince themselves that some other kind of people aren't as good as they themselves are. It's a measly kind of thinking, but there is always a deal of such self-congratulating going on.

What army the Federal Government still had about that time must not have had much to occupy their time, for it wasn't too long before Whynot was swarming with bluecoats trying to sign up the local men to form a militia to help out when they went to drive out the Indians. The soldiers didn't have much trouble getting volunteers for that militia, either, for a lot of those same men had been marching on the green when the British came back in 1812. Naturally none of them had ever heard a shot fired in anger during that ruckus and it all seemed like a lark to them. Besides, there wasn't much in the way of entertainment available thereabouts.

Only Jacob Staples stood calm and not saying much on either side of the question. I have always suspected that it was because he had been forever trading gunpowder and lead and suchlike to the Indians on the sly and the old bandit hated to see such good customers slipping away.

Next time I rode out to Powatawa's village was my last. The Shawnees were already packing up, getting ready to move — where, I didn't know, and they themselves weren't altogether sure, either. Just somewheres west.

They all wore long faces and there wasn't anybody cracking jokes, like they usually did, which even if you didn't understand what had been said, you could tell by the quick burst of laughter afterwards. Mothers scolded their children more than I recalled and everybody was scurrying about picking up this or that bit of property and holding it up in the air whilst they considered whether or not they should take it along or leave it behind, shaking their head the while, then putting it down. Then they would grab up some other item and do it all over again.

The Shawnees owned quite a number of wagons and some draft-horse teams and here and there in the village you might see a wagon standing beside somebody's wegiwa piled high with household plunder, then a little later it would contain no more than half as much. Powatawa's band had lived in that village for I don't know how long and it wasn't easy for them to decide what to take along with them. Standing there watching them scurry about like so many frantic ants, I could have cried, if the Shawnees hadn't disapproved so of a man doing such a thing right out in the open where they could see him.

Powatawa took me aside and we walked out to a grove next to the village, to see to his horses, he said, but when we were far enough away from the village he stopped and turned to me and said, "You wonder, Temple Buck, why the Shawnee do not stand and fight. Why we run like women."

I allowed that the thought had crossed my mind. From what I had seen and the little I knew of their reputation, I reckoned the Shawnees could have whipped that sorry bunch of bluecoats and their rag-tag militiaman gang and made them all turn tail and run, and I said as much to Powatawa.

"It is true, Temple Buck," he said, and the look in his eyes right then told me that he was remembering battles in his past and possibly the thrill of fighting just for its own sake, besides fighting for what he believed was right. He went on,

"The bluecoats would not stand two days before us. The volunteers would run to their homes like rabbits to their holes before the first sun sets. The Shawnee know well how to fight. The Shawnee warrior loves battle as the babe loves the milk of his mother. We would take many scalps and the rest would run like whipped dogs." There wasn't much to say to that, so I stood silent, waiting for him to go on, and he did. "We would win one fight, maybe two, maybe three. But there would be more, forever more, for there is little for the bluecoats to do now and they must have work to fill their hands.

"Leaders of all Shawnee bands nearby have met in council. We have learned from our past, from a time when our people lived far to the south, where we bathed in water that tastes of salt. In that land it is forever warm. We could not remain there. White men drove us from our land. My grandfather, then just a boy, was there and he remembered well how it was. We fought well and we could have fought more, but our women and children would have died. Without children there can be no Shawnee people."

He paused for a moment, maybe thinking of that distant land they had lost, that he himself had never seen, and I recalled that Ma had told me that the Shawnees used to live faraway in Florida. Powatawa commenced speaking again. "The Shawnee came north. We fought Choctaw, Creek, Cherokee as we passed through their country, until we came to this land called Ohio and here we lived well and our numbers increased." He paused again, his face tight-lipped and grim, and then he continued. "The white men came again, this time from the rising sun, and once again there was war, bloody war for forty years. Then peace came and we have lived beside white men, not as brothers, but in peace. Now again they offer war.

"The council has decided and I agree. Tecumseh is gone. The power of the Shawnee is broken. If we stay and fight, our women and small children will die. A few stubborns will stay. Most Shawnee will go. No, we journey west, to the dark land, where the sun sleeps. Perhaps we will find a good home there."

There was nothing to say after that, for either him or me. We walked back to the village in silence.

I stayed with them for the best part of a week, until every last wagon was loaded to where the axles were groaning and the spare horses and mules were packed to a faretheewell, panniers bulging and all manner of truck tied to the packsaddles. I helped wherever

I could, but what I remember most was this heavy stone in my chest where my heart should have been.

෨   ෨   ෨

I was standing in the village street holding the bridle reins of my Kumskaka horse, watching the file of lurching wagons and pack animals wind out of the village, whilst a few men with torches darted from one wegiwa to the next, burning them to the ground, leaving nothing for the white soldiers. My heart had returned to my breast, but it was breaking.

Powatawa rode up from behind me and stepped down from his horse, as graceful as a drifting leaf. His face was grave but he managed a kind of smile before he said, "Do not be sad, Temple Buck. We shall meet again. This thing that we do now is best." Then he reached his hands behind my head and draped a small quilled poke on a thong around my neck. I knew what it was, a medicine pouch, a parcel of charms to protect me and bring good fortune. Then his eyes bored into my very soul, if I own such a thing, and he said, "Temple Buck, I will always remember you by your Shawnee name, which I give you now. You will be called by us Sauwaseekau. Your name means A-door-opened. Keep that name forever close and safe in your heart."

I clasped my hands tight on his arms like I would never let go and then I turned him loose. He stood back, tall and proud and handsome as any man I have ever seen. Then he did a most un-Indian-like thing. He bent forward and kissed me on the forehead. He straightened then and swung up onto his horse and rode off, not once ever looking back.

I knew Methotasa was standing somewhere behind me. When her father rode out of sight, she came up to me and stood in front of me, staring into my face for what was all of a full minute before she reached out and stroked the bear-claw scars on my arm, her brown eyes brimming with tears but not really weeping. She bowed her head for a moment and then she just about leaped at me and pressed her cheek against mine. I hugged her close, wishing I knew the Shawnee words to say to her, but if I did I couldn't remember them right then. Then she broke away and ran to where her horse was standing, grabbed up his trailing reins and ran into the crowd of people filing past. She was soon lost in the bustle of wagons and carts and people and horses.

I had just about given up on Chiksika when I saw him threading his way through the welter of people and critters, like a fish swimming upstream, riding tall and proud, his musket balanced on his thighs. We had discovered that he was a year younger than I was, but he looked every inch a man that day. He came off his horse in one fluid motion and stepped up to me, holding out his hands palms up. His eyes were troubled but he wore a crooked kind of smile. I don't know what my face looked like, but it couldn't have appeared happy.

He grunted something in Shawnee that I didn't understand and then he said, "No look bad, Tempo — Sauwaseekau. You, me, brothers now. Always. You, me, hunt together some time. You see. That day come."

I have no idea what I said back to him, but I tried to say it in Shawnee, even though his English was better than my Shawnee ever was. Whatever it was that I said, I reckon he understood what I meant and his smile got broader. He reached out and we gripped each other's arms just above the elbow, like Shawnees do. We stood there in the midst of creaking carts and wagons and bawling cattle, women scolding and babies crying, men putting a brave face on it, grunting or laughing or shouting advice, some of them looking cheerful and some of them grim, everybody heartbroken at losing the only home that many of them had ever known. Chiksika and I stood there gripping each other's arms, staring hard into each other's face, silently swearing never to forget the friendship we had built together. And then he was gone, galloping into the rainbow swirl of the Shawnee retreat.

I sat on my nervous horse and waited in the street, feeling the blistering heat of wegiwas burning and crumbling all around me, until the last dog had chased the last wagon out of sight. Then I gathered up my reins and rode home.

≈ ≈ ≈

Pap was grinning like a cream-poaching cat when he saw me riding up to the cabin. He had a pretty fair idea about where I had been, but he didn't know what had been happening there. He was well aware, howsomever, of what the bluecoats and the militia ruffians were preparing to do.

He came ambling up from the still and stood there grinning whilst I tethered my horse in front of the cabin. Then he said, "Yew about ready to jine up, Temple? You're — how old is it now? — jist about eighteen an' old enough to lend a hand with the militiamen, drivin' them thievin', murd'rin' savages off'n our land. It's long past time ye done your duty." He cogitated a spell about what he had just said before he added, "Yep, yer bounden duty as a white man an' a God-fearin' Christian."

I looked him hard in the eyes and then I shook my head, not really answering what he had said, just letting him know that I didn't side with him in this or much of anything else. He started to say something more, but I never heard him. I yanked the reins off the rail and swung myself up onto Kumskaka's back and rode out of the dooryard at a lope, headed for Uncle Ben's. Leastaways I wouldn't need to listen to such talk over there. Ben was never one to mix into other men's affairs, one way or another.

The next year went by pretty fast. It was springtime again and the county was as peaceful as ever it was. It had been nearly a year since the bluecoats and the militia had mounted their Grand Expedition, as Pap was fond of calling it, against the Shawnees. What they found, for the most part, was nothing but piles of ashes and cinders and little else. As Powatawa had said, there were still a few small villages of the stubborns, as he called them, who had refused to retreat, and the tatterdemalion army hiked off to attack them with a great deal of enthusiasm, which enthusiasm quickly ran out when they came up against those Shawnee warriors.

Afterwards the county possessed several more widows than there had been and I reckon Pap did his level best to console every one of them in their grief.

Howsomever, the little army prevailed at last and they came riding and marching into Whynot, claiming a Grand Victory, some of the militiamen waving bloody Indian scalps until their wives caught them at it, after which they tucked them away out of sight. Pap did his share of crowing, when he wasn't consoling, although he never picked up a musket during the entire affair.

There wasn't a Shawnee left in the county, as far as I knew, except a couple of half-breeds, so I expect that God Almighty was smiling down on us right about then. Leastaways, Pap said so.

I passed my time doing pretty much what I had always done, hunting and trapping alone or with Uncle Ben, working some at home, and hiring out with the neighbors. I spent as much time as I could talking with Ma to keep her from feeling lonely when she wasn't teaching her pupils and Sarah and I continued to sneak off whenever we could to hold each other close and maybe kiss from time to time and talk about a future that didn't appear to be getting any closer. I still couldn't get hold of a clear idea about what I wanted to be doing with the rest of my life.

I was spending more and more time over at Uncle Ben's. They made me feel right welcome, Ben and Aunt Penny, too. She was always pushing food on me, telling me I never ate enough and that I needed to eat if I was to grow up big and strong.

Fact is, I had already turned nineteen and although I have always been of a lean and somewhat slender build, I was nearly six feet tall, taller even than Uncle Ben, and strong for my size and age. Still, Penny always fussed over me and I reckoned it was on account of they had never had children of their own and she was thinking of me as the son she never had.

On this particular occasion I was out on Kumskaka, riding in the general direction of Uncle Ben's, not doing much of anything, just musing over words, which is a habit of mine. I got to thinking about the name of my horse, Kumskaka, Cat-that-flies-through-the-air. He was aptly named for he was cat-quick, able to spin about on a shilling-piece, and when I leaned over his neck and touched my heels to his sides he fairly flew. I had rather more trouble with my own name, Sauwaseekau. I knew it was Shawnee for A-door-opened, but I had no idea what that might mean.

I noticed it was getting near sundown and I was thirsty, so I turned Kumskaka into the lane that led to Ben and Penny's place. Aunt Penny must have heard me coming, for she came out onto the stoop as I rode up to the cabin. She wore a big smile on her face and she waved when she saw who it was.

"Temple! How good of you to drop by." She talked as if I didn't spend half my time with my feet under their table, but that was just her way. She was a lively little person, still pretty as a spring flower, and she loved company and all the talk that goes with it, which Uncle Ben, for all the virtues I saw in him, could never provide.

"How do, Aunt Penny?" I called out. I noticed the dogs were nowhere to be seen. "Uncle Ben around?"

"Why no, Temple, he's not. He's out hunting somewheres with his dogs. Don't know when he'll be back and I don't reckon he does, neither. You know how he is." She smiled again and then she said, "Get down and put up your horse. Come on in and set a spell. I just brought some cold buttermilk up from the spring house. Now won't that taste grand?"

I allowed that it would indeed and I walked Kumskaka out behind the house and put him up in the shed they had for their horses. I tethered him and pulled off the hair-pad Shawnee saddle I was still using and forked some hay into the manger before I walked around to the front door of the cabin and went in. I stood my musket in a corner before I sat down at the table and said, "Cold buttermilk is better than I deserve, Aunt Penny, but I'll happily accept it anyhow."

She sort of giggled and said, "Oh, Temple, you needn't be always calling me Aunt Penny. Just Penny will do." Then she added, "I'm not that old."

Fact is, she wasn't. Looking at her there in the fading daylight with the candle on the table pushing back the shadows, she didn't appear to be much older than I was. And I told her so, which made her giggle again.

As she poured a big earthen mug brimful of buttermilk, she sort of simpered and said, "Oh, Temple. You always say the nicest things. A lady always enjoys it when she receives compliments from a gentleman."

I didn't know precisely what to say to that, so I just looked up at her and grinned. The buttermilk was tart and thick and cold as ice and I drank nearly half of that big mug before I set it down on the table. Quick as scat she filled it up again.

About then I noticed that Aunt Penny had loosened the strings of her bodice and was in danger of spilling out whenever she leaned across the table to pour me more buttermilk, which she kept on doing whenever she saw that I had drunk some of it, even just a mite. Howsomever I didn't reckon that it was proper for me to mention anything about such a thing, so I held my peace, even though my eyes kept straying in that direction. Then she snatched off her mob cap and shook out her curly red hair. Her face was flushed to a rosy color and her bright blue eyes fairly sparkled in the candlelight.

"What are you thinking right now, Temple?" she asked, her mouth curved in an impish smile, like a schoolgirl. "I'll give you a penny for your thoughts." She giggled and then she said, "Or maybe I'll give you a penny anyhow. Would you like that?"

My face was burning red and Aunt Penny could see that it was, of that I am sure, for she came around the end of the table and stood real close, just over me, so that I had to look up at those milky mounds first if I was to see her face.

Now it is one thing for a young man to sneak a peek at a young mother suckling her child, but this was a whole lot different from a woman giving pap to a babe. This was a grown woman with considerably different intentions. And besides, she was my aunt, the wife of my Uncle Ben.

Right then she caught me behind the head and pulled my face into her bosom. Her bodice had slipped down and I was staring straight at her nipple, looking like nothing so much as a ripe red raspberry on a snowbank. She twisted sideways and crammed that nipple up against my mouth and there didn't seem to be much else for me to do but open my mouth for it, which I did.

I felt Aunt Penny shudder. Her hands clamped down hard over my ears, but I could still hear her voice up above me, sounding like an echo, saying things like, "Oh, Temple, how long I have wanted you, to feel your young strength and manhood, to teach you the ways of love," and other such nonsense.

I have no idea how long we might have stayed like that, but I daresay that time passed rather swiftly, considering the situation. Then Aunt Penny took a step backwards and her nipple popped out of my mouth. She stooped and caught my hands and tried to drag me up from the chair. I started to rise but then I realized that I shouldn't, considering the sizable bulge in my britches at the moment, which I didn't think would be seemly.

Aunt Penny didn't seem to mind it at all. Fact is, she appeared to admire it. She tightened her grip on my hands and tugged me out of the chair and, without stopping, dragged me right on through the doorway of her and Uncle Ben's bedchamber. I'm not sure if I tried to resist much or not, but she swung me around and pushed me backwards onto the bed. Then she jumped right onto me and started covering my face and neck with kisses.

Her breath was hot, downright steamy, I would say, and her lips were wet and all of it felt mighty good to me, but I was brought up properly and I knew there was a whole lot that was wrong about all of this, although at that precise moment it was hard to remember what. I twisted my head somewhat sideways and choked out, "This can't be right, Aunt Penny. You're kin!"

She commenced kissing my mouth and eyes again before she said, "Pshaw! I ain't blood-kin to you, Temple! I'm jest a girl from Tinnissee and I want you right now!" And then she went to tugging at my britches.

I considered what she said with what I had left in the way of thinking at the time — which was more than somewhat addled, I must confess — and I reckon I decided that she might be right.

Aunt Penny snatched off my moccasins and she had tugged my britches nearly off when I heard her gasp, "Oh, Temple! This is too good to be true! More than I hoped for!"

Next thing I knew she hiked up her skirts and leaped up onto the bed and right onto me and before I knew it I wasn't a boy anymore.

              ≈   ≈   ≈

Aunt Penny was a good teacher besides being a powerful persuader. I must grant her that. The first time didn't last very long at all, as you might expect, but by the third or fourth time it was taking considerably longer and it was rather more pleasurable, too. But when she wanted to go again I found that I wasn't nearly as strong as I had been, which, I must admit, was something of a disappointment to the both of us.

Then Aunt Penny did the most remarkable thing. She stripped off my shirt and started kissing me all over my chest and down to my belly and then she did something that I had never even thought of. It was quite a surprise, I sincerely warrant.

              ≈   ≈   ≈

The way it all ended was Aunt Penny was riding me like a half-broke horse and howling like a passel of wild Indians when the bedroom door slammed open and I heard Pap's voice roaring, "What's goin' on here? Who's that? It ain't Ben! He's gone!"

Aunt Penny threw herself over me so that Pap couldn't see who it was and then I heard an explosion like a thousand thunderclaps. I scrambled sideways and peeked around Aunt Penny's shoulder and saw Pap standing in the doorway holding one of Uncle Ben's fowling-pieces in his hands. The room was still boiling with smoke from the gunpowder, but I could see Pap's face looking more than somewhat dismayed. I don't reckon that he truly meant to fire off that charge, but Pap was always more than somewhat excitable.

I wasted no time. I wriggled out from under Aunt Penny and snatched up my shirt and britches — no time for moccasins — and dived straight through the window, which happened to be open because of the warm spring weather. I landed on the ground rolling and never stopped running until I got to Uncle Ben's woodlot, where I slipped into my clothes.

I just stood there for a spell, breathing hard and wondering what to do next, when I heard a thing that I dreaded even more than Pap busting into the bedroom. It was Uncle Ben and he was shouting, "Lorenzo! Lorenzo! That yew? What's going on 'round here? I heard a shot!" and other such remarks, all at the top of his voice.

I reckoned that Pap had come out of the cabin and by now he must be telling Ben all about me and what he had seen. I started running again, hardly knowing where, just anywhere to get away from those two. I forgot everything I ever knew about traveling through the woods and I kept bumping into trees and falling into brambles and getting my hide all scratched and bruised.

When I thought my lungs would surely come bursting right out of my mouth, I dived into a thicket and tarried there for a spell, long enough to get my breath and set my thinking somewhat straighter. I knew that Pap could get lost in our own dooryard, but Uncle Ben was the best tracker by far in those parts. And he had dogs, besides.

My brain must have frozen solid just about then, for I started running again, running anywhere, just so it was away from Uncle Ben's, until I stumbled into the crick.

I lay there in the cool water, trying to catch my breath and gulping down water when I could, when I thought I heard dogs barking. I was up and running before I realized that I was, crashing through the brush like a crazy blind man, running first on one side of the crick, then the other, running as best I could in the water in the crick bottom for a spell to throw off the dogs, then jumping onto the bank and running on, always downstream, away from Uncle Ben's.

&ebdkl;   &ebdkl;   &ebdkl;

I have no idea how long it was that I kept on running, but when I opened my eyes and looked around, I knew where I was. I was lying on the bank of the only big water in those parts, the Ohio, and there was Kentucky, the Dark and Bloody Ground, on the other side, just like I had seen it first, misty and mysterious in the early morning fog. Daylight was just breaking and when I got up on my knees I made out a dim shape rolling gently in the water. It was a keelboat anchored not far from shore and nothing was moving on it.

I stood up and saw that my shirt and britches were in tatters. My feet were torn and bloody and my arms and legs were slashed with scratches and oozing blood. I was groggy from that long run and not getting any sleep to speak of. I knew that I couldn't run any more right then and that I had to hole up someplace until I could start running again.

I waded into the chill gray water and started swimming toward the keelboat, knowing it was the only place I was likely to find where I could hide myself. The water, cold as it was, soothed the rips and scratches and drained the ache from my muscles.

Once I came alongside the boat, I caught hold of the anchor rope and then the rail and pulled myself over the side. I rolled onto the deck with a thump and lay there not moving, fearful that I might have awakened somebody, but no one stirred. There was a small cabin at one end of the boat and I could hear some really loud snoring, but there was no other sound or movement.

I crawled to the far end of the boat, away from the cabin, and scrooched myself in behind some bales and chests and curled up with my head resting on a coil of heavy rope. And then I let everything go — the fear and the pain and the guilt and whatever else I was feeling. I turned it all loose, letting it flow down the Ohio River to wherever it wanted to go.

Chapter II
The Ohio

Pain shot through my thigh and I felt myself lifting off the deck, then slamming up against something hard. Bewildered with sleep and numb with pain, I struggled to get my eyes open, but as soon as I did I found myself squinting them almost shut against the bright sunshine that flooded everything around me. I was sprawled against a sharp-edged crate and lying almost flat on my back, the hurt spreading out of my leg and into my belly bad enough to make me sick. I forced my eyes open and tried to see who or what was causing me all that grief. A thought flitted through my brain that perhaps I was in hell to pay for my recent sins, but for all the preaching that I had had to listen to from Pap, I couldn't recall that he ever mentioned anything about there being any sunshine in hell.

Standing over me, his back to the sun, was a man, and even from where I was I could tell that he was a big man. Looking up into the sun like I was, I couldn't see his face, but I could hear him growling something way down in his throat. I saw him turn his head and I shifted my own head sidewise into a scrap of shade, so I could get a look at him. Then I heard him roar, "Lookee here, boys! We got oursel's a goddamn stowaway!"

With that he reached down and grabbed what was left of my shirt and hauled me to my feet. I stood tottering in front of him when I saw his fist coming up fast towards my face, his other hand still gripping onto my shirt. I might have tried to jerk away, maybe not, but right then my shirt tore and I went flying headlong to the deck, his fist just grazing the side of my head. I rolled away from him as best I could and fetched up against the rail and huddled there, my knees up around my chin, expecting another blow.

When I dared to look up, he was standing above me, hands on his hips, an ugly scowl creasing his face, his hard blue eyes fairly scorching me. "Who the hell are ye, boy? What ye doin' on my boat?" His voice sounded like it was coming straight out of hell.

I tried to say something but nothing came out. I just sort of gurgled at him. He started to reach for me but then he stood up again and bellowed, "Can't talk? That it? Or won't! I reckon we'll jes' see 'bout that!" He swung his open hand down and cuffed me alongside the head, but it didn't hurt much, leastaways not half as much as I expected.

Then he stood back and bellowed like a breeding bull, "Ye know who I am, boy? Ye know who?" I didn't, of course, and I wasn't equipped right then to tell him even if I did. I reckon he didn't expect an answer anyway. He just went on in that bull-roaring voice of his. "I be Mike Fink, that's who! Best damn boatman on the Oh-hi-oh — an' the Miss'ippi, too! Yer damn right I am! From the Monongahela clear to N'Orleens, where they all talk French an' they wear their Sunday duds ever' goddamn day! They all know Mike Fink! Best damn river boatman anybody ever seen or ever even heard tell of, too!"

I was looking up at him, not wishing to appear disrespectful, but I wasn't saying anything. He didn't need any help. "Yer damn right I be Mike Fink! Half alligator an' half hoss! An' two-thirds curly-tail sheep-killin' wolf, besides! That's what I sartinly be!" He paused for a moment, warming to what I took to be his favorite subject, and then he started in again. "Mike Goddamn Fink! I loves the wimming an' I chokes the men an' drinks their likker, too!"

Fink, for by now I reckoned that I knew what his name was if I ever would, paused to take a breath before he went thundering on. "Mike Whoreson Fink I be an' don't ye never fergit it! I eats li'l black nigger pickaninnies fer my breakfast an' I washes 'em down wid the whole goddamn Allegheny! I makes pie out o' whole passels o' heathen Injuns, too, an' I serves 'em up fer Chris'mas to my frien's!" He cleared his throat and spat over the side before he said, his voice going as flat as his eyes, "Jist ye remember ye this. I be Mike Fink. I don't talk much, but ye had oughter damn-sure better hide yerse'f when Mike Fink gits hisse'f on the prod!"

I reckoned that was the best advice I had heard so far, but I refrained from telling him so. I wasn't saying anything at all. It seemed to me that he had said all this a time or two before and that he didn't appreciate being interrupted.

About then Fink reached out and snatched me by the arm, yanking me to my feet and half-dragging me towards the rear of the boat, where I saw two men, one standing at the tiller, steering, the other hauling on the square sail that bellied in a fresh breeze blowing down the river valley. Fink's keelboat was big, sixty feet or more in length and maybe twenty wide, with high pointy ends.

Fink bounded up onto a part of the deck that raised up about four feet and ran pretty near the whole length of the boat, cutting off at about a dozen feet in front of the man at the tiller. I learned later that this was the cargo box, where they carried freight. He dragged me up after him and headed for the two men in the stern, muttering something like, "C'mon along, boy. Time ye met yer shipmates."

He hopped down off the cargo box and pulled me after him. Then he swung me around to face his two companions. The man at the sail had tied off the line and had ambled back to the tiller. Fink shoved me forward a step and announced, "Boys, meet our stowaway! This li'l bastard thinks he's come aboard fer a free ride, but he sure-as-hell has got another think or two comin'!

The two men standing on the platform at the tiller looked down on me, unsmiling, their eyes as hard as Fink's, taking stock of me like as if I was some sort of bug or a critter they had fished out of the river that they had never seen before. They were both big men, as big as Fink, bare-chested and brown from the sun, and they looked to be as strong as any men I had ever seen. Fink was, too, and with a power in him that put you in mind of a painter that would kill a cow or a bull just for the fun of doing it.

Fink poked me in the back and said, "That'ere be Carpenter, him at the rudder. T'other be Talbot." Neither man spoke. They just kept on staring at me. Fink pulled me around to face him and asked, "So what do they call ye, Laddy Buck?" I almost gasped. Laddy Buck, a name come back to haunt me.

I found my tongue about that time and stuttered out, "Buck. My name is Buck."

Fink scowled and swung his hand up so fast it blurred, fetching me a stinging blow on the cheek that sent me reeling sidewise. I somehow stayed on my feet and I turned back to him and said, "I told you my name is Buck, and it is. Go ahead and call me something else if you've a mind to."

Fink's face creased in a grin, but there was no happiness in it. He laughed out loud and said, "So, ye can talk after all. An' talk back, too! So be it. Buck it is an' Buck it'll be." He turned to the two men in the stern and called out, "Hear that, boys? He calls hisse'f Buck." For all they let on, they might not have heard what he said.

Now that Fink had let me talk it seemed to me to be a worthy thought to get off that keelboat as soon as I could, so I said, "I'll thank you, Mister Fink, if you'll just put me ashore when you can." I saw a hard look forming on his face and I stumbled on, saying something like, "I mean to cause ye no bother. I can swim. I'll just swim ashore." I made a move towards the side and Fink's hand shot out like a copperhead striking and grabbed my arm again.

His face wore a look of hurt surprise that didn't look to me to be very sincere. "Swim? Ye think ye'll swim ashore, do ye?" His voice started to climb. "An' what about yer passage? Who's to pay fer that? Fer you ridin' on my boat? Ye got money to pay?" I shook my head and glanced sidewise away from him and saw the other two men watching us. They were smiling now, thin, evil smiles.

"Well, then, ye'll hafta work it off, I reckon!" He was roaring by now. "There be no free ridin' on any boat o' Mike Fink's, by God! I warrant ye'll know a keelboat stem to stern afore I get shut o' ye."

His fist came out of nowhere and I felt my jaw crunch under it and then I was reeling backwards into deepest night.

ॐ ॐ ॐ

By time I returned to myself it was dark on the river and I could feel and hear the water lapping at the side of the boat. Water ran into my eyes and I squinted up at the face of a black man, a Negro.

He was squeezing water onto my face from a rag he kept dipping into a pail at his side. I struggled to sit up and I felt a tug at my ankle and I heard something clink. I moved my leg and I realized that it was a chain. I was shackled like a slave to a cleat sunk into the deck.

My mouth was dry, but before I could ask for water, the black man put a dipper up to my mouth and I drank deeply and gratefully. It had been nearly a full day since I had tasted water. I reached for the dipper and found that my wrists weren't shackled, just one leg, but that was enough. A burning resentment flowed through me and I wondered why Fink or anybody would do a thing like this.

I heard the Negro scuttling around behind me and the sound of clinking chain told me that he was shackled, too. He plopped a basket down in front of me and said, "You hongry, Marse? It's vittles. Ain't much nor much good, neither, but it's vittles."

I reached into the basket and felt around in it. There was a broken loaf of dry bread, some greens, and what I took to be some kind of smoked meat by the smell of it. I recollected that I hadn't eaten since I couldn't even remember when, so I broke off a chunk of bread and started to munch it. The pain in my jaw when I bit down recalled the last glimpse I had of Mike Fink and his fist and although I was a boy who had never known harsh treatment, except maybe at the hands of some schoolboy bully, I began to understand for the first time in my life the meaning and the use of revenge.

As I sat chewing dry bread and bits of meat I looked around me, taking stock of where I was. We were in a corner of the cargo box across from the cabin and outside I could see, through a couple of splintered boards, a nearly full moon shining down on the empty deck. The sound of powerful snoring coming from the cabin nearly rattled the whole keelboat. I could see, too, the chain wrapped around my ankle, fastened with a rusty padlock. I strained at the chain, trying to pull it loose from the cleat in the deck, but it wouldn't budge.

I could tell that the boat was tied up for the night by the feel of it swaying out into the river, then shuddering to a halt as it strained against the ropes, then swinging back shoreward again, still tethered, just like I was.

The Negro was sitting beside me, not saying anything. I couldn't see much in the near dark inside that cargo box, so I had no idea of his age or how big he was, but I reckoned that it wouldn't hurt to get to know him, considering that we were both in the same pickle. I started by asking him his name.

"Micah, Marse, dey call my name Micah." There was a careful tone in his voice, as if he were apologizing, not sure of how I might take whatever he said, even just his name.

"They call me Temple Buck," I said. "You can just call me Temple and leave off calling me Marse. I don't own you or anybody else." I thought for a moment and then I said, "I'm not sure if I even own me anymore."

No one around Whynot, nor in the whole county, that I ever heard of, owned slaves. Where we lived wasn't that kind of farming country and I had rarely even seen a black man, much less talked to one, just once in awhile when the rough-looking men that folks called Patrollers would come through herding chained-up runaway slaves back to plantations in Kentucky or Virginia. Ma didn't hold with slavery, even though she came from Virginia, where she told me they keep a lot of slaves. She said it wasn't right for one man to own another and her feelings just naturally rubbed off on me.

Micah didn't offer to say anything more, so I asked, "How long have you been with Mike Fink? Does he own you?"

"Don' ezzackly know how long, Marse Tempa. It been a spell. Oh, yeh, it been a spell." I could tell that Micah didn't precisely trust me, so I reckon he kept on calling me Marse just to be on the safe side.

"All right," I said, "but does he own you, proper and legal-like? Has he got papers on you?"

Micah was silent for a long time and I wondered if he had heard my question. I was about to ask again when he said, "No, I don' reckon he do, not propah. He fish me out de ribbah when de boat go down an' I like to drownded in de watah. Marse Fink he say ain' nobody 'roun' he kin see lookin' like dey own me, so Marse Fink he say he reckon he jes' keep me foh a spell."

That sounded like Fink, little as I knew of him, keeping another man's slave that he saved from drowning, much as he might have kept for himself a box or a barrel that he found floating in the river. I asked one more question. "Well, if he doesn't own you, did ye ever try to run off, to go up North?"

Even in the darkness I could feel Micah sort of shudder before he said, "I try one time. Marse Fink he cotch me an' whup me sumpin' scan'lous. I don' dast run no mo'. Marse Fink he say nex' time he hunt me an' cotch me an' kill me sartin'. No mo' runnin' foh Micah."

I couldn't think of anything to answer to that, leastaways nothing that Micah could have used. I lay back and stared upward into the darkness, thinking that being halfway well-brought-up and polite with my elders and knowing what little I did about wild critters and the woods wasn't doing me a whole lot of good in this particular situation. I realized that the only teacher who could show me how to live through all this was Mike Fink himself and I would need to learn from him. And that wasn't an especially happifying thought. Suddenly I felt very tired and I didn't want to think anymore. I let my eyes fall closed and before I knew it I didn't know anything at all.

I heard the rattle of the hatch cover being shoved aside, but before I could sit up the chain jerked taut on my ankle and I was dragged out onto the deck. It was just daybreak. Upriver the sun was barely above the trees, daubing the clouds and the river mist orange and gold. Fink was looking down on me, a hard smile curling his lips. "Time to shine like the sun, Laddy Buck! Enjoy yer nappin', did ye?" I don't suppose he expected a reply, for he dropped to one knee and fitted a key to the lock at my ankle. The chain dropped away and I rubbed blood back into my ankle before I rolled onto my feet and stood shivering in the early-morning damp as he released Micah. I could see now that the black man was somewhat smaller than I was and likely close to the same age. Fink cuffed the Negro on the shoulder and said, "You, Micah, ye black bastard, rustle us up some grub fer breakin' our fast! An' be quick about it! There be a lot o' river bottom we aim to be passin' afore this day's done!" Micah disappeared around the cabin and Fink turned to me. "An' you, Laddy Buck, sitcherse'f down on the box here, where I can keep an eye on ye. There be chores aplenty ye'll be learnin' this fine day."

I did as I was told and Fink went into the cabin. A moment later Talbot came out, barefoot and rubbing his eyes and yawning, and then Carpenter. Talbot picked up a bucket with a rope tied to the bail and threw it over the side. He hauled it aboard and the two men splashed water on their faces and sluiced it over their shoulders before they went back into the cabin. Fink came out and, ignoring me, turned back to yell through the door, "Move yer arse! It's past time we be castin' off and headin' out! River's runnin' high! We kin make Limestone afore dark."

I was wondering how they could possibly make limestone when Fink barked at me, "Git off yer arse, Buck, an' go give the nigger a hand!" He glared at me and added, "An' don't be tryin' none o' yer tricks!"

I trotted around behind the cabin and found Micah crouched in front of a big iron trough filled with burning charcoal. Coffee boiling in a big copper pot sitting in the coals flavored the air with a smell that took me back to mornings in Ma's kitchen, but this was a long way from that pleasant place. Micah was frying sowbelly in a big iron spider. He threw slabs of potatoes into the sputtering grease and then he broke at least a dozen eggs into the simmering mess.

He sat back on his heels and watched it cook, stirring it from time to time, before he reached into a box beside the fire and pulled out several tin plates and spoons and a croker sack half-filled with cornpone. He tossed a couple-three pones onto each plate and ladled gobs of sowbelly, eggs, and taters onto the plates and handed two of them to me, jerking his chin as if to tell me to take them to the men on the other side of the cabin.

With a plate and spoon in either hand I went out to where Fink and his men were sitting side by side on the cargo box. When I got there I stopped, confused as to which two I should serve first. I started towards Fink, but he looked up and snarled, "Them two eat afore me. They got work waitin'!"

I handed the plates to Talbot and Carpenter, neither of whom bothered to look up, and trotted back for Fink's breakfast.

When Fink took his plate from me, he glanced up and growled, "An' where the hell's the coffee? Don'tcha know nuthin'? Git the goddamn coffee and git a move on!"

I hotfooted it back to Micah and brought the coffee pot and three tin cups to Fink and his men and set it all down beside Fink. Without looking up, he said, "G'wan back an' eat the leavin's. Ye'll need your strength this day, Laddy Buck."

When I got back to Micah I saw that he had filled two more plates and a couple of tin cups of coffee for the two us. He was sitting cross-legged on the deck, scooping up his breakfast as fast as he could bolt it down. He jerked his head towards the other plate and I didn't needed to be in*Vite*d twice.

I wasn't half finished wolfing down those greasy vittles when I heard Fink roaring my name. I crammed what I could into my mouth and tried to gulp coffee around it and came running around the side of the cabin.

Fink's back was turned to me, but he made a swipe at me and missed as I ran past and halted in front of him, just out of his reach. I didn't say anything, just stood there looking at him, waiting for his orders. That was the first time I ever really looked at him. I saw that he was maybe a hair shorter than I was, but bulkier, not a smidgeon of fat on him, with muscles bulging and rippling over all of his body that I could see. He was a lot older than I was, but not old, and halfway handsome, too, save for his mean blue eyes and a mouth that was almost always curled in a sneer. All he wore right then was britches chopped off below the knees. I could see what I took to be knife scars showing white on both arms and one big one that ran clear across his belly.

He bent down and picked up a long pole and threw it to me. "Here, grab this. Git ready to push off the bank." He picked up another pole and went to the rail, where Carpenter was standing ready with a pole of his own. Micah was already there, his pole dangling over the side, waiting for orders.

I took a place at the rail where a wave from Fink's hand told me where to stand. Talbot ran along a narrow walkway above the cargo box to a rope that was tied to a tree on shore. He reached out and caught the tag end of the rope and hauled on it until he pulled loose a kind of slip-knot and the rope came free.

Quick as scat Talbot ran towards the stern to a second rope and I heard Fink roar out, "Quick, now, lads! Push away!" Out of the corner of my eye I saw the other three stabbing their poles into the bank. I shoved the end of the pole into the soft mud until it hit something solid and then I leaned on it with all my strength, pushing the keelboat away from the bank. Talbot had released the second rope and was coiling it on the deck when I saw the prow swing out into the current, pointing downriver. All four of us pushed at the bottom until the boat broke free of the bank and commenced to float downstream.

Fink and his companions knew their work well. Without a word Carpenter jumped up to the tiller and Talbot ran a small square sail up the stubby mast. The keelboat picked up speed and soon we were well out in the river, making good time to I knew not where.

Micah had disappeared, most likely behind the cabin to finish his breakfast chores. I was alone with Fink, careful not to get too close. He threw down his pole next to Carpenter's and snapped, "Put 'em wid the others." I followed his eyes and for the first time I noticed a neat pile of a score or more poles like the ones we had used, each about a rod long and equipped with a knob at one end, stacked on the cargo box. As I stooped to pick up the poles that he and Carpenter had dropped, I heard Fink say, "Well now, Laddy Buck, we might make a boatman of ye yet." It was the only thing that came even close to being halfway civil that I ever heard from Mike Fink. Then he erased the slight compliment with, "If'n I don't kill ye first."

❧   ❧   ❧

I don't mean to retail here every blow and insult that Mike Fink
bestowed on me. I assure you there were many of both. It should
be said, here, howsomever, that it was Mike Fink who taught me
the use of hatred and there were many times when I would have
killed him if I could. He was a capricious man who enjoyed cruelty
for its own sake, who cared not a jot or tittle for anyone or
anything but himself. Mike Fink was a consummate, arrogant
bully.

ᔥ   ᔥ   ᔥ

The rest of that day, like so many others on that journey, blurs in
my memory. All that I recollect is running from one chore to
another and jumping at Mike Fink's commands, doing my best to
dodge his random cuffs and blows, moving and stacking crates and
boxes, demijohns and kegs and barrels, and straining with Micah
to hoist bales atop other bales. As the sun commenced to dip into
the downriver trees, Micah and I were fastening together the sides
of what looked like a hog pen in one corner on top of the cargo box.
It smelled like it, too, and Micah muttered, "Reckon we gwine stop
foh hogs come Limestone." It occurred to me then that Limestone
was a place and not some kind of rock.

About then, I heard Fink call out to Carpenter at the tiller and
Talbot, who was leaning against the mast. "Moon's comin' full,
lads. An' river's runnin' high. No use stoppin' this night. We'll
ride on through an' break our fast in Limestone come mornin'."
He walked to the rail and peered down at water rushing past before
he shouted to Talbot, "You, Talbot! Get to the bow an' keep yer eye
peeled fer snags! I'll tend sail."

For all his inbred evil, Mike Fink knew the river, every island,
shoal, and snag and dangerous riffle. This was his work and his
pride, his skill that earned him the respect of men who otherwise
would merely have feared him as a reckless bully.

I knew nothing of boats or rivers, but I could feel the current
running stronger and stronger under the boards and see the dirty
gray sail bellying out as the twilight wind freshened and swept

down the river valley. Fink was leaning out over the rail, the wind ruffling his hair and flapping his shirt, his eyes seeking out landmarks on shore and river islands he knew, barking and bellowing orders to Carpenter at the tiller, keeping the keelboat running in safe channels ever westward.

ॐ   ॐ   ॐ

It was almost dark with a nearly full moon riding halfway high in the sky when Fink left the rail and yelled, "You, Buck! Git yer arse down here! It's cradle time for you an' the nigger!"

When I jumped down from the cargo box I saw that Micah was lying inside, his leg already chained. Fink pushed me down and wrapped the other chain around my ankle, snapping shut the lock as he said, "This'll keep ye put. It's a kindness. Don't wantcha gittin' foolish thoughts, Laddy Buck, 'bout jumpin' overboard. River's runnin' high an' quick an' ye'd sure-as-hell git yerse'f drownded." With that he stood up and slid the hatch cover into place and snapped another padlock shut.

Micah had spread out some dirty blankets on the splintery deck. I couldn't see them but I could smell them. Still, it was an improvement on the night before. Micah had squirreled away some dry cornpone and scraps of salt meat from supper and we lay there munching our sorry fare, too tired to talk and with littleto say if we hadn't been, grunting instead of using words.

Afterwards I curled up, my head on my arm, hearing the rush of water past the bottom and wind beating at the sail above. From time to time I could hear Talbot call out a warning from the bow to Fink and hear Fink yell an order to the ever-silent tillerman Carpenter. Almost for the first time I let my mind stray back home, to Ma and Sarah, Uncle Ben, and Aunt Penny's surprising behavior, my horse Kumskaka, and even Pap.

About then a thought occurred that if the keelboat should run onto a snag and sink, Micah and I would be fish bait for sure. I wondered if Fink had thought of that when he was telling me what a kindness it was to chain me to keep me from jumping overboard. I mostly decided that he had, for there was little or nothing that I would have put past such a man. Howsomever, I was young and dead tired, so I put such thinking out of my head. There was nothing I knew how to do to change any of it, anyhow. I reckon I was thinking about savage Shawnees and civilized white men like Mike Fink when I crept off into sleep.

The sudden, mournful blast of a boat horn followed by a grating sound, then a jarring thump woke me and I rolled to the hatch cover, brought up short by the chain on my ankle. Gray dawn was just breaking and I could see trees overhanging the deck. I saw that we were on the Kentucky side of the river. Fink was yelling to Talbot to secure the bow line and I could hear the sound of running bare feet slapping on the deck above.

Micah was already awake, hunched up in a corner, hands clasped around his knees, shivering in the early morning damp. He rolled his eyes shoreward. "We's in Limestone." Micah had left off calling me Marse, but now he didn't call me by any name at all and he hardly ever said anything to me.

Before I could reply I heard the rattle of the hatch cover and Carpenter's voice for the first time. "Hop to it, lads," he said, his voice every bit as harsh as Fink's. "There's cargo needs movin' this mornin'!" He knelt and quickly freed Micah and me of our chains. He stood to his full height, which was greater than my own, and said in a voice like cutler's steel, "Foller me. I'll show ye what'll be goin' off here."

Micah and I padded after him to a cargo bin near the bow and we spent the best part of the forenoon lugging boxes and crates and rolling barrels and kegs meant for Limestone down the length of the boat, over a pair of wide planks that spanned the water, and onto a rickety dock. Fink and Carpenter left the boat and disappeared amongst a scatter of shacks that made up the town of Limestone. Only Talbot remained aboard to keep an eye on us and from time to time to shout an order from where he lounged on the tiller deck in the stern.

During the morning several men from the town came out onto the dock to pick up goods that we had stacked there. They were all pretty much alike, it seemed to me, generally dirty,unshaven, bleary-eyed, and rawboned, dressed any whichaway in too-big tattered britches hanging off their galluses and patched-together shirts, most of them barefoot and smelling of strong spirits. Altogether a shiftless lot, from the look of them. They didn't appear to be the kind of folk who might aid me if I tried to run off from Fink in their neighborhood, so I put that thought aside for the time being.

They pawed through the stack of merchandise we had piled up there, dragged out a box or two and maybe a keg, and then counted out an amount of money and handed it to Talbot, who counted the money again and nodded. Then the man would haul his goods away off the dock. Nobody had a receipt or a piece of paper that showed the merchandise belonged to him and most likely none of them, including Talbot, could have read it if they had. They totted it all up in their heads and everything appeared to work just fine.

In the course of the morning another stack of goods accumulated on the other side of the dock, brought there by many of the same men. Talbot walked over each time a new batch arrived, listened to what the man told him, carefully counted the money the man handed him, and then returned to his perch on the tiller deck.

~ ~ ~

Micah and I were stowing the new cargo and the sun was well past noon when Fink and Carpenter strolled across the dock and stepped onto the boat. They were each carrying a jug and Fink was even louder than usual. I daresay he had been drinking more than somewhat, but you couldn't tell it by his walk. They said something to Talbot and he hopped down from the tiller deck and left the boat, heading into the jumble of shacks that called itself Limestone.

Carpenter and Fink climbed up to the tiller deck and sat there draining their jugs and chatting. Now and then as I passed by on my way to and from the dock I could hear them talking about the "wimming" in town and bragging to each other about whatever came to mind.

Then I saw Fink jump down and go into the cabin. He came out a minute later carrying a rifle and his powder horn and bullet pouch. He climbed up onto the afterdeck and leaned against the tiller, surveying the shoreline. I followed his gaze and saw, about fifty yards from where Fink stood, a huge brindle sow surrounded by eight or nine suckling pigs. Fink caught me watching him and he roared down to me, "Hey, Laddy Buck! D'ye wish to see some superfine shootin', now do ye?" I nodded, hoping the while that he didn't have me in mind for a target. Fink roared even louder. "I want pig! I got me a pluperfec' yearnin' fer pig an' I by-god mean to eat me some pig this day!" He brought his rifle down and commenced to pick his flint, all the while yelling about what a good shot he was. "They call me Bang-all in Pittsburgh Town, they do, 'cause Mike Fink's the best goddamn rifle shot any of ye ever did see or even hear of, by God, an' they won't even 'low me to shoot agin 'em no more, 'cause I'm that goddamn good, I am! They jes' natcherly give me the fifth quarter ev'ry time, the hide an' taller, an' I spends it all on wimming an' whiskey an' drams fer m'friends, I do, 'cause Mike Fink's the goddamn best there ever was!"

Fink's hollering brought a fair-size crowd out of the shacks. Soon a throng of townsfolk clustered on the bank, watching and waiting for what Fink might do next.

Fink swung himself around and looked again at the sow and her brood. He raised the rifle and prepared to take aim, when an old man stepped out of the crowd and called out in a pleading voice, "Please, Mike! Cap'n Mike! Fer the sake o' Baby Jesus don't ye go an' shoot my pigs! Them'ere's gonna be some prime hogs when they be growed an' I truly wish ye wouldn't be doin' me like thet'ere!"

Fink paused a mite, as if he was considering the old man's request. Then he shook his head and said, "Naw. Gonna do it anyways." He raised his rifle and pointed it towards the sow again. I should mention here that even though the keelboat was tied up close and snug against the dock, the river was running high and fast and the deck was rolling and pitching under our feet, the boat bumping against the dock and shuddering from time to time as the mooring lines strained taut against the current.

Fink peeked sort of sidewise at the old man as he drew a bead. Then he said, "Wal, mebbe I'll jes' trim 'em up fer market fer ye then." With that he took careful aim and squeezed off a shot. One of the young pigs squealed and jumped into the air and we saw that Fink had neatly clipped off its tail up close to its rump. The pig was not harmed otherwise.

Fink laughed aloud and drained a deep swig from his jug. Carpenter was grinning. The old man couldn't make up his mind whether to laugh with relief or to keep on worrying, for Fink was loading his rifle again.

Fink continued to shoot and reload and pull at his jug until he had docked the tail off every one of those pigs without really injuring a one of them. The old man who owned them, on the other hand, was in a sorry state of agitation from worry and concern for his property.

After Fink completed his final shot he laid his rifle aside, looked down at me, and gave me a broad wink, as if to say that if I chose to run off I had best arrange to give myself a long head start. I had already been thinking much the same thing.

I was tidying up and lashing down a stack of new cargo and Micah was behind the cabin boiling pork for barbecue. The old man who owned the newly-docked pigs had donated a quarter or so of a half-grown hog to express his gratitude to Fink for not killing all of his young pigs. I myself had seen and smelled about all the hogs I ever wanted to, considering that we had spent the rest of the afternoon chasing down and loading and penning a score of hogs up on the cargo box. They were bound for Cincinnati, the next port on our downriver trip, along with two passengers who owned the hogs, and a passel of goods we had loaded in Limestone. I finished tying off a rope and stepped back and nearly bumped into Fink, who was standing just behind me. I jumped sidewise away from him and stood there waiting for him to say something. From the look on his face he appeared to be in a better frame of mind than he usually was, possibly because of his successful shooting that afternoon. Whatever the cause, he said, sounding almost kindly, for him, "I been keepin' an eye on ye, Buck." I had no doubt in my mind that he had, but I didn't say anything and waited for him to go on. "Ye've shown yerse'f to be able an' willin' to do the work. Ye don't know nothin' but I see ye're tryin'."

He paused and gazed out over the river, maybe watching the big uprooted trees twisting and thrashing and rolling in the current, before he said, "We're bound fer Saint Looie, we are, an' ye're goin', too, like it or not." He paused again and studied my face, as if he was weighing something in his mind before he went on. "Now ye kin go like ye been doin', a pris'ner, chained up nights like a dog, or ye kin go about like a man o' my crew an' no chains. The choice is yer own." I waited for him to go on. I certainly didn't trust him and he knew it. "I take ye fer an honest lad, Buck. Gi' me yer word ye'll stay aboard an' no runnin' off. If ye do, I warrant I'll track ye and find ye and then I'll jes' natcherly kill ye. An' ye got my bond on that!"

I never doubted for a moment that he would do just that. There didn't appear to me to be a great deal of choice, so I nodded and said, "You have my word." And he did have it. I reckon he could read that in my eyes. Little as I knew him, I reckoned, shrewd as he was, he could judge a man's character.

Fink bobbed his head and without another word to me he spun on his heel and walked back to the stern, shouting orders to cast off and get under weigh for Cincinnati.

As I trotted forward to cast off the bow line I marveled at how Fink could read me the way he had, how he knew that once I gave my word I would hold to it. There was no way to tell, but he was right. It appeared that I was going to see Saint Louis town. I wondered what it would be like.

ȣ ȣ ȣ

The work was no easier than it had been and Fink was no gentler. He was quick to punish, his hard hands stabbing out in a punch or a slap, and even quicker to curse, often with words I had to ponder before I understood their drift, but more and more I began to feel as if I somehow belonged on that keelboat, on it or to it, a part of it all. Talbot and Carpenter, too, seemed less on their guard whenever I came near, better able to tolerate me, now that I wasn't chained up at night like some wild critter.

I never did see Cincinnati, except for what little I could make out from the docks when we tied up there to unload and take on more cargo for downriver. We were traveling day and night now under a full or early waning moon, snatching a few winks here and there when we could, grabbing a mouthful to eat now and then. Fink decided to trust me enough to let me spell Talbot in the bow, calling out a warning whenever I saw a snag or floating trees drifting near.

The Ohio was running high in spring flood and it broadened as we drove ever westward. I was standing at the rail marveling at the breadth of it and the might of it when I heard Fink's voice at my shoulder. "It's somethin', ain't it? But this ain't no more but what a mare can piss, nex' to Mississip! Ye'll see." He turned and walked off to the stern. I continued to stare at the gray-brown chop of the mighty stream that was bearing me off to a place I had barely imagined and a life I wasn't at all sure I wanted.

આ આ આ

Once I gave my word to Mike Fink about not running off, he quit chaining up Micah at night as well. I never learned why. Maybe he just lumped the Negro and me together in his mind as both of us being slaves, which wasn't too far off the mark. Whatever the reason, life was better for the both of us now and Micah became downright cheerful at times. We still slept in our cubby hole in the cargo box, but we found a chance to wash our blankets and we were eating better. We talked more, too, and I discovered that Micah was far from stupid. He couldn't read or write, but he paid

mind to what he saw and heard and he remembered just about all
of it. I reckoned I could teach him how to read.

Naturally there was no privy on the keelboat. All there was for that
purpose was a big bucket with a rope on the bail that you threw
overboard into the river when you were finished and a little bucket
with a lid that was stuffed with some tattered old books with the
covers torn off and half the pages missing, sometimes a couple of
newspapers, and a few corncobs for whoever preferred them.

Reading is a strong habit, hard to break, and I had started
sneaking off with what was left of this or that book, reading,
whenever I could snatch a few minutes to myself, the bits and
pieces that hadn't already disappeared into the river.

One day when I had finished off my chores for the time being I
was in the bow reading some pages of what I recall was the
Pilgrim's Progress, when a hand came out of nowhere and
snatched the papers away. I turned and saw Mike Fink standing
behind me, wearing a look on his face that was somewhere
between a scowl and a sneer. "What the hell d'ye think ye're at, ye
measly pup? Not work enough fer ye to do, Laddy Buck?" There
was no proper answer to either question, so I kept quiet and just
looked at him. "Readin', is it? An' what good is yer readin' to ye
now, ye scurvy punk, ye ragged-arse river rat?"

By that time I knew him well enough to guess that he was off on
one of his yelling sprees and I wasn't mistaken. "I'll tell ye what
such trash as this is good fer, Perfessor! Fer arse-wipe an' nothin'
else, that's what!" He went on like that for a minute or two, getting
red in the face and stamping his bare feet on the deck, before he
ripped the pages to shreds and scattered them over the rail. Then
he cuffed me on the head and stalked off, still grumbling about
books and reading and no-account perfessors and such.

Fink started calling me perfessor after that, when he wasn't
calling me Laddy Buck or worse. I continued to sneak off with
whatever I could pilfer from the little bucket, but I was a lot more

careful where I did my reading. And whenever we were safe in our cubby hole, I commenced teaching Micah how to read.

❧   ❧   ❧

After Cincinnati we made several stops along the Ohio at little places that maybe didn't even have a name, just a rickety wharf sticking out into the river and a shack or two on shore, where we would stop for an hour or less to drop off cargo and maybe pick up goods or critters to take downriver.

Then one morning I noticed that the boat was crowding more and more to the left, the Kentucky side, and when we swept around a bend I saw a town spread out on the southern shore.

The blast of a trumpet came near to splitting my ears and I spun around to see Mike Fink standing on the cargo box with a boat horn at his lips. He gave another blast before he shouted to Carpenter in the stern, "Looieville! It's by-god Looieville, Carp! An' two days sooner than ever we done it afore! I warrant we're first down the river this year! We'll be havin' the pick o' the hands this fine day!"

Carpenter grinned back and leaned his hip against the tiller to steer us closer to the bank. Fink kept blowing on his trumpet when he wasn't yelling and he waved Talbot and me to the bow, so we could be ready to fasten the bow lines to the wharf. I stood up on the prow and marveled at the size of the town. There must have been a thousand people living there. I had heard folks tell of Louisville, but I never guessed it was so big.

❧   ❧   ❧

After we got the boat snugged up fast against the wharf, Micah and I set out the planks so that we could unload cargo. Fink, Talbot and Carpenter walked across and stepped down onto the dock. Fink called back, "Belay unloadin' fer now. We'll be takin' on some helpin' hands here."

We watched the three of them swagger the length of the dock. I saw that all of them were wearing boots now and they were clad in

Sunday-best shirts and caps, their britches belted snug and proper, each one of them with a knife at his hip, and Fink had a pistol shoved under his belt.

Micah and I finished up our chores, hurrying so that we could get to work on Micah's schooling, now that we found ourselves with a little time away from the prying eyes of Fink and his crew. I was teaching Micah his letters and I must admit that I was taking some extra satisfaction from spiting Fink by doing it. Micah told me that where he came from in Kentucky it was against the law to teach a Negro slave how to read.

We had been at it for maybe three hours when I looked up and spied Carpenter and Fink coming across the dock, walking with that peculiar rolling gait that boatmen use when they are ashore. Carpenter was carrying a jug and they would stop every few strides and pass it back and forth, each man drinking deeply before he gave it up. They were laughing and joking as they came aboard and you could tell they were fast friends, one as bad as the other, except that Fink was noisier.

Micah stuffed the papers we had been using under his shirt and we both stood up, as if awaiting orders. Except that his face was somewhat flushed, Fink looked to be as sober as a parson — leastaways a parson like Pap. Carpenter looked much the same.

They barely glanced at us and went into the cabin and came out a minute later, each carrying a rifle and slinging on their shot pouches and powder horns. Fink glared at me and ordered in a loud voice, "Hey, Perfessor! Git along wi' ye an' foller up! Ye kin fetch the jug."

I picked up the jug, which felt to be no more than half full, and followed them onto the dock and into the town. They made their way past stores and sheds and houses like men who knew the way. They halted when we came to a building that looked like a store, except that all there was inside was a halfway dignified-looking old man seated behind a table that had books stacked on one end, an inkstand and a cup stuffed with quills, a whiskey jug, and papers strewn all over it and scattered on the dirty floor around it. He was a portly man with a red face and white side-whiskers and I recall that he wore a flowing green cravat spilling out over a dirty white shirt. Fink stopped at the door and told Carpenter and me to wait there.

Fink stepped through the doorway and I heard him call the man Judge as he threw himself into a chair in front of the table and sprawled there, his rifle propped between his knees. I couldn't hear anything else that they said except some mumbling and occasional laughter, but I saw the white-haired man rummage amongst the papers on the table and then he handed a large sheet to Fink. I recall that the paper was a yellow color and that it looked heavy and there was a black stripe on it that ran cater-corner on one side of the top of it and a blob of red wax at the bottom. The fat man smiled and leaned back in his chair, hands folded on his belly, whilst Fink scanned the document. Before long Fink commenced smiling, too. Then he fingered into his belt poke and came up with several large coins and some paper money and slapped it all onto the table. The judge, if that is what he was, smiled even broader, and pushed the jug over to Fink. They both took a long swig and Fink shook the man's hand and said something that made the both of them laugh before he made his goodbyes and joined Carpenter and me outside.

Fink was still grinning when he said to Carpenter, "I got it. Signed, sealed, and sartin. He's mine fer sure now." He folded the paper and shoved it into his pouch. About then he must have noticed the look on my face, for he added, giving me a hard stare, "No, not you." Then he said to Carpenter, "Let's git on wid it."

We continued on through one corner of the town until we came to a grove on the river bank and there I saw perhaps forty or fifty men, most of them young or not far from it, gathered around a keg, splashing whiskey into tin cups or standing in bunches, eating barbecue. Two young Negroes crouched at a fire, ladling out meat and what I took to be hunter's stew onto tin plates.

They all fixed their eyes on us when we came into the clearing, as if they were expecting something. Fink stalked to the center of the group and thumped the butt of his rifle on the ground before he shouted, "Hear ye, lads! I promised ye a show an' a fine show ye'll have, too! An' after that we'll be comin' to biz'ness! Drink up and pleasure yersel's!   There's plenty more vittles an' drink where that come from!"

There was a general rush of men to the keg and the sound of their voices mingled with the clang of cups against the spigot, when the roar of Fink's rifle, followed by Carpenter's, brought everyone up short. Fink and Carpenter were blowing smoke out the breech of their rifles, measuring powder, and ramming home rifle balls. Fink swung about to face the gathering crowd and said in a loud voice, "It's time we sky a copper to see who'll hold the whuskey!" He searched about in the poke at his belt and brought out a big English penny, which he flipped to Carpenter.

"Call it, Mike," Carpenter said as he sent the penny spinning in the air. He caught it on its way down, slapping it smartly on the back of his hand.

"Tails, I say!" said Fink, grinning broadly, but his expression never changed when the coin showed heads.

Without another word, Fink laid aside his rifle and picked up a full cup of whiskey. Then he stalked sixty paces out to the river bank and turned to face Carpenter, who was picking his flint and wetting his thumb to wipe the frizzen.

Fink removed his cap and shoved it into his belt. Then he placed the whiskey cup carefully on his head, all the while wearing an easy smile as he gazed at Carpenter.

Carpenter cocked, pressed the frizzen down, and raised his rifle to draw a careful bead. Every man there, including me, drew in his breath and held it there as we watched Carpenter's finger tighten on the trigger. I caught myself wishing that he would miss his shot and I blushed out of habit, hardly from conscience, but nobody noticed or knew why if they did.

The ring of the cup bounding towards the river bank blended with the blast of the rifle charge and through the gray smoke we could see Fink wearing a broad grin and wiping whiskey from his brow, then licking it from his hand as he strode briskly back to the crowd.

"Good shootin', Carp," he said, no trace of excitement in his voice. "An' now it's a case o' turn about's fair play." He reached to pick up his rifle leaning against a tree.

Carpenter nodded and handed his empty rifle to me. Then he went to the keg and filled a cup before he walked out to where Fink had stood. He was adjusting the balance of the whiskey cup on his head as he turned to stare at Mike Fink, who was busy with his rifle and paid him no attention. I tried to read the look on Carpenter's face, but to me he appeared as unconcerned and matter-of-fact as he always did.

About then I noticed Talbot standing out of the way, at the edge of the fringe of trees, his eyes fixed on Carpenter, his face strained with a worried look.

Fink readied his rifle, wet his thumb and wiped it over the front sight and the frizzen, then he raised it to his shoulder, his look as carefree as Carpenter's, as if he planned to shoot at a squirrel that he didn't really need, a hard grin curving up his mouth.

Carpenter stood tall, not moving at all, one thumb hooked over his powder horn, the other in his belt, and even at sixty yards I could see his pale blue eyes watching Fink, calm and steady.

Fink drew a careful bead, not the slightest tremor showing along the long rifle barrel. Then he fired and sent the whiskey cup flying. Carpenter never changed expression. He just ambled back to the keg, picked up an empty cup, and drew himself another ration.

When the powder smoke cleared, I looked back to where Talbot had been standing, but he was nowhere around that I could see.

Fink leaned his rifle against a tree and turned to face the men gathered there. "Show's over!" he yelled. "But the fun's jest about to commence!" The crowd tightened up somewhat around him. "I need a score o' hands fer Saint Looie! An' Mike Fink allus takes the best! The best of ever'thin' there is! Whuskey, wimming, an' workin' hands! Same work! Same wage! An' ye know Mike Fink pays prompt an' proper! Some o' ye been on the river afore wid me, so ye know I'm talkin' true. We're likely first down the Oh-hi-oh fer the year an' the Saint Looie whores'll be fresh an' ready an' waitin' fer ye!"

He keyed his voice up a notch or two and roared, "If ye're game fer Mike Fink's boat an' Saint Looie, jes' line yersel's up an' we'll commence the pickin' an' choosin'!"

A few men drifted off but most of them stayed and formed themselves into a ragged line. Fink and Carpenter walked in front of them, choosing some they already knew and picking likely men from amongst those that they didn't. If Fink fancied a man's size and what he took to be his strength, he stopped and looked at Carpenter. If Carpenter approved, he nodded. If not, he didn't say or do anything and they moved on to the next man.

Choosing the crew didn't take a great deal of time. Before long a knot of some twenty men stood off to one side and Fink turned to the others and shouted, "Sorry, lads! Can't ship the whole lot o' ye, but fill yer cup now and drink to the health o' Mike Fink an' calm waters on the river!"

No one seemed to object to that and the vicinity of the keg was quickly crowded with jostling men. Fink turned to the score of men he had chosen and bellowed, "All right now! Ye're all o' part o' Mike Fink's crew! I'm boss an' don't ye never fergit it! Carpenter here an' Talbot are the mates! Most o' ye know what to do an' them as don't kin learn from the others!

"We'll be leavin' in three hours time. Git on home fer yer plunder an' be on the boat as quick as ye can! Fill yer cup now and drink to Saint Looie!"

A ragged cheer went up from the gathered men and they rushed to the keg to fill their cups and gulp and then to fill them again. Soon they were trotting out of the grove in various directions, headed for their homes to pick up their possessions and to say their goodbyes.

Fink turned to me and said, "Fetch the keg, Laddy Buck, an' foller us." He reached into his poke and threw a few coppers to the black boys at the fire before he turned on his heel and marched out of the grove.

        ℞   ℞   ℞

When we got back to the keelboat Fink ordered me to stow the mostly-empty whiskey keg in the cabin. I'm not sure what I expected, but I was surprised at how prim and tidy it was in there. Bunks were snugly made and the brass hardware of a dozen or more well-oiled rifles and fowlers gleamed in a corner. I even saw a few books stacked neatly on a sea chest next to one of the bunks and I wondered which of the three was their owner.

Inside of hardly an hour the first of the new crew straggled across the dock, bulging haversacks and skimpy bedding slung from their shoulders, several with muskets or rifles dangling from one hand or a pistol shoved into their belt, most of them ill-clad and barefoot. All in all, howsomever, they appeared to be a cut or two above the Kentuckians I had seen at Limestone, which isn't saying much in their favor.

Talbot had returned to the boat before we did and as soon as some of the new crew members arrived he put them to work with me, off-loading cargo bound for Louisville and stowing goods stacked on the dock that we would carry westward. Talbot had a curiously high-pitched voice for a man as tall and sturdy as he was and his commands cracked like a teamster's whip as he called out orders to the new crew. Carpenter posted himself on the dock to oversee delivery and receive new merchandise, carefully counting every coin. Fink remained in the cabin.

The new men were willing enough and we made short work of the cargo chores. *Merci*fully we took on no hogs at Louisville, but some of the new crew smelled about as bad.

Talbot had provisioned the boat while Fink and Talbot were busy in the grove and the back and one side of the cabin were piled high with flitches of bacon and sacks of beans and flour, croker sacks stuffed with pone, some with charcoal, and jugs of sorghum. Micah was already stoking up his fire trough to prepare the evening meal and naturally I pitched in to help him.

As we worked side by side I asked Micah why he thought Fink had hired so many hands. The five of us had done just fine so far. Micah just shrugged and said, "Don' need 'em now. We gwine down de ribbah. We come to de Falls, we need 'em. On de Mis'sippi, we's gwine up. We sho'ly need 'em den."

I didn't really understand why we would need all those men then, but I held my peace. It was just another case of wait-and-see. There had been a lot of those lately.

The next two days passed quickly, for there was little time left to Micah and me to do more than prepare three meals a day for the crew — mostly beans and sowbelly — even with the aid of a couple of the new men whom Talbot had ordered to help us. There was little work for most of the new hands to do, and when Talbot and Carpenter ran out of chores for them, they lounged on their bedding all over the cargo box, playing at cards or dice or yarning and spitting tobacco juice over the rail.

The river kept on broadening with each crick and river we passed and running higher, the current getting stronger. The easterly wind held and the sail was stretched near to bursting as we scudded downriver.

Near evening of the second day Carpenter steered the keelboat in close to the right-hand side of the river and several of the crew secured lines to stout trees on the bank, always under Talbot's watchful eye.

Fink emerged from the cabin and vaulted to the tiller deck, where he turned and shouted to the men lounging on the cargo box and along the walkways on either side, "Now ye'll commence earnin' your wage! Bright an' early we'll be strikin' the Falls an' ye'd best look lively, ev'ry man-jack o' ye!"

The sound of many feet slapping and pounding on the cargo deck above woke me up and by time I rolled out of the cubbyhole I could see men scurrying everywhere in the half-light just before dawn. They were stacking more pushpoles on deck and hauling long oars out of storage bins in the cargo box and fitting them into the rowlocks positioned below the catwalks.

Excitement laced the air that morning, flavored with healthy fear and spiced with bravado. You could hear it in their voices. Men who had worked on keelboats before bragged on it and sought to terrify their less experienced comrades with warnings of how difficult and dangerous it was to run the Falls of the Ohio, especially in early spring when the river was running high and fast. Those who had never been on the river had little to say.

They just stood calm and quiet, working up their courage to deal with whatever might happen next. As usual, my feelings were more than somewhat mixed. I surely didn't want to die, but aside from that I had nothing to lose and if Mike Fink lost his boat he would have no further use for me, as far as I could see.

"Cast off the bow!" Talbot's voice cracked over the length of the boat and several men scrambled to yank the bow lines loose. Talbot himself stood ready to release the final stern line as the prow swung out into the current, a half dozen men near the bow meanwhile pushing away from the bank with poles. Carpenter threw his hip against the tiller and steered the keelboat farther out into the stream, whilst Talbot trotted forward to the mast and ran up the sail.

Fink was everywhere, positioning men with poles on the righthand catwalk and half a dozen oarsmen on either side, cursing everybody and everything, mostly for no better reason that I could see than because it gave him pleasure just to be running his mouth. An extra man stood beside Talbot at the mast, not doing much of anything, and I reckoned he was there in case Talbot was needed elsewhere. I picked up a pole and joined the other men at the bow, for there was hardly anything that riled Mike Fink more than seeing a man standing idle.

The morning was chilly and damp, the gray sky reaching down into a heavy mist that hung just above the gray-brown river, the wind whipping whitecaps across the choppy water and big trees floating and churning and bumping downstream as we passed them by. Once we were under weigh, men in twos and threes trotted to the stern to snatch a mouthful of breakfast and gulp strong coffee before returning to their post to spell their comrades. There was little to do right then, but every man aboard was strung tight as a fiddle string, each one steeling himself to be ready for the Falls.

I heard it long before I saw it, the rumble of water crashing over rocks and against the river bank. Fink and another man had mounted to the tiller deck and stood beside Carpenter, all three of them leaning their weight against the tiller to guide the keelboat northward, close to the righthand bank. Talbot had left the mast and was screeching at the oarsmen to pull for the northern bank, while those of us with poles stood ready to keep us from crashing into the rocky bluff once we got there.

There must have been a channel on the north side of the river, for I could see white water boiling and foaming against rocky shelves on the bottom at our left, looking for all the world like a wolf's teeth snapping at us as we swept past. The bow tilted downwards as we entered the Falls in earnest, the oarsmen now pulling like men possessed, now shipping oars when Talbot screamed out still another command. Fink was yelling orders from the tiller deck, half of which were lost in the wind and the roar of the rapids. For me it was a nightmare of shuddering jolts and aching muscles as I stabbed the pole at the bluff with every ounce of my strength, scrambling with the other men to shove us away from the rocks and river trash that littered the shoreline.

A shout from a man at the bow jerked my head around and I saw that the keelboat was heading into a huge uprooted tree swirling in the channel, its branches sweeping over the catwalk and the deck. Talbot was suddenly beside me, a long pole in his hands, leaning out over the rail, stabbing at the tree trunk, trying to push it far enough away for us to slide past it.

I got my pole on the tree right next to his and leaned on it with all the strength I had. It was a pretty sight indeed when I saw that tree slipping towards the stern. Just then Talbot appeared to leap upwards, as if he had been suddenly summoned to Heaven, which, now that I reflect on it, wasn't all that likely. Fact is, one of the upper branches of the tree had caught in his shirt and snatched him off the catwalk as we sped under it. Almost without thinking I lunged for him and caught his belt and hung on for dear life, my feet braced against the rail, until I heard his shirt rip and we fell together in a heap on the deck.

Talbot wasn't hurt, just scratched up considerably about his face and arms. When we untangled ourselves, he stood up and gathered what was left of his shirt about him and gave me a curt nod before he walked away. He didn't smile and he didn't say thankee, just stalked off without a backward glance.

The keelboat bucked and kicked like a green colt as it shouldered its way through the rest of the Falls. Every man aboard put in a week's worth of work that morning, rowing or poling or doing whatever it took to keep that big boat more or less pointed downriver and in the channel, but at last we found ourselves on the downstream side, in fairly calm water, with hardly any damage. We had lost a few poles and some of the oars were splintered and broken when we rammed up against the bank a time or two, but except for such measly items we had survived the Falls of the Ohio better than most keelboats ever did. I have that opinion directly from Mike Fink, who was stalking around the tiller deck crowing and bragging on what a magnificent pilot he was and how nobody else could have done it. To give him his due, he might have been right.

৵   ৵   ৵

The town of Clarksville lies on the north bank of the Ohio River just below the Falls and you would have thought we had just won another war fighting the British, the way the townsfolk carried on when we tied up at the dock just after midday. They all knew Mike Fink and his boat, but nobody expected even his keelboat to come through the Falls for at least another month or so, until the spring floods receded. Fink made the most of it, bragging and swaggering and strutting and drinking bumpers with anybody who offered to stand him a drink. There were quite a few townsmen who did. Carpenter was, as you might expect, right by Fink's side, not bragging nearly as much but matching him swig for swig. Talbot stayed back on the boat and kept the crew busy tidying up the deck and unloading cargo bound for Clarksville before he turned our rag-tag navy loose for a spree in town.

Naturally I stayed aboard with Micah. I had no money to spend and I was ashamed to be seen by proper folk in my ragged clothes. Besides, I wasn't sure if Fink would have allowed me to leave the boat. He had hardly wasted a word on me since Louisville, which I didn't regret at all. Then, too, Micah and I always ate better than usual when Fink and the others left the boat whenever we stopped at a town.

Another thing we did was to keep on teaching Micah how to read whenever no one else was about, when we were alone on the boat or at night in our cubbyhole. Micah had pilfered some candle nubs from the cabin and we would huddle in a corner under the cargo deck in the flickering light, poring over odd pages torn from books. He was eager to learn and quick at it, too, and I reckon he took as much satisfaction from cheating Mike Fink at that game as I did.

After the last of the crew had crossed the dock, Talbot tossed the water bucket into the river and dragged it aboard. He drenched himself and washed off most of the dried blood from his scratches and threw his torn shirt overboard before he went into the cabin. When he came out he was wearing a clean shirt and he carried a bundle of clothing under his arm. He walked over to me and threw the clothing onto the deck in front of me and then, without ever saying a word, he stepped onto the dock and went into town. He never did say thanks, but then I never expected him to do so.

Raised the way I was, I had never cared much about clothes, except for the quilled and beaded buckskins the Shawnees gave me, but those too-big hand-me-downs from Talbot did wonders to lift my spirits. I commenced to think more and more about what I would do when I got to Saint Louis. Until then Fink had my word, but after that I had no idea what I would do, except that Mike Fink wouldn't be included in any plans of mine.

One day of drifting down the Ohio was pretty much like another and except for cargo stops here and there along the way, the only change was that the river kept getting broader as we passed scores of small cricks on either side and the Wabash flowing in from the north and then the Tennessee and the Kentucky from the south. The crew had little or nothing to occupy them and they passed the

time at cards or yarning. Now and then a fight broke out amongst
them, but Fink or Carpenter and sometimes Talbot were quick to
step in and settle it. Fact is, the three of them took so much
satisfaction from settling those fights and they did it so thoroughly
that the crew soon quit giving them an opportunity to thrash them.

℞ ℞ ℞

A few days after Clarksville — I don't recall precisely how many
days — Fink called out from the tiller deck, "Fort Massac, lads!
Last port on the Oh-hi-oh! Ye'll commence earnin' yer wage quick
enough now!" A loud groan mixed with a spatter of laughter went
up from the men sprawled around the cargo deck. I was standing
at the rail and I saw on the northern shore a rough-looking
stockade surrounded by huts and sheds and horse paddocks and as
we drew closer to the shore I could make out blue-clad men going
about their business.

We tied up at a sturdy wharf at the foot of a muddy path that led
up to the fort and the crew made short work of off-loading cargo
destined for the Army stationed there. When the work was done
some of the crew ambled on up towards the fort and a few scruffy
soldiers wandered down to the dock and lounged on the crates and
barrels we had stacked there. None of them looked to be in any
hurry to move the cargo up to the fort.

Seeing the soldiers, one of our crew, a tall, rawboned, slat-
ribbed, stubble-bearded fellow they called Tuttle Thompson, bared
his big yellow teeth in a grin and commenced to shuffle and fan out
a deck of greasy cards before he unwound himself from where he
was propped against the mast and stepped onto the dock,
mumbling the while about how he surely aimed to shear those
bluecoats like his own personal flock of sheep. I was thinking that
if these soldiers were anything like the shiftless bunch I had seen
around Whynot, their fleece would be very sparse indeed and that
they, instead, would more than likely relieve Tuttle Thompson of
the few coppers that rattled in his poke.

Whilst I was watching Thompson chatting up a card game with the
men on the dock, I noticed a big burly-built soldier coming down

the path. He looked to be somewhat older than the others and I saw that he was a sergeant, judging by the broad yellow stripes on the sleeves of his dirty blue tunic. Like the others, his uniform was far from complete. He wore buckskin britches and knee-high moccasins and a battered felt hat and his jaws surely hadn't known a razor for a week or more.

He barely glanced at the men huddled around Tuttle Thompson as he made his way across the dock and stepped onto the boat. Then he walked directly to the cabin like a man who had been there before. Fink hadn't gone ashore with Talbot and Carpenter. He was inside the cabin. The sergeant rapped on the door and called out something I couldn't quite hear from where I was sitting on the bow deck. A half-second later Fink stepped out of the cabin, a broad grin slicing across his face. Fink said a few words to the sergeant, who commenced smiling, too. The two of them strolled the length of the boat, chatting in low tones that I couldn't overhear, and ended up at the cabin again. Fink went inside and returned a moment later with a leather pouch that looked to be of considerable weight. He slapped it into the sergeant's outstretched hand and they both appeared to be pleased with their transaction, whatever it was.

The sergeant, still smiling, stuffed the pouch into the waistband of his britches and smoothed his tunic over it, shook hands with Fink, and returned to the dock. On his way to the path he stopped and broke up the card game and I could hear him order the soldiers to tote the goods we had piled there up to the fort. Then he marched up the muddy path without a backward glance, his back straight and shoulders squared, like a man who was satisfied that he had accomplished his mission. Once he was out of sight, the soldiers resumed their gambling with Tuttle Thompson.

Fink went back inside the cabin and I sat in the bow wondering what it was that I had witnessed. Considering Fink was a part of it, I was sure that it was dishonest and, recollecting Pap and his Holy War with the Government, I mostly decided that Fink was bootlegging whiskey on his boat and that he had just paid a bribe to the sergeant not to catch him at it.

An hour later we cast off from Fort Massac and proceeded downriver until dusk, when we tied up to trees along the bank, ate supper, and settled in for the night.

≈ ≈ ≈

We cast off when the eastern sky showed a bare glimmer of silver gray and what we could see of the river looked like galena. I was in the bow with Talbot, watching for snags and floating trees and such. Whenever I saw anything that looked like it might be a danger to the boat I would mention it to Talbot and if he thought so, too, he would call back to Carpenter at the tiller, but he spoke nary a word to me.

When the sun broke through the upriver trees I could see the broad expanse of the Ohio running high in the spring flood, looking like an ocean, the shores on either side showing only the tops of distant trees and nothing else.

When one of the crew came up to the bow to relieve me, I went back behind the cabin to help Micah with the breakfast chores, ladling out beans and sowbelly and pouring coffee into what seemed like a never-ending river of tin cups. The heat from the fire trough was welcome after the chill damp breeze in the bow. Micah, too, was a comfort, for he was the only friend I had on that keelboat. "Dis de las' day on de Oh-hah-yo. T'morra we gwine up de Mis'sippi," Micah muttered, glancing around, careful that Fink was not nearby. "Den come de hahd wuk."

He was more right than I could have realized right then.

≈ ≈ ≈

We spent that night out on the river, the boat moored to the upper branches of drowned trees, for in that flood there was no way that we could bring the keelboat into the shore.

At first light we cast off, the keelboat soon riding the swift current, the sail straining in the downriver breeze, the whole boat looking like an anthill with men running every whichaway to add extra lashings to the deck cargo and dragging oars to the rowlocks.

My first sight of the Mississippi nigh took my breath away. It appeared to stretch right over the end of the earth, but then I made out a fringe of trees on the far side and I knew that it was a river and not a sea. The powerful Ohio River current swept us nearly halfway across the big river, coffee-brown water churning and boiling under us, the keelboat heeling over as the force of the Mississippi smashed against the side of it.

Mike Fink was fairly dancing on the foredeck, roaring orders spliced with curses, first to Talbot at the sail, trying his best to catch an upriver breeze off the Mississippi, then to the oarsmen, two to an oar, who stood ready to pull the boat upstream and free of the Ohio River current. I marveled that twenty-five men could even hope to win a battle against all that water.

I was standing beside Tuttle Thompson, both hands gripping an oar, wondering if we would be carried all the way to the southern sea, when I felt the keelboat swivel in the stream and saw the prow swing shoreward towards the Illinois side.

"Pull, ye bastards, pull!" Fink's voice boomed like a cannon and Thompson and I dipped the oar deep and strained to pull it even with ourselves, then to do it again and again. Lift, dip, pull. Lift, dip, pull. I could hear men grunting behind me as they strained against their oars and see Carpenter and another man braced against the tiller, fighting to keep the boat headed towards the shoreline.

Sweat stung my eyes and my arms and belly ached from hauling against the oar. Thompson, too, was gasping with the effort, planting his big bare feet on the deck and heaving his body backwards, the sinews in his arms popping out like cords as we fought the clutching current. Then I felt the boat break loose from the pull of the Ohio and the keelboat began to move steadily towards the shore, still heading upstream. Rowing was a mite easier now and I saw that we had moved under a headland jutting out into the river.

Fink was crowing like a rooster as he capered about the foredeck. "We done it, lads, we done it! We're shut o' the Oh-hi-oh now an' we're on the Mississip! Now it's but a hop, skip, an' a jump to Saint Looie an' all o' them juicy whores jest a-waitin' thar

and a-pantin for ye! Waitin' wid open arms! An' open legs, too, I
warrant!"

*   *   *

Mike Fink's idea of a hop, skip, and a jump is not my own, nor that
of any sane man. It was brutal work to haul sixty feet of heavily-
laden keelboat up the Mississippi. The Father of Waters, running
in spring flood, grudged every inch and a snail might have made
swifter progress.

We used every weapon we owned in our battle against the
Mississippi current. If there was the slightest breeze from the
south we tacked across the river, aiming for the calm water that lay
behind each headland that poked out from the shore, then crossing
the river again to do it all over again, zig-zagging back and forth,
rowing crosswise and upwards against the flow, always watching
for snags and floating trees that could have stove in the boat and
drowned us all.

When the wind died and the sail hung useless from the mast, we
poled the boat upstream. I can still feel the butt of that long pole
gouging into my shoulder, as I and a dozen other men shoved the
boat forward a foot at a time, shuffling in a line along the catwalk
towards the stern, then moving back towards the bow and doing it
all over again.

Worst of all was the towline, a rope attached to the top of the
stubby mast, which a score of us employed to pull the boat forward
whilst we trudged on shore or waded in the shallows, clouds of
mosquitoes swarming about, stinging us, swelling our eyes nearly
shut, so that we could barely see the sweating red neck of the man
in front, sometimes up to our necks in muddy water, feet sinking
into the muck on the bottom, shoulders raw from pulling on the
rope. At first I worried about what I might tread on down there in
the muck, but it wasn't long before I really didn't care.

Years before, Ma had given me some books to read that told
about the galley slaves of ancient Rome and I thought about such
things as I fought against the towline. Their work couldn't have
been a great deal worse than what we were doing right then, but

we, except for Micah and maybe me, were free men, not slaves. But then I reflected that perhaps we weren't free at all. Making a living working for other men can make some powerful demands on a man and his freedom. I commenced to wonder, as I sweated and struggled and cursed, what I might do to earn my way in the world and still remain free.

I had generally avoided as much as I could the men we had taken on at Louisville, but working alongside Tuttle Thompson at the oar and hauling on the towline and listening to his wild good humor made me come to like him. For all the slat-sided skinny look of him he was powerfully strong and no matter what came along nothing appeared to dampen his spirits. There was a kindness in him, too, that belied the swagger he put on when he was amongst the other men.

Sometimes when we lay exhausted on the deck after a day at the oars, poling upstream, or on the towline, he would talk of the little farm he owned in Kentucky and how his wife and two children had all died of the cholera three years before. His eyes would close and his voice would soften as he spoke of them and then he would catch himself up and say something outrageous about Fink or Talbot or one of the other men. It had been a spell since I had done any laughing and I came to look forward to my palaver with Tuttle Thompson.

Tuttle was maybe five years older than I was and he had already been to Saint Louis twice before, working on keelboats, since his family died. He said it was as good a way as any to pass the time but he couldn't see any future in it. He allowed that he would rather be shooting squirrels or deer, but there wasn't any future in that, as well, and no cash, either.

He had noticed how Fink and the other two treated me differently from the rest and he asked me what I was doing on the keelboat, since I surely wasn't a riverman and it didn't look to him as if I wanted to become one. I told him how I came to be aboard, naturally not mentioning the matter of Aunt Penny and Pap and

Uncle Ben, and he said it was a crying shame but now it would be just as well to wait until we got to Saint Louis before I tried to change matters. I agreed. I had come this far and I reckoned I might as well get to see Saint Louis. Besides, I had given my word to stay with the boat until then.

ॐ   ॐ   ॐ

There is no way for me to reckon just how many days we rowed and poled and hauled our way up the Mississippi, but at last we tacked our way across to the west side of the river and tied up at Cape Girardeau, an old trading post owned by a most remarkable trader, Louis Lorimier. We arrived in the forenoon of a sunny day and the old man came down to the wharf to greet us, looking downright stately in his quilled and beaded buckskins. Lorimier was surely pushing eighty years, but he stood tall and erect and alert as a hawk. His most remarkable feature was his hair, white as snow but thick and worn in a braid that fell nearly to his heels. His Indian wife stood by his side, dressed in the fashion of eastern white women, and one time I heard her speak to him in what I took to be Shawnee. When he answered her in the same tongue I was sure of it and I made up my mind somehow to ask her if she knew anything of Powatawa and his band.

Lorimier had brought several of his people down to the dock with him and together with our crew we soon had his cargo on the dock and the goods he was shipping to Saint Louis stowed in the cargo box. What he was sending with us was mostly fine furs — fox, mink, otter, muskrat - and I saw the name CHOUTEAU lettered on the bundles. I had heard that name mentioned in talk I overheard amongst Fink, Carpenter, and Talbot, but at the time I had no idea who that might be. Now I reckoned that he must be some kind of fur trader in Saint Louis.

Lorimier, most likely with a trader's sharp eye always out for possible customers, inVited the whole crew up to his post for a drink. Then he announced that there would be horse racing in the afternoon and it was hard to tell which one inspired our men most, free whiskey or the prospect of showing off their knowledge of fast horses.

Tuttle Thompson prided himself on being an excellent judge of horseflesh and corn whiskey, both. He was one of the first off the boat and I watched him trotting up the path to Lorimier's trading house, long arms waving and shirttail flapping, his loud laughter echoing off the water and making everybody smile.

I hung back with Micah and helped him haul fresh drinking water from Lorimier's well to the barrels they kept on the boat. When the barrels were full and with everybody else off the boat, the two of us settled down to work on Micah's reading. He was learning like a house afire, maybe spurred on by thinking about the time to come when I wouldn't be there to teach him. Once he had mastered his letters and learned the sounds they made, I noticed that he commenced to talk more like the book pages he was reading — not too well, but much better than before.

We had been at the schooling for something more than an hour when I noticed a half-scared, half-guilty look come across Micah's face that warned me that Fink was coming. I glanced over my shoulder and saw that Mike Fink and Carpenter were on their way back to the boat and Tuttle Thompson wasn't far behind them. When they stepped across the plank and headed for the cabin, Fink barely nodded and Carpenter stared right through us.

Tuttle's long legs scissored across the dock and he fairly leaped aboard. He brought himself up short in front of us and let a grin slide across his whiskery red face. "Temple, what in the name o' pluperfec' hell are ye still doin' on this damn ol' stinkin' tub? Thought ye'd have your fill of it by naow! The ol' Frenchy's givin' whiskey away up thar an' fixin' to race some hosses, too, an' hyar I find ye consortin' with thish'yere darky!" He bestowed a good-natured grin on Micah and Micah smiled back.

It was obvious that Tuttle Thompson had not let Lorimier's free whiskey go begging. He was weaving slightly as he looked down at us sitting on the cargo box, book pages safely hidden, apparently doing not much of anything.

"Well, Tuttle, I don't rightly know if Fink'll let me off this boat. I can't read his mind and he sure ain't inclined to tell me much."

"Well, hell's fire, Temple! If he ain't said no, I reckon thet's gotta mean yes! C'mon, let's git on up to the post."

Just then Fink stepped out of the cabin. He had his rifle in his hand and his powder horn slung across his chest, bullet pouch and a long knife in a sheath hanging from his belt. He glanced our way and barked, "Hey, you, Buck! Git yer arse ashore! Carp an' me, we aim to be playin' our li'l game! P'raps ye need some remindin'!" He ignored Tuttle and Micah.

Carpenter had appeared behind Fink, his rifle cradled in one arm, his powder horn and bullet pouch dangling from his other hand. Fink growled across the space between us, "C'mon along, then. An' see ye be stickin' close, mind ye."

I was wearing the shirt and britches I had from Talbot, and though I was barefoot, I felt halfway respectable, leastwise not looking like a scarecrow. I stood up and followed them, Tuttle trailing on behind.

At the trading post Tuttle ducked inside and reappeared a moment later carrying two tin cups brimming over with clear white spirits. He shoved one at me and I took it gladly, relishing the rough scald of it as it burned its way down my throat and into my gullet. Now I had never acquired a taste for strong spirits, even though there was certainly enough of it around at home, stilling corn being Pap's main occupation as it was, but there are times when a man needs a drink and this one was certainly long overdue. But even as I gulped and coughed, I kept an eye on Fink and Carpenter hiking out towards a clearing behind the trading post. I drained the cup and laid it aside on the stoop and trotted after Fink and his ever-present companion.

I was already feeling light-headed when Tuttle and I arrived at the clearing. A mob of the roughest men I had ever seen, even counting the bunch at Limestone, milled around a rude race course, a stretched-out circle scraped into the turf that looked to be about half a mile in length. I heard them shouting rude curses and laughing and drinking from earthen jugs or gourd cups. Here and there a fistfight broke out, quickly quashed by the crowd moving between the fighters, most of whom apparently forgot the cause of their disagreement before they managed to find each other again.

Fink and Carpenter, sunshine glinting off their well-oiled rifles, were strolling out to the center of the track, pausing now and then to accept a cup or hoist a jug offered by the ruffians who clustered around them. About then I saw Louis Lorimier and his fine-looking Shawnee wife seated on a bench on a little raised platform at the edge of the track, apparently waiting for Fink's entertainment and the horse racing to commence. The drink that Tuttle had given me must have lent me a passel of dutch courage, for I walked up to them and greeted the wife in Shawnee.

The Shawnee words coming from the mouth of a white-eyes ragamuffin startled her. She leveled a piercing stare at me, her mouth half open, but she said nothing. I plunged on, in English now, fearing that she and Lorimier would have me run off for my rudeness, but they didn't. "Sorry, ma'am. I don't mean to be disrespectful, but you bein' Shawnee and all, I was wondering if you might know the whereabouts of a Shawnee chief name o' Powatawa and his band. They headed out this way from Ohio about a year or so ago and maybe they settled in somewheres hereabouts." I am not sure if I said it just that way, but it was something close to that.

The Indian woman just stared at me, saying nothing, her expression unchanging. Then she turned to Lorimier and spoke to him in a language I didn't understand. He looked thoughtful before he replied and then he said something to her and shrugged his shoulders. She turned back to me and said, "No. No Powatawa. No Shawnee come this way from Ohio, many winters now."

With that she shifted in her chair, her face away from me, and stared straight ahead. Lorimier paid me no mind at all, as if I had been no more than a bothersome mosquito or somesuch nuisance.

I don't know what I had expected to hear, but I was feeling pretty bad about not learning any news of Powatawa and the liquor I had drunk was surely disturbing my judgment. As I turned away I saw Tuttle standing nigh, a smile on his face and a cup of whiskey in his hand. He offered the nearly-full cup to me and I snatched it from him. All the days and weeks of putting up with Fink and his bad treatment and now not finding Powatawa, although I had no good reason to suppose that I would, seemed to crash down on me. I drained the cup to the bottom and handed it back to Tuttle. Then I made my way out to the edge of the race course, my legs feeling somewhat more than a trifle unsteady and my head even more so.

Fink and Carpenter were getting ready to play their game. Fink roared out something and Carpenter waved the crowd away from them. I sidled closer and heard Fink holler, "All right now, hear ye this! Me an' Carp here, we aim to show ye how we does our shootin' up Pennsylvaney way! Stan' back now an' keep yer distance if'n ye don't want a galena pill to cure what ails ye!"

He flipped the big English penny to Carpenter and said in a loud voice, "G'wan, Carp, sky the copper an' I'll call!"

Carpenter spun the coin high in the air and caught it just as Fink called out, "Tails!" Tails it was and Carpenter, without a word or a change in his face, handed his rifle to Talbot, who was standing near. Then he took a full whiskey cup from one of the men at the edge of the crowd and marched out sixty paces and stood facing Mike Fink, the cup balanced on his head, just as he did in Louisville.

Fink wiped the frizzen with his thumb and pressed it down, wet the front sight, and raised his rifle as he called out, "Hold yer noddle steady, Carp, an' don't be spillin' the likker!"

Carpenter stood calm, arms folded across his chest, not a flicker of concern or even interest showing on his face. Fink leveled his rifle and cocked it in one smooth motion. The blast of the charge and the ring of the cup blended in a single sound. Carpenter stood unhurt and unfazed. As the cloud of gray smoke drifted skyward, I could see men crowding around Mike Fink, slapping him on the back and shoulders, and I heard his throaty chortling laugh echoing above their shouts of approval and admiration. For my part, I reckon I admired Carpenter's calm courage more than Fink's marksmanship.

I stayed where I was and after a time I saw Fink coming towards me. The smirk on his face should have warned me, but the whiskey I had drunk had dulled my good judgment. It must have loosened my tongue as well, for when he marched up to me and stood with his hands on his hips and demanded, "How now, Perfessor, what d'ye think o' that?" I replied quite honestly, "Well, sir, if I had my way — if it was my own way, mind ye — Carpenter would've won the toss and he would've missed his mark and he would've blown your damned head off!"

Next thing I knew was Tuttle Thompson leaning over me and saying, "'Bout time ye be comin' 'round. Hosses are fixin' to commence runnin'." When I finally got my eyes focused on his face, he added, "What in pluperfec' hell did ye say to Fink thet he went and walloped ye like thet?"

I mumbled something about how I reckoned it was worth it, but I didn't mumble much, for my jaw was aching something fierce.

Tuttle hauled me to my feet and more or less dragged me along with him through the crowd and up to a paddock where a number of horses were tethered along the fence. As we passed along the line of horses, Tuttle showed off his judgment of racing horseflesh with remarks such as "a leetle too up-an'-down in the pastrens" or "back's plumb too short fer speed" or "sickle-hocked an' puny in the laigs" or "he's got no gaskins a-tall" or "don't like the look o' thet eye, hard to keep 'im runnin' straight" and other such nonsense, or maybe it wasn't.

Men gathered around each horse, currying backs and bellies and little else besides, throwing on saddles and snugging up girths, or just standing back appraising the qualities of the sorriest collection of horsehide I could ever recall seeing. The Shawnees back home would have eaten every last one of them. At last we came to what I reckoned was the least promising specimen of them all, a dark-brown nag with a hide like a hedgehog, its winter coat only half shedded out, long sweat-stiff hair sticking up in tufts all over him, dull eyes, lower lip drooping, ewe-necked and cow-hocked, and a mite shorter than any of the others.

I couldn't tell his age from where I stood, but I reckoned that he had acquired that woebegone patient look from a long lifetime of disappointment.

Tuttle dropped his voice to a confidential tone as he catalogued the virtues of this particular horse. "Lookee now, Temple, this'un's a winner. Jest ye mark my words. They be callin' 'im Whiskey an' he ain't no beauty, thet's a fact, but ol' Whiskey hoss he be a sure-'nough fust-place winner."

I mentioned the ewe-neck that made a body think of a camel, but Tuttle had a ready reply. "Why thet never be no kind o' blemish nohow! Lends 'im balance when he's runnin'."

Whilst I was at it, I pointed out that the horse was cow-hocked, too, well-nigh deformed. Tuttle almost sneered when he replied. "Jest goes to show how leetle y'know 'bout runnin' hosses! Why, jest look how them cow hocks 'low his hinder legs to come 'round on the outside o' the front ones when he runs an' thetaway they give 'im a longer stride 'thout any extry effort! This'un'll go the course 'thout even breathin' hard!"

I realized that Tuttle Thompson had an answer for everything and I had no wish to discourage him. About then a young Indian-looking fellow, nearly as tall as I was and somewhat plump, walked up and commenced brushing the horse's back. Tuttle drew me a step or two away and whispered, "See 'im? Thet be the feller gonna ride 'im."

"Him?" I said, surprised. "He's too big."

"Thet's all ye know, Temple. Thet'ere lad be the ol' Frenchy's gran'boy an' thet be the ol' man's hoss! An' thet ol' man ain't about to run no hoss what cain't win!" He fell silent before he added, "If ye don't know the hosses, bet the rider."

I was still shaking my head in wonder and disbelief when Tuttle caught my arm and dragged me into the crowd, meanwhile calling out, "Got a bet ri'chere! Anybody wanna wager?" and other such invitations. Close up, the local residents were even more fearsome-looking than at a distance. Most sported long, tangled, tobacco-stained beards spread over dirty shirts and long knives and pistols shoved into their belts, some wearing shapeless soft wool-felt hats, others with a kerchief tied around long greasy hair. Most were barefoot and all of them were rank with sweat and strong drink. I doubt there was a sober man amongst the lot and most of them looked like they could wrestle a bear and take pleasure in the opportunity.

As Tuttle threaded his way through the mob, calling out his wish to wager, men would approach him and ask which horse and how much. "Whiskey's his name an' two dollars in silver says he's game fer winnin'! An' last I heard, odds be three-to-one agin 'im, mebbe more, but I'm willin to settle fer three-to-one."

At least a dozen men in that crowd had looked at the sorry brown nag and decided, just as I had, that such a horse would be lucky indeed to make it across the finish line, so Tuttle had no trouble in making a dozen wagers at three-to-one.   Each man showed his money and the deal was made without benefit of a stakes-holder, just a quick hand-shake.

Somebody started blowing on a boat horn and the whole mob flowed towards the starting line, then strung itself out along the track. The race was about to begin.

Tuttle was in high spirits, grinning and rubbing his big hands together as he stretched his long legs into a shambling lope, eager to get to the starting line.   As I trotted to keep up with him, I couldn't help asking, "Tuttle, you just wagered a lot of money. You got that much?"

"Sure," he said and held up two silver dollars.

"But you made a dozen wagers! What if he loses?"

Tuttle grinned before he replied, "He ain't gonna do no sech a thang." He paused and looked thoughtful before he said, "But ef'n he does lose, them fellers'll jist natcherly kill me." He appeared to reflect for a moment before he added, "Mebbe yew, too, seein' as how they likely know ye be hyar with me."

The boat horn blasted once again and we saw the horses backing into a ragged line in front of Lorimier's little platform, some of them fairly dancing and half-rearing in their excitement as their riders fought to calm them. The little brown horse stood quietly on the outside of the track, head hanging down, legs splayed out, looking downright dejected. The Indian lad on his back appeared to tower over him.

A big man wearing a rusty top hat and carrying a pistol in his hand stepped out of the crowd and walked to the outside of the starting line. The riders did their mostly unsuccessful best to keep their horses somehow abreast, tugging on the reins to back them and gigging them forward to get them into formation. The Indian boy sat silent and unmoving, staring straight ahead, a stout club dangling from his right hand.

The man in the topper must have decided right about then that the horses were as close to an even line as they were ever likely to get, for he raised his pistol in the air and fired it off. He must have had it double-charged. Half the horses shied and nearly fell down at the roar of it and the rest of them scrambled to get past them. Only the brown nag appeared undisturbed. He bolted straight ahead, the Indian boy standing in the stirrups, bending low over his neck, heading for the inside of the track, the club dangling unused by his side.

The horses at the starting line finally got themselves untangled and commenced to gallop, straining to close on the little brown horse, who didn't appear to be pushing himself at all. The pack was about three-quarters around the track when a big chestnut passed our Whiskey horse and it wasn't much later that three more horses overtook him, too.

I let out a groan and turned to Tuttle, but he just stood there grinning, intent on the race. As the pack swept towards the start-finish line I could see that most of the horses were running wild-eyed, sweating, and lathered, except for the little brown horse running in the middle of the bunch, hugging the inside, calm and steady and commencing to move to the front, but too late!

I groaned again and turned my eyes away, not wanting to see the finish. Then I felt Tuttle's hand on my shoulder and I looked up to see his face wreathed in a smile as he said, "I reckon I neglected to mention, Temple, this'n's a miler."

The horses pounded past us on their second circuit of the track, the little brown horse slowly edging his way up to each of the leaders and forging ahead of them. In the backstretch he broke out in front, still in that easy gallop, still crawling ahead. At the final turn, the Indian boy stood up and swung that wicked-looking club around his head and the little horse saw it.

You would have thought that critter had turned into a centipede, the way his legs were churning in a pluperfect blur, so fast you couldn't tell which was which, head down and shoulders pumping, streaking across the finish line an easy eight lengths in the lead.

Tuttle Thompson let out a loud guffaw and punched me lightly on the arm. Then he leaped into the crowd, intent, no doubt, on collecting his winnings.

I had nothing better to do, so I wandered over to the finish line. The Indian boy had dismounted and was walking the little brown horse in a wide circle, cooling him out. Old Lorimier was at his side, smiling and slapping him on the shoulder from time to time, chattering away in a language I didn't know. The Indian lad looked as grave as ever.

I stood there enjoying their happiness and feeling good about Tuttle Thompson's good fortune, too, when I felt a plucking at my sleeve. I turned to see Lorimier's wife looking up at me, her face as sober as her grandson's. She spoke directly, with little or no expression on her face or in her voice. "You. You seek a Shawnee man they call Powatawa. I know him not. I will seek him also. You come here one time more. Plenty Shawnee come here. Somebody know him. If Powatawa here, we find."

She turned away, taking the arm of a pretty young woman who might have been her daughter, and walked off, erect and dignified. I called my thanks after her and promised to return when I could.

Lorimier's grandson was leading the little brown horse away and I saw the old man join his wife near the platform where they had watched the race. She took his arm and they walked towards the trading post, looking downright regal, the old man's long white queue swinging gently behind him. The crowd had pretty much drifted away from the race course by then and since I didn't really know anybody anyhow, I set off in search of Tuttle Thompson.

I expected to hear Tuttle before I saw him, so I was more than somewhat surprised when I felt his big hand clap me on the shoulder. I swung about and saw that his big horse-toothed grin was still in place but one of his eyes was fast swelling shut and his cheek was scratched and oozing blood. So were his knuckles. He saw the look on my face and explained, "All but one of 'em paid up prompt an' proper. Last'un, though, he figgered to run off, likely countin' on me havin' to pull out with the boat. Caught 'im in yon

woods, howsomever." He waved towards a line of trees that
bordered the river. "Put up one hell of a fight, fer a fac', but it
done him no good a-tall." He jingled coins in the poke on his belt
and crowed, "Got my money jest the same!" And then, in a
jubilant tone, "I'm rich, Temple, rich!"

We passed the night sprawled on the stoop of the trading post,
backs propped against the wall, backsides resting gingerly on the
splintery planks, Tuttle pulling from time to time at a jug he
purchased with some of his winnings. Now and then he would
offer the jug to me, but I reckoned I had had quite enough of that
popskull to last me for a spell.

All manner of thoughts were going through my mind, about
what Mike Fink might do when I returned to the keelboat and what
I might do if he did, about Saint Louis and what awaited me there,
and what I would do once I got shut of Fink and his bully boys.
Naturally there was no telling about any of it, so I just stared up at
the stars and half-listened to Tuttle Thompson telling me about
what to look for in horses and how to bark a squirrel and other
such valuable lore, until I drifted off to sleep, still sitting propped
up against that wall.

ﾂ   ﾂ   ﾂ

My body felt stiff as a plank when Tuttle shook me awake at dawn.
Somebody was blowing a boat horn and I slowly realized that it
was coming from Fink's keelboat. Tuttle was on his feet and
tugging at me to get up and follow him. "C'mon, Temple, time to
rise up an' shine! Jist a couple more stops an' then it's Sain' Looie
sure'nuff!"

Drowsy as I was I knew it was past time to get a move on. Fink
was likely feeling ugly enough about the day before and holding up
his boat would just make matters a whole lot worse.

We trotted down to the dock and I saw Fink standing on the
tiller deck getting ready to blow his horn once again. He barely
glanced at us as we scrambled aboard, the look on his face
completely unreadable.

It was nearly an hour later when the last of the crew straggled down to the dock and stumbled aboard. Fink was hopping mad and Carpenter and Talbot, who had been out searching for the missing men, were scarcely less irritated, but none of them singled me out to show their displeasure. Fact is, for most of the rest of the trip upriver it was as if all three of them were looking plumb through me and not seeing me at all.

A brisk breeze was blowing from the south when we cast off. Rowing to the far side of the river was easier than it had been. It was just as well, too, for most of the crew was not in what you might call prime condition. Most were pale and bleary-eyed, tousled and shaking from too much drink the night before, but they all put their backs into it and tugged manfully on their oars as we commenced our seemingly endless tacking back and forth, inching the keelboat painfully upriver.

There is no profit in retailing here every jot and tittle of the journey after that. I can't recollect most of it, anyhow, except a sweaty, muscle-aching blur of rowing, poling, and hauling on the towline from dawn to dark, sinking up to our knees in Mississippi muck, and lying exhausted on the deck when we tied up at dusk. Fink mainly showed his dislike of me by rousting me from my resting amongst the crew after a hard day's work and ordering me to help Micah with the cooking chores. Beyond that he said and did little else to me.

Fact is, it pleasured me to work with Micah whilst I helped him with the way he talked, teaching him to say his words like a white man would say them and hearing how he would switch from one way of talking to the other, depending on who was within earshot. Then at night in our cubbyhole in the cargo box he would light a candle nub and we would continue teaching him to read, both of us aware that the learning would soon be at an end.

The last two cargo ports before Saint Louis were Kaskaskia, an Army post on the Illinois side, and Cahokia, which was also in Illinois, where most of the folks spoke French and little or no English and dealt mainly in furs, from what I could tell.

It was after dark and I was leaning on the rail, gazing across the river at the lights of the town that Tuttle had said was Saint Louis, wishing I could sprout wings and fly into it and disappear, when I heard a boot scrape on the deck behind me. I turned and saw that Fink was standing there. Even in the dim light I could make out a smile on his face, but I couldn't be sure what it might mean. You could never be sure of anything with Mike Fink.

I shifted away from the rail and put what I hoped was a safe distance between us. I heard him laugh before he said, "Stand easy, Laddy Buck. I've not come to harm ye. If I had, ye'd be layin' senseless by now." He chuckled to himself before he went on. "No, I've come to tell ye that on the morrow ye'll complete yer bargain. We'll be in Saint Looie an' that's the end of it.

Ye've kept yer word, damn fool that ye are. I'll keep my own an' good riddance to ye!"

As he turned to go he said over his shoulder, "Nex' time, I trust ye'll be a mite more careful about whose boat ye're doin' yer trespassin' on."

With that he walked off and I returned to the rail, thrilled at the thought that this was the last dealing that I would ever have with Mike Fink. I watched the muddy, snag-strewn river rolling on to some unknown wherever. Which was all I knew about what I might be doing next.

Chapter III
St. Louis

I reckon that final morning was the only time in my life that I took the least mite of pleasure from pulling on an oar. Tuttle Thompson and I stood side by side, bare feet planted against the deck, grunting and tugging for all we were worth against the might of the Mississippi, forcing the keelboat upstream of the dock on the Missouri side so that we could drift into position to tie up. I could hear men all around us straining at their oars, breath whistling through clenched teeth as we all struggled to yank the boat inch by inch through the muddy water boiling at the bow. Now and then their groans would be pierced by a rippling cackle of high-pitched laughter when somebody would call out some remark about whores and whiskey waiting in Saint Looie Town and you could feel the boat lurch forward just a little faster as the men redoubled their efforts at the oars.

Talbot stood at the mast, lines in hand, trying to snare in the little square sail whatever breeze might push us forward, and Carpenter strode up and down the cargo box, barking orders to the rowers on this or that side to ship oars or dig deep in order to slide the big boat into position at the dock. Fink was at the tiller, mostly silent, his face a mask of concentration, intent, I reckon, on showing whoever might be watching from shore what a master boatman he was.

We docked at last, the long keelboat tugging and shuddering like a nervous horse against the ropes secured to the massive pilings that supported the wharf, the hull bumping gently against the planks as the Mississippi rushed past on its southward journey.

You would have thought the keelboat had caught on fire, the way the crew threw themselves into unloading the cargo, and I was as eager as the rest, most likely more so, to get that chore behind us. Soon the wharf was stacked high with crates and chests, casks, kegs, barrels, and bales and boxes bound for Saint Louis and I saw that the cargo box was completely empty, except for one part of it that was always shut up tight with a big rusty padlock. I had never seen it opened.

That was most likely one of the happiest days that I will ever see in my life, except for the pain I felt at bidding farewell to Micah. I felt downright guilty for being so happy at being free again, knowing the while that he could be neither.

Fink was paying off the crew when I crawled into the cubbyhole to change into the clothes Talbot had given me. I was pondering whether I should take my old rags along with me and deciding that I wouldn't when Micah slipped through the hatch and crouched beside me. His face in the dim light betrayed a mixture of grief and loving friendship and his voice was husky when he said, "Marse — Ah mean t'say Tempa, Ah gwine t'miss seein' ya sumpin' scan'lous an' dat's a fac', but dis ol' Micah he be plumb happy dat you, leas'away, be gittin' out o' dis ol' tub an' gwine home t'yo' kin."

He bowed his head and I could see his thin shoulders shaking and now and then I heard him sob. I was feeling more than somewhat choked up myself by then and I said something like, "Micah, I don't know what I can do to help you right now. Nor my own self, either. But I promise you on all that's holy, I'll do whatever I can whenever I can."

He looked up at me then and I could see tear streaks on his cheeks, but his eyes were alive and almost dancing. He grinned before he said, "Dass awright, Tempa. You awready he'p me plenty, more'n enuf. Ah kin read now!" His grin broadened and he came near to laughing. "Not so good, but Ah kin read! Ah'll nevah quit! You gwine t'see, Tempa, ol' Micah he gwine make ya proud!" He chuckled, mostly to himself. "Don' know how. Don' know when, but you gwine be proud o' yo' job o' learnin' Micah! Ah kin read! You don' own nuthin' yo'ownse'f, but you gib me dat! Ah kin read!"

It was true. I never did have anything to give him, but now he could read somewhat and scrawl out his letters and cipher a little. I knew he was smart and given half a chance, slave or not, he would go on to something better from there. Precisely what and where and how, I hadn't any idea.

I heard moccasins padding towards us and a moment later Tuttle Thompson knelt down and peered in at us through the hatchway. "Thar ye be, Temple! Ready to go?" A grin split his whiskery face. "C'mon, lad. Shake a leg! Time to be gittin' a move on an' git your arse off o' thi'shere slop bucket!"

He was right and I knew it. I leaned across to Micah and pulled him to my chest. It was the first time in all my life that I had ever hugged a man, besides Powatawa, but it seemed to me to be the proper thing to do. I blurted out some nonsense, such as, "Take care, Micah. We'll be meetin' up again sometime." Whatever it was that I said, he understood what I meant and he squeezed my arms in a silent farewell. The feel of his hands on my arms made me recollect my goodbyes with the Shawnees and I wondered then if I would ever see them or Micah again.

Tuttle was getting impatient. "C'mon naow, Temple. I ain't leavin' without ye! No tellin' what sorta evil ol' Fink'll be hatchin' up. It's long past time we be goin'!"

That did it. I scuttled through the hatchway and rolled onto my bare feet, trotting towards the gangplank and the dock, never stopping until I reached the far end of the wharf, where I could feel honest landlubberly dirt between my toes.

Tuttle caught up with me there, his powder horn and bedroll slung criss-cross from his shoulders, deer rifle in one hand and a pair of moccasins dangling from the other. He swung the moccasins towards me and said, "Hyar ye go! They likely be a mite big for ye, but ye cain't be goin' about barefoot in a highfalutin town like Sain' Looie. 'Tain't proper!"

I thanked him as I took the moccasins and slipped them on. They were indeed much too big for me and considerably worn at that, but just being shod made me feel proper and somehow respectable, poorly clad as I might be otherwise.

Tuttle was already heading away from the wharf and into the fringe of buildings at the edge of the town. Before I followed him I turned and looked back at the boat. Fink still stood on the tiller deck, Talbot and Carpenter nearby, a little cluster of men looking up at him from the cargo deck. They were too far away for me to hear what was being said, but Mike Fink most surely must be doing all the talking.   I breathed a silent prayer to I'm not altogether sure just who and I promised myself that this would be the last traffic I would ever have with Mike Fink or with keelboats either.

☙   ☙   ☙

When I caught up with Tuttle he was swinging along briskly, like a man who knows precisely where he's going. He was several inches taller than I and as I tried to match my stride to his I came to realize that he was mostly legs. I had leaned out and muscled up considerably from all the heavy work I did on the keelboat, but it had been a long time since I had done any amount of walking and I was hard-pressed to keep abreast of him.

We hiked through muddy streets crammed with more stores and workshops than I would have thought that a single town could hold, mercantiles and fur sheds, harness and saddle makers, smithies and farriers, apothecaries and drapers' shops, gunsmiths, bootmakers, tailors and dressmakers, and a power of dramshops sprinkled throughout the lot like raisins on a Christmas tart. The roadway fairly boiled with people, blue-coated soldiers and rough-looking men in hickory shirts and torn britches, others wearing buckskins and fur caps and carrying rifles, young men and boys with slicked-down hair and black bombazine sleeves over their white shirts scurrying from one doorway to another, dignified gentlemen sporting beaver toppers, silk cravats, and gold-knobbed walking sticks, fine ladies mincing around puddles and clutching their skirts away from the mud, kids of all sizes and ages, dressed to the nines or some just barely covered, a variety of Negroes, most in rags, a few dressed like gentlemen with shopping baskets on their arm, and Indians draped in gaudy, tattered blankets slumped against storefronts, drunk or sleeping or both, all of us scattering like startled quail whenever heavily-laden wagons drawn by sweating, lathered teams squeaked and clattered and rumbled through the mob, the teamsters' warning curses well-nigh lost in a bedlam of voices and noisy confusion.

Tuttle seemed hardly to notice all of those wondrous sights as he trudged onward, chin held high, jutting like a prow, eyes fixed straight ahead, half a smile curling his lips. I was near to trotting just to stay up with him and finally I asked, "Where're we goin', Tuttle? You lose something around here?'

He halted then and his smile broadened, "Why, Temple, di'n't I mention? We be headed for the Veed Poach an' the sooner we be gittin' thar the better. I been buildin' one hellacious thirst this long while."

I knew no French at all at that time of my life, so the name meant nothing to me. It was only later that I learned that Vide Poche meant Empty Pocket in the French tongue and referred to a particularly seamy section of Saint Louis. It also most likely described the lack of wealth of its inhabitants, as well as most of its visitors after soon after their arrival there.

Tuttle started off again and as I trotted at his side I saw from between the buildings, high on the hills beyond, broad green lawns dotted with shade trees and sliced by drives sloping up to houses that looked to me like the fairy palaces Ma had told me about in her stories, glistening white in the sunshine, their tall pillars stretching up to two and even three storeys above wide verandahs. Tuttle acted like he didn't even see them nor to care if he did. He just kept trudging on like a man who knows precisely where he means to go.

The road forked and Tuttle led me down a steep and twisting little lane that threaded its way through a tangle of rude wooden buildings that bordered the river. The people I saw there looked to be a great deal harder than those I had seen in the upper part of town, their faces closed like shuttered windows. Sunlight was dim here and river smells mingled with the odor of rotting meat and vegetables and bones that littered the narrow alleyways. Even the slat-ribbed dogs and mangy cats wore a wary look.

Tuttle halted and stood still, sniffing the air like a critter that had finally found its prey, before he announced, "Hyar we be, Temple lad. This'll be the Veed Poach."

Before I could reply he ducked through a low doorway and disappeared into the gloom beyond it. I followed him inside and when my eyes grew accustomed to the darkness I found myself in a long room with a low ceiling, lighted by a few flickering candles and shafts of feeble gray sunshine that filtered through slits chopped through the outer walls. Tuttle was already standing in front of a counter of rough planks propped on a couple of large casks, chatting in a friendly way with a stout, baldheaded, one-eyed man who appeared to be the proprietor of this particular den of iniquity. Ma had warned me about dens of iniquity and told me to avoid them. And though I didn't see any iniquity going on right then and wasn't altogether sure just what it was, anyway, I reckoned this would be a likely place to find it.

Tuttle waved me over to where he was and I hastened to join him, bumping my way amongst rude plank tables and benches that cluttered the hard-packed dirt floor. Here and there about the room, I could see several knots of three or four commonly-dressed men seated at the tables, talking in low tones and drinking what I supposed was whiskey from bottles and jugs. In one corner was a ragged circle of a half-dozen or so bearded, leather-clad men sprawled on the floor, playing at cards, a whiskey jug in their midst. Now and then one of them would say something in a tongue I didn't know and the rest would burst into loud guffaws.

When I got to the counter Tuttle shoved a cup of what I took to be whiskey towards me and said, "Drink up, Temple, an' meet Shanghai. This be his place o' bizness, naow thet he ain't aimin' to go to sea no more." I looked to the proprietor, expecting to see a welcoming smile, but his whiskery face remained as blank as a barn wall. Tuttle went on, "Yep, ol' Shanghai hyar he been jest about ever' place wu'th seein'. He been to China an' France an' gawd-knows-whar-else, but he says naow he be shet of all o' thet nowadays, 'cause he plumb found a home ri'chere in the Veed Poach. Ain't it so, Shanghai?"

It was plain that I would have to take Tuttle's word for it, for Shanghai said nothing. Only his single eye straying over the room from time to time showed that he was alive and it betrayed no more of what he was thinking than did the black patch that covered the other one.

Tuttle slid his cup towards Shanghai and motioned for him to fill it again. Then he lifted it high and gestured for a toast. "We'll drink to Sain' Looie, Temple!" He raised his voice to a shout. "To Sain' Looie an' freedom an' fer all tyrants bein' double goddamned to hell!"

Recalling Fink, I found no fault with drinking to any of those sentiments. I raised my cup and gulped a mouthful of what felt like liquid fire. I spat out all of it that I could and bowed my head in a fit of coughing before I sputtered out, "My God, Tuttle! What in hell was that?"

"Why, it's rum, lad! Ol' Shanghai's own makin's, ain't it, Shanghai?" Tuttle finished off what remained in his cup.

The one-eyed man behind the plank broke his silence then. He uttered a single word. "*Absinthe.*"

Tuttle looked into his cup and replied, "Yer damn right it's absent! Plumb empty! Fill 'er up agin!" He threw a few coins onto the plank and Shanghai poured the cup full again. I asked for whiskey and he filled a fresh cup for me, which I continued to sip while Tuttle proceeded to get thoroughly drunk on Shanghai's hellish concoction. Rum or *Absinthe* or bottled fire, whatsoever they might call it, it was surely no drink for me.

At last Tuttle leaned his back against the counter and peered owlishly around the dimly-lit room. The French fur traders, for that is what Tuttle said they were, still shuffled cards and smacked them on the earthen floor, laughing and drinking the while, every so often singing out a line or two of some ditty that I took to be French. Most of the other men, rivermen and stevedores, according to Tuttle, had drifted out and the place was nearly deserted.

Tuttle squinted at the empty tables and announced, "This ol' hole be dead enough fer undertakin'! Ain't no wimmen nohow! Ain't hardly nobody else hereabouts, neither! Time we go, Temple!" He started for the door, dragging his rifle beside him, weaving more than somewhat but staying on his feet.

I followed him into the street and saw that it was already dark. Tuttle stood tall, swaying like a poplar in the wind, his eyes scanning the street ahead. Here and there yellow light splashed through open doorways and I could hear fiddles scraping, mixed with high-pitched laughter of women and the gruff voices of men. Clusters of three or four men together and now and then painted women alone or in pairs roamed along the walls of ramshackle buildings on either side of the street before they disappeared down narrow alleyways on the right and left.

Tuttle straightened his long, lank frame and squared his shoulders like a man who had made up his mind. He turned back to me and called out, "Temple, we need to be goin' to Madam Matilda's an' thet's a sartin fact!" Saying not another word, he loped on up the street and there was nothing else for me to do but trot after him.

I realized that Tuttle wasn't nearly as drunk as I had thought, for he led me through one narrow alley after another, burrowing ever deeper into the maze they called the Vide Poche, until I was sure that I could never find my way out again. Then he halted abruptly in a puddle of lamplight spilling through an open door. Inside I could hear screechy music and women laughing. Without turning around he called out to me, "Thi'shere be the place, Temple! Madam Matilda's!"

A big Negro halted us at the door and I heard Tuttle say, "Well, you jest g'wan an' tell 'er it be Tuttle Thompson an' I be a-rarin'!"

A moment later a very large woman, her face all powdered and painted and her bosom nigh bursting her shiny black dress, shouldered the Negro aside and planted herself in front of Tuttle, a thin smile on her lips but not in her hard black eyes. "Tootle, *bienvenue!* Eet been long times we 'ave not feasted ze eyes on you." I didn't know much at the time, but her eyes did indeed look hungry. Then they narrowed when she asked, "You 'ave of the *monnaie*, Tootle?"

Tuttle laughed aloud and dragged his poke from under his belt. He jingled it next to her ear and her smile broadened instantly. "Oh, but yes, my leetle Tootle, mon vieux, you are welcome 'ere always! Come, my leetle cabbage! For what you are standing yourself at the door?" She grabbed his arm and dragged him inside, his rifle trailing from one hand, his poke clutched in the other. The big Negro took a step backwards and I followed them. Madame Mathilde, for that is what I learned she called herself, was pushing Tuttle into a chair at a small table when I caught up with them.

Tuttle looked up at me and grinned, his eyes bright with pleasure and strong drink. "Temple, meet Matilda! She runs the bes' damn whorehouse in the Veed Poach! Mebbe all o' Sain' Looie! I dunno. I ain't tried all of 'em yet!"

I was shocked at his language in front of a lady, but Madame Mathilde just ran her eyes over me as if she meant to buy me for beef. Most likely she recalled Tuttle's jingling poke about then, for she gave me a quick, cold smile and dragged up a chair for me and then a couple more. She leaned down then and gave Tuttle a quick hug before she moved off, calling out in French and snapping her fingers. Faster than a body could expect, two women, both of them a lot younger than Mathilde but neither one any prettier, slid into the empty chairs at our table, each of them bringing with her a bottle and a couple of real glasses. They poured the glasses full for all four of us and commenced talking a mile a minute, mostly to Tuttle, which I didn't mind at all, since I could barely make out their Frenchified talk above the fiddle music and the palaver all around us. Besides, you couldn't blame them. Tuttle had all the money.

Whilst I sipped at my glass of whiskey, which appeared to stay brimful, I studied the women and took in what I could see of the noisy room in which we sat. I reckoned both women had been sort of pretty once, but now their skin had a puffy, fish-belly look, what you could see of it under layers of cracked powder and rouge and dark paint around their eyes, like sunshine was a stranger to them. They positively clanked with gaudy necklaces and huge finger-rings and bangles and dangling eardrops flashing in the lamplight. Wrinkles were only half-hidden under caked-on powder on throats and blue-veined bosoms, nearly bare and ready to fall out of flimsy dresses, which they propped on the table as they leaned in towards

Tuttle, who was paying all four of those items no small amount of attention. But I wasn't and I wondered why not.

Ma had warned me away from fleshpots, too, and even if I couldn't be precisely sure what a fleshpot was, I reckoned I was most likely sitting in one right now. Considering the flesh being offered, howsomever, I reckoned I had as lief pass on it.

Finally Tuttle half-rose out of his chair and declared, "Temple, I be horny as hell! Never been hornier! Cain't wait no longer! Choose yore pick o' these yere beauties and we'll go up them stairs an' git oursel's laid!"

I told him I didn't feel altogether right about it just then and, drunk though he was, Tuttle appeared to understand. His eyes were dancing and his whiskered face was flushed beet-red as he said, "Well, don't ye fret none a-tall, m'friend. I'll jest take 'em both!" He started away from the table, a woman under either arm, then turned back to say, "Jest set right thar an' he'p yorese'f to the booze. Ye kin expec' me when ye see me!"

I did as I was told. The bottles were half-full and the whiskey, raw as it was, tasted good on my tongue and warm in my belly. I kept on drinking, slowly but steadily, feeling happy about being free of Mike Fink, and letting my mind roam back to Whynot, thinking of Ma and Sarah and Powatawa, Uncle Ben and Aunt Penny, my horse Kumskaka, and even Pap and Jacob Staples's store. Half a dozen times one or another of Mathilde's ladies drifted by the table and offered to join me, but I just smiled and waved them all away. It felt good just to sit there and sip whiskey and watch the shapes and colors of the changing crowd and listen to the Negroes playing music and tinny laughter and loud talk in tongues I mostly couldn't understand, until I wasn't watching or hearing much of anything at all.

఼   ఼   ఼

I woke up on a hard wooden bench, my head on Tuttle's bedroll and his rifle and powder horn gouging my side. Sunshine streaming through an open doorway stung my eyes and I squinted through half-closed lids to see where I was. The crowded, noisy room of the night before was deserted and the big Negro was sweeping the floor. Madame Mathilde, wearing a faded wrapper, her hair tied up in a bandanna, was perched on a high stool at the counter, scratching with a quill in a big ledger book. She looked up when she heard me turn over and fixed her black eyes on me in a long, appraising stare, before she cackled, "So! Ze leetle rat awakens himself! No more dreams, hein?"

I nodded and rolled off the bench, then stood half-crouching, wondering how I might ask her which way to go. She understood and waved me towards a back door.

I found the outhouse in a small, well-kept garden behind the establishment and when I emerged I almost ran over one of Madame Mathilde's ladies. She stepped back and smiled before she asked, "You are ze friend of Tootle, hein?"

I smiled back at her and nodded and then I asked, "Do you know where he's at? Tuttle, is he all right?"

She laughed gaily and rolled her eyes towards the upper storey of the house. "Oh, 'e ees well. 'E is ver' well! 'E ees, 'ow you say, too well! Truly, I 'ave nevair seen Tootle quite like zis! Nevair!" She laughed again and then she ran back inside the house.

When I got back to the main room Madame Mathilde was sitting at a table, sipping her coffee. She waved me into a chair at the table and poured a cup for me. "I t'eenk you 'ave need of ze *café*, pair'aps, leetle rat, *hein*?" She rolled her eyes. "Too much of ze veeskey for you yesterday night, *hein*?"

I allowed that she was more than somewhat right about that and drained my cup in a single gulp. Mathilde poured me another and without turning around she snapped her fingers and called out, "*Café complet!*" A moment later the big Negro brought a tray loaded with a steaming coffee pot, warm milk, a mountain of rolls, butter, and little stone pots of preserves. Mathilde jerked her head towards the food and said, "Eat! Eat! You 'ave need to eat!" I fell to with more enthusiasm than I had ever been able to muster for the rough fare on Fink's keelboat.

Mathilde helped herself and the two of us munched away in silence, until I couldn't contain either any more breakfast or my concern about Tuttle's whereabouts. I waited until she had poured herself and me still another cup of coffee and milk and lighted a slim cheroot for herself, blowing out a cloud of smoke with obvious satisfaction. Then I asked, "Excuse me, ma'am, but what's happened to Tuttle? Is he all right?"

Her laughter burst out like a rifle shot and she kept onlaughing until her cheeks were running with tears. She dabbed at her eyes with her napkin and then she replied, "Ah, *oui*, Tootle ees, 'ow you say, all right. Truly! 'E ees *fou*! 'Ow you say, crazy! Tootle ees *formidable*! Een jus' one night Tootle 'ave bed all my leetle *pigeons*! Some of zem two-t'ree times! 'E continue even now!" Laughter overtook her again and it was a full minute before she could go on. She looked at me inquiringly and asked, "What ees eet zat eet ees zat Tootle eat before you come 'ere? Or drink, pair'aps?"

I told her that the two of us had eaten hardly anything the day before and then I recollected the fiery rum Tuttle had been drinking like water at Shanghai's. "He called it somethin' like 'absent,' as I recall."

"Aha! *Absinthe*! And so much!" She burst out laughing, her fat rolling and shaking inside her wrapper, dabbing at her eyes, until her face settled into a wicked smile. "Now I comprehend! So zat ees 'ow, zat ees ze reason Tootle 'e become like a 'orse, *un cheval, un étalon, un éléphant terrible!*"

Mathilde never did explain why and how Tuttle had suddenly become a man among men. She just sat there chuckling to herself until a fearsome racket erupted above us. I looked up to see Tuttle Thompson chasing a naked woman along the balcony. He was naked, too, and when she ran into a room and slammed the door, he stopped and turned and saw us looking up at him. His face was flushed and he appeared to be somewhat leaner than he had been. He dropped one hand over his private parts before he called down to us. "Mornin', Matilda! Mornin', Temple! See ye made it through awright. I be what ye might call sorta occupied right naow, as ye kin see. I'll ketch up with ye arterwhile."

Tuttle turned his back on us and commenced pounding on the door and I stood up and thanked Madame Mathilde for the breakfast.   She was laughing wildly again and calling out something in French, most likely asking for volunteers.

There wasn't anything for me to do around there and it didn't appear that Tuttle would be joining me soon, so I left his rifle and possibles with Madame Mathilde and strolled out to see the sights of Saint Louis.

The sun showed that it was well past noon, but I had nothing better to do than to find my way out of the Vide Poche and then up to the main part of town, keeping track of landmarks the while, so that I could retrace my steps to Madame Mathilde's. I wandered here and there for a time, stopping now and then to look into saddle shops, to chat for a spell with a gunsmith, or just to stand in the roadway and soak up the marvel that was Saint Louis, a wondrous place for a boy raised up in Whynot. I would not have been at all surprised to meet fairy kings and queens.

My meandering took me by chance back to the riverfront and I found myself looking down at the wharf where Fink's keelboat was moored.   The deck was deserted.   Nothing moved anywhere aboard, but I noticed a squad of blue-uniformed soldiers patrolling the dock around the boat.

I was curious about the soldiers and the deserted keelboat and wondering, too, if it all had anything to do with the cargo hatch that was never unlocked, when a rough hand grabbed my shoulder and swung me around to face the cold blue eyes of Mike Fink. Carpenter and Talbot stood on either side of him, flanking me, so I knew that it would do no good to run, even if I could.

Fink wore the same sneering look on his face that he usually did. It matched his voice when he said, "Lookee here, boys! The perfessor's come back fer a visit!" Then to me, "Pinin' fer us, are ye?   Feelin' lonesome fer us, Buck?   Thought you'd'a had yer bellyful o' keelboatin' by now!"

I shrugged his hand off my shoulder and stared at him before I said, "You're damned right I have! I kept my word to you — just why I did, I'll never know — but it's over now. Just you let me go and I'll be givin' you no trouble."

His laugh put me in mind of a barking dog. "Trouble is it? An' what kind o' trouble d'ye think ye'd ever be causin' Mike Fink, ye scrawny li'l river rat?" He dropped his right hand to his side and I braced myself to duck his punch. Then his eyes went about halfway blank, as if he were running an idea through his head. He caught my arm once more and jerked his head as a signal to Carpenter and Talbot, telling them to follow, and started walking away from the river, dragging me along with him.

He explained himself as I stumbled along beside him. "Come along, Perfessor, an' step lively. I've a task for ye. Ye kin read, I know that — an' write yer name, too, I warrant. I needs ye fer a witness. Chouteau sez we gotta have a witness of our own. It'll be takin' but a mite o' time an' then I'll be lettin' ye go on yer way fer good an' be damned."

There was nothing else in it but to do as he said, so I nodded my agreement and Fink turned loose my arm. We hadn't walked very far at all when we turned in at a big red-brick building, two storeys high. A big brightly-painted sign over one large double-doored entrance proclaimed *Berthold et Chouteau et Cie., Maison de Commerce.* We went on to a smaller door, where a small brass plaque on the wall beside the door read *Berthold et Chouteau, Commerçants.* Fink shouldered his way through the doorway and I followed him, Talbot and Carpenter trailing behind.

Inside the building the light was dim and a dozen or more clerks were perched on stools, scribbling with quills in big ledger books or on papers that littered their work tables. All was quiet save for the sound of pens scratching on paper and parchment and here and there a muffled cough. From somewhere beyond the room in which we were standing I could hear a buzz of voices in the mercantile and smell the unmistakable odor of cured furs mingled with a hundred other aromas of goods stored in the warehouse — oiled leather and new rope and a power of spices, corn and wheat flour and oil for cooking, coffee beans roasting and tea and the sharp fragrance of cheeses and smoked and salted meats, whale oil for lamps and for keeping guns clean of rust — smells that came from farm and forest land nearby and of goods that had been carried here on ships from faraway lands all over the world. Familiar smells that I had learned as a boy in Staples's store, but here so many more.

One of the clerks slipped off his stool and approached us, his eyes questioning our purpose in being there and looking none too approving of whatever that reason might be.

Fink shattered the quiet of the room when he barked, "Tell Chouteau Mike Fink's here! An' be quick about it!"

The clerk retreated and disappeared through a doorway at the far end of the room. A minute or two later a man carrying some papers in his hand emerged and walked towards us, the clerk following at his heels. The man was tall, black-haired and black-eyed, and as he approached I somehow knew that here was a man who was used to getting his own way, no matter what.

Fink's manner visibly softened into something like courtesy as he stepped forward, his hand outstretched. Pierre Chouteau, le Cadet, for that is who he was, halted and bowed slightly, coldly, I would say, but he didn't shake Fink's hand. Fink dropped his hand and tried to recover his customary bluster as he said loudly, "How d'ye do, Mister Chouteau. We got bizness to do. Let's be gittin' to it."

Chouteau nodded and when he spoke his English was good, but with a strong French flavor. "Yes, M'sieu Feenk. I believe the papers are in order." I gathered from that remark that Fink and Chouteau had already settled the details of whatever business they were about to complete that day. Chouteau walked behind a counter and spread out the papers he had carried from his room. An inkstand and quills stood on the counter.

Chouteau selected one of the papers and handed it to Fink, who, for all his braying about how useless reading was, was more than somewhat handy at it. Whilst he pored over the paper, pursing his lips and pushing his finger over the lines, his two bully-boys and I stood back, saying nothing. At last Fink looked up and crooked his finger at me, motioning me to join him at the counter. Whilst I stood beside him he pointed at words and phrases here and there on the paper and told me to tell them what they meant to me, which I did as well as I could.

What I saw on that paper truly amazed me. Mike Fink was selling out! Everything! Even his treasured keelboat. All sorts of items were written there on the heavy parchment — large sums of cash, various goods and gear, and one entry that was listed simply as "Mdse" with a big number next to it. Then I read an entry that made my gorge rise. Fink was selling Micah, too. I glanced at the other papers strewn on the counter and saw a heavy yellow parchment that bore a black stripe across one corner and I knew then, for sure, the business Fink had concluded in Louisville. The fat man with the green cravat had forged an ownership paper on Micah. Now Fink was selling him to Chouteau.

For some reason they were leaving all their money with Pierre Chouteau, to be collected at a later time. Just when, the paper didn't say. I don't recall the precise amounts of money assigned to each item listed there, not even Micah's price, but it all added up to what appeared to me to be a king's ransom, more money than I imagined any one man could own by himself. Fact is, I saw that the three of them, described there only as the undersigned, owned equal shares in the whole shebang and if one of them died before they collected their money from Chouteau, his share went to the other two, or just one of them if two of them died. There was no mention of heirs. I reckoned they hadn't any.

When Fink finished reading through the paper he grunted what I reckon was his approval and motioned Talbot and Carpenter to come to the counter. I stepped back and waited while each of the three, in turn, took up a quill and scratched his name on four copies of the document. Fink signed first, then Carpenter, and Talbot was last. After Fink put aside the quill, he commenced telling something to Chouteau, not paying any mind to the other two, but when he saw that Talbot had laid down the pen, he snapped his fingers at me and waved me up to the counter. He shoved the papers at me and snarled, "Here, Perfessor! Write yer name right there, where it says Witness!" "An' be quick about it!" Then he turned away to face Pierre Chouteau.

I had shuffled the papers into a stack and dipped the quill into the inkpot before I saw that Talbot had made his mark where I was supposed to sign as witness. I riffled the pages sidewise and saw that he had made his mark in the same place on all four copies. My first thought was something like childish satisfaction on learning that Talbot the arrogant bully didn't know how to read nor even how to sign his name. Then it occurred to me that the only place left for me to sign was his. When I tried to call Fink's attention to Talbot's error, he just growled at me over his shoulder and I thought better of disturbing him just then. Instead, I dipped the quill again and wrote my name, Temple Buck, as bold as ye please, right under Carpenter's, on all four copies. Then I backed off from the counter. I had learned sometime earlier that it was not wise to stand too close to Mike Fink for very long.

When Chouteau saw me step away, he left Fink and picked up the papers. He glanced at each one, making sure that all four copies had been signed. Then he signed them all himself and dusted them with powder to set the ink.

Whilst I waited for Chouteau to hand a copy of the agreement to each of the three bullies, I was hoping that none of them would notice where I had signed my name, leastaways until I got free of them. I knew that Fink, by his own words, hated reading anything, no matter what, and I had never seen Carpenter with a book. I wasn't concerned about Talbot, for now I knew that he couldn't read anything at all.

Before he handed over the copies, Chouteau slipped each one into an oilskin pouch and sealed each one for protection, as such valuable documents warranted. I breathed a sigh of relief.

As we prepared to leave, Pierre Chouteau, standing tall and straight behind the counter, said to us, "*Merci, M'sieu* Feenk, *M'sieu* Charpentier, *M'sieu* Bock. Eet 'as been *mon plaisir.*" I noticed that he didn't mention Talbot, but then, he couldn't know how to pronounce Talbot's mark.

Outdoors in the roadway I prepared to hike off, but Fink grabbed my arm again. "Hold on, Laddy Buck! I got jes' one more thing to ask ye. Dependin' on what ye say, ye kin go to hell fer all I give a good goddamn or mebbe I'll be sendin' ye there meself!" Naturally I thought right then that Fink had, after all, seen where I signed the papers. I looked for a place to run, but Talbot and Carpenter still blocked my way. Fink turned to them and said, "We'll be goin' on to Lucy's. This be thirsty work!" Without waiting for a reply, he yanked my arm and all four of us set off in the direction of the Vide Poche.

Just before we came to the road that turned down to the Vide Poche, Fink stopped in front of what looked to be just another big red-brick house. Then, still pulling me along, he walked up to the entrance and rapped loudly on the door.

The door swung open and I beheld a tall, square-shouldered Negro, his head completely shaved, wearing the clothes of a gentleman, but dandified, everything, save his ruffled white shirt, in eye-scalding colors fit to pop your eyes. Comical as you might think he looked, he didn't. There was not a trace of a smile on his face when he said, "Y'all wait heah." He pulled on a cord that hung inside the doorway and settled back as if he were waiting for something, his right hand snugged under his bright green coat.

Oddly, Fink said nothing. He just waited with the rest of us. A minute or two later there appeared behind the Negro one of the prettiest women I had ever seen. I shall never forget how she looked right then. She was slim and neither short nor tall. I couldn't guess her age, but she looked to be older than a girl and younger than the authority in her manner would lead you to expect. Her hair, piled high in ringlets, was dark, nearly black, and her dark eyes fairly smoldered against her buttery skin. She wore a bright corn-yellow dress, ruffled and tucked all about and cut low enough in front to make me blush.

She wasn't smiling as her eyes swept over the four of us. The big Negro spoke to us first. "This's Madame Lucette and this's her house." Then he turned to the woman and said, "This'n's Mike Fink. Don' know the others, leas' not the names." He looked to me and added, "This'n I don' know nohow."

It appeared to me that her jaw firmed up somewhat before she said, "Ah, Feenk, *le bravache*, 'ow you say, ze bully!" I turned my head away from Fink and smiled and she saw me do it. She truly knew what he was. She went on, "Ah, I recall you now, Feenk. You love ze fighting, *hein*? But not 'ere, nevair in zis 'ouse. You do so 'ere and 'ere you will do ze dying. Better you go on to Vide Poche.

If I permit you to enter you will conduct yourself as a man of good manner, a gentleman, or you will leave, forevair." She looked over the rest of us, her eyes resting on me a little longer, I thought, than the others, before she added, "Forevair!. All of you."

Mike Fink mumbled something that sounded surprisingly apologetic and reassuring and he actually took off his cap as we filed inside under the disapproving eyes of the tall Negro, who never removed his hand from under his coat. Madame Lucette led the way into a large room and waved us to a table in a corner before she disappeared through a doorway at the far end. Fink sat himself down and jerked his thumb at the chair beside him, telling me to sit there.

A Negro waiter appeared as if by magic and Fink ordered two bottles of whiskey before he lapsed into a brooding silence.

Whilst we waited for the waiter to return I was able to look around the room. It appeared to me like it had been plucked right out of a fairy tale. Whatever windows there might have been were draped with rich red velvet hangings that dropped all the way to deep woolen carpets with curious designs, covering the floor from one end to the other. A rainbow of painted pictures festooned the walls and all the tables were covered in white napery and sparkled with crystal candlesticks and glasses that reflected the light from what I reckoned must be a thousand candles burning in a huge chandelier hanging from the high ceiling. Four or five Negroes with fiddles large and small, on a little deck raised off the floor in a far corner, were playing sweet soft music of a kind I had never heard before. Finely dressed gentlemen were drinking and talking quietly at their tables on a mezzanine at the top of a wide wooden staircase. Here and there, upstairs and down, pretty women in colorful dresses, bare shoulders gleaming in the soft candlelight, sat with men at tables. It was truly a wondrous sight.

I noticed, too, that we were seated as far away from the other patrons as the confines of the room permitted, which didn't surprise me at all, considering Mike Fink's reputation and the sorry look of the four of us, especially next to the quality folks thereabouts. All three bullies were wearing their Sunday Best, which was still only the rough style of river boatmen, and I, of course, had only Talbot's cast-offs to cover me.

Another thing that caught my eye was a rank of maybe a dozenwaiters dressed in plum-colored livery, standing with folded arms at one side of the lower room. They were all big, muscular black men who looked more like stevedores than what might be required to fetch and carry bottles and glasses.

When the waiter arrived with two bottles of whiskey and real glasses on a tray, Fink shoved one bottle over to Talbot and Carpenter and sloshed whiskey into two glasses on our side of the table before he swiveled around to me and snarled, "Drink up, Perfessor! It could be yer last!"

I lifted my glass and sipped whiskey that was better than I had ever tasted or even imagined. Fink drained his glass in a single gulp and poured another. Then he faced me and said, "The boys an' me, we been havin' a mite o' trouble an' I been wond'rin' if mebbe you might be at the bottom of it all."

My first feeling was relief. What he had in mind most likely didn't have anything to do with where I signed the papers. Then I realized that it was something even more serious. I held my peace and he went on, "Some sonofabitch tattled to the sojers." He drew a deep breath and I could see that it bothered him to tell me anything about his affairs. He changed his tack and barked, "Whaddaye know 'bout what's in the for'ard cargo box, what's under lock an' key?"

His gunmetal eyes bored nearly through me, seeking to read my thought before I spoke. Fink was a bully and a loudmouth, but he was no fool. He knew what made men tick. I looked straight into those icy-gray eyes of his and said, "Not a damned thing. You never opened the hatch, leastaways not when I was about." I didn't dare let my eyes waver from his, for I knew that he placed much less stock in what I might say than what he could divine from my eyes. I never saw him blink during what was maybe a full minute that he stared at me. Then he turned away and poured himself another glassful and tossed it off in a single swallow before he swung back to me and demanded, "An' the nigger tol' ye nuthin'?"

The two of us went to staring again before I said, "No, Micah told me not a thing about your damned cargo box." Then I asked him, "What's in there, anyway?"

Fink just grunted and settled down in his chair. I reckoned he was satisfied, leastaways for now, that I hadn't informed on him. He filled his glass again and for some reason I picked up the bottle and poured my own glass full to the brim. It was an act of bravado, to be sure, but I felt that I had to do something to show him that I was my own man again. Fink appeared not to notice. He was lost in thought.

Fink continued to drink at an increasing rate and I must admit that I kept right on sipping as well, feeling ever more reckless the more I drank, but I held my peace and said nothing. When his bottle neared empty, Fink snapped his fingers and the waiter brought two more bottles to the table. Carpenter and Talbot were as silent as they usually were, drinking steadily but not talking even to each other. None of them appeared to be drunk but I myself was feeling more than a little light-headed.

I had seen, back at Chouteau's, that the three bullies shared everything in common, but one thing that Mike Fink didn't share with the other two was his everlasting need to be talking. He started in again. "So, Perfessor, now ye know I'm put ashore! Chouteau owns the boat an' all that's in it! An' ye know why?" I didn't, of course, and right then, sitting that close to Mike Fink, I wouldn't have said so if I did. His voice grew louder, more angry. "'Cause somebody snitched to the sojers! Tol' 'em what's in the for'ard cargo box! Made me sell out — lock, stock, bar'l an' boat! Chouteau's got it all! He kin handle the sojers! I can't an' he knows it!"

Fink was nearly shouting now and I saw Madame Lucette, looking vexed, threading her way among the tables, heading for us, four of the big black waiters following at a short distance. When she halted near our table, Fink saw her, and before she could speak, he roared, "Lucy, by God! We needs some goddamn wimming here! Fine way to run a goddamn whorehouse! Where's yer goddamn wimming! Git a move on an' fetch some o' yer whores!"

I shoved my chair backwards, as if to show that I had no part in what the other three might say or do, and Fink saw me do it. His hand blurred as he dealt me a stinging blow on the side of my head that lifted me out of my chair and threw me to the floor. As I was shaking my head to clear it, I heard him growl, "No whores fer the rat there! He ain't wid us!"

Lucette's voice was flat and cold when she said, "And zere will be no ladies for you, M'sieu Feenk. No more anysing! You will depart now. *Immédiatement!*"

I was still on the floor when I saw Fink ball his fist and commence to rise from his chair, as if to attack Lucette. Before I knew it myself, I jumped to my feet and lunged at him, swinging my fists, feeling all those miserable weeks on his keelboat pouring out in a white-hot, hazy-red torrent of rage and hate, wanting nothing so much as the pleasure of smashing that sneering red face to a pulp. I landed just one punch on the side of his head before I went numb from a blow to my neck from behind. My knees buckled and as I began to sink I saw all at once Madame Lucette's look of alarm and Fink's red face twisted with anger and all of the plum-colored waiters sprinting towards us and the green-coated doorman waving a pistol and Fink's arm swinging upwards. Then his fist exploded in my face.

੨੦ ੨੦ ੨੦

The sound of water falling pulled me out of the darkness. I forced one eye open, the other wouldn't obey, and I saw three young black women bustling around a big fiddle-shaped copper tub, pouring pails of steaming water into it. They were all dressed alike in short black dresses and frilly white caps and dainty white aprons.

I lay there unmoving for quite a spell, watching out of one eye those pretty black girls busy at their chores. After a time I tried to open the other eye, but it was no use. It was swelled shut, but I was happy to learn that it was still there. About then I came to realize just where I was — or leastaways where I might possibly be.

I was stretched out on the prettiest red counterpane a body ever saw, in a four-poster bed that looked to me as if it spanned an acre or two, with lacy hangings overhead and stacks of soft pillows piled at the head of it. I had never seen or imagined such a bed, much less slept in one. The best I had ever known was a corn-shuck mattress or a pallet of hides.

The bedchamber was big, but it was much more than a sleeping room. It was furnished with colored carpets strewn over a polished wood floor and pictures on the walls, some of them of naked women, which was quite a revelation to me, padded chairs, a divan and a settee, a not-so-big dining table and chairs that matched it, a power of carved wooden and painted screens and chests and little tables scattered here and there, and looking-glasses hung on the walls and some standing upright. Whale-oil lamps cast a soft yellow glow over it all. It looked to me as if there ought to be a queen somewhere in such a room.

Fact is, one wasn't long in coming. A door opened softly at the far end of the chamber and Madame Lucette entered quietly, still wearing her corn-yellow dress, so I reckoned that I hadn't been unconscious for very long. The maids all snapped to attention but she just waved them back to their work and walked directly to the side of the bed. Up close, even looking at her through just one eye, she was even more beautiful than I remembered.

When she saw that I was awake, she smiled down at me, a smile that felt like sunshine warming me and bathing me all over. "So, *mon chevalier*, my defender, awakens." Her tone was bantering but I could read concern for me in her soft brown eyes. I tried to smile back at her, a rather lopsided smile, I warrant, considering that one eye was sealed shut, before I said something like, "Shucks. I reckon I never got to do much to help out." Her smile broadened and she replied, "Perhaps not, but your *effort* was *admirable*. I am, 'ow you say, grateful, truly, for zat."

It didn't seem right for me to be lying there whilst we spoke and I tried to rise from the bed, but she pushed me back against the pillows, saying, "No, rest zere. Do not arise just yet." She turned to a little table beside the bed and poured a glass full of some sort of liquor from a sparkling glass bottle and handed it to me. "Dreenk zees, *mon ami*, eet weel restore you. Eet ees *cognac*, from France. Ze ver' best." Then she rattled a string of French to the maids who were hovering around the big copper tub, still steaming in the middle of the chamber.

Propped against the pillows on the bed I sipped the best of brandy a body could wish for, liquid sunshine if ever there was such a thing. I could feel it warming my throat and then my belly and all the way to my toes, even draining away the throbbing ache from my eye. When the maids had left the room Madame Lucette returned to the bedside and proceeded to massage my bruised eye gently with some sort of unguent. She asked in a low voice, "'Ow ees eet zat you call yourself, *mon ami?*"

"Temple, ma'am, Temple Buck." Then for some reason I said, "From Ohio. Ohio, ma'am. I'm not from around here."

She chuckled softly and replied, "No, not from 'ere. Zat is *évident.*" She pronounced my name aloud a time or two before she said, "I call myself Lucette Papillon. You may call me Lucie." She paused and then she added, "Jus' Lucie. You need not call me 'ma'am.' We shall be friends. I weel not address you as *M'sieu* and you need not say Madame."

My bruised eye was feeling better already and I swung my feet off the counterpane and stood beside the bed, surprised that I felt as shaky as I did.

When she saw me on my feet Lucette pointed towards the bathtub and said, "Come. Eet ees time for your bat', before eet cools." Then, when she saw me hesitate, wondering if she meant for me to take off my clothes right there in front of her, she took my hand and led me to one of the screens, behind which I found a stool and a chamber pot and a silken robe all padded and quilted. I used all three and left my clothes there. When I came out, wrapped to my chin in the robe, I saw that the tub was surrounded by screens. Lucette was still there, standing by the bed. She waved towards the tub and I went behind the screens.

The soapy water was hot and soothing to my body, drawing away my aches and pains in a cloud of perfumed steam that rose from the tub. I stretched out and relaxed and let my mind drift away into those steamy clouds, thinking of nothing in particular except a general marveling at all the pleasant things that had somehow befallen me and wondering when I would wake from what certainly had to be nothing more than a delightful dream.

I woke up fast enough when I felt a soft hand on my shoulder. Perfumed oil cascaded onto my head and spilled onto my brow. It was Lucette and she was kneeling beside the tub, an apron protecting her pretty yellow dress. I was horror-stricken that she would see me in my nakedness, but she seemed unconcerned, as if she were bathing a puppy instead of a grown young man. She kneaded the soapy oil into a thick lather in my hair, which fell to my shoulders even then, and then rinsed it off with warm water from a big ewer that stood nearby, all the while crooning a little tune but saying no words to me that I could understand.

Old as I was, I was coming twenty, I had grown very little hair on my body and hardly any beard. Nevertheless Lucette lathered my face and opened a razor case and shaved me, still crooning her little French tune and bending close to my face as she worked, so close that I feared that I would fall headlong into those beautiful liquid brown eyes.

I commenced to relax, enjoying the feel of her hands on my face and neck and the warmth and fragrance of the water and her breath, enjoying it so much, in fact, that my horror returned with a rush when I realized that I was about to be unpardonably rude! Without thinking I clutched my private parts under the water, lest they declare their presence above the surface.

Lucette laughed gaily and rose to her feet, smiling down at me as she said, "Fear not, Temple Bock. I depart." She pointed to a stack of bath towels and, still laughing, slipped away behind the screens.

Wrapped head to foot in the silken robe I went to retrieve my clothes, but they were gone. When I came out from behind the screen I saw Lucette seated at the little dining table gleaming with china plates and silver and sparkling goblets, candles casting a soft light over all of it. She beckoned to me and as I approached I saw that a supper had already been laid there and a large green bottle rested in ice in a silver bucket at one side.

Still feeling uncomfortable about being naked under the robe, I took a seat on the opposite side of the table as she poured two bell-

shaped glasses full of a pale yellow liquid that foamed and fizzed
and at last bubbled endlessly from the bottom of the glass. Lucette
raised her glass in a toast and declared, "Welcome to *Saint Louis*,
Temple my friend! May your fortunes improve always!" I lifted
my glass in response and drank the best of all wines, dry on the
tongue and tingling in the throat. She chuckled at the pleased look
on my face and said, "Eet ees *champagne*, ze ver' best of all ze wine
of *France*." I smiled and nodded my agreement, even though I
knew nothing at all of France or its wines or brandies or much of
anything else about that far-off land. She refilled my glass and
then she commenced to heap a plate with slices of crisp ham and
wild fowl and tiny sausages and cheeses and hardboiled eggs and
greens and bread better than any I ever tasted. She handed the
plate to me and prepared a less generous one for herself. She ate
sparingly but with good appetite and she saw to it that our glasses
were never empty, chatting the while about Saint Louis and
answering my questions about the things that I had seen there.

As we ate and talked I saw the three black maids enter the
chamber at the far end and busy themselves removing the screens
from around the bathtub and then rolling it out the door on little
wheels attached to its bottom. They made hardly any noise at all
and soon they were gone. Lucette appeared not to notice them at
all and when she finished eating she pushed her plate away and
looked at me with a serious look on her face and said, "Tell me
now, 'ow ees eet zat you find yourself wiz such a peeg as Mike
Feenk? You are not one of zem, *certainement!*"

Everything conspired to loosen me up and wash away my
shyness — the wine and the brandy, the bath and good food, her
striking dark beauty so close to me across the table, and the
warmth of her obvious friendship. I told her everything that came
to mind, even about Aunt Penny and Pap and Uncle Ben and how I
came to be aboard Fink's keelboat and how I had pledged my word
to stay with him until we reached Saint Louis. I didn't dwell on
Fink's ill treatment of me, but I reckon she could guess that part. I
told her, too, about befriending Tuttle and how Fink had sold out
to Pierre Chouteau, his keelboat and all of its cargo, at which she

nodded and smiled impishly and said, "Ah, *Pierre Cadet*, 'e knows 'ow an' when to seize ze bargain, *hein*?"

All my talking and her attentive listening, not to mention the brandy that she continued to pour when the champagne bottle was empty, made me bold enough to ask, "Tell me, why are you being so kind to me?"

Her smile grew pensive and then she replied, "Why indeed, Temple Bock?" She fell silent, her expression thoughtful, before she continued. "Because my life 'as not been always as you see eet now." She waved vaguely at the room in which we sat and perhaps the whole house. "No, zere 'ave been many 'ard times, times when I 'ave 'ad even no shoes, nor to eat, when I 'ave known the cruelty of men like Feenk, and women, too." She paused, her face reflecting remembered unhappiness, and then she smiled and said, "But I 'ave overcome. Now eet ees *possible* for me to aid some of zose zat are as I was. Eet provides me pleasure to do so." She looked me full in the face, her dark eyes seeming to probe into my very soul, and said quietly, "You, Temple, were *misérable*, as I once was, yet you rose to defend me. I 'ave *gratitude* for zat. An' zat is why I aid you now."

With that she stood up and took my hand and led me to the bed. All sorts of thoughts were going through my head right then, mainly wanting to take her in my arms and kiss her and heaven knows what else after that. But I didn't.

And just as well, too. She pulled back the covers and gently pushed me down onto the bed. My head almost disappeared amongst the soft pillows as she lifted my feet and pulled a silken quilt over me. Then she bent swiftly and kissed me gently on the forehead, murmuring, "Sleep well, my brave Temple. I am, after all, *une femme d'affaires*. I must see to my *établissement*. *Fais dodo*. Goodnight, my friend."

I wasn't sure if I was disappointed or relieved as I lay there watching her retreat. She snuffed the candles on the dining table and then I heard only the rustle of her skirts as she moved across the chamber in darkness, then the door closing softly behind her, then nothing but the sweet image of Lucette smiling at me in the glow of candles.

I fell asleep with a silken pillow hugged to my breast.

᷿   ᷿   ᷿

Dreaming can be a marvelous thing, especially if your dreams come true. That night I drifted into dreams of Lucette, of falling ever downwards into the liquid, luminous depths of her dark eyes, spiraling down to a place where she awaited me with arms as soft and smooth as silk, yet strong enough to clasp me close to her, pressing my face against her flesh, fragrant with the clean, fresh, exciting smell of her, her husky voice murmuring from a faraway place words that I could barely understand. Then I was struggling to breathe, to gulp mouthfuls of air flavored with the musky scent of woman, as I swam back to realizing that my face was pressed into the yielding curve of her throat and Lucette was crooning soft words in French, then in her charming English, her lips brushing my ear as she spoke.

When she saw that I was awake, she chuckled deep in her throat and said, "Ah, my Temple, *mon brave*, you 'ave awaken. Ees eet zat your dream eet 'as come true?"

I answered her honestly when I replied, "I reckon not. I gotta still be dreamin'." Just the same, I tightened my arms and pulled her close to me. She was naked and her hair was damp, as if she were fresh from her bath, which she was, and her only perfume was the scent of Lucette herself.

I surprised myself by my boldness and then I was embarrassed, for I felt something growing between us and I tried to slither my body away from hers, but she wouldn't allow it. She hugged me closer to her and bent her head to kiss my lips, her damp hair tumbling free and brushing my face. It was a long kiss, sweet and pulsing and open-mouthed. Her tongue found mine and we melted into one in that kiss, a kiss like I never thought a kiss could be, a kiss that was molten gold and paradise come true. We were breathless when at last she broke away and pushed my head down between her breasts. Warm and firm and smooth they were, just-ripe pears luscious with promise, tiny taut nipples brushing my cheeks, inviting me to nibble. Which naturally I did.

When she rolled over and pulled me to her it was as if I had been with her a thousand times before, natural and right and inevitable, gentle at first, then building to a fiery explosion that left the two of us gasping.

Young as I was, the first time didn't take long at all, as you might imagine, nor did the second. After the third we lay sprawled in each other's arms, breathing hard and nuzzling and making sounds that nobody in the world could understand but the two of us. Then she scooted out of bed and I could hear her scampering across the room and soon the sound of water splashing. When she returned she bathed me with warm, moist, scented towels before she slipped in beside me. It was right about then that I came to realize that Aunt Penny hadn't invented that thing she did, after all — and whilst we are on that subject I also learned that it is better to give than to receive. Well, almost.

We slept hardly at all that night and the sun was sneaking in past the heavy draperies as I lay propped against the pillows, Lucette's dark head cradled on my chest, her hair all tousled and her beautiful face calm and childlike, her arms still around me, her soft regular breathing telling me that she had fallen asleep at last. My mind strayed back over the days and weeks just past and I reckoned that, brutal as they had been, this night had pretty much made up for the most of it.

I awoke to a room filled with sunshine. The heavy red drapes had been pulled back and lacy white curtains billowed in a soft spring breeze. Outdoors I could hear faraway sounds of Saint Louis busy at work, a buzz of voices and the clatter of wagons rumbling and rattling in the streets below, the ring of a hammer on an anvil, birdsong, and somewhere a church bell tolling. Lucette was gone and I lay naked beneath the red counterpane. The bed, so rumpled the night before, was tidy and neat and only a bowl of flowers rested on the table that we had left littered with the remains of our supper. A drinking glass and a cut-glass pitcher filled with water and ice stood on a little table beside the bed and I drank deeply.

I looked about for my robe. It was nowhere to be seen. Modesty soon lost out to other urgencies and I rolled out of bed and raced naked for the screen that hid the chamber pot, after which I washed my face and bathed as best I could in a basin of barely-warm water I found there, then scurried back to bed, content that my modesty, what was left of it, had been preserved.

I lay there drowsing and remembering and wondering if the night before had really happened and deciding that it mostly had, when the door opened softly and Lucette slipped inside, carrying my robe folded neatly on her arm. When she saw that I was awake, she laughed gaily and pranced across the room and jumped onto the bed. Her hair was damp from the bath and her smiling face fairly glowed. She wore only a light silken wrapper, which fell open as she leaned down to kiss me, revealing tiny pink nipples smiling out from her tawny breasts. I rose to the bait and then I pulled her down beside me. I wanted her right then as much, maybe more, as I had the night before. She buried her face in my throat and giggled before she murmured, *"Bon jour, bel-ami,* ees eet not time zat we break our fast?" I agreed that it was, and we did, after which it was time to see about something to eat.

She led me through the filmy white curtains onto a terrace overlooking a garden, a rainbow of blooming springtime flowers and well-pruned trees ranged along high red-brick walls. We sat on lacy white-painted iron chairs at an iron table, where coffee steamed from a pot already waiting there. Lucette poured two cups before she rang a little silver bell that was on the table. I had hardly got the cup to my lips before one of the young black maids appeared carrying a tray laden with our breakfast, a fresh pot of hot coffee and a pitcher of boiled milk, white sugar and golden honey, a mound of crisp and flaky horn-shaped rolls lighter than summer clouds, sweet butter, and a variety of preserves in little pots. I was suddenly mindful of just how hungry I was after our night-time exertions. I attacked those delicious vittles with tremendous appetite. Lucette sat smiling approvingly across the table, nibbling daintily but steadily. Before long she tinkled her little bell once again and another maid arrived bearing a china platter heaped with a huge fluffy omelette smothered with crisp bacon, spicy little sausages, and what I took to be broiled lamb chops. Not wishing to appear ungrateful, I did justice to it all, whilst Lucette beamed and encouraged me to eat more and more so as to keep up my strength.

When I couldn't manage even one more bite I pushed my chair back from the table and sat smiling at my hostess, marveling at her beauty and the goodness that appeared to glow all around her, vaguely wondering why all this good fortune had been visited upon me. Considering everything that had happened to me since I ran off from Whynot, howsomever, I was not inclined to examine such matters any too closely. Good and bad things just seemed to happen to me, without much effort or intention on my part, and that was somewhat troubling, but what was past was past. Now it was time that I myself take charge of the fortunes of Temple Buck, but how I might accomplish that I had no idea.

I was still naked under that soft, quilted robe and, fine as it was, I was feeling fairly uncomfortable about my lack of proper clothing. A man needs his britches.

I needn't have worried. When she was sure I had finished my breakfast, Lucette rose from the table and said, "Come, mon ami, eet ees time for you to dress." I stood and she led me back through the curtains. Inside I could see that the room had been tidied up in our absence. The bed was made up prim and proper and laid out on a fresh yellow counterpane was a gentleman's suit of clothes, a ruffled white shirt, even a silk cravat and stockings, everything, and a pair of tall, shiny boots standing on the floor.

I glanced quickly around the chamber to see if there might be another man in there somewhere, waiting to get dressed. Lucette saw me do that and she understood. Her laugh was purest crystal, then she said, "No, my Temple, zey are for you. Your ozzers, I 'ave 'ad zem burned."

The boots were a mite too big but they fitted me well enough. The rest of the outfit might have been made for me before the weeks of hard work and poor food aboard Fink's boat had stripped me down to not much more than muscle and bone. Lucette insisted on dressing me, as if I were a favorite doll, adjusting the embroidered waistcoat and tying the dark-blue cravat just so. Nobody that I ever knew had owned, let alone worn, a cravat and I would just as soon have gone without, but Lucette declared that no gentleman would be caught dead outdoors in Saint Louis without one, so I went along with her on it, even if I did feel as if I was being gussied up like a prize pony.

When she was satisfied with her fussing and combing and adjusting, Lucette led me to a tall pier glass and let me view the result. I hardly recognized the man in the reflection. Only my hair, which was long even then and fell past my shoulders, looked familiar. The rest was pure Saint Louis dandy. I wasn't at all sure that I approved, but Lucette stood beside me, beaming and chattering about how handsome I looked, so proud of her handiwork that I made no objection.

Then she stood on tip-toe and kissed me lightly on the lips before she pushed me towards the terrace, saying, "Go now, M'sieu, *mon beau garçon*, and 'ave your *café*. I mus' call my maids to prepare me."

Hot coffee awaited on the table and beside the steaming pot and a single cup was a long clay pipe, tobacco, and flint and firesteel. I poured a cupful and although I had rarely used tobacco up till then I filled the pipe and lighted it, feeling that I looked every inch a gentleman as I reclined in my chair and also feeling like an intruder in a world where I had no proper business to be.

The sun showed that it was early afternoon before Lucette emerged through the flowing white curtains, breath-taking in her dark beauty, her hair in high-piled ringlets once again, wearing a low-cut frock of pale green, the color of lily pads, her eyes sparkling. She leaned to kiss me and then sat opposite me at the table, preening herself in the sunshine, as a pretty woman who knows she is pretty will do. When she saw that I had finished both my coffee and my pipe she stood up and took both my hands, pulling me to my feet, and said, "Come, Temple, *mon cher*, eet ees time zat I show to you my *établissement*." She paused and added, "And you to zem."

Lucette took me on a grand tour of her large house, introducing me to all of its residents, including Israel the doorkeeper, smiling today and resplendent in a bright red frock coat, and most of the waiters, all of them taller than I and muscle-bulky under their plum-colored uniforms. The grand salon was nearly deserted, but in spite of the early hour there was a sprinkling of gentlemen at the tables on the mezzanine, chatting amiably with some of Lucette's ladies. She introduced me to several of the ladies who were not occupied at the moment and I was struck by their comeliness and polite manners. Lucette noticed my appreciative looks and she said, "You may look, my Temple, *mon bel-ami*, but do not touch. You are mine." The look in her eyes as she said that made me wonder if the previous occupant of the fine clothes I was wearing had failed to heed that advice.

Lucette's establishment was huge. We visited the gaming rooms, the kitchen and the laundry, the smokehouse, the garden, the dairy and the springhouse, the storerooms, the stables and the carriage house, and the musty, cobwebbed, dirt-floored cellars where casks and crates of wine and kegs of whiskey and brandy and heaven-knows-what-else were kept. In each place Lucette tarried to talk with whoever was in charge, chattering away in French and giving what I took to be orders in a pleasant but definite voice, whilst I stood shifting from one foot to the other, feeling more than somewhat useless.

One part of the house that we did not tour was where Lucette's ladies stayed and plied their trade. I didn't mention it, of course, but Lucette seemed to be able to read my mind. "Zere now," she said, reaching up and pulling me close for a kiss, "you 'ave seen enough. Eet ees enough zat you know to find your way to my *chambre*."

The next couple-three days passed pleasantly enough. Whilst Lucette was busy elsewhere, I spent the days reading books in English that she brought to me, on the terrace in fine weather, deep in a padded chair if it was raining, or rattling around the big house and grounds, chatting with Israel the fine-feathered doorkeeper, who appeared to have an inexhaustible wardrobe of brightly-colored frock coats and britches, or loitering in the stable, admiring Lucette's excellent carriage horses.

The nights were best. After I had turned down the lamps and retired, Lucette would return from her duties and come to bed, fresh from her bath, as hungry for me as I was for her, endlessly inventive but all the while with an innocent quality about her that belied the experience that I knew she must possess. I didn't dwell on such thoughts. For the time I was content to lose myself in her arms, her infinite charm, the delicious natural perfume of her warm, firm flesh.

Each day slid effortlessly into another, but it wasn't long before I commenced to feel restless, useless, rather like a pampered lapdog, a stud horse, or maybe just a teaser. That picture of myself didn't suit me at all. All I had ever known was hard work in the outdoors and, much as I thought I loved Lucette right then, I knew that I could never be content simply to be Lucette's knight of the bedchamber. It was a pleasurable occupation, to be sure, but not altogether respectable.

So it was that one morning after breakfast I announced that I wished to stroll through the town, alone. At first Lucette objected, saying that Fink and his bullies were still in Saint Louis and that she feared what they might do if I met up with them. Howsomever when she saw that I was determined to go out on my own, she fell silent, and then she asked me to wait there for a moment whilst she attended to some business.

When Lucette returned a few minutes later she carried a tall beaver hat and she looked less unhappy than she had a few minutes earlier. She stood tip-toe to kiss me, then stepped back and drew a short double-barreled pistol from inside the hat. I must confess that for a moment I wasn't altogether sure what she meant to do with it, but she handed it to me, saying, "*'Ere, mon amant*, zees weel protec' you from Feenk and ze ozzer *bravaches*." She reached into the hat once more and handed me a leather purse heavy with coin. Then she popped the topper onto my head and adjusted it to what she considered to be a properly rakish angle.

When she was satisfied that I looked something like a gentleman she kissed me again and said seriously, her eyes more troubled than her voice, "You are of great value, my Temple. Come soon to me." I folded her in my arms and kissed her long and hard and promised that I would do as she asked.

Once out in the street, I was uncertain which direction to walk. At first I thought of going into the Vide Poche in search of Tuttle, but I reckoned that it was more likely that I would meet Fink down there instead of Tuttle. Instead, I found myself walking towards the town, feeling very much a gentleman under my beaver topper, comforted by the solid weight of the pistol in my belt and the purse in my pocket.

Without exactly meaning to, I found myself in the neighborhood of Berthold & Chouteau, which was most likely where I had been aiming to go all along. My joy at being free of Mike Fink had been marred by having to say farewell to Micah, still a slave and subject to the whims of a master. I needed to see him at least once more, if I could.

I didn't have long to wait. As I approached the entrance of Berthold & Chouteau's mercantile I caught sight of Micah fetching boxes and sacks of merchandise from inside the store and loading them onto a dray in the street. He hadn't seen me yet and it warmed my heart to see a smile on his face as he joked with the black teamster sitting on the wagon. There hadn't been many smiles for either of us aboard Mike Fink's keelboat.

I waited at a distance until he finished with his task and stood waving at the driver rumbling up the street. As I made my way towards him I saw that his woolly hair was neatly cropped and that he wore a fresh hickory shirt and clean britches, not a patch showing anywhere, and there were shoes on his feet. He saw me then and a huge grin split his face as he came trotting towards me. "Marse Tempa, dat you? My, ain' you sumpin'!" He stopped in front of me, hands on his hips, taking me in from head to foot. "You lookin' lak quality folks foh shuah!"

I reached out and hugged him, mumbling something like, "No, Micah, not yet. Most likely never. It's just the clothes." I stepped back and held him at arm's length, happy to see him again and pleased that he looked to be happy, too. "Tell me now, how goes it with you?"

His grin grew even wider as he said, "Marse Tempa, dis de bes' Ah evah been! Dis niggah gotta wuk foh sumbuddy, das a fac', an' de bes' sumbuddy Ah could evah wish foh he be Marse Shoe-toe, 'ceptin' mebbe you. He fin' out Ah kin read an' he don' min' nohow! Marse Shoe-toe he say if Ah learn to talk French he gonna larn me how to be a clark! 'Magine dat! Ol' Micah clarkin'! Ain' dat sumpin'?"

His words came tumbling out almost too fast for me to understand what he was saying, but what I drew from it all was that now Micah enjoyed decent treatment and he had clean clothes, a clean bed, three meals a day, books to read, and time to study them. Forbidding as he had looked to me when I had seen him last, Pierre Cadet evidently had a heart as well as a sound head for business. I felt grateful to him on Micah's account.

A black man appeared in the doorway of the mercantile and waved at Micah, telling him to come inside. We made our farewells and I promised to come to see him whenever I could. We hugged one last time, then Micah trotted up to the door and disappeared inside.

I stood looking after him. Then as I was about to turn away I heard someone call my name. It was Chouteau, tall and very well-dressed and smiling. As I moved towards him I heard him saying, "Ah, M'sieu Bock, you 'ave come to visit your student." His smile broadened. "You 'ave done well. You 'ave chosen well zis black man. I 'ave much 'ope for 'eem 'ere, your Micah."

I expressed my thanks for his good treatment of Micah and then I asked him, right out, "How did you know that Micah could read?"

Chouteau looked puzzled at my question and then he said, "But of course, M'sieu Feenk said eet was so." A slight frown flitted across his face before he continued. "And because of zat ability 'e insisted on a greater price. Feenk ees, 'ow you say, an 'ard bargainer. But I 'ave receive good value."

So Fink had known all along that I was teaching Micah how to read. It was not surprising. Fink was no fool, whatever else he might be. All I could say was, "Fink certainly is that, a hard bargainer, amongst some other things."

Chouteau went on. "Yes, you 'ave chosen well zat man for an associate. Feenk weel make you *riche*." He paused and looked me over, obviously taking note of my fine clothes. "Already you 'ave an air of *prospérité*. *Saint Louis* appears to be agréable for you, *hein*, M'sieu Bock?"

Without explaining just why, I allowed that Saint Louis had so far been very agreeable and we chatted about not much for a minute or two more before I took my leave. I still recall his parting words. "Concern yourself not, M'sieu Bock. Ze money eet weel work 'ard. *Au revoir.*"

He made a short bow and I did my best return it. Then he turned on his heel and marched into the mercantile.

When I turned to depart a sudden movement caught my eye and I saw two of Lucette's waiters disappearing around the corner of a building. I almost laughed out loud. Lucette was taking no chances, either with Mike Fink or with me.

ॐ   ॐ   ॐ

I hadn't been gone half a day but when I got back to Lucette's a body would have thought I was the prodigal son returned from half a lifetime spent wandering the earth. Even Israel at the door looked relieved to see me and when Lucette came fluttering through the grand salon she covered my face and neck with kisses, right there in front of the servants and everybody.

Supper that evening was even better than usual, which I hadn't thought was possible. So was the champagne. And when Lucette led me to bed we commenced such a night as I don't reckon I am ever likely to forget.

ॐ   ॐ   ॐ

Next morning measured up to the night before. After breakfast we even took a bath together in the big copper tub, laughing and splashing and doing it one more time, which commotion likely vexed the black maids when they came in to mop the floor and trundle the tub out of the chamber.

There is a saying that from eating comes appetite, and not only for making love. It wasn't too long after I was dressed and drinking one more cup of coffee on the terrace that I felt an itch to walk abroad in the town again. I laid aside my book and went to find my hat. The pistol and the purse were still inside it, where I had left them the evening before. I pocketed the purse, tucked the pistol into my belt, gazed unbelievingly one final time in the looking-glass, and left the bedchamber.

Lucette was busy with her accounts and so as to avoid another tearful scene I walked straight to the front door and asked Israel to let me out. He looked troubled but he did as I asked.

As soon as I stepped into the street I felt a curious sense of elation, like a bird freed from a cage, even though that particular cage was the best thing that had ever happened to me.

I glanced towards the Vide Poche, thought better of it, and sauntered in the other direction, towards the city, satisfied and content in every way that I could think of, but still hungry for I knew not what.

I stopped by a saddler's shop and chatted awhile with the men there, bought a poke of sweets from a pedlar in the street, and peered into a dozen shop windows, marveling at the variety of goods to be had in Saint Louis. I was standing in front of a farrier's barn, watching the thickset smith at work and thinking of my horse Kumskaka and wondering how he fared, when a strong hand gripped my shoulder. My hand stabbed for the pistol in my belt and I spun around to see Tuttle Thompson's big horse face laughing at me. Tears were streaming from his eyes and he was nearly doubled over with laughter, pointing at me and trying to choke out words I couldn't understand.

When he finally got halfway control of himself he stood gasping and still pointing and saying, "Lookee yew, boy! Kin thet be our

Temple? Our ragged-arse Temple I useter know on Mike Fink's hell-boat? Why, no! Cain't be! Ol' Temple's gone an' died an' this'n be some angel jest sorta looks like 'im, come down from heaven to bless all us sinners!"

I waited, saying nothing until his humor had run its course, happy to see once more his scarecrow frame and his whiskered face. At last he ran out of words, almost. "My gawd, Temple, what in pluperfec' hell happened to ye? You're a Saint Looie fop fer damn sure! Tell me now, ye find yerse'f a gold mine somewhars?" Then he stood back and surveyed me head to toe, shaking his head in wonder.

I told him the story as best I could, leaving out bits and pieces about signing the documents at Chouteau's and just how close Lucette and I had become. I didn't want to come off a braggart and besides, I wasn't especially proud of being Lucette's fancy man, for that is what I knew myself to be. Then, mainly to keep Tuttle from prying into details about my life at Lucette's, I asked him, "And what about you? Last time I saw you, Mister Tuttle Thompson, you stood in a fair way to be declared champion stud horse of all time."

Tuttle actually blushed and then he stood tall and said proudly, "An' I reckon I done it, too! Leastaways thet's how they be tellin' it down at Matilda's. Cost me all my money, but it was wu'th it. Whooeee! What a fine time thet war!"

I winced at a vision of a naked Tuttle chasing the naked lady around the balcony. I laughed out loud and said, "I reckon it was and I reckon you did." Then, more seriously, I asked, "So what'll you do now? Your purse is flat and Fink sold his boat. What's next?"

Tuttle's face lighted up like summer sunshine. "Ain't goin' back to Kaintuck, leastaways not fer a spell yet. Nosirree! Gonna go up the Missourah, trappin' beavers an' fightin' Injuns an' gittin' rich! An' I was hopin' ye might choose to come along, if'n I could find ye in time." He reached into the pouch at his belt and brought out a tattered page of newspaper and handed it to me. "Hyar," he said, "it be in thar somewhars." I was reminded that Tuttle couldn't read.

I saw that the paper was from the *Missouri Republican* and when I found what Tuttle was talking about I read that a man named William Ashley was seeking a hundred enterprising young men to go all the way up the Missouri River for a year or two or three. It didn't say what for but it did say that somebody called Major Henry would be the boss and that he would supply the particulars. It also said that he could be found at the lead mines in Washington County, wherever that was.

A whole new world appeared to open up for me. I saw a way out of a life that, comfortable as it was right then, made me feel foolish and surely couldn't last anyway. My questions came out in a rush. "Hey, Tuttle, is there still time? Where's the lead mines? Where's Washington County? How're we goin' to get there?"

Tuttle's grin threatened to break his face. "So ye wanta go! I knew ye would! No need to go traipsin' up to Potosi. The Gen'ral's ri'chere in Sain' Looie, out on the edge o' town. Let's git a move on, afore it's too late!" With that he started off, rifle on his shoulder, powder horn banging at his waist, his long legs eating up the street fast enough to make me trot to keep up with him.

The route Tuttle took passed the dock where Mike Fink's keelboat had been moored, but it was no longer there.

As we marched through Saint Louis the shops and the people blurred into patches of color, without form or meaning. All I could see were pictures that Tuttle's words conjured up in my mind as he talked of trapping beaver and the sights that he had heard folks tell about of the unknown country that lay in the far reaches of the Missouri. It was a life I knew I had been born and raised for, a life in the wilderness. And getting rich at it didn't hurt either.

Tuttle's quick-stepping soon brought us to the outskirts of town. After that it wasn't long before he turned into a yard in front of what looked to be a warehouse. A clean-shaven, tallish, spare-built man was seated beneath a blossoming apple tree, talking with a bunch of young men crowded around him. Just about everybody there was young and strong-looking, except the well-dressed man seated under the tree, who was neither young nor old, but he looked sturdy enough.

Tuttle and I stood for a moment on the fringe of the crowd, but Tuttle soon grew impatient and shouldered his way past the men standing there, dragging me with him. His voice rang out above the buzz of conversation. "Gen'ral! Gen'ral Ashley! I gotcher man ri'chere! This'n be Temple Buck, Gen'ral, a man what's teetotally right fer yore ex-pee-dishun!"

Ashley stood up as Tuttle yanked me forward. He surveyed me with a cool eye and his voice had a steely edge to it when he said, "Oh, do you think so, Thompson?" He ran his gray eyes the length of me, taking in my fine clothes, my tall, well-brushed beaver hat, and the cravat that Lucette had carefully tied for me that morning. Then he addressed me directly. "And why, young man, do you suppose that you are fit to join this expedition? A journey filled with danger and hardship. It will be no church picnic, I assure you." A ripple of laughter ran through the crowd and Ashley appeared to warm to his subject. "There is no place for fops and dandies on the Missourah, sir. Have you been recently disappointed in love or did you, perhaps, lose a wager, which brings you to us?"

A burst of laughter from the crowd burned my ears and I saw my new-found dream slipping away. I fought down my anger and then I blurted out, "You can make sport of my clothes if you like, General. They're the only clothes I've got. But I'm no fop!" Then I shoved my hand out to him and said, "Would you shake my hand, sir?"

Ashley looked surprised and then he took my hand in a firm grip. I returned his grip and then I released his hand and turned up my palms before his eyes. I was feeling reckless about then, reckoning that all was lost anyway. "And what do you find there, General? Callouses! That's what! And a damn sight more than you've got!" I am not altogether sure just what I said after that, but it went something like this. "I've worked hard all my life, on a farm and on a damn ol' keelboat, and I can shoot as good as the next man and ride a horse better'n most! I never trapped a beaver 'cause there ain't any where I come from, but I can learn 'most anything you can teach!"

Ashley looked perplexed at first, then he smiled a thin smile and said calmly, "Well now, perhaps we shouldn't judge this book by its cover." He sat down and looked up at me with a different light in his eyes. Then he said, "I'll tell you what. Major Henry is expected here today. Wait here and we'll see what he thinks. If he approves of you I will enlist you to accompany the expedition. Meanwhile, get yourself something to eat." He cleared his throat and stifled a grin, but I could hear him chuckling as Tuttle and I moved off to stand in line behind a passel of men waiting to be served barbecue and beer.

Whilst we waited our turn Tuttle told me that Ashley was a general in the Missouri Militia and Andrew Henry was a major. Tuttle told me, too, that he had heard that Henry was no newcomer to the trapper's trade, that a dozen years before he had led an expedition to the headwaters of the Missouri and that even though Indians had forced him out, he had managed to turn a profit on the beaver furs they trapped and traded for.

The barbecue was tasty indeed and whilst Tuttled sprawled against a tree afterwards, smoking his pipe and sipping a cup of beer, I shucked my frock coat, stuffed my cravat into a pocket, and laid my topper aside, determined that Andrew Henry wouldn't see me as a dandy. There wasn't anything I could do about my ruffled shirt and stylish tight britches, but I hoped that Ashley might put in a good word for me with the Major.

When Andrew Henry finally showed up from Potosi in the late afternoon he looked to me like he could have been Ashley's brother or leastaways a cousin, rather tall and lean and craggy-faced. They both put me in mind of pictures I had seen of Andy Jackson. He wasted no time in putting us new recruits to the test. When it came my turn he asked me my name and age and where I was from, dipping a quill and scribbling down my answers in a ledger book he held on his knee. I told him I was called Temple Buck, that I was nearly twenty, and that I came from Whynot in Ohio. He cracked a brief smile and said, "Why not?" I reckon I liked him from that moment on. A man would need a sense of humor in the line of work that he proposed that we would be doing. Then he asked me what I had been doing the most of my life. I told him about the farm and hunting and running a trapline with Uncle Ben and even about coming to Saint Louis on a keelboat, though I didn't mention how that came about or whose boat it was.

Then it was time for the testing. I borrowed Tuttle's rifle and shot tolerably well for never having shot it before. Both Henry and Ashley watched how fast we could shoot and reload and we each got three shots. Mine fell just a hair outside of Tuttle's and when I sneaked a peek at the two bosses after my last shot, I saw them smile and nod at each other.

Next they wanted to see if we could ride. The horse they gave me was about half-broke and cranky, but I kept his head up and put him through his walk-trot-canter before I busted him out through a field at a gallop, turned him back, and came thundering into the yard, pulling him to a stop and stepping off all at once. The two of them nodded and smiled once again.

Whilst we waited for Henry and Ashley to make up their mind about who would be allowed to go and who wouldn't, I got to talking with a fresh-faced young fellow who said he was a blacksmith. He looked it. He was big, broad-shouldered and brawny and maybe a year or so younger than I was. He said his name was Bridger and he was called Jim. Then he told how he wanted the trapper's life more than anything else in the world, how he hated the smoke and grime and closeness of the smithy and how he longed for the clean air of the wilderness. I had no trouble understanding that.

They called his name before mine, but when they finally did I trotted up to sign the ledger book, bursting with joy at being picked, and saw that Bridger had signed with an X. Tuttle's X was already there amongst several simple marks. Maybe that is why I signed my name with such a flourish, just to show that I knew a little something. Henry looked up and said, "Oh, you can read." I nodded and he made a note next to my name, but I couldn't see what he wrote. Then he explained the terms and conditions of employment, the most of which, I must admit, went in one ear and out the other. I was so happy to be accepted that I most likely would have agreed to work for nothing. As it was, he said that we would be working on shares and that we were expected to furnish our own firearms, bedding, and personal gear. If we didn't have those things they would be supplied and the cost of them would be deducted from our wages. That part stuck in my mind, for I had nothing more to my name than the fancy clothes I was standing in and I didn't even properly own those. Henry asked me then if I had any questions and I said that I hadn't any and that is all there was to the event that changed the course of the rest of my life.

The men who hadn't been called commenced to drift away, but Ashley called them back and announced, "Gentlemen, we are supremely grateful for your interest and we regret that we cannot accommodate all of you. Remember, however, that this is merely the first of our expeditions. There will be more such ventures in future and Major Henry and I hope that you will once again respond to our call for service when it comes. Please wish us good fortune and to all of you, godspeed!"

Then Ashley and the Major assembled all of us who had been enlisted that afternoon. There were some thirty of us gathered there under the trees and I wondered about the other seventy or so they needed to make up the party. Ashley soon cleared up that question. He stepped onto a bench and when his voice rang out we all fell silent. What he said went something like this. "Gentlemen, it is truly written that many are called but few are chosen! You are indeed the Chosen Few! Major Henry and I have sifted through many good men in our effort to assemble the best possible company to pursue our aims in the mountains of the Upper Missourah. Our choice has fallen upon you. We believe that you, each of you, will prove equal to the arduous task that lies ahead, that you will triumph over hardship and danger and reap the rewards of your labor. And be sure, gentlemen, there will be much of both hardship and danger, from the elements and from the Indians and the wild creatures that you will encounter in that country, like nothing you have ever experienced, I assure you, but we are confident that you will cope successfully and overcome all such difficulties." Tuttle nudged me, along about then, and whispered that Ashley was a politician and I had no trouble believing that. The General went on in that high-flown, Fourth-of-July style for a spell and then he got down to brass tacks, telling us mainly that Major Henry was the man in charge and that discipline would be as hard and rigid as you might find on a naval ship or in the army. I had no experience of either, but I reckoned I knew what he meant.

He explained, too, that the other seventy-odd men who were to make up the party had already been spoken to and that all of us were expected to show up in front of Berthold & Chouteau's Mercantile at six o'clock in the morning the day after tomorrow.

Andrew Henry said a few words, *Merci*fully few, afterwards, which I don't recollect precisely, but the gist of which was that he was the only man amongst us who had any experience of the mountains and that he intended to keep us all alive long enough to learn enough to keep on living, which sounded like good and welcome commonsense to me.

The General wished us godspeed, too. Then the meeting broke up and the men wandered off in their several directions. Just as Tuttle and I were about to leave I chanced to find myself alongside of Andrew Henry and I asked him, "Beg your pardon, Major, but where will we be meeting up with the horses for our journey?"

Henry looked startled at my question. "Horses? Oh, not for quite a spell yet. When it's time, we'll trade for horses with the Indians, a long ways up the Missourah. Till then we'll be traveling by keelboat."

      ૎   ૎   ૎

As Tuttle and I made our way back through Saint Louis, he to Mathilde's in Vide Poche, I to Lucette's, I was a battlefield of mixed feelings. On the one hand I was overjoyed to be on my way to being master of myself again. On the other, I felt miserable about saying farewell to Lucette. Nobody in my life, except Ma and maybe Sarah and Uncle Ben, and Powatawa perhaps, had ever cared as much about me as she had shown she did and here I was running away from her, just as I had run off before. Still, if I stayed, wouldn't she come to despise me as much as I would despise myself for being a useless hanger-on, some sort of parasite, really no better or much different from one of the ladies who worked for her? And then I thought of Ashley and Henry's great adventure and all that it promised to men with grit enough to undertake it. Like I said, I was whipsawed about my feelings, but I reckon I knew all along that when the expedition started up the Missouri I would be a part of it.

I only dimly heard Tuttle prattling on about beaver and wild Indians and getting rich. It appeared to me to be an easy matter for him. From what I could tell, Tuttle was giving up nothing that he valued. With me it was different. It seemed to me that I was always leaving pieces of me behind.

We were passing a draper's shop when I called out to Tuttle to hold up and wait for me. I ducked inside and bought a hickory shirt and britches with some of the money Lucette had given me the day before. Somehow that simple act made up my mind and sealed my decision. I would be going with Andrew Henry and nobody would take me for a fop in such clothes.

We parted in front of Lucette's and agreed to meet there day after tomorrow, if Lucette didn't kick me out that night, in which case I would join him at Madame Mathilde's. As Tuttle turned to go I caught his arm and shoved Lucette's purse into his hand. "Here, Tuttle," I told him, "take this. Get what you need for the journey and drink up the rest. It'll likely be a long dry spell."

He grinned at me, hefted the purse, and dropped it into his belt pouch before he replied, "Yep, likely so, but naow there be time an' money enough to moisten up consid'able afore we go."

I stood in the road watching his gangling frame disappear in the gathering dusk as he hiked down the lane that led to the Vide Poche, happy that I had at least one friend to whom I wouldn't have to say goodbye. Then I squared my shoulders and marched up to the door, ready as I would ever be to face the music.

When Israel let me in his face was solemn and Lucette was nowhere to be seen. I reckoned that her spies or bodyguards or whatever they were had got there before me and reported what they had seen out at Ashley's and that she was sulking somewheres, mad as hell about what I had agreed to do. It was early evening and the grand salon was already filling up, the Negro musicians playing soft, sweet music, candles casting mellow light, waiters bustling, and the ladies' polite laughter tinkling in response to the pleasantries, humorous or not, of the paying guests.

I made my way through the salon, up the stairway, across the mezzanine, and down the corridor to Lucette's chamber, all the while craning my neck to catch sight of her. I could have been invisible. Nobody frowned, but nobody said good evening either. The door was unlocked and I let myself in. The room was deserted, neat and tidy, but quiet with a silence that was painful. It was the same room where we had romped and laughed and made love, but right at that moment there was no comfort for me in that room.

I felt hot and sweaty and guilty as all the souls in hell. I tossed the parcel that contained my new hickory clothes behind the screen that I had been using and shucked my beaver hat and natty frock coat and poured myself a big glass of French brandy, thinking the while that I would likely never drink liquor anywhere near that good again, which wasn't too far off the mark, come to think of it.

I was sprawled in a chair on the terrace, staring down into the garden without really seeing it, the brandy bottle nearing empty, when Lucette stepped through the curtains and stood staring at me, saying nothing at first. Then she fairly exploded. "So, you weesh to leave me! You love not your Lucie! What 'ave I done to make you go? What 'ave I not done to make you stay wiz me? For what do you weesh to live wiz ze *sauvages peau-rouges*, ze redskins, and ze great gray bears?" She went on like that for quite a spell, mostly in French, now and again straying into English, but I held my peace, not knowing which question to respond to first and then realizing that she didn't really want to hear any answers to any of them. Several times she told me to leave right then if I had a mind to, but whenever

I started to rise from my chair she would push me back down again and keep right on yelling. I reckoned it was best to let the whole thing run its course.

When at last she ran out of breath, leaning into my face, her eyes snapping, I reached up and pulled her down and kissed her hard. She bit my lip.

But then she threw her arms around my neck and snuggled close and commenced to sob. I held her tight, crooning to her and wondering what in the world I could say to her to make her understand why it was necessary that I do what I surely knew I must do if I was ever again going to be able to walk like a man.

I never got a chance to tell her anything at all that night. After she cried herself out, she rested there in my lap for a spell, pressing her face into my neck, and then she slipped out of my arms, stood up, pulled me out of my chair, led me inside to the bed, and pushed me down onto it. I was glad to lie down. All that brandy had made me unsteady on my feet and I knew, the way I was, that I could never explain myself properly right then.

There was no need and no opportunity. Without a word, Lucette spun on her heels and stalked out of the room.

Somehow I scraped off my boots and wriggled out of my snug britches and burrowed under the bedclothes, my head buried in silken pillows that bore the sweet, exciting fragrance of Lucette.

It might have been hours or perhaps it was only minutes before I drifted halfway out of a dreamless sleep and realized that she was there beside me, her arms around me and straining me to her, saying nothing because there was nothing to be said. I turned and took her precious naked body in my arms and held her close to me throughout that night.

                        ❧   ❧   ❧

I woke up with a condition common to young men and, I reckon, most men of whatever age. Howsomever Lucette was understanding. You might say she possessed a firm grasp of the situation. She chuckled deep down in her throat and then she said, "Eet would be a pity to waste such a gift, *n'est-ce pas?*" I agreed completely, recollecting the old saw, 'Waste not, want not,' which appeared to me right then to be among the wiser mottoes.

Fact is, we neither wasted nor wanted through most of the forenoon, by which time breakfast was welcome indeed.

We ate like a herd of horses and we drank champagne and at last we talked, facing across the lacy iron table on the terrace in soft springtime sunshine. Lucie never looked so beautiful as she did right then, her face still flushed from our lovemaking, her dark eyes soft and thoughtful and understanding. I tried to explain why I had to leave, but she held up her hand and said, "I understand, *mon bel-ami,* better zan you can know. You mus' go. Zat I accep'. Eef I keep you 'ere, zat in you zat I love ze mos' weel die, as a bird of ze fores' mus' die in ze *cage. Je t'aime* too much for zat." Tears glistened in her eyes, but she stood up and shook her head and laughed, rather too gaily it appeared to me. "But come, *mon amant,* let us make of zis, our final day togezzer, *un grand souvenir!"* She pulled me to my feet, kissed me, and said, "Come! Eet ees time for our bat'!"

After our bath together I went behind the screen and put on my hickory shirt and britches. When Lucette saw me a fleeting frown clouded her face, but she said nothing about it.

Lucie's duties kept taking her off to other parts of the house and grounds. She returned each time as soon as she could, smiling and laughing, but her smile was fragile and her laughter somewhat strained. There was no need for me to leave the house that day, so I didn't, contenting myself to spend the time when she wasn't there in reading or daydreaming on the terrace.

Whenever she returned she brought me little treats, a plate of sweets she called *bonbons,* a dusty bottle of fine wine or brandy from the cellars, or pastries still warm from the oven. We were much in each other's arms that day and through the early evening. Then after a supper that surpassed all the others she took me to bed.

We slept very little if at all that night. Our lovemaking was by turns tender or playful or frenzied with a heat of passion that would surely burn itself out if there were time to do so, but time was one thing we didn't have.

It was still dark outdoors when a light tapping at the door of the chamber roused us from a shallow slumber. Lucie started up, then strained me to her and kissed me fiercely, reaching for me and whispering a plea for one more time. Which I naturally did not refuse.

As we lay gasping and hot and sweating I realized that time was running out and Tuttle would soon be waiting in the street below. I rolled to my side and gave Lucie a final peck and scooted for my screen, where I washed my face and bathed what I could in the basin there. Then I slipped into my hickory britches and shirt and came out carrying my tall boots in my hand.

Lucette had lighted a couple of lamps, which bathed her in a golden glow. Standing completely naked as she was, it was a picture that I reckon I shall always carry in my mind. She smiled when I appeared and said, "Oh, Temple, *mon amant*, please remove your clos'ing." I must have looked downright scared, for I certainly was. Up to then I had always been equal to the occasion, but after that last day and night I feared I would likely be something of a disappointment. Lucie saw me hesitate and laughed as she said, "Please, my Temple, for me."

I did as she asked and shucked out of my clothes, sorry to bid her farewell with a failure. When I looked up she was beaming as she came to me, holding out a beautiful suit of buckskins the color of fresh cream and fringed to a fare-thee-well. She stood on tip-toe and kissed me and then she said, "Put zem on. Eet ees not *propre* zat you go to ze *forêt* in ze *costume* of *un cultivateur*, 'ow you say, ze farmer."

When I pulled on those leather britches and wriggled into the long shirt it was like diving into a churn full of butter. They were soft as sunshine and they clung like a second skin. Memories of Powatawa and his family and the *wegiwa* swam into my mind as I stood swinging my arms and admiring the graceful fringe. When I looked up I saw Lucie holding a rifle that was nearly as tall as she was. She leaned it towards me and I took it up, hefting the light weight and perfect balance and carrying it to a lamp where I saw engraved on the barrel close to the lock the name *Melchior* and the number *.52*. It was of Pennsylvania workmanship of a quality that Uncle Ben would have envied. Lucie saw my dumbstruck look and she laughed and clapped her hands like a child on Christmas morning. Then she took my hand and led me behind a screen that stood near the door. There on the floor was a heap of plunder all ready to be bundled up. I saw a powder horn and a belt complete with pouches, a bedroll and a hooded coat made from a woolen blanket, and a pair of bulging saddlebags. I tossed my hickory clothes onto the heap, recalling what a grubby job working on a keelboat could be, certain that such clothing would likely come in handy before long.

Lucie reached into the pile and brought up a dark-red woolen cap that looked much like a stocking with a tassel at the top. She reached up and pulled the cap down to my ears, then stepped back, hands on her hips, and regarded me approvingly. "Eet ees *une tuque*. Now you 'ave ze look of *un voyageur français, mon chevalier de la forêt! C'est propre!*"

I had hardly any French at that time, but I reckoned I caught her drift, that I was her knight of the forest and the cap somehow tied me to her as long as I wore it.

Then she led me to the little table where my books were stacked. "Take what you weesh, *mon amour*. I 'ave learn how important eet ees for you to do ze reading." That mark of thoughtfulness impressed me as much as all the other plunder she had amassed for me. I selected two books, Homer's *Iliad* and his *Odyssey*, and slipped them into the bedroll.

Day was breaking and the clock on the mantel showed just past five. Lucette stepped to the door and called out, "*Café complet, s'il vous plaît!*" Then she took my hand and led me to the dining table, picking up her wrapper from the bed and shrugging into it on the way. A moment later two of her maids entered with trays piled high with enough breakfast for half a dozen people. She chattered almost without stopping whilst we ate, but her eyes were bright with brimming tears and her smile was brittle.

I tried to talk of common things, but I, too, was choking up. Finally I said, mainly just to be saying anything at all, "But how did you know what I needed, what to get? That rifle, for one thing...." I trailed off uncertainly.

"Oh, zere are many men 'ere een *Saint Louis* zat make trade with ze *Indiens*. Zey know *la forêt, le désert*. I sink zey know what ees require. Zey 'ave chosen well?"

I replied honestly. "They certainly did. I reckon they know a whole lot more about it than I do. My thanks to them." Then I tried to say thanks to her, but I couldn't think of words to tell her what I felt.

I reckon she read it in my eyes, howsomever, for she leaped up, ran around the table, and threw her arms around my neck, covering my face with kisses and hot tears that mingled with my own. Then she ran to the heap of plunder near the door and came back with a pair of beaded moccasins that looked to be of Shawnee design, but I couldn't be sure. She knelt and commenced to put them on my feet. I tried to stop her but she insisted on doing it, so I quit resisting and let her do as she wished.

I won't try to tell of our leave-taking. I've said too much as it is. We parted there in her bedchamber, neither of us trusting ourselves to say farewell in front of other folks. We made no promises nor did we express regret. We both knew what we were feeling and words were not required.

At the downstairs door Israel and I clasped hands. His face was grave but his eyes were soft with good wishes and he and I had no need to say anything either.

Chapter IV
The Missouri

I stepped into the street, rifle in hand and burdened with plunder enough to cripple a mule. Tuttle was waiting a short distance from the door and when he saw me he let out a loud guffaw. "Oh, Goddlemighty, do presarve us!" he roared. "Jest look at ye! If'n ye ain't one sort o' dandy, ye're another!" He circled around me, cavorting like a scarecrow come alive and pointing in mock wonder at my gleaming buckskins, the overstuffed bedroll slung from one shoulder and the heavy saddlebags from the other, the hooded overcoat that Lucie called a *capote* draped over all. He ran on with remarks such as, "If'n ye don't look like Mizzuz Washin'ton's pet pony!" and other such foolishness. I held my peace. I confess that I did look a mite shiny. He, on the other hand, looked like he always did, plumb scrofulous.

When I reckoned I had heard more than enough of Tuttle's jibes, we set out for Chouteau's, hustling through the nearly-deserted early-morning streets, the both of us anxious not to be tardy. It had rained during the night and we had to dodge around pools of muddy water that stood in the unpaved streets. When we chanced upon a big puddle, I halted and dropped my burdens to the ground and handed my rifle and powderhorn to Tuttle. He stared at me, saying nothing, obviously wondering what I meant to do. He hadn't long to wait to find out. I braced myself and ran into the puddle, threw myself down, and rolled to the far end of it. When I got to my feet, dripping muddy water from head to foot, I glared at Tuttle and said, "There! That suit ye?" He said never a word and I picked up my plunder, took back my rifle and horn, and continued on the way to Chouteau's. Nobody was likely to call me a fop after that.

ॐ   ॐ   ॐ

Folks were schooling like feeding fish when we arrived in the street in front of Chouteau's big mercantile. Not just the men who were to go upriver but also their friends and families and lady friends and even some black servants. As soon as we got in amongst them I regretted my roll in the mud puddle. Some of those young men who were signed up to go with the expedition were togged out in a much more dandified manner than I was, or had been, with spotless new buckskins and bright shirts and silk scarves and hats and caps of every style and color, new rifles glistening with oil, the most of thcm standing beside piles of plunder too great for one man to carry all at once.

Everybody wasn't dressed like that. Most were wearing hickory clothes, like Tuttle, though I didn't notice any of them who were quite as dirty as he. Some wore home-made moccasins and others were shod in square-toed boots. Their plunder was skimpy, their bedrolls slim, and no more than half of them were equipped with winter coats, but almost all of them had a rifle or musket, powder horn and pouches, and a knife or two tucked in their belt.

I spied young Bridger amidst the crowd, bright-eyed and smiling and trading quips with the other men, though I couldn't hear what they were saying. I was happy to see him there. He was getting his wish, just as I was realizing my own.

Before long Major Henry appeared, threading his way amongst the waiting men, halting now and then to chat with this or that one, smiling mostly but sometimes looking grave and thoughtful when he replied to some man's question. When he came near Tuttle and me he looked me over head to foot before he said with a grin, "Mornin', Brother Buck. Sleep in a swamp last night, did ye?"

I was still more than somewhat damp and muddy and wishing that I hadn't risen so quickly to Tuttle's jibes, but I grinned back at him and replied, "No, sir. I daresay I slept more comfortable last night than I'm like to do again, leastaways for a spell yet."

Henry chuckled and said, "I daresay you're right about that, Mister Buck, but I reckon you'll manage." He wished Tuttle a good morning and exchanged some pleasantry with him before he moved on. I watched him making his way through the crowd, slim and wiry and square-shouldered, a tall beaver hat atop his head, dressed in well-worn buckskins that I took to be left over from his early days in the Missouri River wilderness. He halted in response to a hail from a big, rough-looking man sprawled against a bedroll, his rifle across his knees, who appeared to be more than somewhat older than the rest of us, his deeply-seamed face the color of old saddle leather and his square-cut black beard streaked with gray. Even from a distance his piercing blue eyes looked mean. The buzz of talk around us kept me from hearing what he said to Henry, but I saw the Major frown and make a short reply. Then he shrugged and continued on his way.

Tuttle touched my arm and said in a low voice, "Thet'ere be Hugh Glass an' he be a hellion fer sartin sure. I seen 'im a time or two when he be on the prod down in Veed Poach. He's got hisse'f an orn'ry streak a yard wide. Even Matilda won't let 'im in her place no more."

I totally trusted Tuttle's judgment in such matters. I nodded and determined to avoid Hugh Glass.

Tuttle fell silent for a spell and then he asked, "Ye got any money, Temple?"

"I don't rightly know," I replied. "Lucette gifted me with all this plunder just this morning and I ain't sure just what I do have. Why're you askin'? You still thirsty?"

Tuttle grinned at me and I could see no shame in his eyes. "Hell, Temple, I'm allus thirsty, but thet ain't what I got in mind right naow." He paused for a moment, a smile on his whiskery face, most likely recollecting last night's spree at Matilda's, before he said, "No, I'm thinkin' we be needin' a mite o' tradin' plunder afore we go up the river, fer swappin' with Injuns. Some o' them Frenchy traders down at Matilda's tol' me to take some along, but I went an' drank up an' poked away all o' what you gave me. Ye got any more?"

I didn't bother to reply. Instead I unbuckled the straps on my saddlebags and spilled the contents onto the ground between us. First thing that I saw was the small double-barreled pocket pistol Lucette had lent me earlier. I picked it up, saw it was loaded and primed, and shoved it into my waistband under my shirt. Still lying there were two bullet molds, one for the pistol, the other, larger one for my rifle, spare flints, a bullet pouch full of rifle balls, a clasp knife, firesteels, a hone, soap and a razor, a small silver flask that I was sure was filled with Lucette's good French brandy, two briar pipes and a full tobacco pouch, and a passel of other useful odds and ends that I can't recall. But no money.

Tuttle was already spreading out my bedroll and wondering aloud why I didn't offer him some of that brandy. Which I didn't, leastaways not just then. The bedroll produced, besides three thick woolen blankets, three fine linen shirts and some brightly-colored silk scarves, my hickory clothes, a long, slim, double-edged knife in a sheath, a heavy-bladed butcher knife, a light tomahawk, an extra pair of moccasins, mittens, a full bottle of brandy, my two books, quill pens, writing paper, and an ink block. But still no money.

Tuttle was looking ever more disappointed, downright reproachful, as if Lucette and I had conspired to deprive him of his trade plunder. I paid no nevermind to his sulking and unbuckled my outer belt to add my belt knife, bullet pouch, and molds, when it came to me that I hadn't looked into the possibles pouch that was hanging off my middle all the while. There it was, a snug deerhide purse, heavy with coin. Tuttle's trade plunder was assured — and my own as well.

We left our possessions in Jim Bridger's care and trooped into Chouteau's mercantile, peering this way and that at the wonder of merchandise hanging on the walls and stacked on the counters. Even though we had a power of possible choices, it took hardly any time at all to make our purchases, for we knew that whatever we bought we would most likely have to carry on our backs and thanks to Lucette I already had more than enough plunder for one man to pack.

Soon enough there was a tidy pile of likely trade goods on the counter — a score of long tobacco twists, a dozen butcher knives coated with hog fat, a double handful of little round mirrors, six dozen steel awls, fish hooks, a pound of cone-headed brass tacks, a couple dozen packets of vermilion powder, scissors, red trade cloth and bright-colored ribbons, and several hanks of those little white, black, red, and sky-blue beads Indian women are fond of sewing onto shirts and moccasins and just about everyplace else they can think of to fasten them. I recalled then how the Shawnee women had prized those sky-blue beads above all other colors whenever I used to bring gifts to the village, so I tossed an extra fistful onto the pile.

Tuttle had moved off to another counter and when I looked over his shoulder I saw that he was admiring a big, heavy-bladed knife with a shiny brass handle, so I bought it for him. Cash money wasn't likely to be of much account once we commenced our journey up the Missouri.

The counter-jumper was stuffing our purchases into a croker sack and Tuttle was gazing longingly at a fine, well-oiled saddle when I reached into my belt pouch for my coin purse. My fingers touched something else instead. I pulled out a silver locket on a heavy silver chain. When I snapped open the lid I saw a tiny portrait of Lucette, her dark eyes deep and glowing against tawny skin the color of *café-au-lait*, her generous lips curved in a half-smile, her expression seeming to ask if I was really sure of what I was doing, if I truly wished to leave her.

Fact is, I wasn't altogether sure of anything at all, but I was pluperfectly determined to go ahead and do it anyhow.

Tuttle was still staring at the saddle, his back towards me. I slipped the chain over my head and dropped the locket inside my shirt before I fumbled coins onto the counter to pay for our trade goods, thinking the while that every good thing that had happened to me since I left home I owed to that lady with the quizzical smile.

I was still counting my change when Tuttle swung the sack onto his shoulder and started for the door, anxious, I reckon, to get into the sunshine once again, for Tuttle was rarely at ease indoors, unless he was with a woman. As I turned to follow him I spied Micah coming through a doorway, a heavy sack of what I took to be some sort of grain draped across his shoulders. I called out to him and when he looked up a grin of pure delight split his dusky face. I was grinning, too, as I stepped forward and helped him drop the sack to the floor. He took a step backward and surveyed me from head to toe before he said, admiration in his voice, "My oh my, ain'

yew a *propah koo-ruhr-day-bwah* now, Mist' Tempa!   Yew
sho'nuff gwine up de rivah wid de Mayjah, lak dey bin sayin'." He
rattled on about Indians and bears and beavers and getting rich or
maybe killed and how I needed to take good care of myself and
come back safe and sound and a passel of other trash that folks say
when they want to tell you that they love you and don't rightly
know how to get it said.

As I half-listened to his words spilling out, I was aware that
Micah had changed, was changing even then and there as we
spoke, that here was a man who was realizing that he was indeed a
man. I saw hope in his eyes and heard it in his voice, where there
had been none at all before. I reminded myself that he was still a
slave, another man's property, but I saw, too, that he was growing
into every nook and cranny of whatever small freedom that was
allowed him.   I wondered if Pierre Chouteau knew what was
happening with Micah and I mostly decided that he did.

A big Negro, an older man, came to the doorway and called out
something to Micah in French. Micah nodded and grinned at him
and stooped to shoulder the sack he had been carrying. When he
straightened up he shoved out his hand and took mine in his. His
grip was firm and tears glistened in his eyes when he said, "Yew
take care o' yohse'f, Mist' Tempa, an' keep yoh eye peeled foh dem
Injuns." He choked up about that time and then he said, "Ah loves
ya, Mist' Tempa, but Ah reckon you awready knows dat." Then he
shuffled through the entrance doorway and disappeared amongst
the drays and wagons and carts in the street.

I don't recollect what my own parting words were but what I
wanted to tell him was that one way or another I would see him a
free man one day or die trying to make it happen.

Tuttle was sprawled against our piled-up plunder when I made my
way through the crowd of waiting men and hunkered down beside
him.   Bridger was on his feet and peering out across the river,
trying to see the keelboats coming to pick us up, as if he feared that
something might happen to prevent our departure. I admit that I

shared his worry, groundless as it might have been, for this great unknown adventure had become the most important event in my young life and I daresay in Bridger's as well.

Howsomever I had no time to dwell on such doubts and wonderments for it came to me that I couldn't put off any longer writing a letter to Ma and telling her what I was about to do. She deserved at least that much from me, even if she despised me for doing what Pap and Uncle Ben had almost certainly told her that I had done.

I nudged Tuttle aside and dug out from my bedroll some writing paper, pens, and the ink block, shaved off some ink powder and moistened it with brandy, and commenced scribbling a letter that tried to tell Ma where I was and what I aimed to do and roughly where I expected to do it, without explaining why I had left home in the first place or what I had been doing since then. That letter, lame as it turned out, was most likely the most difficult task I had ever attempted. I was drowning in guilt and there was nothing I knew how to say to excuse it, so I didn't try. I just told her that I loved her and that I loved Sarah, too, even though thoughts of Lucette swam into my mind when I wrote those words and made me feel even more guilty. I was too young then to understand that a body can love more than one person in the same way at the same time.

I finished off by telling Ma that she could probably write to me, if she still wanted to, in care of Pierre Chouteau at Berthold & Chouteau in Saint Louis, as he would be most likely to know how to get a letter to wherever I might be. By time I got to Your Dutiful Son and scratched Temple underneath it, my eyes were too blurry with tears to write a separate letter to Sarah, even if I had known what I could possibly say to her, which I surely didn't.

Whilst I was scribbling those uncertain words I happened to glance sidewise at Tuttle and knew that he saw the tears in my eyes, but he never said a word about it. Rude and crude and loud and unlettered as he certainly was, Tuttle Thompson had a sense of respect for another man's dignity that many a so-called gentleman could afford to copy.

I folded the sheets and wrote Ma's name in care of JacobStaples's Store in Whynot, Ohio, hoping the while that somebody knew where that was and how to get a letter there. Then I went back inside the mercantile to have it sealed and posted.

The clerk was dripping hot red wax to seal my letter and I was counting coins to post it when I looked up and saw Pierre Chouteau standing beside me. He pushed my coins back to me and took the letter from the clerk, saying, "I shall myself attend to zis, M'sieu Bock." He glanced at the inscription and asked, "Zis is your wife?"

"No, sir, my mother." I thanked him for his kindness and told him what I had written about sending her letters in his care. He smiled and said that he would be happy to assist in every way. He was wishing me *bon voyage* when we heard a shout go up from the men waiting outside, announcing the arrival of the keelboats. Excitement surged through me and without thinking I spun around and made for the door, checking myself in mid-stride and returning to shake Chouteau's hand and mumble my thanks one final time. The man they called le Cadet laughed out loud and waved me away and stood beaming as I scurried outdoors.

Everybody outside was on his feet and cheering as the two keelboats swept downstream towards the wharf, the rowers straining mightily at their long oars to bring them shoreward. Boatmen stood in the bows, coils of rope in their hands, ready to heave mooring lines to the men on shore. Another shout went up from the crowd as the first line snaked through the air and was grabbed by a dozen men, who snubbed it around a post and tied it fast. Soon the air was laced with flying ropes and before long the two keelboats were riding snug against the wharf, bumping gently in the Mississippi River current.

Eager to lend a hand, I wormed my way through the press of men on the wharf. As I broke through the front rank I saw Tuttle Thompson already there, craning his lean neck to watch the mostly short but sturdy, swarthy men aboard the keelboats going about their work, dropping the square sail from the stubby mast, making lines fast, and shoving wide planks into place between the boats and the wharf. I sidled over to Tuttle and heard him say, a tinge of distaste in his tone, "Frenchies. Frenchies what they shorely be. Canucks down from up North'ard."

I noticed that nearly all of the boatmen wore a dark red stocking cap like my own and most sported a bright-colored sash around their middle. They seemed to me to be a good-natured lot. Smiles showed through their dark beards and here and there I caught a snatch of song in a tongue I now knew to be French.

My gaze roamed over the deck of the nearest keelboat, which had the name St. Pierre painted on the bow, and on to the second boat, the *Bonhomme*. My heart sank. My eyes were locked into the steely blue glare of Mike Fink, his lips curled into that sneering half-smile I had come to despise. Behind him bulked the familiar shapes of Talbot and Carpenter, those inevitable shadows that seemed never to be more than half a step behind him.

Quick as a cat, Fink vaulted over the low rail and landed on the wharf, his heavy boots ringing on the planks. He shouldered and shoved his way through the milling men and halted in front of me, hands on his hips, his face set in a mirthless smile, venom dripping from every pore. "So now, Laddy Buck! Yer nigger wench t'run ye out? Ye fail at pimpin', too?"

I was too stunned to understand more than half of what he said or to make any reply at all. Without thinking I shoved my hand under my leather shirt, reaching for the pistol in my belt, when I felt Tuttle's iron grip on my wrist and heard his calm, dry voice saying, "Hear ye now, Mike Fink, neither'n us work fer ye now. Thet's past. From now, ye leave this lad be."

I saw Talbot and Carpenter moving through the crowd towards us and I reckon Tuttle did, too, for he went on, "Ya'll'd best tend to yer own biz'ness an' let us get on with our'n. An' let thet be an end to it."

Fink's surprise at Tuttle's words and the flat, deliberate way he had said them showed through his customary smirk. His bully's mask dissolved for an instant as he fought to regain his customary bluster. I had never thought I'd see Mike Fink at a loss for words. Howsomever it didn't last for long. His voice exploded in a roar. "Ye makin' this your fight, too, Thompson?"

"I reckon I am. If'n it's a fight you're wishin' fer, I reckon I'm in it." Tuttle's tone remained calm and matter-of-fact, but he kept his grip on my wrist and I could feel his muscles tighten, tense as a hammer-spring at full cock.

Fink opened his mouth to reply but I cut in. "What in hell were you sayin' about Lucette, Fink? You've no call to be talkin' about her like that."

Talbot and Carpenter were by now standing on either side of Fink, which appeared to restore his swagger. "Mike Fink sez what he damn pleases an' I'm choosin' to tell ye now she's nuthin' but a high-yeller whore out o' N'Orleens what's made it rich runnin' a Sain' Looie whorehouse an' you're nuthin' else but her goddamn fancy-boy!"

I lunged forward and fought to yank my pistol from my belt, but Tuttle's hold on me remained firm. In spite of my struggles Tuttle's voice was almost tranquil when he said, "I reckon the three o' you had oughter go on back to yer boat, lest I turn the lad loose an' then we're all goin' to be sorry."

Before Fink could reply, the iron voice of Andrew Henry rang out. "Do as he says, Fink. Return to your boat. Now! You other two, Carpenter and Talbot, you go with him. Immediately."

Fink wasn't used to taking orders from anybody, but there was something in Henry's tone and in his stony face that made the bully falter, then turn away, grumbling under his breath. The Major raised his voice and announced to everybody within earshot, "I'll tolerate no brawling amongst the members of this expedition! None! Any man who violates this order will be discharged immediately and set afoot to return as best as he can! Let that be understood by one and all! There will be no fighting amongst this company! None whatsoever!"

Although Fink's back was turned I could see his muscles quiver under his shirt as he fought to control himself. He wheeled and threw a dirty look at me. Then he glared long and hard at Tuttle, surely promising to even the score, before he turned and made his way through the crowd, flanked by his companions.

It was only then that Tuttle turned me loose and I was rubbing the numbness from my wrist when Major Henry stepped in front of us and said, "You two will travel aboard my keelboat, the *Saint Pierre*. Understood?" We both nodded and he bent a thoughtful, penetrating gaze on me before he continued, "Avoid those men as best you can, both of you. Especially you, Mister Buck. I have learned something of your history with Mike Fink, but I cannot allow anything to interfere with the conduct of this expedition. There will be excitement aplenty as we proceed to the mountains and no need at all to borrow more of it."

I grinned and mumbled my agreement and Tuttle did the same. The Major allowed himself a brief smile and said, "I reckon the two of you will do all right. Men need to stick together in the mountains." Then he turned on his heel and was quickly lost amongst the throng of men on the wharf.

I had plenty to think about during the next couple of hours as Tuttle and I pitched in to help with toting and stowing all sorts of cargo aboard the two keelboats. Without saying anything about it, we both avoided Fink and his men and I noticed that they were keeping their distance from us as well.

It was mindless work, grunting under the weight of sacks of flour and dry beans, bundles of steel traps, powder kegs, galena pigs for casting rifle and musket and pistol balls, crates of rifles, muskets, and trade guns, a power of saddles, cordage, blankets, boots and clothing, a forge and blacksmith tools, kegs of salt pork and sacks of bacon flitches, spades and axes, adzes, and carpentry tools, crosscut and ripping saws, bales of goods for trading with the Indians upriver, and besides which I truly don't know what all. In the meantime my mind was gnawing at what Fink had said about Lucette and what I had just learned about the character of Tuttle Thompson.

I had thought I knew Tuttle passably well, a footloose, happy-go-lucky Kentucky woodsman interested mainly in horses, whiskey, and whores, roughly in that order. I had regarded him as a friend, to be sure, but up till then I hadn't thought much at all about how deep that feeling might run, either on his side or my own. Now I knew that he was a sight more than just a friendly companion. He knew Mike Fink and his bully-boys as well as I did, yet he had dealt himself into a deadly game in which he had no stake. The feud was mine, not his, but now he was in it up to his neck. I never had a brother, as you know, but I felt like I had one now.

What Fink had said about Lucette stung like a nest of hornets. All sorts of notions buzzed around inside my brain, bumping into each other and cancelling one another out. Maybe Fink had been lying outright, but maybe not. And if not, what did it matter anyway? He had called her a nigger, but she was as white as I was, maybe whiter, and even if she was what Fink had said she was, why should that change the way I thought of her? As for his calling her a whore, that didn't trouble me overmuch. After all, being a schoolmarm or somesuch wouldn't equip a body to run an establishment like Lucette's. You'd have to know what makes the clock tick. No, the bothersome part was about her being Negro, even just a mite, and I pondered on why I should find myself caring anything at all about such a matter anyhow, asking myself who could have planted such a notion in my head and when it might have happened. I'm not sure just when I made up my mind, maybe not right then, but in the end I decided that Lucette was well-worth my loving her and the likes of Mike Fink should never have a say in what I thought about anything or anybody.

෴ ෴ ෴

Many hands make light work, like they say, and it wasn't long before the mountain of supplies on the wharf had dwindled down to nothing, all of it safely stowed in the cargo holds of the keelboats. The Frenchy boatmen had overseen the work, smiling and pointing and rattling out throaty commands that only some of the Saint Louis dandies understood, but somehow getting the idea across to the rest of us about what was supposed to go where. I made up my mind then and there that I would learn to talk French. And in the course of time I pretty much did so.

The sun was high in a mid-morning sky when Major Henry called us all together and assigned us to six-man messes, which meant that the men in a particular mess would camp, cook, and eat together, that rations would be issued to each mess and divided by an elected leader amongst its members, and that each of us would be responsible for the well-being of the other five men in our mess. It all sounded reasonable to me, especially when the Major called out the names and we found that Tuttle, Jim Bridger, and I were assigned to the same mess. We didn't know the other three, John Smiley, John Fitzgerald, and Padraic McBride, but it didn't take long to get a handle on them. Smiley rarely ever smiled and Fitzgerald and Paddy McBride proved that all Irishmen are not alike.

As we listened to the Major reading out the names I was impressed with how much he already knew about us, how he sorted the men into messes that would likely get along with one another. When he called out Mike Fink's name I was sure that Talbot and Carpenter would soon follow. And so it was. I wondered who their other three messmates might be and I was not surprised when I heard the name of Hugh Glass added to their number. I daresay Henry reckoned he could keep a closer eye on the bullies and troublemakers if they were gathered together in a single mess.

The Major gave us all time to seek out our messmates, which wasn't all that easy amongst a mob of nearly a hundred men, but we managed to find the other three, none of whom knew the others, as it turned out. At last we stood together, our plunder in a single heap, and waited for the Major's next order.

Waiting gave us time to take stock of one another. John Smiley was a Pennsylvanian, a man who wasted no words, as tall as Tuttle and lean, almost gaunt, older than the rest of us, most likely somewheres about thirty, sober and grave. He made a body think more of an undertaker than a trapper, but his eyes were sharp as a lancet and when he easily shouldered his considerable plunder we could see that he was no weakling. His weathered face and calloused hands, well-worn leather clothing, and his fine Pennsylvania rifle, scarred and scratched from hard use but gleaming with oil, bespoke him to be a man who was no stranger to the wilderness and the life that goes with it.

Paddy McBride was a whole different matter. Short, stocky, red-headed and freckled, with a quick, sharp tongue and twinkling blue eyes, Paddy hailed from Ireland by way of Boston. He owned little more than the clothes on his back, but there was nothing apologetic about him. He said that he'd come to America to make his fortune, but Boston was "divil a place fer doin' that, so it's up the High Missourah an' turnin' furry critters into spendable gold fer the needs an' wishes o' Paddy McBride!"

John Fitzgerald was a stew from quite a different kettle. He told us he was from "back East" and little else, nothing about a trade or what he might have been doing up till then and naturally we didn't ask. I'd say he was in his mid-twenties, tall, broad-shouldered, looking like he had muscle enough, with an Irishman's ruddy complexion. It was his eyes that bothered me, for they would shift away when he talked to you, as if he feared that you might read his thoughts if you looked him full in the face. His clothes were citified but he was no dandy and he carried no rifle. From the first he distanced himself from McBride, anxious, it seemed, that we wouldn't think of him as just another Irishman. I reckon he succeeded, for none of us ever lumped the two of them together.

The blast of a boat trumpet called our attention to Andrew Henry standing at the rail of the *St. Pierre*. We were already gathered nearby, for Tuttle and I had told the others that we would be traveling in Henry's boat. The Major wasted no time in getting us aboard. He called out one name from each mess and directed that group to the first or second keelboat. When Tuttle's name rang out we hoisted our plunder and tramped across the planks and onto the boat. Tuttle led us to a spot atop the cargo box sternward behind the mast, next to the catwalk that the Frenchies call the *passe-avant*, and we heaped our plunder there. Whilst we waited for the rest of the expedition to board we went ahead and elected our mess captain. By unspoken common consent, Jim Bridger, Paddy McBride, and I were left out of the running, maybe because we were considered to be too young, and Tuttle declared right off that he didn't want the job. That left John Smiley and Fitzgerald and when we finally spoke up and voted, all of us voted for Smiley, except for Fitzgerald, who didn't vote for anybody. I reckon he wanted the job for himself, but there was something about the man that didn't inspire a great deal of confidence.

As each mess bunch filed aboard their assigned keelboat there was a flurry of action on the wharf as mothers and fathers and sweethearts and even the black servants of those men who had such relations present moved to embrace them and offer farewells and final gifts. Afterwards, when all of us were aboard, we could still hear a parcel of sobs and wails and all manner of lamentations, mostly from the women. Tuttle and I stood at the rail and watched it all, but there was nobody crying for us.

Andrew Henry's voice cut through the air and we turned to see him standing on the stern deck of our boat, motioning the men on both boats to gather closer. William Ashley stood beside him.

Henry spoke first. "Gentlemen, it is time to set off on our great expedition. We have supreme confidence in the success of our enterprise and in you, the men who will make that success possible. Hardship and peril will be constantly at your elbow, to be sure, but the rewards to be gained will amply compensate all of you who meet with courage, discipline, and honest effort the challenges that lie ahead." He went on in that vein for a considerable spell and Tuttle nudged me and whispered one word, "Politician!" I sniggered under my breath and fought to keep from grinning as I pictured Pap's highfalutin sermonizing on the Sabbath.

The Major finally tied up his remarks and then he announced, "It gives me inestimable pleasure to inform all of you today that the success of our venture will be further insured by the presence of my esteemed friend and valued colleague, General William Ashley, who has determined to lend us his presence and accompany us on our journey upriver!"

Henry made a little bow and waved the General forward and when Ashley spoke I was even more reminded of Tuttle's whispered "Politician!" for it appeared to me that what he said was tailored a great deal more to the gentry on the dock than to those of us who were going to the mountains with him. Howsomever none of it made no nevermind to me. I just stood there enjoying the warm spring sunshine on my back and watching the stiff breeze ruffle his hair when Ashley doffed his tall beaver hat to bow to the folks standing on the wharf. I recollect, too, thinking how like a pair of hunter hawks those two appeared to be, standing side by side up there on the stern deck, and I reckoned that the two of them were worth following just about anywhere they wished to lead us.

When the word to cast off came at last, Tuttle and I grabbed up a couple of boat poles and helped the Frenchy boatmen push us away from the wharf. As we drifted into the current I looked up for one last glimpse of Saint Louis, where my life had turned a somerset but left me standing on my own two feet. My gaze roved along the waterfront, the dock a riot of color and movement, still crowded with well-wishers waving farewells. My eyes shifted to the road above and I felt a sudden stab of pain, for there in front of Chouteau's Mercantile I saw Lucette's landau with Israel on the box, whip in hand. She was perched on the rear seat and Pierre Chouteau was standing in the street beside her, leaning languidly against a high yellow wheel. So she had come to bid me farewell after all.

Our eyes met across the water and when she saw me wave, she smiled, then turned away, dabbing at her eyes with a lacy white handkerchief. She looked up again and I could see a strained smile on her pale face as the current swept us farther out into the stream. Israel raised his whip above his cockaded coachman's topper in a goodbye gesture and Chouteau waved a casual farewell. Behind me I could hear the sail bellying and flapping in a brisk breeze and the Frenchies laughing and cursing good-naturedly as they strained at their long oars. I paid none of it no nevermind. I continued to stare at Lucette, my heart churning the while, until her features dissolved in the distance.

๛   ๛   ๛

We made hardly any progress at all that day, just across the river and a little ways upstream before we moored on the Illinois side and waded ashore to make camp. The skies had turned cloudy and there was a skimpy drizzle falling as Tuttle struggled with flint and steel to get a fire started. John Smiley went off to get our supper rations and Bridger, Paddy McBride, and I rustled up firewood. Then we fashioned a rude bower of leafy branches to help keep us out of the weather. I didn't notice Fitzgerald doing much of anything.

After a spell Smiley returned, loaded down with a kettle, wooden bowls and spoons and such, and a croker sack half filled with sowbelly, beans, and flour, which he and Tuttle proceeded to turn into a passable supper. It was nothing like what I had been getting used to at Lucette's, mind you, but it stuck to the ribs and was somewhat better than most of what I'd lived on before then or that we'd likely be getting to eat later on.

Dusk was falling rapidly into night and there was neither moon nor stars to relieve the darkness. All of us crawled under the bower and spread our bedrolls, glad to stretch out and gladder still to be on our way to the mountains. All of us except McBride. He just stood outside, saying nothing. He had no bedroll, no blankets, nothing more than what he stood up in, but he had no voice for complaining, or begging either.

Tuttle stared at him for a spell and then he grunted, "Aw, c'mon in hyar." Paddy ducked inside and crawled into the space between us, mumbling thanks. We shared our blankets with him and soon enough we were grateful for the extra warmth. I curled into a ball, my head on my possibles and my rifle cradled in my arms, my mind drifting back over all the happenings that had crowded that day, until sleep overtook me and I bathed in soft tears spilling from the liquid brown eyes of Lucette.

The blast of a boat trumpet roused me from my slumbers. I opened my eyes to gray early-morning light glinting dully through mist rising from the river. Tuttle was already at the fire, coaxing tiny tongues of flame from last night's embers. Smiley squatted nearby, waiting to warm the kettle that held last night's uneaten vittles. I rolled out of my blankets, jostling McBride as I rose. He awoke yawning and stretching and licking his lips, a smile already on his beard-stubbled face. As I dodged out of the bower I saw Jim Bridger stepping out from the trees, carrying an armload of firewood, and on the other side Fitzgerald coming from behind a bush, still buttoning his britches.

I stepped behind a tree and by time I returned to the fire the trumpet sounded again and we heard Major Henry's voice announcing that all men who required clothing, blankets, or firearms to report to his boat in a quarter-hour to receive an issue of such as they needed.

"I reckon the Majah be talkin' to you, Paddy," Tuttle called from the fire. "Time fer ye to mortgage yore soul an' git yorese'f an outfit o' yore own. Cain't tolerate no more o' yore snorin' in my ear all night!" Paddy blushed outright and then he laughed aloud. Tuttle went on. "Yew, too, Fitzgerald. Git yorese'f a shootin' iron. Ye'll be sure to be needin' it 'fore long, I solemnly opine." Fitzgerald hesitated and Tuttle barked, "G'wan naow! The two o' yew! We'll be savin' some o' these yere vittles fer when ye git back."

McBride favored us all with a broad grin, rose to his feet, and trotted towards the keelboat. Fitzgerald trailed after him, walking tall and not very fast, as if his slower gait somehow preserved his dignity.

Tuttle turned to Smiley and said, almost shyly, "Hope ye don't mind my buttin' in thetaway, John, but them boys had oughter git what they need an' bein' fust in line, they jest might git to choose their pick."

Smiley nodded and allowed that it made no nevermind to him who said what, so long as the job got done. Then he asked, "And you'uns? Ye got all ye'll be needin'?" Jim Bridger and Tuttle allowed that they had and so did I, especially me, for I reckoned that with all the plunder Lucette had bestowed on me I had more than enough. Fact is, I would likely need an extra packhorse, once we left the keelboat.

We were scraping the last of breakfast out of our wooden bowls when Fitzgerald strolled up to the fire, a couple of blankets draped over his shoulder, a long smoothbore musket cradled across his arm, and sporting a new powderhorn, leather belt, butcher knife, and bullet pouch.   Paddy McBride wasn't far behind him, chattering like a magpie and looking like he had looted a mercantile, burdened as he was with blankets, clothing, and a pair of square-toed boots, a musket in the crook of his arm, and a powderhorn, belt, and all manner of plunder slung about his neck.

"Would ye be lookin' at all o' this beeyootiful trash, would ye now? Young Padraic McBride's become a gentleman, lookin' rich beyond all measure, I am! Sure'n 'tis a paycock indeed I'll be!" He paused for breath and then he laughed, a wild, good-natured laugh.   "O' course, like ye say, Tuttle, I had to mortgage me immortal soul an' that o' me first-born son, as well, to git all o' this, but 'tis worth iv'ry pinny, fer now no man'll be after callin' Paddy McBride a ragged-arse mick! 'Tis the clothes that're after makin' the man, don't ye know? An' now I'll be goin' in style to god-knows-where to trap all o' thim beavers wid the best of 'em!" With that he dumped all of his plunder on the ground, kicked off his broken shoes, and shucked out of his ragged clothes, right there in front of us, and when he had dressed himself in his new hickory-cloth finery we realized that Paddy's words were mighty close to the mark. Not only did he look different, he *was* indeed different, confident, cocksure of himself, ready to rise up to any challenge.

Whilst Paddy and Fitzgerald wolfed down their breakfast and I was rolling up my bedroll, I thought about the changes that the expedition was making in the men around me and in myself as well. Here we were, nearly still in sight of Saint Louis, and already I could see alterations taking place. Tuttle, who never took the lead in anything, was speaking up whenever he took a mind to and Paddy McBride had just grown at least a foot taller right before our eyes.

Another trumpet call split the air, followed by the Major calling us all to gather at the boats. When the last of the men straggled out from the trees, Henry commenced speaking. This time we heard a speech that was considerably different from what he and Ashley had said the day before at the wharf in Saint Louis, when friends and family were present. This morning there was iron in his voice and he came directly to the point. He let us know right off that the expedition would be conducted on military lines and that it was for our own good, that democracy didn't work on the river or in the mountains, and that he was the boss and he, and only he, would be giving the orders and every man-jack amongst us was expected to obey those orders, no matter what.

William Ashley stood next to him, but he said nary a word, just stood there looking halfway grim and totally determined, lending authority to the Major's every word.

Henry went on to name his lieutenants and to lay down some rules, namely that every man was expected to keep himself and all of his equipment clean, especially our firearms. A groan went up from many of the men when he announced that drinking strong spirits and gambling would not be permitted and that we would all be required to shave regularly, that Indians despised bearded faces and we would need their respect and occasionally their support. Tuttle looked downright sour when he heard that, but it made no nevermind to me. I had never taken to cards or dice and I hadn't much of a beard anyhow.

Henry's tone softened somewhat at the end, when he explained that his rules, stern as they might appear to be right then, were needful if we expected to survive the country we were heading into. Fact is, he proved to be plumb on the mark.

– – –

Traveling upriver, leastaways at first, was rather much what you might expect on a keelboat. We all took our turns rowing and poling and sometimes hauling on the towrope the Frenchies called a *cordelle.* I found that I didn't mind the work nearly as much as I had on Mike Fink's boat, for this time it was my own choice to be where I was, but I was nonetheless happy when Henry told Tuttle and me that we would be hunters, along with a number of other men considered to be good shots. He picked Smiley and Bridger, too, but half the time he kept Jim busy at a forge he had set up on deck, repairing odds and ends and fashioning stuff he decided we needed. I reckoned it was just as well that I never learned a trade, for I dearly loved to hunt.

A pair of light skiffs trailed behind each keelboat and most days Tuttle and Smiley and I, along with a Frenchy boatman, pushed off for shore in a skiff to go perform our hunting chore. Once I got the sights tweaked just the way I wanted, I plumb fell in love with my rifle. I called it Melchior, after the name on the breech, and at first I marveled at the way that heavy ball could knock down a deer in its tracks. The rifle balls Uncle Ben and I used weren't much more than half that big.

Once we left the Mississippi and started up the Missouri, the settlement shacks were few and far between and the deer a lot more plentiful. Each of us hunted alone and after we shot a deer we gutted it on the spot and toted it down to the riverbank and left it for the Frenchy boatman to pick up and load into the skiff. Most days, if I say so myself, our skiff was riding low in the water, loaded with deer meat, by time we caught up with the keelboats laboring their way upriver.

Nobody remained idle for long if the Major had his say — and he always did. The top of the cargo box fairly buzzed with bunches of men busy skinning and butchering and scraping and tanning deer hides for clothing and moccasins. Strings of jerked deer meat drying in the clean Missouri air festooned the decks and crews of men sat under them, stitching buckskin shirts and britches and leggin's with sinew. Andrew Henry wasted neither time nor materials and all of us learned from one another the skills we would need to survive in the wilderness.

It wasn't all work, howsomever, and oftimes in the evening when the weather was fair Henry would sit outside the stern cabin he shared with General Ashley and play upon his fiddle, gay country airs and lively reels and soft, pleasant music of a kind I had never heard before, whilst we sprawled on the deck or on the shore and smoked and talked in low tones or just let the music steal us back to other times and faraway places and faces.

Most nights we camped ashore, gathered in our separate messes, cooking our vittles and performing daily chores such as cleaning and oiling rifles, refilling powder horns, casting rifle balls, and repairing moccasins and such by firelight, all the while chatting about a hundred different things, mostly about what might await us upriver and in the mountains. John Smiley rarely joined in such talk, but he listened. Fitzgerald, on the other hand, sat apart, saying and likely hearing nothing.

Sometimes, especially when a particularly bad stretch of river lay just ahead, we made camp early and there would be enough daylight for us to practice shooting at a mark or to play at throwing tomahawks and belt axes and butcher knives at a tree trunk. I learned to be rather handy at throwing the light tomahawk and the heavy butcher knife Lucette had given me, but right then such skills amounted to no more than a pastime.

Oftimes on such occasions Tuttle and Smiley and I would take Paddy McBride to a clearing away from camp to teach him how to shoot. We discovered that Paddy had never fired a gun before. It was high time that he learned. He took to it readily enough, howsomever, and we kept him at it until we were satisfied that Paddy could make a killing shot with his musket. Like I said, none of us had any idea of what might lie ahead, but we reckoned an extra gun might be just what was needed to save our skins.

ॐ   ॐ   ॐ

The Missouri is not what you might call a friendly river. In springtime especially it boils and surges with water running high and fast and thick with mud, the channels fraught with snags and sawyers that can rip the bottom out of a boat as clean and fast as you can peel a hardboiled egg. Most of us started off thinking the Frenchy boatmen were something of a joke, with all their funny talk and laughing and singing and dancing and such, but it wasn't too long until we came to admire their skill and to rely on it. The Frenchies understood keelboats and they knew the river and its channels, how to avoid snags and sawyers, and just when to use sail, oars, poles, or the *cordelle*.

As you might suppose, not everybody admired the Frenchy boatmen. Mike Fink was certainly and loudly one of those. It was, as you might say, a matter of professional jealousy.

It all came to a head like a festering carbuncle somewheres above the Kaw and just below where the Osage River joins the Missouri, when we hadn't been on the water but a couple of weeks, if that.

It was late in the day and a chill spring rain was drizzling down, drenching everyone and making tempers short. Tuttle and I were at the oars in the skiff and Jean-Luc L'Archévêque, our Frenchy boatman, was handling the tiller and the skimpy little sail. Loaded as we were with three fat deer and a couple-three turkeys, our progress upriver was slow but still faster than the two keelboats, which were cautiously threading their way through a thicket of snags and sandbars and sawyers, whole trees anchored in the riverbed with branches reaching up through roiling muddy water like the clutching hands of an executioner.

Our skiff was just drawing abreast of the *Bonhomme*, which was following the Major's keelboat through the channel, its sail bellied out to catch the stiff upriver breeze and oars dipping on both sides, when I caught sight of Mike Fink on the stern deck, waving his arms at the tillerman. I couldn't hear what Fink was yelling, but his red face and menacing manner were evidently enough to make the steersman cower on the far side of the heavy tiller arm. Then Fink's arm shot out and his fist caught the tillerman full in the face, knocking him to the deck.

The tiller arm swung free and slammed into Fink's midriff, driving him to the rail. Before Fink was able to grab hold of the tiller, the *Bonhomme* slewed in the heavy current, the sail went slack, and the keelboat smacked sidewise into a sandbar, splintering oars and catapulting half a dozen oarsmen over the side. The current grabbed the keelboat and dragged it off the sandbar, whirling out of all control and threatening to capsize. The deck tilted wildly and we could see the jagged shaft of the broken tiller break out of the water and men scrambling like ants to reach the high side of the deck as the keelboat swept downstream like a matchbox bobbing in a brook.

Tuttle and I nearly bent our oars in two as we dug deep to keep the skiff clear of the wreck. L'Archévêque breathed a fervent *"Sacré merde!"* but he stayed calm enough and guided our skiff into a little backwater, from where we watched the crippled *Bonhomme* spinning and lurching downstream until it smashed into a huge sawyer, a proper granddaddy of an oak tree rooted in the riverbed, and broke in half.

The two halves of the keelboat hung in the branches of the sawyer for what seemed a considerable spell but most likely wasn't very long at all, whilst we watched men scurrying about what was left of the decks, some snatching up what they could of their plunder, others diving straightaway overboard. Then first one half of the *Bonhomme* washed clear of the sawyer, then the other, and the two ends went tumbling downstream, scattering wildly thrashing men their wake.

My heart was racing but Tuttle remained his customary undisturbed self, leastaways as far as I could tell. Jean-Luc could speak a little English, very little, but Tuttle wasted no words. He motioned for L'Archévêque to drop the sail, which he did, and then we rowed to the riverbank, where we pitched our day's bag, three deer and the turkeys, onto the shore. Tuttle's only comment was, "'Pears to me them boys're gonna need a hot supper tonight. Them as don't git drowneded, thet is."

We returned to the oars, Jean-Luc left the crumpled sail where it was, and we headed downriver to help as best we could. The skiff, relieved of its burden, rode high in the water and we made good time, sweeping past the riverbank clotted with men already ashore and others scrambling to safety through the shallows. Dark heads bobbed in the deep water like so many corks and L'Archévêque hoisted the sail and dropped the keel deeper and swung his tiller to skew and slow the skiff in the current so that Tuttle and I could grab hold and drag coughing, cursing men aboard. The river was running too fast for us to pick up all the men we passed, but I saw the St. Pierre's other skiff with Smiley and Bridger aboard doing the same as we were. Fortunately the *Bonhomme*'s two skiffs had also been off on hunting chores that day, the same as we were, and they joined in the rescue.

We continued to drift downriver until we could spy no other survivors. Just as we were about to turn back, I saw a man's head bobbing in the water. Leastaways I thought at first it was a man swimming with the current, but in the gathering dusk I couldn't be sure. Then it appeared to be a drifting stump with a broken-off branch sticking up above it. I yelled to Jean-Luc to steer close to it, bringing us broadside to whatever it was. As we drew nigh, we saw it was indeed a man. Tuttle sculled oars and I leaned out and hauled him into the skiff. What had appeared to me to be a branch was his rifle slung across his back on a strap. The man was a dead weight and the weapon banged me alongside the head as I struggled to get him aboard.

By that time we had collected half a dozen shivering, water-logged, groaning, cursing survivors in the skiff, but the last one appeared to be worse off than his fellows, which was no surprise, for he had been in the water the longest. He lay on his belly, not talking or groaning, just spitting up river water from time to time. I saw he still wore a belt loaded with his possibles. Then he rolled onto his back and stared up at us with nary a flicker of expression on his face. I gasped and Tuttle groaned. It was Talbot and he uttered not a word of thanks, not then or anytime after that.

ॐ   ॐ   ॐ

It was long past nightfall by time we hauled the skiff ashore and joined the men already on the riverbank. We realized there was no profit in our looking for the St. Pierre until daybreak. The rain had quit and somebody had contrived to kindle a fire. I sincerely warrant you never saw a sorrier pack of drowned rats than the bunch huddled around that fire's warming blaze.

After he secured the skiff to a stout tree trunk, Jean-Luc went off to search out his friends and we saw no more of him until the following morning. The survivors had nothing to eat and neither did we, so Tuttle and I hunted up Smiley and Bridger, who had come ashore earlier, and the four of us rounded up half a dozen more men to hike upstream to retrieve the meat we had put ashore earlier.

By time we got back to the main bunch, our several deer and turkey carcasses swinging off sapling poles, several small fires were blazing. The men who huddled beside them, shivering and staring blankly into the flames, were a legion of lost souls. The heart had gone plumb out of them. Satisfied appetite is a marvelous curative, howsomever. Soon after we butchered up the game and offered meat all around, they brightened considerably. Hardly anything cures a young man's blues like filling his hungry belly. Soon you could hear men laughing and joshing one another and before long somebody commenced singing and then it took no time at all before a dozen hoarse voices were raised in song.

Whilst we were butchering the carcasses and setting out cuts a fallen log, Carpenter appeared out of the darkness and helped himself to a couple-three chunks. He spoke not at all, nor was there a trace of a smile or a thankee on his face. Without so much as a nod or a by-your-leave, he picked up the meat and strolled back to his fire, where Fink and Talbot sat cross-legged and silent. I wasn't at all surprised to see that all three had survived. Luther Pike, one of the Major's lieutenants aboard the *Bonhomme*, squatted off to one side, but I couldn't be sure if he was part of Fink's bunch or not. I didn't see Hugh Glass amongst them, but I would have wagered heavily that the old pirate had made it to safety. Folks say that only the good die young.

Tuttle had put aside a couple of tender backstraps from the butchering and after we finished that chore, he and John Smiley and Jim Bridger and I kindled a fire and cooked our supper. All we had was meat, but so long as there's a plenitude of meat, a hungry man doesn't need much else.

It had been a busy day, for we had pushed off from the St. Pierre before dawn to set out upon our hunting chore. Then what with fishing folks out of the river and all, the four of us were plumb tuckered. It wasn't long before all of us stretched out around the fire and soon I could hear the others snoring. I cradled Melchior in my arms, wishing that I could swap him, for just a brief spell, for the lady who had given him to me, but before I hardly knew it, I didn't know much at all.

❧   ❧   ❧

Morning sneaked in past a heavy mist rising from the river and the marshes, muffling the sounds of the camp, which was just coming to life, like trying to hear with your ears stuffed full of cotton fluff. I rolled to my feet and saw that Jim Bridger was gone. His rifle lay next to Smiley's, so I reckoned he was off gathering firewood, so after I attended to personal matters I tramped off to hunt up dry twigs and branches, too.

When I got back the whole camp was on its feet and Tuttle and Smiley were cooking the last of the backstrap on green willow sticks propped over the fire. Whilst I waited for my share, I tried to count noses amongst the bedraggled survivors of the shipwreck. There was no telling how many had been drowned, but from what I could see, most of the *Bonhomme*'s complement had made it to shore.

The crowd scattered along the riverbank was what you might call a mixed bag. Saint Louis dandies, nigh a score of them, sat apart from the rest, most of them sullen and depressed, looking like they wished they were anyplace else. The French-Canuck boatmen, on the other hand, appeared to take the wreck in stride — all in a day's work, as ye might say. One of them had managed to grab up his little musical squeezebox before he went over the side. Now he sat amongst his comrades coaxing cheerful ditties out of it, although the music sounded more than somewhat soggy.

At another fire alongside the Frenchies were half a dozen Indians, Iroquois from the East and down from Canada, Smiley said. Not one of them looked at all discomposed and they all had their firearms still with them, as well as several with bows and quivers besides, and enough hardware slung over their shoulders and hanging from their belts surely to sink a white man.

We carried four or five Delaware Indians aboard the St. Pierre. I reckon the Major had thought it best to keep the two tribes on separate boats in order to avoid a war, which proved to be an unnecessary precaution. The rest of the men were about what you might expect, some Kentuckians from Fink's keelboat crew, mostly tall, rawboned hunters who put me in mind of Tuttle Thompson, a

handful of Scots and a few Irishmen, three or four Englishmen —
limeys, Tuttle called them, though I never knew just why and when
I asked him, he didn't know either — some quiet men from the
East, a German or two, and a couple of ill-tempered complaining
men that Smiley said hailed from New York — altogether a mixed
bag. None of them was very old, but that morning they all looked
considerably the worse for wear.

When the meat was halfway cooked, we wolfed it down, then
prepared to launch the skiff. Earlier, Jean-Luc had conveniently
wandered up to our fire, rubbing his belly, just in time to share our
skimpy breakfast. After he belched and wiped his greasy hands on
his britches, we trotted down to the skiff and shoved it off from the
bank. Tuttle and I settled down to the oars and when we were
clear of the shore Jean-Luc ran up the sail. We headed upriver, for
it was doubtful that Henry would have risked the St. Pierre by
coming downstream in the dark.

Sure enough, not far above the wicked stretch of river that had
destroyed the *Bonhomme*, we saw the St. Pierre moored on the far
bank and the smoke of half a dozen cooking fires on shore curling
above the trees. Smiley and Bridger and their boatman were
trailing close behind us and soon our two skiffs bumped alongside
the keelboat.

The morning mist had cleared by then and golden springtime
sunshine spilled onto the river, warming our backs and our spirits,
too. Howsomever when we looked up and saw Andrew Henry's
face peering down from the afterdeck, his expression was anything
but warm and sunny, more like Grim Death itself.

"Thompson!   Buck!" he barked, "How fares the *Bonhomme*?
What of the men?"

Tuttle appeared to be having trouble with his speech, so I spoke
up first, though I hated to be the one to deliver ill tidings. "She's
lost and gone, Major, but the men are all right — the most o' them
anyways, close as we can tell."

Henry muttered a curse half under his breath and then he said,
"Get ashore and find yourselves some breakfast. Then get back
there and fetch the men up here."

We did as he ordered. Warm sowbelly and beans and steaming coffee black as Egypt's night never tasted so good before and rarely since. Afterwards we scudded downriver and passed the rest of the morning ferrying boatloads of men up to the St. Pierre. We had the use of all four skiffs for the job, so we made fairly short work of it.

Then Henry sent us down again to see what we might be able to salvage of the *Bonhomme*'s cargo along the riverbank and on the sandbars. There was no trace of the *Bonhomme* itself and except for a crate of muskets that had spilled onto a sandbar and a couple sodden bales of what we took to be Indian trade goods we found little worth retrieving. The other three skiffs fared hardly better. The Missouri is a hard-fisted tax-collector and like most who practice that trade, it gives little or nothing back.

When we returned to the St. Pierre we learned that not a single man had been lost in the river. It appeared to be something like a miracle, but just the same, a cloud of gloom hung over the entire company. Most of the survivors, especially the dandies from Saint Louis, were short-tempered and surly, and even the French-Canucks were quiet, as if they believed themselves disgraced by the loss of their boat.

The St. Pierre was crowded, for now we had twice as many men aboard as before, until we reached Fort Osage, an Army post on the Missouri, a couple days afterwards. Once we got there the burden was lightened considerably when a number of men who had been on the *Bonhomme*, mostly the Saint Louis sons of what some people called the "best families" — as if our families weren't as good as theirs, except for Pap, naturally — requested and were granted their discharge from the expedition. Even some of the Saint Louis gents aboard the St. Pierre asked to be released and the Major agreed to that as well.

"Good riddance!" was what Tuttle had to say of the matter. "Don't need no snivelers pukin' an' whinin' on thi'shere ex-pee-dishun!" And John Smiley nodded his assent.

All of the Kentuckians stuck and all of the Indians, too, Iroquois and Delawares alike, and most of the foreigners as well. It was rather like winnowing grain and, little as we knew of what lay upriver, all of us were certain that we didn't need any chaff up thataway.

Ashley and Henry arranged with the officers at the fort to send the quitters downriver next time a supply boat came up. Henry sent most of the Frenchy crew of the *Bonhomme* with them, too, for he didn't need all of them for just one keelboat. One thing he did that didn't seem quite fair was that he discharged his chief lieutenant from the *Bonhomme* and sent him back to Saint Louis for failing to control Mike Fink, which was rather like asking the man to keep a halter on a cyclone. The other officer, Luther Pike, he kept, which I daresay Henry lived to regret.

Your guess is as good as mine why the Major didn't order Mike Fink to be taken out and shot for what he did on the *Bonhomme*, or leastaways to send him packing, but he didn't. It's true that from then on Fink did his share, and maybe a shade more, of pulling an oar and hauling the *cordelle*, but that was all the punishment he suffered, leastaways that we could see.

Paddy McBride told us he heard Ashley and Henry talking about how they had lost ten thousand dollars worth of goods when the *Bonhomme* went down, but that didn't stop them nor hardly even slow them down. Two days later we were on the river once again, resupplied from Army stores, still headed for the mountains.

                                    ❧   ❧   ❧

Traveling up the Missouri on a keelboat was, for me, a tedious experience, not that there weren't some moments of excitement and some occasions of downright enjoyment, too, like stepping into the trees along the riverbank early in the morning, taking in all the rich forest smells and sights and sounds, treading softly and seeking out game critters, mainly deer and turkeys and now and then a bear, and the farther up we got, keeping a watchful eye out for Indians who might not take kindly to our trespassing on their hunting grounds.

It wasn't all hunting for Tuttle and me, though we would have preferred it that way. Some days the Major would send out other hunting parties and keep us aboard for other duties. All of us did our fair share of rowing, poling, and hauling and now and then Henry would recollect that I could read and write and put me to work as a clerk, copying out his journals or counting the stores. Because of all we lost when the *Bonhomme* went down, now he kept an even closer eye on what we used of the cargo.

We still had upwards of seventy men, not counting the Frenchy boatmen, so Henry had need to be stingy with the food stores, which meant that he sent out all four skiffs almost every day, carrying hunters ashore and hauling game back to the boat. Mike Fink and his pals were often amongst the hunters, for everybody knew what crack shots they were and passing fair at tracking game, too. But we noticed early on that the Major never sent anybody from our mess out on the same day Mike Fink went ashore, which I reckon was just as well.

Days slipped into weeks and stretched into a month, then two, until it seemed to me sometimes like we had all died and gone to hell, doomed to spend eternity on that miserable keelboat. I learned from copying out Henry's journal that he meant to get to the Falls of the Missouri before autumn, but I had no idea where that might be nor how long it might take to get there. As it was, we amused ourselves by counting the rivers and streams that we passed on our way north and west, the Chariton and the Grand, the Kaw and the Osage, the Kansas, Platte and Little Sioux, Floyd's River, the Big Sioux, the James, and a couple hundred smaller streams whose names I never learned, if they even had any.

Somewhere between the White and Bad Rivers, the Major kept the hunting parties aboard and we had to make do with jerky. He told us that we were passing through the country of the Little Missouri Sioux and that we would avoid trouble with them if we could, but for all of us to keep our rifles and muskets loaded and handy to prime in case we couldn't.

It was there, one forenoon, that I saw my first wild Indian. The Shawnees I had known surely didn't count, for they were a sight more civilized than most of the whites around Whynot. The few Indians we saw downriver didn't count, either, for most of them had been corrupted by whiskey, their bands and tribes shattered by white settlements spreading ever westward.

We were under sail with a good wind astern and just enough oars out on either side to avoid snags when we rounded a bend and came upon what looked like a couple hundred Lahcotah warriors spread along the riverbank and up a slope that lay behind it. They were a colorful sight, what with their painted faces and breasts and feathers in their hair and leather shirts and leggin's bedecked with quillwork and bright beads enough to make a body squint, most of them mounted on ponies gussied up as much as their riders. They fairly bristled with lances and clubs and bows and muskets gleaming with brass tacks.

Ashley and Henry were seated on the afterdeck, chatting and taking in the soft morning sunshine, when we came in view of the Indians. The Major stood up and signaled to Hamish Davidson, his lieutenant on the St. Pierre, a Scotsman who said little but who left no doubt that he meant whatever it was he did say. Davidson barked out a command in French and a couple boatmen heaved the bow anchor overboard. In the same breath, the oars were shipped, the sail lowered to the deck, and the St. Pierre came to a halt, swinging in the current twenty yards offshore.

Davidson's big voice rang out again, in English this time. "Prime your pieces, gentlemen, but don't anybody shoot! Nobody! I'll tell ye when, if need be!" Rumor was that Davidson had been a partisan for the Nor'west Company in far western Canada and, true or not, he wore his authority like a favorite coat.

There was a general rush to our bedrolls to grab up our rifles and powderhorns and such. Then we all high-tailed it back to the rail and the *passe-avant* to see what might happen next.

The sudden appearance of that many men and all those rifles and muskets discomposed those Indians rather more than somewhat. There was a flurry of activity on shore. A howl went up, horses cavorted, and there was considerable shaking of muskets and lances in the air. It all quieted down, howsomever, when one of them I took to be a chief held up his arm, then brought his hand down to his knee. His horse stood with his front feet in the water, sidewise to the river, as if he meant to block our passage. Which he had, for it was plain that the chief meant to parley, either that or there was likely to be bloodshed.

The chief was a fine-looking man, near six feet tall, from what I could tell with him sitting astride his horse. He wore no paint or feathers and his long black hair was bunched in back, held in place by a chain of shiny brass plates of diminishing size that dangled nearly to his waist. He was bare-chested and badly scarred on either breast, but his coppery skin was otherwise smooth, glistening with what I took to be bear grease or somesuch. A buffalo robe, belted around his waist, had slipped off his shoulders and rested on the cantle of his saddle, which was of a curious design, both pommel and cantle a foot or more high. His horse wore no bridle, only a horsehair cord knotted around the lower jaw and looped back over his neck for reins. The chief's leggin's and moccasins were bespangled with fine quillwork and he carried in the crook of his arm a musket bedecked with shiny brasswork and a power of tacks. It was hard to think of such a leader-like man as only a simple savage.

Something bumped on the far side of the keelboat and when I turned to look I saw that only Ashley remained on the afterdeck — just the General and three men who were pulling a canvas cover off a little brass cannon mounted up there, then training it on the crowd of Indians milling about on the shore.

About then one of our skiffs pulled into sight. Andrew Henry, wearing his tall top hat and a brass-buttoned green tail-coat over his buckskins, stood in the bow and Jacques Leclerc, the patron, the chief boatman, crouched beside him. Leclerc looked to be about half-Indian himself. He was a veteran boatman on the Missouri, which is likely why the Major picked him to help out with the parley. As the skiff neared the shore I studied the chief, whose face appeared to be carved out of stone. Andrew Henry's expression didn't look a great deal different from the chief's right then.

When the two of them were about a dozen feet apart, Henry raised his hand and the oarsmen commenced sculling their oars to hold the skiff in place. Henry spoke first.

Without looking at Leclerc he said, "Tell him we wish him a fine day and a long life and that we come in peace." Leclerc stood up then and began making signs, now and then grunting out words that I took to be Lahcotah.

I likely should mention here that the Sioux don't call themselves Sioux. Only white men and that tribe's enemies call them that. Their proper name is Lahcotah and there is a passel of different tribes and bands of Lahcotahs, each one called by a particular name. It's not a tribe. It's what you might call a nation and the ones farther south call themselves Dahcotahs, but they are all of the same general breed. This bunch was of the Little Missouri Lahcotahs and they had earned a reputation of being river pirates, collecting taxes from anybody who passed by on the Missouri and attacking those who refused to pay.

The chief, who was neither old nor young, sat his horse with calm dignity and never spoke a word. He used signs instead and Leclerc supplied the words in broken English to the Major. I could hear most of it, but I won't try to put down here precisely what Leclerc said to Henry. I'll do my best, howsomever, to render the gist of what passed between Henry and the chief.

First off, the chief said that a large boat such as ours must be very rich and before he could allow us to pass we must gift the Lahcotahs with twenty muskets and much powder and lead, many knives, and to show our good intentions, plenty tobacco and two kegs of whiskey.

Henry's face never changed. You might have thought that he hadn't heard what Leclerc was telling him. The chief went on, hands flying like a covey of bobwhites. He explained that his woman and all the women of his band were very poor and that they yearned for red cloth and warm blankets, trinkets — Leclerc used the word *fanfreluche* — beads, mirrors, ribbons, and such and that he was sure that the rich white chief would not disappoint them.

When the Major replied, he spoke very slowly in a loud, firm voice, and the expression on his face never changed. As near as I recall he said something like this: "We come in peace and we desire friendship with the mighty Lahcotahs. We have no wish to stay in your land. We are traveling to a place far from here, to the land of your enemies, the Crow, Absaroka, the Shoshone, and the Blackfoot, Seekseekah, and the Ahtseenah." Henry paused and let

Leclerc catch up with what he had been saying, then he continued: "We wish only peace, not war, although I have many warriors at my back and we do not fear you." He swung his arm towards the keelboat and the chief's eyes followed. What he saw was three score and more men, every one of us armed with a rifle or a musket pointed at him and his boys. Besides the cannon at the stern, the swivel gun on the bow deck was by now uncovered, as well, with three men, one holding a smoldering match, to man it. But if the sight of all that hardware impressed the chief, he never showed it.

When Henry pointed back at us, my eyes just naturally followed. I saw Hamish Davidson step up to Mike Fink and relieve him of his rifle. Fink had cocked his gun and was squinting down the barrel. Hamish was taking no chances on a hothead starting a war just then.

Henry had fallen silent and the two leaders stared at each other. It was time for somebody to blink, but neither one did. The warriors along the shore grew restless and commenced to murmur and curvet their horses. Hamish Davidson walked behind the men perched on the *passe-avant* and spread out along the rail, growling, "Be ready now, but don't ye dare fire 'til I give ye the word."

You could have cut the air with a dull knife. Then Henry, still standing stiff and erect, his hands clasped behind him, snapped his fingers. Jacques Leclerc bent down and dragged a heavy bundle wrapped in croker sacking from the bottom of the skiff, propped it on the side, then hopped into the shallow water and lugged the bundle to the shore. He laid it on the sand next to the chief's horse and as he retreated, he slit the sacking with his belt knife and pushed it aside, revealing all manner of trade goods — tobacco twists and half a dozen butcher knives, a couple-three shiny tomahawks, strings of bright beads, vermilion packets, several pigs of bullet lead and a couple powder horns, some red trade cloth, little mirrors, and I don't know what all.

The chief glanced down and a flicker of a smile flitted across his face. The deadlock was broken and his dignity was intact.

Leclerc splashed his way back to the skiff and clambered over the side before Henry spoke again. "We are happy to bring gifts to the noble Lahcotah, but we will pay no tax or tribute. Let us part in peace and friendship." Leclerc's hands were shaking more than somewhat as he signed and grunted what Henry said, but still it looked like he put the idea across. When Leclerc quit waving his hands the chief sat straight and still as a post on his horse for a long moment that felt like half a day. Then he raised his hand, palm outward, and swept it in the direction of upriver. Which we took to mean that we could go on our way in peace. Which it did.

Andrew Henry neither bowed nor nodded. He just stood there in the bow of the skiff, hands behind his back, a paper-thin smile frozen on his face, and snapped his fingers once again. Leclerc growled something to the rowers and, without turning it around, they sculled the skiff, stern foremost, away from the shore and back to the far side of the keelboat. Henry continued to stand in the bow, his eyes locked into those of the Lahcotah chief, his hands still clasped behind his back, until he disappeared from the Indian's view behind the boat.

I never learned if Andy had a pistol tucked into the back of his britches under that tail-coat, but I wouldn't be at all surprised if he did.

The skiff had no sooner bumped against the stern of the keelboat than I heard the bow anchor thump onto the deck and the creak of the sail being hoisted to the top of the mast. The oarsmen were already in place and as soon as Henry appeared on the afterdeck, Hamish Davidson roared out the order to proceed upriver.

Ashore, several Indians had dismounted and were rummaging through the trade goods spread out on the beach — under the watchful eye of the chief, I noticed, who evidently meant to get his share. There wasn't enough to go around, naturally, and a good many warriors followed us a-horseback along the riverbank, until a big patch of marshland got in their way and they had to turn back.

That night and for several more, until we were well out of Little Missouri Sioux country, we slept aboard, anchored in mid-channel well away from either shore, and sentries were posted during the dark hours, lest we receive a visit from our Lahcotah landlords. There was no hunting on shore during that time, for we could see

Indians we took to be Lahcotahs on the hills and amongst the trees, and Henry meant to avoid a fight if he could.

One day when we were lazing around Jim Bridger's forge, Tuttle and I casting rifle balls and the others just smoking and talking nonsense, Hamish Davidson came by and squatted down in our midst. He ran his cool gray eyes over each of us and then he said, "Well now, lads, what lesson did ye learn from our brush wi' the Sioux back there?" Nobody spoke up and he continued. "Amongst many things, it's this ye should bear in mind. Never willingly step into a fight ye're not sure o' winnin' and never show fear to a redskin. They'll have ye for vittles if ye do." He paused to light his pipe, then went on. "Bear in mind, as well, all o' ye, that Injuns o' no matter what stripe, hate losin' even one man. It's a disgrace to the chief an' to them all, for they're all related, one way or another. At the least they're neighbors an' friends in the village — not like us, mind ye, who come from the four corners o' the earth an' keep on comin' an' don't hardly know one another from Adam's off ox."

He drew deeply on his pipe and blew out a cloud of blue smoke that whisked away on the upriver wind. "That's mainly the chief's p'int o' view I'm speakin' of, mind ye. As for this or that buck warrior, he's been raised all o' his life to think he's brave an' he'll astonish ye with what he'll try in a battle — an' often get away with, too!" He drew on his pipe again and added, "Aye, the aborigine is truly excitable when it comes to a fight. Never sell 'im short and I advise ye to learn all about 'im that ye can as quick as ye can." Davidson cleared his throat and spat over the side as he stood up. "And one last thing. Don't ye be supposin' that you're dealin' wi' a pack o' stupid, ignorant savages. Some're smart an' some're wise beyond belief. They're raised different from the most of us, but a man's a man for a' that." He chuckled and said as he turned to go, "Those're not my words, mind ye. Bobbie Burns owns 'em."

In the following days and weeks I thought long and hard on what Davidson had said to us. I recalled Powatawa and how wise he had been and even though the Shawnee weren't Lahcotahs by a long shot, they were the only Indians I had known. I reckoned it was best to learn whatever I could wherever I could, which is how I came to make friends with Brass Turtle, a Delaware Indian — he called Delawares *Leh-nee Leh-nah-pay* — from somewhere east of Ohio, though I'm not sure just where.

Brass Turtle looked much the same as the other four Delawares who were along with us — brown-skinned and usually bare-chested, hawk-nosed and lean and muscled, long braided hair with a feather in back, quilled and beaded leggin's, britch-clout, and moccasins, and a power of necklaces — but he was remarkably different from the rest. For one thing, Brass Turtle loved to talk and what he had to say would make you laugh at first and then, later, it made you think. His English was at least as good as my own and he used it a whole lot better than I did. He had a sharp wit and a wicked tongue and nobody was safe from either one, but he could get you to laughing so much that it took the sting out of most of what he had to say.

I wondered how he had learned to speak our tongue so well and he explained that he had been more or less adopted when he was a small boy by a white militiaman and his family after the militia burned his village and slaughtered his mother, much as you might decide not to drown a particular puppy from an unwanted litter. But puppies grow into dogs and not all dogs are well-loved. As he grew older he found that the white family was treating him more and more like a household slave and less and less like one of their own, so when he was about twelve or so he gave up a promising career of slopping hogs and chopping weeds and set out to find his people, which he finally succeeded in doing, in Missouri, where a lot of Delawares had gone when they could no longer hold on to their tribal lands in the East. After I heard all that, I understood his bitter wit a whole lot better.

The Delawares and Iroquois we had aboard didn't mix much at first, but the one thing they shared was their early-morning bath. Whether we were camped ashore or cooped up aboard the boat, you could find all of those Indians diving and splashing in the river every morning of their lives. Which made me wonder why our generally unwashed white men called them "dirty Injuns."

I took to inviting Brass Turtle to eat with us in our mess. At first Tuttle Thompson kept him at arm's length, as you might expect a Kentucky backwoodsman to do, suspicious as they are of all redskins, but Turtle's joking ways and Tuttle's sense of humor soon prevailed. Laughter opens up your pores and it wasn't long before Tuttle took to him about as much as I did. Paddy McBride and Jim Bridger weren't far behind. Paddy, coming from Ireland as he did, had no experience with Indians, so for him Brass Turtle wasn't much different from the rest of us Americans. Jim Bridger, on the other hand, once he heard Turtle's history, no doubt recalled his own hard apprenticeship at the blacksmith's forge and soon accepted the Delaware as an equal. Smiley's lifelong, bred-in-the-bone distrust of all Indians kept him from being outright friendly, but he was quietly civil, as he was with the most of us. Fitzgerald didn't like anybody, so what he might have thought didn't amount to much.

ॐ   ॐ   ॐ

The day after we passed the Cheyenne River the Major told us that we were out of Lahcotah country and could commence our hunting once again. It was a joy and a relief to get off the keelboat, spending most days combing through the woods for deer and nights camped ashore around a warming cookfire. I reckon I despised keelboats more than most, for my own reasons, but none of the others liked being cooped up on that crowded deck any more than I did, roasting in the summer sun all day or huddled under a flimsy canvas when it rained, which it did all too often.

Each day as we pushed and pulled and dragged that infernal keelboat upriver the country around us grew flatter and the fringe of trees that bordered the river became scantier. Deer were scarce and nobody had seen a bear anywhere above the Cheyenne. Along about then there was more sowbelly and beans than game meat in the cookpots.

It so happened that Hamish Davidson was out hunting with Tuttle and me on the prairie when I saw my first buffalo. At first I didn't know what it was, a great shaggy brown bearded beast with horns that put you in mind of a cow, but much bigger and more fearsome. This one was upwind of us and busy rolling on his back in a muddy hollow, so he didn't see or smell us coming up on him.

Since leaving Little Missouri Lahcotah country we had been hunting in pairs and threes. It was safer that way in case we ran into Indians. We were just topping a low rise when we looked down and saw the buffalo. Hamish dropped to his knees in the tall grass and dragged Tuttle and me down with him, exclaiming in a hoarse whisper, "Saints be praised! Buffalo at last!" We crawled back up to the crest and peered through the grass at the great hairy creature, who had by then got to his feet, standing broadside to us, shaking his enormous head and sending spatters of muddy water flying in every direction. Hamish tapped my shoulder and hissed, "Buck, ye might as well learn now. Take him in the body, never the head. Neither high nor low, through the lungs, a hand behind the heart. Think ye can do it?"

I nodded, completely unsure of where all those innards might be located on a critter that I had never seen before. My hands were trembling as I poked Melchior through the grass and did my best to draw a bead on where Hamish had told me to shoot him. Busy as he was with shaking the mud off and downwind as we were, the buffalo didn't hear me cock my rifle and once I was halfway sure that I was aiming at the right spot, I squeezed the trigger. Somehow in the stillness the sound of my shot sounded louder than ever before and set my ears to ringing. When the smoke commenced to drift off I saw the buffalo spinning around in his tracks, taking a dozen faltering steps towards us, blood gushing from his nostrils, before he sank to his knees, folded over onto his side, legs shuddering and sticking out straight, little angry red eyes staring but unseeing, then all was still.

Tuttle was beside himself with joy, pummeling my shoulder and muttering compliments about my shooting, when Hamish reached over and shushed us both, pointing beyond the dead buffalo to a little draw where we saw three more buffalo straggling into the hollow, grazing and grunting as they approached their fallen comrade. They were upwind of the carcass, so they couldn't smell the blood.

I slid back down the slope to reload, dumping powder down the bore and ramming home the ball as quietly as I could. I was still spilling powder into the pan as I wriggled my way back to the ridge, in time to hear Hamish whisper, "Take your aim now, all three of us at once. I'll take the bull on the left, then you, Tuttle, then Buck. Ready now?" He didn't wait for a reply. Out of the corner of my eye I saw him drawing a careful bead.

Then I heard a whispered, "Now!"

Three rifles going off at once was like a thunderclap on that grassy hillside and bits of flint from Tuttle's lock stung my cheek. When the billowing black smoke lifted I saw that one of the bulls was already down, coughing blood through his mouth and nostrils. Another was staggering towards us, head down, beard dragging, weaving uncertainly. The third one, the buffalo I had shot at, was scampering back towards the draw and I cursed myself for making a careless shot. Hamish heard me and said, "Don't ye fret, lad. Ye hit 'im square enough. I warrant he won't be travelin' far."

Which he didn't, for we found his carcass not far up the draw. Tuttle was crowing like a rooster, as happy as I was at killing his first buffalo, the biggest critter either of us had ever seen. Hamish, too, was pleased. His grin was a yard wide as we set about skinning and butchering our kills, rolling each critter onto its belly and yanking the legs outward to hold it upright whilst we slit the woolly hide down the backbone, slicing out the backstrap, then the tongue, and finally the fleece fat and hump ribs, all according to Davidson's directions, of course, for this was a new thing for Tuttle and me.

As the three of us staggered back to the river, each of us under an impossible load of bloody meat, Hamish was saying, "I was wond'rin' if we'd ever see buffalo this year! We should've seen 'em long since, as far down as the Platte, mind ye, and likely before that, but that's buffalo for ye. Expect 'em when ye see 'em, that's the rule, an' there ain't no other rule that applies." He halted long enough to wipe sweat and blood from his brow with the back of his hand before he said, "These're all young bulls driven out o' the herd by the old man, the seed bull, the boss. They ain't fat cow, but they'll do to start with. Once ye've eaten buffalo, even bull, ye'll never love deer meat again, long as ye live!"

By time we arrived at the skiff on the river all of us were sweating and grunting and gasping for breath, but the grin that lit up Jean-Luc's face when he saw all that buffalo meat made up for all the hardship of lugging it. We sat and rested then, smoking and reliving the thrill of our first buffalo kill, until we saw John Smiley and Jim Bridger and their Frenchy boatman Yves Dureau scudding towards us from the far bank.

When they reached the shallows, Bridger jumped out of the skiff and hauled it onto the strip of pebbly beach where we sat. He was grinning when he called out, "Happy to see ya'll're still healthy!" As he came closer he said, "Didn't know what to make of all that shootin'. Thought it might be Injuns."

Tuttle could hardly contain himself. "It's buffler, Jim! We kilt ourse'fs some buffler! Four of 'em! Temple here got two of 'em all by his-ownse'f! You ever even seen a buffler, Jim?"

Bridger allowed that he hadn't and Tuttle went on to say, "Well naow, thet hole in your eddicayshun had oughter git filled up, so we're gonna 'low y'all to he'p us tote the rest o' them bufflers on down hyar to the boats, seein' as how we be feelin' plumb gen'rous today."

John Smiley had strolled up meanwhile, a gentle smirk on his craggy face as he listened to Tuttle's bombast. His expression settled into something like Sunday-parson serious, but his eyes were twinkling when he said, "We'uns'd hate to deprive you'uns of your en-joys, Tuttle, but if you'uns are insistin', we'uns'll lend yew a hand. Jest where be them buffler critters?"

Hamish, Tuttle, and I, recollecting our recent labors, scrambled to our feet, glad to have help. Tuttle yelled, "Thisaway!" and started back to where the buffalo carcasses lay. Howsomever Hamish checked his departure and before we made a return trip we cut saplings from along the riverbank and equipped ourselves with rope from the skiffs, which made it a whole lot easier, and cleaner, to transport the remainder of the buffalo meat.

When we arrived at the hollow where the buffalo lay, white wolves were already drifting in around the carcasses. They retreated reluctantly when we showed up, snapping and snarling but backing off nevertheless. The wolves didn't go far, howsomever. Instead they slunk up the hillsides, where they sat whining and slavering, hard yellow eyes staring, until we departed.

L'Archévêque had joined us to help with our chore. He had already seen buffalo on earlier journeys up the Missouri, but just the same he stood with Smiley and Bridger and marveled at the great shaggy beasts we had slain. Even dead the brutes were impressive.

Six men with sharp knives and hearty appetites, especially with Hamish calling out instructions, made short work of butchering out the rest of the buffalo meat. Two trips to the river, great slabs of meat swinging from the poles, completed our chore. Our two skiffs were perilously low in the water as we plied our way slowly upstream and it was almost dark when we caught up with the St. Pierre, already moored for the night, the cooking fires on shore burning bright.

We received a hero's welcome when the company saw the meat that we brought. The roars of approval were even louder when it was roasted and we all feasted on it. Most of us there had never seen a buffalo, much less tasted its flesh, the flavor and texture of which made all other meats we knew pale and puny stuff by comparison. The two skimpy deer that the other hunters had brought in were left uneaten that night. Hamish Davidson was right. I have never savored deer meat from that day on.

Somehow the appearance of the buffalo brightened the spirits of the entire company and the heavy labor of hauling the *St. Pierre* up the Missouri seemed lighter now. Men joked and laughed even as they rubbed their shoulders raw on the *cordelle* or strained at the oars or dodged one another on the narrow *passe-avants* as we poled our way through swift-running shallows, striving to shove our bulky old ark yet another yard, rod, chain, furlong, and mile upwards against the river's stubborn current.

Nights on shore were more cheerful as well. Campfires blazed higher and later into the night, too, partly to roast great gobbets of buffalo flesh that dripped rich fat onto the firewood and enveloped the entire camp in a delightful fragrance, but mainly to fend off the clouds of mosquitoes that grew ever thicker the farther we traveled upriver.

General Ashley and Major Henry had taken to spending their nights ashore, no doubt to be near the fires and thereby escape the mosquitoes, but whatever the reason it was good to have them amongst us, for their presence seemed to weld the men of the expedition more solidly together. The Major would often take out his fiddle and play merry tunes on it, moving from time to time from one mess to another, and the men would follow him for the sake of the music. Once there they mingled with one another and broke down the fences of unfamiliarity, forging new friendships and strengthening the bonds that were sorely needed to protect and defend our little company against the hostile forces of that unknown wilderness.

The Frenchy boatman who had saved the little musical squeezebox he called a *concertina* when the *Bonhomme* was lost brought it out now and often joined the Major in his campfire entertainments, lending depth and flavor to the music. Then it wasn't long until a quiet, crabby man who hailed from Tennessee, Anse Tolliver by name, overcame his shyness and produced his homemade fiddle and was soon scraping duets with Andrew Henry. Even Brass Turtle dug out a Delaware flute and piped along with the others, although his fellow tribesmen frowned and grumbled at first at what they might have considered sacrilege.

Those of us who couldn't play music sang along with the tunes we knew and learned new ones from our fellows. The camp rang out night after night with music and singing and hearty laughter enough to put you in mind of a picnic, but our rifles were rarely out of our reach, for most of us never forgot where we were and who might not favor our intrusion into their lands.

Not everybody joined in. Fink's mess sat apart, apparently absorbed in one another and occupied with hatching out evil schemes, by my reckoning. The Iroquois, too, remained aloof, for whatever reasons they had, but I realized even then that you can't apply white men's thinking to Indians.

But for the rest of us, music it was that glued our expedition together, more than anything else, even greed.

જ્જ જ્જ જ્જ

Buffalo became more common the farther we traveled. Hunting became a routine chore. We commenced to be downright choosy, seeking out fat cows when we could find them and ignoring old bulls. That wasn't a simple matter, howsomever, for the cows usually stayed with the large herds, under the protection of big, strong bulls that guarded their harems like jealous sultans. It was much easier to pick off stray young bulls who had been run off from the herd or old patriarchs who had lost their harems to stronger, more youthful husbands. Such outcasts usually ran alone or in small bunches, haunting the fringes of the main herd.

One day Hamish Davidson overheard me complaining to Tuttle and Brass Turtle about the difficulty of shooting cows that stayed with the larger herds, which were quick to spook whenever I tried to creep up on them.

Hamish cut in and said, "Rest yoursel', Temple lad, an' be content wi' what ye're doin' now. You're still afoot an' stray bulls are your proper meat. Later on, when we get some horses, all o' ye will learn how to run buffalo a-horseback, Injun-style, gettin' into the herd and choosin' the fat cows an' killin' the best of 'em. But for now, the strays'll do nicely."

When I heard that magic word, I spoke up. "Horses? When'll we be gettin' horses, sir, an' gettin' off this boat?"

Davidson looked vague and although I reckoned he knew just when and where we would be getting horses for the expedition, he was not at liberty to tell us. Instead he replied, "The Rees have horses a-plenty and the Mandans and Minatarees, too, but it's not for me to say. It's solely the Major's business and none o' my own."

I must have looked somewhat crestfallen, for he added, "Ye'll be livin' on dry land soon enough, Temple Buck. In the meantime, ye can be preparin' yoursel' by gettin' hold of a pistol or two — big pistols, mind ye, big enough to kill a fat cow. And a couple o' holsters for your saddle, as well. Ye'll be needin' 'em 'fore ye know it."

That night my head buzzed with enough thoughts to rival the swarms of mosquitoes that harassed the camp. Pictures, too, swam into my mind and I saw myself skimming across the prairie on a horse very much like Kumskaka, laying waste to entire nations of fat buffalo cows.

಄   ಄   ಄

Twice, by the time we reached Moreau River, the keelboat was forced to anchor in midstream for half a day or more whilst we waited for an endless procession of buffalo, sixty or seventy critters wide, to swim across the Missouri. The water and the riverbanks were black with their shaggy hides and the air was clotted with the sound of bawling calves and the frantic cries of cows seeking their errant offspring.

Hunting was easy then and it continued so until we arrived at the mouth of the Grand River. A hunting chore that would have kept us combing the woods for deer from dawn to dusk was often completed with abundance in the forenoon and there was plenty of time for lazing and smoking and yarning. I dug out my copy of the *Iliad* and let Homer steal me away to Priam's kingdom and adventures with Hector and Achilles outside the walls of Troy, stumbling over unfamiliar words and sometimes reading a single line a dozen times until the meaning came clear. I was in no hurry to finish, for I owned only two books, and each adventure that I read provoked a dozen more in my imagination.

Overmanned for just one keelboat as we were, there was time, too, for just being shiftless, lying on my back in the late afternoon sunshine, listening to the curlews call across the water, the creak of rusty oarlocks and Frenchies laughing and cursing and shouting words that had no meaning for me just then, the little sail flapping against the stubby mast as a boatman sought to catch just a little more wind in the canvas, and the ring of Bridger's hammer on the anvil at the forge. It was a time for remembering, too, recalling dear, familiar faces that had once made up all the world I knew. Even without closing my eyes I could see Ma in all of her humors, troubled and tranquil and girlishly happy and tenderly loving me, too. I reckon I had always known that it was her strength that gave me my love of life that was often hard but always happy because of her. Ma's face would fade into Sarah's smile and once again I felt the thrill I had always known when she was near. Sarah fresh and clean and soft and strong, wise and knowing far beyond her years, loving me for what I was and asking only for my love. Which always brought to mind Lucette and all the raw excitement of the love I felt for her as well, the naked passion of our last embrace and all her changing moods embedded just the same in what I surely knew was love. I wished and tried to separate the two, but both of them were intertwined and knotted close together deep within my heart.

Memories of Whynot always brought to mind those happy days with Uncle Ben, learning how to track and trap and shoot and know the ways of critters, plants, and weather in all the seasons of the year. But naturally then I'd see Aunt Penny, too, and all my guilt came flooding back and poisoned all the good things I recalled. At such times I'd force my mind to dodge and shift away to somewheres else, like Jacob Staples's store, where I'd wallow in remembered smells of well-oiled traps and harness, saddles, guns and knives and garden spades and rope, lamp oil and medicines and foodstuffs, spices from all the corners of the world, yard goods, and crusty, sweaty farmers who spat upon the stove. Which always brought me back to Pap and wondering just why it was that a wall always stood between the two of us and why it was that I wished neither to climb over it nor tear it down.

A young man mostly lives in the here and now and what's next is far more important to him than what was. It's just as well, too, for Whynot was a long way from where I was right then and returning there someday was hardly even a dream.

The Major started sending out more hunting parties than usual and he kept a crew of men busy drying buffalo meat until the keelboat looked like a butcher's shop or the Fourth of July, festooned as it was with string upon string of strips of red buffalo flesh curing in the dry prairie air, looking like festive bunting. He doubled the size of the hunting parties and he cautioned us all to keep a sharp eye out for Indians, telling us to avoid a fight if we could but not to get ourselves killed either.

We did see a few Indians here and there, flitting amongst the trees near the river or standing watchful on a bluff, but they gave us no trouble and we didn't court any with them.

When I asked Hamish Davidson what might be happening, he looked grave, but all he said was, "Rees. Ye'll be findin' out soon enough." Which at the time told me nothing useful at all.

❧   ❧   ❧

The morning we passed by the mouth of Grand River the Major ordered all hunting parties to remain aboard and he called the men together in the space below the afterdeck. General Ashley was at his side, but he said nothing, which must have been hard for him, politician that he was. Hamish Davidson and the lieutenant from the *Bonhomme*, a man we knew as Luther Pike, stood behind them, the both of them looking serious.

Andrew Henry stepped forward and without ceremony began to speak in that high crackling voice that bespoke his Pennsylvania origins. "Gentlemen, we are at this moment entering the territory of the Arikara Indians, the Rees. We anticipate no trouble with them, but the Arikaras are notorious for their treachery and I wish to have as little to do with them as possible.

"There will be no hunting parties sent ashore until we are well out of their neighborhood and all hands will remain aboard this vessel at all times during that time, as well. That is to say, there will be no camps on shore for the next several nights."

A general groan went up from the men assembled below, for all of us had come to enjoy our evenings ashore, what with the feasting and music and singing and all.

Henry raised his hand for quiet. "Mister Davidson and Mister Pike here will post a guard day and night and it is required of every man to keep his weapons clean and loaded and close at hand at all times. Your powderhorn and your bullet pouch will both be full.

You may cast rifle and musket balls at Jim Bridger's forge and Mister Davidson will issue whatever supplies of powder and lead that you require.

"There is no reason to be alarmed, gentlemen, but readiness forestalls regret!" Henry cleared his throat and went on in a less severe tone. "This is not a military expedition, gentlemen, but I expect you to conduct yourselves as if it were. I don't trust the Rees, not as far as I can throw 'em, and I intend to see that they don't catch us napping!"

All of which explained the vast quantity of jerked buffalo meat the Major had been storing up against a time when we wouldn't be able to kill fresh meat every day. What it didn't explain was how in creation Luther Pike ever got to be named a lieutenant. Hamish Davidson was a natural prime choice for the job. If the Major hadn't appointed him, all of us most likely would have elected him. But Luther Pike was the last man I would have picked even to accompany the expedition, let alone to be in command of other men.

As you might imagine, there is gossip aplenty when you coop up seventy or so men aboard a single keelboat, especially when one of them isn't required to do his fair share of work and then shirks most of what he is supposed to do. That was the character of Luther Pike, a down-at-heels Southern aristocrat from Georgia come to repair his bankrupt family fortunes by making it rich in the fur trade. Now you don't get a Luther Pike overnight or by accident. No, it takes generations of inbreeding unworthy stock to manufacture such a paragon of arrogant Southern virtue.

His appearance was bad enough. He was halfway tall but stoop-shouldered and scarecrow-skinny. His clammy white complexion that only burned and never browned in the sun was adorned with a pair of close-together pale-blue marble-hard eyes that framed a knobby nose which hung over his pursey mouth and hardly any chin that was thinly disguised by a scraggly brown beard that he was allowed to maintain in spite of the Major's orders that all of us shave at least every other day.

Still, it was what Luther Pike had to say that made me despise him most. He didn't like anybody very much and he regarded most of us as barely human white trash, certainly his social inferiors. He outright hated Indians and his bloodless lips would curl in distaste whenever he looked upon the Delawares and Iroquois in our company. One day I overheard him talking to a bunch of men who had taken to hanging around Fink's mess and I wasn't at all surprised to hear him pronounce, "Injuns! You got to show 'em who's boss! We been runnin' 'em out o' Jawjah fer years, all of 'em — Cherokees, Choctaws, Creeks, all o' them dirty redskins squattin' on good farmin' land what rightfully b'longs to white folks! Ain't no better'n niggahs! Wuss, in fact! Got no respec' fer nuthin'!" There was a general murmur of agreement from his listeners and I reckon Pap would have joined right in on that kind of talk if he had been there.

I suspect it was General Ashley who fostered Pike's promotion, whatever his reasons, for the Major seemed too level-headed to entrust any part of his expedition to such a man. Our two leaders didn't always agree, as I learned one day when David Jackson, the regular clerk, was busy elsewhere and Henry had me doing scribbler's work on the afterdeck, scratching out a copy of his journal. Ashley and Henry were seated not far off, engaged in conversation conducted in low tones but considerably heated nonetheless. Naturally I strained my ears to hear what they said, meanwhile keeping my eyes downcast as I scribbled.

It appeared to me that Ashley was trying to persuade the Major to trade with the Rees for horses if he could and Henry was steadfastly refusing to do so. The General's point was that the sooner we got horses the faster we could send some of our men overland to the Yellowstone and set up a headquarters. Henry agreed that although that was a worthy intention it was too risky to traffic with Arikaras. He had been here before, which Ashley hadn't, and he was familiar with their treacherous ways. Besides, he said a trader named Pilcher had warned him, just before we left Saint Louis, to beware the Rees this particular year. Henry wanted no part of them and he was satisfied that he could trade safely for horses with the Mandans and their neighboring tribes, once we arrived at the Mandan villages.

Their talk ended without any agreement that I could hear but I reckon that Henry prevailed, for a day or two later when we arrived at the Arikara villages, we tried to sail right on by. It didn't quite work out the way the Major had planned, howsomever, for when we rounded the bend just below the village a passel of Indians in dugout canoes swarmed towards us from shore and even more of them, all of them armed with muskets and bows, were gathered on a low island just offshore, within a fair musket shot of the channel.

We were favored with a decent breeze and every oar we owned was digging deep in the water, but just the same the dugouts gained on us steadily. The brass cannon was pointed sternward over the trailing skiffs and the swivel gun on the foredeck commanded the shoreline. Every man who wasn't occupied with rowing lined the rails and *passe-avants,* armed, loaded, and primed. Half a dozen men with rifles were stationed in the bow with the swivel-gun crew and our mess was ordered to the afterdeck, where Ashley and Henry awaited the dugouts, which were fast closing the distance.

I saw Mike Fink with Talbot and Carpenter crouched on the *passe-avant* with their rifles leveled shoreward and for once I was content that they were part of our company.

I had time to observe the village or rather both of them, for there on shore, on the lefthand bank, were two large stockades, one of them on a hill above the other, each enclosing a large number of round-topped earthen lodges, at least three score in either one. The stout logs of both palisades were a dozen feet tall or more and the Rees had dug broad ditches outside each of them. It was plain to see that these Indians devoted a lot of thought to warfare and that they knew pretty much what they were doing. I could see women working in the cornfields that stretched away on either side of the villages and for a moment my mind flicked away to Whynot and my early labors in support of Pap's whiskey still.

The Arikara dugouts were drawing nigh, four or five Indians on each side ploughing their paddles fast and deep, making their canoes fairly leap forward against the current. I chanced to glance back at the cargo box below and saw that Luther Pike had herded our Iroquois and Delawares into a tight huddle at the foot of the mast. Brass Turtle was on his feet, shouting something I couldn't quite hear and Pike was waving his arms and shouting back at him. I moved to the edge of the afterdeck in order to hear them better and the Major saw me do it. He took in the commotion below and ordered, "Get down there, Buck, and find out what in hell is going on."

By time I reached the deck Hamish Davidson had joined the brawl and I heard him roar, "What in the name o' goddlemighty's happenin' here? Why're these men not at their posts?"

Brass Turtle subsided and Pike swung about as if he had been stung. "Well now, if it's any o' yer business, Mister Davi'son, I'll tell ye! These're Injuns an' I don' trust 'em nohow. 'Twere up to me, I'd pitch 'em all in the river right now. They're jist as like as anythin' to throw in with them hostiles out there, soon as the fightin' commences!"

I saw Hamish draw a deep breath, as if he were fighting to control himself. Then he must have given up that fight as useless, for he fairly exploded. "Are ye daft, man? Don't ye know nothin'? These Injuns are Iroquois from the East and Delawares, by God! They'll do a better job o' slicin' up Rees than any man aboard this tub! I wish to God we had twenty more!"

Pike took a step backwards in the face of Davidson's rage. His mouth fell open and his eyes bugged out but he made no reply. Hamish clapped Brass Turtle on the shoulder and said in a gentler tone, "Tell 'em to get back to their posts an' mind ye take your orders from me from here on. There's a good lad."

Turtle grinned and said a few words to the Indians. They all sprang to their feet and trotted off, muskets in hand, powderhorns bouncing, each of them lugging enough razor-edged hardware on his person to stock a cutler's shop. Davidson watched them go and then he turned to Luther Pike. "Pike, I'll tell ye once and only once. Ye'll not abuse my men. If ye do, it's betwixt you and me. Understood?"

Hamish was a big man, as Scotsmen tend to be, and the humor that usually twinkled in his bright blue eyes was gone now.

Luther Pike's customarily loud mouth was clamped shut. He merely nodded, turned his back, and slunk away. Which was one of the few sensible things I ever saw him do.

Davidson saw me standing nearby and he glared at me, but before he could speak I scooted up to the afterdeck. Once there, I stood behind the Major until he snapped, "Yes?"

"All composed, sir. No problem," I replied as soberly as I could, though I felt a grin tugging at my mouth. The Major grunted and turned back to watch the Arikara canoes and I hastily dodged around the cannoneers and rejoined Tuttle and Paddy McBride at the rail.

The canoes had nearly caught up with us and we could clearly see the Indians in the closest ones. They weren't pretty. The Lahcotahs downriver, fearsome as they were, were by and large a handsome lot. These Arikaras looked downright evil — short, squat men, light-skinned but pockmarked and muddy-looking, their greasy hair bedecked with shells, their faces and bodies naked to the waist bedaubed with paint.

One dugout forged ahead of the others, coming nearly to the sterns of the skiffs bobbing behind our boat. A paunchy Indian struggled to his feet and stood unsteadily in the bow, whilst his paddlers labored to maintain the distance. Even from that far away, there was a shrewd and scheming look about him, especially when he flashed a gap-toothed grin and held up his hand in a sign of peace.

"That's old Gray Eyes," I heard the Major mutter to Ashley. "The worst of 'em all." Howsomever Henry returned the salute as he instructed us in a low voice, "Keep your sights on 'em, lads. If they try to hook the skiffs I'll let ye know when to fire, but ye dast not shoot 'til I tell ye."

All six of us knelt at the rail, three of us on either side of Jacques Leclerc, the tillerman, and trained our sights on the canoe that was out in front of the others. Paddy McBride was beside me and I heard him whisper, "D'ye think we'll be after havin' a donnybrook wid 'em, Temple?" His voice was excited but steady and when I glanced at his face he was actually grinning.

I replied as honestly as I knew how. "Don't know, Paddy. You scared?"

Paddy guffawed, then looked sidewise to see if the Major had noticed. When he turned back to me, he said, "Didja iver see a Mick as didn't love a fight? Sure'n it's been iver so long since the last'un!" A grin spread over his face and he added, "An' this time I got me a gun!"

I chuckled under my breath and decided that Padraic McBride would do to take to the mountains or 'most anywhere.

Kneeling at the rail, my rifle aimed squarely at the paddler in the stern of the dugout, I wondered about myself, if I was scared or just excited, for the muscles in my thighs were jumping like bugs on a griddle. I glanced sidewise at Tuttle, but his faint grin told me nothing about what he might be feeling. At last I reckoned it was best not to think about it at all and just watch the fun as it unraveled.

The wind behind us had freshened and most of the rowing right then was being done by our Frenchy boatmen — they called themselves *bateliers* — who were wasting neither will nor skill nor effort to get us past the Rees. We were making better time than ever before, but we couldn't gain on the Arikara dugouts. Old Gray Eyes' canoe moved even closer and a second Indian stood up behind the chief and waved his arm.

"That's Little Soldier," Henry said to Ashley, "a cowardly wretch and a sneak to boot." Henry casually waved back. "Speaks a little English he does, but the slimy little bastard never learned to tell the truth in any tongue."

Little Soldier signaled to the other canoes and they fell back a mite. The chief's canoe forged ahead and came abreast of the skiffs, almost under our stern, just outside our wake. We could see the paddlers' muscles rippling and straining as they fought to maintain their speed against the heavy current. Gray Eyes steadied himself against the prow and yelled something to Henry in a harsh, downright jagged, tongue. A smiling Little Soldier shouted from behind him, "Our leadah, chief, say velcome! Ve 'ave 'orses, plenty much 'orses trade vit' you! 'Rik'ra need 'bacca, powdah, boollet, veeskey! You got? You vant 'orses? Ve got plenty 'orses! Ve trade!"

Henry's face was a solemn mask as he shouted back, "Don't need 'em! Not here for trade! No time! We need the wind!" He waved his hand towards the bellying sail.

Little Soldier spoke rapidly to Gray Eyes before he yelled, "Much trouble in ribbah! Dere!" He pointed upriver. "Too many much too plenty trees! You stop! Ve eat, talk, smoke, trade! T'morra, ve send men, show you vay!"

Henry stood tall and proud, unsmiling, coattails flapping, tall hat wedged firmly on his brow, shoulders square. "We'll take our chances! Thanks for your help! Farewell and godspeed!" He snapped his fingers at Hugh Toomey, the gunner, who was crouched beside the brass cannon. Then he said in a low voice to Ashley, "I'll risk every snag and sawyer in the whole Missourah before I'll put my trust in these sons-o'-bitches! They're too goddamned anxious!"

Toomey meanwhile had gone to the rail carrying half a dozen carrots of tobacco, which he tossed down into the dugout. A couple of the forward paddlers scrambled to grab them and the canoe slipped back somewhat. Henry called out, "Farewell! Smoke for us! Wish us fair winds and good fortune!" He allowed himself a brief smile and said, half under his breath and to no one in particular, "And go to hell!"

Old Gray Eyes was scowling as he resumed his seat but Little Soldier remained standing, waving his arm, a smile pasted on his wolfish face but not looking at all happy nevertheless. Their canoe slid back with the others and soon they all turned and made for shore.

We had by then reached the upper end of the village, where the channel cut sharply to the right, well away from the village and out of rifle range from that side but close to a well-forested bank, where any number of Indians might be lurking. Toomey and his gun crew trundled their cannon to that side and I saw that Davidson had already ordered the swivel gun in the bow to be trained in that direction. A number of men scurried across the deck and the cargo box and took up positions on that side, rifles and muskets poking out like bristles on a hog. We saw a few brown skins flitting amongst the trees, but the sight of that much hardware must have discouraged them. Not a shot was fired from either side and soon the Arikara village slipped out of sight.

That night and for several nights thereafter we anchored in mid-channel, a heavy guard posted on both sides of the keelboat. Davidson and Pike patrolled the decks throughout the dark hours, making sure that every sentry was alert.

You might wonder how it was that Tuttle and I had so little traffic with Mike Fink and his cronies, cooped up as we were on the St. Pierre, which, big as it was, was still crowded with nigh a double complement of men. I reckon the reason was that Fink wanted no more to do with us than we did with him. Just the same, I was hardly ever without the comfort of my pocket pistol snugged in the waist of my britches.

The day after we got past the Rees, the Major called me to the afterdeck and I spent most of the day riding a pen, making a copy of his journal entry concerning our encounter with the Arikaras, amongst a passel of other observations. Whilst I was shaving ink and scribbling I overheard still another rather warm discussion between our two leaders. The General still wasn't convinced that the Rees had posed a serious threat to us. No matter how hard Henry tried to change Ashley's mind, the General steadfastly maintained that we could have bought horses from them without any danger. At last the Major just clammed up and stalked off, shaking his head, and said nothing more.

The more I thought about it the surer I was that it hinged upon the General being a general and Andrew Henry being just a major, which meant William Ashley had to have the last word.

                                                ≈   ≈   ≈

It wasn't until we passed Cannonball River and got halfway to Heart River before the Major allowed us to resume hunting and to camp on shore at night. Even then he and his lieutenants cautioned us to be on our guard, for the Hidatsa villages were not far above us and the Hidatas were a fickle lot, sometimes friendly, sometimes not at all, who prided themselves on their skills at warfare and thievery.

Even so, it was good to stretch our legs on the prairie, to gather around our cookfires and sink our teeth into slabs of juicy buffalo hump and meaty ribs, and afterwards to listen to the Major scraping happiness out of his fiddle, joining in now and then to sing out the choruses of old and new-learned songs, although our rifles were rarely but a hand-reach away from any of us. The Lahcotahs and the Rees had taught us to be wary. After dark, men went now in pairs and threes and fully-armed to do their business outside of camp.

I was sick and tired of the keelboat, but that was nothing new. And after I saw in the distance, one day whilst I was out hunting, a bunch of what I took to be Hidatsa hunters running a small bunch of buffalo a-horseback, the aching hunger I felt for the feel of a horse between my legs once again was plumb pluperfectly painful.

Tuttle felt the same way I did, likely even more so, and after I told him what I had heard the Major say about getting horses from the Mandans, both of us were on pins and needles.

As you must have gathered by now, most of us in Andrew Henry's expedition were green as early grass when it came to the country we were in, but not all of us. Onesuch was Ned Godey, a sometime trapper but mostly a skin trader, up from somewheres in Missouri, who had worked for Pierre Chouteau and a fellow named Manuel Lisa for several years on the Upper Missouri, swapping various plunder with the Indians for furs, mostly beaver hides — he called them plews — until it became plain that there had to be a better way to harvest beaver fur than waiting for the Indians to get around to trapping the critters and curing their pelts. Ned said that once an Indian buck had got himself a musket and a sufficiency of powder and lead, a few brass tacks and maybe some trade cloth, beads, and trinkets — he called such truck foofurraw — for his woman, the Indian completely lost interest in trapping more beaver, which was no way to run the fur business.

That is where Ashley and Henry came in, according to Ned. Their scheme was to rustle up a bunch of likely greenhorns such as ourselves and haul us up the river and teach us to trap beaver on wages and skimpy shares, counting on our ignorance and greed to keep us at it until we got good at it or got ourselves killed, in which case it wouldn't matter much anyway, for there was always a goodly supply of enterprising young men who yearned to try their hand at the wilderness.

It was something of a shock to hear Ned put it baldly like that, but thinking it over, Tuttle and I agreed that it was just about what Ashley and Henry had offered in the first place.

Ned Godey knew the country and he knew the Indians and the critters that lived thereabouts. We didn't, which was the best reason we could think of to stick close to Ned and learn enough to keep our hide in one piece and our hair where it belonged.

Hamish Davidson knew such things, too, but he was always busy doing the Major's bidding. Ned Godey, on the other hand, had no such responsibilities and once we got past his distrust of smart-aleck greenhorns he proved to be a true and worthy friend.

Ned looked every inch what I supposed a mountaineer should be, medium-tall and not an extra pound on his lean and wiry frame. His buckskin clothes looked well-worn but clean and he was the only white man aboard who wore a britch-clout and leggin's. His brown hair brushed his shoulders and his sharp features were clean-shaven, passably handsome, and deeply tanned, but it was his eyes that caught and held you. Deep blue they were, squinted from a lifetime in sunshine and glaring snow, alert and knowing, promising both patient understanding and unyielding judgment.

The morning we arrived at the Hidatsa village, not long after we passed Heart River, before we anchored, Andrew Henry called Hamish Davidson, Leclerc, and Ned Godey to the afterdeck and told them he wanted them to help with his meeting with the Hidatsa, that he wanted to buy horses but not just yet, and that he would tell the Hidatsa he would be trading for horses when we got to the Mandan villages and they should fetch their best stock up there if they wished to make trade.

Henry had considerable experience with Indians and he understood the importance of ceremony, which is likely why he was decked out once again in his bright green tailcoat, brass buttons gleaming, and his tall beaver topper perched upon his head. The General was even more splendid in a bright blue tailcoat, creamy britches, and shiny black knee-boots, with a gleaming military sword belted around his waist.

Jacques Leclerc was named the chief hand-talker, Hamish in charge of the skiff that would take them to shore, and Ned Godey was to look after the customary gifts that Henry would present to the chiefs. Ned picked Tuttle and me to help him with his chore.

Tuttle and I had just finished stowing two hefty sacks of presents in one of the skiffs when the keelboat rounded the bend below the Hidatsa village. I saw a couple dozen boats, looking for all the world like big brown soup bowls, bobbing out from the shore. I stood marveling at the queer craft, when I heard Ned call down from the deck, "Them're bullboats, what the Injuns up thisaway mostly use on the water. You'll be seein' a lot o' them an' likely you'll be learnin' how to build 'em, too."

The St. Pierre drew up abreast of the village and dropped anchor in the channel. There was already a goodly cluster of Indians, men and women of all ages, and children, too, on the riverbank, with more and more of them boiling out of their big beehive mud-and-thatch houses and coming down to get a look at us. Even from where I stood on the deck I could see that they were by far a more comely lot than the Rees downstream. They were taller and straighter and a great deal cleaner, besides being a sight better dressed.

Hamish piped on a little whistle he carried around his neck and Tuttle and I clambered down into the skiff, our rifles slung across our backs. I might mention here that when I saw how Fink and his pals and several others had saved their rifles when the *Bonhomme* went down, I wasted no time in fashioning a rifle strap for Melchior and Tuttle did likewise.

Four *bateliers* were already at the oars. Tuttle and I went to the bow, ready to cast off the towline. Godey soon joined us, then Hamish and Jacques Leclerc, followed by Henry's clerk, Davey

Jackson, an older man likely in his thirties, who was quiet but friendly enough. The Major was last to step into the skiff. He quickly settled himself on the stern seat and waved us on our way. General Ashley remained standing on the afterdeck, arms folded, cape falling from his shoulders, looking for all the world like some sort of emperor. The oarsmen bent to their task and the skiff slid smoothly out from behind the St. Pierre.

By that time the beach was milling with Indians and as we drew nigh to the shore the hubbub was deafening. They looked to be good-natured enough, but just the same I glanced at Ned and Hamish, who appeared to be enjoying it all, which reassured me more than somewhat. The Major, too, appeared relaxed and a faint smile wreathed his craggy features.

The bow grated on the gravelly beach and Tuttle and I leaped into the shallow water, caught hold of the prow, and dragged the skiff forward onto dry land, to save the Major the discomfort of wet boots. Henry made his way past the *bateliers* and stepped out onto the beach, followed by Leclerc, Hamish, and the others. Tuttle and I hoisted the gift sacks onto our shoulders and fell in behind Ned Godey. The boatmen slid the skiff back into the water and waited there.

When Andrew Henry strode forward a few paces and halted, a hush fell over the Indians. I wondered if his green tailcoat and shiny brass buttons had surely worked a charm, but then I saw their ranks part like the sea before Moses and make way for the most magnificent Indian I reckon I will ever see.

He stood well over six feet tall, handsome of face under his paint, muscles rippling on his coppery bare arms and chest, a quilled and painted buffalo robe thrown across his broad shoulders, his britch-clout, leggin's, and moccasins crusted with bright quillwork. Most impressive of all, howsomever, was his headdress, a huge round bonnet made of magpie feathers, black and white and fluttering in the breeze, looking like an exploding rocket, topped by a lone eagle feather and a short cape of hawk feathers that ran to the back and fanned out over his shoulders. Standing there in front of Henry, holding his staff and a sort of wand, he looked as if he ruled the world.

Ned Godey took half a step backward and whispered, "That'n be Buffalo Calf, one o' the head chiefs." Ned looked up to see if he was interrupting anything, which he wasn't, then he added, "He be Dog Society, but I reckon he won't be traipsin' back'ards today. This be business, not medicine." I hadn't the slightest idea of what Ned might mean by that, but I nodded sagely nonetheless.

The Major held up his hand, palm outward, as a sign of peace, and the chief lifted his staff in reply, saying nothing but looking affable enough. The Major commenced talking in a loud, slow, speech-making sort of way, saying all the things you might expect about coming in peace and our being friends of the Hidatsas and wishing them well and other such nonsense. Leclerc, who already knew what the Major was going to say, had his hands flying and fluttering as soon as Henry opened his mouth, but the chief kept his eyes fixed on the Major, barely noticing the Frenchman's sign language. Then Henry got down to brass tacks concerning the horses. A murmur of approval rippled through the watching throng of Indians, most likely because they were pleased that we hadn't traded for horses with the Rees.

It occurred to me about then that the sign language was a handy thing to know, for anybody who could see Leclerc's hands knew what he was saying, no matter how much noise there was, and a crowd of Indians is never precisely orderly.

When the Major got to the part about waiting to trade until we got to the Mandans, howsomever, I heard a muffled groan rumble amongst the Hidatsas when they learned that they wouldn't be the only horse traders. Buffalo Calf, the chief, merely tightened his lips a mite, but otherwise his expression never changed. Henry went on to tell him that the business would be conducted three days hence at the Mandans and that now it was time for us to show our respect for the Hidatsas. He snapped his fingers behind his back and Ned jerked his head, telling Tuttle and me to bring our sacks forward, which we did, laying them on the beach in front of the chief, slitting them open, and spreading out the various plunder, much as we had seen Leclerc do with the Lahcotahs.

This time the Major had been rather more generous with his gifting, but the merchandise was much the same — tobacco, butcher knives, belt axes, vermilion powder, beads, and suchlike. Buffalo Calf glanced at the plunder, allowed himself a brief smile, nodded, and then he spoke, haltingly. "You come good, White Chief, to Hidatsa. Hidatsa know you, Henley, from ago. Is good, look on you. Hidatsa horse plenty. Hidatsa horse plenty good. No need Mandan horse, plenty bad." He paused a moment, then continued. "Hidatsa come three sun. Plenty horse. Eat. Smoke. Three sun." He held up his hand, three fingers extended, and smiled, likely with satisfaction at his own speech. "Peace."

Henry made a short bow and smiled, uttering some sort of sociable nonsense I can't recall, and we retreated to the skiff. Once we were afloat I had a chance to admire the Indians on the beach. The chief had departed by then, but those who remained were a fine-looking bunch, prideful in their dress and handsome in their persons, men and women alike. I was wishing, too, that we had more time to look at the women, but there wasn't. I was able, howsomever, to examine the bullboats. They were more or less round, eight to ten feet across, a couple feet deep, made of green buffalo hides stretched on a frame of willows lashed together with sinew.

Andrew Henry was in a jovial mood, pleased with his meeting with Buffalo Calf and confident that the horse-trading would go well. He positively cackled when he announced, "Now we'll have some competition goin' amongst 'em when the trading commences! They don't like it much, but they'll come! It's time to sharpen our wits and drive some hard bargains, eh, Thompson?"

Tuttle jumped when he heard his name, startled that Henry should mention him, but he sounded calm enough when he drawled, "Thankee, Mayjah. We'll do 'er right an' get us some good'uns."

❧   ❧   ❧

It was the third day of July when we arrived at Knife River and the Mandan village. I know this is so because the General announced that the morrow would be Independence Day, the Fourth of July, and proclaimed a holiday for all hands.

We moored the St. Pierre on the left bank, the south side of the river, just below the Mandan village, which was really more of a town, with row upon row of beehive earthen houses stretching out to cornfields and squash patches, good reason to suppose the Mandans, like Hidatsas and Rees, were Indians who preferred to stay put. Ned Godey told us that the Mandans had lived in that neighborhood since long before any white man could remember.

We set about pitching camp, pulling down our canvas awnings on the keelboat and stretching them over brush bowers we built on shore. We camped more or less according to our messes, but men had long since begun to sort themselves out, like to like, according to their general humor. Brass Turtle and Ned Godey were spending more time in our mess than in their own and John Fitzgerald had drifted into the fringes of Mike Fink's crowd.

Once the shelters were up we foraged for firewood and that night the fires burned high and bright. We gorged ourselves on fresh buffalo meat we had shot the day before and generally soaked up the cheer and good feeling that came from knowing our river journey was drawing to an end, although what was in store after that few of us could even hazard a guess.

Ashley and Henry passed the evening amongst us, visiting one mess after another at first, but after a time we all merged together. The Major got out his fiddle and soon Anse Tolliver, the quiet man from Tennessee, was scraping away on his. The little Frenchman, Yves Dureau, pumped his squeezebox and Brass Turtle tootled his Delaware flute and Paddy McBride leaped to his feet and flung himself into a wild Irish jig. Ere long a dozen men were prancing and cavorting in the firelight, whilst the rest of us roared with laughter that warmed a body clear to the bone.

Sparks floating into the sky from our bonfires, the music, and the general merriment in camp must have caught the attention of Indians in the village, for when darkness fell it wasn't long until we could see shadowy figures standing at the edge of the forest, silently taking in our noisy behavior. It wasn't long, either, before, here and there, men commenced to slip off amongst the trees and return sometime later with a satisfied smile on their face. Ned Godey must have caught my longing look as I watched them leave and come back to the fire, for he grinned and said, "Hold on if ye kin, Temple. These're Mandans an' they ain't no strangers to white-eyes traders. An' they ain't strangers to the clap an' the pox, neither. Wait, if ye kin, 'til ye come acrost an Injun maid who ain't met up with a passel o' whites, which ain't likely hereabouts."

That was a sobering thought, for I had heard a lot of talk during my time on the St. Pierre about such ailments, especially the clap, about which some men bragged, "You ain't a man 'less'n you had it!" I reckoned if it came to that, I'd just as lief remain a boy.

Hamish and Luther Pike were busy that evening threading their way amongst the men gathered at the fire, tapping this or that one for a spell of sentry duty on the St. Pierre. Camped as close as we were to the village, they were especially wary of thievery. Ned advised, "Keep a close eye on yer possibles. Injuns are jist natcherly thieves. It ain't a sin ner a crime with them. It's more a matter o' pride to git away with it."

I have no idea how long the merry-making went on that night, but the camp was still throbbing with good-natured noise when I crawled into my blankets to sleep and dream of a woman who was sometimes Lucette and sometimes Sarah and sometimes a copper-colored maiden I had never seen.

అ   అ   అ

I awakened next morning to the big bass voice of Hamish Davidson, striding through camp and roaring, "Hear ye now, me buckos! 'Tis time ye're rousin' out o' your robes! 'Tis your great Hamerican holiday! Your Day of Independence from the bloody Sassenachs! A time for rejoicin'! The Major says ye're all to be shavin' this day an' to put on your Sunday Best, if ye own any, so's to look spruce for the Mandans! Shake a leg now an' join the Gen'ral an' the Major at the boat in an hour's time!"

I trotted off to the woods and when I returned I saw Jim Bridger and John Smiley squatting at the fire, a kettle of water bubbling in the coals. They looked happy. Jim Bridger was laughing his boyish laugh and even John Smiley permitted himself a pleasant grin at something young Bridger had said. Tuttle knelt nearby, peering into a sliver of mirror propped on a bush and cursing softly as he scraped his razor across his blue-stubbled cheeks.

I ran barefoot to the river, stripping off my hickory shirt as I went, and dived into the chill water, less muddy this far up the river than down below. I splashed and dived as long as I could stand the cold, then raced back to camp, where I shucked off my dripping britches and slipped into my buckskins, considerably weathered by now, but still the best I owned. Shaving didn't take long. It never did, for my beard, what there was of it, was slow to grow, which bothered me not a mite.

By time I put on my best pair of moccasins and tied up my bedroll, Tuttle had sauntered into camp wearing a long red shirt I had never seen before. As he stood preening himself, freshly shaved and hopefully bathed, garbed in his bright new shirt, belted now with his big knife, possibles bag, and bullet pouch around his waist, I had to admit that Tuttle wasn't nearly as homely as I usually told him he was.

"So, Temple, what d'ye think?" he asked, squaring his shoulders. "Ain't I somethin' now?"

I just had to get even. "Well, now, talk about Missus Washington's pet pony! Ain't you something to conjure with? 'Pears to me we had oughta find a mud puddle!"

Tuttle brayed like a jackass, then he sniffed. "Envy, Temple, be mebbe the worst o' the Seven Godawful Deadly Sins.Thought yew, a preacher's boy, would be knowin' thet!"

I couldn't keep from laughing at the prissy-pious way he said that and of course he joined in. Laughing was a thing that Tuttle did best and admired most. Then it came to us that it was past time that we get down to the boat. We slung our rifles, hoisted up our bedrolls, and left camp at a trot.

Most of the company was already there when Tuttle and I ran onto the keelboat, stowed our gear, and joined the others on the riverbank. A blind man could have found that place, just by following his nose. Our leaders had conscripted the Frenchies to prepare a holiday feast for us and the air was rich with the fragrance of boiling coffee, fresh-baked bread, bacon frying, hams roasting, and two huge cauldrons of spicy beans and another of corn porridge bubbling over the coals. Nigh a side of buffalo was turning on a spit, whilst Leclerc ladled and laved a thick red-brown sauce over the roasting meat.

We all fell to and stuffed ourselves like a passel of Christmas geese, then sat back smoking a morning pipe and drinking up the rest of the coffee whilst the General stood up on a fallen log and delivered his inevitable Fourth of July oration, which no matter how overlong and overblown it was, was still meager payment for the excellent vittles we had just consumed. Naturally he went on about the virtues of democracy and the valor required of all citizens to keep our young nation strong and free and other such claptrap without which you can't be a politician unless you have a pocketful, but when he raised his arm and pointed to our flag fluttering from the mast of the St. Pierre, I daresay there wasn't an American there who didn't feel his eyes itching with prideful tears. Then he told us that all of us gathered there were true patriots, for we were establishing American rights to the territory claimed by General Clark and that other fellow a decade and a half before. He said a lot of other things, some of them more than once, it seemed to me, and at last he ran down like an unwound clock. I reckon the cheers and huzzahs and clapping when he finished were more for the completion of his oration than for the speech itself.

Naturally Andrew Henry had to have his say, but his message was a sight shorter and rather more welcome than the General's. He stepped onto the log and waved a big wooden mallet for silence. When he had our attention, he said, "I reckon the General has said it all better than I ever could. I join all of you in saluting our flag and our nation!" He pointed to the stars and stripes waving from the mast and then he roared, "So it's time now to drink a toast to Old Glory!" With that he jumped off the log and trotted over to a keg that the Frenchies had rolled up to the fire and set on end. Henry swung the mallet and caved in the lid, then picked up a gill measure and yelled, "Who'll be first to drink to liberty and our success in the mountains?" He had a lot of takers. All about me men spilled their coffee into the dirt and surged around him, waving their cups and cheering the Major in a manner that the General must have envied.

He was well into the second keg by time I got to the front of the queue. Henry sloshed a full measure into my outstretched cup and said with a broad smile, "Drink hearty, Mister Buck! Tomorrow you'll have your wish! Horses!" I grinned back at him and allowed that I would happily drink to that worthy cause.

The whiskey wasn't the best, not nearly as good as what I had drunk at Lucette's, but it was welcome indeed. Even so, I spilled a good half of it into Tuttle's cup, which was nearly empty by then. That, too, was soon gone and Tuttle hustled over to where the Iroquois were selling their ration to the highest bidders.

Tuttle went with some other men into the Mandan village, where they had heard that some white traders were selling whiskey. I chose not to go along and spent the rest of the day with Mister Homer outside the walls of Troy, thinking now and again how much Thersites brought Luther Pike to mind. At length I closed my book and went aboard the St. Pierre to retrieve Tuttle's bedroll and my own and hauled them back to camp.

Only John Fitzgerald was there, his back propped against a tree, his eyes glazed and a silly smile on his lips. He hailed me with unaccustomed cheerfulness. "Hey now, Misther Buck! Drop yer traps now an' take a load off yer feet. Set yerself down an' we'll be takin a dram together fer the sake o' the Glorious Republic!" I noticed that his brogue was much more pronounced than usual and his hand fumbled as he reached inside his coat. He drew forth a fairish-sized flask and shoved it at me. "Here now, Misther Buck, we'll drink to the everlastin' glory o' the Red-White-an'-the-Blue an' piss on England's Cruel Red!"

That seemed to me to be a fair-enough proposition, so I unscrewed the top of his flask and guzzled down a generous mouthful of whiskey that was better than I had any right to expect thereabouts. I thanked him and handed back the flask. Fitzgerald helped himself to a sizeable pull, wiped his lips with the back of his hand, set the flask in the dirt between us, then regarded me with rheumy eyes. He cleared his throat and spat and said, "I'm s'posin' ye've been wond'rin' what's after bringin' a man like meself, John James Fitzgerald, Esquire himself, all the way from Noo York to a godforsaken, uncivilized place like this." I hadn't, but I nodded just the same, so as not to disappoint him. "Well now, seein's this is after bein' the Farth o' July, the greatest holiday in all the world, I'll be after tellin' ye."

Fitzgerald picked up his flask, took a long swig, and continued, "Well now, not long ago I used to be a politician in Noo York, the greatest city in all the world! Oh, I wasn't one o' them Grand Naybobs like the Mayor or an alderman or nuthin' like that, not yet! But I was what ye might call a Risin' Star, maybe still just a wardheeler, gettin' out the vote fer the Party and gettin' 'em to vote the ticket right so's our candy-dates was sure to be elected, an' natcherly acceptin' little favors in return, don't ye know. But I was a Risin' Star wid a future as broad an' bright as the shinin' sea, livin' the good life an' lovin' the work I was doin'! Not a ragged-arse Mick the likes o' Paddy McBride!" He took another pull and shook the nearly-empty flask. "An' then we lost the election an' all hell broke loose! Next thing we know, the Opposition is after callin' fer arrestin' us fer takin' graft, like as if there ain't honest graft and dishonest graft, but 'twas all the same to them. I told 'em, John Fitzgerald seen his opportunities an' he took 'em! But it made no diff'rence to the likes o' them. I was forced to get out o' Noo York on the run an' here I am in god-knows-where in the wilderness, tellin' me tale to the likes o' you on a glorious Farth o' July, when John James Fitzgerald should be marchin' proud as ye please on the bricks o' Broadway!"

Fitzgerald drained the last of his whiskey and his chin dropped onto his chest. Just as I rose to leave, I heard him mumble, "I seen me opportunities an' I took 'em."

I shared some warmed-over buffalo ribs with John Smiley and Jim Bridger at the fire before I turned in, just as darkness fell.

Later I was awakened by Tuttle staggering into the bower and fumbling with his bedroll. I could hear a drum beating from somewheres up near the village and I reckoned the Hidatsas had shown up with their horses. Paddy arrived not long afterwards, somewhat the worse for wear, and soon the peaceful snoring of my whiskey-sotted companions mingled with the comforting rhythm of the drum and lulled me back to sleep.

ॐ ॐ ॐ

Buying horses from the Mandans and the Hidatasa took up two whole days. I learned a lot about sound horseflesh from Tuttle and even more about shrewd bargaining from the Major, who proved to be as hard as flint in a horse trade.

There was no nonsense about Andrew Henry when it came to judging horses. He had a practiced eye himself and he relied on Tuttle Thompson to see what he himself might have overlooked.

Tuttle missed very little. First he would pry open the horse's mouth to learn its age by looking at its teeth. Then, too, he could tell a surface crack from a crippling split in a hoof or spot a bowed tendon that had been fired to shrink it short again and there was many a groan from both the Mandan and the Hidatsa horse-traders when he hiked this or that horse's hind leg up to its belly and held it there, then slapped it on the flank to make it run, in order to detect a hidden spavin in the hock.

Naturally the Indians first offered their blemished horses for trade, but after Tuttle had turned thumbs down on the first half dozen, I saw Indians leading several horses away without even trying to pass them off as sound.

The Hidatsa chief Buffalo Calf led his people to the horse-trading, but he took no part in the haggling. He was dressed that day in simple buckskins, no paint on his face, and his hair was braided on either side and unadorned. Ned Godey commented wryly that this was business, not ceremony. The Mandan chief who was overseeing matters for his people was called Four Bears, a fine-looking man, slighter of build than Buffalo Calf but equally impressive, a hawk nose and penetrating, intelligent eyes staring out above his painted cheeks, his long buckskin shirt painted with a record of his deeds in bright colors. He wore his long hair loose and around his neck was a necklace of huge bear claws, bigger than any I had ever seen, the original owners of which, Ned assured me, Four Bears had certainly killed.

I learned a lot that day, not only about Missouri River Indians, but mainly about horses. Tuttle Thompson had high standards. After he was assured that a particular horse wasn't too old or damaged, he looked for qualities that made for strength, endurance, and handiness. He insisted on a wide, deep chest that told him the horse had big lungs and a lot of wind. He was a good teacher, for he would go over each horse, front to back, pointing out to me what he was looking for. "Here now, Temple," he would say, "y'oughter be lookin' fer big, wide-apart eyes. Keeps 'em from spookin'. Makes 'em kind, too. Head hadn't oughter be too big an' the neck oughter be purty straight, though I seen some ewe-necks thet're right handy. A deep barrel'll give ye a long ride an' a short back won't break down. Ye want lots o' muscle in the flanks an' a short stifle fer a long reach, fer coverin' a lot o' ground 'thout a lot o' effort. An' a lot o' muscle in the gaskins'll let 'im climb all day an' turn about on a shillin' piece. Pastrens oughta be long, but not too long fer fear o' breakin' down, an' slopin', fer a soft ride. If'n the pastrens be short an' straight-up, he'll likely rattle yore teeth right outa yore head."

Once Tuttle was satisfied that a horse possessed the qualities he desired, he would hoist me up onto the horse's bare back and send me off on a gallop around the trading ground, whilst he watched the horse's action. When I returned and pulled the horse to a halt in front of him, Tuttle would first put his ear to the horse's mouth, then press his cheek close to the throat, to see if its breathing was ragged and broken. If so, he knew that the animal had damaged lungs or a scarred-up windpipe. Wind-broke, Tuttle called it. Watching the horse gallop let him value the horse's stride and his way of going. Sometimes he would say, "Jest a leetle cow-hocked but it don't hurt nuthin'. Lets 'im reach way up 'thout interferin'."

Like I said, I learned a great deal that day. Some of it I had heard before, for Tuttle dearly loved horses and he dearly loved to talk about them, but it was much better when the horse was right there in front of us.

Once Tuttle nodded his approval of a particular animal, it was Andrew Henry's turn to haggle the price. We had hauled up a big heap of trade goods that morning and all the Indians had big eyes for the plunder stacked and spread around behind the Major. He drove a hard bargain, but a fair one, evidently, for when he reckoned he had named the right price and grabbed up a pinch of brass tacks to seal the bargain, the tacks were rarely refused.

Sometimes, howsomever, the horse-owner would stand his ground and turn down Henry's price. When that happened, say with a Hidatsa, the Major would tell Tuttle to call up a horse from the Mandans and the whole rigamarole would commence all over again, whilst the Hidatsa eyed the dwindling heap of trade goods. When it was his turn again it didn't take long for him to come to terms. Henry never cracked a smile, but you could hear the satisfaction in his voice when he said, "Ye see? Like I said, competition is a good thing."

Ned Godey was Henry's hand-talker for the horse-trading, for he knew horses better than Leclerc did. Watching Ned's hands flutter and slice and dance in the sign language would just about make you dizzy and the different looks on his face when the Indian horse-owner presumed to argue with him were truly a sight to behold.

By day's end we had bought a score and more horses and all concerned, Indians and whites alike, appeared to be satisfied with the dealing. General Ashley had joined us in the late afternoon and he and the Major, with Ned to do the hand-talking, went off with the Hidatsas to eat and smoke and palaver. They had been with the Mandans the night before. Smiley and McBride and Jim Bridger helped us load up the remaining trade goods on some of the gentler horses and Tuttle and I drove the rest back to camp.

Once there we made hobbles from rope we got off the St. Pierre and set our new mounts out to graze under watchful guards, for Ned had warned that he wouldn't put it past either Mandans or Hidatsas to steal them back again.

Next day we were back at it, but this time I noticed a lot more piebald horses being led to the trading circle. The first day the horses had been mostly solid-colored, bays and chestnuts and line-back duns. I mentioned this to Ned Godey and he replied, "Today we come to the close bargainin'. Injuns up thisaway prize them spotted ponies more'n the others, not jist 'cause they're purty, but 'cause you cain't hardly see 'em at a distance. The spots break up the outline an' they don't look like nuthin' much a-tall from far off. Comes in handy fer a war party an' keeps 'em from gittin' stole sometimes, too."

Ned was right about the trading being tougher. The horses offered for trade on the second day were generally a whole lot superior to those we had bought the day before. Now and again Ned would say, "That'n's a buffler hoss, sure'nough." Then, proving what Ned had said, I'd see Tuttle allowing himself a sly smile as he passed the critter on to the Major for the bargaining to commence. The price was higher for such animals, but Andrew Henry always saw to it that he got his money's worth.

We finished up with forty-eight horses, all of them serviceable, some better than others, but I didn't see a one for which I would have swapped my Kumskaka horse.

๖ะ ๖ะ ๖ะ

I woke up next morning eager but bleary-eyed, for I had slept badly, excited as I was at the prospect of spending the next day a-horseback. The Major had picked Tuttle and me to go along with the horse herd on the south bank of the river whilst the keelboat forged its way upriver. He had also chosen Ned Godey, who knew that part of the country well, and Brass Turtle, too. Hamish Davidson was in charge of our horse detail, which also included three men whom the rest of us knew hardly at all, Saint Louis French aristocrats left over from the batch of quitters that returned downriver from Fort Osage. These gentlemen knew some English but they usually talked a sort of high-class French to each other that even the *bateliers* could barely understand and they pretty much kept to themselves when they could, like white trash and Indians didn't belong with the exalted likes of themselves. One of them was named Longchamps. I don't recollect what the other two called themselves.

All that made no nevermind to me, howsomever, for I was in my glory when I threw a dragoon saddle onto a handsome bay horse, buckled the girth snug, and slipped the bridle over his ears. All of those horses were skittish, raring back, white showing in their eyes, whenever we got close. Ned Godey said they didn't like the smell of white men but he reckoned they would get over it in time. Only Brass Turtle appeared to have no such trouble, which sort of proved the truth of what Ned said.

The first three days went better than a reasonable man could ask for. The weather held good and the country we traveled was generally flat and treeless, covered with belly-high grass that provided plenty of graze for the horses. Eight men moving only forty herd-broke horses makes for an easy chore. We didn't need that many drovers, of course, but there was always a chance of running up against Indians. As it was, there was plenty of time for jawing and jesting and just plain reveling in the feel of a good critter under your backside. The Saint Louis dandies rode mostly up front with Hamish or out on the flanks. The four of us brought up the rear, gathering strays and pushing the herd.

There was time, too, to judge how the other men rode. Hamish was workmanlike but stiff, like a willing but awkward bridegroom on a dance floor. Brass Turtle and Ned were what you might expect, fluid as a rippling brook, melting into their mounts and becoming one with them. I was forced to grant our three aristocrats grudging credit for their horsemanship, for formal as it was, their riding proved that they had spent a lifetime in the saddle. Howsomever it was Tuttle who astonished me. Gangling and ungainly as he was afoot, aboard a horse he was as graceful as a delicate maiden. His huge calloused hands spoke gently to his horse's mouth and his coaxing voice and calm manner appeared to soothe even the most fractious critter in the herd. I was mightily impressed and I told him so, but he just blushed and brayed like a mule and replied that I ought to see him with a woman sometime, an observation that I would just as lief pass on. I had come entirely too close to such an experience, as it was, that morning at Mathilde's in the Vide Poche.

Nighttimes we hobbled all the horses just outside camp and kept a heavy guard on them. We were in Indian country and Ned Godey said, "If'n it be a matter o' choice, Injuns'll take a hoss over a woman any time. You git yourself hosses enough, ye kin git jist about any woman ye're wantin'."

Naturally our three aristocrats didn't stand horse guard, but Smiley, Bridger, and McBride happily took their place. Anse Tolliver volunteered as well and so did little Yves Dureau, the batelier who played the squeezebox. Anse allowed that he didn't care much for horses, but, he reckoned, since we were lackin' mules so far, he could put up with horses for the time being. As he put it, "Mules're smart. Oncet ye git to knowin' mules, a body cain't hardly tolerate them damn dumb hoss critters."

The morning of the fourth day we ate a hasty breakfast and saddled up, ready to commence pushing the herd west, as soon as the St. Pierre got underway. Godey said we would likely cross the Little Missouri that day, so we had best get a move on. The water was too deep to cross at the mouth of that river, which meant that we would need to move upstream, away from the Missouri, and then we would most likely need to swim the horses across, at that.

We had taken to riding different horses each day, in order to gentle as many as we could. Hamish had so far failed to show up, so Brass Turtle and I caught up a likely chestnut and put Hamish's saddle on him, so as to save time when he arrived. The Saint Louis dandies had mounted by then and all of the horses were free of their hobbles, milling in the grazed-over field, tended by Tuttle and Ned. But still no sign of Hamish.

We were all getting impatient, horses and men alike, when I beheld a sight that sent my heart sinking to my moccasins. It wasn't an Indian war party. It was Luther Pike trudging through the tall grass, rifle slung across his back, a hard smile frozen on his meager lips.

"Mornin', men. I'll be givin' orders today." His Georgia drawl cracked like a blacksnake whip. "Time we git to movin."

I handed him the reins of Hamish's horse and without thinking I asked, "Where's Hamish?"

Pike tried to wither me with a superior glare, focused somewhere just above my eyebrows. It didn't work, but he tried. "Mistah Davi'son is othahwise occewpied! Doin' what is none o' yo' goddamn beeswax!" He shoved a boot into the stirrup and swung himself up, then announced to everybody there, "Like I said, I'm givin' the orders an' I'll be takin' no back-sass!" Then he reined his horse around and jammed his sharp little spurs into the pony's flanks.

When the chestnut finished pitching and generally trying to turn himself inside out, Luther Pike was somehow still aboard, but he was red-faced and breathing hard and he had lost his topper somewhere in the tall grass. Nobody offered to go look for it. Pike smoothed his ruffled hair and tried to regain his composure by shouting even louder, "Awright! Let's git these'ere animals movin'!"

I rode out to the herd and got myself between Tuttle and Brass Turtle, where I nearly fell off my horse laughing. Pike took his place at the head of the bunch, flanked by his fellow aristocrats. Ned Godey was out in front, scouting the best place to cross the river. The St. Pierre moved out from shore and commenced to move upstream, oars dipping and the little square sail hanging mostly slack. The wind nowadays was almost always from the west, which meant a lot more back work for the men still aboard. We got the horses moving along the riverbank, halting now and then to let them graze, waiting for the keelboat to catch up with us.

We usually tried to stay in sight of the St. Pierre, just in case we ran into Indians, but when we neared the Little Missouri, Ned Godey rode back and waved us southward, away from the Big Missouri, then rode off in search of a decent place to ford the Little Missouri. We continued to push the herd to the south a couple-three miles until we finally saw Ned ride out of the brush and signal us to come up to him.

When we got there we saw that he had found a passable fording place. The river was wide at that spot and it ran deep enough for swimming water in a few places, but none of that offered much of a challenge. Godey was talking with Pike and the Saint Louis dandies were pressing the flanks of the herd towards the center.

Brass Turtle and Tuttle and I were bunching them up from behind, ready to push them into the water, keeping them together so we could get all forty horses across at one time, when I heard Tuttle gasp, "Christamighty! Injuns!"

Sure enough, when I looked up I saw painted redskins on both sides of the river, fine-looking men, most of them bare to the waist, mounted on excellent horses, carrying muskets over their arm or bows and quivers slung across their back. Ned said a few words to Pike, then rode around the herd back to us. Tuttle and I had by that time unslung our rifles and Brass Turtle was spilling powder into his priming pan. When Ned rode up he called out, "Assiniboins! They're makin' friendly sign an' mebbe that's what they be. Don't shoot yet, but git ready." Then he rode back to Pike.

The loose horses stayed pretty well bunched and we edged our way forward amongst them so we could hear what was going on. By that time one of the Indians who appeared to be the boss had ridden up to within a rod or two of Pike and Godey and commenced making sign. Ned raised his voice so we all could hear when he told Pike what the Indian was saying. Pike didn't need to raise his voice when he answered back. He always talked loud enough to wake the dead. Ned told him, "The chief here says the Assiniboins be friends o' the white brothers. Says they wish only peace an' they want to help us howsomever they kin." Ned cleared his throat and spat into the river. Then, still smiling, he said, "I say he's likely a no-good sonofabitch an' I wouldn't trust him no fu'ther'n I kin throw his hoss!"

Now if Luther Pike hadn't gone and disgraced himself that morning by nearly getting pitched off his horse and losing his hat in front of all of us, matters might have turned out somewhat differently. As it was, his contrary streak bulged up and blocked out the little good sense he had. "See here, Godey, you listen to me an' listen up good," he snapped. "I'm the man in charge ri'chere and you jes' keep on makin' yore li'l hand-signs and do what I'm tellin' ye!"

So far I had counted at least a dozen Indians and those were just the ones that I could see. For all we knew there could have

been that many and more back in the trees and brush that
bordered the river. They looked pleasant enough. Fact is, they
looked too happy. They all had big smiles smeared across their
faces and they were laughing and calling out things to one another
that provoked even more laughter amongst them.

Pike was talking again. "Awright, Godey. You jes' tell the chief
here we thank 'im fer his he'p an' if'n he'll put his men yonder
downstream thar whilst we drive our critters acrost, we'll be much
obliged."

Ned Godey was a patient man, but this was something that ran
up against everything he had learned by hard experience. He made
no hand signs. Instead he looked Luther Pike straight in the eye
and said, "Mister Pike, I'll be doin' no sech a thing. These here be
Assiniboins — we mostly call 'em Rocks — an' they ain't your
readin'-writin', harness-broke, civilized Cherokees an' Choctaws!
These here be wild Injuns! You make a stand ri'chere an' now an'
tell 'em no-thankee an' good-bye or they'll be takin' ever' head o'
stock we got an' likely our hair in the bargain!"

Even from a distance I could see Luther Pike's face turn red as a
turkey gobbler's. He swelled up like a toad and screeched, "Lookee
here, Godey! I'm lootenant here an' you ain't! I know Injuns! I
was raised amongst 'em! They was all around us 'til we run 'em
off! All ye got to do is show 'em who's boss an' they'll come lickin'
yore hand! These here Sinny-boyns or whatever ye call 'em know
oh-thority an' soo-periority when they run up agin it! They're jes'
like chir'ren! Now do like I tol' ye an' be quick about it!"

Ned turned hard as iron and cold as ice. He fixed his gaze
squarely on Pike's face and said, "Nossir. Won't do it!"

The Assiniboins were watching all this with considerable
interest. They had quit laughing and joshing one another and
instead were staring at Pike and Godey in wonderment, now and
again rattling off something in their tongue that made them
chuckle. Then Tuttle spoke up, "Y'oughter listen to 'im, Pike. Ned
here knows the country. We don't!"

Pike spun around in his saddle and barked, "You jes' shet yore
pie-trap, Thompson, or I'll charge y'all with mutiny!"

It was too much to ask for me to keep on holding my peace, so I chimed in. "He's right! Ned's the only one of us who knows what we're dealin' with here. Listen to what he says!"

I had no sooner shut my mouth when Brass Turtle sang out. "They're right, Pike! You don't know nothin' 'bout Injuns! I reckon I oughta know! You play with these brothers an' they'll have the britches off your arse — an' your balls for boot!"

Pike fairly exploded. For a moment there he just sputtered noises, making no sense at all. Then he screamed, "Enough! Ye're all charged with mutiny! I won't have it! Won't tolerate it nohow! Git off them horses right now an' git back to the boat! You! Buck an' Thompson! An' take yer uppity li'l redskin with ye! I'll deal with y'all later!"

Choleric as we knew him to be, this came as a surprise to all of us. Cutting his horse guard in half was patently an invitation to the Assiniboins to help themselves to whatsoever they wanted. I looked to the Saint Louis dandies to see how they were taking all this, but they appeared remote, you might say disinterested. To this day I have no idea what they might have been thinking, whether they just didn't understand what was going on, which isn't likely, or whether they agreed with their fellow aristocrat that the Assiniboins meant well by us.

When I returned my gaze to Pike he looked mean as cat spit and his voice was a rusty razor. "Awright, Ned Godey, what'll it be? You gonna do like I say or you jinin' these others?"

Ned's voice was calm and steady when he said flatly, "I awready told ye. Don't let these Injuns help with nuthin'. They'll steal ye blind."

Surprisingly Pike didn't scream this time. His voice was more like a hiss. "So be it! Git off o' that hoss an' carry yore buckskin arse on back to the boat!"

Godey didn't bother to reply. He merely reined his horse away from Pike and waved to the three of us. "C'mon, fellers. We'll cross over here. The boat's likely past this river by now." Then he plunged his horse into the water and picked his way towards the other side.

Brass Turtle, Tuttle, and I didn't linger. Without a word or even a look at Pike we followed Ned into the river, our horses scrambling through rocky shallows and swimming in the deep places until they lunged up the far bank, not far behind Ned.

Pike's voice shrilled over the water, "You leave them hosses right thar, dammit! They ain't yours! They b'long with the rest!"

Ned had already unsaddled his horse and slipped off the bridle before we got out of the river. He was tethering his mount to a tree with a halter-shank when we rode up to him. He sounded almost tired when he said, "Y'oughta do likewise. Might's well save what we kin. Them Injuns'll git the rest."

We did as Godey said, meanwhile keeping an eye out and rifles ready for the Indians on our side of the river. I could see half a dozen of them through the trees, but they offered no harm right then. Fact is, they looked sort of puzzled at what we were doing. Godey noticed it, too, for he said, "Reckon they don't have no English a-tall. Cain't quite figger what's happenin', but they'll cipher it out soon enough. C'mon! Let's git a move on!"

He slipped his bridle over his shoulder and swung the saddle onto his back, picked up his rifle, and trotted off towards the Big Missouri. You can wager that the rest of us followed suit in no time at all.

A dragoon saddle doesn't weigh very much, so we were making good time as we hustled through the woods, but we hadn't gone but a quarter mile when we heard a shot, then another, then what sounded like a ragged volley. Ned skidded to a halt and dropped to one knee, listening, but we heard nothing more.

Godey frowned and then he sighed. His tone was steely when he said, "Damn! I hate bein' right, right now!" He looked thoughtful, then he said in a flat voice, "Reckon I'll go on back. Come along if ye like, but ye don't hafta."

Naturally we all did. We cached the horse-tack and trotted back on a different trail, lest the Assiniboins were feeling inclined to make a clean sweep of all our plunder. As it was, howsomever, forty-eight horses and all the property of our four aristocrats apparently satisfied our helpful red brothers.

We found the four of them on the riverbank, wet and bedraggled, a passel of drowned rats, but alive and still wearing their hair. Longchamps was bleeding from a head wound and so was Pike. Ned set about washing and bandaging the Frenchman and Brass Turtle did the same for our cranky leader, whilst Tuttle and I crouched in the brush and kept our eyes peeled for Indians.

Brass Turtle's hands weren't gentle and his tone was tart when he asked Pike if he still wanted help from those little red children. He ripped off the back of Pike's shirt, tore it in strips, and wound it around the bleeding wound, saying as he tied it fast, "It's surprisin' the chief didn't make ye his wife whilst he was about it! Or did he?"

Pike didn't even grunt a reply and Turtle commented wryly, "No. Reckon not. That Injun looked entirely too smart to swive the likes o' you. No tellin' what ye might be carryin'."

The Assiniboins had picked our four aristocrats as clean as a parson's plate — rifles, powder and bullets, even their coats and hats and boots — so they weren't at all encumbered when we retreated to the Missouri, taking still another trail through the trees. We dug the saddles and bridles out of our hasty cache and kept on moving as fast as we could towards the river.

Longchamps was reeling, doubtless dizzy from his head wound, and wincing whenever he trod on sharp stones with his bare feet. It showed some bedrock virtue in Brass Turtle when he draped the young Frenchman's arm over his shoulder and helped him along, even though he himself was burdened with his rifle and horse gear and half a mercantile of cutlery around his middle.

↪   ↪   ↪

We discovered the St. Pierre anchored in the channel not far upstream from the mouth of the Little Missouri. A shout went up from the deck when they saw us duck out from the trees and soon a skiff was making for shore.

Andrew Henry didn't wait for the skiff to ground. He stepped out into knee-deep water and splashed his way to shore. He glanced swiftly at the injured Pike and his lip curled, then he turned to Ned Godey and demanded, "What in bloody hell happened to my horses?"

Ned regarded him calmly and replied quietly, "I reckon you oughta be askin' your lieutenant 'bout that." Henry bristled and was about to demand a reply when Ned added, "Let's see what he has to say. If it's the truth, ye'll know. If not, we'll sure 'nough be tellin' ye."

The Major stared long and hard at his sorry-looking officer, bloody and drooping and hanging his head. Then he looked up at the rest of us and said not unkindly, "Let's get aboard. We can get to the bottom o' this back on the boat."

❧   ❧   ❧

We hardly had time to dump our horse gear on the deck before the Major summoned the four of us to his cabin. The General was there and so was Hamish Davidson, both looking sober as a brace of undertakers. Luther Pike sat on a low stool, bloody bandaged head bowed, chin on his bony chest, saying nothing.

Henry jerked his head towards Pike and broke the silence. "I can't get a sensible word out of this man." "Tell me now, what in the name o' Christ happened out there?"

Ned Godey took half a step forward and said, "Well now, if Mister Pike hyar cain't, or won't, tell ye, I reckon I must. They was yore hosses an', 'pears to me, ye got a right to know. It ain't tattlin', jist fact."

Ned launched into an account of the whole shebang, leaving nothing out and embroidering not a whit, and he told it all in a lot less time than I just did. When he was finished he said, "An' that's the simple truth of it. Ye kin ask the others here or ye kin ask them Saint Looie fops about it or ye kin ask yore lieutenant hyar, if he's o' mind to speak up, but if it's truth ye're lookin' fer, ye jist heard it."

Andrew Henry threw a hard look at the three of us still standing against the wall and we all nodded at once. Only Brass Turtle spoke up. "Onliest thing Ned left out was, eight guns could'a kept them Injuns peaceable. No hoss-raidin' party's willin' to lug home that many dead bodies. Only white men are willin' to fight like that an' that's jest 'cause they don't give a damn fer each other. Which is jest as well."

The Major favored us with a curt nod and muttered a word of thanks to us before he turned to Luther Pike still drooping on his stool. As we filed out I heard Henry roar, "What in the name o' God were ye thinkin', ye addled sonofabitch? Forty-eight horses ye cost me! Four dozen, ye dumb bastard! D'ye reckon I'm made o' money? An' where am I to get more of 'em? Tell me that, ye sorry whoreson heap o' shit!"

≈   ≈   ≈

Our camps were quiet for the next several nights. The Major was not of a mind to be making merry music and Anse and Yves weren't about to provide any, either. A pall hung over the entire company and we tied up late in the day and cast off early each morning, as if there was a new urgency to complete our journey.

The buffalo were still plentiful as we passed through the flat prairie land that bordered the river. Tuttle and I went back to hunting with Ned. The three of us, along with other hunting parties, supplied more than enough meat for the company, but the gloom that prevailed ever since the day we lost the horses seemed to taint the flavor and steal away our appetite.

The little square sail was all but useless now, for the wind was almost unfailingly westerly, and most times the stubby mast stood bare, useful only to suspend the *cordelle* when we dragged the St. Pierre upstream through the shallows. Every man in the company had by now learned to be sure-footed at scampering along the *passe-avants* and leaning his weight on a pole or putting his back into pulling on an oar. Whenever we weren't sent off on a hunting chore, Tuttle and I naturally pitched in with the rest and lent our strength to pushing that dreadful old scow just a little closer to the mountains.

≈   ≈   ≈

It was mid-day when we came in sight of the Yellowstone spilling its clear waters into the murky Missouri. It was hot, the sun a cauldron of molten gold sending heat shimmers vibrating over a grassy prairie flat as a table top.

As we pulled even with the mouth of the Yellowstone, Andrew Henry came out of his cabin and climbed to the afterdeck. The General and Hamish followed close behind him. Henry stood there a moment, surveying the landscape on either side of us. Then he nodded to Davidson, who brought a shiny brass boat horn to his lips and blew a loud blast on it before he announced, "Hear ye now, gentlemen! The Major here's about to tell ye some'at ye'll likely wish to hear!"

Every hand not occupied at the oars crowded aft, eager to hear some good news for a change, whatever it might be. Hamish stepped back and Andrew Henry came to the low rail. He stood looking down at his assembled men for what seemed to us a mighty long spell. Then he squared his shoulders and said in a loud voice, "Take a good look at it, gentlemen! This is the last mile you'll be traveling on the Missourah on this voyage! We've arrived!"

Standing amid the closely-packed men, the cheers and huzzahs were enough to make a body deaf. Several men rushed to the row stations and crowded in to lend a third pair of hands at the oars, eager to wrest that final mile from the Missouri as quickly as they could. You could positively feel the St. Pierre lunge forward against the current with a new energy. Andrew Henry remained at the rail for a spell, looking down at those of us still standing there, a wry smile on his lips.

Ere long we came abreast of a long, forested tongue of land that thrust itself out from the south bank. Standing high on the passe-avant, you could see the Yellowstone on the far side. Hamish blew another blast on his trumpet and the tillerman swung the St. Pierre shoreward. A moment later the bow and stern anchor chains rattled overboard and the keelboat came to rest.

Henry stepped to the rail once more and announced, "We've arrived! Our river journey has ended! Now the real work commences! This is where we'll build our fort!"

Chapter V
The Yellowstone

First thing I did when we got ashore was shinny up the tallest tree I could get my arms around. I climbed just as high as I dared, halting only for fear that the puny branches up higher were like to break under my weight, and peered out in every direction, looking for the Shining Mountains, but all I saw was sun-scorched golden prairie rolling out forever, the Missouri winding down from the west, and the Yellowstone straggling in from the southwest. There was nothing you could take for a mountain anywhere in sight.

When I got back to the ground I hunted up the Major and when I saw that he had an idle moment, I stepped up to him and said, "Pardon, Major. I thought you said we were headed for the Shinin' Mountains. But I don't see any mountains hereabouts."

Henry chuckled and replied, "Oh, you'll be seein' mountains aplenty 'fore you're done, Mister Buck. Indians, too. And God-knows-what-else." He pointed towards the west and swung his arm southwestwards. "They lie out yonder, range upon range of 'em, but we can't proceed without horses." He must have seen the troubled look that clouded my face at his mention of the stolen horses, for he clapped a friendly hand on my shoulder and said, "Nobody's blaming you, Buck. I reckon we all know where the fault lies."

I mumbled my thanks for his time and backed off, headed for Tuttle and the rest of our mess, who were setting up camp, when Henry called out, "Don't worry, Buck. We'll get ourselves more horses somehow and we'll get the job done. I warrant ye that!"

That night was better even than the best of times on our long river journey, for we knew that particular purgatory was finally

ended. After supper, Henry broke open a keg and ladled out half a
gill to every man, calling for a toast to the safe and successful
completion of our voyage up the river. He didn't mention the loss
of the *Bonhomme* or the horses. He got out his fiddle, too, and ere
long the whole camp was rollicking with music and singing and
roaring with approving laughter at Paddy's nimble jigs and the
men who joined him in the firelight.

When the camp quieted and most men had gone to their beds
and only a few small groups remained near the fire, talking of what
lay ahead, I wandered out onto the prairie and stood looking up at
stars flung like diamonds on black velvet, straining my mind's eye
to see those longed-for mountains, conjuring pictures of
adventures I might encounter there. Romance beckoned, but then,
please recall that I was still only nineteen years of age and green as
early grass.

                    ❧   ❧   ❧

It was just early-August and Ned Godey said it was far too early to
be trapping beaver. Their fur was much too sparse in summer and
wouldn't be prime until it thickened up with the frosts and snows
of autumn and early winter. There was plenty to do, howsomever,
for Andrew Henry meant to get his fort built before trapping
season. Not a man was idle, except for Luther Pike most of the
time. Most of the company shunned him now, though nobody
offered to harm him. The only place he appeared to be even
halfway welcome was in Mike Fink's mess, for I reckon those
watermen didn't harbor a great deal of affection for horses
anyhow.

After all the cargo was carried ashore, the Major put a crew to
work tearing out the cargo box from the deck of the St. Pierre, for
the sake of its lumber, which was needed for cabin walls and
furniture in the fort. Timbering crews pushed the forest ever
farther outward from the clearing atop a low hill where the fort
would stand, mindful that open ground would help to keep Indians
from creeping near.

Some men were put to work stripping sinew and fleshing and tanning the hides of buffalo we managed to shoot for food and others were taught the fine art of pounding buffalo fat, bone marrow, and bits of meat together with dried chokecherries to make trail rations Godey called pemmican. Others were busy digging a deep well inside the fort.

Jim Bridger's forge smoked and hissed with steam and rang with anvil-clang from morn 'til night as he and his helpers fashioned door-bolts and hinges, hasps, and all manner of useful hardware for Andrew Henry's fort. I daresay Jim must have often questioned why he had traveled all that way up the Missouri just to be swinging a blacksmith's hammer once again.

Three score and more of men possess amongst their numbers a passel of trades and skills. It took no time at all for them to sort themselves into crews that were handy at the different jobs needed to build the fort. Nobody in our mess possessed any particular skill that was called for, so all of us did our share of donkey toil, grunting and sweating at chopping trees, hauling the trunks to the clearing, stripping bark, gathering rocks for the masons, and digging trenches for the stockade walls.

Relief came only whenever Hamish came strolling by to assign us a hunting chore for the next day. Buffalo weren't as plentiful thereabouts as they had been earlier in the year and farther downriver, so even poor bull looked good to us, especially when we came upon a straggler not far out of camp. We missed our stolen horses even more than usual whenever we found ourselves staggering back under a load of bloody meat, swatting flies out of our eyes and cursing the day that the thieving Assinboins and Luther Pike were born.

Tuttle and I got to be halfway handy at ripsawing lumber, taking turns at hauling on a big two-handed rip saw either from above or down below in the saw pit, slabbing planks and boards from the arrow-straight lodgepole pines that shared with massive, shaggy cottonwoods the spit of land that poked out between the two rivers. Working below in the saw pit was the worst part of the job. August in that country is hot as the hinges of hell and working in the saw pit, forever hauling downward on the ripsaw, sweating like a horse under a never-ending shower of sticky sawdust that burned my eyes and clogged my breath, almost made me long to be up to my neck once again in chilly Missouri River water, straining against a *cordelle,* much as I had hated it at the time.

After the first day or two I made myself a britchclout out of trade cloth and that is all I wore when we worked at that particular chore. Tuttle did, too. It helped, but not much.

Still and all, that particular time in our lives was the cleanest that I can recollect that Tuttle ever was, for at the end of the day we would race to the river and throw ourselves in, splashing and scrubbing off sweat and sawdust that smarted the skin like a fieldful of nettles.

Then sometimes after supper and camp chores, Tuttle and I fetched willow poles over to one river or the other and caught catfish out of the Missouri or big silvery fish called trout out of the Yellowstone for a breakfast treat. The fishing was good but the palavering was better. Tuttle was easy to talk with. He was especially good at listening. He would take in all I had to say and then cap all my opinions with a pithy remark that summed up all my thoughts and some I hadn't even thought of. For instance, I told him how working in the saw pit made me feel like a slave, sweating and suffering and being punished for doing no wrong. Tuttle thought on it for a spell and then he said, "Yeah, but the diff'rence be thet fer us thar's an end to it."

He was right. The end was drawing nigh. Henry's fort was taking shape. Every day we'd be called away from our ripsawing chore to help up-end peeled logs a dozen feet long and drop them into the ditch, then mortise them in with river rocks and dirt. Inside, carpenters braced them together and went to building rooms against the outside walls. By September the stockade was pretty near complete, with watchtowers and gun decks at the four corners and storerooms, a forge, a big trade room, a couple of privies, and lining the outside walls, quarters for the Major and skimpier ones for the men. The whole job would have been a sight easier if there had been horses to help with the heavy hauling, but even though we built paddocks and pens, we still had no horses and no prospect of getting any.

≈∕   ≈∕   ≈∕

Daylight was getting shorter and there was a nip in the early-morning air when General Ashley made up his mind to return downriver to Saint Louis. The fort was all but finished. The stockade was complete, the last gate had been hung, and the swivel gun taken off the St. Pierre now commanded the upper end of our land spit. Rumor was that trapping would soon commence.

The St. Pierre rode high in the water now, stripped as it was of the cargo box and all of our freight, carrying only enough provisions to see the crew through to Saint Louis. That was just as well, too, for it was late summer and the Missouri was running a whole lot shallower than it was when we came up.

The three Saint Louis dandies, Longchamps and the other two, chose not to stay and the Major made no objection to their going. Luther Pike, too, was ordered to go with the General, like it or not, and nobody shed a tear when we learned of his departure.

Yves Dureau and Jean-Luc L'Archévêque begged Andrew Henry to be allowed to stay on with us and finally he reluctantly agreed to let them remain as *engagés*, camp helpers.

I had heard the Major say more than once that in time the Crows or maybe the Assiniboins would come to us to trade for horses, but we hadn't seen hide nor hair of any Indians in the nearly two months since we had landed. I was getting downright desperate for the feel of a horse under me and a chance to go buffalo-running, which recalled Hamish's advice to get hold of a big pistol or two, which I still hadn't been able to do. Then, a day before the St. Pierre was due to cast off, Ned Godey called me aside and asked, "Ye still lookin' fer pistols?" I assured him that I certainly was and he replied, "Well now, I reckon you had oughter be seein' that Longchamps feller afore he gits away. He's got hisself a pair o' beauties I reckon he won't be needin' back in Saint Looie."

I thanked Ned and hot-footed it over to where the Saint Louis dandies were camped. They looked a lot less like fops nowadays, considering how the Rocks had stripped them down, but they still kept to themselves and maintained their uppity ways.

Longchamps was neighborly enough, howsomever, and once he saw the gold coins I still had from Lucette, it took hardly any time at all to strike a bargain for his pistols. Word was that our Saint Louis Frenchmen were all from rich families. Even so, but like Uncle Ben used to say, "Rich ain't jist makin' money — it's keepin' it." Once Longchamps saw those gold coins of mine, he just couldn't resist a chance to turn a profit.

Ned hadn't lied. The two pistols were handsome indeed, long-barreled on a sturdy frame, with fine silver chasing around the lock, of a somewhat larger caliber than Melchior. Longchamps named his price and we haggled for a spell, until he threw in the bullet mold, a priming flask, and a pouchful of pistol balls. We shook hands on it, both of us satisfied.

I trotted on back to camp and when I got there I tossed one of the pistols to Tuttle, saying, "Here ye go. Now we both got a pistol for buffalo-runnin', if we ever get horses again."

Tuttle smiled and looked the pistol over, admiring the heft and balance and the fine silverwork. Then he handed it back to me and asked, "Ye still got money left?" I said that I had and tossed him the purse, somewhat lighter now but still full enough of coins to make a healthy clink. Tuttle shoved the coin purse into his belt and strode out of camp without a word, headed for the Saint Louis Frenchies.

He returned half an hour later, a long-barreled pistol dangling at arm's length and a triumphant grin on his face. He plopped the purse, not much lighter than it had been, into my lap and handed over his pistol for me to admire. It was plainer than my own but of fine workmanship and what looked to be the same caliber. He grinned broadly as he said, "Now I got me one o' my own an' I daresay a sight cheaper, too." He chuckled and went on, "Thet Creole dandy jest got hisse'f a lesson tradin' Kaintuck-style. 'Twas gold what done it. Once he seen the color o' yore money, t'other'n jest couldn't keep hisse'f from tryin' to skin me, too!" He laughed aloud. "But I reckon he di'n't!"

I gathered from what Tuttle was saying that I had paid too much for my pistols, but it made no nevermind to me. I had what I wanted and money was likely to be of little use where we were.

࿇ ࿇ ࿇

A skim of frost whitened the ground the morning the St. Pierre commenced its journey downriver. A brisk wind was blowing from the west and the keelboat tugged and shuddered at its anchor chains. The quitters were already aboard. There was a sight of hugging and kissing on the cheeks when the *bateliers* bade farewell to Dureau and L'Archévêque, but it didn't mean anything personal. That's just how those Frenchies are.

The whole company was gathered on the beach, some of us lucky ones huddled inside our capotes, the rest clutching blankets around their shoulders, all of us shivering in the early-morning chill. General Ashley made a thankfully short speech to us all, telling us that he would return next year and wishing us good health, divine protection, and success in our trapping, the last of which I reckon he considered most important. Then he shook hands with the Major and Hamish and Louis Prudhomme, our new lieutenant, a long-time French trader from Saint Louis, before he stepped into his skiff and had himself rowed out to the St. Pierre.

Andrew Henry called out his good wishes for fair winds and Godspeed as Ashley climbed aboard. We heard the anchor chains rattling and the St. Pierre, riding high in the water, went bobbing downstream, the little square sail bellied out nigh to bursting and the brass cannon on the afterdeck glinting in the feeble morning sunshine.

General Ashley, swathed in a bright blue greatcoat, standing tall beside Jacques Leclerc at the tiller, waved a final farewell as the St. Pierre swept around a bend in the river and was lost to view.

Tuttle, standing beside me, grunted and opined, "Well naow, thar she goes. T'aint likely we'll be grievin' over the absence o' thet stinkin' ol' tub ner all thet speechifyin' — ner the sight an' society of ol' Luther Puke neither!"

࿇ ࿇ ࿇

It wasn't but a day or two after the departure of the St. Pierre that we were blessed with a passel of visitors and welcome indeed they were. It was late in the day and Ned, Tuttle, and I had just lugged back to the fort the last of the meat from an old bull we had killed out on the prairie south of the Yellowstone. The three of us were sprawled outside the stockade wall, smoking a pipeful, tired, sweaty, bloody from the meat, soaked to the waist from wading the river, and totally out of sorts, but our spirits lifted more than somewhat when Ned looked up and said, "Well, lookee thar now! Crows! Absarokees come fer tradin' hosses, I'll wager!"

Sure enough, there on the prairie on the far side of the Yellowstone, where we had just come from, was a band of Indians, whole families of them, setting up camp, by the looks of it. The women were unloading all manner of goods off their pony drags, a pair of long poles cris-crossed in front of a saddle and allowed to trail on behind the horse, toting a heap of plunder in a buffalo hide slung between the poles — *travois*, Godey called them. Here and there four long poles lashed together near the top would arch into the air and before you hardly knew it the women would spread them out and lay a dozen or more poles onto them and stretch a covering of buffalo hide all around, top to bottom, then stake the whole shebang to the ground.

Ned saw me watching them, mouth agape in wonder as the big cone tents, some painted in wild colors, some plain brown, sprang up in curving rows, doorways facing east, like wildflowers blooming in springtime. "Tipis, Lahcotahs call 'em," Ned said. "Don't know how ye say it in Crow, but tipis'll do."

It wasn't an hour before a whole village stood on what had been empty prairie. Women bustled about their chores and girl children scurried about the riverbank picking up firewood. On the far side of the Crow village we could see a sizeable horse herd put out to graze under a guard of young boys. Under the trees beside the river little groups of colorfully-dressed men sat cross-legged, smoking and palavering, now and then making sign-talk. It was truly a sight to conjure with.

Brass Turtle, Bridger, and Paddy had joined us, all of them armed and looking halfway anxious. Ned noticed their concern and said, "I wouldn't be frettin' overmuch. These're Absarokees an' they ain't much fer killin' white-eyes. They'll trade the pecker off'n ye an' they'll steal ye blind, but they mostly do their fightin' with other Injuns — an' they're purty good at it, too."

All the sweat and blood from packing buffalo meat had commenced to get unbearably itchy, so Tuttle, Ned, and I left our rifles and possibles with Brass Turtle and trotted over to the Missouri side and jumped into the river, clothes and all. By time we got back to the fort, dripping wet but feeling a whole lot better, half a dozen Indians had crossed over the Yellowstone on horseback and were making hand-talk with Hamish, who was interpreting to Andrew Henry what they had to say.

Those Absarokas were an impressive lot, big men, almost all of them over six foot, astride some of the best-looking horses I had ever seen. All of them sported painted faces and feathers stuck in their top-knots. They were dressed to the nines in quilled and beaded buckskins top to toe, most with painted and quilled buffalo robes slung across their shoulders, a couple of them draped in bright red blankets instead. None of them quite equaled the Hidatsa chief Buffalo Calf for finery but they weren't far off the mark.

What struck me most, howsomever, was their hair, especially the Crow who was hand-talking with Hamish. He was big and he packed a deal of muscle, handsome of face but hard-looking and prideful, older than I but not old. He had the longest hair I had ever seen on anybody, except maybe old Louis Lorimier back on the Mississippi. He wore it loose and sitting on his horse as he was, it spilled down over the high cantle of his saddle and flowed back over the crupper and blended with his horse's tail. It was hard to believe a man could grow that much hair and I made note in my mind to ask Ned about it.

Right then wasn't the time, for we were trying to listen in on what Hamish was telling the Major. Ned's guess had been right. The long-haired Indian was telling Henry that the Crows had horses, plenty horses, for trade. He went on to say that he could see that Henry was very, very poor in horses and that he could remedy that problem if we had muskets and powder and lead, blankets, and what-all to swap. The Major allowed that we did indeed have such plunder and they agreed to meet next morning to commence the trading.

I was listening with half an ear to what Hamish was telling Henry but most of my attention was on the horse that the long-haired Indian was sitting on. He was a tall, fine-boned dapple-gray gelding, pushing sixteen hands, a dishy face with big, wide-apart, kind eyes, and from what I could see of him under the high Crow saddle and the fancy quilled saddle pad Ned called an apishamore, he was everything that Tuttle demanded that a horse should be.

Quick as Henry and Long-hair set the time for the trading, the Indians wheeled their horses and galloped back to the Yellowstone. I stood watching the big gray gelding as he ran, his long, rolling stride keeping him easily out in front of the others, dodging smoothly around badger holes and river trash and such, until they all disappeared amongst the fringe of trees along the riverbank. I reckon I fell in love again right then.

Tuttle's big, hard hand clapped me on the shoulder and I heard him say, "Hey thar, Temple. Ye look like ye never seen a hoss afore. It ain't been thet long."

"No, reckon not," I replied, still straining my eyes to watch the Indians climb the far bank. "What'd ye think of ol' Long-hair's big gray?"

"Handsome critter." Tuttle looked across the river to watch the Indians riding into their camp. "Yep, he'll do fer looks an' he be right handy, too." Then he regarded me with a quizzical eye. "Why d'ye ask?"

"Cause I mean to have 'im, an' that's a fact."

Ned Godey had joined us and stood listening to what we were saying before he chimed in. "That critter's Purty-on-top's buffler runnin' hoss an' ye'll be doin' some hard dealin' afore ye get 'im — if'n ye ever do. Still an' all, if'n the price be right, that'ere heathen'd sell his own mama."

Hearing the name Pretty-on-top called to mind the question I meant to ask Ned, so I did. "How is it these Crows have such long hair, Ned? I've never seen the like."

"Well now," he replied, "it be a custom 'mongst Absarokees fer chiefs an' sech to wear their hair as long as they kin git it. It's their pride an' joy. Problem is, ain't hardly no man, ner woman neither, kin grow their hair that long." He chuckled, then went on. "Jest wait'll ye see some o' the Crow women close up. The most of 'em don't have hardly enough hair to cover their ears." Ned laughed again. "Ye see, the men cut it off an' have it plaited into their own. Ol' Purty-on-top he be a mite excessive, but 'most all of 'em do it."

Our mess was still camping outside the fort, due mainly to Tuttle's dislike of indoor quarters, unless booze and whores happened to be part of the parcel. As we prepared to return to our camp, Ned called out, "Ye'd best be sleepin' inside the walls, leastwise whilst the Crows be hyar. They'll surely steal the britchclout right off'n yer arse."

That appeared to be reasonable advice, so after a moment's thought and considerable grumbling from Tuttle, we moved our plunder inside the stockade walls. After a supper of fresh buffalo meat and little else, we bedded down in one of the little sheds — except for Tuttle, who spread his blankets just outside the door. Beating drums and high-voiced, wailing chants drifted across the Yellowstone and soon carried me into dreams of a tall dappled buffalo horse and then a short-haired dusky maiden who had never known a white-eyes.

      ‽   ‽   ‽

Horse trading commenced early next morning. About half an hour after breakfast the Absarokas drove a score or more horses across the river and hazed them up to the fort. Major Henry met them outside the gate and after he and Hamish and Prudhomme and Ned and half a dozen important-looking Crows had smoked and palavered nonsense for a spell, the business was begun in earnest.

The trading went pretty much like the last time, with Tuttle turning thumbs down on the first half-dozen or so horses, pointing out spavins and incurable wervils and such, and the Crows grumbling and driving the horses back across the river, only to return with more and better horses. The main difference was that the Crows were easier to deal with than the Mandans and Hidatsas, who had considerably more experience with white men, living right on the Missouri as they did. The Major was even more of a skinflint than he had been the first time, mindful as he was of his dwindling stock of trade goods.

Brass Turtle and another Delaware called Little Mountain and I shared the riding chores that day and when I wasn't busy with that employment I sat off to one side, stitching a pair of pistol holsters to fit onto my dragoon saddle. Pretty-on-top had ridden his big gray buffalo horse over to the fort and left him in the care of one of the herd-boys whilst he smiled and ranted and cajoled and raved his way through the horse-trading. With each horse, he started off as hard as English flint, but gradually he retreated to a pose of reasonable reluctance. Each swap commenced with his scornful refusal and ended with a grudging acceptance of the Major's offer. I eyed the big gray as much as I dared but I was careful not to show too much interest, for I knew that would surely boost the price out of my reach.

The trading lasted all day, all through the second, and well into the third day, but Tuttle remained just as pernickety with the final horse as he was with the first. Horse-judging was a matter of pride with him and he beamed near to bursting each time the Major complimented him on his skill.

At the end of the first day Pretty-on-top in*Vite*d Andrew Henry and Hamish to visit the Crow camp to eat and smoke. Then he waved casually to the rest of us and in*Vite*d us to visit, too. Henry accepted and afterwards he picked a score of us to join him, insisting that first we must shave and wear our best clothes, so as to make a good impression on our Absaroka hosts.

After supper we swung up onto some of our new horses and crossed over the Yellowstone. The rest we penned for the night. We rode bareback, except for Henry and Hamish, for the Major reckoned it was best not to tempt the Crows overmuch by putting saddles within their reach. When we arrived at the camp, Hamish detailed half a dozen of us to stand horse guard, to be relieved after an hour or so. Ned, Tuttle, and I were on the first watch. Whilst we waited, Ned told us some of what he knew about

Absarokas. He warned us not sell them short as warriors, but then he went on to say, "Fact is, Crows'd ruther let a white-eyes live, if'n they kin, after they steal his hosses. They reckon we'll come back agin next year with more hosses, if'n they don't kill us, so's they kin steal them new hosses all over agin."

When the horse guard relief showed up, we strolled into the Indian camp for a look-see. The noise was something scandalous — dogs barking and naked kids yelling and scampering underfoot, women screeching after the both of them, somewheres a couple-three drums beating and far-off voices raised in plaintive singing. Cooking fires blazed out front of nearly every lodge and here and there short-haired women squatted at their chores, cooking meat or chipping buffalo hides or tonging hot stones intobig bladders hung on rickety tripods, jumping to their feet from time to time to chase after kids or dogs or tend to some task inside their tipi.

The fragrance of an Indian camp for the first time is an experience to be reckoned with, though this one, after only a couple of days, wasn't nearly as heady as some of longer standing. I did my growing up with hogs living under the house, but the smell nigh took my breath away when we first entered camp. Tuttle, howsomever, appeared to be unmindful of it and it was likely nothing new for Ned.

As we strolled amongst the lodges the women darted swift glances at the three of us, then jerked their gaze away, tittering and squawking amongst themselves. Dark-skinned young men, some with painted faces and feathers in their hair, wrapped to the chin in painted robes or colorful blankets, eyed us with suspicion from a distance, but they made no hostile moves. Still and all, it was reassuring to feel the weight of the big pistol in my belt. Then, as we neared the big council fire burning in the center of camp, I saw the tipi of Pretty-on-top. I knew it was his, for picketed outside was the big gray gelding, munching at a heap of prairie hay. The lodge was painted in gaudy colors, pictures of a sun with its rays flowing outward, a bolt of lightning, a crudely-drawn buffalo with a broad red arrow running through it, and I don't recollect what else. Next to the doorflap was a tripod supporting a painted shield festooned with what I took to be scalps, an unstrung bow and otterskin quiver, and a feathered lance. There was a passel of painted lodges in camp and many other such tripods, but Pretty-on-top's was the showiest of them all.

Godey was looking to trade for some new moccasins, so we halted at one of the cooking fires, where Ned hand-talked his wishes to the women gathered there. They giggled and chattered one to another for a spell and then a couple of them skittered off amongst the tipis. Soon a number of women appeared from behind the lodges and Ned commenced to bargain for his moccasins.

I stood back, watching Ned's hands flying like barn swallows and enjoying the sound of the women's voices talking in Absaroka, a throaty yet flowing and musical tongue, when I felt someone tugging at my sleeve. Startled, I turned and found myself staring down into the biggest, blackest eyes I had ever seen in one of the prettiest faces I could recall. As soon as she got my attention, she commenced to rattle off a positive Missouri River of words, not a solitary one of which could I understand. Howsomever it made no nevermind to me, for it was a pleasure just to look at her. The crown of her head barely reached my shoulder, but I saw that under her soft deerskin dress was a grown-up woman indeed, full in the breast and slim at the waist and brimming with life. I saw, too, that her black hair was long, loose and flowing nearly to her waist, and I was certain that it looked a whole lot better on her than braided into some buck's top-knot. Her black eyes were dancing and white teeth flashed between full red lips in her dusky face as she chattered away like a magpie. I couldn't help bursting out laughing, which only made her natter and sputter the more.

Godey heard me laughing and when he finished his dealings with the woman who agreed to make his moccasins, he stepped away from the fire and came over to discover what was going on. Ned couldn't speak Absaroka — nobody that I knew of in our company could — but the hand-talk is rather much the same all over the plains and in the mountains. He signaled some sort of whoa and then I reckon he asked her what was her problem. She never did stop talking, smiling and laughing the while, but her hands commenced fluttering like a bushful of butterflies. Ere long she needed to stop to take a breath. Ned, laughing now as much as she was, turned to me and said, "The lady hyar says ye be the handsomest man she ever laid eyes on, Temple, but she says ye're lookin' downright shabby. Says ye be sorely in need o' new clothes an' she's jist the lady what kin make 'em fer ye." Then he went to laughing again.

Now I had done just as the Major ordered and dressed myself in the best I had, the buckskin suit that Lucette had given me. It was true. howsomever, that those clothes were more than somewhat seasoned by then, after all the wear and tear of our journey up the Missouri. Still, it rather hurt my feelings that she singled me out and called me shabby. Tuttle always looked much worse. On the other hand, I had always been fond of nice clothes, the few times I managed to have any, from the very first outfit that Powatawa's wife made for me. So when Godey finally got hold of himself, I said, "Well now, that just might be an idea. I've got some trade goods I can spare."

"Oh, that oughtn't to be a problem," he replied. "These Crows're greedy, it's true, but they don't see a lot o' white men, livin' where they do most o' the time, so she'll likely be fairly modest 'bout what she's askin'."

"Well, then," I told him, "tell her to go on ahead and make me pretty as she pleases, providin' I can afford it. As ye know, I expect to be doin' some tradin' for a horse and I sure don't want to spend it all on clothes."

Ned grinned and said, "I reckon ye got a sufficiency fer both." Then he turned to the woman, who by now was chattering at Tuttle, and once he got her attention, commenced his hand-talking once again. When she answered him, he turned to me and said, "She wants some little beads, blue ones if'n ye got 'em, an' some o' them little lookin'-glasses, a firesteel, some shiny tacks an' a couple o' awls an' some trade cloth an' 'specially a knife. Ye got all o' that?"

I allowed that I did, for neither Tuttle nor I had done any great amount of trading up until then. Ned said, "I reckon ye got yerse'f a trade." Then he turned to the woman and told her that I agreed. Her hands fluttered and darted again and Ned said to me, "She says fer you to stand up straight and quiet. She needs to take yore measure."

I did as I was told and the little woman commenced to put her hands all over me, thumbs together to span half my waist and to get the size of my neck, then her hands outside the top of either arm to measure the breadth of my shoulders, and so on for the width of my chest and the length of my arms and legs. I thought she lingered rather long when she measured the inside of my leg for length, but I saw no good reason to object to that. Fact is, I was halfway disappointed when she went on to measure my feet for moccasins. Whilst she went about her chore I couldn't help but look at the curve of her cheek, the sheen of her shiny black hair glinting in the firelight, the swell of her thigh when her dress hiked up as she bent to her task. When she finished and stood up, I asked Ned to find out her name. Ned waved his hands a time or two and when she answered back, her hands dabbing at her face, he looked puzzled and asked her again. At last he said to me, "Near as I kin make it out, they call her Eyes-o'-night or Night-eyes or mebbe Evenin'-eyes, somethin' like that. Cain't be sartin sure, but I reckon that be close."

"If ye don't mind, Ned, would you ask her how is it she still has her long hair? Most of the other women don't, 'ceptin' for the old ones, as you can see."

Ned grinned. "You surely are the curious one, ain'tcha, Temple? But I'll ask her." Which he did.

Her reply took up quite a spell, what with her hands flying and words neither Ned nor I understood spilling out like a bubbling spring. When at last she settled down and stood silent, Ned turned back to me and said, "The short of it 'pears that she's a widder. Her man got hisse'f kilt by Lahcotahs a year or so ago on a hoss raid. She's been livin' in her sister's lodge since then an' they been tryin' to marry her off. Problem is, she's barren. Got no young'uns. Mebbe cain't have none, neither. Crows're big on kids — most Injuns are — so that kin be a real problem. The sister's husband don't want her, so they been leavin' her hair be, hopin' some buck'll come along an' think she's purty an' take 'er off'n their hands."

I thanked Ned for his help and when I turned to her and made sort of half a bow, I caught her looking at me with a softness in those big black eyes that made me want to take her in my arms. I didn't, naturally, mindful as I was of the Major's orders for us to be on good behavior thereabouts, but I surely wanted to.

About then we heard a call for us to return to our horses and I saw Hamish and the Major coming out of a big tipi and passing by the council fire, heading for the grove where our critters were tethered. I looked about for Tuttle but he was nowhere to be seen. I was no little disturbed by his absence but Ned just grinned and started off for the horses. As we left the circle of firelight I glanced back and saw Night-eyes watching me, a soft and thoughtful look on her face. I smiled and waved my hand and then I trotted off to catch up with Ned.

We were already mounting up when Tuttle shambled through the trees, yanking his belt tight and grinning like an ape. I have never seen an ape, mind you, but I recall reading somewheres that they grin a lot.

Splashing out of the water on our side of the river, I asked Tuttle where he had taken himself off to. His reply furnished no information I could use right then. All he said was, "Hell, Temple! Ye don't need to talk an ye don't hafta be purty. Jest bein' sociable an' willin's enough, I reckon." And that is all he ever told me about it.

Trading for horses next morning went rather much like the first day. The horses were of better quality and the bargaining grew sharper, but the Crows badly wanted our trade goods and they were willing to pay for it with saddle and pack animals that we sorely needed. They even brought a number of mules for trade and Tuttle called on Anse Tolliver to help with the judging, for Anse had often quietly and solemnly proclaimed that the only two things he knew or really cared about were fiddles and mules, but he knew those two things better than 'most any man he had ever met.

We were getting together quite a large herd, so whilst the trading continued, Major Henry ordered a crew of men to build more horse pens onto the ones we already had. Another crew was sent out to gather prairie hay for feed. I stayed busy riding out the stock that passed Tuttle's first judging, but with the help of Brass Turtle and Little Mountain what I was called on to do that day didn't tax me overmuch.

After supper I was lazing in front of our quarters inside the fort, smoking a pipeful and reading how Polypoites smote Damasos with a spear, right through his bronze helmet and all, and scattered his brains, when Ned Godey called me to the gate. Outside I saw Night-eyes standing at a little distance from the stockade, looking small and halfway frightened, holding a bundle that I took to be the clothes she had made for me. "Seems like she's got your duds all ready for ye, Temple," Ned said. "Best ye collect yore plunder an' we'll go find out."

I waved to Night-eyes and trotted back to our sleeping room, where I scissored off a couple yards of bright red English woolen cloth, scattered onto it the goods she had mentioned, and rolled it all into a bundle. When I stuffed our remaining trade plunder back into the croker sack, I saved out a few little mirrors and some more strings of tiny blue beads and dropped them into my possibles pouch, in case I needed them to even the deal.

Ned was standing out on the prairie, hand-talking with Night-eyes, when I came through the gate and trotted out to join them. She was even prettier in the soft evening light than she had been the night before. Her smile was quick and her eyes lit up when she saw the red cloth under my arm and she commenced to babble Absaroka words in the soft gurgle they use for a language.

Ned hailed me with, "Yep. She's got 'em all ready. Says she wants ye try 'em on, so's she's sure they fit." I turned about and took a few steps towards the stockade before I recalled that the Major had issued strict orders that no Indians were to be allowed inside the fort. I halted, confused, and I heard Ned laugh. "Nope. Cain't go thar. Don't reckon you're wantin' to show yore bare arse out'chere, neither." He chuckled again. "Whyn't y'all go down to them willers 'longside o' the river? That'll do fer a private place."

I nodded my willingness to do so and Ned explained in hand-talk to Night-eyes what we meant to do, but when I started towards the Yellowstone, she caught my sleeve and pulled me in the direction of the Missouri. One side appeared to me to be as good as the other, so off we went, me leading the way, she trotting on behind clutching her buckskin bundle.

When we neared the riverbank Night-eyes plucked at my sleeve again and headed for a dense thicket of willows. Naturally I followed her inside and when she came upon an open space carpeted with thick grass she halted and turned back to me, her great black eyes shining and her full red lips parted in a smile. She held out her buckskin bundle and I handed over the red woolen one I carried under my arm. She laid it on the ground without even opening it up and commenced to point at the buckskins, chattering the while in Crow, at last tugging gently at the leg of my britches, by which I understood that she meant for me to try on my new duds right there in front of her.

I must have blushed, for she started in to laughing and pushed me towards the willow bushes that circled the little clearing. When I reckoned I was more or less screened by the willows, I kicked off my moccasins, shucked out of my leather britches, and unrolled her bundle, all the while taking care to keep my back towards her. For some reason I had expected her to make me a new pair of britches, but she hadn't, for making trousers of any sort is beyond the skill of just about any Indian woman I ever knew. Instead she had built a beautiful pair of leggin's with long fringes and a little bit of quillwork on the sides, a britchclout of soft blue stroud, a braided leather belt, a long deerskin shirt that reached nearly to my knees, and a pair of Crow moccasins that came up over the ankles, decorated with quills over the toes.

I had just slipped on my new leggin's and was reaching for the britchclout when I felt her hand where my britchclout should have been. I jumped and she giggled, but she didn't let go. Instead she led me back to the little clearing. Her grip was gentle but firm and I was naturally becoming rather firm myself as time went on, as you might expect. Once there, she sank onto the soft grass, still not letting go, and pulled me down beside her. I took her in my arms and pressed my mouth to hers, my lips seeking her own. She pulled away. It was then I knew that she had never been with a white man. She didn't know how to kiss.

She learned quickly enough, howsomever, and she took to it with remarkable enthusiasm, licking my cheeks, then gently biting and sucking on my lower lip until she got it halfway right. It was a different sort of kissing, but I saw no reason to complain.

My hand had strayed to the goal and she never let go her grip. Just when I reckoned I couldn't hold out any longer, she rolled over onto her hands and knees, critter-like, and guided me home. What was surprising was, powerful as she had been when she pulled and tugged at me earlier, now it felt like she had never loosened the grip of her hand, though I knew she had.

As you might imagine, after all those months on the Misssouri, the first time took hardly any time at all. The second lasted a sight longer. After we collapsed in a heap, shuddering and panting and gasping for air, I rolled her onto her back and kissed those big black eyes and crooned I don't know what-all into her tiny ears. She looked startled when I slipped between her thighs, uncertain about what I meant to do, but she smiled and giggled outright and rose to my thrust, her fingers tangled in my hair, pulling my face close to hers and laving it with kisses, once she caught on to more white men's ways.

I have no notion at all how long we lay there, rising from time to time to bathe in the river, only to return to the grove for more. Her appetite at least equaled my own and it seemed our hunger would never be satisfied. A sliver of a waning moon rode high in the sky when at last we rolled apart to bathe and search for our clothes and other belongings, flung every whichaway into the bushes, interrupting ourselves over and over again to kiss and caress each other.

Later, when we stood outside the fort, embracing, both of us reluctant to end that night, she pushed me away at last and held out her red woolen bundle, still unopened, saying no words but nonetheless telling me to take it back. I pushed it back to her and crushed her in my arms one more time, glorying in the warm woman smell of her and feeling the strength of her sturdy body flowing into my blood. Then we broke apart and she trotted into the darkness whilst I stood watching her dwindling figure in the starlight and the feeble rays of a high-riding moon.

Tuttle, sleeping outside our quarters, rolled onto one elbow as I approached. Even in the dim moonlight I could see him grinning. "Been swimmin', have ye, Temple?"

I knew what he meant, but all I said was, "You're right, Tuttle. There be times when there be no need for talkin'."

ॐ   ॐ   ॐ

The Crows showed up early next morning, herding fewer than a score of horses up to the fort and driving harder bargains than ever before, for these were the best they had offered so far. Even Tuttle was impressed, but just the same I didn't see a one of them that was as good as Pretty-on-top's gray gelding.

The Crows wanted muskets and powder and lead. They got their wish, but Andrew Henry made them pay dearly in horseflesh, trading shrewdly and hard as a gimlet before he consented to give up each musket. At last the trading came to an end. We had bought a hundred and eighteen sound horses and a sprinkling of mules for less plunder than we had paid the Mandans and Hidatsas for fewer than half that number. I could tell that Pretty-on-top wasn't pleased with the way the business had gone. The Major had bested him in their haggling and although Pretty tried to smile and act friendly, his natural haughtiness showed through.

Henry called for food and sugared coffee to be fetched from the fort and soon the Absaroka chiefs and the Major and his lieutenants were all sitting together, eating and waving their hands in sign-talk. I waited until afterwards, when they were smoking, before I knelt beside Henry and said in a low voice, "Pardon, Major, but I wonder if you'd mind if I try to buy just one more horse off these here Crows."

Henry looked up, startled at my request, but then he cracked a smile and said, "Well now, Mister Buck, it appears to me these Crows have emptied their poke, but if you think you can pry one more out of them, do so with my blessing!" He looked thoughtful, then he asked, "D'ye have the wherewithal to trade?"

I assured him that I did and he nodded and said, "Well then, good fortune to ye!"

As I backed away from the circle I heard Henry say to Hamish, "Tell ol' Pretty there that Mister Buck wishes to trade for one more horse. He'll let 'em know which one."

I scurried off to our quarters and came back a few minutes later with our sack of trade goods, which was hardly lighter than when we started up the river. Then I stood with Ned and Tuttle, waiting for the Crows to finish their smoke.

Indians on the plains and in the mountains are great gamblers. Horse-trading, which is a mixture of gambling and bluff anyway, is hardly less appealing to them, so it took no time at all until the Crows rose to their feet and came over to where I stood. When Ned signed that the horse I had in mind was the tall gray gelding that belonged to Pretty-on-top, their hands flew to their mouths, which is how they show surprise, or in this case, downright astonishment. Even Andrew Henry looked startled. Ned repeated what he had told them, telling them, too, that no other horse would do.

Now Andrew Henry might have been the better horse-trader, but no man on earth excelled Pretty-on-top at strutting and bluster. He positively raved, declaring that nobody but he could ever own that horse, that the gray gelding could actually fly, if he, Pretty-on-top, asked him to, that the horse was gentle as a doe and wiser than Grandfather Buffalo, swifter than a prairie goat, handier than a hawk, and strong as a whole herd of buffalo. Then he asked how much I was willing to pay.

I started off small, realizing that this would be no quickly-finished business. I didn't know the Absaroka tongue, but sneering needs no translation. I upped my first offer by laying a shiny steel tomahawk on the pile of beads and awls, tobacco twists, and vermilion I had started with, then a big butcher knife, then another, and finally the only bright red blanket I owned. Then I stood without saying a word, my arms folded across my chest, and waited for Pretty-on-top to reply.

His face remained as blank as a barn wall. I could read greed and connivance in his eyes, but he said nothing either by word or by sign. Then I asked Ned to tell him that there lay my offer but there could be no trade until I had a chance to ride the horse myself. Pretty called out something to the herd-boy holding the gelding and when the lad brought him up, Tuttle stripped off the high-backed Crow saddle and apishamore and carefully inspected the horse from ears to hocks, lifting each hoof and peering into it like a palmer reading a fortune. When at last Tuttle straightened up and nodded, his face a blank, I brought out my bridle from the trade sack and tossed the reins over the gelding's neck. He bridled a mite at the unaccustomed bit, but then he settled down and let me slip the headstall over his ears. I wasted no time. I grabbed a fistful of mane and swung onto his back, nudging him with my heels and leaning over his neck. Almost before I knew it we were flying out across the prairie towards the Yellowstone, the horse so smooth under me that I hardly felt the light and even thud of his hooves on the sun-baked earth. I turned him and whirled him, stopped and doubled back, jumped a driftwood log, and sent him into a gallop from a standstill, zig-zagging amongst imaginary trees at full tilt. He seemed to know what I wanted him to do before I did.

I fought to straighten my face and hide my excitement as we trotted easily back to the fort, the gelding breathing not even hard enough for me to tell. I knew that if I betrayed even a tenth of my pleasure with him, I'd never be able to afford him.

Pretty-on-top's face was stony as ever, but his eyes glittered like sparking flint when I rode into the circle, swung off, and retrieved my pistol from Tuttle. I shoved it into my belt and said to Ned, "I reckon he'll do. Ask him if we have a deal."

Godey's face was blank as a rock, but I knew he was fighting to hold back his laughter. I saw him swallow hard before he looked over to Pretty and commenced to wave his hands. Tuttle had said nothing, which told me that he totally approved. The other Crows muttered and murmured amongst themselves, but there was no telling what that might signify. Pretty-on-top stood silent, unmoving, arms folded. His face might have been carved out of hickory. Only his black eyes moved, shifting from the heap of trade goods to the horse, to me, and back to the trade plunder, then to me again.

At last he spoke, barking out a word or two in Crow, and shot out his arm, stabbing his finger towards my middle. Then he drew himself up and signed something to Godey before he stood tall and crossed his arms and resumed his silence.

I feared that Pretty's finger-pointing was sign-talk that meant he intended to have my private parts before he'd sell his horse, but instead Ned muttered, "Ol' Long-hair hyar says he'll take yore plunder but he wants yore pistol, too, afore he's willin' to give up his hoss." Godey cleared his throat and spat before he added, "I reckon that's as fur as he'll go."

I hated to give up that pretty pistol, but I reminded myself that I still had another one, so without another word I walked over to the trade heap and laid the pistol on top. Then I took the reins from Tuttle and led the gray gelding inside the fort. I was nigh to bursting inside with satisfaction at the deal I had made. The pistol and the trade goods had cost only money — and money has never made no nevermind to me.

After the Crows returned to their camp, lugging home bright red and dark blue blankets bulging with plunder and cradling new muskets on their arms, a few of them with iron kettles dangling from their wrists, Pretty-on-top astride one of the herd-boys' ponies, the Major let me use the afternoon working my new horse, getting him used to my smell and accustomed to the dragoon saddle, the heavy bridle, and how I moved on his back.

Good-natured though he was, the gray was full of fire and power. Without hardly thinking about it I commenced to call him Chiksika, after Powatawa's son, the closest thing I had ever had to a brother before I met Tuttle. Then the more I thought about it the more proper it appeared to be, for Chiksika had owned such a fiery nature as my horse possessed and it was he who had taught me how to ride and who had been first to hand me the reins of my never-to-be-forgotten Kumskaka.

After supper I made sure that Chiksika had plenty of hay. I was pleased to see that his easy-going disposition didn't extend to the other horses.   He guarded his feed like a jealous husband. Whenever another horse strayed near he laid back his ears and bared his teeth, squealing and kicking until the intruder nigh rolled over backwards getting out of reach of those flailing hoofs. Satisfied that he could look after himself in the pen, I returned to the fort, doused myself with a pailful of water, dressed in my new buckskins, and rolled up some foofurraw and various useful truck in a length of red cloth, noticing the while that Tuttle, too, had been doing some trading from our store of plunder.   Then I moseyed over to the willow grove.

I had no way of knowing if she would be waiting there, but she was, a rolled-up buckskin bundle at her feet. We had no words between us, but we didn't need any. She pulled me down to the grassy earth and I slipped her dress over her head, burying my face between her breasts and marveling at her strength and the clean woman fragrance of her, my fingers gently tweaking her nipples until they stood like tiny soldiers at attention.

The love we made that evening was slower, more thoughtful, less urgent, than the night before, but nonetheless powerful. When we lay exhausted for a spell, clasped as tightly as two young trees grown together, murmuring nothings in each other's ear, each in our own tongue but understanding the other nevertheless, she wriggled away to retrieve the bundle she had brought. When she rolled it out I saw another pair of leggin's, fringed and quilled more elaborately than the first pair, moccasins, and a britchclout of bright red stroud.   Then she rummaged under the heap and drew out a tiny quilled buckskin poke on a loop of sinew and slipped it over my head, pulling it straight and patting it in place, so that it covered the silver locket that I wore, as if she knew that the image of Lucette was hidden there.

I sought to put such thoughts and memories away from me and reached for the bundle I had brought, but she swept it behind us and caught me close to her, nibbling my ear, her hand straying downward. I abandoned all remembering and common thoughts and gave myself up to her wants and needs, for I shared them all.

At last we lay unmoving, our bodies pressed tightly together, each straining to become one with the other, our grassy grove illumined only by starlight from a cloudless sky. In time, though, we rose and went to the river to bathe one last time. Then we dressed and gathered our belongings and walked hand in hand past the fort, where we parted without an uttered word but with a final kiss that spoke entire libraries.

Inside the fort, I merely grunted in respose to Tuttle's cheerful greeting. I could still hear him chuckling as I burrowed under my blankets and forgot all else but the sight and the feel and the delicious taste of the woman called Night-eyes.

            ~   ~   ~

I was watering horses in the Missouri next morning when I first heard it — or rather, felt it — a low rumbling that shook the ground as if a giant were trying to burst from his earthy tomb. Chiksika felt it, too. His ears pricked up and he snorted and tossed his head. I gathered the halter shanks into a firmer grip so as to lead the four horses in my care back to the pen. We hadn't traveled but a rod or two towards the fort when I heard somebody yell, "Buffler! Buffler! Goddlemighty, jist look at 'em! Buffler 'til hell won't have it!"

When we reached the slope that led up to the fort I could see men running every whichaway, brandishing rifles and dragging saddles, bridles, and ropes and yelling, "Buffler! Buffler!" I leaned over Chiksika's neck and thudded my heels against his ribs, yanking the other horses into a gallop, and sped up the slope and into a whirlpool of excited horses and cursing men. From our low hilltop I could see beyond the Yellowstone the prairie black with buffalo and the Crow camp boiling with running Indians and rearing horses, looking for all the world like a kicked-over anthill.

Tuttle had already saddled the tall bay he called Ready and I saw that he had fetched my weapons, powder horn and possibles belt, and my saddle and pad. I slipped off Chiksika and saddled up, my fingers fumbling with the girth, overcome by the sheer excitement of it all. I looped the horn-strap over my head, slung Melchior across my back, and swung into the saddle just as Ned Godey rode up and said, "Best we let the Crows have first go.

They're apt to git a mite tetchy if'n we bust in an' scatter the herd." He let his eyes roam out over the plain, black and rippling with thousands of shaggy backs. "'Pears like there be a sufficiency fer all." Then he turned his gaze full on Tuttle and me. The look on his face was dead serious when he said, "Jist keep an eye on the Crows. They'll be showin' ye how it's done. An' don't git yorese'fs kilt. Runnin' buffler ain't fer kids."

The Major and Hamish were bustling about, separating the company into four groups — horseback hunters, indifferent riders but crack shots — the likes of Fink and his river cronies — who would ride over and then go afoot to shoot stragglers, another bunch to follow up and butcher the kill, and finally the sentries and swivel-gunners who would stay behind to keep the fort secure.

We took what Ned had said to mean we three were amongst the horsebackers. I was buzzing with excitement and Chiksika felt it. His ears were pricked and he snorted and stamped whilst we awaited the order to move out. The whole arrangement didn't take five minutes and soon Louis Prudhomme signaled us horseback hunters to follow him down to the Yellowstone. As we started for the river I could see the Absarokas pouring out of their camp like swarming bees, galloping out to the herd.

Trotting down the hill and splashing through the river, I spilled the priming out of my pistol and rifle and poured fresh powder into each pan, taking pains to keep it dry, for I reckoned a misfire could be dangerous when we rode in as close to buffalo as we expected to do. Tuttle was riding beside me and Ned caught up with us as we scrambled up the far bank. "Keep yore eyes peeled now," he cautioned. "Watch the Crows. Learn from 'em. They kin teach ye plenty." Tuttle and I both nodded and hurried our horses to keep up with Prudhomme, who had put his mount into a slow gallop and was fast closing the distance between us and the buffalo sweeping past.

Absaroka hunters, some with muskets, some with short bows, most with both, were already in the midst of the herd, riding in close on the right beside their prey, standing in the stirrups and aiming downwards for a killing shot in the heart or lungs, horse and rider a single being as they sped across the plain. Watching them was useful, but I knew the only real way I was likely to learn that particular skill was by doing it.

Prudhomme reined in his horse a short distance from the edge of the herd. He was quickly surrounded by his hunters, all of us eager, some laughing aloud, others serious and intent. Jim Bridger rode up in company with the Delawares, Brass Turtle on one side, Little Mountain on the other, followed by a chunky young fellow by name of Stone Bird and an older man called simply Foot. They all commenced chuckling at something Turtle said, but I was too far away to hear it. I saw that our Delawares, like many of the Crows, carried both muskets and short bows and quivers stuffed full of arrows.

The Absaroka hunters were by now far in advance of us. Louis Prudhomme stood in his stirrups, swung his arm towards the herd, and called out, "*Messieurs*, zere is your dinnair! I weesh all of you *bon appetit! Bonne chance! Allons, enfants! Prenez garde!* Make meat!" His ringing laugh was more of a battle cry as he put spurs to his horse and plunged into a sea of shaggy brown backs. Chiksika, already impatient, tossing his head and champing and rattling his bit, half-reared when he saw Prudhomme depart and next thing I knew, I, too, was amid an avalanche of huge horned heads and pounding hoofs, flaring nostrils snorting snot, and glaring little red eyes. I confess I commenced to question if this was going to be as much fun as I had thought.

A running buffalo herd, once you're inside it, is not the solid mass it appears to be from the outside. Considerable gaps develop between one bunch and another, each bull running behind his harem of cows to haze them together and protect them.

Chiksika was a good teacher. Fast as the buffalo were running, the gray was easily faster, stretching into a flat gallop low to the ground, smoothly dodging critter holes and sagebrush, jumping shallow gullies and pulling alongside a fat cow running all out, her tail sticking stiffly straight up as she plunged ahead. I hardly used the reins, for Chiksika seemed to know the business much better than I. I slid my pistol from its holster on the pommel, cocked it, and swung it out at arm's length, aiming for a spot just in back of and below her pumping right shoulder. Chiksika cut in close and held steady behind and just out of reach of her swinging horns. I scarcely heard my shot amid the bawling, bellowing tumult, but I saw the cow take no more than a stride and a half before her knees folded under her and she skidded chin foremost to a shuddering stop, blood gushing from her mouth.

My own blood was singing in my ears, roaring triumphal anthems against a deafening chorus of pounding hoofs and squeals and grunts and rasping breath as the red-brown sea of woolly humps and massive heads and clattering horns plunged ever onward. I shoved the pistol into its holster and unslung my rifle, laid the barrel across the pommel, and brought the muzzle to bear on another cow. Chiksika divined my every thought. He crowded closer and held steady just a shade behind her shoulder, his flat gallop smoothly matching the speed of her plunging gait. I squeezed the trigger and thought I had missed, until I saw her break stride and stumble and freeze, then tumble onto her horns.

Naturally all this was new to me. I didn't know how to reload at a gallop, carrying spare balls in my mouth, dumping powder down the barrel, and seating the ball by slamming the butt of the rifle against the pommel. Maybe some of our people knew how, but I didn't.

I slapped the right rein against Chiksika's neck and leaned leftwards towards the outside of the herd. I could feel his unwillingness to abandon the chase, but he moved away from the bunch we had been pursuing, vaulting aside to avoid a vicious swipe of the horns of a herd bull who managed to close the distance as we swerved outwards. Once we were in the clear we threaded our way at a gallop amongst bunches of running buffalo until we emerged on the fringes of the herd. I reined him in and commenced to load and prime my weapons as quickly as I could, meanwhile keeping half an eye on what was happening amid the herd. Far out in the middle I saw Tuttle. He looked like an addled scarecrow aboard his big bay, arms flapping, rifle banging on his back as he closed on a running bunch, reining his horse ever closer for a shot with his pistol. Ned Godey and Jim Bridger trailed not far behind. Then all of them were swallowed up in a blanket of dust churned up by the fleeing buffalo. The Delawares swept past, riding more or less abreast, rifles slung and leaning over their horses' necks, their short bows pulled nearly double and arrows nocked as they each pursued a different bunch. At first I wondered why one or another of them shot an arrow into dead and dying buffalo they passed, but then it came to me that they were marking them, staking claim, in case the Crows sought to declare the carcass was one their own kills, for each man's arrow markings are somewhat different.

Chiksika's patience was stretched nigh to breaking whilst I reloaded. He fairly sprang into the thinning herd when I gave him his head and touched him with my heels. The herd was meager and scattered now and we raced to overtake a likely bunch. I held my rifle aloft as we gave the herd bull wide berth, then darted in ahead of him and held steady at the side of a fat cow that I shot from no more than a foot away. I slung my rifle, jerked the pistol from its holster, and flew in pursuit of another bunch, which I reduced in size by one fat cow before I checked Chiksika and headed him towards the left-hand side of what was left of the herd.

Whilst I reloaded my weapons I saw that we had come out just below half a hundred or more Absaroka women and kids waiting to run out and butcher the buffalo their men had killed. The last rags of the herd disappeared into a dust cloud. The prairie was strewn with black blobs of dead buffalo, shaggy crumpled lumps, legs poking out stiff and straight, unmoving in the crisp morning sunshine.

I let my gaze wander amongst the Crow women, seeking a glimpse of Night-eyes, but if she was there, I didn't see her.

The Absaroka hunters were drifting back now, some riding alone, most in small groups, laughing excitedly and shouting one to another, doubtless bragging on their skill. I couldn't blame them if they were, for I felt very much the same.

One of the Crows broke away from his bunch, kicked up his horse, and headed straight for me. As he drew nigh I saw that it was Pretty-on-top, plastered with dust and riding a tall chestnut that was lathered to a fare-thee-well. Chiksika was barely sweated. When I was able to make out his face I could tell that Pretty wasn't feeling precisely neighborly right then. His black eyes were squinted and cold and hard as pebbles, his lip curled in scorn and dislike, his face a thundercloud. I raised my hand in greeting but he ignored that friendly gesture. He just sat in his tall saddle and stared as if his eyes could break my bones, letting his gaze stray to Chiksika from time to time, then back to me. At length Pretty-on-top jerked his horse's head about and rode off at a trot, his back poker-stiff, with nary a farewell look or sign.

I peered out onto the prairie, seeking my companions, but at first all that I saw were scores of dead buffalo and here and there packs of white wolves worrying at the carcasses. I saw, too, a huge silvery bear, bigger than I thought a bear could be, nearly as big as the buffalo he was trying to drag off, but I had no wish to mess with such a critter then or ever. At last Tuttle, Godey, and Jim Bridger appeared out of the sagebrush and I rode out to meet them. Jim, his dust-caked face wreathed in a smile, called out first, "Hey thar, Temple! How'd'ja do? Got me a couple o' fat'uns!" His face showed only beaming approval when I allowed that I had shot four cows.

Ned Godey looked purely relieved when he saw that my horse and I were whole and sound and Tuttle was chortling fit to strangle himself as he recounted the thrill of chasing buffalo and killing three of them. Then he said, seriously, "Thought ye was a goner thar when thet hoss o' your'n up an' jumped plumb inter thet'ere buffler herd. Which one o' you two was it done the decidin' when to go?" I confessed it was mostly the horse's idea but declared that he had a lot more sense about buffalo than I did. Tuttle nodded and said, "Yep. He ain't short o' brains, thet'un, ner nuthin' else thet I kin see. He'll sartinly do."

Godey smiled and bobbed his head in assent when I told them I was well aware that Chiksika was the only trained buffalo horse amongst us and credit for my four kills mostly belonged to him, as well as for keeping me from breaking my neck.

Butchering crews leading horses dragging *travois* poles were making their way towards us across the plain. We were watching them from a distance as we walked our horses back to the Yellowstone when we saw that several crews were making haste to a single spot. The four of us nudged our horses into a trot and we learned all too soon what had drawn our men to that place. Lying in the midst of a circle of men was what was left of the body of a man, shredded and smashed to strawberry jam and well-nigh unrecognizable. A rod or so behind him was his horse, trampled to rags, his foreleg still jammed into a badger hole. Nobody spoke. Nobody wanted or needed to.

Finally Tuttle broke the silence. "Thet be Jake Yancy. From up aroun' home. I knowed 'im. Best we git 'im on back to the stockade."

The men on the ground tied the battered body somehow onto a *travois* and Tuttle led the horse back to the stockade, where we told the Major what had happened. Then we returned to the prairie to help fetch in the meat we had made.

We worked all afternoon, helping out with the skinning and the butchering and hauling meat back to the fort, our earlier excitement and satisfaction drowned in gloom at the death of a comrade. I hadn't known Jake Yancy, but I remembered him as one of Fink's crew on the Ohio and that vague kinship made his death hurt all the more.

೩೨   ೩೨   ೩೨

Supper that evening was a quiet affair, in spite of fresh buffalo tongue, juicy fleece fat, and tender hump ribs still smoking from the fire. Jake Yancy's death was on everybody's mind, though few said anything about it. He was the first in our company to lose his life and the way he died called to mind how fragile all of us were in that still unknown wilderness.

Even Tuttle was glum, his customary good humor drenched, I reckon, by memories of home and good and bad times shared.

After supper I walked down to the Missouri and bathed, scrubbing off the dirt and sweat and blood and buffalo snot that caked my body like a shell, washing away in the chill water, too, some of the gloom that clung like cockleburrs to my spirit. Afterwards I put on clean buckskins, rolled up my reeking hickory shirt and britches, and headed back to the fort.

On the way I stopped by the willow grove, hoping that Night-eyes might be there, but she wasn't.

It was still broad daylight when I entered the fort but most of the company had already turned in. Only a few small bunches of men sprawled in front of their quarters, smoking and talking more quietly than I had ever known them to do. I walked to the cookfire, still flickering and smoldering from supper, and tossed my bundle of ragged hickory clothes onto it, thinking as I watched it crumble in flame and smoke that this simple act signified one more step into the life I had chosen. I knew it to be a good life, for all its dangers, for I could already taste the freedom that it offered to those who could embrace it.

When the final shred of cloth flared and disappeared I walked out to the horse pens to make sure that Chiksika had hay enough to see him through the night. He nickered when he saw me and came to the fence, propping his chin on the top rail, inviting me to scratch his ears and stroke his velvety muzzle, which I did.

As I turned to leave I waved to the Iroquois sentry that Brass Turtle called Owl, seated on a fence rail, musket on his knees, his unstrung bow and quiver slung across his back. He nodded solemnly but spoke not a word, which was how those Iroquois mostly were with us whites up till then.

Above on the watchtowers I could hear muffled voices and the thud of boots and moccasined feet as the sentries chatted and moved about, no doubt bored and yearning for their relief at midnight. The Major had doubled the guard when the Crows arrived, but so far there appeared to be no good reason for it.

The fort was too quiet. A feeling of foreboding hung over everything and everybody in it. Leastaways that is how it felt to me. I didn't want to go back inside and, tired and muscle-sore as I was after a long hard day, I knew that I couldn't get to sleep if I did. Instead I strolled down to the willow grove, thinking the while of Night-eyes and the pleasures we had shared there, somewhat surprised that I felt no guilt about those favors freely given and accepted. That surely was not the way I had been brought up to consider such matters.

She was there, as I had hoped she would be. But she wasn't the way I expected and wanted her to be. She was sitting at the edge of our little clearing, her back to me, facing the willows, huddled inside her blanket, scrunched into herself, silent, and looking small and childlike and somehow pitiful.

I went to her and threw myself down beside her, gathering her in my arms, and tried to turn her face to mine, but her strong little body was rigid as iron. She pulled away and clutched her blanket tighter about her head and I heard a deep sob struggle in her throat. I caught her by both shoulders and turned her to me. The blanket fell away and in the gathering dusk I could see her great black eyes, tear-stained now, one of them swollen nearly shut. Bruises and deep scratches marred her cheeks. Then I saw that her beautiful long black hair had been cropped as close as a town boy's.

When she realized that I had seen her shame, she fairly shrieked and buried her face against my throat, sobbing and shaking and clinching me close, murmuring words I couldn't understand, then breaking into sobs again.

I have no idea how long I held her in my arms, there in our willow grove, crooning nonsense into her ear, trying to comfort her, knowing the while that even if I could speak her tongue I knew no words to wash away the shame she felt. At last she lay quiet and silent in my arms, her face pressed against my breast, her strong young hands gripping my waist and pulling me ever closer to her.

It was pitch-dark and a light rain was drizzling over the prairie when we rose from the wet grass and made our way slowly and silently to the fort. She crowded close to me as we walked, her head bowed and her blanket pulled over head and nearly to her eyes.

At the gate I called out to the sentry and asked him to summon Godey. When Ned appeared I asked him to fetch a lantern, for I sorely needed to know the long and short of what had happened with Night-eyes.

Standing next to the stockade wall in the yellow glow of the lantern I learned the how and the why of it all. Ned's hand-talk was quick and precise, but Night-eyes, with eyes downcast and muffled in her blanket, waved her hands excitedly, talking the while in a voice that jumped from sorrow to anger and back to sorrow again. Over and over, Ned made the sign that asked her to repeat herself. At last she grew silent and she pulled her hands back inside the folds of her blanket.

When Godey turned to me his face was grave and his voice was strained. "Y'ain't gonna like what ye're gonna be hearin', Temple. Jist hear me out fer now an' don't ye be thinkin' o' doin' nuthin' foolish." I nodded my assent and Ned went on. "'Pears as if ye be at the bottom of all o' her trouble. Ol' Purty-on-top's the bastard what done her harm, but jist why he done it might be a mite hard to swaller."

I felt the blood rush to my temples, but I merely nodded and Ned continued. "Seems like he's stiff as a poker 'bout you buyin' that purty gray hoss off'n him." He held up his hand as I started to protest. I bit my tongue and he went on. "I know. Ye traded 'im fair an' square an' he's a growed-up man what made the deal, but sech-like makes no nevermind to the likes o' him. Ye got his buffler hoss an' he don't. That's what's stickin' in his craw an' li'l Night-eyes here jist got in the way. He's madder'n hell 'bout the hoss an' when' he found out 'bout you an' her, he jist natcherly knocked her about an' cut off her hair to spite ye!"

I couldn't hold my tongue. "Are ye sure, Ned? All this about a horse? A horse I paid his price for?" Another thought occurred to me and I said, "Are ye sure it ain't about me an' her passin' time down by the river? Maybe they've got some rules an' such about such doin's."

Ned chuckled. "Oh, they got rules, all right, but jist like the most of us, them rules go purty much by the board when there's plunder to be had!" He paused and I could see him grinning in the feeble lanternlight. "Hell, Temple! Y'ain't the onliest one here been passin' time with a Crow woman, but ain't nobody over there offered to beat hell out o' the rest of 'em!" The grin disappeared and he said earnestly, "No, it's pers'nal 'twixt you an' him, Temple, an' li'l Night-eyes here says he's talkin' like he ain't through yet."

Night-eyes had been growing more and more agitated while Ned was talking to me and now she commenced to jabber and flitter her hands at him, bobbing her head the while, until the blanket fell away and Ned could see her bruised and swollen face, the jagged scratches, and the ragged remains of her hair. Ned said nothing, but the pain and anger that showed in his eyes and the grim look that settled on his face bespoke a side of him I hadn't seen before, a side of which I heartily approved.

He laid a gentle hand on her shoulder and then he stepped back and commenced hand-talking to her. When he finished, she was silent and still, standing with her head bowed and her eyes downcast. He turned to me then and said, "Temple, I'm gonna tell ye the same as I jist told her. Let it be. No gittin' even. Ye cain't win. Ol' Purty'll git his comeuppance. Don't know how or jist when, but he'll git it, be sure."

A hundred protests boiled up inside me, but all along I knew he was right, there was nothing to be done, so I swallowed hard and said nothing. Ned gave me a light punch on the arm and said, "So be it then. Ye'd best be takin' this li'l lady on down to the river, but ye dast not cross over with 'er." I nodded and was turning to go when he saw that I was unarmed. He drew his pistol from his belt and said, "Here, jist in case, but don't ye use it 'less ye hafta."

Our leave-taking at the river's edge was more tender than it had ever been. She hugged me 'round the middle till I thought my ribs would break and I replied in kind. Then we kissed one last time and she slipped her dress over her head, rolled her moccasins in it, and waded into the river, holding the bundle aloft, and faded into the darkness.

It was still drizzling a fine, cold rain when I got back to the fort, wet, bone-weary, and seething with anger. Tuttle had brought his bed indoors and I could hear his steady breathing and occasional snores as I lay wide-eyed and rigid, picturing impossible scenes of revenge until they dissolved into a fitful doze.

❧   ❧   ❧

I must have slept more soundly than I thought I could, for daylight was breaking when Tuttle shook me awake and I heard men shouting and cursing and saw Paddy McBride and Smiley, weapons in hand, collide in the doorway as they struggled to get outside. I shook the sleep from my head and the noise jelled into meaning. A score of angry voices cursed and yelled. "They stole the hosses! Sumbitches went an' stole the goddamn hosses! An' they kilt the Injun! Skelped 'im, too! Who the hell was pullin' sentry-go?"

I grabbed up Melchior and dashed through the doorway and out the gate, barefoot and clad only in my shirt. As I rounded the end of the stockade I saw that the horse pens were empty, the gate-rails removed and laid neatly alongside the fence. On the far side of the pens men were clustered around something lying on the ground. I trotted over to them and squirmed my way to the front of the crowd. It was Owl, an arrow stuck clean through his neck, the top of his head a bloody mess where his top-knot had been sliced off.

Numbly, I backed away and when I was clear of the crowd I looked across the river. The Crow village was gone. Only a few smoldering fires testified that it had ever been there.

A riot of random thoughts and feelings churned in my brain as I stumbled back inside the fort, until they congealed into a single image, the hard, haughty face of Pretty-on-top, sure as hell the author of all this misfortune. As I stood staring unseeing at the rough plank walls of our little room, I felt my sorrow freezing into cold resolve to make him pay for his greed and arrogance. My dark thoughts were interrupted by Tuttle shouldering through the low, narrow doorway. He looked puzzled. "Temple, whadda'ye make o' them Injuns, all of 'em, Dellerwares an' Eeriequahs alike, pickin' up an' hot-footin' it 'crost the Yellerstone like all o' the imps o' hell was a-bitin' on their arse?" For a moment Tuttle appeared to be lost in thought. Then he said, suspicion in his eyes, "An' ol' Brass Turtle a-leadin' 'em, too. Ye don't s'pose our Injuns was in cahoots with them Crow Injuns, do ye?"

I did not for a minute suppose that such a thing could be so and I said as much to Tuttle, adding, "You just wait an' see. They'll be back an' they'll be givin' ye a good reason for their goin', too." I couldn't really fault Tuttle for his suspicions, though, for he had been brought up amongst folk who considered all Indians to be treacherous, if not much worse.

Sure enough, it wasn't but an hour or so before we spied all nine of our redskins break out of the brush that fringed the Yellowstone and come trotting up to the fort. When Brass Turtle saw Tuttle and me, he called out, "Hey, Temple! Ye want your purty gray nag back?" Without waiting for a reply, for he certainly knew what it must be, he said, "If ye do, c'mon along!"

We followed behind the Indians to the Major's quarters, where Turtle rapped on the door, then gestured to the rest of us to be quiet and let him do the talking. Andrew Henry himself swung the door open and I could see Hamish and Ned and Louis Prudhomme crowding behind him. Brass Turtle wasted no time on hellos. "Major, if ye want your hosses back, I reckon we can do 'er! Tracks're plain as your palm — hosses, trav-wah drags, the lot! Mud makes fer easy trackin', but we had better oughta get a move on!"

The Major nodded, his face hard as iron, and turned back to confer with the men standing behind him. It wasn't a minute before he faced Brass Turtle and said, "I reckon you can do it, Turtle, if anybody can. Take Prudhomme an' Godey here along with ye. Who else d'ye want?"

Turtle said that he wanted all the Indians, Delawares and Iroquois alike, and then he named Jim Bridger, Tuttle, and me. I took it as quite an honor and Tuttle grinned. From in back of the crowd I heard Anse Tolliver's drawl raised in an unaccustomed shout. "Hold on thar, Turtle, damn ye! Thar's mules 'mongst them critters an' I want 'em back! Ain't no man here kin handle mules like me! Ye'd best be takin' me 'long to yore shindig!"

Henry cocked an eye at Turtle and the Delaware nodded and flashed a grin before he shouted back, "Awright, Tolliver, you kin come! Bear in mind, howsomever, it's all flat out thar! Ain't no hills to run around!" He was referring, of course, to the old jest that all mountain folk possessed one leg shorter than the other and were apt to fall down on level ground.

Anse just grinned and spat and drawled, "Ye'd best be lookin' after yore ownse'f! Thi'shere ol' boy'll be standin' proud an' upright 'til the last dog is hung!"

So there it was, fifteen men bound to take on the whole nation of Absarokas, if need be. I wasn't thinking about any peril that might be involved, which I admit wasn't altogether too smart. All I wanted was my horse Chiksika and perhaps a chance to settle a score with old Pretty-on-top.

Getting ready to go didn't take much time. I left Melchior with John Smiley and took only my pistol. Tuttle did likewise, for we knew that we faced a long hard journey afoot and the less and the lighter we toted the better. Hamish issued each of us a small sackful of pemmican and jerky, which together with spare moccasins, powderhorn and a pouchful of pistol balls, a single blanket, and a couple of ropes was all we would need. I stripped everything extra off my belt and left on it only my possibles pouch, a big butcher knife, and my dirk. At last, when I thought I had taken everything I would need, I recalled the little double-barreled hideout pistol from Lucette. I dug it out of my saddlebags and dropped it, along with a handful of little pistol balls to fit it, into my possibles pouch.

John Smiley, meanwhile, was outdoors cooking breakfast, which was a sort of thick porridge laced with bits of roasted buffalo meat from yesterday's supper, served up with steaming strong coffee, thick and black as mortal sin. I recall that that breakfast very well, for I longed for such a meal many times in the days to come.

Before we departed, the Major called the whole company together for the burial of Jake Yancy and Owl. The Iroquois held whatever ceremony they might have performed off by themselves and Brass Turtle and the other Delawares went with them. The Major asked Tuttle Thompson to say a few last words for Yancy, seeing as how he was the one man amongst us who knew Jake best. Tuttle looked like he would rather swallow castor oil than make a speech, but he did as he was told. What he said went something like this: "We be gathered hyar to bid fare-thee-well to ol' Jake Yancy. I reckon I knew ol' Jake better'n most, ri'chere an' back yonder, too, when we was growin' up. Best I kin say fer 'im is, Jake had a purty fair eye fer a hoss an' he warn't allus as bad as he mostly was. Like I tol' ye, Jake an' me warn't kin ner nuthin', but I knew Jake passin' fair, boy to man, an' I'm sartin sure if ol' Jake hadn'a gone an' got hisse'f kilt, he'd'a told us to plant 'im quick an' git on with fetchin' them hosses back!"

Tuttle stepped back from the open grave and Andrew Henry, head bowed to hide a grin, spaded a shovelful of dirt onto the canvas-wrapped body. I made up my mind then and there that if I died out there and somebody asked Tuttle to deliver my elegy, I'd just as lief pass. I don't recollect much of what the Major said to send us on our way, but I do recall the words "one hundred and eighteen horses and mules" were mentioned more than once.

It was still in the forenoon when we trotted single file down the slope to the Yellowstone, running somewhat higher after the rain, and waded across, holding our packs and firearms above our head. When we climbed up the opposite bank, Little Mountain and an Iroquois called Acorn streaked arrow-straight across the prairie to a spot where the Absarokas' tracks led out of their trampled campground and onto their southwestward trail.

We traveled pretty much at a dog-trot, strung out single file, keeping to the low ground and brushy bottoms where we could, halting every hour or so to catch our breath and adjust our gear, every man amongst us keeping an eye peeled for Crow scouts watching their backtrail. Tuttle and I ran near the back of the pack, learning what we could from the Indians, who ran mostly up front. None of them carried firearms, just unstrung bows and quivers bulging with arrows, besides a power of knives and axes and clubs with stones thonged onto them.

Following the trail wasn't hard, for besides a maze of horse tracks sprinkled with manure, *travois* poles grooved the muddy earth with sign enough for a blind man to follow. Besides, a whole village on the move, no matter how canny their warriors might be, scatters enough trash in the form of lost and worn-out moccasins, kids' toys gone astray, gnawed-on bones, and such-like to make the trailing job downright easy.

Even so, when night fell, moonless and cloudy, we had to halt and hunker down and wait for daylight, knowing all the while that the Crows suffered no such restriction. This was their country and they knew where they were headed. We didn't.

We bedded down in a brushy hollow alongside a little crick. Naturally we couldn't light fires, for fear of prying Absaroka eyes, but even so, it was welcome indeed to slake our thirst, gnaw on some jerky, smoke a pipeful, and roll into a blanket spread on the damp ground.

As I was reaching out for sleep I heard Tuttle ask in a low voice, "By the by, Ned, jest who was it standin' guard up thar las' night?"

Godey spat and replied, "Thought ever'body knew. 'Twas Fink an' his mess an' yore New York Irisher 'long with 'em."

Tuttle cursed softly and muttered, "Ain't surprisin'. Them goddamn watermen don't care nuthin' fer hosses ner fer tryin' to unnerstan' Injuns neither."

So there it was. Mike Fink and Pretty-on-top made a perfect match, to my way of thinking, a sure-fire recipe for misfortune. Troubling as such a thought might be, howsomever, even my growing hatred of those two scoundrels was no match for the fatigue that closed my eyes and pushed me into a deep, dreamless sleep.

ન્ટ્ર   ન્ટ્ર   ન્ટ્ર

Morning came all too soon. It was still dark when Brass Turtle roused us from slumber. We were already on the trail when dawn's silvery fingers first poked into the eastern sky. That day and the days after melded into a leg-weary, thirsty, hungry, angry blur as we trotted across table-flat prairie, avoiding prickly pear when we could, wincing and cursing when we couldn't, straining our eyes out to the horizon, seeking horsemen and pony-drags that never came into view. I could hardly believe how fast the Absaroka camp was moving, encumbered as they were with old folks and kids and dogs and everything they owned, but their cookfires were a long time cold by time we found them and the Crows were nowhere in sight.

I learned to eat pemmican on that journey and I learned, as well, not to chew too much of it at once, for even a little ball of it swelled into a mouth-filling mass that nearly choked me the first time or two. I was astonished at how just a mite of that mixture of buffalo fat and slivers of meat and chokecherries took away my hunger pangs and gave me strength enough to keep on putting one foot in front of the other as we pursued the Crows to what threatened to be the end of the earth.

Then in late afternoon of the fourth day, Acorn poked his head up out of a little ravine and waved us to him. Little Mountain soon joined us as we huddled in the scant brush alongside a trickle of water meandering down to the Yellowstone. The two scouts jabbered and flung their hands about for quite a spell, telling Brass Turtle all about whatever it was, before the young Delaware turned back to us, a hard smile on his face. The Iroquois and the other Delawares were grinning, too, nudging one another and laughing quietly, for they understood what the scouts were reporting. Turtle chuckled softly and then he said with a grin, "'Pears we got 'em jest where we want 'em. They been settin' up their camp a-hind them little hills yonder. Reckon we'll be hittin' 'em arter dark."

I recollect wondering what he might mean by "got 'em where we want 'em," considering that we were but fifteen men afoot against a whole village of Crows with horses, but I held my peace and simply nodded along with the others.

We stayed put until dusk, talking quietly and readying our weapons, Anse and Tuttle forever honing their knives, already sharp enough to shave with, although neither one of those worthies was hardly ever of a mind to dull his cutlery in such an occupation, unless they were required to do so. Brass Turtle had gone off with the scouts and a couple other Indians, returning just as twilight turned the prairie purple and hazy gold.

My moccasins were in tatters and I was just tying on a new pair that Night-eyes had made for me and recalling her charms when Turtle wriggled his way down the bank. When he stood up, his face wore a look of undiluted glee. "It'll soon be time to git movin'. We can do 'er jest fine but don't nobody do nuthin' 'less'n I say so.

We'll hit 'em quick an' hard an' be gone with ever' hoss they own 'fore they kin git off o' their womenfolk!"

Whilst we waited for darkness we cached our food pokes and whatever else we didn't need to carry right then near the top of the bank, hopefully to retrieve such truck on our way back to the fort. I replaced the priming in my pistol and knotted one of my ropes into a Crow-style bridle and shoved it under my belt, along with the other rope for a lead if I should need it. I kept my blanket, too, for I reckoned it would help me blend in at the Crow camp and cover up all the hardware I was carrying on my belt. Then I settled down with Jim Bridger for a smoke. Neither one of us offered much in the way of conversation.

It was not quite dark, that time of day when it's harder to see even than at midnight, when we crept out of the gully and trotted towards a low range of hills that lay to the west. When we got to the place where the hills sloped up off the plain, an Iroquois called Fish and the old Delaware Foot led us up a narrow draw, until we were nigh the top, when the word was passed along for us to get down on our bellies and crawl to the ridge.

Once there, I slithered through what grass there was and fetched up behind a sagebrush, overlooking a bowl more or less hemmed in by low hills like the one we were on. Directly below was the Absaroka camp, tipis glowing like paper lanterns and fires burning outside most of them, women cooking and chasing kids, men moving into and out of the firelight, here and there a horse tethered near the doorway. I strained my eyes to find Chiksika, which I couldn't, and then to see where the horse herd was, which I couldn't see either, but I reckoned it must be somewheres on the far side of the little crick that meandered through the camp.

I never heard Brass Turtle approaching before he touched my arm and whispered, "Are ye set an' ready, Buck?" I allowed that I was, leastaways as much as I ever would be. Then he asked, "Ye still aim to git yer gray hoss back, don'tcha?" He was vaguely visible in the starglow, so instead of speaking I nodded. He went on. "If'n ye do, ye'll hafta march right on through the camp, proud as ye please. No sneakin'. They'll ketch ye sure as hell if ye do. Kin ye do it?."

Right about then, I wasn't at all sure that I could even stand up, but I told him I was ready to deal with whatever came my way. Whether he believed me or not, Turtle pointed out the best way to get down the hillside, about where in the camp I was likely to find my horse, and which direction to ride out of there, once I got hold of him. Then he said, "Rest yerse'f. Mebbe even git some sleep. I'll be tellin' ye when to go. We got a long wait 'til them Crows git to their robes." Then he crawled off as silently as he had come.

I surprised myself by actually going to sleep. I jumped when Turtle touched my arm and growled, "It's time." Down below, the camp was mostly dark and quiet, cookfires smoldering, most of the tipis barely visible. Here and there a dog barked and once or twice I heard a voice raised in a quavering chant.

Turtle was still by my side and I couldn't help but ask him, "Turtle, you ever done anything like this before?"

Even in the darkness I could see the white flicker of his grin before he replied, "No, but I always wanted to." He paused a spell and then he said, "Onliest thing could make it better was if we was stealin' that white-arse step-dad o' mine purely blind, 'stead of these-here measly Crows."

There was no time to ponder what he said. Turtle stood up and as I fumbled to my feet and was shoving my pistol into my belt, he reached behind him and handed something to me, saying, "Here, ye better take this along. It don't make so much noise." It was one of his Delaware war clubs, a foot-and-a-half-long stick with a hefty rock thonged onto the end of it. I mumbled some kind of thanks, though I wasn't at all sure if I knew quite how to use it, slipped the loop around my wrist, pulled my blanket around my shoulders, and followed him downward into the darkness.

The hillside was not as steep as I had feared it might be and besides, Turtle led the way until we nearly reached the bottom. Then he said in a low growl, "Ye'd best be goin' into camp from 'bout ri'chere. I'll be goin' fu'ther up, but you'll sure as hell be hearin' me comin' back!" He chuckled as he squeezed my arm, then faded into the hillside.

When I got to the bottom I hadn't taken more than half a dozen steps until I realized where I had come out in the Absaroka camp.

The sharp tang of human dung stung my nostrils and I froze in my tracks, hoping and praying to nobody in particular that I had stumbled into the men's, and not the women's, private place. I recollected the Shawnees had been very pernickety about such matters.

I squatted and pulled loose the string I used to tie my hair back and shook it loose. It fell well past my shoulders now and I hoped that it would help let me pass for an Indian, like Pap used to say I could. Then I pulled the edge of the blanket over my head and commenced to thread my way amongst a passel of Absaroka mementoes, careful to toe in my moccasins, Indian-style, and not thump my heel down first, like white men do.

The midden was located downwind on the edge of camp and I recalled that, at the fort, Pretty's lodge had been fairly close to the middle, so I headed that way, muffled in my blanket and shuffling halfway fast, like I knew where I was going, keeping my eyes peeled for Chiksika and Pretty-on-top's painted tipi. Here and there I saw what I took to be buffalo runners tethered outside this or that lodge, but none of them was mine.

I reckon the Crows were as tuckered as we were after their forced march away from the fort, for I saw hardly anybody lingering in the alleys between the lodges as I made my way towards what I was hoping was Pretty's neighborhood. The few that I did see were men relieving themselves and naturally I was too polite to disturb them. I did suffer one bad scare when a couple-three scrawny dogs charged out from amongst the tipis, snarling and snapping, but I kept on walking and after they got close enough to sniff, they backed off whining and went their way, reassured, perhaps, by the smell of Night-eyes' leggin's and moccasins.

Chiksika it was that I saw first, head down, nosing into a heap of hay, then the sun and lightning bolt on Pretty's lodge. My heart bulged into my throat but I fought myself into keeping a steady pace until I was abreast of my horse. Then I went to him and stroked his neck and scratched his ears, reminding him of the feel and the smell of me. He nickered deep in his throat but he stood steady, not offering to pull away. I was just about to cut his tether when I heard somebody moving around inside the lodge. My innards froze within me. I dodged behind the tipi and crouched there, huddled in my blanket, making myself small, unmoving, not daring to breathe, waiting.

I didn't have long to wait. Pretty-on-top, looking big as a buffalo, naked, long hair streaming, a big knife in one hand and my pistol in the other, came around the side of the lodge and stood for a moment beside Chiksika. He yanked on the tether to make sure it was tied fast, peered into the darkness to discover whatever had disturbed his horse, then advanced, half-crouched, pistol pointing, seeking the intruder if there was one.

I reckon he wasn't a yard away when I swung Brass Turtle's war club the length of my arm and caught old Pretty, full force, on the side of his head. He went down without even a groan, the only sound the thud of his big body hitting the ground. My first thought was to cut Chiksika loose and run for it, but action begets action, and as I looked down at Pretty-on-top my fear gave way to a simmering rage against all that this man had done, killing Owl and beating my woman and shaming her by cutting off her hair and stealing my horse and all the other horses to boot. Anger boiled into my throat and nearly choked me. I snatched up his knife and grabbed a handful of his hair and commenced to hack and slice all of it away from his skull, cursing under my breath the while, until hardly a wisp of it remained. When I leaned back on my heels to stuff it all under my belt, I heard his faint breathing and knew that I hadn't killed him. Then I saw in the dim light that in my haste and fury I had sliced half of his left ear nearly off. It was hanging by a mere thread of skin. So I did what I was sure that old Pretty would have done for me. I sliced it completely off and stuffed it into the little medicine poke Night-eyes had given me. It appeared to me the proper thing to do.

Then I knew it was surely time to decamp. I tossed Pretty's knife into the darkness, picked up his pistol and shoved it into my already overloaded belt, and stepped over to Chiksika, who was nickering nervously and pulling back on his tether, no doubt more than somewhat disturbed by all the commotion and the smell of blood. It was the work of only a second or two to slip on his rope bridle, cut the tether, toss my blanket over his withers, grab a handful of mane, and swing onto his back, even burdened as I was by all the hardware and such hanging off my belt.

I had hardly touched heels to my horse when I heard and then saw Brass Turtle come a-whooping and a-hollering and waving his blanket behind a dozen or more horses galloping through camp, scattering cookfires and tipping over meat racks and tripods, knocking tipis askew, and colliding with even more horses being hazed by Stone Bird and Foot and Little Mountain, Jim Bridger laughing his fool head nearly clean off, and at least one of the Iroquois.

I fell in behind Turtle and commenced waving my blanket, too, crowding the loose horses together, keeping them running more or less straight between the lodges. Naked men came boiling out of the battered tipis as we swept past. Women, too, but there was no time to enjoy it. At last we broke clear of the camp and ran into an even bigger bunch of horses driven by Prudhomme and Tuttle, Godey, and the other Iroquois from our company. As we galloped the herd towards a saddle in the low hills I saw Anse Tolliver astride a tall mule and leading a gray mare on a rope halter, a score or more of mules chopping along right after her, determined, it appeared, not to let the gray mare out of their sight.

Godey and Prudhomme knew the country best, so they rode forward on the flanks, keeping the herd pointed where we wanted them to go. The rest of us spread out onto the wings and rode drag behind, keeping the horses bunched as much as the broken country allowed. When we drew nigh the place where we had cached our plunder, Brass Turtle galloped to the front and he and Prudhomme headed off the herd leaders and turned them back. The rest of us meanwhile rode circles around the horses, crowding them inwards, until the whole herd commenced to mill and finally settled down somewhat to graze on what puny grass there was out there. These weren't wild horses, mind you. They were all herd-broke and used to being driven in a bunch.

I was rummaging through the cache, handing out pemmican sacks and whatever other plunder to whoever claimed it, when Brass Turtle rode up, swung off his horse, and slapped him on the rump, sending back to the herd. He was quickly joined by three Iroquois and a couple of Delawares, all of whom did the same. Ned Godey appeared out of the darkness about then and, still straddling his horse, inquired, "A mite early to be changin' critters, ain't it, Turtle?"

Brass Turtle laughed aloud. "No it ain't, Godey. We'uns aim to get some o' the best'uns this go-'round. Buffler hosses, most likely." Turtle took a step backwards to include me in what he was saying. "Ain't likely we got all their hosses. I know fer sure we di'n't. Them Crows're sure to be mad as hell, not thinkin' straight, an' hot on our arse by now. We'uns aim to in*Vite* 'em to a li'l sociable fer their trouble." He laughed again, a flint-hard laugh that had little good humor in it. "Ye'd best git the herd movin', quick an' fast as ye kin. We'll ketch ye 'fore daylight." He turned away then and jabbered a spell in his Indian tongue to the other redskins. Then they all melted away, purely vanished, in the darkness.

I tossed a pemmican sack to Godey and swung up onto Chiksika, pausing only to call out "Good luck!" to Turtle, but he had disappeared as well.

We pushed the herd hard that night, mostly at a gallop, halting only long enough to swap our tired horses for fresh ones, which is the main advantage horsethieves enjoy over their pursuers, who usually don't have spare mounts. I rode several different horses that night, but I never turned Chiksika loose, preferring instead to let him run by my side on a lead rope. Besides, he was considerable help to me, once he caught on to what was needed. I was riding drag and Chiksika would nip the laggards and drive them forward into the herd.

Daylight was just breaking over the eastern rim of the prairie when the Iroquois Fish, riding out on the right-hand wing, yelled and pointed back. Less than a mile behind us was a bunch of horsemen, I couldn't tell how many, riding fast, closing the distance. By that time I was hoarse from yelling at horses and my arm was sore from waving my blanket to haze them into the herd, but yell and wave I did with a will, leaning low along my horse's neck and beating my heels against his barrel. Still, no matter how hard we pushed, the bunch behind us continued to close the gap.

Then I saw Prudhomme pushing the leaders to the right and Godey turning them back and I realized that they meant to halt. As soon as the herd commenced to mill and settle down somewhat, I reined in my horse, slipped to ground, jerked out both pistols, and dusted fresh powder into the priming pans, determined to be as ready for a battle as I knew how, if it came to that.

Tuttle rode up about then and grinned down at me. "Don't fret yorese'f, Temple," he said. "Thct bunch yonder be only Turtle an' his Injun frien's. Cain't see no Crows amongst 'em."

Sure enough, as the horsemen drew nigh I could see that it was indeed Brass Turtle and his five comrades, driving half a score of prime horses before them. When they halted before us they were grinning and laughing like schoolboys home from a lark. Tuttle was first to speak. "So, Mister Turtle, back safe an' sound an' welcome. An' I see ye got yorese'fs some leetle keepsakes, too."

At first I thought he meant the fine-looking horses they had captured. Then I saw the bloody hair hanging from the belt of every one of them. Brass Turtle snorted out a short, hard laugh. "Reckon they won't be needin' 'em no more," he said flatly, jerking his thumb towards his belt. "An' I reckon they won't be pickin' on no more greenhorns fer a spell, neither." His eyes shifted to my middle and he burst out laughing. "Speakin' o' sech, thet's sure some fancy britchclout ye got yourse'f, Temple! Let's get these critters to water an' ye kin tell us about it!"

I looked down and commenced laughing myself. All our hard riding overnight had worked old Pretty's pride and joy — one of them, leastaways — around to my front and looked for all the world like a hairy black britchclout that hung nearly to my toes. I shoved it to one side and swung onto my horse, putting him to a lope to catch up with the rest of the party, who appeared to be in no particular hurry now.

ৰ্ষ   ৰ্ষ   ৰ্ষ

Horses dawdled in a little feeder crick of the Yellowstone and grazed up and down its banks, half of our party tending them, whilst Tuttle and Godey and Anse and Jim and Brass Turtle and I lazed about a little fire, gnawing on jerky, smoking a pipeful, and swapping lies concerning the pony raid. Most of it wasn't lies, howsomever. There was no need, for there had been excitement enough that night for a passel of good yarns.

I told them how I got Chiksika back and about the business with Pretty-on-top, even telling how scared I was, when I recalled that I still had Turtle's war club. I started to hand it to him when a better notion occurred to me. Instead I handed him the pistol I had taken off Pretty. "Here y'are, Turtle. 'Pears to me this oughta be yours. 'Thout your club I reckon I'd be wolf bait by now."

Turtle cracked a smile and replied, "Oh, I reckon you'd'a thought o' somethin'. But I'll take thi'shere iron anyways. An' thankee."

Godey roused himself, reached into the fire and pulled out a burnt stick, and swiped two black marks across my right leggin'. Before I could protest, he said, "Them're coup stripes, Temple, how Injuns up thisaway show they done somethin' special. You counted coup twicet, stealin' a buffler hoss from right in front of a lodge an' skelpin' ol' Pretty 'thout killin' 'im. Most of 'em set a heap more store on shamin' than killin', ever' time."

Then they all went on to tell about all the killing that did go on. Not a single shot had been fired by any of us. Our Indians had crawled in amongst the main herd and killed the four herd-boys with arrows, whilst Tuttle and Godey, Prudhomme, and Anse waited for their signal to come on in and get the herd gathered and moving. In the meantime Brass Turtle and Bridger and the rest of our Indians were sawing almost through the tethers of all the good buffalo horses they could get at, so they could bust loose when the uproar commenced. It appeared to me that a passel of coup stripes was deserved by all. For a moment I felt sorry about the herd-boys, but then I recalled Owl lying dead and bloody, his top-knot ripped off. I reckon those herd-boys would have happily favored any of us in like manner.

The ambush, the way Turtle told it, was pretty plain to imagine. When the Crows came busting through, all bunched up, chasing us, they ran into a hailstorm of arrows. A good Indian bowman can shoot fast enough to keep three or four arrows in the air at once and half a dozen Indians can create an absolute blizzard of flying flint. A few of the Absarokas got away, but, like Brass Turtle said with a wicked grin, our people wanted to leave some for seed.

Fifteen men driving some three hundred herd-broke horses and a score of mules makes for an easy chore. The country was generally flat to rolling and the weather held fair. Anse Tolliver, still leading the gray mare, kept his mules in the drag, where I mostly rode, leading Chiksika and pushing the slower horses forward into the herd. I was pretty young and green back then and I hated to show my ignorance by asking questions, but at last my curiosity got the best of me. I asked Anse about the gray mare and why he kept her with him on a lead. He didn't reply at first. Fact is, he looked downright perplexed. At last he said, "Wal, now, I don't rightly know the *why* of it, but the *haow* o' doin' it is becuz mule critters'll jest natcherly foller a gray mare to hell an' back. Pap tol' me 'twas so an' I daresay his pap afore 'im tol' him an' it allus gits the chore done, so I reckon I'll jest keep on a-doin' it." Which seemed fair enough to me and I told him so.

It was late afternoon the next day when we got to our crossing on the Yellowstone. The Delawares and Iroquois all cut willow staves and tied onto them the scalps they had taken on the raid, which gave me an idea. I gathered old Pretty's hair together at the top with a thong and just before I swung onto Chiksika I knotted the tag ends together around my neck and let that hairy waterfall stream down my back like a cape. It was a grand moment for me to come riding back to the fort mounted on my own horse again, sporting a trophy I had taken from the scoundrel who had stolen him. Of course I was only nineteen at the time.

经 经 经

Naturally Andrew Henry was beside himself with joy and
merriment when he saw all those horses and mules come busting
out of the brush along the Yellowstone.   He declared that a
celebration was in order. After a supper that was more like a feast,
he broke out a keg of whiskey for the occasion. The fifteen of us
who went on the pony raid got a double ration. Tuttle drank his
own and the best part of mine and most of the Indians sold theirs
to the highest bidders.   Henry brought out his fiddle and Anse,
tuckered though he must have been, joined him in scraping out
merry tunes, whilst Yves Dureau filled in the gaps with his little
squeezbox. I stumbled off to our quarters, tossed my prize from
Pretty-on-top into a corner, and dropped onto my blankets as if I
had been shot.   I fell asleep wondering if I could ever sort out
Night-eyes' hair from amongst all the others. Which I never did.

ঌ   ঌ   ঌ

After he picked out a couple-three buffalo horses for himself and
Hamish, the Major rewarded all of us who had gone on the raid by
giving us first choice of the others for our personal saddle horse.
Chiksika didn't count. I already owned him myself.

Tuttle never hesitated. He picked a tall, leggy bay gelding, one
of the buffalo runners, and he called him Amen. I asked him why
that name and he just smirked and replied, "'Cause thi'shere Ay-
men hoss be the pluperfec' *las' word* in hossflesh, thet's why!"

I chose another buffalo runner, a stout line-back dun gelding, a
shade shorter than Chiksika and chunkier, with the same kind eye,
handy and willing, and with fire a-plenty if you asked him for it. I
called him Jake, for it appeared to me only fitting that our
departed Jake Yancy should be remembered — and from the little I
knew of him, Jake Yancy would have approved of a truly good
horse carrying his name.

Chapter VI
The Musselshell

When ice started crisping up the edges of the cricks that fed the Missouri and the Yellowstone, Andrew Henry declared it was time that we set ourselves to the chore that had brought us all that long, hard distance up the Missouri, namely trapping beaver.

First off, he split the company by sending a score or more of our men under Louis Prudhomme farther up the Missouri to the Musselshell. The rest of us he kept at the fort, which we were calling Fort Henry by then, sending us out in parties of ten or a dozen men for a week or so at a time to trap the streams that fed the Yellowstone and the Missouri. Henry himself was itching to journey up to the Great Falls of the Missouri, but as Hamish pointed out, it was too late in the season for such a journey, so that part of his plan would have to wait until spring.

The original messes had pretty much sorted themselves out into bunches of men who enjoyed or leastaways tolerated one another's company. John Fitzgerald had long since attached himself to Mike Fink's crew and Ned and Anse and Brass Turtle along with his Delawares spent most of their time with us. The Iroquois went over to the Musselshell with Louis Prudhomme, on account of his speaking French, which was a language some of them more or less understood. L'Archévêque and Dureau went with him, too, for much the same reason. Henry sent Fink and his followers to the Musselshell with Prudhomme, as well. I myself was glad to see that last bunch go, as you might suppose.

Except for Paddy McBride the most of us in our bunch had done our growing up in the woods, hunting and fishing and trapping muskrats and skunks and now and then, when we got lucky, an otter or mink, but beaver was a whole new thing for us, except for Ned Godey, who had done some beaver-trapping on his own hook when he wasn't trading for furs with the Indians along the

Missouri. Like they say, in the Kingdom of the Blind the one-eyed man is king, so Ned just naturally got himself elected by the rest of us to be our teacher.

Time was, beavers were bountiful in the East, buffalo, too, and elk, what the old-timers and the Indians in those parts called wapiti. Howsomever that was before any man amongst us was even born. Uncle Ben never spoke of it, so I reckon it was before his time, as well. Back then, to hear old folks tell of it, every stream and crick and brook was clogged with beaver dams and country boys and men in every place where it was cold enough to grow good fur kept themselves in ready cash by trapping those big flat-tailed, web-footed rats for the making of gentlemen's top hats. Problem is, the appetite of the hatters and their customers in New York and Danville and London and Paris and god-knows-where-else feeds on itself and keeps growing ever larger. There will never be enough good beaver fur to satisfy their hunger for it. In time, all the beaver critters got pretty much wiped out in all the streams and cricks east of the Mississippi.

Which is how I came to be freezing my arse, hip-deep in icy water, a couple-three rods above a beaver dam on a little crick that fed the Yellowstone, learning from Ned Godey how to fool a buck-toothed rat into letting me send his hide off to be turned into some London dandy's topper.

I had best explain how the matter is accomplished. The Major issued each man half a dozen steel traps with jaws about the width of a grown man's hand, a spring on either side of the jaws, a trigger-table dead center of the jaws, and a four-foot chain with a two-inch ring at the end of it fastened to one of the springs. Six such traps, proper bait, and complete indifference to discomfort was all a beaver-trapping man needed to become wealthy. Leastaways that's the way my comrades were telling it at the time.

Now I need to tell how a beaver thinks or leastaways how we think a beaver thinks, which brings us to the matter of bait. Beavers are jealous landlords. They can't abide some other beaver coming nigh a dam they've built nor will they tolerate a stranger swimming in the pond behind it. Hospitality is unknown to those critters. Then comes the matter of groceries. Beavers eat tree bark and maybe some tender roots and shoots. That is all they eat and you can't tempt a beaver with meat or fruit or suchlike, even if you happened to have some such truck on you. They prefer young saplings but they will happily gnaw down trees a foot or more through at the trunk and they almost always fall them towards the water, most likely with a mind to building bigger and higher dams and storing up more and more bark for their winter feed.

All of which brings us around to the business of bait and how to coax a beaver into your trap. Giving him food won't get the chore done. He prefers to forage for himself, so you have to trade on his bad manners, his lack of hospitality.

Castoreum is the key to the puzzle. Up betwixt a beaver's hind legs is a pair of glands that contain a godawful creamy-looking, evil-smelling, orangey-brown mess, a single whiff of which is sure to clear your sinuses for at least a week. It is called castoreum and every beaver's castoreum smells a mite different from all the others, — not to me, but I reckon it does to other beavers.

Ned carried a little dram-bottle of that awful stuff that he still had with him from a previous journey up that way and he showed us how to peel a fresh twig and dip it into that mess, then plant it on the edge of the bank near fairly deep water in a place where we could see plenty of beaver sign, or best of all, a beaver slide, where those playful critters ride their backside down a muddy bank and splash into the water, for all the world like skinny-dipping kids.

Next we place the trap, all cocked and ready, under water in the shallows, right in front of the baited stick, then stake it to the pond bottom at the end of the chain. After that, we hike a fair piece in the water before we come out onto dry land, so as not to leave our own smell anywhere nigh the trap and the bait.

When everything works right, and it often does, Mister Beaver — or his missus or one of the kits, for that matter — comes swimming by, maybe looking out for trespassers, and gets a noseful of castoreum that certainly didn't come from anybody in his family. He bustles right on over to that smelly little peeled stick, ready to defend his hearth and home. If all goes well — for us, not him — he sticks a foot into the trap and it snaps shut on his leg. Now a beaver is a water animal and water is his best defense, so when he's scared and hurt he just naturally dives for deep water, dragging the trap with him, which, heavy as it is and staked on the chain as it is, holds him under and in one place until he drowns.

That is pretty much what beaver-trapping is all about. What keeps it interesting, howsomever, is all the things that have nothing directly to do with trapping beaver, such as bears and painters, bull wapiti in rut and on the prod, and unfriendly Indians come to pay a visit whilst you are busy with your traps or skinning out your catch. As you might suppose, all of us were on our guard during those early days on the Yellowstone, looking out for Absarokas coming back for their horses and a passel of revenge, but they never did.

Cold water was the worst of it. I found myself shuddering at the thought of it, even before I got to some icy beaver pond and waded in to look after my traps, then shivering my way through the skinning if I caught anything. Ned Godey helped some by showing us how to make leggin's from our woolen blankets. Buckskin holds the chilling damp and buffalo robes make for warmer sleeping anyhow. But it was Brass Turtle who made the difference for me, telling how you could just put the cold aside and not think about it — rise above it, so to speak, and get on with what you had to do. It didn't work for me at first, but in time I found that I was able to put a distance between my body and my mind, so that cold and hunger, thirst, and pain — and sometimes even fear — became less important than before and couldn't touch the core of my being. I came to think of it as the Indian Way, perhaps because it was Brass Turtle who told me of it, but by whatever name such thinking goes, it helped me survive the cold and many another hardship after that.

                            ≈   ≈   ≈

You might call it beginner's luck but our beaver-trapping in the general vicinity of the fort was successful beyond all reasonable expectations, thanks to the teachings of Ned and Hamish Davidson and sometimes Andrew Henry himself. Even Paddy McBride was soon bringing in his fair share of pelts — plews, Hamish and Ned called them, a French word they use for beaver hides in the fur trade — and commenced to whittle down the debt he owed to Ashley & Henry. The fur harvest was so successful, in fact, that each of our trapping expeditions was forced to range farther and farther afield along the cricks and streams that flowed into the Missouri and the Yellowstone.

Matters weren't going nearly so well on the Musselshell, howsomever, and because the fur harvest was petering out where we were, the Major decided to send our crew up there to help out with the trapping before the winter freeze-up. Ned Godey knew that country better than any man amongst us, so Andrew Henry named him to lead our party. Ned was a proper choice for many reasons. If Henry hadn't appointed him, we would have elected him. Ned was an easy boss, a leader not a driver, and most of us had been doing as he said ever since we first got to know him. He knew how to listen and he never let on that he knew it all, but he knew a damnsight more than the rest of us right then.

Packing up wasn't much of a chore. Nobody owned much in the way of plunder anyhow. So early next morning we rode off from the fort and headed up the Missouri to the Musselshell. I reckon the happiest man amongst us was young Jim Bridger, for he had worried that the Major might keep him on at the fort on account of his smithing skills, but the most of that work was already done and Jim was a natural at trapping beaver, as he was with 'most anything he put his hand to, except for reading and writing, which wasn't much called for in our line of work.

Tuttle was astraddle of Amen and leading his bay for a packhorse. I rode Chiksika and used Jake for a packhorse, loading him with my sleep robes and other plunder, which, skimpy as my worldly goods were at the time, didn't overburden him nohow. Most of the others led packhorses or mules toting their own property and supplies that Henry was sending up to Louis Prudhomme's trapping camp. Anse Tolliver rode one of his tall mules and led another, his fiddle strapped on behind his saddle. Ours was a happy company and there was much singing and joking and horseplay along the way, but our rifles were never out of hand's reach — afoot, astride, or asleep — for all of us remembered the Assiniboin horsethieves all too well and nobody was altogether sure that the Absarokas were finished with us yet.

Snow wasn't deep and lightly-loaded as we were, we arrived in camp in the forenoon of the fourth day. Prudhomme was happy to see us, both for the supplies and the extra help, but otherwise there was a dismal feeling about that camp, like smoke where you can't see the fire. Men were quiet, well-nigh sullen. You couldn't put your finger on it, but somehow you knew there was a deal of unhappiness thereabouts. I expected to see Mike Fink, for he could throw a wet blanket with the worst of them, but we learned that he and his mess were trapping elsewhere.

We bedded down for the night around the trade cabin Prudhomme was building and rode out early next day, headed upstream on the Musselshell to a slice of country that Prudhomme said was thus far untouched by his trappers. It took nearly two days of steady riding through heavy forest, but when we got there, we found that he hadn't lied. The harvest thereabouts promised to be even more bountiful than our best days on the Yellowstone. The feeder cricks and brooks were jammed with dams and, from all the sign we could see, swarming with beavers.

Before we commenced trapping, howsomever, we set up a proper camp, for it was plain from all the beaver sign thereabouts that it would take a tidy spell to trap that country dry. Ned passed up several likely spots before he settled on a clearing in a grove of sweet cottonwoods, not far from water, with plenty of deadwood handy for fires. All of us fell to and scraped patches of ground clean of snow and built over them bowers of willow saplings driven into the earth, bent nearly in half and laced together at the top in roughly a three-quarter circle — facing east, for the wind almost always blows from the west up thataway. Then we covered them with swatches of ship's canvas scrounged from the fort, then bark and fir boughs piled atop that. Such a shelter is by no means a mansion, but with a fire burning in front it makes a halfway warm and snug hideaway from the weather.

We ran our traplines early morning and late afternoon, generally in pairs and sometimes three men together, partly for the company but mostly for protection. Three pairs of eyes and ears are more likely to discover what might be hurtful and three guns are a sight better than one if trouble comes calling.

Trouble might arrive from several quarters, mainly Indians out to steal horses and whatever firearms and other plunder they might lay hands on and critters big enough and hungry enough to make a meal off an unwary trapper, such as painters and bears.

Godey told us about the Indians around there. "Hereabouts ye're like to find mostly Rocks, what they call Assiniboins, them as stole the hosses the fust time, an' Crees, too. Crees ain't much diff'rent from Rocks — concernin' white-eyes, that is to say. Neither'n takes a shine to us comin' onto their huntin' land — trespassin's the way they see it — but they won't likely send out no war parties, neither, seein' as how we'll be trappin' fer jist a spell an' then movin' on."

Ned looked thoughtful and then he said, "Reckon I oughta tell about Blackfoots whilst I'm at it. This ain't precisely their country, but Blackfoots kin be 'most anywheres, thievin' hosses, takin' scalps, an' gen'rally makin' a godawful nuisance o' theirse'fs. Keep yore eyes peeled. Blackfoots don't hardly never give you much warnin' ner a second chance."

There was plenty to do when we weren't running our traplines — gathering deadfall for the fires, scraping beaver hides and stretching them on willow hoops to cure, hunting for game enough to feed a dozen always-hungry men, and forever peeling the bark of sweet cottonwoods to feed the horses.

We lived mostly on beaver meat that early winter, cooking it in stews with tender roots and frostbitten berries that Ned told us would keep the scurvy from rotting out our teeth. Now and then somebody would shoot a deer or maybe a wapiti, a tender cow if we got lucky. Once we came upon four bull buffaloes, outcasts from some herd, pawing for grass in the snow and paying us no nevermind whilst we crept in close, downwind, took careful aim, and killed every one with a single volley. We feasted on hump ribs, fleece fat, and tongue that night, but at the last we ate everything off those critters but the beller and the squeal.

Ned showed us, too, how to skin out beaver tails and slice and fry them. Some said it tasted like sowbelly, but I never thought so.

Our main business, howsomever, was trapping beaver and trying to keep warm, forever drying out soaked and frozen leggin's, britchclouts, and moccasins, and gathering enough in the way of vittles to keep body and soul together. We all did a heap of learning, too, not only from Ned Godey but from the Delawares as well, for even though they were strangers in this new land they carried with them plenty of how-to that generations of their people had learned in the eastern forests and passed down to them. Uncle Ben often told me that a good idea don't care where it comes from and I saw no good reason to differ with that notion now.

~ ~ ~

Winter kept on tightening its icy grip on the land until at last it brought the trapping to a halt. Snow was getting deeper and the cricks were frozen nearly solid. Even if we could break through the ice, beaver quit rising to the bait, preferring instead to stay snug and warm in their lodges and live off the bark they had stored there. Game in that neighborhood was scarce as a parson's charity and cottonwood bark for the horses was nearly used up thereabouts. Grandfather Winter owned the country now and he was not a benevolent landlord.

So it was that one morning Ned Godey announced it was time to break camp, saying it was best we return to Prudhomme's headquarters and turn in our plews. He was mindful, too, that there is safety in numbers and Ned said that even though we were a dozen men, the larger camp was a better place to be if a party of Blackfoots came roaming through the neighborhood. None of us except Ned had ever laid eyes on a Blackfoot but nobody differed with his counsel.

It had taken us less than two full days to get to our camp on the upper Musselshell but the trip back stretched into nearly five, afoot and leading our horses loaded with our plews and plunder and taking turns breaking trail through heavy snows, digging out balls of snow and ice that packed into the horses' hoofs, cursing chilblains and chewing the last of our pemmican, huddling around puny fires after dark, peeling cottonwood bark for the horses, and working up our courage to forego the fire's piddling warmth and stretch out on our packs and saddles to snatch sleep enough to renew the strength we needed to keep on slogging through that white wilderness for yet another day.

෨෭   ෨෭   ෨෭

Cookfires twinkling in the twilight beckoned like Circe's sirens. Prudhomme's headquarters camp looked as delightful as Saint Louis to our dozen hungry, exhausted trappers when we stumbled out of the snowy woods and into the firelight. A welcoming shout went up from Prudhomme's men as they straggled out of the bowers that surrounded the rude trading cabin that Prudhomme had completed in our absence. It looked like a mansion to me. A few greeting shots fired in the air brought Louis Prudhomme out of the cabin. Released from the Major's discipline, he had let his beard grow out. Strong white teeth flashed in his sun-browned, wind-weathered face. He wrapped Godey in a bear hug and roared, "*Joyeux Noël, mon vieux!*" Then, beaming at all of us, he thundered, "*Bienvenue, mes amis! C'est la veille de Noël!* 'Ow you say, ze Eve of Chris'mas! All of you are indeed welcome!"

There was no mistaking that Louis Prudhomme had already partaken of a fair share of Christmas cheer, but not a man amongst us could begrudge him that when he in*Vited* us all inside to do likewise. Several men stepped forward to help us unsaddle and drop our heavy packs to the ground, then led our horses off, promising to water and feed them well.

Prudhomme herded us all into the cabin, where a hot fire roared and fairly rattled the mud-and-stone hearth at one end of the big room. Prudhomme's bed and heaps of trade goods piled behind a counter occupied the other end. The simple warmth of that place was nearly as welcome as the generous ration of whiskey that Louis ladled into our cups, but not quite. This time I didn't offer to share mine with Tuttle and I noticed that the Delawares weren't selling off theirs, either. There was an air of gaiety in that room and Prudhomme led the merriment, inspired, I suspected, as much by our successful trapping as by the Christmas spirit. His canny trader's eye could not have missed the size and weight of our bulky packs, which meant a sizeable slice of profit for him.

Soon it seemed that everybody was talking at once, laughing and recounting our adventures upriver, even the most painful of which appeared humorous now — everybody, that is, except for the four Delawares and me. We sprawled on the hard-packed earthen floor, backs propped against the log wall, grateful for the warmth and relishing the creeping fire of raw whiskey in our bellies. Dimly I heard Brass Turtle and Tuttle vying for attention to their whoppers, Prudhomme's hearty bass laughter, and John Smiley's high-pitched cackle, when the thought came to me that if this was Christmas Eve then my December first birthday was already long past. I drained my cup in a silent toast and congratulated myself on surviving this most unusual year of my life, as well as the fact that I was now twenty years of age.

I awoke still slumped against the wall. All of the Delawares were gone and Louis Prudhomme lay snoring on his rumpled bed. The other half-dozen of our crew were flung about the room like so many rag dolls discarded by a careless child, felled in their tracks by John Barleycorn. In the gray early-morning light I made out Jim Bridger, his ruddy features wreathed in a good-natured smile, even in sleep, snoring gently, dreaming perhaps of those longed-for distant mountains, just as I often did.

The heavy door banged open and Brass Turtle and his Delawares trooped inside, stomping snow off their moccasins and joshing one another in their own tongue, their long hair dripping icicles and ruddy skin glowing from their morning bath. I shuddered at the thought and made up my mind, Indian Way or not, that I would pass on such foolishness for the time being and stay dirty.

After the rest of us straggled outdoors and relieved ourselves, we took breakfast with Prudhomme and prepared to settle in for the winter. First off, each of us turned in the plews he had taken and Louis Prudhomme graded them with a practiced eye. Late in the season as our trapping had been, most of our fur rated prime and I recollect thinking that, even at only a dollar a pelt, I could make more money in a day's trapping than I could earn doing farm chores in a month or more back home.

When the counting and grading was finished and Louis had scratched our tallies into his account book, Tuttle spoke up. "Looie, I reckon you won't be mindin' if'n Temple hyar takes a leetle peek at yore ciphers — jest fer makin' sure, don'tcha know."

Prudhomme reddened for an instant, but then he smiled broadly and spun the big ledger around on the counter and shoved it towards me. I could feel myself blushing, too, but I dutifully called out each man's tally, all of which were correct, then returned the book to the trader, who beamed on me and said, "So, M'sieu Bock, you know to read an' to write. P'raps you weel asseest me wiz ze accounts and wiz ze *journal, de temps en temps, n'est-ce pas?*" I blushed again and assured him that I would be happy to help out whenever he wished.

Brass Turtle rescued me from my embarrassment by calling out, "Hey, Godey! We found us a good place to winter up, 'bout a furlong from here, close by water an' thar be firewood an' sweet cottonwood aplenty." Ned smiled approvingly and nodded, as happy as I was to change the subject, and we all filed out of the cabin with Prudhomme's *Joyeux Noël!* ringing in our ears.

We collected our livestock from the various camps and thanked the men who had cared for them overnight, then saddled up, loaded our plunder, and trooped off to Brass Turtle's campsite. It was all that he said it was, near the river, thick with sweet cottonwood for the horses, and plenty of deadfall for fires. We spent that Christmas day preparing to hibernate for what promised to be a long winter. This time, after we built our bowers, we borrowed spades from Prudhomme and dug into the frozen earth a foot or two inside and stacked the soil on the outer wall, which helped keep the cold wind from sneaking in and stealing away the fire's warmth. After that there was little to do besides keeping ourselves and our horses fed, waiting for springtime and the start of a new trapping season.

        ॐ   ॐ   ॐ

You might suppose that passing a long, cold winter, cooped up in such close quarters, would be dull, maybe maddening. It wasn't. Besides hunting for game critters and fetching firewood and gathering roots and berries and such truck, there was plenty to keep a man occupied. For one thing, there was learning the hand-talk. Ned Godey led it off, but it was no time at all before the Delawares picked up the differences between what they knew from home and the way it is done out west.   Then all six of them commenced teaching the rest of us how to talk sign. Jim Bridger, who couldn't read or write, was quickest of all, moving his hands and curling his fingers swiftly and smoothly and even learning naughty, humorous signs that made the Delawares hold their sides with laughter. Paddy McBride, too, was an apt pupil. I reckon he needed so much to talk that any language would do.

John Smiley, Anse, and Tuttle were the slowest, although none of them was what you might call dumb. In time I chalked it up to their breeding, trained as they had been from birth to distrust and despise all things Indian, lest they lose a particle of their fragile pride in being white men. I held my peace, but I silently thanked Ma, and Uncle Ben, too, for steering me away from such foolishness.

Howsomever, after a spell, all three of them joined in and learned with the rest of us. They just about had to do so, for some days nobody spoke hardly a word, except perhaps to explain a new sign, and just sat around making hand-talk.

Naturally there was endless yarning as each man told as much as he chose to reveal of his boyhood, the people he had known, the place where he had grown up, and the stories he had learned there. Paddy often spoke wistfully of Ireland, for time and distance were dimming the hardship he had known in that far-off land, and he told wondrous tales of the Little People, leprechauns he called them, and the treasures and tricks with which they tempted and foiled the greedy. He spoke, too, of ancient Irish warriors and brave and noble kings and sometimes I was able to close my eyes and hear my mother's voice in his.

Naturally we visited men we knew in the other camps and they came to ours, drawn most likely by Anse's fiddle and Turtle's flute.

Little Mountain soon joined in with his own flute and Yves Dureau often came with his little squeezebox concertina to swell the music and the merriment.

Dureau and Jean-Luc L'Archévêque were frequent visitors in our camp that winter, whenever they could get away from the chores they owed Louis Prudhomme. Jean-Luc spoke a little English, very little, and Dureau wanted desperately to learn. I had made up my mind back on the keelboat, and even before that, with Lucette, that I would someday learn to speak French and this appeared to me to be an excellent time to do it. Neither of the *engagés* could read or write, so learning was all by ear, which made it easy for Jim Bridger to join in and learn along with us, which he did at least as well as I, most likely faster and better, for, because I could read, I kept trying to spell French words in my mind, although I had no notion at all how to do it.

Louis Prudhomme helped. From time to time, as he had warned, he called me into his headquarters camp to help him with his accounts and the journal, which he scribbled in French and then explained to me in his haphazard English so that I could write down in English a daily record of what was happening amongst his crew. Little by little those garbled, guttural Frenchified noises jelled into meaningful words and phrases that made sense to me and after a time I was able to make myself understood, not very well, but enough to get by.

Now and again I saw Mike Fink, usually but not always trailed by his pals, strutting around the headquarters camp. He had lost not a jot or tittle of his swagger and his bull-roaring voice was louder than ever. A time or two he came into the cabin to demand some item or favor from Prudhomme whilst I was bent over the ledger or journal, but we exchanged not a word between us. His glare, on the other hand, was as menacing as ever it had been. Each time we met I was glad of the comforting weight of the little pistol in my belt, but I never needed to use it.

≈ ≈ ≈

One morning, a week or two after Christmas, Tuttle awakened me with a shout and a shove, shaking my shoulder and crowing, "Hey thar, Temple Buck! Roust yorese'f outa them robes an' let's be gittin' on! We got ourse'fs some comp'ny!"

I cracked one eye barely open and saw that the buffalo robe flung over his shoulders was dusted with new-fallen snow. Tuttle was fairly dancing with excitement. Still groggy with sleep, I managed to mumble, "Company? Who? What?"

"Dunno, 'zackly. Injuns? Frenchies? Sorta crossed betwixt 'em. They got some queer-lookin' carts an' cattle."

Still not sure what he might be telling me, I was fumbling for my pistol when Ned Godey dodged into the bower and announced, "Métis. Breeds. Cree an' French-Canuck, most likely. Mebbe Scotch. Mebbe both. Likely no harm in 'em, 'less'n ye rile 'em." I saw that he was smiling. Then he said, "Hell, Temple! What're ye waitin' on? Let's go see 'em!"

I snatched up my moccasins drying by the fire, stuffed in some loose buffalo hair, and yanked them on. There was no need to dress, for it was always much too cold to undress. Ned and Tuttle were already outside. I shrugged into my capote, shoved my pistol into my belt, and trotted out to join them, pausing only to rub the sleep out of my eyes with a handful of snow.

We went afoot, floundering through snow that was too deep for horses until we reached headquarters camp, where the ground was pretty well trampled and a clear trail led out to the Missouri. A quarter-mile farther on that trail alongside the river we came upon the camp of the Métis.

It was a wondrous sight. Thirty or forty impossibly high-wheeled carts were drawn into a ragged circle, big buffalo-hide tents stretched off their sides and pegged out to the ground, cookfires burning in front of every one of them, colorfully-dressed women squatting or scurrying about their chores, boys and girls of all sizes running every whichaway, some of them diving over the riverbank and scrambling back up with armloads of driftwood for the fires. Even from a distance we could hear fiddles scraping and bagpipes and musettes tootling lively tunes and see a sizeable herd of horses and oxen along the treeline.

A good half of our trappers had got there ahead of us and were wandering in twos and threes amongst the tents or hunkering down beside cookfires, warming their hands and trying to talk with the women. As we entered the circle of carts and tents I could feel the eyes of the women taking our measure, regarding us with a cool, direct stare, not like the Crow women who had peeked at us when they thought we weren't looking and giggled and glanced away whenever we caught them at it.

By and large these were a handsome people, clear-eyed and self-assured, with a quiet dignity that bespoke hard experience in dealing with whatever came their way, leastaways the ones we had seen so far, which were mostly women and kids. That was my first thought about them and I never after saw any good reason to alter that judgment.

The fiddle music drew us to the carts ranged alongside the riverbank, where I was not surprised to discover Anse Tolliver perched upon a wagon-tongue amidst a gaggle of Métis fiddlers and pipers, actually permitting himself a satisfied smile once in awhile as he scraped in tune with the rest of them. Yves Dureau knelt nearby, coaxing truly astonishing squeaks and groans from his little squeezebox and gabbing away a mile-a-minute, obviously ecstatic to be surrounded by so much music and able to speak French with one and all.

A scraggly-bearded man wearing a tasseled red stocking cap like my own touched my elbow and hooked his thumb towards a nearby cookfire, murmuring, "*Café? Tu es bievenue.*"

I nodded and smiled and managed to mumble, "*Merci*," and walked to the fire, loosing my cup from my belt as I went. A sturdy woman about Ma's age was seated on the far side of the fire. She smiled, showing strong white teeth in a sun-browned face, when I squatted down to dip a cupful of bubbling brown liquid from the iron kettle nested in the coals. She said nothing but waved her hand to show that I was welcome. I grinned and grunted my thanks in return. The coffee, if that is what it was, was delicious, thick enough to be called chewy and flavored with all manner of herbs and spices. No matter what might have been in it, the brew was hot and wet and welcome and I was grateful to hunker down beside the fire, sipping from my cup and watching all that was going on.

The woman clucked to get my attention and handed over a wooden bowl filled with what I took to be bits of bone marrow, breaded and browned to a turn and spiced to a fare-thee-well, a delightful dish for breaking my fast. I smiled in gratitude and she smiled back, saying nothing, just beaming on me, her hands clasped over her belly, rocking contentedly on her heels.

Like I said, those Métis were a handsome lot, neither quite white men nor Indians but a successful mixture of both. There were blue eyes and gray aplenty amongst them, but mostly they were brown-eyed. Their long hair, too, ranged from tawny brown and curly to straight and black and, naturally, gray amongst the older men and women, framing faces weathered brown by sun and wind, and here and there ruddy features that testified to a Scotch or Irish forefather. Swathed as they were in colorful blanket capotes, buffalo coats, and blankets girdled with bright sashes, it was hard to gauge their general build, but they all looked sturdy and lively and brimful of strength. Men and women alike pitched in together to finish setting up camp and tend to chores, unlike what I had seen in the Absaroka camp downriver, where such tasks were left solely to the women.

Two things especially caught my eye. One was the great variety of headgear worn by the men. Besides fur hats and caps of every size, shape, and color, I saw many tasseled woolen caps that the French call a tuque, like the one Lucette had given me, and here and there, in spite of the ear-nipping cold, tam-o'-shanters perched on the heads of men apparently determined to claim heritage from some long-ago but not forgotten Scotch ancestor. The women mainly wore round fur hats or bright-colored turbans.

The other item that claimed my interest was their footwear, bulky moccasins made of thick buffalo hide that reached nearly to the knee and tied snug with thong. They looked to be warm, a lot warmer than my own footgear, and I made up my mind to own a pair of them ere long. Indian Way or not, I hate cold feet.

Red Cap appeared from amidst the scattering of men gathered around the fiddlers and spied me still squatting at his fire, whereupon he half-danced his way across the snow, blear-eyed and grinning and certainly tipsy. When he halted in front of me, he reached inside his capote and hauled out a little stone jug, which he plopped into my lap by way of invitation and which I happily accepted. No sooner had I tipped up the jug and taken a swig, which burned like heavenly fire, than Tuttle showed up, thirsty as usual and anxious to share in this newfound hospitality. Which he proceeded to do repeatedly, as you might expect of Tuttle.

All of us did, including and especially our host. After he departed to refill his jug, Godey approached the fire to warm his hands and inquire what we thought of the Métis so far. Tuttle was quick to voice his approval. "Fust-rate folks they be! Neighborly an' gen'rous an' free with their likker! They got all the Christian virtues what count fer aught!"

I nodded my agreement and then I asked Ned if he thought I could get myself some winter moccasins like the ones the Métis wore. He chuckled and replied, "Course ye kin. An' why d'ye reckon they're bein' so friendly? Tradin's what they like most an' do best. Jist tell 'em what ye be after an' they'll please ye best they kin — fer a share o' yer poke, natcherly."

Tuttle's gaze had been roaming about the camp circle, resting now and then on one female or another. I knew that look all too well by now. Then he asked, "An' wimmen? How they be feelin' 'bout their wimmenfolk?"

Ned caught his drift. "Well now, I'm no judge, but I reckon the womenfolk do much as they please, providin' they ain't married, o' course, an' even then it's anybody's guess, like anyplace. Ye dassn't try to force 'em, mind ye. The menfolk don't tolerate nothin' like that. But if a widder, say, takes a shine to ye, well, it's most likely 'twixt jist you an' her."

The fiddlers had fallen silent, doubtless taking time to wet their whistle, and clumps of Métis sprinkled with our trappers stood around passing jugs and laughing and waiting for the music to commence once more. For all their apparent good nature, they looked to be as tough and warriorlike as any men I had ever seen. Their colorful sashes fairly bristled with knives and pistols and here and there a belt axe. Ned might have read my mind, for he

went on, "Like I tol' ye, don't ye even think o' forcin' none o' the
women here. These hyar breeds be mostly happy-go-lucky, s'long
as ye mind your manners with 'em, but they kin be meaner'n
painter scut if'n they git on the prod. Even Blackfoots steer clear
of 'em if'n they kin an' they mostly end up more'n halfway sorry
when they don't."

"What're they doin' here, Ned?" I asked. "They live around
these parts?"

Godey looked out across the Missouri before he replied. "Naw.
This bunch is jist waitin' fer the river to freeze solid enough to git
their carts acrost. They mostly live in Red River country, north an'
east o' here, up in Gran'father's Land, but they go to tradin' an'
chasin' buffler all over hell's half-acre when the weather's warm.
Thi'shere year ain't been cold enough yet to let 'em git acrost an'
git on home fer wint'rin' up."

I shivered and huddled inside my capote and wondered just how
cold that might be.

Ned stood up to greet Red Cap, who just then came weaving out
of his tent, waving his little jug, his face split in a welcoming grin.
After the jug had made its rounds, Ned and Red Cap exchanged
some words that sounded mostly like French but not altogether,
amongst which I thought I heard all of our names mentioned, but I
couldn't be sure. Then Godey turned to us and said, "Thi'shere's
Belette — means *weasel* in the French lingo. Says he's glad we
come to camp an' do we want'a trade? I tol' him you be takin' a
shine to his moccasins an' he says his daughter's jist the lady kin
fix you up, providin' you got trade plunder fer swappin'."

I allowed that I had some trade goods and when Belette heard
that, he laughed aloud and sent the jug on its rounds again. Then
he led me around to the far side of his high-wheeled cart, where a
second tent was pegged out from its side, a fire burning in front of
the low doorway. Belette crouched down and peered inside, calling
out, "Simone! Simone! *Es-tu là?*"

A mumbled reply issued from the darkness and a moment later
a woman's tousled head appeared in the opening. She was young
enough to be Belette's daughter, as he had said she was, and more
than halfway pretty, leastaways to my way of thinking at the time.

A blush reddened her coppery cheeks when she saw me standing there and she hastened to smooth her hair, then smiled when Belette rattled off a string of words telling her what it was I was after.

She beckoned me to come inside, which I did after partaking of a farewell nip from Belette's jug and thanking him, as best I could, for his kindness. Once my eyes got used to the feeble light inside I saw another small aspen wood fire at the far end of the tent, vented by an open flap in the roof, flanked by a couple of willow backrests next to the back wall that covered the big cart wheel. On one side was a pallet made up of buffalo robes and coverlets of what I took to be soft-tanned wolf and fox and beaver pelts stitched together. On the other was a scattering of Indian-painted rawhide boxes the Frenchies call *parflèches*, a big bundle of tanned furs, and rolls of buckskin, stroud, and buffalo hide, some of it with hair on, some grained clean. It wasn't a mansion, but it was warm. Compared with our damp, dark bower back in camp, it looked like a sultan's palace to me.

Simone, for that was her name, seated herself and drew her legs under her, then motioned for me to step onto a chunk of buffalo hide lying in front of her. She pulled a charred stick out of the fire and swiftly drew the outline of each foot, measured to my knee, and made a couple of quick squiggles on the hide. Then she leaned back on her heels and stared up at me.

It came to me that she expected to commence trading for the moccasins right then and there. It struck me then that I hadn't brought any trade plunder along with me. I was still too shy and uncertain of my French to be using it in real life, so instead I commenced to babble nonsense in English with a French word or two thrown in here and there, backed up with half-remembered hand-talk signs, trying to tell her that I would run back to camp and get my trade plunder and return, but all the while wishing nothing more than that I could kiss those full red lips and fall headlong into her shining deep brown eyes.

After she let me make an utter damned fool of myself, she commenced laughing and waved me towards the doorway, sputtering away in her Frenchified tongue and making hand-signs telling me to go and then return.

I can't say that I exactly hot-footed it back to camp, for the snow was too cold and deep for that, but I made good time. Tuttle and Ned were already in our bower, rummaging through trade goods and palavering like a pair of schoolboys. As I ducked through the doorway, Tuttle looked up and laughed. "'Bout time ye be comin' back, Temple. What kept ye?" He laughed again. "Gotta say, howsomever, ye got yorese'f a spankin' good idee consarnin' them mockersins. Yep, gonna git me some o' them mockersins fer my ownse'f." He cackled once more and cocked his thumb towards Godey. "Ol' Ned here, he's gonna git hisse'f some mockersins, too!"

I started to tell them that I was sure that Simone would be happy to make moccasins for them as well, when Tuttle held up his hand and said, not unkindly, "Hold on thar! We got cobblers of our own, thankee. No need to fret yorese'f nohow, Temple. Jest tend to yore own chores. We be lookin' after our'n."

I reckoned I knew what he was getting at, so I let it be and wished them well. As they left, Tuttle called back, "Wish me a good fit on muh mockersins, Temple!" Which I did.

I had chores of my own to do. After I visited for a spell with Little Mountain, Stone Bird, and Foot, who were keeping an eye on the camp, I led my horses down to the Musselshell, broke through the ice to water them, and filled a kettle with water whilst I was at it. Back at camp I built a fire and put the kettle on to heat whilst I fed the horses a hefty armload each of cottonwood bark from the heap we kept outside the bower, then sorted out some trade plunder — little mirrors, some awls, a butcher knife, a good firesteel, a few strings of blue beads, vermilion, and suchlike — and finally, cold as it was, I shaved my measly beard and scrubbed under my britchclout, just in case.

It was gathering dusk by time I got back to Weasel's camp and scratched on Simone's tent. I heard her call, "*Entrez!*" so I dropped to my knees and crawled inside. She, too, had been busy. One moccasin looked to be half-finished and an iron kettle of stew that she called *ragout* was bubbling on the coals. She had taken time to make herself presentable as well. She was wearing a snug doeskin dress that showed her to be very much a desirable woman and her long dark-brown hair was brushed smooth, spilling over her shoulders and gleaming in the firelight.

I commenced to untie my bundle of trade plunder, but she frowned impatiently and pushed it aside, motioning for me to sit down, which I did. She filled a wooden bowl with steaming, fragrant stew, plopped a buffalo horn spoon into it, and handed it to me, then filled one for herself. I mumbled "*Merci*" and set to with a will. Hungry as I was, it was no time at all until I was scraping the bottom of the bowl and she filled it again. She, too, ate with good appetite, but considerably slower than I, taking time to name in French the things around us, such as *cuiller* for spoon, *bol* for bowl, which was easy, *chaudron* for kettle, and so on, coaxing me to repeat each word and giggling when my tongue fumbled the sound.

By time I finished off my third bowl of her delicious *ragout* we had grown easy in each other's company. Sharing food and the fire's welcome warmth and laughing together at my gibberish had rubbed smooth the brittle edges of our earlier strangeness. Outside a frigid wind howled and tugged at the tent and snow rattled against the buffalo hides billowing with every gust. I shivered at the thought of making my way back to the bower.

When I unrolled my stock of trade plunder she laughed like a child and exclaimed over each item, peering closely at this and hefting that, until she made her choices. Enamored as I was, I never thought of haggling, but she was exceedingly modest in her demands — a couple of steel awls, some beads, a firesteel, and little else — and when she finished deciding, she rolled up the remainder and placed the bundle beside me.

I hated to do it, but at last I reached for my capote, resigned to return to camp, but she frowned, then smiled, then took it from me and tossed it aside. Without rising she caught my arm and tugged me towards her bed. You can safely wager that I didn't hang back. Unequipped with words as the two of us were, there was no opportunity for coquetry, which was just as well, for I had no talent for dealing in such niceties and she apparently felt no need of it.

Underneath her furry coverlets she slipped out of her dress and relieved me of my clothes, letting her fingers stray and linger where they would. Her hands were hard from daily chores but they were gentle and nimble, too, and soon my loins were raging with a welcome fire. I kissed her eyes and mouth and nibbled at her rock-hard nipples and buried my face between her generous breasts, glorying in her musky woman smell and the luscious taste of her. When at last I entered her I knew she was no virgin girl, but she wasn't what you'd call a loose woman, either.

What we had together all that night wasn't love, for we had met only that day and couldn't even speak, but it was more than merely lust, for we shared a common, honest need for warmth and being close that can be known only by a man and woman locked in that tight, penetrating and enveloping embrace. Maybe critters know it, too, and for their sake I hope they do.

ॐ   ॐ   ॐ

I awoke to the aroma of boiling coffee, or what passed for coffee in that Métis camp. No matter how they made it, howsomever, it was a tasty brew. Simone was already at work beside the fire, stitching a moccasin, looking shy and somehow uncertain. That look exploded into hearty laughter when I scrambled naked out of her bed, trotted to the fire, and kissed her soundly on the lips.

By time I returned from outdoors she was frying meat in a spider and chattering French at me as if I could really understand her. After we broke our fast I tried to explain, mostly by signs, that I had work to do, feeding horses and such. She understood and pushed me to the door, making it clear, howsomever, that she wanted me to return.

As I came around the back of the cart I saw Belette, the Weasel, Simone's father, huddled beside his fire. I greeted him but he replied only with a brief smile on his stubbled face and by rubbing a gritty forefinger alongside his bony nose, looking for all the world like the critter whose namesake he was.

The trail back to headquarters was by now well-traveled and trampled mostly smooth both by our visiting trappers and Métis who were toting furs and tanned buffalo robes to trade with Prudhomme. I was trotting past the cabin when Louis Prudhomme spied me and called out, "Bock! I 'ave need of you! Zese Métis, zey bury me wiz zere plew! Come 'elp me wiz ze comptes!"

I told him I would help out with the books after I saw to my horses and such and continued on my way to camp, where all was well. The four Iroquois had moved in next to the Delawares, which was reassuring, for you can count on an Indian over 'most any white man any day to keep a sharp eye out for thieves.

Moreover, ever since our pony raid against the Crows, there was a quiet, friendly understanding and trust amongst those of us who had risked our lives together in that venture.

Jim Bridger was coming up the path when I led my horses to water. His always good-natured face lit up when he saw me and we tarried a spell to chat. I learned that he, too, had been getting measured for moccasins. After we parted and I went on down to the river, I reflected that everybody's humor had improved immensely in the last day or so. The arrival of the Métis had indeed been a blessing.

Matters were somewhat different, howsomever, with Louis Prudhomme. He swung like a pendulum between elation at the unexpected windfall of trade that had come his way and short-tempered exasperation with the horde of Métis and trappers who crowded his counter, clamoring to be served. Trader-like, he loved haggling, but the Métis were easily his match, flint-hard in their dealings and insistent on receiving fair value for their furs and robes. Our trappers, too, were loud in their protests at the outrageous prices he charged them for trade goods they wanted for swapping in the Métis camp, ten times or more the original cost in Saint Louis. Naturally they had to pay his price or do without, but they weren't the least bit shy about voicing their unhappiness when they saw their earnings from the fall hunt melting away in a single day.

That day it came home to me as never before that it is the trader, never the trapper, who makes a fortune in the fur trade. I silently thanked Tuttle Thompson for his foresight, accidental though it likely was, in convincing me to buy a passel of trade plunder in Saint Louis before our departure.

I learned, too, more than I had even guessed about the furs of the Upper Missouri. Louis judged and graded each pelt, then called out the name of the critter and what he was trading for it, whilst I scribbled what he said in the ledger. The counter overflowed with tanned buffalo robes, otter, marten, mink, wolfskins, the little prairie wolves he sometimes called *loups de prairie*, other times, *coyotes*, skunk, muskrat, big white flat-footed rabbit skins, white weasels he called *hermine*, and a few beaver, although the Métis didn't appear inclined to trap beaver as much as other furs.

I also recorded debits against each trapper's account when they bought trade goods from Prudhomme. At day's end, when the cabin was nearly empty, curiosity got the best of me and I flipped through the ledger to the pages where the accounts of Mike Fink, Talbot, and Carpenter were recorded. From the look of it, you'd suppose all three Ohio River bullies were far and away the best trappers in the outfit. Their tallies were almost twice as great as anybody else's, even more than the most successful trappers amongst my own crew. I reckon I knew right then what caused the rest of Prudhomme's men to be so sullen. Fink and his pals certainly weren't above robbing another man's traps and then daring him to do something about it.

If the matter was that plain to me, who knew practically nothing of the workings of the fur trade, then such a thing could not go unnoticed by Prudhomme, shrewd and experienced as he was. Howsomever, from where he stood, it was his job to gather plews for Ashley & Henry and it mattered little to him who got paid for them. Then, too, he was only one man pitted against three touchy powder kegs and maybe a couple more besides, with nobody to back him up. Louis Prudhomme was a good trader and mostly sweet-tempered to boot, but he was no martyr and no leader of men.

Whilst I was at it, I looked up the work rosters of trappers assigned to winter chores such as building the cabin and the fur press, baling plews, guarding the fur shed, and suchlike. Fink, Carpenter, and Talbot were not amongst them and neither was Hugh Glass. Somehow I was not surprised.

When I was looking at their accounts, I saw that all three bullies had instructed Ashley & Henry to deposit their earnings with Pierre Chouteau in Saint Louis, just as Tuttle and I had. That was reassuring, for it reminded me that as much as Fink hated Chouteau for depriving him of his keelboat, he nevertheless trusted him with his money.

After I watered and fed my horses I trotted back to the Missouri, thoughts of Simone hastening my steps. Our own camps were quiet and well-nigh deserted as I passed by. Only a few men remained to stand watch against thieving. The Métis camp, on the other hand, fairly buzzed with music and laughter and songs roared out in raucous French and Scotch-flavored English. Fires blazed high, sending showers of sparks skyward whenever still another stout log was thrown onto the embers for light and warmth. At the far end of camp, half a dozen fiddlers, musettes and Scotch and Irish bagpipes, flutes, and a drum or two scraped and tootled and whistled and pounded out wild melodies, whilst tipsy trappers and Métis men and women cavorted around huge bonfires.

The Métis don't dance the way Indians do. They jig, alone or in pairs or in something like quadrilles. That night the crown prince of them all was Paddy McBride, leaping high in the air and kicking his heels over his head, his stocky little body fluid and flowing wherever the music might lead him, spurred on by the cheers of admiring Métis and trappers, too. Whenever exhaustion forced Paddy to halt to catch his breath, a pretty little dark-eyed Métisse, caught up in his enthusiasm, would hug him and plant ardent kisses on his flushed and sweating face. I had no doubt that

Paddy, too, would be measured for moccasins before that night was over.

A plucking at my sleeve caused me to turn and face Belette, the Weasel, his inevitable stone jug extended towards me, inviting me to drink. Which I did, naturally. Then he proceeded to insinuate in a whining voice that it was only fair that I reward him for introducing me to Simone, which stung me, not because of the pitiful mite of plunder that would have satisfied him, but rather for his willingness to stamp his own daughter a common whore.

I was trying to marshal my smattering of French into a suitable reply when I felt a firm grip on my elbow, pulling me away. It was Simone, eyes flashing, sputtering a fusillade of angry words at her father, who positively cowered in the face of her attack. I didn't resist and she led me off to her tent, still growling her displeasure at his actions.

Inside, she pushed me down against a backrest, then rummaged in one of her *parflèche* boxes until she found the trade goods I had swapped with her the night before. She threw those things at my feet and launched once again into a torrent of denunciation, the most polite words in which were *canaille, cochon,* and *maquereau.* At first I thought she was calling me a rascal and a pig, a pimp and a passel of other Frenchified unpleasantnesses, but then I realized it was Belette, not me, who was the object of her ire. You may wonder how I could understand what she said, feeble as my French was at the time, but anybody who ever picked up a language by ear knows the cusswords come first.

I rose to my feet and embraced her, mumbling nonsense the while. Ere long her anger dissolved into hot tears and at last she kissed me hard on the lips, shoved me back to my seat, and commenced ladling out our supper, another tasty *ragout* thick with meat and parched corn and I don't know what else. My appetite has never needed encouragement and it wasn't long before Simone was grinning her satisfaction at my compliments on her cooking. After supper she presented me with my new moccasins, really more like boots, sturdy and warm, an excellent fit, and beautifully made. I kissed her then, returned her trade goods and added still more, daring her to object. Which she didn't, for the Métis are a practical people.

I have heard it said that a new language is best learned in the dark and so it was with Simone and me. Lying there in her bed under the soft quilted furs, that night and many more thereafter, murmuring loving nonsense to each other, I reckon I learned to speak common French faster and certainly more pleasantly than ever I learned my native tongue. She taught me, too, to use the word *Mih-chif* instead of Métis when I spoke of her people, explaining, mostly by sign, that Métis are any people of mixed Indian blood, no matter where they live, but that her people from Grandfather's Land are properly called *Mih-chif.*

It wasn't long before 'most all of our trappers were sporting new winter moccasins, some of them bragging on how they got measured, others just pleased to be enjoying warm feet, no matter the cost. We were all pretty green, that first winter on the High Missouri, and nobody had come prepared for the bitter cold that hangs on for months in those parts.

Most of our weather came out of the southwest, bringing snow aplenty and cold, too, but nothing like the bone-breaking chill we learned to hate when the wind swung northwest one night and slammed us with Grandfather Winter's icy fist. Trappers huddled inside makeshift dugout shelters or scurried to whatever Métis tents where they might be welcome. Tree limbs popped and tempers grew short because of the cold and the idleness it enforced. Fights broke out and knives came into play when Métis men objected to some of our trappers making rude overtures to their wives and young daughters. Nobody got killed but our men soon learned to treat the *Mih-chif* at least as equals.

Every day you could see *Mih-chif* men out on the frozen Missouri, testing the ice to see if it were thick enough yet to support their carts and livestock, then returning glum-faced to report that it was still not ready.

Game was scarce as a preacher's pity and we were hard-put to keep body and soul together. One morning Fortune smiled when Tuttle and I came upon a cow elk and her yearling youngster about a mile outside of camp. We shot them both and I went back to get horses to haul in the meat. By time I returned, Tuttle had shot three wolves out of a pack that refused to back off. They hung out near the timber, snarling and glaring, fidgeting to get at the carcasses. We shot a couple more before the rest of the pack finally slunk away. Naturally we took the wolves for meat, too.

Later that day I dragged a hindquarter off the cow and the five wolfskins over to Simone's tent. She called in Maman and Belette and I rustled up Ned and Tuttle. They fetched their lady friends along and we had a grand feast, well-lubricated by the Weasel's apparently bottomless jug. Cold as it was, nobody went home that night. They just slept where they fell, spooned in pairs for warmth, most of them snoring, until morning.

Keeping our horses fed, peeling cottonwood bark, was well-nigh a day-long chore, when I wasn't called to headquarters to help Prudhomme with his books and journal. Men took to hanging about the cabin, inventing excuses to get inside for a few minutes' warmth. Mike Fink was often there, loud-mouthed and foul-talking, declaring that he had a right to be anyplace he damn well pleased. Louis Prudhomme never challenged him and although I wished that he would, I really couldn't blame him.

Word was that Fink and Carpenter had had a falling-out over a woman. From the gossip that came my way, I gathered that Fink had been entertaining a woman of his own until he abused her so badly that she ran back to the *Mih-chif* camp screaming and swearing that he meant to kill her, which I had no doubt he might have done, given time enough.

Now Fink had always been cock o' the walk amongst his pals, so it appeared to him that it was only right and proper that Carpenter would just naturally hand his own woman over to Fink, but Carpenter balked. Perhaps it was the long, cold nights and the thought of sleeping alone, the equality and independence that beaver-trapping fosters, the general idleness, or the lack of a keelboat holding them together, but whatever it was, Carpenter refused to give her up and went so far as to move out and build a shelter of his own. Fink was fit to be tied. Trappers in nearby camps heard them wrangling and roaring and cussing at each other, mostly Fink, for he was forever running loose at the mouth, but it ended with Mike Fink sleeping single in his robes.

Talbot wasn't mixed up in it. He didn't have a woman, nor did he ever appear to want one, as I recalled from the Ohio, but it was safe to wager that whatever sympathies he harbored in his cold, black heart belonged to Carpenter, whom he always followed around like a faithful hound dog.

Matters came to a head one cold January morning. The wind had died and sunshine glistened on the snow outside. I was busy at the books, keeping half an eye on Talbot, who was waiting for Carpenter to finish haggling over trade goods with Prudhomme, when Mike Fink swaggered into the cabin and yelled, "Hey, Carp! It's past time we bury the goddamn hatchet. Life's too short fer all o' this! Time we be frien's agin!"

Carpenter swung about, a puzzled look on his face, then halfway grinned when he saw Fink brandishing a whiskey jug. Fink allowed himself a thin-lipped smile and said in a loud voice, "C'mon over here, Carp, me ol' river chum! Sit yerself down! It be time we bury our quar'l an' seal our frien'ship wid a draught o' good whuskey!" Then he plopped down on one of the rude benches that flanked a splintery deal table.

Carpenter hesitated a mite, then, drawn perhaps by the whiskey or perhaps a wish to compose their differences, or maybe simple curiosity, he strode to the table, untying his cup from his belt as he went, and sat down opposite Fink, who sloshed whiskey into both their cups and proposed a toast. His raspy voice fairly shook the walls. "Drink up, Carp ol' chum! We'll drink to the River an' ol' frien'ships, what're best! An' to hell wid wimming what prises good frien's asunder!"

They drained their cups at a single draught and Fink was quick to refill them. They drank more slowly then, talking in low tones and chuckling once in awhile — over some remembered villainy they had shared, I daresay.

Both their faces were flushed with the whiskey and the warmth of the cabin and they were well into their fourth cup when Fink skidded his bench back from the table and bellowed, "By God, Carp, it's good as gold, us bein' frien's agin! Tell ye what! What'say we play our game agin? We ain't done it fer ever so long! Let's you'n me show these here greenhorns what proper Pennsylvaney shootin's all about!"

Carpenter's grin vanished and his face wiped into a mask. He spoke not a word but merely nodded his assent and rose from his seat at the table. Talbot had been leaning against the wall near the counter all the while and Carpenter went to him. They spoke in low tones for a spell, then Carpenter picked up his rifle and walked outdoors, where Fink awaited him.

Word of the contest spread through camp like a house afire. Men came trotting into the clearing in front of the cabin, eager to witness the marksmanship of Carpenter and Mike Fink, whose repute stretched from Saint Louis to Pittsburgh and beyond.

Our whole camp straggled up, Tuttle and Ned and John Smiley the first of our bunch, Bridger and Anse and Paddy not far behind, with Brass Turtle and all but one of our Indians bringing up the rear. Trappers streamed in from all the camps and a scattering of Métis drifted in. Soon most of the brigade, nigh a double score of men, gathered in a ragged circle around Fink and Carpenter.

Anxious as they were to see the spectacle, a curious hush hung over that crowd, like as if they already knew that this would be no ordinary shooting match.

Louis Prudhomme, struggling into his capote, a troubled look on his face and clucking his displeasure, hurried out of the cabin and joined our crew. We were standing just behind Carpenter, close enough to hear Fink say, "Well now, ol' chum, let's sky a copper an' see who'll be goin' first."

Carpenter spoke no words. He merely nodded and stepped back to watch Fink flip the big English penny high in the air, calling out "Tails!" as it fell to the ground and buried itself in the snow. Fink stooped to brush away the snow and when the coin lay exposed, he called out, "Tails it is, Carp! Looks like ye'll be first to hold the cup!" Then he deftly snatched up the coin and dropped it into his pouch.

Carpenter's expression never changed. He turned to Talbot at his side and said in a voice loud enough for us to hear, "The sonofabitch has gone an' got me now, but I'm damned if I give 'im the satisfaction o' seein' me crawfish!" He passed his rifle to Talbot, then his pistol and powderhorn, and finally his belt and pouches. Then he reached under his shirt and unbuckled what I took to be a money belt. Talbot's hands were full by now, so Carpenter dropped the money belt at his feet. It looked heavy and I heard a dull clink as it struck the hard-packed snow.

Then Carpenter looked past me to Louis Prudhomme and said in a level tone, "I'm leavin' all of it, the whole shootin'-match, to Talbot here — plunder, earnin's, the lot. Unnerstan'?" Prudhomme nodded and Carpenter, without so much as a final handshake with Talbot, turned on his heel and strode to where Mike Fink was loading his rifle and picking his flint, the whiskey jug and a cup in the snow beside him.

Carpenter filled the cup and, never uttering a word that we could hear, walked out with his wide-legged sailor's stride sixty paces, placed the whiskey cup on his bare head, and turned to face Mike Fink. He stood tall and erect and absolutely calm. His face could have been carved from marble or the toughest hickory, for all the emotion that it betrayed.

Fink swung his rifle up and took a bead, then lowered it and, with a broad grin splitting his face, yelled to Carpenter,

"Hold yer noddle steady, Carp, an' don't ye be spillin' the whuskey! I'll be wantin' a dram presently!" Then he brought his rifle up once more, cocking as he swung, and fired.

The ball hit Carpenter squarely in the forehead, an inch and a half above his eyes, bowling him backwards to lie full length, unmoving, in the snow.

Mike Fink set the butt of his rifle on the ground and coolly blew the smoke out of the barrel, never taking his eyes off the body of his longtime friend the while. Then, reaching for his powderhorn, he bellowed, "Goddammit, Carp, ye went an' spilt the goddamn whuskey!"

Shock faded from the crowd and a chorus of voices commenced yelling that Carpenter was dead, that Fink had killed his friend.

Fink's expression grew stern and he raised his voice to declare, "It's all a mistake! A goddamn mistake! I took as fine a bead on the nick in that cup as ever I took on a red squir'l's eye!" He kicked at his rifle and cursed it and the lop-sided bullet and, at length, himself. Hardly anybody was convinced but nobody was inclined to question what he said.

Fink guzzled a deep swig from his jug and passed it to Hugh Glass, hovering at his shoulder. They traded the jug a time or two, then hiked off in the direction of their camp, whilst Smiley and Tuttle and I helped Talbot carry Carpenter's body to the fur shed, where it remained until the earth thawed enough to bury it. Talbot never said thankee but nobody was surprised.

As we hiked back to camp, John Smiley pronounced in his preacher-like way, "The wages of sin is death."

Tuttle was quick to reply. "Yep. An' the Almighty was more'n a trifle tardy payin' up what He owed! Them wages was long overdue!" He cleared his throat and spat. "An' if I'd'a had muh druthers, they'd'a both of 'em put a cup on their noggins an' they'd'a both of 'em blowed t'other'n to Kingdom Come!"

Try as I might, I could find no fault with Tuttle's solution to a long-standing problem.

Brass Turtle had fallen in with us on the way. Now he asked why we had bothered to help Talbot tote Carpenter's body to the fur shed. Tuttle jumped in first, grinning as he drawled out, "Well, naow thet ye're askin', Turtle, I jest wanted to make damn sure thet goddamn mis'able sumbitch was really an' truly dead!"

Turtle grinned his approval, then he sobered. "'Pears ye'll be gittin' your wish, Tuttle. This early mornin', Foot seen two o' them big black birds — ravens, ye call 'em — walkin' on the snow, headin' fer the camp where them rowdies're holed up. One of 'em flew over the camp. T'other'n jest kept on walkin'. 'Tain't over with yet."

ช   ช   ช

Next morning I discovered a bloodstain on one of my new moccasins, where blood had dripped from the fist-sized hole in the back of Carpenter's head when we toted him off to the fur shed. I sat quietly on Simone's pallet, staring at the dried blood, remembering Carpenter's harsh treatment of all who came near him and the unwavering loyalty he had always rendered to Mike Fink. I was still appalled, in spite of every evil thing

I knew about Carpenter, at Fink's almost casual execution of the only friend he had, for Talbot was, as you might say, no more than Fink's friend once removed. Talbot had been devoted only to Carpenter, not directly to Mike Fink.

Simone, too, was quiet that morning. We sipped our coffee in silence and when I rose to return to camp, she pulled me close and kissed my eyes, but she said nothing. There was nothing to be said, for even I couldn't be sure of what I was feeling.

It was almost a relief when Louis Prudhomme called me to come help him with accounts that day. The hubbub of business at the counter was a welcome distraction, although our trappers talked of little else besides the shooting, making sure beforehand that neither Talbot nor Fink was within earshot.

Talbot was rarely seen outside his camp. Word was that he had moved into Carpenter's shelter and sent the woman back to her people. Fink, on the other hand, was more visible than ever, bragging and swearing and pushing men around, proving that he was still boss alligator, as he was fond of referring to himself.

I recall thinking at the time, howsomever, that Mike Fink had shot a leg off his three-legged stool of power — most likely two legs. Hugh Glass and John Fitzgerald were no proper candidates to replace Carpenter and Talbot. Glass was totally ungovernable, obeying orders from no one, not even the Major. Fitzgerald was too self-concerned to be anybody's true disciple and was likely a coward to boot. Still, there is always a ready supply of toadies for every schoolyard bully and Fink made the most of his authority amongst such men.

Whatever shock there was wore off soon enough and I became occupied once more with Simone and little else, each day savoring memories of the night before and eagerly anticipating the night to come. Our love-making became even more intense, if that were possible, for we knew that it must end when the Missouri froze solid enough to permit the *Mih-chif* to travel homeward. She pleaded with me to come with them, but although my words nigh choked me, I refused and tried to explain that I must get to the mountains. Maybe someday, but not before I saw the mountains.

When I wasn't with Simone or doing horse chores or hunting game with Tuttle or Ned or Bridger, I was usually scribbling accounts or journal entries for Prudhomme. There was leisure time for reading, too, and, in time, Homer's heroes and villains became as familiar to me as most of our trappers were.

Louis encouraged my reading when there was nothing else to do. One day he presented me with a little book called *Candide*, written by some Frenchman named Voltaire. I was purely baffled by the spelling, all those unsuspected letters in words I thought I already knew. Simone was no help, for she could neither read nor write, and neither could Dureau nor L'Archévêque. Prudhomme was some help, but not much, and it was years before I got through it all. Howsomever I kept the book anyway.

&ebp;   &ebp;   &ebp;

A week or so after the shooting, Talbot came to the cabin. That week had exacted a terrible toll on him. He had shed more than a few pounds from his already lean frame and his bright blue eyes glittered as if with fever. His short hair was neatly brushed but a scraggly beard cluttered his customarily clean-shaven face. His firm, deliberate stride was unchanged, howsomever, and his features betrayed no feeling of any kind, nor did his high-pitched voice when he called Prudhomme to the counter.

Ordinarily Louis was what you might call languid in responding to trappers' requests for service, but that time he fairly bustled about in search of what Talbot asked for — a block of tea, a pound of gunpowder, a galena pig, some English flints, and not much else. After he called out to me the items and the charges to be entered in the ledger, Louis did a most unusual and completely uncharacteristic thing, for him. He offered Talbot a cup of coffee from the kettle he always kept on the hearth. And, surprisingly enough for anybody who knew him, Talbot accepted. Prudhomme filled his cup and Talbot seated himself, facing the door, along with some other trappers, at the table that stood in the middle of the room.

It wasn't but a couple-three minutes until Mike Fink slammed open the heavy slab door and burst into the room, red-faced from the cold, a hard smile pasted across his features. He stomped across the earthen floor and casually brushed the other trappers away from the table like so many pesky flies, leaned his rifle against the bench beside him, then sat himself down across from Talbot and hauled his whiskey jug from inside his capote. He undid his cup from his belt and poured it full, then thumped the jug onto the table and said in a loud voice, "T'row that swill out, Talbot, an' let's me'n you have ourselfs a real drink! Fer ol' times an' more o' the same! An' fer lettin' bygones be bygones! Whaddaye say?"

Talbot hardly moved and he neither spoke nor changed expression. He simply laid his palm across his cup and continued to stare at Fink. Silence was a thing that Fink could not abide. It was alien to his nature. Talking was as essential to him as breathing and violent action. He drained his whiskey in a single swallow, nigh choking in his haste and gathering rage, and splashed his cup full again. His red face grew even more flushed and he exploded. "What the hell d'ye want from me? It were a, uh, accident, goddammit! Ever'body saw it! You was there! 'Twas bitter cold an' I flubbed the goddamn shot! Whaddaye askin' o' me?"

Talbot made no reply. He merely maintained his steely staring into Mike Fink's eyes, his face a stern mask, showing not a flicker of what he might be thinking.

From where I perched behind the trade counter I was able to watch both their faces, meanwhile keeping my hand on the butt of the little pistol in my belt. Prudhomme came over to stand beside me, convinced, even as I was, that something serious was building. Trappers who had been loitering behind the two men, likely hoping at first to be in*Vit*ed for a drink, shuffled to the far end of the cabin. Most of them slipped out the door.

Silence hung like funeral crape between those two strong men who faced each other across that rough-hewn table. Neither man spoke for at least a full minute. Such restraint must have cost Mike Fink a supreme effort. Talbot remained coldly serene.

Fink erupted at last. His round blue eyes bugged and the cords in his muscular neck stood out like hawsers straining at a dock. Spittle gathered on his lips and sprayed foam when he bellowed, "An' who the hell d'ye think ye be? Sittin' judgment on the likes o' me! You, Calvin Talbot, what done as much sinnin' as I ever done! An' now ye won't drink wid me?" Fink paused and took a deep draught directly from the jug. It seemed to calm him somewhat. When he spoke again his voice was mean and deadly. "So, now! Ye're judge an' jury, too, are ye? Judgin o' Mike Fink, what's been like father an' mother to the both o' ye! Seein ye t'rough the thick an' the thin! An' now ye're sayin' I kilt yer goddamn fancy-boy a-purpose? That it?"

Talbot spoke at last, his reedy voice level, cold as ice. "I been sayin' nuthin', Mike. Did ye?"

Fink spilled more whiskey into his cup and drained it at a gulp. He slammed down the cup and laid his palms flat on the table, shoulders hunched, his china-blue eyes hard as agate, slitted to slivers, looking for all the world like a painter crouched to spring. When he spoke, his voice was a snarl. "I be Mike-ye-goddamn-betcha-Fink an' I do what I goddamn please! Ain't no man kin say me nay! Not Carpenter! Not you, neither!"

Talbot sat up straighter now, letting his capote fall open, saying nothing, waiting for Fink to go on.

Fink got caught up in his own speechifying, like he usually did. "Don't ye s'pose ye kin be sittin' there, Calvin Talbot, lookin' parson-pious, givin' Mike Fink the fish-eye an' judgin' yer betters! I done what I done an' I kiss no man's arse fer aught I ever done!"

Talbot spoke again, a bare tremble in his voice, "Like I asked ye before, Mike Fink. Did ye kill Carpenter a-purpose?" He swallowed hard and added, "On account o' the woman?"

Fink grinned like Satan coming out of Hell. "Ye're goddamn right I done it! Shot 'im clean through the noddle, I did! Ain't no man kin cross Mike Fink an' live to tell it, goddamn it! Shot yer bloody sodomite clean outa yer bunk, I did, Calvin-fancy-boy-Talbot, an' I be goddamn glad I done what I done!"

Talbot's thumb was already cocking the pistol as he drew it smoothly out from the folds of his capote. He swung the muzzle a mite left of Fink's breastbone and dropped the hammer. The explosion was ear-splitting inside that little cabin. Through the billowing smoke I saw Mike Fink flung backwards, the bench tumbling over with him, his rifle clattering to the floor. I daresay he was dead before he hit the ground.

Talbot's face was blank. Only his eyes moved, resting first on Fink, then darting about the cabin to the rest of us, then returning to Fink, who lay unmoving. Talbot blew smoke out of the barrel and casually reloaded and primed his pistol, the only sound in the room the clink of the ramrod as he tamped home the charge. When he stood up, the few remaining trappers jostled one another getting out the door. Prudhomme and I were nailed behind the counter. Talbot stepped around the table, leaned over Fink, unbuckled his belt, and tossed it — knives, possibles, pouches and all — onto Fink's rifle. He rummaged under Fink's shirt, pulled out a money belt, and slung it over his shoulder. Then he gathered up all the hardware, retrieved his own rifle from where it stood against the wall, and walked out without a word or even a glance at Louis and me.

Prudhomme breathed a fervent *"Sacré merde!"* and I could think of nothing to add. That said it all.

I wondered if old Foot's raven had quit walking and taken wing that morning. I reckoned it had.

Mike Fink's death caused a ripple of excitement in camp, but that didn't last long. Most trappers agreed with what Brass Turtle had to say after Talbot did for all of us the only favor he likely ever did for anybody. A bunch of us gathered in our bower afterwards, chewing the fat about the killing, when Turtle blew out a cloud of smoke and summed it all up. "Times change an' circumstances alter cases. This ain't the Ohio River an' Fink jest couldn't believe it warn't. He wouldn't — mebbe he couldn't — change. He got out o' step with the time an' the place an' the circumstances an' he went an' got his righteous comeuppance. Thi'shere's a whole new job o' work an' there ain't no rules, less'n ye make 'em up yer ownse'f as ye go along."

One of the new rules appeared to be that nobody was inclined to punish Talbot for what would have been called a cold-blooded murder downriver. There was no law on the Upper Missouri and nobody that I knew of wanted any, either. Fink had meant to kill Carpenter, which he did, and Talbot had just naturally killed Fink for doing it. The most of us reckoned it was good riddance to bad rubbish. Besides, Talbot was mean as a grizzly bear, short-tempered and ruthless, with more than enough muscle and gristle to back his play, no matter what Mike Fink might have said about a tender tie between him and Carpenter. From a practical point of view, it was best to let sleeping dogs lie.

Speaking of practicalities, I'll tell what happened right after the killing. As soon as Louis Prudhomme got his breath back after Talbot stalked out of the cabin, he yelled for Dureau and L'Archévêque to drag the body out and stow it in the fur shed alongside Carpenter's corpse. Which they did. Then it wasn't but a quarter-hour before Talbot came striding out of the willows, rifle in hand, face like a storm cloud, heading for the fur shed. He rattled the chain on the door a spell before he busted the lock. Then we heard the door slam open and a moment later the thud of a body being thrown onto the roof. Louis said not a word. I reckon he thought it best to let the matter be.

Next morning Mike Fink was naked as a new-hatched sparrow. Trappers had picked him clean — capote, moccasins, leggin's, the lot. Even his britchclout was gone. He remained pretty much like that on the fur shed roof until spring thaw, except for what ravens and magpies picked off.

❧   ❧   ❧

Matters continued to heat up between Simone and me. She waxed ever more insistent that I come along with the *Mih-chif,* but I dug in my heels just as hard and refused to go. She coaxed me with presents — mittens and leggin's of soft warm stroud, a new britchclout and moccasins, a knitted sash and leg ties, and a couple of butter-soft buffalo robes. I heaped nearly all my trade plunder on her in return, but I couldn't bear to utter the words she wanted most to hear. Much as I cherished her, the Shining Mountains were a lodestone that couldn't be resisted.

One night as we lay naked in her bed, she stroked and kissed the scars on my bear-clawed arm and asked me how I had got them. My French had improved somewhat by then and I told her as best I could the story of the bear and how Powatawa had saved my life and carried me home with him and how I had come to know and love him and his family and the other Shawnees. When my halting words trailed off she remained silent for a spell and then she said how fortunate it was that Powatawa had been standing by, almost as if *le bon Dieu* had meant it so. I allowed that it had indeed been a handy happening, but I wondered to myself where the Almighty had been when I sorely needed Him aboard Fink's keelboat.

She asked me, too, about my family and I told her about Ma and how she had raised me up, forever telling me wondrous tales and teaching me my letters and all, and the quiet love she had always poured out to me. I told her, too, of my growing-up years with Uncle Ben, as well, although I got a lump in my throat when I recalled that final night in Whynot, which I didn't mention. When Simone asked about my father I nearly gagged, but I told her honestly how I felt about Pap, how there was no love lost between us and no regrets at leaving him behind in Ohio.

She was quiet for a long time then and when she spoke at last she said she understood about Pap and me, for she, too, had such a father, which I believed was so, although I held my peace. Then she said it was a pity that Powatawa hadn't been my father instead and I silently agreed once more.

It was a time when she told me it was not proper for us to make love, so that night I just held her close, breathing in her fragrance and glorying in the sleek length and strength of her body next to mine, until we drifted off to sleep, I thinking the while that our quiet talking and just being close to each other was almost as good.

>   >   >

The cold out of the north had never let up and the Missouri was frozen solid as ever it would be. Simone and I knew that our days and nights together were fast dwindling. Then one morning when I returned to the *Mih-chif* camp after chores I discovered that the time had come to say farewell. The whole camp put me in mind of a kicked-over anthill. Women and kids, rosy-cheeked from the cold and shouting and laughing, darted and scurried hither and thither, gathering up their belongings and stowing them in their high-wheeled carts. There was hardly a man left in camp. They were all out hunting, seeking to pile up provisions enough for the journey back to Red River country.

Maman caught me just outside Simone's tent and asked me once again if I would go with them. There was a hint of tears in her eyes and her pretty round face looked troubled when I told her that I couldn't do that, blushing the while and scuffing my toe in the snow like a schoolboy.

Simone must have overheard what I said to her mother, for she never again asked me to come along with her. Instead she hugged me tight and kissed my eyes and mouth — and whenever tears gathered in her eyes, she brushed them away and tried to say some humorous thing to make me laugh.

That night was pretty near sleepless for us, as you might fancy. We didn't talk much, but we didn't need to, for we had said it all before and more talk just causes needless pain.

It was just breaking daylight and I was thinking about getting up and stepping outdoors for a short spell when I heard the first shot, then another. I dived for my rifle and possibles, groping in the darkness for my moccasins and capote, sure that Blackfoots were attacking the camp, when I heard men's voices roaring, "*Bisons! Bisons! Regardez! Nom de Dieu! Une foule de bisons!*" A moment later some of our trappers joined the chorus. "Buffler!

Christamighty, jist look at 'em!   Buffler!   A goddamn river o'
bufflers!"

I yanked on my moccasins and nearly strangled getting into my
capote, then ducked past the tent flap, possibles belt and
powderhorn in hand, dragging my rifle behind me. Outside, half a
hundred men and women, with more still bursting out of their
tents, milled and pointed at a hairy torrent looming out of the
darkness on the far side of the Missouri and shambling across the
river ice, just downstream of camp.   They weren't running, for the
snow was far too deep to let the leaders do more than flounder
through the drifts.   Men were already shooting, kneeling and
taking careful aim with their ancient fusils and rifles, dropping a
buffalo with almost every shot.

I hastened to join them, plodding through deep snow and
regretting that I hadn't taken time to put on my britchclout and
leggin's, but there was no time for such concerns right then.   I
shouldered into line amongst a ragged string of eager, laughing
Mih-chif and as I dusted fresh powder into the pan, I saw out of
the tail of my eye at least a score of trappers streaming out of our
camp, headed for our firing line.

I learned later that at least as many more remained in camp,
shooting buffalo passing through, trying pretty much in vain to
keep that hairy avalanche from crashing through the shelters and
trampling plunder on their journey south.   Happily they missed
our camp, tucked off amidst the cottonwoods as it was.

A light touch on my shoulder made me turn.   Simone was
standing behind me, lips parted in an eager smile, eyes dancing
with excitement.

The mainstream of the herd was some forty yards across and
about that same distance from where we stood or knelt, choosing
cows when we could be halfway certain, aiming carefully for a sure
heart or lung shot, then calmly reloading for another.   There was
little of the excitement of running buffalo in that methodical
slaughter.   It was rather like shooting fish in a barrel.   We were
simply making meat.

Nothing swayed or swerved that woolly horde.   They seemed
unmindful of the blood that spattered the snow, merely swinging

their massive, bearded heads, red eyes glaring, stepping past the carcasses of their fallen comrades and blindly following the leaders into the trees. They could have charged and wiped out all of us assassins in half a minute, if they had taken a mind to, but they didn't. Whilst I was reloading, what I was seeing out there brought to mind an antic thought — the tobacco-spitters gathered around Jacob Staples's stove, how they allowed men like Pap to lead them into all manner of wicked, hurtful foolishness. Such men are no smarter than herd critters. I promised myself that from then on I would do my own thinking, wrong as it might sometimes prove to be. I am not prepared to say whose picture I had in mind when I fired my next shot.

At last the bawling, bellowing procession dwindled and disappeared into the trees. The bloody, trampled snow was littered with a hundred or more huge carcasses, some still trying to heave themselves onto shaky legs, coughing out their life blood, then sagging and collapsing to lie stiff-legged in death.

Simone darted out into the shambles, intent on tying colored rags onto the horns of buffalo that she had seen me shoot, claiming our kills. I trotted after her to help, but when she looked up from her chore she burst out laughing, her eyes riveted upon my mid-section. My capote had fallen open and when I looked down I saw that my manhood had shriveled disgracefully in the cold. She fairly shrieked with laughter and cried out, *"Tom-pool! Tu as l'air d'une jeune fille!"*

I hastily covered myself, all the while insisting that, considerably foreshortened though it was by the temperature, still I didn't look precisely like a young girl! Just the same, I left her to her chores and sprinted back to the tent.

By time I returned Maman and Belette had come to help Simone butcher out our kills. They worked with a will and long-practiced skill, skinning and slicing and spilling the guts out onto the snow, saving out useful innards in a heap, all the while laughing and cracking jokes to one another in a home-grown French patois I still didn't understand. It was too much to hope that my recent embarrassment wasn't being bandied about.

As if to reassure me, when her parents were out of earshot, Simone drew near and whispered in French, "Have not of the fear, Tom-pool. He will return when we have need of him." Then she chuckled wickedly and ran off before I could swat her.

Later I fetched my horses from our camp and we hauled and dragged four quartered-up buffaloes to Belette's camp. My people had killed more than enough for our needs and were already swinging quarters up into the higher limbs of the cottonwoods, out of reach of wolves and other such varmints, by time I got there, so I gave all I had killed to Simone, Maman, and Belette. The Red River country was a long way off and they would need a plenitude of good meat for the journey.

The *Mih-chif* look after their own. Widows and old folks got their fair share of the kill. Nobody ever goes hungry amongst those people if there is food to be had.

By late afternoon the work was pretty much done and the weather suddenly warmed considerably. A chinook wind had come out of the southwest like a blessing, inspiring even higher spirits amongst the Métis and the trappers who swarmed throughout the camp, sharing jugs and kettles with new-found friends grown dear, haggling over last-minute swaps, and a few snatching a final few moments with their departing light-o'-loves.

Bonfires blazed and cookfires glowed, hissing and flaring as great gobbets of buffalo flesh turned on spits in front of nearly every tent and black iron kettles stuffed with tongue bubbled on the coals. Children nattered and chattered and got underfoot, pleading for treats, a sliver of juicy fleece fat or succulent hump or a mouthful of *boudins*, grass-filled buffalo intestine simmered and browned on hot coals and which tastes better than you might think from its description.

Every fiddle in camp was scraping as loud as catgut and horsehair allowed, a grinning Anse Tolliver sawing furiously in their midst, making the most of this final get-together. Jugs passing freely inspired even more merriment and lent more energy to a score or more of men and women jigging like souls possessed in the flickering firelight. To be sure, Paddy McBride was foremost amongst them, kicking his heels high over his head and basking in the loving admiration of his dark-eyed inamorata.

Simone and I sat side by side on a log in a circle of smiling Métis and trappers, all of us gorging on impossibly large chunks of buffalo meat and yards of crispy *boudins*, laughing at jokes I only half-understood but which seemed to me nonetheless hilarious at the time, tipping up a jug whenever one came around, which was often, and putting out of mind for the moment the sure knowledge that this must be our final night together.

Looking around that circle of *Mih-chif* and trappers mixed all together, eyes bright with booze and good-fellowship, cheeks and beards glistening with buffalo fat from the never-ending feast, teeth flashing in the firelight as they laughed at some humorous sally or raised their voices in half-remembered song, joined in their simple humanity, no matter their origin or what they supposed their native blood to be, I couldn't help but recollect the crabby disdain with which Pap and his like-minded cronies regarded all Indians and breeds of any degree. Right then I might have felt sorry for Pap and his kind, but I didn't.

The celebration was still going at a gallop when Simone and I sneaked out of the circle and retired to her tent. I tarried a spell outside for personal business, enjoying the unaccustomed warmth of the chinook and moonlight filtering through the clouds, when Tuttle and Ned appeared out of the darkness and halted to chat. The two of them were more than a mite tipsy and loud in their laments at the departure of the Métis next morning.

At last Tuttle peered at me owlishly and demanded, "Whatcha doin' out'chere, Temple? I'd'a thought ye'd be inside thar afore now, gittin' yore Frenchy larnin' done whilst ye still kin!"

Before I could reply, Ned cut in. "An' how'd'ja know he ain't been?" Ned's tongue was thick but his tone was pleasant. "Ye gotta take a breather once'tawhile if ye're aimin' to run a long race! Ain't it so, Temple?"

I chose to let such talk be, for I knew I couldn't win, and merely grunted amiably. Tuttle giggled and said, "Speakin' o' which, le'ssee if'n we kin larn a word or two our ownse'fs. Time we be gittin' on, Godey. Daylight's comin' 'fore ye know it."

They disappeared into the gloom, weaving uncertainly and joshing each other as they went.

Simone was already snuggled underneath her fur quilts when I entered the tent. Flickering firelight threw dancing shadows on the walls as I shucked off my clothes in a blink and dived in beside her. She shivered at the touch of my icy skin and I daresay she shivered a time or two after that. So did I, but not from the cold. Our frissons were of a warmer kind, as shudders go. It was a night for thrilling and not for French lessons. We practiced what we had learned together until we got it right, reaching near perfection just before the break of day, when the stamping hoofs of horses, bawling oxen, and the creak of ungreased axles signaled the end of our dalliance.

We ate a hasty breakfast of porridge which had been warming on the coals throughout the night, then scurried about the tent, gathering up her belongings, most of them already packed for the journey, and toting her parfleche boxes and bales of cloth and furs out to Belette, who stowed them in the high-wheeled cart. The tents were swiftly struck and rolled, stakes bundled up together, and fires scattered in the snow. Belette and I piled raw buffalo hides atop the load, then quarters of meat, and lashed it all down to the high sides of the cart. Almost before I knew it, the little camp was gone and all stood ready for the journey to *Le Pays de Grandpère*, the Red River country they called Grandfather's Land.

I gave them each a farewell gift — a butcher knife for Belette, red wool and awls and beads for Maman, and a China silk scarf for Simone. Such a soft and flimsy thing was much too fine for me and I knew in my heart that Lucette would approve.

Maman hugged me to her bulging bosom and kissed me through her tears. Even Belette's eyes were wet as he pulled me to his scrawny chest and kissed my cheeks, muttering the while a plenitude of *sacrés* and words I had yet to learn. The *Mih-chif* are a sentimental people, a quality hardly known in the neighborhood of Whynot, Ohio, ever since the Shawnees left.

Simone never cried and she said not a word of farewell, but her dark eyes were brimming as she kissed my eyes and lips, then climbed to the high seat beside Maman. She blew me a final kiss and tossed at my feet a little buckskin bundle, then stared straight ahead and never looked back.

Belette led his brace of oxen, their nostrils spouting steam in the frosty air, straining into the yoke, in a wide arc and joined the procession of squeaking carts that was already making its way across the river, relays of horsemen in the lead, breaking trail through the snow, then up the gentle bank beyond.

I watched them out of sight, straining my eyes into the glistening white landscape, seeking one more glimpse of Simone, until not a creaking axle could be heard and the final straggler disappeared over the snowy bank.

I was suddenly overtaken by an almost desperate urge to leave that empty place strewn with camp trash, discarded moccasins and shattered earthen jugs, charred embers still smoldering in the snow, tender memories, and not a few regrets. I slung Melchior across my back, snatched up Simone's bundle, and trotted back to camp, thinking once again how I was always leaving pieces of myself behind.

❧   ❧   ❧

Winter was harder to bear after the *Mih-chif* departed. Weather was much the same and chores no more nor less demanding, but all of us felt an emptiness at losing the warmth and fellowship of those trail-seasoned wanderers, their women in particular.

I was reminded of Simone every day, for her little buckskin bundle contained a wolf-fur hat that never froze and a roomy shooting bag encrusted with fancy quillwork. Those two useful items never failed to kindle pleasant memories.

When word of the Carpenter-Fink-Talbot matter reached Major Henry on the Yellowstone, he journeyed up to the Musselshell to learn the how and why of it for himself. Louis Prudhomme called me to the cabin to bear witness when the Major showed up, but there was nothing I knew to add to what Louis had already told him. Henry wasn't slow to divine the sense of relief we all felt at the passing of those two bully-boys and he most likely shared that feeling, for I overheard him mention to Prudhomme that it was

Ashley, not he, who had engaged the trio in the first place. His final comment was, "I could've happily killed Fink myself for wrecking my boat." In any case, he let sleeping dogs lie and returned to his fort on the Yellowstone.

I passed more time with Dureau and L'Archévêque, honing my French, and Prudhomme and I hardly spoke English between us if we could help it. Louis helped me, too, to prune out Cree Indian words that Yves and Jean-Luc kept slipping into their French without knowing the difference.

Brass Turtle and Ned kept us at the sign-talk, as well, for it would likely be of more use than French could ever be in dealing with Indians. There was time for reading, too, and Mister Homer's people, Achilles and Hector, Priam and Nestor, Patroclus and Menelaus, became familiar neighbors there alongside the frozen Musselshell.

Days were getting longer. Grandfather Winter loosened his icy grip and his frosty breath now and then mellowed into a warm chinook. Tree branches quit popping from the cold. The little cricks and feeder streams were still frozen, but out on the Missouri ice was breaking up with the ear-splitting crack and rumble of cannonading. Huge chunks piled atop one another, broke loose, and floated downriver like so many enchanted islands.

Back home we always knew that springtime was not far off when crocus flowers poked their heads up through the snow. Signs are somewhat different on the Musselshell. One early morning, right about daybreak, our slumbers were shattered by a gunshot, a painful squeal, the crackle of tree limbs breaking, then a heavy thud just behind our bower. Godey and Tuttle and I fairly flew out of our robes, clawing for our rifles and bowling one another over in our haste to get outside, Ned yelling the while, "Rocks, goddammit! Look to the hosses!"

The three of us tumbled out of the bower and landed in a tangle in the snow, scrambled to our feet, rifles cocked and ready, and looked about for something to shoot at. All we saw at first was Paddy McBride, calmly reloading his musket, a satisfied grin pasted on his homely Irish mug. He uttered not a word, merely winked and jerked his head sidewise. We followed his gaze and saw a huge black bear sprawled at the foot of a big cottonwood, twitching in its final throes, one eye blown clean away where Paddy's ball had ploughed through its skull.

"Faith an' that'ere critter would'a been after eatin' yer supper an' p'raps yersel's if not fer Paddy McBride respondin' to the call o' nature this airly mornin' an' spyin' 'im climbin' up to poach our buffler swingin' in yon tree!" Paddy struggled to appear matter-of-fact but he failed, breaking at last into a loud guffaw and cackling, "But sure now he's after bein' ready to make a supper fer us hisownself!"

After our Delawares and Iroquois, faces grave, with troubled eyes, had smoked and muttered what I took to be prayers over the fallen bear, skinning and butchering took hardly any time at all. The meat was sweet and marbled with fat, a welcome change in our daily fare, but our Indians stuck with buffalo.

Godey dragged the hide and leaking bladder around and through the camp, claiming that such doings marked a territory and would keep other bears away. I don't know if this were so, but we had no more bears in camp that spring. When he finished his chore, Ned declared, "Winter's breakin' up. Bears be quittin' hivernatin'. Rocks an' Crees an' Blackfoots, too, I warrant. They'll soon be prowlin' round fer hosses. Best we double hoss watch, nighttimes, from here on." Which we did.

For several days thereafter John Smiley busied himswelf at his iron kettle, rendering bear fat into grease to keep the damp from soaking through our moccasins. Our Indians wouldn't eat bear meat, but I noticed that they smeared the grease onto their moccasins, just like the rest of us.

᪥   ᪥   ᪥

Springtime is a fickle visitor to that High Missouri country, forever breaking its promises to return, but at last the trees commenced to leaf and bud and cricks and streams shook off their icy shackles. Just the same, many a morning we awoke to behold our camp completely blanketed with snow, until we all despaired of ever seeing spring again.

Howsomever it was time to get to the business that had fetched us there. The shock of splashing into marrow-freezing water was more than somewhat balanced by the thrill of harvesting prime beaver plews thicker than we had ever seen in the fall hunt. Grandfather Winter rewarded our hardships in his house with rich and close-haired beaver fur.

Naturally I quit clerking for Prudhomme. Trapping was my intended trade and I harbored no love for pens and inkpots. I took my pay for my winter work in trade goods, replacing most of what Tuttle and I had happily squandered on the Crows and Métis. What I got for boot was a better grasp of proper French than ever I could have done in camp with Yves and L'Archévêque, or even with Simone. Thereabouts, leastaways for teaching French, Louis Prudhomme was the one-eyed man in the Kingdom of the Blind.

The spring harvest was rich, but soon the branches and ponds in our neighborhood were pretty nigh exhausted. We struck our camp and split into smaller bunches, trapping ever upward on the cricks that feed the Musselshell. We trapped in pairs, one man in the water, busy with his traps, whilst the other stood watch, keeping an eye out for hostile Indians or bears.

Brass Turtle, Ned, and Tuttle and I just naturally fell into a single bunch, trapping together with whoever was ready first in the morning, whilst the other two remained to guard the camp. Then when the first pair returned to warm at the fire and skin and scrape and stretch the morning's catch on willow hoops, the other two rode out to run their own traplines. Most times we rode a-horseback, but sometimes we went afoot, depending on the country, how thick the brush, and how steep the banks down to the beaver ponds. I much preferred to ride, not only for the comfort, but if a horse should chance to catch a whiff of any unfamiliar scent — a painter, bear, or Indian that he doesn't know — he nickers out a warning that could likely save your life.

All in all, it was an easy way of living, for all the ice-cold water and sometimes scanty grub, always moving camp, and never being sure what might be lurking up the trail or just outside of camp. There was time for much palavering, smoking good tobacco, sharing recollections of foolish things we'd seen and done and men

and women we had known, and dreaming of the mountains that we
swore we'd see someday.

Then came the morning when I reckon I did a mite of growing-
up. Ned and Tuttle had ridden off to tend their traps and Brass
Turtle and I were back in camp, the both of us busy skinning out
our catch, a brace of beavers each. We were in high spirits, making
jests and joshing each other, like we mostly did, when Turtle
leaned back on his heels and commenced to hone his skinning
knife, his face gone hard and solemn. When he spoke, his voice
was low and strained. "Hark! Temple, don't ye be lookin' 'round
jest yet, but we got ourse'fs some comp'ny!"

I continued to fiddle with the beaver plew but I was mostly
calculating how to reach my rifle, a full two paces distant, propped
against a fallen tree. Our half-a-dozen horses, picketed at the edge
of camp, commenced to neigh and whinny and haul back on their
ropes, rearing and striking at a shadowy figure flitting amongst
them.

Turtle actually blurred in my sight as he streaked past me,
headed for the horses. I reckoned it was now or never and I dived
for my rifle, but just as I flung myself headlong, the biggest Indian
in the world, at least a dozen feet tall, exploded out of the brush
behind the log and jumped on top of me, knocking me backwards
and pinning me to the ground. His painted cheeks were but an
inch from my eyes. His hot breath nigh burned my lips. He
grunted and raised up, his knife hand cocked, then his breath left
him in a whoosh and he collapsed over me, quivered a mite, and
lay still, heavy as a horse.

I struggled like a snapper turned turtle, arms and legs flailing,
struggling to get out from under the dead weight of that big Indian.
And that's what it was, dead weight, for when I wriggled free at last
and shoved him off onto his back, I saw my skinning knife sunk to
the hilt in his chest. I tried to yank it free, but it was hung up on
bone in there, so I let it be and grabbed up Melchior, thinking the
while how that big Indian had gone and committed suicide and
how it certainly served him right.

I looked for Brass Turtle, but he was nowhere to be seen.

An Indian lay on the ground nigh the horses but it wasn't Turtle and neither was the other Indian who leaped out of the brush just then and sprinted towards the horses. I can't precisely recollect bringing up my rifle and squeezing the trigger, but I do recall the tiniest mite of hangfire, then the charge going off. When the smoke lifted, the Indian was slowly staggering in a circle, like a schoolboy's top running out of spin, then collapsing in a rag-doll sprawl. I was already spilling powder down the bore when I heard a shot from the cottonwood grove behind the horses. I rammed home the ball, scattered priming into the pan, and hot-footed it towards the horses. Before I got there, howsomever, Brass Turtle appeared from amongst the trees, pistol dangling from one hand, a bloody scalp in the other, a wry grin creasing his features.

As I drew near, he shoved his pistol into his belt and stooped beside the Indian who lay near the horses. They had settled down somewhat, reassured no doubt by our presence. Turtle caught the dead man by the hair, pulled out his butcher knife, swiftly drew a circle around the crown, and yanked. The scalp came free with a sucking, liquid plop and Turtle swung it aloft, blood dripping down his arm. His voice was flat, almost toneless, when he spoke. "Thar ye be, ye murd'rin' hossthief! Mebbe now yer frien's won't be so damn set afire to go messin' 'round the likes of us no more!"

I said nothing, merely stared at the body and the deep chop into the liver where Turtle had swiped him with his tomahawk as he flew past to save the horses. I saw then that it was the body of a young man, a boy really, not yet as old as I. Turtle must have read my mind. "Yep, he's a young'un, thet's a fact. But old enough to go hoss-thievin' an' surely old enough to die if'n ye ain't good at it."

We were looking at the body of the Indian I had shot when we heard the pounding of hoofs, Tuttle and Ned come whooping back to camp. I saw that my shot had hit the Indian in the neck and blown out his throat. The silly thought occurred that I must be shooting a trifle high, for I had meant to aim for the big part of his body. Only then did I admit to myself that I had killed this man, a thing I had never done before. Turtle's only comment was, "Right fancy shootin', Temple. Be proud of it." I neglected to mention that I had nearly missed.

Ned and Tuttle roared out of the brush just then, rifles ready in their hands, and reined their horses to a r'aring halt. Tuttle's look of alarm slid into a grin as he swung to the ground and said, "Well naow, lookee hyar, won'tcha! Ain't thet jest like the two o' you? Hoggin' all the en-joys whilst Ned an' me's out workin'!"

Ned stared long and hard at the face of the man I had killed. Then, addressing the corpse, he said, "An' so we meet agin." He turned to us and added, "Thi'shere's one o' them Rocks what took our hosses from Pike an' t'others. Time he got his comeuppance! Who kilt 'im?"

Brass Turtle jerked his chin in my direction and said, "So's the one out thar in the trees an' I wouldn't be a tall bit surrounded if'n t'other'n Temple kilt war amongst 'em, too."

Ned and Tuttle looked surprised when they learned that I had killed not one but two horsethieves, so naturally we had to mosey over to the body that lay behind the fallen tree. Losing all that air so fast must have shrunk that gigantic Indian more than somewhat, for by time we got back to him he wasn't a great deal taller than Tuttle, whose only comment as he surveyed the dead Assiniboin was, "Purty clothes." We all agreed that this one, too, had been in the bunch that robbed us of our horses on the Little Missouri.

Brass Turtle summed up the feelings of us all when he said, "Glad we he'ped 'em break the habit."

Nevertheless I was feeling more than a little shaken, knowing that I had killed two men, leastaways one of them. The first one might be reckoned a suicide. I walked out of camp and hunkered down near the crick, reflecting on how far I had come in the past year, not only in distance I had never even dreamed of traveling, but also how I felt right now and what I was prepared to do if need be. I was wondering what Ma might say about all this, when two bloody scalps landed in my lap, spattering my already bloody shirt. Without even looking up I knew that Brass Turtle stood behind me. He squatted at my side and said, "Git used to it, Temple. Them're your'n. Ye earned 'em. Ain't never gonna be much differ'nt up thisaway. Do what ye must an' don't be slow about it." He let his eyes rest in mine for a spell, then he grunted, rose to his feet, and returned to the fire.

Brass Turtle was practical, if nothing else. So were Ned and Tuttle. By time I returned to the fire, the bodies were stripped naked, their clothes and weapons heaped nearby. Tuttle was already trying on the big fellow's moccasins, chortling about how well they fit, and laying claim to the rest of his clothing. Ned and Turtle had scoured the nearby woods and retrieved the muskets, capotes, and other plunder the horsethieves had cached out there. They took time as well to drag in the body of the Assiniboin Turtle had slain. Now they were sorting all the plunder into heaps according to fit. At first I felt a mite squeamish about wearing a dead man's clothes, but then I recalled how pleased I had been to get Talbot's seedy hand-me-downs aboard the keelboat and I straightway put aside such delicate notions. What we didn't want for ourselves, we kept for trade plunder.

Breaking camp this time was a greater chore than usual. We dumped the bodies into the crick and let them wash downstream, buried the fire, broke down the bower and tossed the boughs and saplings into the brush, raked the campground with branches as best we could, scattered horse manure after we saddled up and packed our plunder onto the spare horses, and said a prayer for snow or rain to cover up or wash away what we couldn't hide.

That afternoon we headed upstream and gathered our traps, then farther up we forded the crick, climbed over a stony ridge, and descended into another little valley. By nightfall we were snug and reasonably safe in a new camp. Somebody's prayers, not likely my own, were answered. It snowed that night, covering our tracks, but just the same, sleeping was fitful and all of us kept a wary eye over our shoulder in the days to come.

≈   ≈   ≈

From time to time, whenever we had harvested a sufficiency of plews, half a bale or so for each of us, the four of us cached our camp, loaded the horses, and rode down to Prudhomme's to turn in our catch and draw supplies, mainly gunpowder and galena, coffee, tea, and sugar. Such visits were good for our spirits, getting in amongst the other men, renewing friendships, and brushing away the cobwebs of irritation that must accumulate amongst a handful of men living cheek by jowl for weeks at a time, no matter how much they might like and trust one another. Each time we made that trip, we returned to our trapping grounds in high spirits, our vigor replenished, happy to be together and back at work once more.

On one such visit in early spring we encountered Andrew Henry, bound upriver with a score of men from the fort on the Yellowstone. The Major was still convinced that a multitude of beaver awaited him in the country around the Great Falls of the Missouri and beyond and nothing else would do but that he proceed there with all possible haste and harvest them. I reckon he had another reason, too, for a dozen years before, Blackfoots had kicked him out of that country. Such memories are bound to rankle until they are laid to rest.

We fell in with his party and rode along with them to Prudhomme's camp, renewing old acquaintance and bragging on our wintertime experience and our mounting tally of beaver plews. Once, when I chanced to be riding nigh the Major, he cocked an appraising eye at me and remarked, "Well now, Temple Buck, it appears ye've wintered well. Ye've taken to the trapper's life, have ye?" I allowed that I had but I said little else. Henry looked thoughtful for a spell and then he asked, "Would ye care to join us on our expedition, Mister Buck?"

A small voice somewheres inside my head told me to say no, which would have been rude, so I simply held my peace and stared straight ahead, avoiding his eyes. Henry didn't ask again. He merely harrumphed, put spurs to his horse, and rode to the head of the column. Naturally he could have ordered me to go along with his party, but that wasn't Andrew Henry's way.

Two days later the Major led his men out of Prudhomme's camp and headed up the Missouri. They were all in high spirits, saddle horses sleek and frisky from a lazy winter, sturdy packhorses and mules laden with provisions, traps, and trade goods, the men happy to be released from winter confinement at the fort, eager to see new country.

We watched the column disappear into the trees alongside the river, some of us envying them their adventure, some not. Brass Turtle, his features solemn, his tone sober, summed up my own feelings when he pronounced, "Grant the Sperrit let's 'em be so gleeful comin' back."

The small voice inside my head nagged for a spell and then it was still. It was not for me to judge such matters.

By time the wapiti were gaining fat, beaver plews were running thin and poor and hardly worth the taking. Snow had long since gone and summer was at hand. At last we quit trapping altogether and passed our days stalking game or dawdling over chores in camp, feasting every night and living lazy, until all four of us were forced to confess it was time to return to Prudhomme's on the Musselshell. It was a hard choice to make, for lax and light as Louis Prudhomme's discipline was wont to be — so long as we fetched him gobs of beaver plews — the utter freedom of our trapping camp was not easily forsaken.

It wasn't but a day or two after we returned to the Musselshell when Jean-Luc came running into camp, shouting, *"Attention! Tout oreilles! Le patron est arrivé! Viens! Viens!"* The Major had returned.

The most of us swung aboard our horses bareback and loped up to the cabin, just in time to witness a bedraggled Andrew Henry and what was left of his men straggle into the clearing that surrounded the cabin. They were a sorry bunch, not so many now, some riding double, some afoot, many wounded men bound with bloodstained rags, arms in slings, all of them haggard, hungry-looking, staring out with vacant eyes. Godey said it all with just a single word. "Blackfoots."

So it was. Henry and his party had hardly arrived at the Great Falls of the Missouri when they were attacked by a huge force of Blackfeet, how many nobody knew for sure. Four men were killed and most of the rest wounded more or less seriously. Several saddle horses and baggage animals were killed or run off by the Indians, as well. Henry had no choice but to retreat downriver. The Blackfeet hung on like cockleburrs, stealing horses by night when they could and sniping from cover by day, until the party dragged itself far enough downstream into Cree country to make the Blackfoots give up their sport, lest their old enemies take sides with the Major and give them a drubbing.

Henry's party rested three days on the Musselshell, letting horses and men regain their strength and treating the wounded, which was most of them. Old Foot and Little Mountain were busy from dawn to dusk and half the night, digging out musket balls, stuffing in spider webs to stanch the blood, cleaning old wounds, and laying on poultices of herbs and such that they gathered thereabouts. Some of the wounded were leery about letting Indians, even our own, tend to them, but their reluctance didn't last for long, for those two redskins were the only surgeons we had — and as it proved out, likely the best to be had anywheres.

Andrew Henry was anxious to get back to his fort on the Yellowstone, so on the fourth day after his arrival on the Musselshell and well before his men had mended, he mounted up his cripples, half of them on fresh horses he took from Prudhomme, and set out downriver. Louis sent our camp of fifteen men along with the Major to look after the wounded and tend to the pack animals loaded with plews harvested by our people in the spring hunt. Our bunch had never quite meshed with Prudhomme's original crew, preferring as we did to stay off by ourselves, so I reckon we were his logical choice.

In spite of the sunny June weather, the trip down to the fort took considerably longer than our trip upriver in the fall. The wounded men tired easily, so we often started late and made camp early each day. It was slow going for the pack animals as well, heavily laden with furs as they were. The rich spring harvest of plews was all that served to lift Henry's spirits. Otherwise he was sunk in gloom, grim-faced and short-tempered, wrapped in his own brooding thoughts.

Our bunch, on the other hand, was enjoying what you might call care-free good humor, sort of a holiday feeling. None of us had got ourselves hurt and the spring hunt had gone even better than in the fall. Even Paddy McBride had got himself out of debt and jumped onto the credit side of the ledger. Horses are quick to divine a rider's temper and ours were frisky and willing, happy, I daresay, to be free of the tether and working every day.

Three or four days along the trail we came upon a small bunch of buffalo and half a dozen of us galloped off to run them. Jim Bridger killed a cow and Tuttle and Brass Turtle each got a young bull. I didn't, but it was all the same to me, for the thrill of the chase, feeling the warm summery wind in my face, and the power of Jake surging betwixt my thighs pumped new vigor into my blood and nigh made me dizzy with delight.

Fresh buffalo meat roasted to a turn is a cure-all for just about any ailment. That night we feasted on hump ribs, hot fleece fat, and tongue aplenty. It was purely magical the way simple gluttony gratified was able to sweep away the pall of ill humor that had hung over the Major's company since their return from the Great Falls. After everybody was stuffed to the gills, Anse Tolliver fetched his fiddle and commenced scraping out merry tunes. It wasn't long before the Major joined in with his own, his grim features softening in the firelight as the music worked its spell. They were still at it when I rolled into my robes and drifted into dreamless sleep.

Next day on the trail, Tuttle and I made out half a dozen Indians a-horseback on a ridge on the far side of the Missouri. I immediately rode back to inform the Major of what we had discovered. Henry studied the Indians through his glass for a spell before he pronounced, "Crees, most likely. Maybe Rocks. Not Blackfeet. They won't likely trouble us, as many as we are." His judgment proved to be correct, for a few minutes later they melted into the brush.

I remained where I was, riding beside him, observing that his craggy face had smoothed out considerably since the day before.

Then, without precisely looking at me, he asked, "Tell me, Buck, what made you decline my invitation to join us on our journey to the Falls?"

His question flustered me more than somewhat, so I had to answer honestly. "Well, sir, I don't rightly know, but somethin' kept tellin' me it wasn't the best thought you ever had."

A wry grin settled on his features and his blue eyes took on a faraway look when he replied, "No, Buck, it wasn't, not by a long shot." He fell silent for a spell, then he said, "I suggest you continue to listen to that something, whatever it is. It might help you keep your hair."

I nodded and held my peace, happy that I hadn't made him angry with my honest reply. I took his advice to heart, howsomever, and from that day forward I have never been sorry that I did.

Chapter VII
Arikaras

Life at the fort was a humdrum affair, except for hunting wapiti and the prairie goats some of the men called antelopes and now and then running buffalo whenever a bunch drifted nigh, but that pleasure didn't last long. We hadn't been at the fort but a week or so when a brace of visitors showed up from downriver.

They were a sorry-looking pair when they rode up to the fort, an American and a French-Canuck, half-starved and tattered, hollow-eyed from exhaustion but quivering with excitement, their horses tottering from short rations and overwork. They demanded to see Andrew Henry. Hamish Davidson conducted them directly to the Major.

We weren't long in our ignorance of who they were and what they were about. The American, who was about my own age, was called Jedediah Smith. Ned Godey knew the other one, a Frenchman name of François Villefranche, a long-time trader for Missouri Fur down along the Platte. General Ashley had sent them up to us, demanding that we send reinforcements in a fight he had got himself into with the Rees, the Arikaras, downriver.

From what we could piece together from gossip that day and in the days thereafter, it appeared that Ashley had failed to heed Andrew Henry's advice from the year before and had gone ahead and traded with the Rees for horses, so that he could send a party overland to the Yellowstone. Matters went well enough for the first couple of days or so. The Rees acted friendly and the General got the mounts he was after. He anchored his two keelboats out in the river, just offshore, and was holding the horses with about forty men, Smith amongst them, camped on the big sandbar in front of the Rees' lower village, when all hell broke loose at daybreak of the third morning. The Rees commenced shooting from every whichaway, from their palisades and all manner of cover on both sides of the river.

Greenhorns in the fur trade though they were at the time, the Americans fought back right smartly. Most of the horses were killed outright. Ashley's men dragged the carcasses together and used them for breastworks, shooting back as best they could but doing little damage to the Rees, dug in and well-prepared as those tricky redskins were. Ashley tried to get his two keelboats into shore so as to get his men out of there, but his Frenchy boatmen said *Merci* but no thankee and refused to get any closer to the shooting. I've noticed that a French-Canuck is long on song but generally short on pluck. By time Ashley got a couple skiffs ashore, his men on the sandbar had got their dander up and declared they wouldn't retreat. Only half a dozen or so men, most of them badly wounded, got off in the skiffs.

Guts alone can't always get the job done. Exposed and shot up as they were, with half their number killed or seriously wounded, the Americans were forced at last to give ground, but the keelboats were still anchored out in the channel and neither skiff was anywhere to be seen. They had to swim for it. Several wounded men drowned. The rest were dragged aboard the keelboats, anchor cables chopped free, and the boats drifted back downriver.

Fourteen men were killed that early morning and half the men who survived were severely wounded. Villefranche said the whole battle lasted but a measly quarter hour.

Ashley put into shore on an island downriver, out of reach of the Rees, and tried to rally his people to try once more to pass the Arikara villages, but the men showed more horse sense than greenhorns customarily do. They told him no, not without considerable reinforcements.

The upshot of it all was that Ashley was forced to retreat even farther down the Missouri, build a temporary fort, load most of his property onto just one keelboat, and get ready to send the other one back to Saint Louis carrying the wounded and a passel of men who had got into more fight than they had belly for, whom I reckon you might call deserters.

Ashley was left with just thirty men out of a hundred or more and five of those were Frenchy *bateliers*. He needed help in a hurry and Henry's men had been elected. Villefranche told us that Ashley was trying to get the Army to help him, too, but at the time he and Smith had ridden out of Ashley's camp, nobody was sure if the soldiers would come to his aid.

Somehow I wasn't much surprised by what they told us.

Andrew Henry wasted no time. Within an hour he despatched Godey and Brass Turtle with orders to Prudhomme to abandon camp on the Musselshell and bring all his trappers to the fort. When Tuttle and I stepped forward and asked to go with them, Henry simply grunted and nodded. We took that for a yes and flew out of his quarters.

We made the journey to the Musselshell in less than two days, riding one horse and leading another, changing back and forth several times a day, munching jerky whilst we rode, snatching sleep only in the time it took to let the horses graze for a spell and restore their legs — and even then two of us stood watch for horsethieves.

Louis Prudhomme bounded into action when he heard our message. He called in his hunters from the prairie and rode around the camp, shouting, "*Allons! Allons! Vite! Vite!* You mus' 'urry, *mes gars!* Come, my lads! Le Major of us 'as need of us! *Tout de suite! Immediatement!*" and other such macaroni.

In less than half a day the Musselshell bunch was saddled up and packed and ready for the trail. It wasn't really much of a chore. Nobody owned much of anything and most of the spring fur catch had already been sent down to the fort. Talbot was the only one who was even slightly burdened. He had inherited all the plunder of both Carpenter and Fink and I reckon he meant to hang onto it. Instead of one packhorse, he led two.

We departed in the early afternoon and rode until dusk, forty-odd men and more than twice that many horses snaking down a trail that ran roughly alongside the bank of the Missouri. Our journey was pleasant enough in the soft summer sunshine, except for swarms of mosquitoes that rose up in clouds out of marshy bottoms nigh the river at our approach, but mosquitoes and such were a common nuisance in those parts and hardly anybody paid them much mind.

Now and again we spied Indians a-horseback keeping an eye on us from the ridges on the far side of river, but they were considerably more than a long rifle shot distant from us. Besides, they didn't appear to be disposed to mess with a party as big as ours.

Talbot mostly rode alone, silent and glum, but such behavior wasn't a great deal different from the old days when Carpenter and Fink were so chummy and Talbot mostly tagged along behind his friend like a devoted dog. Only Hugh Glass attempted to be companionable with him, now and again, when the old scoundrel wasn't straying off on his own, but I never saw Talbot exchange a single word with him.

Each day we quit the trail near dark and rose before daybreak to hurry downriver. Rations were scanty, mostly jerky and pemmican, for there was little time for hunting. Louis Prudhomme was anxious to answer the Major's summons promptly and most of his men appeared to welcome a change of place and routine, no matter what might lie ahead for them. The four of us felt pretty much the same way, for there was talk that after the business with the Rees we would travel to the mountains in time for the fall hunt.

In the forenoon of the fifth day our Musselshell crew straggled into the clearing that surrounded the fort. A glum-faced Andrew Henry, Hamish at his side, greeted our arrival. Men from the fort were bustling about bundling up packs of provisions and beaver plews that Henry meant to take along when we went to Ashley's aid. Looking at that mountain of baggage, I wondered what the Major would have done for transport if our bunch hadn't captured as many Absaroka horses as we did the previous fall.

No time was wasted at the fort. Early next morning Major
Henry's relief column was on its way south and east down the
Missouri and often cross country to assist Ashley's battered little
brigade. An impressive column it was indeed, some threescore
trappers and a packtrain that appeared to stretch back forever.
Except for Hamish Davidson, who was left in charge of the fort
along with the wounded veterans of Henry's venture at the Great
Falls and very few others, no more than a score in all, Henry's
expedition against the Arikaras included nearly every able-bodied
man we had and most of the horses as well, loaded with provisions
and bulging packs of beaver plews.

The first day out was slow, as it always is, with frequent halts to
repack loads and snug up pack ropes and such, but after that,
Andrew Henry set a rapid pace for so large a caravan, pushing men
and critters, and himself as well, to the limit of endurance.
Jedediah Smith mostly rode beside the Major, somehow assuming
rather more authority than you might expect an express messenger
to warrant. He appeared to me to be a trifle forward for one so
young and new to the beaver trade, but I told myself that it made
no nevermind to me. Which it didn't at the time.

Two days before the celebration of American Independence we
arrived at a pitiful collection of log breastworks that Ashley had
ordered his men to throw together some miles below the Arikara
villages. The Rees hadn't bothered to follow up their first attack
and Ashley's two keelboats were still tied up to trees on the shore,
the wounded men strewn about the deck suffering considerably in
the summer heat. The rest of his company were a dispirited lot
when we got there. Their humor improved, howsomever, when our
rowdy crew filed into camp, calling out rude jokes, roaring with
laughter, bells jingling on the pack animals. Some of Ashley's men
fired off their rifles and muskets to signal our arrival. They were
all strangers to me except for Davey Jackson, Ashley's clerk, whom
I recalled from the year before.

It was easy to tell Ashley's people from our own. I wouldn't have thought that a single year on the High Missouri could have altered us so much. Henry's trappers were, by now, lean and rawhide-tough, squinted and browned by sun and wind, long-haired and dressed more like Indians than white men, and even as tattered and tired and dirty as all of us were after nearly a month on the trail, you could see honest pride and a knowledge of self-worth in their bearded and stubbled faces and in the way our men walked and bestrode their horses. Most of Ashley's newcomers were pink and pasty by comparison.

The General wasted no time in getting our furs loaded aboard one of the keelboats and sending it downriver to Saint Louis with the wounded, Jedediah Smith in charge of the cargo. Before its departure, several of our trappers, Tuttle Thompson foremost amongst them, swarmed aboard and proceeded to swap Indian and Métis trinkets, clothing, and suchlike for whatever whiskey the quitters and the wounded men had smuggled up from Saint Louis and hadn't already drunk up. It was only later that I discovered that my trophy hair from Pretty-on-top and my two scalps were missing. I reckon Tuttle guzzled them in good health and with hearty appetite and I never regretted their loss. I still had the memories, for good or ill.

We hung around Ashley's sorry little fort for a couple of weeks, doing little more than providing meat for the company. Then one morning when we returned from hunting, we were met with a scene of confusion that became downright customary in the weeks to come. Word had arrived that soldiers from Fort Atkinson were coming upriver in keelboats to help us punish the Arikaras. This was welcome news indeed, considering that the Rees outnumbered by some ten to one our combined force of about fourscore trappers and were safely forted up inside their palisades to boot.

General Ashley was excited beyond all measure at the news and nothing else would do but to abandon that camp, which was no great loss to anybody, and for all of us to go downriver to meet the soldiers. Ashley sent his remaining keelboat farther downstream and ordered us all into the saddle, mounting the new hands on packhorses that had been relieved of their packs of beaver and loading fresh provisions on the rest. It was all the same to us, for it was summertime and any excitement at all was better than lying around camp waiting for the fall hunt.

We were on the trail by mid-afternoon, traveling at a brisk pace set by General Ashley, who was fairly trembling with anticipation of exacting a just revenge on the Rees. As usually happens on such a journey, I found myself riding in company with various men, first Tuttle and Ned, later with Brass Turtle and his Delawares, and then in the late afternoon with two of the new men who would come to rank amongst my favorites in the fur trade. The older one was Jim Clyman, more than half again my age, a lean six-footer, thin-lipped and narrow-faced, dark brown hair worn long, a quiet man with smoky blue eyes that bespoke thoughtfulness and which missed nothing. The other man was Tom Fitzpatrick, my senior by a couple-three years, an Irishman by the sound of him, shorter than I and wiry. His face was open, somewhat lantern-jawed, with quick, intelligent blue eyes, a shock of curly black hair spilling from under his cap. It was plain to see by the easy way they rode that neither one was a stranger to horses.

Fitzpatrick spoke first. "'Tis a foine animal ye're ridin', lad. Ye must be proud of 'im." I was riding Chiksika and leading Jake, who was packing my plunder and a quarter of elk we had shot that morning. I nodded at the compliment but said nothing, struggling to keep my face straight, much too aware for my own good of my recently-acquired status as a hivernant, that is, a trapper who had wintered on the High Missouri. Fitzpatrick let his eyes stray over both my horses, before he said, "An' t'other'n, as well. Ye're well-mounted indeed." He turned to Clyman and asked, "An' wouldn't ye be sayin' as much, Seamus?"

Clyman flicked his eyes over the horses and then onto me. He allowed himself a brief approving smile and said, "Good stock. Where'd ye get 'em?"

"They're both of 'em buffler runners," I replied, intending to let it go at that, but they had discovered the key to unlock my reserve — horses. Ere long I was telling them how I had bought Chiksika from a Crow chief and then about the pony raid, pointing out my companions in that adventure, and in no time at all we were exchanging names and other bits of the sort of information which builds bridges amongst strangers. By time we made camp at nightfall, I felt that I had made two new friends. Which was so.

~o   ~o   ~o

Two nights on the trail brought us to our destination, a broad flat alongside the Missouri that some wag chose to call Fort Recovery. What greeted our eyes was a scene that possessed all the military precision of a kicked-over anthill. Dirty, unshaven bluecoats in mismatched uniforms, together with what looked to be Saint Louis townsmen, buckskinned trappers, and traders from down along the Platte were swarming amidst a cloud of Lahcotahs bristling with muskets and bows, all painted and feathered for war, astride ponies gone half-wild from all the noise and hubbub, r'aring and capering and scattering the unwary who ventured too close. Four keelboats lay at anchor in the Missouri and rows of tipis stretched over the ridge. A cluster of dirty white soldier tents cluttered the shoreline and a couple-three big brass cannons on wheels and a swivel-gun or two glinted in the soft morning sunshine near the riverbank. Indian women swathed in bright wool blankets wandered amongst the whirling throng and their half-naked kids darted every whichaway, snatching up plunder of more or less value whenever and wherever they could.

As I said before, the picture that we saw there looked for all the world like a kicked-over anthill. All I can relate of who and what was there and what occurred then and later, as well as the how and why of it all must be from the viewpoint of just one single ant — and not a very important ant at that.

General Ashley was leading our column, making a beeline for the soldiers' camp, cutting a swath through the milling mass of humanity and overheated horseflesh. As we approached the tents, a tall, spare man stepped out of the crowd and strode towards us. If Ashley and Henry put you in mind of a brace of hawks, this man was an eagle. I was admiring his fine, quill-bedecked buckskins when I saw him wave a casual half-salute to Ashley, then walk directly up to the Major, a hearty grin breaking through his black and silver-sprinkled beard. "Andrew! How very good to see ye!" he shouted above the noise of the crowd. Henry smiled in recognition and cried out, "Pilcher!" and swung down from his horse, beckoning me to approach and hold his fretting mount, which naturally I did. The two men embraced, as old friends will, then stepped back to survey each other, before breaking into volleys of questions and replies. I missed most of what they said, but at last Pilcher swung his arm in a broad arc and asked, "What d'ye think o' my Injuns, Andy? Nigh five hunnerd Lahcotah bucks, give or take, an' natcherly all o' their kin! I fetched 'em up for fightin' Rees, for nobody hates Rees worse'n Lahcotahs do, 'ceptin' you an' me!" They palavered on for a spell before Pilcher inVited Henry to supper, then took his leave and melted back into the crowd.

Ashley had disappeared amongst the soldier tents. The Major turned our column around and led us back the way we had come, into a grove of trees that bordered the river, where we dismounted and made camp. As we were riding back, Henry, obviously pleased at meeting his long-time friend, told me that Joshua Pilcher was president of Missouri Fur, headquartered somewheres along the Platte, and that Pilcher had even more reason than Ashley to punish the Rees. They had attacked one of his trading posts that early spring and killed a number of his people. Then directly afterwards, Blackfoots destroyed one of his big trapping parties on the Yellowstone, killing the leaders, men name of Immel and Jones, and making off with all their furs and horses. When Pilcher learned of Ashley's disaster, he got himself appointed Indian Agent and gathered up this passel of Lahcotahs, along with a double score of his own men, and come running to settle accounts, leastaways with the Rees.

Making camp was no chore at all. Fine weather let us simply spread out our sleep robes and build a cookfire for the elk meat. We hobbled the horses and kept them in sight, mindful how Indians of whatever stripe can never resist pilfering ponies. Clyman and Fitzpatrick came along for supper and ended up spreading their sleep robes amongst our own. They both talked good sense, which was enough to make any man welcome in our camp.

After we ate, Tuttle sidled by and said, "Temple, I'd be beholden if'n ye'd borry me some o' yore cash money 'long about now." He riffled a greasy deck of cards in his big hands and explained, "Thar be sojers hereabouts, as ye see, an' sojer-boys allus got whuskey an' they be allus ripe an' ready fer cards." I didn't even bother to reply. I just started digging in my pouch. Tuttle laughed aloud. "An' don't ye fret none, neither. Ye'll get yore money back with boot an' a jug to cap the bargain!"

I slapped a handful of silver in his palm and tossed a gold piece on top of it, saying, "Go get your en-joys, Tuttle, an' don't you fret. Win or lose, we won't be needin' cash money in the mountains, if we ever get there."

Tuttle hiked off in the direction of the military encampment with a purposeful stride, his shoulders squared, like a man launched on a sacred mission, which in a way for Tuttle it was. I truly believe he fancied himself to be some sort of patriotic avenging angel, divinely ordained to separate Our Boys in Blue from the twin evils of whiskey and money.

Both Clyman and Fitzgerald had been amongst Ashley's men on the sandbar in front of the Arikara villages and amongst the last to retreat. We spent the better part of the evening with the two of them yarning about that battle, what happened there, who did what, and who didn't. The fight with the Rees had winnowed out the good grain from chaff in Ashley's company. He lost two-thirds of his force in killed, wounded, and quitters, but what remained was a band of fire-eaters who promised to do well in the fur trade or wherever else they might find themselves.

Jim Clyman half-blamed himself for the poor mettle of some of the men, for it was he whom Ashley had assigned to recruit volunteers for the expedition. Word had spread amongst the Saint Louis dandies that the High Missouri was no Sunday school picnic, so most of them declined Ashley's second invitation to adventure.

Clyman was forced to resort to cajoling the boozy denizens of grog-shops and hangers-on at whorehouses and suchlike men to fill the rolls. I took it on myself to reassure him, telling him not to feel too bad about the way matters had turned out, relating how Ashley and Henry themselves hadn't done much better, how nigh a score of men had quit after one of our keelboats sank and still more resigned when the Rocks ran off with our horses.

As often happens with casual palavering, I soon found myself telling again about the Crows and our pony raid, running buffalo, the Métis, and the Assiniboins on the Musselshell. They lapped up such tales like nectar. This was a life they had freely chosen and they wished to learn all about it. The trapper's trade is not for everybody, but it was plain to see that it would fit those two like a glove. I mentioned, too, that last year Henry had warned Ashley not to deal with the Rees, leaving it to these newcomers to reckon which one had been in the right.

It was late at night when Tuttle returned, bearing an armload of whiskey jugs. He showered coins into my lap and plopped a jug on top of them, then stood back grinning, hands on his hips, before he said, "Like I tol' ye, Temple, them sojer boys jest cain't wait to donate! Drink up, all o' ye, fer the health o' yore liver an' the everlastin' glory o' the Yew-nited States of Amurrica an' ever' last one o' the terry-tories!"

I thanked him and took a swig of better whiskey than I had expected, then passed the jug to Fitzgerald and Clyman, who helped themselves most gratefully. In the meantime, Tuttle was rummaging amongst his possibles and cursing under his breath. He evidently found what he required and shambled off to the riverbank, still grumbling. The three of us continued to pass the jug until Tuttle returned, clean-shaven and bleeding, fresh razor-nicks visible even in the firelight. He pawed through our sack of trade goods, picked out what he wanted and shoved it into his pouch, grabbed up one of his jugs, rose to his feet, and stood glaring at us for a spell before he growled, "Awright now, don't ye be laughin'! Thar be times ye gotta swap yore comfort fer yore hankerin' an' thar's a leetle Sioux woman over yonder sez she taken a shine to ol' Tuttle but she ain't about to be havin' no truck with no dog-face! Which is why I pert'near cut my own throat jest naow!"

The three of us just naturally burst out laughing. Tuttle merely snorted, guzzled a swallow from his jug, and stomped off into the darkness, grumbling still, jug swinging from one hand, headed for the arms and charms of his pernickety light-o'-love.

❧ ❧ ❧

A week or so after our arrival, Jim Clyman pronounced over his breakfast porridge, "That'ere French gen'ral Napoleon sez an army travels on its stomach. Mebbe so, but gossip's sure'nough fust-rate axle grease."

John Smiley, squatting beside the fire, looked up from his cooking chores and agreed. "That's a fact. Tongues're waggin' all over thi'shere camp, but don't nobody know nuthin' fer sure. You'uns heard some'at's got some meat on it?"

The rest of us shrugged but said nothing. John was right. Rumors were flying like swallows come back in springtime, but everybody was in the dark about what we would do next and when we might be doing it. All of us hoped our leaders knew more than we did, but it appeared to be problematical that they did.

"Game critters gittin' altogether scarce," Tuttle complained. "Even t'other side o' the river. An' them Injuns got this side combed pert'near clean."

"An' them sojer-boys," Paddy McBride chimed in, "gittin' greedier iv'ry day, demandin half o' what we're after shootin', jist fer rowin' us acrost an' back! 'Tis robbery! An' robbery's a sin, a mortal sin, I'm thinkin', an' a bloody shame to boot!"

Everybody was gloomy at the prospect of deer and wapiti running out, for Ashley and Henry were miserly with their scanty provisions. Ned Godey changed the subject. "Them Injuns must be gettin' mighty itchy, too. Injun bucks don't take to settin' still. Keepin' 'em bunched up together an' headin fer the same place is a chore akin to herdin' turkeys."

Tom Fitzpatrick forced his customary lop-sided grin into an expression of mock gravity. "All right, lads, hear me now! Since ye're after insistin' to be let in on the Grand Scheme, here 'tis! What we're after doin' now is learnin' how to wait. An' waitin's the key to the intire div'lish plan. An' whin we git real good at waitin', we'll be after movin' on up to the village o' the Rees an' there we'll be waitin' some more, until all thim haythen savages die o' creepin' auld age! An' in the meantime we'll be after coaxin' 'em to name us in the will! That's the scheme! Inheritance! Which is likely the only way anyone'll iver be seein' divil a bit o' the plunder thim murd'rin' haythen blackguards stole offa us!"

Fact is, it was hard to dismiss Fitzpatrick's foolery as mere blather, for from where we were sitting there appeared to be no other plan. Another week went by and every man amongst us was restless. Quarrels broke out between Pilcher's traders and our trappers and even more with the soldiers. Indian youths grew ever more daring in their thievery. It commenced to look as if the only war we would ever see would be amongst ourselves. And still Ashley and Pilcher and sometimes Andrew Henry continued to huddle every day with Colonel Leavenworth, the military commander, with no result that any of us could see.

The only benefit of all that leisure was getting to know some of Ashley's new men. Naturally we renewed acquaintance with Davey Jackson and we came to know the Sublette brothers from Missouri. Milton was the younger, a big, blond, bluff, open-faced fellow whose warmth and wild good humor quickly endeared him to our bunch. His older brother Bill was a different kettle of stew altogether. He was tall, angular, sandy-haired, and horse-faced, with sharp, intelligent blue eyes that appeared to measure and weigh everything and everybody. Unlike Milton, Bill was quiet-spoken and stingy with his talk. Milton moved in with us, but Bill mostly hung out with Jed Smith and his ever-present Bible, the two of them tight as ticks. Neither one of them appeared to want to have much truck with the rest of us.

After another passel of soldiers and a couple of brass-bedecked officers arrived from Fort Atkinson downriver, we were all called out to get our marching orders. The soldiers were organized into five or six companies, Pilcher's two-score people made up another one, and our mob, Ashley and Henry's four-score trappers, were combined into still one more company. Josiah Pilcher was named a major and placed in command of his five hundred or so

Lahcotahs, who likely neither knew nor cared about such a title or position. They believed it was every man for himself and had come along solely for plunder and revenge. Military discipline was not in their vocabulary. Nor in ours, either, truth be told.

Characteristically, when General Ashley named his officers, not one was chosen from amongst Andrew Henry's men. Jed Smith, who had returned from downriver, got to be a captain and Davey Jackson a lieutenant, along with a couple of other greenhorns both named Hiram who instantly became captains. Tom Fitzpatrick, who could read, was quartermaster and Bill Sublette was named a sergeant-major. All this made hardly any nevermind to those of us who had already spent a year on the High Missouri, trapping and surviving and some of us fighting Indians, but we noticed it and committed it to memory.

Paddy McBride, howsomever, came close to being a one-man mutiny. Colonel Leavenworth had lost one of his keelboats on the way up the Missouri. A half-dozen of his soldiers had drowned and most of the rest aboard had lost their rifles and equipment, so Leavenworth just naturally called on Pilcher and Ashley to re-arm his soldier-boys, ten rifles from Pilcher and thirty from Ashley. Our politician-general responded in the high-handed manner we had come to expect of him. He started off by picking on Paddy McBride to surrender his musket for the use of Leavenworth's bluecoats.

Mild-mannered Paddy surprised us all by what he told the General. "No, sor, beggin' yer pardon, ye'll not be after takin' this here gun from Padraic McBride himself. Ye sold it to me yerself, an' dearly, an' I paid fer iv'ry inch o' this here darlin' with the sweat o' me brow an' ice on me arse an' any sojer what's after gettin' this here gun'll be after pryin' it from the cold, dead hand o' Paddy McBride — an' divil a chore he'll have o' doin' it, too!"

What Paddy had the courage to say was a capital mark of what a single year on the High Missouri could do to change a greenhorn into a trapper. It reminded us all of who and what we were. The closest we ever came to a proper military maneuver was when our entire bunch, more than a score of us by then, without a word spoken, turned on our heel and walked away, our weapons still in our hands. Ashley never challenged us.

Fortunately the General's remaining keelboat had slipped down the river and arrived at Fort Recovery that afternoon. The required rifles and muskets were made up from Ashley's stock of trade goods and we heard no more about the matter.

Late that afternoon Colonel Leavenworth called everybody together and made a grand speech in which he informed us that from then on our motley assemblage of soldiers, trappers, traders, and war-painted Indians would be known as the Missouri Legion. Jim Clyman privately called it Falstaff's Battalion. The Colonel then ordered a grand feast for everyone, which was notable for a passel of public palavering by whites and Indians alike and which nobody, whites and Indians alike, listened to. Army provisions made for a welcome change in vittles, howsomever, and jugs appeared from everywhere, so Colonel Leavenworth's feast was a rousing success. Afterwards, Tuttle insisted on paying a final visit to the Lahcotah camp and in*Vited* me along to meet the sister of his lady friend, but I declined and remained where I was, chatting and sipping and running a stock of rifle balls with Brass Turtle, Bridger, Godey, and Clyman until after dark.

Riding back upstream was a welcome relief after weeks of doing practically nothing. It was mid-morning before we left camp, headed in the direction of the Arikara villages. Pilcher's Lahcotahs rode well out in front, with the rest of us trying to keep up. Even the Lahcotah women made better time than we did, riding shaggy horses dragging *travois* loaded with all their worldly goods, their kids and old folks, and even their dogs. Most of the bluecoats were afoot, which slowed us more than somewhat. Trundling their heavy cannons and swivel-guns and ammunition wagons through the woods alongside the Missouri didn't help speed our progress either. Word was that the keelboats were traveling upriver with Pilcher's complement of traders aboard.

In the forenoon of the fourth day we halted amongst the trees a mile or so below the Arikara villages to get ready for our first attack. Such preparations made no nevermind to the Sioux, howsomever. They just kicked up their ponies and busted on ahead, hungry for plunder and thirsty for revenge against their old enemies. Then another three hundred or more Lahcotahs showed up, anxious to get in on the fun. I reckon we had some eleven hundred fighting men ready to do battle by that time. It appeared the Rees were about to get their comeuppance.

We rode forward as fast as we could through the trees, trying to catch up with the Lahcotahs, now and then dodging their wild-eyed stragglers burning to join the fight before it was over and the plunder all gone. As we neared the plain that stretched out below the villages we could hear the sharp crack of rifles and the dull thud of muskets and then, as we drew closer, the yip-yip-yip of Indians yelling their heads off. But which Indians they might be, we hadn't a notion.

I was riding Chiksika and leading Jake, who was packing my plunder, and wondering what I was going to do with a packhorse in the midst of a battle, when we came upon a detail of bluecoats stringing picket lines just inside the treeline, which useful chore might have been the one and only well-executed military activity of the entire campaign. Most of Henry's trappers were encumbered with pack animals, just as I was, so we rode over and tethered our extra stock with the army critters, over the protests of the soldier-boys yelling that the picket lines were for army use only. Naturally we paid them no nevermind and galloped off to get in on the fight.

I fell in behind Brass Turtle and his Delawares, galloping when we could, loping and slowing to a trot when we needed to, ducking under low branches that smarted the hide like buggy whips, then breaking out of the trees onto a stretch of prairie and cornfields and a scene that looked and sounded more like a swarm of angry bees than a battlefield. The Rees had mounted up when they spied the Lahcotahs and come out of their stockades to fight them. Screaming Indians a-horseback were criss-crossing every whichaway, shooting muskets and bending bows and swiping with lances and clubs and tomahawks, now and then jumping down to yank a scalp or grab up weapons or clothing or all three, then swinging up again to ride pell-mell back into the fight.

The Lahcotahs appeared to have the matter well in hand, so the most of us reined up at the treeline and just sat watching the fun. It was a colorful sight. Bonneted Lahcotah chiefs, feathers and fringes streaming, would pick out a likely Ree, then ride hell-for-leather up to him and whack him with a coup-stick, then ride on, confident that the single-feathered, half-naked young bucks trailing behind would finish off the befuddled enemy.

The fight appeared to be pretty even, sometimes surging towards the villages, then ebbing back to the treeline whenever the Rees got their forces together, until Leavenworth's bluecoats came straggling out from amongst the trees and a couple of their cannons and swivel-guns lurched into view. A howl went up from the Arikaras and they quit their charge, fell back, and appeared to take notice of our bunch for the first time. Half a dozen muskets swung up and pointed at us, followed by puffs of smoke, but they did no harm. A ragged volley from at least a score of our rifles made them think better about attacking us. A couple Rees slumped over their ponies' necks but none of them fell. They spun their ponies in their tracks and made for the palisades, Lahcotahs in hot pursuit, with our bunch following up.

Bodies and a number of dead horses were strewn over the plain and already Lahcotahs were busy hacking off trophy scalps, hands, and feet from the fallen Rees and hanging them around their necks. Jim Clyman rode up beside me and together we followed the pack almost to the gate of the lower village, taking care to stay out of musket range from the walls.

The Rees vanished inside and the Sioux milled around on the plain, shouting what I took to be insults, taunting the Arikaras for their cowardly retreat, when one Ree warrior ventured forth from the gate. He advanced some distance from the pickets and commenced to trade a passel of tantalizing palaver with the Lahcotahs, daring them to take him on, I reckon. About that time a Sioux on a fine-looking horse sauntered forward, all the while smiling and offering invitations for the Ree to come closer, then whipping up his horse and charging. Quick as lightning, the Ree

laid his pony plumb over his knee and made for the village, the
Sioux hot on his hocks, until they both nearly reached the gate.
Then, his horse in a flat gallop, the Sioux swung up his musket and
fired. By that time, the Rees inside must have fired forty or fifty
shots at the pursuer, clouds of powder smoke billowing from the
walls. Then out of the smoke galloped Mister Lahcotah, laughing
to beat the band, and the Ree's pony loped on through the gate
without its rider. I daresay that particular Sioux earned himself an
extra eagle feather that day.

Clyman glanced over at me and asked, "Reckon ye want to try
doin' somethin' like that, Buck?"

"Mebbe tomorrow," I replied, but naturally that was just a
manner of speaking.

Most of us retired to the treeline to watch the goings-on. Only
our Delawares and Iroquois remained near the village, likely all
fired up for battle and hoping the Rees would come out to fight
again, but they never did.

The Sioux were still picking over the dead Rees when Jim
Clyman called my attention to one old Lahcotah chief who was
leading one of his wives up to an Arikara corpse that lay just
beyond a long rifle shot from the walls. We nudged our horses
forward and reined in just in time to see the old chief hand his wife
a war club and to hear him calling out insults to the Rees inside the
village. The wife rained blow after blow on the body of the dead
warrior whilst the old man berated the Rees for their cowardice in
letting a woman defile their dead comrade within gunshot range of
their palisade.

We were just reining our horses around to leave when a most
peculiar event occurred. We caught sight of a big, heavy-set
Lahcotah, walking on hands and feet, snuffling and grunting for all
the world like a bear, advancing towards the corpse of an Arikara.
When he got to the body he leaned down and commenced to tear
out mouthfuls of flesh from the breast with his teeth, r'aring up
every so often and pawing the air, then returning to his grisly feast,
all in plain view of the village.

Clyman nodded to me and, without words, we agreed that we
had seen enough and it was time to rejoin our comrades. Whilst

we rode back, chewing over what we had seen, there was no dispute betwixt us that it was just as well the Lahcotahs were on our side, leastaways for now.

るン るン るン

Josiah Pilcher was bustling about the picket lines like a mother hen chasing chicks, shouting orders, cracking jokes, coaxing, cajoling, and threatening soldiers and trappers alike, trying to whip some sort of order and commonsense into what was less of an army than an unruly mob. Clyman and I tethered our horses and joined the rest of our bunch, who were more or less gathered around Major Henry. He wasn't saying much. I reckon he thought it best to hold his peace, seeing as how they were both majors and Pilcher was making enough noise for the both of them. General Ashley was nowhere to be seen.

I found Tuttle hunkered down behind a tree, a jug between his knees, keeping out of sight of Major Henry, who disapproved of drinking at such times — fact is, most times. Tuttle's face lit up when he saw me. "Thar ye be, Temple! Sit yorese'f down ri'chere an' take a nip. Thi'shere fightin' be thirsty work!"

I accepted the jug gratefully, neglecting to mention that so far we had fired only one shot apiece and that one in self-defense. I drained a deep swallow, wincing at the harsh bite of raw whiskey, and passed the jug to Clyman, who took a healthy swig, wiped his mouth on his sleeve, and jerked his head in Pilcher's direction as he asked, "He said anythin' wuthwhile?"

Tuttle shook his head and replied, "Nuthin' I could hear. Reckon ol' Leavenworth's the onliest he-dog hereabouts an' he cain't make his mind up 'bout nuthin'. Reckon all we kin do is sit ri'chere an' wait some more."

Which is what we did, passing Tuttle's jug until late afternoon, by which time the keelboats had come upriver and the soldiers fetched more cannons and ammunition onto the shore. Meanwhile the Rees stayed snug inside their palisades, refusing to come out and fight. When we strolled out to the treeline we could see a passel of Sioux tipis already raised on the western ridge and the Lahcotah women in the Arikara cornfields gathering the harvest.

No doubt the warriors were disappointed about the lack of fighting, but the women were making the best of it.

That night we bedded down nigh the picket lines, sharing amongst our bunch what vittles we had carried with us, but mostly going hungry to our robes. Leavenworth's soldier-boys weren't likely much better off.

Early next morning General Ashley loped into the grove, red-faced and halfway excited, and ordered all of us trappers to go afoot to the upper end of the lower village, along the riverbank, to keep the Rees from sneaking out that way. Which we did.

Before we left, howsomever, Tuttle took it on himself to warn the bluecoats stationed there about guarding our horses and plunder. "Don't ye be fergittin' whatcher hyar fer. Don'tcha be lettin' them hosses stray ner them'ere Injuns git a-holt of 'em, neither. An' none o' ye'd best be gittin' long-fingered with our plunder, neither!" The soldiers commenced laughing and looking skeptical, but they sobered up right smart when Tuttle drew out his big brass-handled knife, slapped it softly against his palm, and added quietly, "An' if anythin's missin', hosses or plunder, either one, I reckon I kin skelp ye good as any Sioux kin do."

They must have taken him at his word, for when we returned, nothing was disturbed. On the other hand, the safety of our stock and plunder might have been insured by the handful of silver coins I bestowed on the horse guards before our departure.

The Missouri was running halfway shallow in mid-summer, so we trotted along the shore, keeping cover under the riverbank, past a passel of bluecoats and a cannon or two, until Major Henry told us to halt and find some cover. Which we did.

When the cannons commenced firing in the early forenoon we reckoned the Rees would come running out and the fighting would commence in earnest. No such a thing happened. We learned later that the very first cannonball killed that old scoundrel Chief Gray Eyes and the second one clipped off their medicine flag staff, but the Rees sat tight and never budged. The artillery kept hammering at the palisades, busting holes in the logs, but the Rees just laid themselves down inside and let the cannonballs whistle overhead. Naturally I saw none of this myself, but that is what was said later.

There wasn't much for us trappers to do at first, for there was nothing to shoot at, so we just lay there and watched the cannonballs battering the palisades without much effect. What really got our attention, howsomever, was when Major Vanderburgh, one of Pilcher's men, fired off a cannon from above the upper village and sent a cannonball whooshing right over our heads, landing in the river behind us with a tremendous splash. They moved the cannon elsewhere right after that, so we stayed put until Ashley trotted up and ordered us to advance to a gully not twenty paces from the palisade. Which we did.

Matters heated up considerably about then. The Rees must have thought that we meant to rush the village and they commenced shooting in earnest, some of them climbing up inside the palisade and firing down at us and others crawling outside the walls to get a better shot. Giving the devil his due, I ought to mention that Talbot and Hugh Glass both exposed themselves to harm when they went running to the far end of the gully we were in and shot a pair of Rees who had sneaked in behind us. Glass was winged on his way back, but Talbot returned without a scratch.

I kept on shooting and reloading until my rifle barrel got almost too hot to hold, but I am not altogether sure that I ever hit anybody. Tuttle claimed he shot two Rees that morning, but I wouldn't swear to it.

At length our powder and ball commenced to run low, so Major Henry picked Brass Turtle and McBride and me to run down to Leavenworth's headquarters where the stores were kept. The three of us crawled out of the gully and dodged our way to the riverbank and jumped over. Once there, we were under cover and fairly safe, so trotting on down to headquarters was no hard chore.

Tom Fitzpatrick's quartermaster stores were heaped up right behind Leavenworth's tent, which was well out of rifle range of the village. Bluecoats were running every whichaway, officers and sergeants shouting orders that I'm sure nobody ever heard and certainly nobody obeyed. Whilst Fitz was doling out powder and lead and spare flints, I caught sight of the Colonel and Joshua

Pilcher palavering in a most heated fashion. They were both
waving their arms and Pilcher kept stomping around in a tight
little circle, then thrusting his flushed and sweaty face close to
Leavenworth's and shouting some more.

I had nothing useful to do at that particular moment, so I sidled
nearby and caught the drift of their quarrel. It appeared that the
Colonel wanted Pilcher to bring his Lahcotahs up to both villages
and attack the walls. Pilcher kept telling him that it wouldn't
work, that Sioux weren't cut out for that kind of chore, that they
were willing to fight only in the open, preferably on horseback, and
that setting fire to the villages and driving the Rees out from
behind the walls was the only way the Lahcotahs could be used.
Leavenworth refused to do that, on account of the Arikara women
and children, he said, and Pilcher insisted that there was no other
way. Which was where matters stood when Brass Turtle signaled
and I had to leave.

As it turned out, Pilcher was right. The Sioux wouldn't budge
and for rest of the campaign they were no more useful than a third
stirrup on a saddle.

The cannonading quit about midday, whilst we were threading
our way under the riverbank lugging sacks of powder and lead. By
then Henry's trappers had retired out of the gully and were
hunkered down below the riverbank, a few of them posted to keep
an eye on the Rees, most just lazing about alongside the water. On
our way past, I noticed John Fitzgerald bathing and bandaging
Glass's injured arm, whilst Talbot sat alone nearby, staring
vacantly out across the river.

Major Henry passed out powder and galena pigs and spare flints
himself, making sure each man got what he needed and no more.
Soon the narrow shore was dotted with little fires and huddles of
men casting rifle and musket balls. Every trapper carries his bullet
mold and lead ladle on his belt, for hardly any two rifles or
muskets you are apt to come across are likely to have precisely the
same size bore. Some men collected driftwood for the fires, but
most of us just busted up the Ree canoes and dugouts tied up along
the shore and burned them.

After Tuttle and I filled our powderhorns and ran a stock of rifle balls, he disappeared. I wasn't surprised. Tuttle had a marvelous knack for evaporating into thin air, nearly always for some illicit purpose. I discovered him snugged in behind a big fallen cottonwood, safe from Andrew Henry's eyes, dealing from his greasy deck of cards to a couple of disreputable-looking bluecoats and Tom Shanahan, one of the Musselshell trappers, who by that time should have known better than to play cards with Tuttle Thompson. When he glanced up and saw me peering over the log, Tuttle hailed me with, "Hey thar, Temple! Sitcherse'f daown an' larn how the big fellers do it! Ye don't hafta play. Jest be watchin' an' larn sumthin'."

I was rolling over the top of the fallen tree to join them when a cloud of splinters erupted next to my hand, followed instantly by an explosion and searing pain on my neck from the muzzle blast of a musket fired from the top of the bank, not eight feet above me. As I fell sprawling I caught sight of the spiky hair and painted face of the Ree who had shot at me. Tuttle proved again that his big hands were good for more than dealing cards. His fist was a blur as he yanked his pistol from his belt, shoved his arm straight out, and dropped the hammer. When the smoke cleared, the Ree's head dangled over the edge of the bank, half his forehead blown away. Tuttle blew smoke from the muzzle and proceeded to reload his pistol as he said calmly, "Thar ye go, Temple. Thet's one of 'em ye cain't be 'quivocatin'." At times Tuttle could come up with the most remarkable, if irrelevant, words.

A rattle of gunshots along the bank quickly blended into one continual sputtering noise, seasoned with the shouts and curses of our men. Even as I scrambled to my feet, groping for my rifle, I knew in my gut what had happened. Rees had crept out from the walls and occupied the gully we had held that morning. Now they held a position from which they could freely snipe at our entire line. Tuttle's bluecoated pigeons went scurrying back to their unit, heads down, bent nearly double, and Shanahan was not far behind. I was stepping off to follow them when I caught sight of Tuttle reaching up to the dead Ree, grabbing a handful of hair, and slicing off the scalp with that big knife of his. His grin was wide as a barn door as he shoved the bloody scalp under his belt and slid his still-dripping knife into its sheath, saying the while, "Thar now! Reckon she's baptized proper-like!" Then he grabbed up his rifle and followed me down the shoreline to where the Major was shouting orders, apparently to nobody in particular, for each trapper appeared to be fighting his own little war, Indian-style, finding a proper vantage point and taking pot-shots when and wherever a likely target showed itself.

Problem was, the fight was going nowheres and the longer it continued the more likely it was that some of our trappers would be killed or seriously wounded. Now Andrew Henry was a militia major, sure enough, but more important, he was a businessman, and every healthy trapper he had on hand meant more fur profits for him and Ashley. Naturally I don't actually know his thinking at the time, but what he ordered next made such reasoning on his part appear likely. Right then, we were merely sparring with the Rees. The better course was to wallop those scoundrels with a Sunday punch.

Brass Turtle and his Indians, Delawares and Iroquois both, were gathered around the Major when Tuttle and I came trotting up. When Henry spied us, he motioned for us to join them, so naturally we hunkered down and waited for what he had to say. Before he spoke, howsomever, he hiked along the bank and pried Jim Bridger and Godey out of the hidey-holes they were shooting from and sent them down to us. Henry's final choice was Talbot, which was a surprise to us all, as you might imagine.

The Major's plan was simple, as the best plans are. What he had to say went something like this. "The Rees want to cut themselves a path to the river here so they can escape, but so long as we're here, they can't do it. That's why they've occupied that ravine, to dislodge us and force our retreat. Your chore is to get them out of there." Fact is, he used a passel of terms like enfilading fire and suchlike, but that's the gist of what he said. Henry went on to tell us just how the job ought to be done, but all of us knew, even as he spoke, that precisely how we would accomplish his purpose could be determined only when we got there.

It wasn't but a few minutes until all fourteen of us were dog-trotting upriver under the overhanging bank, seeking a handy place to climb up, a spot far enough away from the village and the gully where we wouldn't attract attention and brushy enough to conceal our movements. Our Indians were all grinning, happy, I reckon, to be doing something besides out-waiting the Rees. Jim Bridger's boyish face fairly beamed with eagerness, as it usually did, no matter the task. Godey and Tuttle looked thoughtful but resolute. Even Talbot's stony features betrayed an unaccustomed satisfaction with our chore. I am not altogether sure what I myself was feeling, but there were several things that I would have preferred to be doing just then, instead.

When Brass Turtle swerved left and glided up the bank, smooth as a snake, the rest of us followed as quietly as we could, burdened as we were with rifles and pistols and all manner of hardware shoved into and dangling from our belts. We found ourselves in thick brush, willows and tall weeds all growing together, but sparse enough here and there to let us make our way back downriver towards the village, treading softly, trailing behind Turtle, trotting when we could, bent over nearly double, silently cursing the stinging mosquitoes and whipping branches and smarting sawgrass in the marshy hollows, all the while peering in every direction, lest there be Arikara pickets posted to warn their comrades of surprises such as ours.

The sound of gunfire grew increasingly loud as we neared the village. Brass Turtle halted and sank to the earth, then motioned for us to come up with him. We wriggled forward on hands and knees and bellies, until we could see below the overhanging branches the upper end of the gully stretching straight out in front of us. Half a dozen Arikaras were shooting towards the river, then dropping down to reload whilst that many more stepped up to the edge and fired in their turn.

We had no plan of attack, but when Brass Turtle brought his rifle up and fitted it to his shoulder, those of us in front remained prone on our bellies, others rose to their knees, and the rest stood up behind them. The thunder of fourteen rifles and muskets going off at once was deafening. The Rees in front wilted like wheat before a scythe. There was no time or reason to reload, for our Delawares and Iroquois jumped to their feet and plunged headlong into the gully, swinging clubs and knives and tomahawks, screaming what I took to be war cries, with Calvin Talbot squarely in the midst of them. When I saw Talbot in there, I must have taken leave of my senses. I left my rifle where it lay and scrambled to my feet, jerking my pistol from my belt and fumbling for my belt axe as I ran to catch up.

Not all the Rees had been killed or wounded by our volley. The fighting in that narrow ditch was close and sweaty, bloody and stinking and very personal. Bridger had got there before me, punching and smashing with his rifle butt, his big blacksmith's arms making it a more terrible weapon at close quarters than ever it was as a shooting iron. Talbot was clubbing with his empty pistol in one hand and slashing and stabbing with a big butcher knife in the other, his sleeves blood-soaked to the elbows, his face wreathed in the only smile I ever saw on his grim features.

I recollect pointing and discharging my pistol at a Ree who appeared from around a dog-leg in the ditch, thinking the while that this was no place for firearms, where we were just as likely to kill one of our own as one of the enemy, when a terrible blow on the side of my head sent me reeling against the muddy wall and knocked me off my feet. Half-stunned, I was groping on the ground before me, trying to find my tomahawk, when a Ree, his face all smeared with paint and mud and blood, appeared before my eyes, a knife cocked in his hand. I clawed under my shirt for Lucette's little pistol, forgotten until now, and snatched it from my belt. I never could have used it, howsomever, if the Ree hadn't slipped on the bloody mud and fallen headlong into my lap as he lunged for me. I but dimly recall earing back the hammers and blowing off the top of his head with both barrels.

When I came back to myself I was slumped against the muddy wall of the gulch, the Ree's broken head still in my lap, thinking stupidly that there really wasn't enough left to make a proper scalp. The hubbub was as great as ever, but it had a different quality from before. Then I glanced up and saw Talbot staring down at me. His smile was gone, so I reckoned the fight must be over.

   ‽ ‽ ‽

The whole operation just sort of fizzled after that. After we gathered up our weapons and returned to Henry on the shore, an order came in from Ashley for us to abandon our position and retire downriver to the headquarters area. Considering what we had just accomplished, such an order didn't make sense, but then, hardly anything did during that entire campaign.

 Brass Turtle and all his Indians had waded into the river and were washing themselves head to foot. I thought it might be one of their ceremonies, but whatever it was, it appeared to me to be a good idea. I was spattered and reeking with blood and brains and stinking from that sticky kind of sweat that comes from being scared out of your wits. I shucked my belt and powderhorn and left my weapons on the shore before I dived headfirst into the river. The cool water worked a miracle, washing away dirt and sweat, to be sure, but also laving my spirit clean, carrying off the smarting shreds of fear and rage that lingered in my soul and restoring whatever innocence I could still call my own.

 Godey and Tuttle were waiting on shore with Jim Clyman when I waded out of the river, buckskins heavy and dripping. Just the same, I felt lighter in body and spirit than I had before, as if the cold river water had baptized my sins away, if indeed they were sins in the first place. Then I heard Clyman say something to Tuttle that let it all make sense.

 Jim was joshing Tuttle about the Arikara scalp tucked under his belt, playfully calling him a savage and suchlike, but Tuttle was feeling no shame about the matter. He just grinned at Clyman and said, "Like Brass Turtle was sayin' jest t'other day, circumstances alter cases. Sech doin's 'pear to be the fashion hereabouts. If'n I hadna took his'n, he'd be sportin' mine by naow. I jest got thar fust."

 Jim looked thoughtful for a spell and then he said, "Ye're likely right, Tuttle. Ye cain't make a civilized man out of a savage in a whole generation, but it don't take no more'n a month or mebbe even less to turn a civilized man into a savage. Course, some of us backslide sooner'n others." He chuckled, mostly to himself, before he added, "Not that I ever seen no Kaintuck folk what ye might be callin' civilized!"

Tuttle took no offense. He merely guffawed and slapped his leg, allowing that he had never met up with any either.

I thought about what Clyman had said as we tramped back down the shore to the headquarters, how a civilized man could become a savage in a very short time, if keeping body and soul together required it, and I mostly made up my mind that it was not a bad thing to do. The old rules didn't get the job done up thisaway and they mostly didn't work back home, either. I recalled the fear and rage I used to feel in those battles with schoolyard bullies when I was little. Matters weren't a great deal different hereabouts. The stakes were simply higher.

∾ ∾ ∾

Leavenworth's headquarters was buzzing like a beehive. Problem was, they were all drones. Nobody was doing anything useful about the Rees. The cannonading had quit and bluecoats parading on the prairie wouldn't likely boost the Arikaras out of their villages. Gold-braided young officers saluted and sirred their superiors in a proper military manner but none of it was accomplishing the chore that we had come here to do.

We hung around headquarters for a spell, but it appeared there was nothing for us to do. At length Major Henry ordered us trappers to return to the horse camp, but just as I turned to obey, he called me back and said, crisply polite as always, "Mister Buck, please stay. Your writing skills may come in handy here. Go help Fitzpatrick in the quartermaster tent."

I wanted to get back to my horses, but naturally I nodded my assent and marched myself off to the quartermasters and told Tom Fitzpatrick what Henry had said. He simply shrugged and replied, "There's nothin' much to be done here, Buck, less'n these sojers are after gettin' their arse movin', but ye're welcome." Then he stepped back and surveyed my blood-stained clothing, still damp from my plunge, and asked, "So ye been chasin' thim Rees all the way into the river, have ye now?" I related what we had done since my earlier visit, which produced an approving smile and the laughing remark, "Well now, let's be after thankin' the Almighty somebody's doin' somethin', even if 'tis wrong! These popinjays could be takin' lessons from the likes o' you an' your redskins!" He looked closely at me then and said, "But ye're lookin' some'at peakèd, lad. Go lay yerself down an' rest awhile. Like I say, there's nothin' much happ'nin' here."

I thanked him for his offer and stretched myself out on a heap of blankets, bales, and such, thinking, as I drifted off, of Jim Clyman's remark, about how little time it took to rub off a lifetime of civilizing and bring us down to our savage bedrock. I thought, too, about the Ree and his broken head resting in my lap and I decided that he had got only what he bargained for, which I reckon more or less proved Clyman's point.

ह्ल   ह्ल   ह्ल

It was still daylight when Fitzpatrick nudged me awake. The sun was slipping below the western hills and cookfires had sprouted all over the soldiers' camp. Hungry, unshaven bluecoats jostled one another around huge steaming black cauldrons suspended on tripods over the fires, rattling tin cups and plates, exchanging greetings and good-natured curses. The soft summer evening air was laden with cooking odors, stirring sharp hunger pangs that reminded me I had eaten not a morsel that livelong day and not much the day before.

Fitzpatrick grinned down at me and said, "On yer feet now, Temple Buck, me lad! 'Tis time we be fittin' on the nose bag! The grand Colonel Leavenworth, in all his gen'rous munificence, has deigned at last to issue rations to the troops!" He snorted and added, "An' about time, too! Two intire days we're here an' divil a crust we've had from his mean hand!"

I swung my feet to the ground and buckled on my belt whilst Fitzpatrick went on, warming to his subject and the sound of his own words as only an Irishman can. "'Tis no wonder these bloody bluecoats are after bein' such a sorry lot, starvin' an' freezin' as they do, whilst their officers loll in the lap o' pagan luxury the while!" I doubted there was a great deal of luxury, pagan or otherwise, available in the officers' tents, but I let it go.

The flow and flavor of Fitzpatrick's invective was much too delicious to permit interruption. At last he said, "Come now, Misther Buck, 'tis time we be shaggin' oursel's on to camp an' partakin' o' the heap o' vittles I was after sendin' over whilst ye were nappin'!" He swelled himself up in mock dignity and pronounced, "I'm not after bein' yer Lord High Quartermaster fer nothin', mind ye! The Almighty helps thim as helps thimsel's an' 'tis past time we be after helpin' oursel's to a grand supper!"

ॐ   ॐ   ॐ

Trappers' camp was brimming over with shouting and laughter and the fragrance of food frying and stewing over a dozen cookfires scattered amongst the trees. John Smiley and Paddy and Anse were squatting by our fire, busy with cooking chores. The rest of our bunch sprawled in a loose circle around them, impatiently awaiting supper. An approving shout went up when they spied Fitzpatrick, applauding his efficient and generous pilfering of Army provisions. He bowed to them all with mock gravity, a lop-sided grin on his face, and found a place amongst them.

Before I joined them, I visited my horses and saw with satisfaction that they were content and well-fed, a generous armful of prairie hay sprinkled with grain in front of them both.

Tuttle's threats and my coins together had proved a winning argument with the horse guards.

After days of short rations or none at all, supper in trappers' camp that night was a feast indeed. Salt pork and army beans, bully beef and pan bread, pork fat and fresh roasting ears gleaned from the fields of the Arikaras, washed down with real coffee, thick and black and steaming in tin cups, rivaled the feasts of Roman emperors, leastaways in the minds of those amongst us who had ever heard of Rome. Fact is, we would have preferred buffalo hump, fleece fat, and ribs, but those shaggy beasts, dim-witted as they are, were wise enough to give wide berth to the pandemonium that reigned in that busy neighborhood.

Fresh tobacco poached from officers' stores by Fitzpatrick complemented our rude banquet and whiskey was still available from amongst the troops for those with guile enough to trade them out of it. Naturally Tuttle was one of those. A freshly-shaved Tuttle and I sat smoking and sipping and recalling the events of the day, until he grew restless at the sound of drums beating in the Sioux camp on the ridge and, no doubt, the remembered charms of one or more of his Lahcotah mistresses. It wasn't long until he took his leave, making sure beforehand that his pistol was freshly primed, his possibles pouch well-stocked with trinkets, the Ree scalp prominently and proudly in view on his belt, and his jug reasonably full. Thus armed for amorous conquest, Tuttle bade me farewell and slipped out of camp, confident of one more successful escapade.

I remained where I was, back propped against a tree, smoking and reflecting on the distance I had come in the past year and a half, how my life had changed, and how my view of life had altered as well. I had killed yet another man that day, likely two, and I found that I wasn't particularly troubled by that fact. I had known honest women who were not ashamed of their desires and I was grateful that I had been privileged to know them. This camp and all its rowdy trappers was for me the only real world and I was happy in it. All else, Whynot and all the people there, even Ma and Sarah, appeared to me just then to be a fanciful tale, a legend but dimly recalled from childhood.

Our Indians had built a sweat lodge on the riverbank, as they often did. The gentle beating of old Foot's drum outside the lodge blending with the strains of a plaintive mountain tune that Anse was coaxing out of his fiddle provided a fitting lullabye for me when at last I retired to my robes.

ꝏ   ꝏ   ꝏ

My slumbers were broken by the shouts and curses of trappers camped at the far end of the grove. Half a dozen horses had been stolen in the night, certainly by the Sioux, who regarded all horses as fair game, even those of their allies. I rolled out of my robes, grabbed up my pistol, and ran barefoot to the Army picket lines, where I found our horses safe and pawing the ground, impatient for their breakfast. Tom Fitzpatrick had arrived before me and was standing beside his mount, currying out caked-on sweat and crooning a soft Irish air into the horse's cocked-back ears as he worked. When he spied me trotting into the clearing, Fitz called out, "Top o' the day to ye, Temple

Buck! Rest yoursel', lad. Our ponies are all safe an' sound. 'Twas thim on the fringe o' camp that got taken off. All's well hereabouts." He paused to run his currycomb under the belly where the girth sets, then added, "Thim bluecoat Johnnies're after bein' good fer somethin', after all!"

I busied myself rustling up hay and Army grain for all of our horses, dispensing a few extra coins to the horse guards as I did so. Fitzpatrick, still busy with his grooming chore, continued to apprise me of the night's events. "Thim Sioux pranksters was after out-doin' thimsel's last night, they was! Hear tell tell they grabbed off half a dozen artill'ry mules an' a passel o' thim little white sojer tents to boot!" He chuckled, mostly to himself, and added, "'Tis fortunate fer thim sojers that britchclouts are all the fashion amongst 'em, else thim bloody haythens'd have the britches off their arse!"

When we returned from watering the horses, Fitz announced, "'Tis time we be after breakin' our fast an' gettin' on up to me tent, 'fore thim long-fingered bluecoats steal me blind. Any poachin's to be done, Tom Fitzpatrick'll be doin' it his ownself!"

By time I got back from my private chore, Smiley and Anse Tolliver had cooked breakfast, a rib-sticking corn porridge laced with cracklings. I filled my cup and joined Fitz and a sleepy-eyed but contented Tuttle sprawled near the cookfire. As I munched my porridge, I marveled for the hundredth time how it was that Smiley, who almost always volunteered to do the cooking, remained so scarecrow slim. This time I spoke up and mentioned it, not really expecting a reply. John Smiley, howsomever, was a serious man. He pondered my remark for a spell and then he said, "Wal, now, us Smileys don't holt with packin' a deal o' taller. We'uns allus say hit's the lean hoss what wins the long race, hennit?" That is all he said, but it was a better reply than I deserved. I held my peace concerning such personal matters from then on.

ॐ   ॐ   ॐ

Headquarters was a-buzz with a passel of activity that appeared to be going nowheres. The cannons were silent but officers and couriers on horseback were all but falling over one another, thundering into camp to report to Colonel Leavenworth, then galloping off in every direction, carrying orders that produced no results that we could see. The Rees were still bottled up within their palisades and there was no reason to suppose that they were about to come out, either to fight or to parley.

After Fitz inspected his stores and found them undisturbed, he dismissed the soldiers who had been guarding the quartermaster tent overnight. After that there was little for us to do except to fill some trapper's powderhorn or to pass out a few pigs of galena, so he and I took turns wandering into Leavenworth's headquarters to learn what might be going on. There was gossip and rumor aplenty, but little information.

Nobody challenged either of us. Dressed as we were in seedy buckskins, we obviously weren't officers. Therefore Fitz and I were men of no consequence, beneath notice and well-nigh invisible. They simply looked right through us. Which made it easy for us to loiter nearby and overhear what was being said, most of which wasn't worth the trouble.

I saw that Jedediah Smith was taking his captaining to heart, chasing about a-horseback with messages from Ashley to the Colonel and back again, and Bill Sublette appeared to be some sort of growth on the General's backside, which is what I reckoned a sergeant-major was supposed to be.

It was mid-morning when an officer galloped up to the Colonel's tent and reported that a Lahcotah chief called Fire Heart had been seen palavering with an Arikara outside the lower village. That bit of news put a burr under Leavenworth's saddle. After last night's theft of our horses and their mules and the mysterious disappearance of the soldiers' tents, the Army worried that the Lahcotahs might join up with their old enemies the Rees and attack us. That fear wasn't far-fetched, for the Sioux had come for plunder and if they couldn't get what the Arikaras possessed, ours would likely do just fine.

Leavenworth sent a party under a white flag up to the lower village, headed by one of Ashley's men, a tall, stern-looking Negro named Edward Rose — Eddard was how he pronounced it — to ask their chiefs to come out for a parley. In the meantime, Joshua Pilcher and the Colonel renewed their wrangling about how best to pursue their little war. Pilcher still wanted to set fire to the villages, claiming that his Lahcotahs were about to go home, or worse, that they might turn on us and take sides with the Rees, but Leavenworth steadfastly refused to burn them out.

Whilst we awaited Rose's return, what I was seeing around me put me in mind of Homer's Trojan War. The Army and the rest of us looked to be like so many Greeks scurrying around outside the walls of Troy, squabbling amongst ourselves and not getting the chore done. The Lahcotahs were no more useful than a passel of Achilles sulking in their tents and the Rees, just like the Trojans, who had started the whole shooting match in the first place, were sitting snug behind their walls and sneering at us. Mister Homer would have burst a gut laughing if he could have seen how little such matters had changed.

When Rose returned at last he fetched with him a dozen or so rag-tag Arikaras with not a chief amongst them. Rose opined that they weren't worth talking to, but the Colonel palavered with them anyway. The Rees looked to be scared to death and they begged Leavenworth to stop the cannon fire, saying their women and children were "all in tears." General Ashley wanted his property returned and Leavenworth told them so. The Rees promised to give back whatever plunder they still possessed but they insisted that all the horses had been either killed or stolen, which didn't please Ashley one bit, for it was horses that he had wanted in the first place.

The whole day got used up with different bunches of Rees coming out to talk peace, but the entire matter was going nowheres. About all Ashley got out of it was a dozen buffalo robes and little else. Joshua Pilcher was fit to be tied. He wanted to fight, but Leavenworth wouldn't allow it. The Colonel told Pilcher to draw up a treaty, but Pilcher told him no, and so did Pilcher's man, Major Vanderburgh. Leavenworth drew it up himself and then Pilcher refused to sign it or to smoke a pipe of peace with the Arikaras, either. Which is where matters stood at the end of that day — precisely nowheres.

Next morning, the entire catastrophe commenced again. This time, Little Soldier, the sneaky little sidekick of old Gray Eyes, came out to parley. He announced first off that since Chief Gray Eyes had been killed, there was no reason to fight anymore. He said Gray Eyes had caused all the trouble in the first place and the rest of them had just gone along with him. Then Little Soldier asked that if the fighting commenced again, could he come over to our side? Leavenworth didn't even bother to reply, so Little Soldier proceeded to tell him just where to aim our cannons in order to do the most damage. Such was the poor excuse for a man with whom the Colonel chose to make a treaty.

Nobody listened to Eddard Rose, who was the only man amongst us who actually knew anything about Arikaras. Fitz had got to be halfway friendly with Rose on their way up the Missouri and had learned that Rose, who was a medley of white, black, and Cherokee, had been at one time a war chief amongst the Crows and had lived a couple-three years with the Rees, as well. He knew their tongue and he understood their ways. Still, as I heard one of the young officers sneer, "Who'd pay heed to a nigger?"

Joshua Pilcher was beside himself. His Lahcotahs were fast fading away, striking their tipis and returning home in disgust at the Army's lack of action, their *travois* loaded with Arikara corn — their extra ponies, too, swaying under huge white panniers made from army tents, were likewise loaded with corn.

Pilcher had good reason to be concerned. Not only were the Rees going unpunished, but now the Lahcotahs were loud in their contempt for the white man's cowardice, as they saw it, not only the Army, but all of us. Such an impression of our courage did not bode well for the future. Even several Army officers sided with Pilcher, foreseeing as they did battles in years to come with Indians who had lost whatever respect they ever had for the fighting ability of white men. Colonel Leavenworth turned a deaf ear to all such protests, howsomever, and continued his palavering with Little Soldier about some kind of a treaty, which, if you think of it, no Arikara could read nor was likely to honor, even if he knew what it said.

The upshot of it all was that Ashley got back three rifles, one very common horse, and sixteen buffalo robes, which appeared to the most of us to be downright measly payment for the lives of fourteen men and a score or more badly wounded, forty or more bought-and-paid-for horses killed, and considerable plunder abandoned on the sandbar, besides pretty much wrecking the second expedition when nearly three-quarters of the men returned to Saint Louis. Ashley and Pilcher were anything but pleased and most of Leavenworth's officers felt the same. Several came right out and argued with him, insisting that he give the order to attack the villages, Sioux or no Sioux. Eddard Rose made one more trip into the villages to see if he could scrape up a few more robes. When Rose returned, he warned that the Rees were set to pull out, but nobody heeded what he said. Leavenworth continued his shilly-shallying. At day's end he declared that he would make his decision overnight and that was that.

The following morning both villages were completely deserted. The Arikaras had flown, taking with them all their plunder and whatever horses they still owned. Only one old woman remained, the ancient mother of Gray Eyes, who was likely too frail to travel. We discovered her in the lower village, sitting peacefully in the midst of a passel of provisions, pretty much unconcerned about the goings-on around her.

Pilcher was outraged and he made no bones about it. Ashley and Andrew Henry were severely disappointed. The Army officers were unhappy and grumbling amongst themselves. Only Colonel Leavenworth appeared tranquil. It was plain to the rest of us that the Rees had won hands down, but the Colonel must have been looking at a different picture. Later on that day he ordered his keelboats to be loaded up with all the cannons and other plunder. The following morning he and his bluecoats set sail down the Missouri to their fort. They hadn't quite reached the first bend in the river, howsomever, before they got a chance to see the biggest bonfire anybody ever saw in those parts. Somebody torched the villages and they burned to the ground. Naturally Leavenworth accused Pilcher of setting the fire. Pilcher denied it, but he said he wasn't sorry that somebody had done it. And that is where matters stood, leastaways as far as I know.

Totting it all up, none of the whites was killed and only a couple of men got creased. The Sioux lost a few killed and wounded, but not many. The Rees lost half a hundred at most, likely fewer than that. Provisions probably didn't cost a great deal and the soldiers would have eaten them up no matter where they were. A body had to wonder, howsomever, just why we went to all that bother in the first place.

The real losers were Ashley and Henry and all the white men who ever came up the river in years to come. The Rees got completely uppity after that summer and set upon every white-eyes they could lay hands on. The Sioux, too, despised the whites for what they reckoned was our cowardice and many a scalp that hangs in a Lahcotah tipi today wouldn't be there if Colonel Leavenworth had possessed gumption enough to do the job that he set out to do. I was there and I saw the most of it and that is what I think of the whole pitiful shebang.

Supper in trappers' camp the night the soldiers left was a grand affair indeed. Tom Fitzpatrick proved himself a worthy quartermaster. Armed with all manner of chits and requisitions which he wrote and signed himself, Fitz amassed a mountain of army beans, white flour, corn meal, salt pork and bacon flitches, kegs of molasses, tobacco twists, gunpowder and galena, and a plenitude of whiskey from the officers' stores. The quartermaster tent was fairly bulging with pilfered wealth. Leavenworth's army stationed in one spot was confusion enough. His army on the move was bedlam and the Tower of Babel put together. Orders were flying every whichaway and nobody was sure who had issued them. Fitz knew how to play such a commotion like an Irish harp.

Joshua Pilcher and his men camped with us in the grove that night, stuffing themselves at our cookfires and joining in the fun afterwards. Ashley and his officers huddled off by themselves, but Andrew Henry, with Pilcher at his side, stayed amongst the rest of us, playing his fiddle alongside Anse Tolliver until long after dark. I reckon that Henry — and Pilcher, too — understood what Ashley never did, that leading a bunch of men meant being a part of them, that all worthwhile authority comes from inside yourself.

We kept our horses close at hand that night and pickets were posted all around the grove, for more than half a thousand unhappy Arikara warriors had slipped off from the two villages the night before and now they could be anywhere, just waiting to pounce. It was past time that we decamped ourselves.

So it was the following morning, right after breakfast and bidding farewell to Pilcher and his people, that Ashley and Henry divided our command into two brigades. The first, under the Major's command, was to go back up the Missouri to Fort Henry and empty it out, then head southwest to the mountains for the fall hunt. The second brigade would proceed directly to the mountains under the command, for some unaccountable reason, of Jedediah Smith.

Perhaps William Ashley saw something in Smith that most of the rest of us didn't. There were several men amongst us who were older and much more experienced in the ways of Indians, the wilderness, and trapping beaver than Jed Smith was at that time, but Ashley was the boss and that was what he decided. Most of Ashley's people from the second year were assigned to Smith's brigade, including Clyman and Fitzpatrick, and so were Tuttle and I, Jim Bridger, all of the Iroquois, and a few more.

Ashley didn't plan to accompany either party. He intended to return aboard his keelboat to Saint Louis, where he had been elected lieutenant governor of Missouri. Jim Clyman told me that the General had a hankering to be the big he-dog of that state and was running for election for governor, which was all right with me, for I didn't intend to live there.

Naturally Tuttle and I hated parting with Andrew Henry, Godey, Brass Turtle, Anse, and all the rest of our bunch, but at the time we thought of ourselves as bound men, engagés, although that situation was getting to be increasingly hard to stomach. Orders were orders, howsomever, and we were obliged to obey.

Packing up never took much time and it wasn't long before we bade our farewells and gathered in two bunches, ready to set out on our separate trails. It was then that I was presented with one of the toughest choices I ever had to make up till that time.

I was mounted on Chiksika and leading Jake, who was packing my plunder and a power of provisions Fitz had supplied, half-listening to General Ashley's farewell oration, when Jed Smith rode up and drew rein, then sat staring first at me and then at my horse. When Ashley finally ran out of breath, Smith spoke up. "You, Buck. I'll be taking that horse. You can have this one." His voice was as flat as his cold, gray eyes and I slowly realized that he wasn't joking.

At first I couldn't say a word. I just sat in my saddle, choked, too stunned to reply, until I felt Tuttle ride up beside me and jam his knee up against mine. That broke the dam and my words tumbled out almost too fast to wrap my tongue around them. "I don't reckon so, Mister Smith! This here's my own horse and I aim to keep him. I bought 'im an' I paid for him an' I stole 'im back from the Crows! I gave a proper haircut to the Crow who stole 'im an' no short-hair Yankee's about to take 'im off me, 'ceptin' over my cold, dead body! You ready?" I didn't actually reach for my pistol, but I knew where it was.

Smith r'ared up in his saddle, eyes bulging, his mouth open, but before he could say a word, Tuttle broke in. "Hold on, thar! Ye're new up thisaway, Smith. We been here a spell. Thet'ere hoss b'longs to Temple Buck. Thet hoss be his'n, bought an' paid fer an' stole back to boot, like he sez. Ain't nobody like to ride 'im 'sides Temple an' thet's a fac'. An' ye kin count Tuttle Thompson in on the fight if'n thar's to be onesuch!"

Jed Smith had no time to reply, for right then General Ashley called out and motioned for him to come over to where he was sitting with Major Henry. Smith threw a hard look at the two of us, then walked his horse over to the General and dismounted. The three of them huddled for a spell before the Major beckoned to Tuttle and me, telling us to follow him, which we did.

Andrew Henry walked to one side of the grove, out of earshot of the others, before he swung about and glared up at us, saying nothing at first, his lips pursed and his eyes scrunched all but shut in a frown. Tuttle and I stepped down from our horses and waited for him to speak first, neither of us with any inkling of which way or how far he was likely to jump. At last he broke his silence. "What in pluperfect hell d'ye think ye're doing, Buck?" Then without waiting for my reply, he swung his flinty gaze to Tuttle and demanded, "And you, Thompson, backing his play! Have you two lost your minds? Have ye any idea what the two o' you just did?"

Henry obviously wasn't precisely posing his remarks as questions, but Tuttle spoke up anyway. "Reckon I do, Majah. Thet uppity yankee grayback was fixin' to steal Temple's own hoss. Hoss-thievin' ain't 'lowed, be it Crow Injun ner Yankee grayback what's still wet a'hind his ears. Time he larns."

The Major's face got remarkably red, well-nigh purple, and he commenced to swell up. I reckoned it was time for me to say something before he actually exploded. "Major, you know us, Tuttle an' me. We've been with you from the first git-along an' you never asked us to do anythin' that we didn't try to get it done, best we could. But you have never been unfair, not once. What that bible-pounder just tried to do was unfair an' you an' ever'body else knows it. He doesn't know men an' I reckon he doesn't want to, neither. Nor much else about this here country, truth to tell."

Before Henry could reply, Tuttle chimed in with, "Ye know we be ready to foller you anywheres, Majah! Allus have, allus will. But thet yankee boy be needin' some serious eddi-cayshun an' I ain't inclined to let 'im use my lily-white Kaintucky arse fer a larnin' slate nohow!"

Henry's rage had simmered down to a healthy boil by then and he commenced to lecture the two of us on discipline and mutiny and authority and suchlike, which mostly went in one ear and out the other, for we knew — and we knew he knew — that the wilderness doesn't precisely abound with second chances and an arrogant, ignorant boss will likely get you killed. All of us had recently got a bellyful of military discipline and the sorry results it produced.

It was like as if Henry could read our minds, even as he was sermonizing. At length he broke off and sighed. Then, still frowning, he said, "You two hold on right here. I'll see what I can do." Then he marched back to where Ashley and Smith were waiting.

It wasn't long before we saw Hugh Glass and John Fitzgerald amble their horses over to Smith's brigade. Andrew Henry waved us towards his own crew, a command we wasted no time in obeying. As we passed by, General Ashley glared holes right through us and Jedediah simply stared at the ground, most likely trying to recall some scripture to help him deal with reprobates like Tuttle and me.

≫   ≫   ≫

The farther we rode up the Missouri, the cheerier most of us became. We knew that after we finished our chore at the fort we would be heading off for the Shining Mountains and the fall hunt in new territory. Fact is, our route took us considerably west of the Missouri, across the prairie. We made a beeline, as best the country allowed, for the mouth of the Yellowstone. Taking into account Henry's disaster with the Blackfoots at the Great Falls, he and the General had decided to abandon the fort and the Missouri trade with Indians and devote all of our efforts to trapping in the mountains.

Not everybody was cheerful, Anse Tolliver for one. He was forever fussing over the welfare of his pack mules, which he insisted were overloaded, mainly by a whole field smithy and a passel of supplies the General had bought at a bargain price from the Army — forge, anvil, tools of every sort, horseshoes, and what all. Such truck made for a heavy, unhandy load and Anse clucked and groused over every sign of a sore back amongst his long-eared charges.

The Delawares missed their Iroquois friends, but, being Indians, they made no big show of it. The absence of Jim Bridger's smiling face and willing disposition was a daily disappointment as well, and we wondered how it was that the smithy had been sent with our brigade and the blacksmith sent off with the other. Howsomever such decisions were not ours to make nor even to question.

Calvin Talbot wasn't cheerful, either, but then, he never was. He rode off by himself, friendless and alone. I reckon he preferred it that way.

Hunting improved as we journeyed farther west on the prairie and away from the Arikara and Mandan villages. Wapiti grew more plentiful and the day before we reached the Teton we came upon a little bunch of buffalo. I'm not altogether sure which one of us was the happiest to get in amongst those woolly critters once again,, Chiksika or me, but I reckon it was him. After weeks of nose-to-tail plodding on the trail and standing tethered on a picket line, Chiksika fairly exploded into action, plunging into the midst of half a dozen cows, keeping clear of the bull behind us, carrying me close beside the hump for my shots, first with my rifle, then the pistol, then darting clear and drawing up to a standstill, the both of us watching our two fat cows stumble to a halt, swaying and coughing blood, then crumple and fall stiff-legged to the ground. It was heart-warming to be doing proper man's work once again and I reckon Chiksika thought so, too.

Army vittles, no matter how plentiful, can never be a match for buffalo cow, rolling fat at summer's end and fresh-killed. When the column caught up with us, several men rode out and commenced the butchering, gobbling chunks of the livers raw, splashed with a mite of gall, glorying in the taste of buffalo once again after weeks of salt pork and army beans, and all too often nothing at all.

Fleece fat and hump and ribs dripping hot grease into sputtering cookfires, wafting a divine fragrance on the evening breeze, improved the humor of the whole brigade more than somewhat that evening. After we gorged ourselves as full as ticks, Anse quit his grumbling and brought out his fiddle to play some lively tunes and not long afterwards the Major joined in, too. The Arikaras and Colonel Leavenworth's fizzling little war were a long way behind us by then and it was time to be thinking of new opportunities and adventures in the mountains.

Even the rain that fell late that night didn't dampen our spirits, although it soaked nearly everything else. Tuttle had sliced several big swatches of canvas out of Fitz's quartermaster tent when the Army departed, so we managed to keep ourselves and most of our plunder reasonably dry. When I came to my robes after standing horse guard, I lay with my head on my saddle, listening to raindrops pattering on the stiff canvas. It seemed to me they were singing songs of sweet promise of the good life that lay ahead in the mountains.

ॐ   ॐ   ॐ

The rain had quit by morning but when we arrived at the Teton we discovered a swollen river running over its banks instead of the peaceful stream we recalled. Ned Godey and Brass Turtle rode upstream and down, seeking a fordable place where the water ran shallow enough to get our animals and men across in reasonable safety, but when they thought they had found such a spot, Anse pointed out that over-burdened as some of the pack mules and horses were, the high water and swift current would most certainly sweep the critters off their feet and wash them downstream to drown.

The Major was in a quandary. He was anxious to get back to his fort and finish the business there, but he was unwilling to risk his pack animals and plunder in the flood. Tuttle and I sat watching him pacing up and down the muddy bank, hands clasped behind his back, frowning deeply, glancing now and then at the roiling waters, and cursing under his breath.

Then a most remarkable event occurred. Calvin Talbot stepped down from his horse, tossed the reins to the man beside him, and strode out to where the Major was standing. Tuttle and I nudged our horses forward, getting close enough to hear Talbot announce in that high-pitched voice of his, "Ef ye hanker to git acrost today, ye oughta be makin' one o' them bullboats. Ef'n ye do, I'll swim a rope acrost an' ye kin haul yer plunder right smart." That was all Talbot intended to say. His mouth snapped shut, tight as a trap, and he stood staring at Andrew Henry, awaiting a reply.

Henry was startled. He looked out across the muddy brown torrent, then back at Talbot, then back at the river, before he asked, "Are ye sure ye can do it?" Talbot merely nodded. Henry shrugged and said with a thin smile, "Thankee then. Go to it." If it had been another man, the Major might have offered to shake his hand, but Calvin Talbot welcomed no such sociable gestures.

The Major gave orders to cut a passel of willows along the bank, which we did. Then Godey and a French trapper called Antoine Leroux showed the rest of us how to bind them together to make a frame, cover it with a fresh buffalo hide we had taken the day before, and lace it snugly onto the frame with fresh sinew.

Completed it looked like a big, ugly soup bowl, but Godey and Leroux assured us that it could get the chore done.

We collected our pack ropes, which tied end-to-end were long enough to span the river twice, with just enough extra length to haul the bullboat back and forth, tied fast to trees on either shore. By early afternoon the bullboat — a length of rope tied to either side of it, one end secured to a stout cottonwood — was bobbing in what passed for shallows in the raging flood.

Meanwhile Talbot had been sitting quietly, saying nothing, watching us at work, smoking his pipe, carefully tapping out the dottle when he finished, no flicker of expression betraying what he might be thinking, if anything.

When the Major pronounced the bullboat fit for the task, Talbot rose to his feet, walked to his saddle horse, and then led all three of his critters to where Tuttle and I were standing. His face was a wooden mask when he handed the reins to me and his distant eyes appeared to be looking through and past me as he said, "Here, you,

Buck. Look after 'em fer me." He shucked off his possibles belt and laid it on the ground at my feet, placing his rifle and pistol on top of it. Then he reached up under his shirt and unbuckled his money belt. It looked weighty and it rattled when he laid it on the heap. When he stood up, his pale blue eyes met mine. I tried to look into them, but I saw nothing there that was warm or human. His high voice sounded hollow, like night wind in a dead tree, when he declared, "Somethin' happens, it's all your'n."

With only that and nothing more, Talbot spun on his heel, shouldered past the men gathered there, walked directly to the river's edge, picked up the rope and tied it around his waist,and waded into a millrace of dun-colored water. I stood dumbfounded, completely confused at his act of trust, watching the water creep higher on his legs, then to his waist, tugging at him as he struggled to keep his footing on the rocky bottom, then washing over him when he threw himself forwards and commenced to thrash his arms and kick his way towards the far shore, which appeared to be a hundred miles away right then.

The current caught him after only a stroke or two and commenced to push him downstream, but he fought back and continued his progress, head down, arms churning, forever angling farther and farther downriver until he disappeared in a watery avalanche.

Suddenly the bullboat leaped off the shore and bounced onto the water. Talbot's rope had paid out and snapped taut, then yanked the bullboat out into the current and sent it bobbing downriver until it jerked to a shuddering stop, halted by the line straining against the cottonwood.

Every man on shore stood frozen, rooted, mystified, fascinated by the wierd antics of the bullboat bouncing on the muddy surface of the river, unwilling to comprehend what was happening, until Andrew Henry's voice cracked out above the roar of rushing water. "Pull him back! Pull 'im in! He's drowning!"

A dozen pairs of hands, then a score, then forty, grabbed at the rope and commenced to haul the bullboat upstream against the awful force of a river gone mad, until at last the clumsy craft was beached and we were able to get hold of the line on the far side of the boat and commence our tug-o'-war against the driving waters once again.

Tuttle, Anse, and Godey labored beside me in the shallows as we strained to retrieve each foot of rope against the grudging power of the river, until at last we saw what was left of Calvin Talbot, the rope snugged around his neck as securely as a hangman's halter, the long length of him twirling slowly in the current.

We dragged the body onto the muddy bank and I looked down into a battered face drained of all color, fish-belly white it was, pale blue eyes staring as vacantly in death as in life.

Anse Tolliver was first to speak. "I allus 'spected he was borned to get hisse'f hung, but thi'shere's a diff'rence, hain't it?"

Tuttle drew a long breath and stared down at the still white face for a spell before he pronounced, "Fer a waterman, a feller what made his livin' on the rivers, ol' Talbot sure as hell never had no luck with water. Water never liked 'im!" I reckon Tuttle was recalling Talbot's brush with death on the Falls of the Ohio and the time we fished him out of the Missouri after the wreck of the keelboat. It was true. Water never liked him.

Ned Godey was customarily practical and equally unsympathetic. "Wal now, leastaways the body's washed all clean fer the buryin'. Time we get 'im planted."

There was nothing for me to add to all that, so I didn't try — but when we were untying the pack rope from around Talbot's neck and waist, I saw that it was my own.

Chapter VIII
The Shining Mountains

It wasn't but an hour until Talbot's body was underground. At first it appeared that the Major was about to ask somebody to say some last words, but I reckon he thought better of it. As for me, the sentiments expressed by my companions on the riverbank summed up the matter better than any parson's eulogy could have done. Whilst a couple of men shoveled dirt and rocks into the grave, Henry stood at one end with a Bible in his hand, but I wager that he was thinking more about the delay in our journey than about the departed spirit of Calvin Talbot.

There was no gloom in camp that night. No one was left amongst us who might have mourned Talbot's passing, if ever there had been. The feeling was relief rather than regret, for Talbot could be grizzly mean if he took the notion and nobody was safe when he was in such a humor.

The fiddles were silent, it's true, but appetites were as hearty as ever, finishing up the buffalo we killed the day before, and the joshing and rude joking was, if anything, louder than ever, as often happens in the neighborhood of death.

We remained three days in that place, waiting for the Teton to settle down, which it did at last. For some reason I refused to paw through the plunder Talbot had left with me until the second day, except for his money belt, which I buckled on first thing, without looking into it, before the body was in the ground. When at last I opened Talbot's packs, the array of weapons put me in mind of a gunsmith's shop. I wanted none of it. My Melchior rifle was all I could wish for, so I gave Fink's big-bore rifle to Tuttle, whose Kentucky-made gun was a trifle puny for buffalo and such. Godey was satisfied with his own rifle, so he got Carpenter's pistol and the rifle went to Brass Turtle. Paddy's marksmanship with his musket was improving steadily, so we helped it along by giving him Talbot's rifle and Anse Tolliver got the pistol. The rest of the hardware — knives and tomahawks and such — went to the other Delawares and whomsoever wanted it. Except for Mike Fink's pistol, which I changed my mind about and kept for myself as a reminder that no matter how bad circumstances appear to be, this, too, shall pass.

≈   ≈   ≈

Hamish Davidson was all smiles when he greeted us at the gate of the fort and his smile grew even broader when he learned that Ashley and Henry intended to abandon the post and move inland to the mountains. Trade with Indians had been slow to hardly-at-all throughout the summer and except for one pony raid by Blackfoots, nothing much had happened or changed since our departure in June. Blackfoots had made off with half a dozen horses, but Hamish had replaced them by trading with Crees and Assiniboins come down from the north to hunt buffalo.

Two of the horses Hamish traded for with the Crees had been our own in the first place, but he bought and paid for them anyway. It was Blackfoots, not Crees, that stole them from us and horseflesh is the universal coin of the prairies. Just how an Indian comes by a particular horse is his own affair — unless you catch him at it, naturally.

Henry's men who had been wounded at the Great Falls were pretty much mended by time we returned and everybody was itching to be off to the mountains and the fall hunt. Clearing out of the fort didn't take but a couple-three days, most of which time our bunch spent hunting summer-fat wapiti and stray buffalo along the Yellowstone. At that time of year, even young bulls made for prime vittles.

When at last every horse was saddled and packed and whatever wasn't needed or was too heavy to tote had been cached in the woods above the fort, Andrew Henry's brigade, now numbering nigh fourscore trappers, bade a final farewell to Fort Henry and set out on a generally southwestward course for the mountains.

Abandoning the fort occasioned no regrets for me, yet as we rode across the strip of prairie to the Yellowstone I recalled with tender feelings the nights I had walked that same path with Night-eyes, returning her to the crossing on the Yellowstone that led to the Crow village after our trysts in the willow grove. Night-eyes was the best part of my memories of that place. She was gone forever now, so when we rode up the far bank of the Yellowstone, I never even bothered to look back.

A couple days out on the trail, I was on horse guard at day's end, sitting alone on the prairie, when I reminded myself that I hadn't yet opened Talbot's money belt. Strangely, I was reluctant to pry into it, although it occurred to me then that he would have suffered no remorse at slitting open my gullet if he was of a mind to do so. That grim thought firmed up my resolve to discover what my legacy might be.

I spilled the contents of the money belt onto the ground and, sure enough, all three oilskin packets, carefully sealed by Pierre Cadet so long ago and still unopened, lay before me, along with a healthy scattering of big gold coins. Calvin Talbot could neither read nor write, but he was no fool. He had understood the value of those documents and he had carefully preserved them — then, for some unaccountable reason, he passed them on to me.

Oddly enough, right then, my discovery was of little moment to me. I was more concerned with what Smiley might be cooking for supper. That night in my robes my thoughts were of the mountains that lay just days ahead, not of the heavy belt snugged around my middle.

    ∾ ∾ ∾

Eddard Rose was our guide, for he knew that country better than any man in our company, even better than the Major, whose travels had never taken him precisely that way. Godey, Prudhomme, Hamish and Leroux, and a couple others were experienced on the Missouri, but the southern mountains were still unknown to them. Rose was a silent man, mostly absorbed in his own thoughts, but quick to see and hear anything out of place on the prairie that rolled out in every direction, broken only by treelines that meandered alongside the Yellowstone and the little streams that fed it. Whether it was buffalo or wapiti or a party of Indians taking our measure, Rose saw them first and quietly informed the Major.

Rose was quiet and he was never what you might call good-natured. A fire burned inside him and he tolerated no disrespect from those amongst our crew who tried at first to treat him like the darkies they had known back home. He was no foot-scraping, cap-doffing slave. Nobody owned Eddard Rose. Nobody could. Word was that he had been a war chief amongst the Crows and before that, a valued trapper and trader for old Manuel Lisa, who had been the first to reach up the Missouri to grab a fistful of beaver plews. There was talk, too, that Rose had started out as a pirate on the Mississippi and nothing I ever learned about him caused me to believe otherwise.

Rose was a big man, well over six foot in his moccasins, lean and strong and hickory-tough, quick and precise in his movements, ever alert and aware of whatever was happening or, it seemed, about to happen, and he wore his quiet dignity like a nobleman's mantle. White, black, and Cherokee Indian blended in his stern features, yet he was none of those. He was a man apart. I have no idea of his age. He seemed eternal.

Men learned to call him nigger only when they were sure that he was well out of earshot, and after a time, not even then.

At first Rose rode alone, well in advance of the party, but as the days wore on he would often ride in company with Brass Turtle and the Delawares, then with Godey and Leroux, whom he knew from when they were Missouri River traders, and after a spell I was admitted to the fringe of his circle. At length he commenced taking his meals with our bunch, but he always slept off by himself, somewhere out past the edge of camp.

Soon after the Yellowstone crooked off to the west, we headed more or less due south. Weather held fair and game was plentiful on the prairie that appeared to stretch endlessly in all directions around us.

Then one early forenoon as I was half-dozing in the saddle as we plodded southward, Antoine Leroux punched my arm and cried out, *"Les Grosses Cornes! Regardez, mes amis!* Ze Beeg Horn! *Les montagnes! Nous sommes arrivés aux montagnes!"*

Sure enough, we had come to the mountains. As my gaze followed his pointing finger I saw in the hazy distance a blue-gray line of hills rising from the prairie. There is no explaining the excitement that welled up and threatened to choke me. I had never in my whole life seen a real mountain and I couldn't properly see them yet, but I felt right then that I was coming home, that out there was where I truly belonged, that Temple Buck was about to become complete.

Leroux was as excited as I was and he chattered on and on about the chain of mountains that lay before us, *les Grosses Cornes*, the Big Horns, named, he said, for a kind of wild sheep that roamed there. For a man who had never laid eyes on either those mountains or the sheep that lived on them, Leroux appeared to know a great deal about both.

When our hunters rejoined the column in the late afternoon their broad grins announced their success, even before we saw their pack animals laden with quarters of buffalo and elk. Shortly afterwards, Eddard Rose rode out in the direction of the hunt, for we learned later that the hunters had reported seeing what they took to be Indians lurking in a crick bottom. Rose went alone and we watched him out of sight, dwindling in the distance until he blended and disappeared into rippling yellow prairie grass and purple sagebrush.

Supper that night was a festive affair. It was a time for rejoicing, not only because we had a plenitude of fresh meat, but mostly because the mountains were dimly in sight at last. We gorged on buffalo and wapiti and merriment reigned throughout the camp, spiced up considerably when Anse brought out his fiddle after supper. Tuttle was carving thin slices from a chunk of buffalo tongue and sharing them with me, when he chanced to glance upwards. His hands stilled, his expression sobered, and he fell silent.   Eddard Rose loomed over us, half-shrouded in the gathering dusk. Neither one of us had seen or heard him coming.

Tuttle, as you might expect, wasn't long in regaining his composure.   He grinned up at Rose and offered him a slice of buffalo tongue dangling from the tip of his big knife. "Evenin', Brother Rose.   Setcherse'f down ri'chere an' he'p yorese'f to vittles."

Rose didn't reply but he allowed himself a brief smile. He took the slice of tongue and squatted on his heels beside us. When he had eaten that tidbit, he went to the cookfire, hacked off a couple-three ribs with a knife as big as Tuttle's, and returned to us. He ate with good appetite, gnawing meat off the bones with strong, white teeth, grunting his satisfaction. When he finished, he threw the bones into the fire, wiped his greasy hands on his leggin's, and commenced to tell us the purpose of his visit. "This'n be a night fer sleepin' light.   Theah be Blackfoots about an' they got a hankerin' fer hosses. Allus do, natcherly, but t'night they got eyes fer our'n."

I believed every word he said, but I had to ask anyhow. "How d'ye know? Did ye see 'em?"

Rose's face never changed expression. "They be theah, rest on it. Could'a picked me off like a ripe cherry, but they warn't o' mind to. That would'a got the wind up." He paused for a moment, choosing his words with care. "It's dark o' the moon. They be comin' late. Close-hobble yer hosses an' stake 'em out tight. Fresh up yer primin' in all yer guns an' keep yer blade loose. Ye'll likely need 'em this night."

He rose to his feet and looked down at us, the slightest flicker of a grin on his lips. "Git yer sleepin' done early if'n ye kin sleep a-tall. We be tellin' ye when ye're goin' on hoss guard." His grin widened considerably when he added, "I reckon we be takin' Blackfoot ha'r this night." Rose faded into the darkness, only to reappear at another cookfire, where he squatted down and commenced talking with another bunch. Tuttle and I did as he told us.

&ed;   &ed;   &ed;

Little Mountain, tugging at my sleeve, pulled me from a shallow slumber and motioned for me to follow him. Tuttle was already awake and ready. I gathered up my possibles, both pistols, and Melchior, crawled out of my robes, and followed him, still on hands and knees, Tuttle trailing behind. Little Mountain led us to the outer edge of the horse herd and pointed to a clump of sagebrush, which I took to be my sentry post. Then he and Tuttle slithered on into the darkness. The ring of sagebrush was dense and scratchy, but I was able to find space enough inside to lie out flat, rifle in my hands, pistols on the ground in front of me, peering out onto the prairie and seeing nothing in the puny starlight, listening with no better success, and wondering how I might behave if and when the Blackfoots showed up.

I had entirely too much time for such wondering, so to dampen down my nerves I let my fancy slip away into Mister Homer's tale, marveling how like old-time Greeks we were, hidden in the belly of a big wooden horse, weapons ready, waiting to pounce on the Trojans. But no Trojans came, nor Blackfoots either, leastaways none that I could see.

My gaze strayed back into camp. Buffalo chip fires burned low, tiny orange flowers blooming in the blackness, barely limning heaps of sleep robes scattered around them, which might or might not conceal our sleeping comrades.

I was thinking that I would prefer fighting to this endless waiting when I changed my mind in a hurry. Out of the tail my eye I caught sight of movement to my left and somewhat behind me and I knew in my gut that it wasn't a stray horse. I was rising to my knees and bringing up my rifle to bear on the shadowy presence when a shot blasted out of the darkness, then a gurgling grunt and a low moan as the figure slumped to the ground. All hell broke loose right then.

A throaty whoop to the right of me made me swing around, still on my knees, rifle stuck out in front of me, just as a mostly naked Indian came charging, swinging a tomahawk in one hand and a big knife in the other. I reckon he never saw me, for he ran his belly right up against the muzzle and knocked me sprawling back on my heels. I just naturally pulled the trigger as I fell and he disappeared in a cloud of fire and smoke.

There was no time to reload, so I dropped the rifle and grabbed up my pistols. When the smoke cleared off I saw the Indian lying spread-eagled on his back, still in front of my sagebrush patch. I was still on my knees and I reckoned it was best to remain that way. Guns were popping off all around me and there was a passel of whooping and hollering going on. Some of it I took to be white men's voices but mostly what I heard sounded like Indian. Standing up would just provide a better target, so I remained crouched down where I was.

I don't know if my eyes had got used to the darkness or if it was the excitement and the blood racing in my veins that made my eyesight keener, but the dark seemed to dissolve into a sort of twilight. I could see Indians, naked save for a britchclout, running every whichaway, some hot-footing it out of the horse herd, others charging up from the prairie, coming to help their companions. One big fellow sprinted out of the herd, heading for the prairie. He was but ten feet away when I aimed my right-hand pistol at the big part of his body and fired, for I was certain he would soon return, better armed than he was right then. The ball caught him low in the back and his feet flipped up in the air and over his head, somersaulting him backwards to lie face down in the grass, twitching at first, then lying still. It was a most remarkable spectacle.

Another Indian must have seen the muzzle flash and smoke from my pistol and reckoned my weapon was empty, for he ran up to my sagebrush hideout and shoved his musket full in my face, his own painted features twisted in a hellish grin. I twisted off to one side, pointed my left-hand pistol as best I could, and dropped the hammer. The double explosion nearly deafened me. White-hot agony seared my neck and right at that moment I knew for certain I would never see the mountains.

As the smoke drifted off I dimly saw my enemy draped over the stiff sagebrush, his musket in my lap, what was left of his face at my feet, dripping blood on my moccasins. My neck felt like I had been branded and blood was running down onto my chest. I still clutched the pistol in my hand and I knew from the heft of it that it was the one I had inherited from Fink. Right then was when I came as close as I ever did to thanking Mike Fink for anything.

Whilst I fumbled powder and ball into my weapons, it appeared the fight was petering out. The heavy gunfire of a few minutes before was sparse and ragged now and the whoops and hollers had a happier sound to them. I peeked through the sagebrush, past the bodies of the two dead Indians, and saw no movement on the prairie beyond. It was only then that I realized that dawn was breaking and soft gray morning light was breathing life into the land again.

The thud of running footsteps on summer-dry earth yanked at my jangled nerves once more. I snatched up a pistol and lay back in my sagebrush nest, ready to defend my life. Tuttle Thompson's face appeared over the brush and it showed, in rapid succession, concern, then relief, then outright fright when he saw my pistol leveled somewheres in the neighborhood of his gullet. "Hold on thar, pard! It be me! Tuttle! Ye still healthy?"

Before I could answer, Brass Turtle, then Ned Godey, poked their heads into view and everybody commenced talking at once. I struggled to my feet, which started my neck bleeding again. My head was spinning but I heard Godey say, "Goddlemighty, Temple! Ye kilt two of 'em fer sure!" referring to the two dead Indians that lay at their feet.

My voice sounded hollow in my ears when I heard myself say, with a mite of pride, I must confess, "That'n's mine, too, yonder there." I recall raising my pistol to point at the Indian who lay face down in the grass, then falling backwards and downwards into total darkness.

಄ ಄ ಄

Old Foot's slow drumbeat and quavering chant, then Little Mountain's round, good-natured face close to mine, at first anxious, then breaking into a grin, assured me that I was still in the land of the living. Little Mountain barked out something in Delaware and the drumbeat ceased. Foot's weathered face appeared and he lifted my eyelid with a calloused but gentle hand. Then he grunted and gifted me with one of his rare, broken-toothed grins, which I'm sure he meant to be reassuring.

I was lying with my head on my own saddle, back in camp, and I saw by the sun that it was still early morning. Whilst Foot fussed with a poultice at my neck, I was able to look past him at a scene of utter frolic in the camp. Brass Turtle and the other Delawares were dancing with a score of trappers around a pole festooned with enough black hair to stuff a mattress. Andrew Henry, Hamish Davidson, and Louis Prudhomme stood off to one side, grinning and chatting and, I reckon, congratulating themselves on giving the Blackfoots some overdue comeuppance. Eddard Rose, who had made it all happen, stood alone at a distance from the others, solemn and thoughtful, excluded from their mutual admiration.

I looked in vain for Tuttle Thompson, but he was nowhere to be seen. Then I heard him before I saw him, which was often the case. "Thar ye be, Temple Buck, back amongst us!" He came trotting up behind me and knelt by my side, grinning down at me and waving a little flask that I had hoped he had forgotten about, which naturally he hadn't. He unscrewed the cap and put the flask to my lips and when he tilted it up I knew once more the taste and the heat of liquid sunshine and my brain flooded over with memories of the warm and ever-blooming presence of Lucette, holding me close and smothering me in the rich woman smell of her, so long ago and so far from me now.

Tuttle, ever generous, held the flask to my lips until I erupted in a fit of coughing and pawed the flask to one side. At length I was able to sputter, "Enough. You have some, too."

Tuttle rocked back on his heels and grinned at me. Then he waved his cup in my face and said, "Naw, thet be your'n, fer sake of ol' times an' sweet ladies recollected." He took a deep swallow from his cup and added, "Naow, this'n hyar be mine." He took another gulp and corrected himself. "Wal, truth to tell, this'n be your'n, too. I awready drunk up muh own!"

I gathered that the Major had rewarded the company with a healthy dram for their efforts of the night before and Tuttle had thoughtfully collected both his share and mine.

The dancing broke up after a spell, but I could still hear a passel of brag and blather amongst the trappers as they retrieved the scalps that each of them had taken. Brass Turtle stepped out of the crowd, a handful of hair in either hand, and made a beeline for me. He hung three scalps, still sticky with blood, on my rifle leaning against a bush, before he grinned at me and said, "Mawnin', Brother Buck, thar be yer prizes, fer all to see." He paused a moment in thought before he continued. "Ye must be gittin' quite a collection. What ye doin' with 'em?"

"Aw, Tuttle keeps sellin' 'em, tradin' for whiskey an' such."

Turtle's grin broadened. "Ain't likely he'll be havin' much luck from here on. 'Pears to me, whiskey's scarce an' hair's a glut on the market hereabouts." He went on to tally up the night's events, nigh a score of Blackfoots killed and scalped and perhaps that many more dragged off by their comrades, no horses lost, and only a few puny wounds like my own amongst our people. He finished by praising Eddard Rose. "We kin be thankin' Rose fer that good fortune. Ain't none of us knows a patch o' what he's awready fergot concernin' fightin' up thisaway." I nodded my agreement, recalling how Rose had used himself as bait and how he had known just when and where to post his guards. Only hard experience teaches such lessons and only a few men are smart enough and brave enough to put such knowledge to use.

I recalled, too, Andrew Henry's disaster at the Great Falls and I wondered how he might have fared if Eddard Rose had been with him. If, in fact, Henry would have listened to a black man at the time, which is doubtful.

Foot returned to change the poultice on my neck. Afterwards he and Turtle chatted for a spell in Delaware. When Foot went off, Brass Turtle asked, "Reckon ye kin ride? Foot sez ye kin. Them Blackfoots're bloatin' bad. Best we git on our way, afore they git to stinkin'. Ain't nobody here about to bury 'em."

Without replying, I reared up to a sitting position and found that my neck hurt hardly at all, just a twinge or two, and the dizziness soon faded. My major discomfort right then was raging hunger. The sight of Smiley and Anse busy at cooking chores promised a ready remedy for that. I grinned at Turtle and told

him, "Count on it. I'll be ready." I heaved myself to my feet and
headed for the cookfire, happy to be alive and amongst my own
kind again.

Tuttle looked after horse chores that morning and by time I
finished surrounding a healthy mess of vittles, he had brought our
critters into camp, saddled and ready to pack. My saddle was on
Jake, which was just as well, for he was a sight less lively on the
trail than Chiksika. Within the hour we filed out of camp, headed
for the mountains, still far off in the blue distance.

As we passed by the bodies of the Blackfeet scattered at the edge
of our horse pasture, I felt a pang of regret that such fine-looking
men should have died for such a paltry purpose. But then I
glanced down at my buckskin shirt, stiff with my own dried blood,
and I reminded myself that it was better them than me.

ॐ   ॐ   ॐ

Two days later we were riding in the shadow of the Big Horns
before we made camp. All day long I had been nourishing my
spirit with the sight of fir-covered slopes blending into craggy gray
heights that framed distant snow-covered peaks beyond, looking
like so many proud white-headed eagles guarding the treasures
that awaited us in those Shining Mountains.

I was not alone in my excitement. Every man amongst us
shared the thrill of reaching our goal at last, each one showing his
pleasure according to his nature. We had served our
apprenticeship on the Yellowstone and the Musselshell and we had
tempered our resolve with the Rees and the Blackfeet. Now it was
time to prove our worth as journeyman trappers.

"Would ye be lookin' at thim mountains now, would ye!" Paddy
McBride said for at least the fortieth time that day. "Crawlin' wid
beavers, I warrant ye! Thick as sov'reigns in a Sassenach's purse, I
warrant ye well! An' all o' thim critters jist beggin' fer Paddy
McBride to come fer the harvestin'!"

Anse Tolliver, prodding his pack mules along the trail, cast a
baleful eye on McBride and said sourly, "Ye'd best be keepin' yore

eye out fer Blackfoots, Irish, lest they be harvestin' that red topknot o' your'n fer their belt. Beaver'll keep."

Paddy refused to be discouraged. He beamed at Anse and said proudly, "Me topknot indeed, Misther Mules! An' wasn't it Missus McBride's lad Paddy what was after takin' the hair o' one o' thim Blackfoots his ownself, not three days past?" He waved a matted scalp at Tolliver and added, "An' me own red mop remainin' exac'ly where me sainted mither was after puttin' it!" It was true. Paddy had held fast the night of the Blackfoot raid and had done the workmanlike chore we had learned to expect of him. Bumptious he certainly was, but Paddy was no longer a greenhorn.

Eddard Rose had ridden in amongst us. He allowed himself a tight smile when he said quietly, "Blackfoots an' beavah, they gen'rally go togethah. We come here fer beavah, that's a fac', but keep yer eyes peeled jes' the same."

Horse guard was no longer a casual affair. Our stock had been close-hobbled and staked fast to picket pins every night since the raid. The guard was double what it had been and every man was alert for Blackfoots come to avenge their defeat. Nobody needed to prod the men to keep their rifles clean, loaded, and primed and most took to sleeping with one eye open, for the Blackfoots had taught us a hard lesson. None came right then, as it turned out. We had whipped them soundly and the remnants of their party were likely still licking their wounds, but nobody opined that we had seen the last of them.

Another week or so carried us across a couple of rivers and farther south and west, climbing ever higher through the foothills, then across a high mountain pass and down into a river valley that Eddard Rose told us was called the Big Horn. We were truly in the mountains, the long-awaited, much-imagined Shining Mountains, gleaming at their frosty summits, rugged shoulders mantled green and hemmed with golden aspens, misty blue valleys threaded with silvery streams, veiled in mystery and promising wealth that could never equal the simple sight of them. I had never seen a mountain but just the same I knew that I had come home at last, that my heart would forever remain here in the bosom of these Shining Mountains.

Nights were getting colder and early morning was crisp with frost. Aspens had turned yellow and beaver sign was plentiful on every crick and stream. The Major called a halt in a grassy meadow sliced through with a little crick and fringed with stands of pine, aspen, and sweet cottonwood. First off, he put us to work building what Hamish insisted on calling a fort. It was really just a big cabin with a breastwork of logs and heavy brush piled around it. Nearly fourscore men made short work of building it and when it was done the Major announced that it was high time that we commence the fall hunt.

There was beaver sign aplenty in that neighborhood, to be sure, but there was far too many of us to trap in one place, so the Major broke us up into half a dozen trapping parties. Our bunch, which had always just naturally stuck together, numbered eleven men. Then Eddard Rose, whose guide skills weren't needed by the Major anymore, joined up with us, making our crew an even dozen. Naturally we missed the cheerful, willing presence of Jim Bridger amongst us, but Rose, with his knowledge of the country and the Indians thereabouts, was a welcome replacement. He had always got along well with the Delawares and since the night of the Blackfoot raid, he appeared to warm up considerably to most of the rest of us as well.

The Major sent out trapping parties in every direction from headquarters. Our bunch was told to go upstream on the Wind River, which we did, traveling three days over tricky mountain trails until we came to a cozy little meadow, lush with coarse dry grass and framed with groves of sweet cottonwoods for horse feed come winter, backed up to a steep mountainside and surrounded by a passel of little streams choked with beaver dams. It looked to us like Eden on the Seventh Day, except there wasn't any Eve, just a dozen dirty, threadbare, saddle-sore trappers, the most of us horny as hell and wishing there was.

Pitching camp was no chore at all and by nightfall we were snug in our bowers and hunkered down by the cookfire, chewing on a fat doe that Smiley had shot along the way that morning, and making plans for the next day's hunt.

We split into three bunches of four, two groups each taking different streams and trapping as far up as we could see beaver sign, whilst one bunch stayed back in camp, doing chores and keeping an eye on our extra livestock and plunder. That first day I rode out to a likely stream with Tuttle and Rose and the Delaware called Muskrat, discovering dams and dens and setting our traps in the ponds behind them. Chill as the water was in that high mountain country, it felt good and proper to be doing useful work once again, instead of chasing wild geese with a passel of bluecoats. Every patch of open water appeared to be swarming with beaver, the banks on both sides spiked with freshly-gnawed stumps. Even the rank, malodorous castoreum we use for bait possessed a comforting fragrance for me on that first morning, like an old friend revisited — sort of like Tuttle, come to think of it.

෨ ෨ ෨

The beaver thereabouts bestowed even more than they had promised. In the early days up there, not one of us ever returned to camp empty-handed. For a spell there, I was coming back to camp every day with a couple-three plews, sometimes four, and now and then an otter hanging off my saddle, after running the half-a-dozen traps on my line. So were the others. Camp was cluttered with beaver plews curing on willow hoops and when they dried, we baled them up, sixty to the pack, about ninety pounds of peltry, two of which make a fair-sized load for a packhorse or mule. Whenever we got together six or eight packs, we loaded them up and a few of us took them down to Henry's little fort, where Hamish graded them and entered each trapper's tally into the account book.

Paddy McBride expressed the feelings of us all when he crowed, "Sure'n thim beavers're after drawin' straws, they are, seein' who's to be first to be gracin' the traps o' Padraic McBride! Gin'rous critters they are, mind ye, wid nothin' more on their wee minds than enrichin' me ownself!"

Or so it seemed. Naturally we were all getting to be more canny as we learned the tricks and wrinkles of our trade, but it was mainly the wealth of beaver teeming in the cricks around us that let us feel like heroes. It was a shining time, but in the mountains, even shining times are not without their shadows.

One early morning I was waist-deep in a beaver pond, rifle slung across my shoulders to keep it dry, searching under finger-freezing water, reaching for the chain on my float-stick, sure that I had a drowned beaver in the trap at the end of it, when that particular beaver became substantially unimportant. The first inkling I had of other, more pressing, concerns was an arrow clanging off my rifle and a second one slicing through my capote, nicking my shoulder, which naturally got hold of my undivided attention. A quick glance behind me revealed what looked like the whole Blackfoot nation, little dabs of paint smeared on their faces, single eagle feathers in their hair, smoky buckskins and all. Fact is, it turned out there was only four of them, but it looked like a mob to me at the time.

I let out a screech, as you might suppose, and I kept on yelling as I splashed and floundered across the pond, hoping that Tuttle and Rose and Muskrat would hear me and come running. Naturally the Indians jumped into the water and came after me, slowed up a mite at first when that chilly water numbed their legs, giving me time to scramble up the far bank and commence running for the timber, dodging through a swath of pointy, foot-high, beaver-chewed stakes that promised to spit me like a lark if I chanced to fall on one of them, thinking the while that the Blackfoots already had my Chiksika horse, so the rascals must be dead-set on wearing my hair.

I dashed into a little clearing, the Blackfoots not two rods behind me, when I saw a clump of willows just ahead. Thinking to hide myself, I ran in amongst those skimpy saplings and immediately thought better of my plan. What I saw right in front of me was a huge old silvertip grizzly bear, tearing up a rotten log in search of ants and grubs and such. He was likely as startled as I was at my sudden appearance in front of him, but, I warrant, not half as scared. I froze in my tracks and the bear rose up on his hind legs to a height of at least a dozen feet, maybe more, and let out a horrible roar, then dropped down on all fours and commenced to scramble over the log to get at me. It was no time to be tarrying. My concerns about the Blackfoots instantly took second place and I fairly exploded out of that willow grove, hotfooting it across the clearing, heading for a skinny lodgepole pine standing at the edge of it.

That grizzly bear must have reckoned it was his birthday, considering all the gifts that were suddenly showered on him, for just then, as I was shinnying up the tree, I caught sight of two Blackfoots come running past the willows, unaware of the new player in our deadly game. The bear saw them first and he nigh took the head off one of them with a single swipe of his paw, claws sticking out like a fistful of razors, then quickly caught up with the other one, who was running for his life, and comnmenced to swat him into a heap of mincemeat.

All that gave me time to climb higher in the tree, until I reckoned the branches were getting too puny to bear my weight. I unslung my rifle, thinking to deal with Old Silvertip, who had turned his attention to me once more and was lumbering across the clearing in my direction, when another Blackfoot, musket in hand, came trotting out of the willows and skidded to a halt, eyes bugging out like a dragonfly when he saw his tattered comrades, his hand flying to his mouth in astonishment and fear of the enormous critter who had settled their hash, in every sense of those words.

That Blackfoot was purely in a quandary, for just then he caught sight of me trying to draw a bead on him from my perch amongst the upper limbs. The bear hadn't noticed him yet and the Blackfoot knew I surely meant to kill him, so he made his choice. Me. He swung his musket up and took aim.

I hadn't had time to freshen my priming and I wasn't altogether sure that my rifle would fire, but as it turned out, it didn't matter. Just then, as I was squeezing the trigger, old Mister Grizzly r'ared up and swatted that skinny lodgepole pine and set it to swaying like it was in a windstorm. The powder fizzled and sputtered in the pan and by time it set off the charge I missed that Blackfoot by half a mile at least. He fired at the same time, but pitching about at the top of that tree like I was, he might have been shooting at a barn swallow.

The two shots melded into a single explosion and the bear still didn't realize that the Blackfoot was behind him. He just snarled and roared and went to clawing at the tree, anxious, I reckon, to make sure of his dessert. I wasted no time in dumping powder down the barrel, stuffing a ball into the muzzle and thumping the butt on the limb I was standing on to seat the ball, then spilling powder into the pan. Naturally the Blackfoot was doing likewise, but luckily I was a hair faster than he was. Just as he was bringing his musket to his shoulder, I drilled him dead center in the belly and sent him out along the Wolf Trail, where proper Blackfoots go when their villainous actions are a shade too slow.

Gutshot as he was, he didn't die right off, howsomever, and his groans and thrashing about caught the attention of Mister Silvertip, who waddled over and swatted at him and chewed on his head until he quit moving, which gave me enough time to reload and settle myself more solidly in the branches, lest my hairy jailer take to setting the tree a-swaying once again.

Now one of Nature's better laws is the one concerning grizzly claws. Fearsome as they are, those bears are not equipped for climbing trees. So if you chance to find yourself up thataway and you see a bear perched up in a tree, you can be sure the bear is black or cinnamon or brown. But if you spy a man hanging on for dear life in the upper branches and something awfully big and hairy is waiting on the ground below, I warrant you that something is a grizzly bear.

That particular grizzly bear was nothing but greedy. He already had three perfectly wholesome redskin carcasses lying dead in the clearing, but still he had a hankering for white meat. When he finished killing the last Blackfoot, he came lumbering back to my tree and went to gashing up the ground and snarling and growling and clawing at the trunk for a spell, before he gave up that chore as useless and sat back on his hams, his claws hooked into the tree bark, forelegs extended upward, and rested his head on them, looking for all the world like a man at his prayers — saying grace in this particular case, I reckon.

Just then still another Blackfoot, an older man by the look of him, sneaked into view at the edge of the clearing. Luckily for him he was downwind of the bear. When he saw the mangled bodies of his three comrades, then spied me perched in the tree, alive and well, and Old Silvertip apparently praying in my direction, the old Indian clapped a hand to his mouth, his eyes big and round as dollars, and backed off, disappearing into the brush without a sound, convinced, I reckon, that I owned a heap of powerful medicine, leastaways with bears, and that it was best not to mess with the likes of me.

When I brought my rifle up, so as to be ready for the old Indian if need be, it startled Old Silvertip into action once more. He r'ared onto his hind legs and commenced to slap and tear at the tree again, sending shudders up the trunk and making the branches tremble, yawping and caterwauling and grunting hollow-sounding snorts and snarls, glaring up at me with blood-red piggy eyes, slavering past a mouthful of long, jagged teeth that looked to me like headstones in a graveyard outside the gates of hell. R'ared up he was, razor-sharp claws swinging wildly as he pawed the air and slapped at the tree trunk, his wicked mouth gaping no more than a yard or so below my feet, roaring threats of painful death. Terrified as I was, I barely recollect shoving Melchior down between my legs, poking the muzzle almost into his wide-open mouth, and yanking the trigger.

An almost human shriek sliced through the cloud of powder smoke and when it commenced to drift off I saw Old Silvertip stumbling in a tight circle, clawing at his throat, then slowly, reluctantly, crumpling to the ground.

I was still perched on a tree limb when Eddard Rose trotted into the clearing, closely followed by Tuttle, both of them with rifles at the ready, looking as if they expected the worst. They inspected the three dead Blackfoots and the carcass of the grizzly bear, still looking huge but not anywheres nearly as big as he had been a few minutes earlier, then looked up at me sitting in the tree. Tuttle was first to speak. He harrumphed and grinned up at me and called out, "Whatcher doin' up thar, Temple? Lookin' fer some more b'ars? Er mebbe Blackfoots? Ain'tcha done enough damage awready?"

I tried to reply in kind, but my voice came out somewheres between a croak and a squeak. "Not nearly! You got more bears an' Blackfoots, bring 'em on!" I handed down my rifle and climbed down from the tree, feeling halfway weak and dizzy when my feet hit the ground.

Eddard Rose gifted me with one of his rare smiles when he clapped a big hand on my shoulder and said, "Ye done good, Brothah Buck. Got yerself three Seekseekahs an' a white bear. Now, le's gut out Ol' Ephraim heah an' git you on back to camp. We kin come back fer the meat aftah."

Whilst we gutted the grizzly to keep him from bloating and spoiling the meat, I retailed my morning's adventures, all of which had occupied not half an hour's time. When I came to the part where the old Blackfoot saw what he thought was a bear saying his prayers to me up in the tree, Rose leaned back on his heels and laughed out loud. Then he said seriously, "If'n we be lucky, he'll run on back an' tell the othahs. Mebbe they be reck'nin' you got big medicine an' leave us be."

I was still half-dazed when Rose led me out of the clearing. A fright like that one takes a spell to pass. Tuttle was busy rifling plunder from the three dead Blackfoots and he had to trot to catch up, the extra hardware clanging and bumping as he came up with us. As we waded through the beaver pond where it had all commenced, I grabbed hold of my float-stick and, sure enough, I felt the solid weight of a beaver at the end of the chain. That did a great deal to restore my spirits, along with the sight of Chiksika, still tethered where I had left him, standing amongst the other horses now and fretting at his tie-rope. When I dragged the beaver up to the bank, Muskrat showed himself from behind a stand of willows and signed that he would look after skinning him out.

Tuttle was more excited than I was. He rode on ahead to spread the news and when Rose and I got back to camp I was greeted with a passel of good-natured joshing and humorous titles such as Bear-killer and Scourge o' the Blackfoots and other suchlike foolery. Whilst Foot was patching up my shoulder, Paddy came running with a cupful of porridge and a chunk of elk meat and when he presented it to me, he swept off his cap, bent himself nigh in half in a deep bow, and proclaimed, "Welcome to our humble abode, Sir Temple, Slayer o' Savages an' Silver Bears an' Ither Sich Varmints. We pray ye be after settin' yerself down, Yer Grace, an' partakin' of our meager horspitality!"

I joined in the general laughter and did as he asked. The porridge was hot and the wapiti tender and juicy and both were welcome indeed. Afterwards I traded on my brief popularity and remained by the fire, smoking my pipe and sneaking a sip now and again from my flask, whilst half a dozen others returned to the clearing to butcher out the bear and haul the meat and the hide back to camp. Before he left, Tuttle dumped a heap of hardware at my feet and said, "Yer gittin' yorese'f a proper arm'ry, Temple, what with killin' Blackfoots like ye been doin'!"

I glanced over the loot Tuttle had scavenged — two battered, tack-studded muskets, a couple powderhorns, several knives and tomahawks, some quilled pouches, and three pairs of winter moccasins — poor payment for such a morning's work but useful nonetheless. I grinned up at him and said, "The workman's worthy of his hire, Tuttle, an' besides, Ma always told me, Waste not, want not." I picked out a couple pairs of moccasins and tossed the biggest ones to him. "These here look like they'll fit ye and these'll do for me. The rest'll go for trade for the two of us." Which, in time, it did.

              ≈   ≈   ≈

We gorged ourselves at supper that night. Each of us whites, which naturally included Rose, took turns at turning a haunch of bear meat over a fire that hissed and spluttered as rich grease dripped onto red-glowing coals. The Delawares cooked wapiti at a separate fire, no doubt saying prayers the while for our bear-eating heathen spirits, which dulled our appetites not a whit. Ol' Ephraim, as Rose called him, was fat as a prize hog, ready for hibernating, and delicious, the rich dark meat marbled with fat crisped by the coals and flavorful with juices.

After we had all come nigh to foundering on bear meat, Anse Tolliver fetched his fiddle and went to sawing out lively airs from his neighborhood in the eastern mountains. I had rarely heard music whilst I was growing up in Whynot. Ma hummed and sang old Irish and English ballads once in awhile, but not often, and Pap's congregation sang hymns at his prayer meetings, but I myself never got the knack. Tuttle, howsomever, took to music and singing like a shoat to a sow. Now, when Anse paused and put his bow aside, Tuttle piped up and demanded, "Anse! D'ye know thet'ere tune they be callin' Fiddle Strings?"

Anse regarded him with a superior air and replied, "Reckon I do." Whereupon he picked up his bow, fitted his fiddle under his chin, and commenced sawing out a song I had never heard him play before. It was a lively tune, but there was sweetness in it, too, and when he had played through a part of it, Tuttle joined in, singing out in a rich, deep voice that didn't sound at all like his customary twangy, Kentucky way of talking. The words went pretty much like this:

"If I could be a fiddle string
 an' you could be a horsehair bow,
 we'd sing the sweetest melodies
 this hard ol' world will ever know."

Anse looked up from his sawing and a dim smile softened his ordinarily stern features. He propped his fiddle on his chest and sang along with Tuttle on the next verse.

"If I could be a fiddle string,
 I'd sing for you a lovin' tune.
 An' you could be 'most anything —
 the sun, the stars, my honey moon."

Anse stepped up the time somewhat for a spell and when he settled down, Godey and Eddard Rose joined in with the first two on what Tuttle later explained was the chorus. Paddy didn't know the words, but he sang along nevertheless, enriching the sound with his high, strong voice.

"Fiddlesticks an' fiddle strings,
 they need to be together.
 True love is what our music brings

in fair or stormy weather."
Tuttle made a sign to Anse and the music slipped back to the first part. This time, Tuttle sang alone, a tiny crack in his voice here and there, perhaps because he was thinking of his wife, long dead but still tenderly remembered.
"If I could be a fiddle string,
  I'd ask you keep my tone in tune
  and never end our song too soon
  whilst we have loving songs to sing."
Then all four of them and Paddy, too, sang out the chorus once again.
"Fiddlesticks an' fiddle strings,
  they need to be together.
True love is what our music brings
  in fair or stormy weather."
When they finished, Anse laid his fiddle aside and all of the singers fell silent, most likely recalling milder times and more gentle companions. My own thoughts drifted back to Sarah Rutledge and our first, fresh, innocent love, then melted into warmer memories of Lucette and Night-eyes and Simone. Each one of them owned a different piece of my heart, but, even sentimental as I felt right then, I had to admit that there was still plenty more left. Whilst I'm confessing, it's only fair to say, too, that my judgment of Aunt Penny had altered more than somewhat during the months since I had run off. Her go-to-hell view of the man-woman thing now appeared to be simply honest and natural. Most of my guilt had blurred and been washed away by time and learning the ways of the world, leastaways the world I was living in.
    Anse was still fiddling when I went to my robes that night, but it was Tuttle's song that kept running around in my head, gratefully fending off pictures of Old Ephraim and the Blackfoots who had died that morning, recalling tender moments spent with women I still loved, and promising pleasures yet to come. Next morning I asked Tuttle to teach me the words to that song. Which he did.

ॐ   ॐ   ॐ

Trapping continued to be rewarding into the late fall. There were beaver aplenty in the cricks and streams that feed the Wind River, but Grandfather Winter was foreclosing his mortgage on the land. It was becoming harder every morning to break through the ice on the ponds to set our traps. We trapped in pairs and threes now, never alone, mindful that Blackfoots could show up at any time, but it appeared that Eddard Rose had guessed right, that word had spread amongst them that one of the white-eyes had got himself a power of grizzly bear medicine and it wouldn't do to mess with any of our little bunch right then.

One evening when we were gathered around a fire, Rose told us this was mostly Snake country, Shoshones, but nobody owned the land and Blackfoots could be anywhere they chose to be, from their proper home in Grandfather's Land to the north and west of us, all the way to Mexico, and when they came through on pony raids and such, most other Indians got out of their way.

Ned Godey nodded his agreement and said, "Tell 'em, Eddard, 'bout the diff'rent kinds o' Blackfoots. Might come in handy."

Rose sighed, for generally he wasn't much of a talker. Then his face grew serious and he commenced to speak. "Like Ned was sayin', theah be mainly three kinds o' Blackfoots — tribes, ye mought be callin' 'em — Pee-koo-nees, Kah-ee-nahs, an' Seek-see-kahs — an' one othah I'll be gittin' to aftahwards. Ye'll be hearin' diff'ernt names fer 'em — like most 'Mericans call Pee- koo-nees Pay-gans an' they say Bloods when they oughta say Kah-ee-nahs an' they don't call Seek-see-kahs nuthin' special, jes' calls 'em Blackfoots, but all o' them be some'at diff'ernt from t'othahs. Onliest thing they likely be agreein' on is not likin' nobody very much, 'spesh'ly white-eyes. Larn what ye kin about 'em, 'bout what makes 'em diff'ernt, one t'othah — 'thout gittin' too close, natcherly. Mought save yer ha'r."

Rose settled back and poked at the fire with a stick, his expression grave, maybe thinking of past battles. Paddy McBride, his blue eyes wide with interest, spoke up then and asked, "An' what about the ither wan? Ye said there's after bein' four kinds o' Blackfoots."

Rose allowed himself a brief smile and replied, "'Deed I did. The othah bunch be Aht-see-nahs, what Frenchies be callin' Gros Ventres an' we be callin' Grovants, Big-bellies. Most Injuns do, too." Rose made a sign in hand-talk with both hands, like a woman with child or a man with a watermelon stuck in his britches. He chuckled and continued. "An' some be callin' 'em Prairie Blackfoots, but they ain't. Ain't even shirt-tail kin to Blackfoots. Don't even talk the same." Rose warmed to his subject as he went on. "Fust off, they ain't hardly none of 'em fat. What they got is a knack o' droppin' in on the neighbors an' hangin' 'roun', mebbe fer two-t'ree weeks, mebbe more, tradin' on Injun welcomin' ways, eatin' up ever' scrap o' food in camp, an' then movin' on, all the time laughin' an' promisin' to come back agin nex' year. An' tha's how come they be callin' 'em Big-bellies!" Rose joined in the general laughter, but then he held up his hand and cautioned, "Now don'tcha be thinkin' Aht-see-nahs cain't fight! They kin! Them Grovants be sneaky-mean as Blackfoots evah was, mean as painter scut!"

As winter gathered, there was more and more time for such palaver, for trapping dwindled off to nothing as winter claimed the land and ice grew thick on the ponds. We were rarely idle, howsomever, for keeping body and soul together was a never-ending chore. We dug shallow caves into the hillside and set up our bowers in front of them, seeking to fend off the deepening cold. Gathering firewood and hunting took up most of the daylight hours but soon game got scarce and our bellies were often pinched with hunger. The Delawares set snares and caught big white splay-footed hares, but as Tuttle complained, "They ain't no greez on 'em! A body be needin' greez agin the cold! What we be needin' is a big ol' grizzle b'ar." Then he looked at me and grinned and said, "Hey, Temple! Why'ntcha setcherse'f out fer bait agin so's we kin be eatin' hardy?"

We climbed the rocky slopes behind us in pursuit of bighorn sheep, but after we shot a few of them, the rest left the country. We combed the meadows and surrounding timber, often wading waist-deep in snow, but wapiti and deer were few and far between. Nobody had seen a buffalo in months. The Delawares fetched in a

couple brace of snow grouse from time to time and Godey shot a
painter up on the slope, the sweetest meat I ever tasted, but it was
gone too soon and we went back to starving once again.

The Delaware Stone Bird discovered a den of rattlesnakes,
wintered up and sluggish with cold, chopped off their heads, and
trotted back to camp with a dozen of them draped over his
shoulders. At first everybody swore they would never eat serpent,
but as it turned out, nobody went hungry that night. The meat was
downright tasty, once you could put out of mind what it was, and
Paddy McBride observed, "P'raps our blessèd Saint Padraic was
after bein' a mite too hasty whin he drove all o' these delicious
critters out of Ireland." Flour and corn meal from Andrew Henry's
stores had long since run out and he had no more to give us. Cold
as it was, a dozen men required more meat than we could bring
down. Starving became a likely possibility.

Our horses and mules fared better than we did. The meadow
was deep in snow, but there was plenty of sweet cottonwood to be
peeled and fed to the critters. Our livestock wasn't precisely
rolling fat, but they were in better flesh than we were, and I'm sure
that many a man cast a longing eye on our precious little herd and
daydreamed of horsemeat roasting over a cookfire.

Such temptations were painfully removed, howsomever, for one
morning Anse Toliver roused the whole camp with a bleating,
heartfelt wail and a string of colorful cusswords, some of which I
had never heard before, which was in itself remarkable.

Every trapper leaped out of his robes, snatching up a rifle or
pistol, thinking we were attacked by Indians, only to discover a far
worse catastrophe. Our horses and mules were gone, every last
head, hide, and hoof.

Our first thought, naturally, was Blackfoots, but after Eddard
Rose combed through the cottonwood grove, he returned to say,
"Snakes! Goddamn Snakes come an' stole the goddamn hosses!"
He led us out to the grove and pointed to a welter of moccasin
tracks amongst the hoofprints in the snow. "Lookee theah! Warn't
no Seek-see-kah ner nobody but a Snake what made that mark!"
He caught sight of my Blackfoot moccasins about then and said,
"Lift up yer foot, Buck. Show 'em." I did as he asked and Rose

pointed out the difference between the footprints, interrupting himself from time to time to cuss out every Shoshone's ancestors and all of their future generations.

The fault was our own, naturally, for we had grown lax about horse guard at night, fooling ourselves that the Blackfoots had been scared off by what they supposed was my grizzly bear medicine. Problem was, nobody told the Snakes about it.

At first, the lot of us was numbed into silence by the loss of our horses. Afoot we were considerably easier prey to marauding mounted redskins and, besides, without critters we had no way to carry plews and plunder. Tolliver was first to voice the question that stood out in all our minds. "Awright, Eddard, what d'ye reckon we oughter do now? I'm hankerin fer muh mules!"

Rose never hesitated before he replied. "Why, we jest natcherly follers 'em an' we takes 'em back an' we kills some Snakes 'long the way."

Scary pictures of our pony raid against the Crows popped into my head, but there was no time for worrying. We had too much to do and not a minute to waste. A snowfall could cover their tracks in an hour and leave us wandering in a white wilderness. First off, we stripped our shelters and picked out what we would take with us — weapons, powder and ball, a sleep robe, a rope or two, extra moccasins, and little else. We had no food, which meant that much less to tote, although I, for one, wouldn't have minded the extra weight, if I had had my druthers.

The beaver catch was already at Henry's little fort, but we cached everything else — saddles, bridles, traps, extra robes, spare powder and galena, such truck as cook pots, axes, spades, and canvas, Anse's fiddle in its case, and the rest of each man's extra plunder — in a hole we dug in the slope behind the cottonwood grove and covered over with bark and branches and snow. It wasn't a proper cache but it was the best we had time for. In less than two hours' time we were ready to travel, a dozen men armed to the teeth and mad as hell, willing, indeed happy, to commit murder if need be.

The Delawares spread out in front of us on the trail, muskets, bows, and quivers bobbing on their backs, and Rose led the rest of us, keeping up a steady trot in the broad track left by twenty-eight horses and mules. The Snakes were keeping to the high ground for the most part, avoiding snow-clogged crick bottoms when they could, seeking to put as much distance as possible between our camp and themselves.

We had neither time nor breath to spare for talk. The lung-bursting pace through the snow numbed the mind as much as it did our legs. Even when Rose called a halt to restore our strength, nobody spoke more than a grunt or two. We trotted until nightfall, the Delawares ranging far out in front, marking trail lest a snowfall cover the tracks, and seeking game that remained safe in hiding that day.

We slept on empty bellies that night, without a fire, most of us doubled up together in our robes for warmth. Only Anse and Smiley slept alone, mindful of back-home propriety. All five Delawares and Paddy McBride huddled together like so many wolf pups in a burrow. If Tuttle snored, I surely didn't hear it.

๑   ๑   ๑

Colorful cursing jarred me from my slumbers and when I poked my head out from under the buffalo robe, the puny light of first dawn revealed that it had snowed in the night, not much, but enough to cover horse tracks. Anse and Tuttle stood face to face, stomping their feet for warmth and trading laments concerning our lost livestock. Eddard Rose was paying them no nevermind, busying himself instead with shaking out his sleep robe and rolling it into a bundle. At length he called out to them, "Time ye quit yer bellyachin' an' git ready to git goin'! I warrant we'll find 'em. Snow be damned!"

I laid Melchior aside, struggled to my feet, and shambled to the trees to perform my morning chore. By time I returned, the Delawares were filing out of the clearing, headed for yesterday's markers, and Tuttle was rolling up his sleep robe and yelling for me to hurry up. Which I did. Five minutes later I was slogging through fresh snow with the rest of our bunch, numb with cold and not sure that my griping belly wouldn't gnaw through my backbone.

Some time after we passed the last of yesterday's marks, Brass Turtle came back to meet us, looking perplexed. Two possible trails stretched outwards down the draw that lay before us. The Snakes might have taken either one and no tracks showed in the snow. Rose paused no more than a blink before he pointed to the lefthand trail and said, "Thataway. They be headin' home an' it likely lies somewheah ovah yondah."

Ordinarily Turtle always made some smart remark, but this time he merely jerked his head in a nod, spun on his heel, and trotted out to the scouts, the rest of us following in his tracks. The trail meandered generally southwestwards, rising steadily on the southern slope and narrowing as we drew nigh a ridge. About then we heard a low yip and saw Muskrat pointing at a tree beside the trail. We shuffled faster through the snow and when we caught up there was a huddle of grinning Delawares clustered around the tree. Their smiles were well-warranted, for a swatch of chestnut horsehair caught in the bark and a faint hoofprint on a patch of frozen mud beneath its boughs assured us that the horsethieves had passed that way. Rose hunkered down, studying the hoofmark for a spell before he pronounced, "It be from yestahday, shuah'nuf, but they ain't too far ahead."

We set off with renewed vigor, although I can't rightly say where that extra strength came from, considering that we hadn't eaten for nearly two days. The trail wound through a low pass and down into a broad, snow-covered meadow, where we discovered a passel of fresh horse sign and the remains of a small camp. Rose and the Delawares prowled about the camp, dropping to their knees from time to time and grunting out their findings, then putting their heads together whilst they thrashed out the meaning of what they had found. At last Rose came to where we were sprawled in the snow and said, "They ain't but mebbe ten-'leven o' them Snakes an' they cain't be far ahead."

Paddy McBride laughed out loud and croaked, "Not more'n a dozen, ye say, Misther Rose? 'Tis no problem indeed! Hungry as I be, I could eat the lot of 'em intirely!"

We all laughed as best we could through parched, wind-dried lips, then bent to shoulder our packs and weapons, anxious to be on the move once more.

It was midafternoon when we heard another smothered yip. All eyes swung to where Little Mountain stood in a little clearing just off the trail, something gray lying at his feet. We rushed headlong through the snow and gathered around a plump young doe, Little Mountain's arrow still sticking through her neck. A single swipe of Turtle's knife opened her from gullet to go-to-hell and when the innards spilled out, everybody grabbed whatever he could lay hands on. Liver and heart were shared around, but after that it was every man for himself. Stone Bird stripped off the hide and knives stabbed into the carcass from every direction, carving out chunks of flesh. Nobody thought of building a cookfire. Hungry as all of us were, that appeared to be a waste of time. Men were cracking bones and sucking out raw marrow and Paddy McBride was scraping bits of tallow off the hide and licking them off his knife blade. He grinned at Eddard Rose and remarked, "Now that I've et, Misther Rose, p'raps only t'ree or four o' thim Snakes'll do fer me supper."

We were on the trail again in less than half an hour, our pace much faster now with fresh meat in our bellies and new blood coursing in our veins. When Rose called a brief halt near a tiny brook, we broke the ice with rifle butts and slaked our thirst with water so cold it nigh froze our teeth. Then, totally refreshed, we resumed our shambling march through the snow.

It was nearly nightfall when Brass Turtle trotted back to Rose and reported that we had reached the end of our journey. The scouts had discovered the Shoshone camp. "They be only jest a leetle bunch o' them hossthiefs, nothin' like a village. No more'n ten or a dozen at most. Cain't know fer sure 'til we git up closer. Best we don't spook 'em in the daylight."

Rose went ahead with Turtle for a look-see on his own, whilst we waited in a hollow at the foot of a low ridge, watching their progress through the snow, keeping to cover as best they could, dodging from one tree to the next, crouching beside big rocks until they could be sure that they were not being observed. At last they disappeared over the crest of the ridge.

The scene that lay before us stirred familiar thoughts. Tuttle leaned towards me and muttered, "Hark, Temple. D'ye git the feelin' we been here afore now?"

Ned Godey spoke up before I could reply. "Ceptin' fer snow, we could be back thar waitin' to jump the Crows."

"Yep, it feels about the same," I said. " Only good thing, there ain't a whole village waitin' over that hill."

Tuttle pulled a long face and looked thoughtful. "True 'nuff. Howsomever it don't take no more'n jest one o' them leetle galena pills to snuff yore candle. Don't make no nevermind jest how many o' them thangs might be flyin' 'bout. Only takes one of 'em. Mind ye keep yore eyes peeled an' yore noggin out o' sight!"

Ned broke in, a hint of tension in his tone. "Here comes Rose, hot-footin' it to a fare-thee-well! Somethin's up!"

A moment later Rose slid down the snowy bank and waved us over to join him. When we were all huddled around him, he told us in a low voice tight with excitement, "Change o' plans. We got comp'ny. Blackfoots. Seek-see-kahs. Score of 'em, mebbe more. Comin' up the crick. Fixin' to grab the hosses, same as us."

Rose paused as Brass Turtle slipped into our midst and hunkered down beside him, then resumed, "Got me an idee. Them Seek-see-kahs don' know we be heah, else they'd be jumpin' us afore now. I'm goin' roun' t'othah side an' try warnin' them Snakes. Don' nobody be shootin' into camp an' don' nobody commence shootin' no Blackfoots neithah 'til ye heah me shoot. Turtle'll be takin' ye up the hill."

Brass Turtle spoke up then. "Leave yer sleep robes ri'chere an' fresh up yer primin' on ever'thin' ye got an' let's git a move on. I'll be showin' ye where ye oughter be."

It was nearly dark by then. I noticed that Rose had slipped off into the shadows whilst Turtle was talking. Two minutes later we were sneaking up the hill behind Brass Turtle, taking cover amongst the trees wherever we could.

A fulling moon was breaking beyond distant peaks by time we got to the ridge. As I followed behind Turtle, crawling on hands and knees, dragging my rifle and taking care to keep snow from clogging the bore, Anse and Muskrat at my heels, I caught sight of a campfire in the Shoshone camp at the bottom of a narrow ravine. Nearly a dozen horsethieves were hunkered down around it. Just as Turtle was pointing to the place where he wanted me to light, I saw the Shoshones jump to their feet and dart towards the shadows on the far side. I reckoned Rose had arrived.

As the moon rose higher I could see below me on our side a bank of broad stony ledges windrowed with snow, stepping down to a measly trickle of water flowing out of a rock slide that boxed in the upper end of the ravine, where the Shoshone camp was. Our horses were milling around inside a brush fence at the lower end and I could just barely make out what looked to be Chiksika's dappled hide. Much more important, howsomever, was what Brass Turtle was pointing at now, a dim figure sprawled full length and motionless in the snow beside a big rock on the ledge below. "That'n be your'n." Turtle barely breathed out the words. "If'n we all git jest one of 'em, they'll likely turn tail." I nodded my reply and he gripped me hard on the shoulder, then crawled away with Muskrat and Anse Tolliver close behind.

Whilst I lay on my belly in the snow, numb with cold, my rifle trained on the back of the Blackfoot below me, I marveled at the courage of Eddard Rose, who had willingly walked into the Shoshone camp to warn them and enlist their aid in fighting the Blackfeet. I marveled still more when I saw Rose and one of the Snakes walk stiff-legged out of the shadows and take a seat by the fire, making themselves easy targets for the Blackfeet hidden in the rocks above them. The two of them sat there chatting and laughing, hands fluttering in sign talk, which Indians often use out of habit, even when they are speaking the same tongue, when Rose suddenly twisted sidewise and threw himself behind a skimpy pile of firewood, at the same time dragging his rifle from under his capote and firing into the darkness below me, whilst his Shoshone companion dived for cover outside the firelight.

My particular Blackfoot r'ared onto his knees and was throwing his musket to his shoulder when Melchior reached out a long finger and poked him squarely in the middle of the back, pitching him onto his face in the snow, his musket flying in the air and falling over the lip of the ledge.

It seemed then as if Satan had flung open the gates of hell. Rifles and muskets cracked and boomed up and down the ravine and orange muzzle flashes blossomed in the darkness. A sliver of memory recalled how that Blackfoot had discovered my whereabouts by the muzzle blast and smoke from my pistol during the fight on the Yellowstone, which prompted me to roll sidewise away from my station by the rock, and just in time, for even through the din of musket fire and yelling Indians I heard a bullet smack against the rock and arrows clatter against its surface.

I pulled one of my pistols from the bosom of my capote, for there was no time to reload my rifle, peering downwards the while onto the ledge, mostly quiet now and nothing moving, moonlight glittering on the snow. A hint of movement caught the tail of my right eye and a soft, now-and-then crunching of snow on the ledge below warned that I had a visitor, most likely an unwelcome one, but I could see no one. Then, not ten feet below where I lay, an Indian, bent over double, scurried out to the body of the Blackfoot I had shot. My blood fairly froze and I hesitated, not certain if it was another Blackfoot or one of our new-found Shoshone allies come to collect a scalp. He knelt by the remains for a second or two, then commenced to drag the body away, which even at that time and with as little knowledge as I had of such matters, I knew that no self-respecting Snake would ever do for a Blackfoot. My pistol was leveled at his head and I squeezed the trigger. Nothing happened. In my excitement I had neglected to cock the hammer and when I did so, the faint metallic click rang out like a bugle call in the still, chill air. The Blackfoot turned loose the body and swung up his musket, seeking his target on the moon-dappled hillside. I dropped the hammer half a blink before he did and the two explosions mingled in the cold night air. Shooting downwards as I was, the ball tore off his chin on its way through his throat to smash his backbone. I reckon he was dead before he fell onto the body of his departed friend.

Whilst I was reloading my pistol, then my rifle, I felt no remorse for killing a man who would have bragged on killing me, but I did feel a certain admiration for that second Indian, who had risked his life and lost it, all for the sake of giving his slain companion a decent burial. I asked myself how many white men would have done the same.

The rattle of gunfire and the yelling slowly subsided. It appeared that the battle was dwindling to a nub. Just the same, I scurried on hands and knees to still another sheltering rock, recollecting Tuttle's sage counsel that it requires but one bullet to put an end to a man's earthly ambitions. I stayed put, lying on my belly and chafing my hands and wriggling my toes in my moccasins to keep them from freezing, until the nearly full moon was riding high in a clear winter sky, all the while sweeping my eyes from one end of the ravine to the other, seeking to catch in the corners of my vision some movement on the slopes that might betray a hostile Indian, but nothing stirred. Then a flurry of gunshots and a passel of whooping and screeching from beyond the brush fence broke the silence, but all I could see was our startled horses racing up and down the hollow.

A few minutes passed, then I saw big branches and small trees in the brush fence being flung aside, making a hole big enough to let a horse pass through, but instead of turning our horses loose, first one, then another horse poked his head through the opening and came trotting in to mingle amongst our herd. In all, nineteen horses, all carrying skimpy hair-pad Indian saddles, crude wooden stirrups dangling, pushed their way past the fence, trailed by men on foot that I knew to be our own, scattered amongst some Indians I took to be Snakes.

Nobody was shooting at them, so I reckoned the fight must be over. I tarried a few more minutes, just to be sure, before I rose to my feet and made my way down into the hollow, mostly by sliding on my backside in the snow, pausing only to pick up the muskets, powderhorns, and bullet molds from my two dead Blackfoots. Such items possessed a sight more value to me than scalps. I reckon it depends on how you view such matters.

Circumstances alter cases, as Brass Turtle was fond of saying, and it was curious how the advent of the Blackfoots had changed our attitude towards the Snakes and theirs towards us. On our way over there, there wasn't a man amongst us who wouldn't have been happy to eat a Snake for breakfast, but now that we had defeated a common enemy together, it was all jubilation and goodfellowship amongst the lot of us, trapper and Snake alike.

The first trapper I came across was Tuttle, who greeted me with, "Evenin', Temple. You goin' into the hardware biz'ness?" Naturally he was referring to the extra muskets I had toted off the hill, but his good humor sounded forced and his voice was a mite shaky. Then I saw the arrow jutting from his shoulder.

"You're hurt! C'mon! Sit yourself down an' we'll get it out o' there!" My voice sounded screechy in my ears.

"Aw, t'aint nuthin' much a-tall. Foot'll git it out. Them Injuns, they git borned knowin' 'bout sich thangs." Tuttle sounded weary, more tired than I had ever known him to be. "I ain't the onliest one. Paddy an' Smiley got theirse'fs a mite scraped up, too." Then, "You awright?" I nodded and tried to smile. Tuttle expelled a satisfied grunt, then glanced towards the brush fence and jerked his chin in that direction. "Lookee yonder. Hyar they come now."

Sure enough, there was Paddy McBride, half carried by Little Mountain on one side and a Snake on the other, his precious rifle inherited from Talbot clutched in one hand, limping through the hole in the fence. As they neared, I could see in the moonlight an arrow embedded in his thigh, the feathers bobbing as he shuffled along. When they got near enough for Paddy to recognize me, he favored me with a lopsided grin and announced, "Well now, Temple Buck, would ye be lookin' at that now! Skewered me like a bloody Christmas joint, they did!" I had no time to reply, for he passed out just then, his rifle clattering onto the snow, and the two Indians dragged him up to the camp.

I stooped to retrieve Paddy's rifle and when I straightened up I found myself staring into John Smiley's face, his lank body slumped against Ned Godey's shoulder. Smiley's eyes were glassy and his jaw was slack. Blood soaked the thrown-back hood of his capote, dripping from a crease that ran from alongside his eye past his ear. I said nothing for he couldn't have heard me anyhow. Ned paused for breath and strangled out, "Fought like devils, they did, them Blackfoots, but we whupped 'em good!" His eyes narrowed and he peered into my face before he asked, "You hurt?" I shook my head and he grunted his satisfaction. Then he said, "Me neither, but it war a near thing, a time or two thar." Ned shifted Smiley's arm around his shoulder and without another word continued up the slope to the Shoshone camp.

Tuttle was weaving in his tracks and it came to me that it was long past time to be getting him up to the camp. I propped my armload of rifles and muskets against a bush, except for Melchior, got my shoulder under his arm to support him, and the two of us shambled our way out of the gully and up to the camp.

The only good thing I know about an arrow over a rifle ball is that it plugs the hole so the wound doesn't bleed so much, leastaways not at first. Problem is, it's a sight harder to get out. By time Tuttle and I staggered into the firelight, Old Foot and Little Mountain were doing just that, shoving the arrow point through the fleshy part of Paddy's thigh, breaking it off, and pulling out the shaft, then laying on spiderwebs and a steaming poultice of herbs and bark and I don't know what all to stop the bleeding and cleanse the wound, whilst McBride tried without much success to crack jokes in a weak voice between his groans and chirps of pain.

When they finished with Paddy the two Delawares commenced to do much the same with Tuttle, who cracked no jokes but merely set his jaw and gritted his teeth, grunting and wincing from time to time as Foot dug the stone point out of his shoulder. When at last they succeeded in stanching the blood, Tuttle grinned up at them and opened his mouth to speak, but he never did. He slumped back unconscious, which was the best thing he could have done at the time.

Feeling useless, I trotted back down the track to retrieve the weapons I had left in the gully. By time I returned, Foot was binding up John Smiley's head wound and Little Mountain was tending to a couple of Snakes who had also got themselves shot up in the battle. Brass Turtle motioned for me to join him at the fire and when I hunkered down beside him, he handed me a steaming gourd half-filled with a rich, thick stew, which I finished off in no more than a gulp or two. I set the empty gourd beside his knee and was commencing to thank him when I saw that his face bore a look more grim than any I had ever seen there and his black eyes fairly glittered in the firelight. His voice was hollow when he said quietly, "Muskrat's gone under." His thin lips snapped shut and he said no more. I made no reply, for there was nothing to add. I merely nodded and recalled with sadness the big young Delaware who had been ever cheerful and helpful, never one with much to say, even in his own tongue, but always eager to lend a hand in camp or on the trail.

My thoughts strayed to wondering how many more of us would suffer Muskrat's fate, but I hastily put such speculations aside.

The hazards of the trapper's trade are many and ever-present and dwelling on them serves no purpose except perhaps to hasten their arrival.

Godey, Stone Bird, Brass Turtle, and I rode back to fetch the sleep robes and other plunder from the hollow where this particular catastrophe had begun that night, all of us alert to the possibility of Blackfoots lingering thereabouts, but nobody challenged us. When we returned to the Shoshone camp, Eddard Rose called all of us together and said, "The chief o' thi'sheah pony-thievin' bunch, calls hisself Drum-singah, says he an' his boys be thankful fer what we done heah tonight an' he says we be welcome to wintah up with theah band o' Snakes south an' some'at east o' heah." None of us made reply and Rose went on. "Fur as I kin make out from the signs, the main band's somewheahs on the Popo Azhieh, likely a bettah camp than our'n. I'm fer it."

Like they say, in the kingdom of the blind the one-eyed man is king and Eddard Rose was the only man amongst us who knew the mountains and the Indians thereabouts. Besides, the more of us against the Blackfoots, the better. All of us nodded or grunted our approval. So it was settled. We would spend the winter with the Snakes.

Old Foot mixed up one of his potions and spooned it into the wounded men, who soon drifted off to sleep. I shared robes with Tuttle and Paddy slept amongst the Delawares. Ned and Anse took charge of John Smiley, who was still somewhat addled and offered no protest about the propriety of sharing robes with other men.

Tuttle's peaceful snoring was a downright comfort that night. Seeing that arrow sticking into him had made it more clear than ever how much like a brother he had become to me.

I was still groggy with sleep when I felt Ned Godey shaking my shoulder and heard him say, "Rise up, Temple. Time we be gittin' on. Time we git on back to camp an' fetch the plunder."

Whilst I attended to my morning chore I heard Old Foot's wailing chant leading the other Delawares in what I knew was a farewell to Muskrat and little as it might be worth I added what I reckon was a silent prayer to help him on his way.

Tuttle was still drowsing when I got back to our robes but he woke up fast enough to protest being left behind when we returned to the Wind River camp. His color had improved somewhat but it was plain to see that he was still too puny to travel. The same with Paddy and John Smiley, who stayed put with Rose and the two Delaware healers. Brass Turtle and Stone Bird went with us three able-bodied whites to fetch the plunder we had cached. We took one of the Snakes with us as a guide, but in fact more likely as a hostage against treachery towards our fellows.

Before we left we broke our fast with a stew of deer meat and roots and dried-out berries that the Snakes cooked up. Skimpy and simple as it was, it was better vittles by far than we had enjoyed for a month or more. Then we saddled our horses with Blackfoot hair pads and headed for the Wind.

Getting our horses back almost made up for all the grief of the night before. Paddy put it in a nutshell when he said, "There's an auld sayin' back home, whin the Good Lord is after wishin' to make a peasant happy, He sees to it the farmer's donkey strays. Thin whin the ass is found, the peasant is joyful beyond all tellin' an' the intire bizness costs the Almighty divil a bit a-tall a-tall!"

Hard riding and little or no feed had taxed our horses considerably, but their hearts were strong and willing. I could feel Chiksika's strength surging into my thighs and my own spirit flowing back into him. Even Jake, trailing on a lead rope, fairly danced at my side, happy, I reckon, to be amongst his own once more.

Riding out of the gully it was hard to believe that a battle had been fought there. I saw no dead bodies, only spatters of blood here and there in the snow. Brass Turtle must have read my mind. "Blackfoots come an' got 'em. Them Snakes took their hair an' plucked 'em clean as baby birds las' night. Reckon the couple-three what got off come back to do right by the dead'uns." When he saw my look of concern upon learning that there were still Blackfoots roaming thereabouts, he laughed and added, "Don't ye fret, Temple. If'n there was still enough of 'em left to fight, they'd'a jumped us agin an' tried to git the hosses. I reckon they be long gone by now."

He was right, for when we returned three days later with our plunder, the Shoshone horsethieves' camp was calm and peaceful. The healers had done their chore well. John Smiley was bright and alert under a bandage that swathed his head like a turban. Tuttle, his left arm in a sling, claimed that he could ride and fight with the best of 'em. And even if Paddy wasn't offering to dance an Irish jig right then, he insisted that he was ready to ride on to the Shoshone camp whenever we wished

Chapter IX
Snakes

Our trail wound generally southwestwards, plunging deeper into the mountains, keeping to the high ground, avoiding snow-choked canyons and gullies when we could, sometimes treading along narrow ledges as we threaded our way through rocky passes watched over by tall snowy peaks.

The Snakes were natural horsemen, merging body and spirit into their mounts, demanding the last ounce of strength and will from their horses and giving back care and understanding. I found myself wondering how they might have lived before they got horses, for even their bodies appeared to be fashioned especially for riding astride. Short-legged and not nearly as tall as other Indians I had seen, they were almost awkward afoot but they brought centaurs to mind once they were in the saddle.

None of them spoke English or French and even Eddard Rose couldn't speak their language, but sign talk served well enough to get our thoughts across. Drum-singer, who wasn't precisely a chief but who was boss of this particular bunch of horsethieves, by the look of it, told us how grateful they were for what we did when we ambushed the Blackfoots, who must have certainly rubbed out that small party of Snakes, as well as for our gifting his bunch with all nineteen captured Blackfoot horses. He assured us, too, that we would be welcome amongst his band, for they had lost several warriors and many horses to the Blackfeet and the Crows that winter. Men were needed for hunting and possibly for fighting if their enemies struck again. Rose signed that we were ready for both and we all nodded our agreement.

We ate well enough on that trek, for Shoshone hunters, using their bows to avoid attracting unwelcome attention, ranged ahead of the main party and nearly every day we came upon a deer or two or sometimes a cow wapiti lying alongside the trail, gutted out with the heart and liver inside, ready for our supper.

Late in the forenoon of the fifth day we topped a ridge and saw below us a frozen stream and a village of a couple score or more lodges, smoke wisping out of the smokeflaps, and a not-so-big pony herd scattered amongst the cottonwoods. A couple of our young Shoshones went yipping down the slope into camp, each of them trailing a pair of Blackfoot ponies behind. Quick as a blink, kids and women and grown men came boiling out of the lodges, shouting and laughing and letting loose that high-pitched fluttering yip-yip-yipping noise Indians make when they're happy.

That didn't last long, howsomever, for a hush fell over that merry throng when the rest of us rode into view. It shouldn't have been surprising, for when I looked down at that sea of clean, smooth, round, rosy-cheeked faces, then back at our dirty, tattered, leathery, hollow-eyed and haggard, bewhiskered bunch, except for the Delawares, even I was halfway shocked at how pitiful we looked.

Drum-singer wasted not a jot of time before he launched into a lengthy harangue, smiling and waving his arms and pointing at each of us and the captured horses, then holding aloft his lance festooned with nigh a score of Blackfoot scalps, all of which appeared to warm the feelings of his people more than somewhat. Ere long they were laughing and chattering again and surrounding us, nearly dragging us off our horses and herding us into a big lodge made of two tipis joined together. It was their council lodge, but I didn't know about such matters at the time. Nobody offered to touch our guns and we hardly had time to turn around before a bunch of young boys dragged in our saddles and packs of plunder. I'm sure that not one of us doubted that wintering amongst the Snakes was going to be a considerable improvement over our hard-scrabble camp on the Wind.

Tuttle was particularly elated. "Hey thar, Temple," he crowed, "didja see thet purty young squaw showin' me the glad-eye out thar? Reckon these hyar'll be some sweet doin's oncet we git settled in hereabouts!" Fact is, I had thought she was looking at me, but then you can never be sure about women and where they might be looking, so I said nothing to dampen his spirits.

Brass Turtle did, though. I reckon he was feeling a mite testy about then, prehaps on account of his thinking about Muskrat, for he said in a flat voice, "Tuttle, my friend, do me a kindness. Quit callin' 'em squaws. That word means cunt in our tongue an' I'd be obliged if ye jest calls 'em women, if'n ye don't mind too much."

Ned Godey looked startled at Turtle's tetchy words, but Tuttle's response was a mark of how close we had all become in the past year and a half. He just grinned good-naturedly and replied, "No offense, Turtle. I never knew thet. Thet be jist a manner o' speakin' back home. I'll be callin' 'em women, like ye say, when I kin remember, but I ain't nohaow pledgin' to change my philanderin' ways about 'em."

Brass Turtle allowed himself a smile and his tone warmed up considerably when he said, "Fair 'nough. Ain't nobody askin' ye do nothin' like that. Ye wouldn't be Tuttle if'n ye could." He clapped Tuttle gently on his good shoulder, then turned away to roll out his sleeping robes while the rest of us did the same.

౼ ౼ ౼

By time Anse and I got back from seeing that our horses and mules were safe and well-fed, which they were, a fire was blazing inside the lodge, which was spilling over with people. Women were carrying in gourds filled with steaming soup and stew, then running out for more. A passel of older men — some kind of chiefs, I reckon — were hunkered down with Rose and Turtle and Godey. Foot and Little Mountain were tending to Tuttle and Paddy and Smiley. Young men muffled head to toe in bright trade blankets and painted buffalo robes stood silent and watchful at the door and a rabble of round-eyed little kids kept getting underfoot, squirming in amongst their elders and sneaking a peek at us dirty, hairy, starveling, sweat-and-blood-smeared newcomers. Everybody was talking and laughing at once but nobody was understanding what was being said, except by hand-talk and smiles and shrugs, of which there was a plenitude.

Early winter night had fallen when the beat of drums outside drew most of the Indians through the doorway, several of them beckoning us to follow. Eddard Rose stood up and stretched to his full height before he announced, "These heah Snakes're fixin' to have themse'fs a scalp dance an' they be hankerin' fer us to git in on it. Reckon we oughta 'commodate 'em."

Only Paddy McBride looked alarmed. "An' whose scalp would that likely be, Misther Rose? Certainly not me own!"

Everybody but Paddy laughed and we all filed through the doorway after Rose. A big bonfire was sending sparks swirling into a clear winter sky, as if to add more stars to the multitude already planted there, and the Snakes, men and women alike, were gathering in a circle around it. The drumbeat quickened when we came into view and a chorus of shouts and yips and howls greeted our arrival. An old man wearing a bear robe fastened about his shoulders appeared to be just finishing a speech as we took our place in the circle, squatting on our heels and leaning on our rifles. When the old man flung his hands skyward and retreated, Drum-singer stepped into the circle and commenced a quavering chant in that high, hollow, nasal voice that Indians use for their singing, all the while doing a shuffling kind of slow dance around the fire and pointing at each of us trappers from time to time. He was dressed in what I took to be his Sunday best and waving his lance above his head, stripped now to but a single scalp fluttering in the firelight. Eddard Rose, looking solemn as a circuit parson, said in a low voice, "Ol' Drum-singah's tellin' what we done fer 'em an' jes' how brave we war. Git ready to rise an' shine."

I was wondering what Rose might mean by that when Drum-singer broke off and stepped out of the circle. The drums grew louder and faster and a passel of young boys ran forward, dragging big branches, and threw them onto the fire, making it blaze higher and brighter, bathing the circle in warm yellow brilliance, revealing a dozen or so women dancing in file on the far side of the fire, each of them waving a staff bedecked with one or more raw Blackfoot scalps.

As the sound and tempo of the drums rose and fell, the women responded with the rhythm of their dancing, now mincing in solemn procession, now flinging themselves into a whirling, stamping frenzy, all the while shaking their staves aloft, broad smiles wreathing their dusky faces as they circled past an audience brimming over with pleasure and approval, many onlookers barking out quick phrases or grunting their satisfaction. The drumbeat ceased for a moment, then rattled out what appeared to be a signal, for the women darted in amongst the watchers and commenced hauling out the men who had taken scalps. I was nigh flabbergasted when a round-faced young woman, black eyes snapping in the firelight, strong, white teeth gleaming between her parted lips, thrust her face close to mine, grasped my hand, yanked me to my feet, and dragged me into the circle. As I stumbled after her I saw two scalps streaming from the staff she carried and I wondered how she or anybody knew that I had killed two Blackfoots that bloody night. But then, Indians don't miss much of what concerns them.

As I shuffled my moccasins more or less aimlessly, trying without much success to match the beat of the drums, she gamboled in a tight circle around me, holding the scalps over my head and making sign with her free hand that I took to mean that I was some kind of warrior to be reckoned with. Tuttle, his left arm still in a sling, cavorted like a colt in pasture, his grin nigh splitting his face, eyes blazing with good-natured lust for the woman who carried the scalp he had earned, the same woman, I noticed, whom he was convinced had given him the glad-eye upon our arrival amongst the Snakes. Tuttle never missed much of what concerned him, either.

Most of our bunch had killed at least one Blackfoot in the ambush or in the running fight afterwards, so only Rose and old Foot sat out that scalp dance. Paddy, still smarting from his arrow wound, tried desperately to jig, lame as he was. Even so, his hobbling gait surpassed my own awkward attempts. Godey and Brass Turtle and the other Delawares showed themselves to be as smooth at dancing as they were in most things. Watching Anse and Smiley reassured me, howsomever, that I wasn't the only one who was about as graceful as a bull buffalo falling out of a tree.

Boys kept running into the circle, heaping wood upon the fire, then scampering out again. My partner, her face flushed and dark eyes sparkling, appeared to be enjoying a wicked pleasure in dancing me ever closer to the blaze, until I feared that my capote would burst into flame, although, truth be told, I wasn't altogether sure if the fire at my back was hotter than the one under my britchclout. Caught up as she was in the spirit and excitement of the dancing, the woman fairly glowed with raw natural beauty and what I commenced to hope was animal lust.

Just as I thought I might be getting the hang of it, the drums fell silent with a final thump. Drum-singer took back his lance from his wife and he and the other Snake warriors melted into the crowd of spectators with the women who had carried their scalps. When I looked for my companion, she had left my side, and I glimpsed her disappearing into the throng, together with the other women who had danced with us trappers, scalps fluttering from the staves they still carried.

Naturally there was feasting and much sign-talk amongst the Snake headmen and our folks in our lodge afterwards, but feeling the way I did about my dancing partner, I had little wish to tarry with Shoshone men just then. I sneaked off to see to the horses, which, I noted with satisfaction, were under close guard by several boys in the cottonwood grove. The feasting and palaver was still going on when I got back, but instead of joining my companions, I slipped into my sleep robes, preferring to dream of black eyes and white teeth and graceful swaying hips.

క్ర క్ర క్ర

Dreaming was the best I could do for several days thereafter, despite my daily efforts to scrape an acquaintance with the dark-eyed woman of the scalp dance. I shaved off the stubble on my cheeks and broke through ice on the Popo-Azhieh each morning, bathing with the Delawares and Snakes, shuddering from bone-deep chill as I donned my best and cleanest clothes, but such affectations availed me nothing. She just looked through me and past me as if I were no more substantial than a winter breeze.

Eddard Rose explained. "That'n be a widdah-woman. See how her hair be chopped off on the one side? That be fer the mournin' time. Mos' likely got slashes on her arms, too. Her man got hisse'f kilt by Absarokas come to thieve hosses jes' las' fall. She ain't ready fer nobody new, no mattah what ye might be wishin' or doin'."

Rose went on. "Mos', mebbe all, o' them wimmen shakin' Blackfoot hair at the dancin' be widdah-wimmen, thankin' you white-eyes fer evenin' up a score, but whethah they gonna bed ye fer it, ye'll jes' hafta wait an' see."

I waited but I could see no hope for my intentions, so most days when clear weather allowed I busied myself with hunting, mainly to use up energy I would have preferred to employ otherwise. Hunting thereabouts proved to be fairly successful and whenever I shot a deer or a wapiti I made sure to leave a haunch or a backstrap at the door of her lodge, but the most thanks I ever got for my trouble was a curt little nod and once or twice a quirky little smile with her eyes downcast, never directly looking at me. I despaired of ever furthering my suit.

That is where matters stood the day I hunted with Ned Godey, Tuttle, Smiley, and Anse and a party of Snakes, ranging rather farther afield than we usually did, without a great deal of success. Which is why I lagged a considerable distance behind my companions as we neared the village on our return, hoping to spy a game critter venturing out to feed at dusk, reluctant to come back empty-handed, lacking a gift for my indifferent light-o'-love.

Nothing stirred at the forest fringe as I made my way stealthily through the snow, concealing myself as best I could behind clumps of sagebrush, so as not to spook whatever game might be lingering thereabouts, angling towards the crick that ran beside the cottonwood grove where young Snakes tended our horses.

Then I saw him, a big man, taller than any Snake I had seen in the village, leading two horses out of the crick bottom, his hand clamped over the nose of one of them to keep him from neighing, eyes darting in every direction to discover a pursuer, but he never saw me, hunkered down as I was behind a sagebrush. I knew him for a horsethief, likely a Crow by the size of him, so I flipped the cow's knee off the lock and raised up my rifle, purely intending to send him off to hell.

Problem was, I couldn't get a clean shot at him, surrounded as he was by hard-to-come-by horseflesh. Keeping low behind whatever cover there was, I scurried towards him, crouching, dragging Melchior through the snow, until by fits and starts I came within half a dozen paces behind him and raised up to fire. Busy as he was with the horses, the first inkling he had of me was when he heard me cock the hammer. He was a Crow indeed and too big to miss. When he heard the click of metal, he whirled about and turned the horses loose before he came running at me, jerking a big knife from his belt as he floundered through knee-deep snow. I had him dead to rights, howsomever, so I was fairly calm when I squeezed the trigger, aiming for the big part of his body, and heard the sickening wheeze and fizzle of damp powder in the pan.

The Crow was nearly upon me before I grabbed Melchior by the barrel and swung the stock at his head, which I missed, clubbing his knife arm instead and knocking his weapon into the snow, which stalled him hardly at all. He hit me like an avalanche, flinging me onto my back and falling onto me, huge hands grasping at my throat, nigh smothering me in the stinking folds of his greasy buffalo coat, grunting and hissing foul breath through clenched teeth as he sought to crush my windpipe.

Swathed as I was in a bulky capote, there was no way for me to reach the pistol in my belt nor the belly gun beneath it, certainly not with the Crow's enormous weight upon me. I was thrashing arms and legs like a turned-over turtle when my fingers brushed the haft of Lucette's poniard — which Tuttle always sneeringly called a toothpick — strapped to my calf. The Crow's big hands had pushed inside the hood of my capote and his fingers were squeezing me into red oblivion when I drove the slim triangular blade to the hilt in his thigh.

He screamed and r'ared up, as much in surprise as pain, I reckon, wrenching the poniard free and giving me a split-instant to roll out from under him and try to scramble to my feet and run. Strong for my size and wiry as I was, I knew I was no match for such as he in a wrestling match.

I barely made a step and a half before he caromed into me again, bowling the two of us over the lip of the gully, flailing arms and legs as we rolled down the slope to the frozen crick below, he punching and slapping and clutching at my windpipe, me stabbing the poniard time and again into his broad back, until we crashed upon the ice with him on top and I felt it crack and part beneath me.

The big man gasped and shuddered just once when the icy water flowed onto him, then slumped lifeless upon my breast, his great dead weight bearing me down like all the Shining Mountains put together, his cheek nestled against my own, as if in a farewell embrace. At first I feared the Crow's enormous bulk would shove my head below the water's surface and I would drown. Then I realized my back was already resting on the bottom of that shallow crick, my head propped up on ice or a rock, and if I weren't able to get out from under that big Indian, death would come more slowly, but just as surely, from the cold.

Each effort to wriggle free of that crushing weight was more feeble than the attempt before. At last I ceased to thrash and splash, admitting that I was in fact a goner, then taking pleasure from the warmth that seeped into my body as the icy water numbed me into blackness.

   ~~~

I recollect I heard the fire first, crackling and popping, but there was no heat, only cold that froze the very marrow in my bones and the dismal thought that Pap had been right after all. I had died and gone to hell, just as he always said I would.

Next I heard a rattling, like dry bones tumbling in a barrel, and I commenced to wonder if the imps of hell always played such music for their guests, until it came to me that it was the chattering of my teeth that was making such a godawful racket and that I was shivering and jerking like a bug on a griddle, r'aring up and shuddering, then falling back to shiver and squirm some more whilst half the fiends of hell peeled the flesh right off my bones.

Once when the shivers grabbed me, I r'ared up and felt strong hands push me gently onto my back again, which wasn't the sort of treatment a body might expect in hell. I cracked an eyelid partway open and saw a fire blazing not an arm's length away, which wasn't surprising in hell, but then I saw in the yellow firelight the face of the dark-eyed woman of the scalp dance and felt her hands soothing my body. It seemed proper enough to me that I had landed in hell, since there appeared to be such a place after all, but I was downright confounded to learn that she had ended up there, too, especially considering that she and her people most likely had never even heard of hell.

I was puzzling over this conundrum when I heard Ned Godey say, "'Pears he's comin' 'round!" Then Tuttle's voice, "C'mon, Temple, you kin do it! C'mon back to us, lad!"

It wasn't the least bit surprising to discover those two reprobates in hell with me, but then, between fits of shivering and through the chattering of my teeth, I heard Brass Turtle's flat Missouri twang. "Hey thar, Temple Buck! Damned if ye ain't the most hellacious stud hoss in all creation! Ye been hankerin' to git yerself into thi'shere woman's robes since ye showed up in these hyar parts an' now ye went an' done it! Mighty peculiar way ye picked fer the doin' of it, howsomever!"

I would have laughed if a fit of shivering and chattering hadn't overtaken me just then. I felt the woman's hands pushing my shoulders back and down and for the first time I heard her speak, in a sharp, commanding voice. Although I couldn't understand a word of what she was saying, I gathered she was shooing my friends out of her lodge. Ned and Tuttle grumbled more than somewhat, but they did as she told them, calling out farewells and promises to return in the morning.

Through slitted eyelids I watched her going about her nursing chores, building up the fire, removing hand-sized flat stones from the buffalo robes that covered me, sprinkling water on the robes, then lifting hot stones from the fire with a pair of sticks and placing them all around me on the dampened robes. Soothing steam and glorious warmth and the simple sight of the dark-eyed woman tending to me transformed that lodge from the hell I had thought it was to all the heaven I could handle right then.

I have no idea how many times I woke up and drifted off again that night, dimly aware of her capable hands chafing my hide to get blood flowing in my chilled flesh and once when she tried to ladle warm broth past my chattering teeth. I do recollect, howsomever, how startled and pleased I was when I woke up another time and realized that it was her warm, naked body clasping me close to her that was making me feel so good.

By morning the only part of me that still appeared to be frozen was my nether parts, which went a long way towards assuring me that I would get well and be healthy again. I needed to answer nature's call, but when I tried to roll out of the sleep robes, I discovered that I was too weak to stand up or even crawl.

That was how the woman found me when she ducked through the door flap, sprawled halfway out of the robes, unable even to roll back in again. She dropped the bundle of sticks she was carrying for the fire and came to me, smiling for the first time and crooning soft words she might have sung to an ailing child. She caught hold of my shoulders and rolled me back onto the pallet, propped up my head on a parfleche box, and pulled the buffalo robe to my chin, then went to the far side of the lodge and returned with an empty gourd, which she shoved under the robe before she discreetly retreated out-of-doors.

By time she returned I was feeling much more comfortable and she betrayed no emotion whatsoever when she carried the steaming gourd out past the tipi flap. I confess I was embarrassed considerably more than somewhat that she had to provide such a service for me. I was convinced that this was no proper way to commence a courtship.

When she returned inside again, she went directly to the fire and laid sticks onto coals heaped around a little iron kettle that I recognized as John Smiley's. As new flame licked at the kettle, she stirred the contents and crooned a quiet, tuneless little song, never quite looking at me, but not hiding her face from me, either.

I saw that she was younger than I had thought, but a grown woman nevertheless, her face not as round as I remembered, her bottomless dark eyes framed by high cheekbones, her generous mouth surely created for laughter, which I could imagine even though I had never heard her laugh. Her coppery skin was smooth and unlined, her face sparkling clean and still rosy-cheeked from the cold outside. I couldn't see her body, covered as she was in a loose deerhide dress and an elkhide cape clasped around her shoulders, but I recalled as through a mist the warmth and the feel of her flesh pressed close to mine in the night and I knew that she was slender but generous where she ought to be, hard-muscled yet yielding, and all the woman a sane man could ask for.

Right now, howsomever, she was all business, ladling broth from the kettle into a gourd and setting it aside to cool. Then, picking up a tiny rawhide box filled with some pasty, evil-smelling herbs, she forced a spoonful or more of that mess into my mouth on a tiny flat stick. It was bitter and made my cheeks pucker but I gagged it down somehow before she laved the foul taste away with thick, fragrant broth that warmed me deep into my belly, her face close above mine, solemn but soft and caring, liquid dark eyes seeming to search deep within my soul to learn what manner of man I might truly be.

When I had gulped down all the broth in the bowl, she laid it aside and commenced brushing my hair with a porcupine tail.

My hair was by then nearly as long as her own where hers wasn't chopped off on one side. She kept on humming and crooning her little song, treating me like some wounded, broken little critter that she had found in the woods. I wanted to tell her that I was strong and brave enough when I had to be and able to take care of myself — and her, too, if need be — but right then such talk appeared not worth the bother and I slipped into dreamless sleep.

Familiar voices and feet stamping snow off moccasins roused me from my slumber. A cold winter sun shone through the smoke flaps above and made me squint as I peered at Tuttle and Godey, Brass Turtle, and Eddard Rose crouching and crowding through the doorway, jostling one another and laughing. Tuttle was first to speak. Fact is, he positively brayed. "Thar ye be, Temple! Come back t' jine us in the land o' the livin'!"

Ned Godey stepped forward, a rifle in his hand, a broad smile on his face. "Hyar be your *Melchior* rifle gun, Temple. Snake boys fetched it from t'other side o' the crick. Thought ye mought be wantin' it."

It was Brass Turtle's turn. He flipped a wad of tangled black hair onto the sleep robes and said with a grin, "'Pears it be giftin' time. That'n be your'n. Reckon ye sure as hell earned it!" I looked down at the mass of long black hair, dried blood crusted on a patch of skin, and felt a certain glow of satisfaction at the sight of it. I had indeed earned that particular trophy, the hardest way I could imagine.

A rustle of leather on hard-packed earth caught my attention and the Snake woman appeared at my side, snatched up the scalp, then retreated to the far side of the lodge.

Eddard Rose dropped to his knees beside me, chuckling as he said, "Reckon she prizes that'n more'n the Blackfoots she danced ye with. 'Twas Crows kilt her man, ye know. Reckon that be why naught else'd do but we carry ye heah to her lodge aftah we drug ye outen the crick. Carried on sumthin' fierce 'til we done like she said." Rose chuckled again. Then he reached into his sash and brought out my poniard and stuck it into the ground beside me, saying, "Heah be yer toad-stickah! Like to nevah got it outen that Crow, stuck in his backbone like it war!"

Tuttle chimed in with, "Thet'n shore was a big 'un! Took the three of us to haul 'im off'n you. Why hell, thet heathen's mockersins be a shade too big fer even me, but I'll be wearin' 'em anyways! Thank ye kin'ly, Temple."

When I tried to laugh it felt like a rusty chain being yanked through my throat, but I managed to strangle out my thankees before I slumped back on my robes, a big, foolish grin pasted across my face, happy to be amongst my own once more. They laughed and joked and joshed me about the perils of going swimming with Absarokas in the midst of winter, until the woman shooed them out of the lodge, laughing at last and sputtering sharp-sounding Snake words, pretending to whip them with the Crow scalp, until the last of them ducked past the door flap with a promise to return.

Her face was flushed and she was still smiling when she turned back to me, merriment and tenderness mixed in her eyes. I commenced to hope that she and I might be a pair in due time. She made me swallow more of her evil herbs, then spooned a bowlful of broth into me to wash the taste away and, I reckon, to make me sleep, for I straightway fell into a deep slumber, furnished this time with pleasant dreams of I reckon you know what I don't need to describe.

I woke again after nightfall and found I was able to pull a robe around me and totter just outside the lodge to answer nature's call. My chilblained fingers and toes still stung, my muscles stuffed with cramp, but I could feel strength commencing to flow into my arms and legs and the giddiness was fast ebbing away. Just the same, weak as I was, I barely made it back to the pallet, where I fell headlong onto the robes.

The woman, busy at the fire, clucked her disapproval at my venturing out of the lodge, then shifted about on her knees and came to my side, bringing with her a gourd filled with bear grease warmed to oil and fragrant with herbs and I don't know what-all. She pushed aside the robe and proceeded to anoint my naked body, head to toe, her strong fingers kneading my flesh, searching into every nook and cranny, probing between my toes and everyplace else you might imagine. I daresay there was a passel of nettles amongst the herbs in that oil, for I felt a prickling, tingling, gently burning warmth all over my hide and deep within me as she laved and rubbed the mixture into my aching, cramping muscles. When she finished with my back, she tried to roll me over again, but I strained to remain on my belly, embarrassed by the result her ministrations had produced. My resistance was to no avail, howsomever, and when she rolled me onto my back, she made that clucking sound again, but this time I detected no hint of disapproval.

Her dark eyes were deep and brimming as she leaned over me to pull the sleep robes into place. I wanted to reach up and pull her to me, but instead I surrendered to the delicious warmth that invaded every pore and penetrated to my very core, hazing me into darkness and sweet dreamless slumber.

When I awoke in the night I felt her naked body spooned against the length of me and saw the soft curve of her cheek limned against the flickering remains of the fire. Her hand had strayed behind her and claimed me gently but firmly for her own. It was enough for now. I cupped her full bosoms in my hand and pulled her close before I let sleep overtake me once again.

෯ ෯ ෯

I followed my nose out of my slumber to the aroma of meat roasting over the cookfire, hardly more than an arm's length from where I lay. The Snake woman knelt at her chore, her face turned mostly away from me, slowly turning half a backstrap skewered on a green willow stick over sputtering flames. Through the open smokeflaps I saw the sun already high in the sky and from outside I could hear laughter and children's chatter and the buzz of common talk, sounds of the village going about its business.

The woman glanced my way when I flung back the sleep robes, then nodded towards my moccasins beside the pallet. I fumbled them on, then, clutching a robe around my shoulders, I made my way to the men's midden and back, all the while marveling at how strong I felt, the ache and numbness mostly gone, my mind clear and sharp as ever it was, and how my belly screamed for solid food.

As I shambled through the village I was aware of many approving smiles and nods from the older Snakes, men and women alike, and shrieks and much finger-pointing by the children, which told me that I had been the object of some interest, if not concern, amongst them since my encounter with the Absaroka horsethief.

When I dodged through the doorway of the woman's lodge I saw my britchclout, leggin's, and deerhide shirt spread neatly upon the sleep robes and I hurried to put them on. As I did so, I was certain that I was indeed restored to health, for my modesty had returned and I was careful to turn my back to the woman as I shrugged into my garments, stubbornly ignoring her muffled titters the while.

The deer meat was tender and juicy and cooked to a delicious turn. The woman refused to share food with me, according to their custom, but she sat opposite me, slicing smoking slabs from the backstrap and refilling a gourd bowl with what I took to be a kind of pease porridge. When at last I was unable to stuff in another mouthful, she fetched my belt and possibles, which thankfully still contained my pipe and tobacco.

Lighting my pipe with a splinter from the cookfire, I blew out a cloud of smoke and leaned back on my elbows, contented as I have ever been, drinking in the sight of the pretty woman who had saved my life, restored my strength, and kindled my desire. She kept her eyes downcast and blushed under my steady gaze, but she brightened considerably when I cleared my throat and, using the hand-talk, asked what her name might be. It took her a couple-three tries before I understood her reply to mean Snowflower. It struck me that Snowflower was an apt name for a woman such as she. I recalled bright yellow crocuses thrusting bravely through late-winter snow back home, triumphing over ice and freezing sleet and promising warm springtime pleasures.

Then she signed that I should tell her my name and for a spell I was confounded. Everybody had always called me Temple, but there was no way that I could get across such an idea in sign-talk. Even I had never actually seen a temple and there was no way that she could ever conceive of such a thing, so at last I made the sign of a he-deer, a buck, complete with antlers, grateful that Pap's name wasn't Schultz or something like that.

The two of us continued to dig for knowledge of each other, she forcing herself to slow down her rapid hand-signs, I fumbling the unfamiliar gestures, both of us sputtering with laughter whenever my fingers misspoke, until a commotion outside the tipi signaled that we had visitors.

I called out a welcome and the doorflap was swept aside, revealing a freshly-shaved Tuttle Thompson, beaming as if his face would split asunder, followed by Godey, Paddy McBride, and Anse Tolliver, all of them rosy-cheeked from the cold and uncharacteristically unbewhiskered.

"Thar ye be, Temple!" Tuttle roared. "We heared ye war up an' about! Lookin' fitter'n a fiddle strang, don't he, boys? Reckon we oughta be thankin' thi'shere li'l lady fer thet!" About then he caught sight of Snowflower retreating to the rear of the lodge, where she turned her back on the lot of us. Tuttle laughed aloud. "Wal, mebbe later!"

Ned Godey echoed his laughter. "An' that ain't all. We be most special grateful fer whatever she's been tellin' t'other womenfolk concernin' the rest of us. 'Pears they jist now fergot how to say no, like they been doin' ever since we got hyar."

Paddy grinned and looked thoughtful before he joined in. "Well, now, lads, don't be after supposin' them widdahs're completely fergittin' the use o' No, but it's becomin' increasin'ly plain fer all t' see, them ladies're after learnin' May-be an' Perhaps as well!"

Anse Tolliver's Tennessee twang cut through the general laughter. "Aw, don't nobody know nuthin' fer sartin, Temple, but the lot of 'em 'pear to be a damnsight more neighborly than they war afore ye took to bathin' 'longside thet hossthief!"

Sifting through their good-natured palaver I gathered that the amorous overtures of my companions, even if not so far successful, were meeting less resistance from their intended light-o'-loves, perhaps because of the example of Snowflower taking me in to nurse me back to health. Perhaps not. Simple curiosity, human need, and the practicalities of a widow's life in an Indian village are powerful persuaders.

After they departed, Tuttle came back dragging my pack of plunder in one hand and carrying a hindquarter of deer in the other. He tossed the pack just inside the doorway and laid the deer meat beside the fire, saying the while, "Reckon ye'd be wantin' to keep an eye on yore plunder yore ownse'f, pard, now thet ye kin agin." Then, glancing at the pack, he added, "Natcherly I he'ped m'se'f to some o' thet'ere trade plunder — jest in case, don'tcha know." He winked and I laughed, fully aware of Tuttle's appetites and how powerful and undeniable they could prove to be.

Snowflower and I passed the rest of the day waving our hands at each other, when she wasn't at her chores and I wasn't cleaning and oiling my weapons, sharpening blades, and taking stock of my possibles, all of which I found to be undisturbed except for Tuttle's forays. When I inquired about her dead husband, she frowned and waved my question away, then asked again why it was that all of us white trappers were so froze to get our hands on beaver plews when buffalo were so much more useful. After a couple of futile attempts, I despaired of ever being able to explain the reason to a woman who had never seen a gentleman's top hat and who had no inkling of the use of money or gold, so I gave up and let her think that we were all somewhat crazy, which idea she appeared to accept with no trouble at all.

After we had eaten again and just as night was falling, a scratching on the tipi cover and a discreet cough announced the arrival of Brass Turtle and Little Mountain, the two of them stripped to their britchclouts, capotes draped over their shoulders. Turtle smiled his approval of my restored condition, nodded to Snowflower, and said to me, "Ye're wanted over at the sweat lodge. Time ye be sweatin' out what's left o' yer white devils, what the woman here ain't scraped off'n ye awready."

I had no idea what he was talking about and even less inclination to join in any religious ceremony, which, white or red, had never been to my liking. Still and all, Turtle was a good and true friend and I had no wish to say him nay. Little Mountain was meanwhile signing to the woman and when I saw what I took to be her nod, I shrugged and said I would go along with them. A few minutes later, stripped even of britchclout and moccasins and shivering in the snowy night air, I crawled into the sweat lodge behind Brass Turtle.

The heat inside hit me like a fist. I coughed and strangled in clouds of steam, seeking to catch my breath. Squinting through my tears I barely made out the dull red glow of heated stones heaped in the center and a naked old man with steam-soaked, glistening hair, a pair of eagle feathers drooping onto his shoulder, sprinkling water on the stones, then disappearing in the steam. Turtle and I crowded in amongst a circle of men who lined the low sloping walls, shoving our backs against the wooden frame, sitting cross-legged, heads bowed, in my case fighting desperately to draw my next breath.

From outside I could hear the tap of drums and old Foot's quavering chant blended with another voice that I took to be

Shoshone, trading song, first one, then the other, rising and falling and losing each other in the hollow beat of the drums. Then Brass Turtle's voice murmuring. "Turn loose of it all, Temple. Let it all fall away, like water comin' down a mountain an' eagles flyin' out acrost a valley in the early-mornin' sun an' night shadders takin' holt o' the land once agin. Go 'long with it all, Temple, an' learn who you be."

Turtle's droning voice and the beating drums, the faraway chanting and the billowing steam must have weaved a spell around me, for I have no idea how long I sat there, head bowed, eyes squeezed tight, soaring and planing over snowy, green-shouldered mountains and misty blue valleys and vast green and golden prairies, borne on the wings of eagles, blown by warm, gentle winds into the sunshine of my very own soul.

I recollect struggling to stay where I was, holding on to peace and contentment I had never known before, washed clean of all concern, and bathed in never-ending bliss, but the dream or vision or whatever it was faded into the dark sweat lodge with all its common sounds and smells. A tiny fire sputtered and flickered at the far end, fed with pungent sage and fragrant sweetgrass mingling with the steam, which had ceased to snatch my breath away and furnished welcome warming comfort now. I closed my eyes, seeking to return whence I had been, but Turtle's voice broke into my thoughts. "Reckon it's time we go." I nodded, unable to form words or to make any sound, and crawled after him through the low doorway.

Outside, naked men from the sweat lodge were plunging into snowdrifts, rolling in the snow, laughing and crowing like schoolboys, unmindful of the dignity they sought to maintain at other times. I saw Eddard Rose and the young chief of the band, a handsome man they called Wah-shah-kee, pelting each other with snowballs. Even the solemn old man who had sprinkled water on the stones was wriggling in the snow like an otter playing on a streambank. I stood watching them, my hide dripping rivers of sweat, commencing to chill in the cold night air, when Turtle bowled me over and pitched me headlong into a snowdrift. I rose sputtering and choking, skin tingling from the shock, determined to return the favor, when Little Mountain caromed into Turtle, the younger man's broad shoulders catching him behind the knees, and the two of them went rolling and thrashing from one drift to another, until they lay exhausted, giggling like schoolgirls.

Tramping back to Snowflower's lodge, I was scarcely aware of myself or the village around me. Cleansed as I was in body and spirit, all that was common and natural seemed to me remote and unreal. Only the crunching snow beneath my moccasins and dimly-heard snatches of Delaware talk called me back to the here and now. I longed desperately to return to the sunlit peace I had known in the sweat lodge.

When I stepped past the doorflap the woman was kneeling at the low-burning fire, stirring steaming liquid in a gourd. She raised her head and looked me full in the face, then motioned me towards the sleeping pallet, moved now from beside the fire to the rear of the lodge. I did as she said, dropping the capote from my shoulders, kicking off my moccasins, and untying my britchclout as I went, all modesty gone and time now only for what was natural and real.

I dropped onto the sleep robes and stretched out full length, then turned on my side and held out my arms to her. She came to me then and crouched beside me, offering the steaming bowl with both hands. I took it from her and drank a deep draught of a delicious tea unlike any I had ever tasted, then held it out to her, inviting her to share it. At first she hesitated, then accepted, sipping with honest pleasure, her unreadable dark eyes watching me all the while. We traded the gourd until it was empty and she put it aside. Then she rose to her feet and slipped her hide dress over her head, revealing herself naked and beautiful, a new copper penny gleaming in the dwindling firelight, raspberry-tipped breasts swelling proudly, deep golden skin flawless and flowing to where she was dark-feathered and plump between strong rounded thighs.

I reached up and caught her hands, pulling her down beside me, and kissed her full on the mouth. Startled at first, she jerked away and her teeth grazed my lip, then she returned her lips to mine and set herself to learn this new white-eyes custom, her growing enthusiasm telling me that she found some of our craziness quite acceptable. My hands in the meantime were not idle, caressing the smooth hard length of her legs and cupping her firm buttocks, roaming the delicious country of her sturdy back and softly rounded belly, delving lower to where she was moist and ready, then pulling my lips away from hers to tease her nipples, stiff as springtime buds, and burying my face in her generous bosom, drowning in the heady woman smell of her and glorying in the clean honest taste of this natural woman.

Her hands were busy, as well, and I commenced to fear that I might arrive too soon. It had been nigh a year since Simone, although right at that moment there had never been a Simone or a Night-eyes or Lucette, and certainly never an Aunt Penny, only this woman, this Snowflower, this Eve created in the Shining Mountains solely for me.

The heat in my loins grew unbearable and would not be denied. I rose to my knees and when she saw my intention she tried to roll onto her belly, in the manner of her people, but I pinned her shoulders to the robes and entered her, kissing her eyes and mouth and twining my fingers in her hair. It was over ere it scarce began. I groaned my disappointment, muttering apologies she couldn't understand, but she was as eager as I. Her appetite matched my own and we soon embarked upon a second journey, more leisurely now but much more delightful, sampling all the pleasures along the way, until we arrived together in shrieking, groaning, clawing, sweet release.

We slept but little that night, dozing off into exhausted slumber, then either she or I toying the other into ardent wakefulness, enchanted with our new-found games, unwilling to postpone our pleasures. There was no need for words, no possibility of misunderstanding, no demand not readily granted, no primal need gone unfulfilled.

Gray early-morning daylight invaded through the smokeflaps when last I stroked her cheek snugged into my shoulder, her soft breathing warming my chest, and I surrendered to contented nothingness.

ও   ও   ও

I slept until mid-morning, when a persistent scratching at the doorflap roused me from my slumbers. The woman was gone and I was alone in the lodge.   I fumbled into my britchclout and hastened to the doorway, where Brass Turtle was calling out in a cheery voice, "Hey thar, Temple, time fer ye to rise up an' shine! Cain't be sleepin' yer life away!"

I pushed the doorflap aside and he ducked into the lodge, sniffing and grinning broadly when he saw telltale welts and scratches on my shoulders and chest that betrayed the lovemaking of the night before. He gazed about the lodge, settling on the bed at the far end, behind the fire. "'Pears to me ye be the big he-dog o' thi'shere lodge now," he said with a chuckle. "'Bout time, too. Took ye long enough."

I mumbled some nonsense in reply and I daresay I blushed, even though I was feeling somewhat proud of myself. Turtle went on. "Reason I come by, ol' Stone Bird he come up on a passel o' buffler this mornin'. We be goin' out to fetch 'em. Thought ye might be wishin' to come along."

I assured him that nothing would please me more — well, hardly anything — then hurried off to the midden to perform my morning chore and scrub my nether parts clean with snow. By time I trotted back to the lodge, Snowflower had returned and was ladling pease porridge into a gourd. When I knelt beside her and tried to kiss her, she brushed me away, but I refused to be put off and kissed her anyway. She kept on with her chore, eyes downcast, but she was smiling, trying, I reckon, to fathom the crazy ways of white-eyes men.   Indians aren't nearly so affectionate towards their women, leastaways not next morning.

I gulped a few mouthfuls of porridge and swigged a bowlful of tea, then busied myself getting dressed for the cold and gathering up my rifle, pistols, and possibles. When I was ready to go, I made sign to Snowflower that I was going with the others to hunt buffalo. She had need to repeat her reply a time or two before I understood her to say, "Better than beaver."

ॐ ॐ ॐ

Tuttle had my horses saddled and ready by time I trotted up to the crowd of men and horses milling in the center of the village. All of our people were there along with half a score or more of Snakes, Drum-singer and the young chief Wah-shah-kee and a couple of herd boys amongst them, the lot of them evidently waiting for me, for they headed out as soon as I swung into the saddle. Stone Bird and a couple others took the lead, breaking trail through knee-deep snow until their horses commenced to tire, then dropping back to let others take their place. The sun was bright but the breeze was cold, keeping the snow crisp and dry and slow to ball in the horses' hooves.

Chiksika surged beneath my thighs like a small tornado and Jake kept running past me until the lead rope checked him, then falling behind, the two of them downright giddy at getting back to work again. I was feeling much the same. Tuttle reined in alongside me, leaned out of the saddle, and slapped me on the back. "Good to have ye back amongst us agin, ol' pard!" he chortled and I wondered if it was the cold that made a tear glisten in the corner of his eye.

Ned Godey, riding on the other side of Tuttle, grinned all the way to his ears and said, "Yep, 't'war a near thing fer ye, Temple, soakin' an' freezin' in the crick like ye war! Ye'd best be thankin' yer stars or yer God or whatever ye hold holy fer that woman o' your'n an' her naggin' an' yammerin' at us to go find ye when ye didn't show up with the rest of us that night." The two of them went on to explain how none of the hunters had noticed my absence and how only Snowflower had missed me, how she had searched the village and the horse herd, and how she had set up a howl when I was nowhere to be found.

Tuttle looked solemn, recalling that night. Then he laughed aloud. "Talk about lookin' fer a needle in a haystack! An' when we did find ye, ye war buried underneath the haystack! Fust off, nobody thought to look underneath o' thet big Crow. We'd'a let 'im lay, 'ceptin' Paddy got to pokin' 'round an' found ye froze up like a goddamn icicle!" I made a silent promise to thank and reward

Paddy McBride for his persistence and if such a thing had been possible, I would have loved Snowflower even more than I already did.

Stone Bird, riding in the lead again, held up his hand and the column halted whilst he swung down and waddled crouching through the snow, keeping low, until he dropped out of sight over the lip of a draw. He reappeared after a short spell and signed for us to dismount and follow him. We turned the horses over to the herd boys and trudged after Stone Bird, clutching at powderhorns and possibles lest they rattle and spook our prey.

By time I got to the rim of a narrow, steep-sided draw and spied perhaps a score of buffalo grazing down below, the Snakes, most of them armed with bows and a few with old muskets, were scurrying towards the bottom end of the draw whilst our Delawares were filtering through the trees and brush on the upper side. Rose led our party down the steep bank somewheres in the middle, slipping and sliding and careening into tree trunks, holding our rifles up and away from the snow whilst we stifled our curses, until we reached a fringe of trees just a mite higher than the valley floor.

Once the firing commenced, it was over before it had fairly begun. Appetite hones a man's shooting skill and none of us had tasted fleece fat and hump ribs in many a moon. After the first volley, I barely had time to reload before the last of the fleeing buffalo were being picked off at the far ends of the draw. Quick as a wink, the lot of us were floundering out to the fallen buffalo, firing killing shots into wounded critters, reloading, then putting our rifles aside and drawing our skinning knives, eager to taste once more buffalo liver splashed with gall, fresh-killed and steaming in the cold crisp air.

Tuttle was laughing like a hyena — though I confess I have never seen or heard a hyena — a bloody chunk of liver in one hand, a length of boudin in the other, his hands and face covered with blood, crowing and cavorting on the blood-spattered snow, proclaiming at the top of his voice that he would bring fresh buffalo meat to his intended widow-woman and thereby seal the bargain. Tuttle was no different from the rest of us in looks or behavior, maybe just a mite louder. It is good sometimes to admit that we are blood kin to the rest of the critters.

The herd boys hazed our horses down a passable trail and we all set to work butchering and packing every useable smidgeon of meat onto pack animals and saddle horses alike. It was winter and there was no telling when we might find buffalo again. I daresay it was slim pickings for the wolves that night. Then we led our critters out of the draw and tramped our way back to the village, as contented as natural men could possibly be, with ourselves and the world we were blessed to be living in.

                                       ~ ~ ~

Shorter nights and lengthening days inched us closer to the spring hunt, but Grandfather Winter showed no intention of loosing his icy grip on the land. The Popo Azhieh and the streams that fed it were choked with ice and there was naught else for us to do but wait for the spring thaw.

The waiting was pleasant enough, howsomever, for there were more than enough amusements to keep us from getting fretful. In good weather we hunted the breaks along the Popo Azhieh for deer and the lower mountain meadows for wapiti and sometimes a moose, now and then coming across little bands of kicked-out buffalo bulls, run off from the main bunch by the bigger, stronger herd bulls. After such a hunt there would be feasting and much merriment in the village, for buffalo meant life itself for the Snakes and, as time went along, for us as well.

Some of us learned the use of the bow, shooting at targets on trees at first, then at willow hoops set to rolling on the snow-covered ground. Throwing knives and tomahawks and belt axes at a target was a pleasant pastime, as well, but we knew whilst we were playing at such games that throwing a weapon away in a real fight was a foolhardy thing to do.

Our trading for clothing and moccasins soon provided the Snakes with a respectable armory of butcher knives and muskets we had taken off Blackfoots and even if you wouldn't precisely call it trading, such foofurraw as glass beads and red cloth and various shiny trinkets cemented many a tender tie betwixt our trappers and their Shoshone paramours.

Snowflower wanted for nothing in the way of foofurraw, for I showered her with all that she would accept. When I presented her with a battered old musket I had taken from a dead Blackfoot, she promptly traded it off for what appeared to be a never-ending supply of soft-tanned deer hides and moccasins and choice foodstuffs.

Naturally there was a great deal of gambling, mostly the hand game, for Indians dearly love games of chance, and naturally

Tuttle was early and often in the thick of it. At first he lost heavily, until he learned the many subtle tricks of switching the pebble or the twig from one huge hand to the other. Then when he produced his greasy deck of cards and proceeded to teach the fascinated Snakes the mysteries of Old Sledge and other pasteboard thieveries, Tuttle stood in a fair way of coming to own the whole village and all that was in it.

There was plenty of time for reading, too, on days when falling snow made hunting and outdoor games impossible. I had read Homer's *Iliad* and the *Odyssey* nearly to tatters and Ned Godey well-nigh finished the job. Ned read intently, lips moving, a blunt finger tracing the lines, and he committed each episode to memory. Ned wasn't taken in by Homer's bias in favor of the Greeks, like when he told me, "That'ere Ash-heels he's got hisse'f a mean streak a whole yard wide! Haulin' ol' Hector 'round the city 'hind o' his buggy whilst Hector's ol' dad is right thar a-watchin' from up on the wall! 'Tain't fittin'! Serves 'im right he got his comeuppance from that'ere arrer in his heel!"

John Smiley owned a Bible and I borrowed it from time to time, glorying in the richness of the language when they weren't begetting. I worked up a real fondness for that tough old bird Isaiah and downright admiration for Jesus and what he tried to tell folks, but the religion part of it failed to rub off on me, just as it always had.

The best part of snowy days, howsomever, was when Snowflower would lean a pair of crossed sticks tied together in front of our tipi door, which told the neighbors not to come scratching. Then she would push the book out of my hand and get to practicing her kissing, which always led to more elaborate doings, until we both lay exhausted on the sleep robes. Fact is, that happened often enough for Snowflower to tell me one day that the neighbors had come to be calling us the cross-sticks people.

That made no nevermind to her, howsomever, for there was not a sliver of false modesty in her, no coquetry. I was her man and she was my woman and that was the long and short of it.

I need to make it clear that Snowflower and I didn't just live off by ourselves. That would never do in an Indian village. Everybody has his nose in everybody else's business and secrets are rare items indeed. Snowflower had a passel of female friends and a whole treeful of relatives and she needed to pass her time with them, as most women do — except for Ma, for the most part. When she wasn't learning the use of herbs and leaves and berries and critter parts and suchlike from Black Otter, the old medicine man from the sweat lodge, and sometimes from our own healer, Foot, Snowflower would be off in one of the lodges of her friends or they would gather in ours, gabbling like a flock of hens and choring at dressing hides or quilling and sewing or making up foodstuffs or whatever it is that women do, not much different from females anywheres, I reckon.

Clannish though we trappers had come to be, the Snakes refused to allow it. Especially after the buffalo surround, they were quick to inVite us to join in their hunts and games and sometimes their councils and ceremonies. I learned from old Black Otter how to lift and point and pass the pipe and on which side to walk in a lodge, taking care not to pass between a seated man and the fire, as well as a passel of other Shoshone etiquette that would never occur to a white man. I even learned some of their words and phrases, but slowly. Mostly I contented myself with the hand signs, happy when I came to understand their humor, some of it downright scandalous, and I brimmed over with pride whenever I was able to make a jest my ownself.

Naturally Anse Tolliver dug out his fiddle and amazed the Snakes with the lively tunes he scraped out of it. Drums and flutes were all the Shoshones had ever known and Anse's kind of music was a whole new thing for them. They came to like it, though, and nigh half the village would gather around his lodge whenever he played. Paddy McBride was a wonder to us all, especially the Snakes, when he danced his high-stepping Irish jigs, once his leg healed. The young men would often fling themselves into the circle and try to out-do him, soon catching on to the unfamiliar rhythms of Anse's eastern mountain music.

Naturally there was a deal of grumbling amongst the whites about shaving nearly every day, but the Snake women were stubborn and unforgiving about dog-faced men, so, like it or not, we cussed and scraped and reluctantly conceded that such discomfort was but a fair exchange for the favors we enjoyed. Shaving was less of a problem for me than it was for the others, for I never sprouted much of a beard anyway.

Every one of us trappers early on had a woman of his own, once Snowflower and I commenced our housekeeping, except for John Smiley. He lived off by himself in a little lodge the Snakes put up for him and he did his own cooking and such, keeping the Snakes at arm's length whenever he could. Fact is, I reckon he would have preferred to put at least a rifle shot of distance betwixt himself and them. John was a fine-looking man and cleaner than most and he owned a respectable stock of trade goods that would have attracted some of the best of the widows. But John had his principles. He couldn't put Pennsylvania behind him. He harbored a bred-in-the-bone distrust of all Indians, except maybe our Delawares, and I reckon he wasn't altogether sure about them. It was plain to see that he chafed under the leadership of Eddard Rose and he was slow to learn new things from our Delawares and the Snakes, things that the rest of us watched like hawks and picked up as quickly as we could, for we knew that such knowledge was apt to save our life and line our pokes. John was a good woodsman, brave, and handy with his rifle, but this was the Shining Mountains, not Pennsylvania. Women aside, John Smiley was too white for his own good.

Life amongst the Snakes that winter was better than we had a right to expect, but it wasn't all rosy. A couple of pony raids, first by Blackfoots, then by Crows, called to mind that we were living after all in the Shining Mountains.

First thing I heard of the Blackfoot raid was when just at dusk Brass Turtle came trotting up to the lodge and in a quiet voice told me to get dressed for the cold and come armed with every gun I owned. He went on to say that one of the herd boys had spied what he took to be a couple Blackfoots lurking in the brush on the other side of the crick. "They'll likely wait 'til dark o' night afore they pounce. We aim to give 'em a proper welcome, but don't ye be shootin' 'til I do." Turtle was grinning, plumb anxious, I reckon, for another good fight and a chance to avenge Muskrat. Then he turned away and trotted off to tell the others.

I dressed as quickly and warmly as I could and gathered up all my firearms, curious, in the meantime, at the bustle I could hear outside in the village. There came a frantic scratching on the doorflap, then without waiting for a response a woman poked her head inside and spoke rapidly to Snowflower before running off. Snowflower reached up and hugged me, her eyes tender, her face strained. Then, tarrying only to fling on her cape, she scampered after her neighbor.

By time I sauntered towards the grove, not hurrying, seeking to appear unconcerned, a huge bonfire was blazing in front of the council lodge, a big drum was beating, and a passel of women and old men were singing their hearts out and dancing in a circle. I was thinking that this was a queer way to defend against an attack when Stone Bird reached out from behind a bush and plucked at the skirt of my capote, motioning for me to get down. Which I did. Then I crept after him through the horse herd and on to the crick, where I found Tuttle and Godey hunkered down behind the scant brush and the few trees that grew along the bank. Stone Bird left me then and I wriggled forward until I was between them, careful this time to keep Melchior out of the snow.

There could be no talking, so we waited in silence, listening to the godawful din coming from the village, trying to filter out any nearby sound, straining our eyes into the darkness, seeking movement in the gloom. I could see nothing.

474   Edward Louis Henry

After what seemed like a year or more, I spied him. A man half rose to his knees, then skittered down the far bank. Quick as scat a shadowy figure erupted out of the snow in front of him and all we heard was a dull slap, a gurgling grunt, then the unmistakable plop of a scalp being ripped off. Then silence and the shadowy killer vanished.

It seemed like no more than half a blink before the far bank came alive with Blackfoots rolling over the lip and sliding down the slope into the crick bottom, which was no more than a dozen yards across. The hardest thing I have ever done was holding my fire just then, but I did. Then the first shot fired from somewheres upstream set off a ragged volley, then a roar of gunfire as every rifle and musket on our side fired into the crick bottom, spliced with the hiss of arrows whizzing down from the branches above us, drowning out the drums and singing from the village. Yells and shrieks and war cries and a snatch of what I took to be a death song boiled up from the crick. Blackfoots were running every whichaway, stumbling over slain comrades and busting into watering holes, where the ice was thin, floundering waist-deep until the rain of bullets and arrows found their mark. Most were trying to scramble back the way they came, but here and there a few climbed up our side to do battle, even if it likely meant their death.

My first shot claimed a late-comer on the far bank, who hesitated a mite too long when the shooting first commenced. I saw him crumple out of sight and laid *Melchior* aside, reaching the while inside my capote for a pistol in my belt. The hammer hung up on my sash and I was tugging to get it loose when a dark figure loomed up in front of Tuttle, first the head and shoulders, then all the way to the waist, a knife glinting in one hand, a stone club in the other. Tuttle grunted and rose to his knees, aiming to use his empty rifle for a club, but the Blackfoot had the edge. By time I yanked my pistol free, his club arm was cocked and I knew I was too late. Then everything stopped. The Blackfoot just hung there, his stone club lifted above his head, whilst I shoved the muzzle into his belly and squeezed the trigger. I scarcely heard the explosion before I saw him double over and collapse on top of Tuttle, an arrow buried half its length in his eye.

Ned Godey and I were still trying to wrestle the big Blackfoot off a squirming, cussing Tuttle when we realized that the shooting had mostly quit. Nobody stood up or moved about, howsomever, lest a parting Blackfoot arrow seek to even up the score. The crick bottom was all but silent. Here and there you could hear a groan or a quavering death-song, but the loudest sounds came from the village, drumbeats and voices raised in song, the brilliant orange blaze of the bonfire lighting up the surrounding lodges.

At length our side of the crick roused into noise and movement, men struggling upright, brushing off snow and stamping numbed feet, trappers calling out good-natured curses and Snakes yip-yip-yipping what I took to be victory cries as they plunged into the crick bottom to finish off their foes and claim their scalps and plunder.

When Godey and I at last succeeded in heaving the big Blackfoot aside, Tuttle scrambled to his feet, shook himself violently, and stuck out his hand to me. "Thankee, pard. Thet'n war a near thang indeed." Just then we heard a rustle and scrape of leather on bark and a boy came shinnying down the tree beside us, his bow slung over his shoulder, wearing a grin big enough to swallow the whole Missouri River.

"I reckon ye'd best be savin' your thankin' for this boy here, Tuttle," I said. "'Twas him as saved ye."

Ned Godey agreed. "That be right, Tuttle. That'ere Injun was awready headin' out on the Wolf Trail afore Temple got his shot off. 'Twar the kid's arrer what done it."

Tuttle stared long and hard at the arrow jutting from the dead Blackfoot's eye. Then he pulled out his skinning knife and handed it to the boy, a lad surely no older than fourteen. The kid wasted no time in grabbing a handful of hair, slicing a generous circle around the crown, and yanking loose the scalp with a sucking plop that was becoming a familiar sound. He grinned even more broadly than before when he offered to hand the bloody knife back to Tuttle, who stared at the knife, then at the boy, and said at last, "Aw, keep it. I reckon ye sure-as-hell earnt it."

Straggling back to the village, we fell in with Eddard Rose and Brass Turtle, the both of them downright gleeful at the results of the ambush. The horses were safe and nobody on our side had got himself killed. The few scratches and gashes our people had suffered was a small price to pay for giving the Blackfoots a drubbing.

The drumbeats and the singing grew louder as we neared the blazing bonfire, but now it had a different, more jubilant sound. Godey posed the question to Eddard Rose before I had a chance to ask. "Rose, what in the pluperfec' hell war them Injuns thinkin' of, singin' an' dancin' an' poundin' on drums like it's Christmas, at a time we got more Blackfoots comin' at us than ye're like to find fleas on a houn' dog?"

Rose exploded with laughter, halting and bending nearly double and slapping his knee with glee. When the fit was over, he straightened up and replied, "That'n was Wah-shah-kee's idee. He reckoned if'n them Kah-ee-nahs reckoned the Snakes was havin' theirse'fs some kind o' selly-brayshun they mought git a mite careless comin' 'crost the crick. Countin' on evahbody bein' at the dancin', don'tcha know?" He nigh collapsed with laughter once again, but he choked it back and strangled out, "An' damn if it di'n't come out jes' like he said!"

Brass Turtle spat and opined, "It ain't all jist standin' fast an' shootin' straight what wins the fight. Gittin' thar fust with proper thinkin' counts the most!"

The rest of us nodded and murmured our agreement, in my own case hoping the while that I could conjure up a good idea of my own next time I needed onesuch.

By time we arrived at the fire, several drums were beating and the dancing was altogether frantic. Word of the victory had got there ahead of us and the Snakes were nigh delirious with joy and triumph. Several warriors pranced in the circle now, flinging themselves about and proudly waving long-haired scalps. Somehow I was not surprised to see Paddy McBride prominent amongst them, outdoing them all with a high-kicking Irish jig, brandishing a clump of bloody black hair, a huge grin pasted across his good-natured ugly mug and his long red locks streaming like molten gold in the firelight.

Suddenly the drumming stopped and the dancers froze in their tracks, The young chief Wah-shah-kee stepped into the circle and commenced to orate in that high-pitched, hollow, nasal voice Snakes use when they speak in council or at ceremonies. The dancers fell silent and folded to the ground, all eyes upon Wah-shah-kee as he told of the defeat of their enemy. Leastaways I reckon that is what he was telling them, for I understood not a word of his oration.

Wah-shah-kee carried a scalp in his hand and from his shoulders hung a long cape of white mountain goat hide spattered with fresh blood. As the young chief spoke it came to me that it had been he who had hidden himself in the snow in the crick bottom, killed the Blackfoot scout, and taken the first scalp.

It was no wonder that, even young as he was, Wah-shah-kee was chief of this particular band of Snakes. His courage certainly matched his cunning and I couldn't help comparing him with Odysseus, who possessed those two qualities in abundance. I reckon Mister Homer would have been proud to know Wah-shah-kee.

As I stood outside the circle, listening to Wah-shah-kee and marveling at his abilities, I felt Snowflower slip her warm hand into mine. I looked into her upturned face and thrilled at what I read in her dark eyes, glistening with relief and need and desire. As soon as the young chief finished his speech and strode off, we hastened to our lodge, scampering through the snow and laughing like schoolchildren freed from their lessons.

No sooner had we stepped indoors and I turned to embrace my woman, when a scratching on the tipi hide announced a visitor. Snowflower pushed the doorflap aside, revealing the young bowman from the crick bank, festooned now with a powderhorn and all manner of belts, bullet pouches, and sundry Blackfoot hardware. Unsmiling and deadly serious, he muttered a few low-voiced words to Snowflower before he shoved a bloody scalp into her hands, then spun on his heel and departed.

I peeked past the doorflap and spied the promising young warrior dragging a musket through the snow with one hand, proud as Lucifer, his precious first scalp clutched in the other. Silently, I wished him well.

Snowflower giggled as she signed that the scalp she held was indeed my trophy, taken from the Blackfoot I had shot when the commotion commenced. The lad had observed it all from his perch high in the tree branches and he felt it was his duty to furnish me with that emblem of my prowess.

Bloodlust and peril thankfully avoided are two powerful elixirs for passionate lovemaking. The Blackfoot scalp proved to be a third, leastaways for Snowflower. Our coupling that night rivaled even our first time together and the sun rode high above the smokeflaps before we collapsed into grateful oblivion.

∾ ∾ ∾

Sometime before winter was ready to turn us loose it was plain to see and smell that the Snakes needed to move the village. Graze for the horses was scant and sweet cottonwood bark in the surrounding groves was all used up, the middens were getting more than somewhat ripe, and as Tuttle phrased it, "Game's gittin' scarce as whores at Sunday meetin'." Once word came from Wah-shah-kee and his council early on a clear and sunny morning, it seemed no more than a blink before the lodges were down and every jot and tittle was packed and stowed on *travois* drags. Horses were in short supply, so even the dogs were set to hauling a pair of sticks loaded with plunder.

Naturally we went along with them. We had nothing better to do and all of us, except for John Smiley, were reluctant to bid farewell to our lady friends. Just before we departed, old Black Otter walked the edge of the old camp, sprinkling water from a gourd with a raven-wing fan and chanting at the top of his cracked old voice, thanking the Great Spirit, as Snowflower told me, for whatever happiness and good fortune the People had known there. Then he climbed onto a load of plunder on a *travois* and signed that we could go on our way. "Jist look at 'im," Ned Godey said.

"Jist a-settin' thar on that'ere trav-wah drag like as if he war the Pope o' Rome." Ned paused a spell, likely chewing over what he had just said, then added, "An' hereabouts, I reckon mebbe that's what he be."

The new camp was eight or nine miles farther up the Popo Azhieh on high flat ground on a bend of the river. Graze was good under windswept, not-too-deep snow and deadfall aplenty cluttered the ground in the nearby timber. By nightfall every lodge stood tall, the ground underneath swept clean of snow, and cookfire smoke curled up from all the smokeflaps. When I offered to lend Snowflower a hand with the chores, she blushed and shooed me off, so I sat and smoked with the other men and watched the women and kids put the village back together again.

Our second day at the new site we knew the place was truly blessed, for hunters came trotting back with news that a passel of buffalo was heading for the river not a mile upstream. Naturally every able-bodied man in camp turned out and that night we feasted on hump and tongue and *boudins* crackled on the coals.

Snow was melting fast each day and even though the cricks and ponds were still choked with ice, all of us trappers got to feeling restless, anxious to commence the spring hunt. Eddard Rose cautioned us, howsomever, that warming weather was not without its perils. "Absarokas'll likely come a-callin', lookin' to thieve hosses an' mebbe take some ha'r. Keep yer eye peeled an' yer gun ready. Now be the time ye kin expect 'em."

And so it turned out. Not three days had passed before one of the Snakes, out hunting early in the morning, sauntered back to camp, then made a beeline for Wah-shah-kee's lodge. He had spied what he took to be a couple Crows sneaking in the brush, heading for the village. Wah-shah-kee called a council and sent for Rose, Brass Turtle, and Godey. The palaver took hardly any time at all. When they came out, Rose called the rest of us together and revealed the plan. "Like I been feelin', they's Crows out theah, come fer hoss-thievin'. They be comin' in afoot. Ain't no way to set up a propah trap, like we done fer them Blackfoots. Ground heah'bouts be too flat an' wide-open fer us to be hidin' an' waitin'. Wah-shah-kee he got a differ'nt idee. Crows'll be creepin' up, diggin' in', waitin' fer dark t'night. We let 'em think we be goin' huntin', ridin' hosses, some ridin' east, some headin' west. When we git beyond 'em, we come back togethah, turn about an' fan out an' then we drive 'em down heah to the rivah." Rose chuckled and added, "Them as ain't awready dead, y'unnerstan'."

It was mid-forenoon by time we mounted up, armed to the teeth, the most of us trappers itching for a fight. Too much leisure amongst the Snakes had made us restless. I, for one, still rankled over Pretty-on-top and the big Crow who had come close to freezing me to death — and our Delawares would never forgive the killing of Owl back on the Yellowstone.

Rose was afoot when he bade us farewell. He had elected to remain amongst the Snakes who stayed behind to defend the village. As he put it, "They's shuah to be a couple-t'ree what gits away. Allus is. An' it's best they don' see me. I mought wanta go back an' live 'mongst 'em sometime." We knew it wasn't fear that prompted his decision. What he said made sense, but it occurred to me that in his own way Eddard Rose was as much a politician as General Ashley ever was.

The doings that morning went pretty much according to Wah-shah-kee's plan. The young chief, Brass Turtle riding close behind him, led us out towards the mountains on the west, as if we intended to hunt wapiti in the high meadows. Drum-singer and Godey, trailing Anse and Smiley, the rest of the Delawares, and a passel of Snakes headed east along the river, looking like they were maybe seeking out buffalo. About half a mile or so out, each party bent back towards the other until we met, like points on an ice-tongs, and commenced a sweep back down to the village on the river bend, a line of Snakes armed with bows up front, the rest of us with rifles and muskets following not far behind.

The snow was only fetlock-deep over most of that ground, with here and there drifts in the gullies and piled up against sagebrush. Bright sunshine turned the slope into a glittering field of diamonds, squinting up my eyes and making it hard to pick out telltale sign in the snow. This was no ordinary hunt and Chiksika sensed my excitement, causing him to prance and strain against the bit, no matter how I strived to calm him. I was riding between

Tuttle and Paddy, the three of us a dozen paces apart, when the Snakes up front flushed the first Crow. Fact is, one of them nearly rode right over him before he jumped to his feet, buffalo coat all matted with snow, trying to aim his musket as he went down in a hail of arrows — "Filled 'im up with arrers like a porkypine" was the way Tuttle told it later — but not before he triggered off his musket and alerted the other Absarokas. All over the plain Crows popped up out of sagebrush clumps, ready to do battle, knowing they were certain to be discovered, preferring to die like warriors rather than being hunted down like varmints.

The Snakes were quick to answer the challenge, rushing pell-mell down the slope, loosing volleys of arrows, some of them standing in the stirrups to fire muskets at the Crows, then swerving their horses in close to wallop their foes with war clubs. Their chief Wah-shah-kee was no laggard in battle. He led the charge, choosing one particular Absaroka horsethief for his personal meat. I fired one long shot at a Crow who stood some distance down the slope, then loped after the chief, trying the while to dump fresh powder down the barrel of my rifle. I looked up just in time to see Wah-shah-kee's horse flounder into a snow-filled gully, pitching the young chief over his head and plunging him headfirst into a snowdrift, not ten feet distant from the Crow, who snatched an arrow from his quiver, intending to finish off his Shoshone enemy.

I slung Melchior across my back and rode straight at the Crow, yanking one of my pistols from its saddle holster and hollering my head off, as loud and fierce as any Indian ever tried to be. Time slowed for me just then. My voice seemed to come from far off. Wah-shah-kee was struggling to get himself upright, tugging at his belt knife, his legs sinking into the deep snow. The Crow, his arrow nocked, bow bent nearly double, glanced my way and paused just long enough to let me level the pistol at his head and blow half his chin clean away.

Chiksika was running too fast to stop right there. He jumped a sagebrush clump and skidded in an arc before I headed him back. By time I rode up to Wah-shah-kee, the chief was standing beside the dead Crow, grinning up at me and offering me the dripping, long-haired scalp. "Ziss yerse," he said. "You take." I did as I was told, confident that Snowflower would be happy to add that trophy to the enemy hair already displayed on the liner of our lodge.

Wah-shah-kee clucked a time or two and his horse picked his way daintily up to us, displaying a somewhat apologetic air, as it appeared to me, concerning his earlier misfortune. The chief ignored his pony's discomfiture, howsomever, and swung himself up. Then, without another word or sign to me, he galloped off to catch up with his warriors.

Rose and the Snakes who remained in the village had come out and caught the few fleeing Crows in a crossfire by time we rode up. A score or more dead Absarokas lay scattered across the snowfield, every one of them scalped and stripped of his arms and whatever else the Snakes considered to be of worth, which was just about everything. Wah-shah-kee beamed at the lot of us, then spoke sharply in rapid Shoshone, swinging up his arm pointing towards the north. A moment later half of his men galloped off to capture the horses of the Crows and take the scalps of the herders. Which they succeeded in doing.

࿇ ࿇ ࿇

That night with Snowflower was as pleasant as you might imagine. Relief at my safe return and delight with visible proof of one less Crow warrior to threaten her people was a sure-fire recipe for passion with her. For my part, hot blood is slow to cool in a man who has been successful in a fight and it was many hours before my excitement finally drained away.

Early in the forenoon, the village crier, a bull-voiced man with a crippled arm, summoned us all to the clearing in front of the council lodge. The whole village was there, dressed in their Sunday best, and off to one side nigh a dozen Crow horses stamped and snorted steam in the chill morning air, hauling back on their lead ropes as herd boys fought to keep them still. Our bunch stood together, as we usually did. I noticed that most of us didn't cut such a bad figure compared with the Snakes, thanks to the artful tailoring skills of our respective ladies.

A murmur of approval rose from the throng when Wah-shah-kee, impressive in brilliant quilled buckskins and wearing a colorful eagle-feathered bonnet, stepped out of the council lodge, flanked by his headmen. As he spoke to his people, he accompanied his words with the hand-talk, as Indians often do, so I was able to understand that yesterday's fight had been a great victory for his band, that more than a score of Absarokas had been killed and their arms and horses taken, with only some minor wounds suffered by the Snakes. I daresay he said much more than that, for he went on at length, as orators of whatever stripe are wont to do, but that is the gist of it.

Then he walked over to the horses and proceeded to lead them out, one by one, and present a horse to each of us trappers, telling the crowd what each one of us had done the day before. When he came to me, he passed by a couple-three horses and took hold of a tall black and white skewbald with a fine small head, a kind eye, and little prick ears. I named him Patch even before Wah-shah-kee pressed the lead-rope into my hands. Then he turned around and launched into another long speech. I couldn't see his hands, so I don't know precisely what he was saying, but I hung my head and blushed anyway.

When it was over and the Snakes commenced to drift away, I started off to where the herd was grazing, intending to turn my new horse out with the rest. Snowflower came running up, black eyes snapping, chattering like a magpie, and snatched the lead rope out of my hand. Then she proudly led Patch through the village lane and staked him out in front of her lodge, where he remained for a week or more, whenever I wasn't riding him. The other trappers' women did likewise. Those people set a heap of store on such honors.

Grandfather Winter at last turned loose the iron fingers that had gripped the land so long, leastaways in the valley of the Popo Azhieh and along the cricks and streams that feed it, but he still held sway amongst the snowcapped peaks, the Shining Mountains all of us had dreamed about, the place we now called home. Withered brown meadows were greening up. Willows and aspens started leafing out and birds commenced singing where only ravens croaked a week or two before. Ice split and cracked and rumbled in the river and streams ran free and full. It was time to come alive again, to commence the only useful work we knew anymore. It was time for the spring hunt.

All of us were gathered outdoors in the warming springtime sunshine, when Eddard Rose looked up from chipping rust off his traps and pronounced, "These las' two wintahs the lot o' ye done passed up thisaway gives ye rights to be callin' yerse'fs 'eevairnahns fer shuah." He paused and thought a spell before he said, "An' now y'all put in one o' them wintahs ri'cheah in the Shinin' Mountains, I reckon ye kin be callin' yerse'fs mountaineahs, right and propah, on the top of it." He chuckled and said again, "Tha's right. Righteous, propah mountaineahs!"

Naturally we laughed at what he said, but not one of us forgot his words — and in the days and months and years to come, those two words, hivernants and mountaineers, came to hold important meaning for every man amongst us. We bore those rude titles as proudly as any duke or baron ever did his own, for we had earned them with blood and sweat and shivering cold.

≈ ≈ ≈

Cold work it was, wading hip-deep in icy beaver ponds, setting traps and harvesting our catch, ever alert and ready to retreat from hostile redskins on the prowl or crotchety grizzly bears come looking for breakfast after their long winter sleep. But it was happy work, as well, for this was what we had come all that long, hard way to do. We honed our skills each day and at night we traded lore and new discoveries around the cookfire, gaining just a mite of pride with each new trick we learned that might increase our stock of beaver plews or keep our hair in place.

At first we trapped the branches and the ponds nearby the Snakes, but it wasn't long until we had trapped them out, forcing us to travel ever farther afield, until at last that valley and all of its tributaries became pretty much barren of beaver. Our absences stretched ever longer and Snowflower commenced to sulk, divining that at length my companions and I would need to be on our way, seeking new country in which to trap.

A powerful argument might be made in favor of a scarcity of common language between lovers. At night in her lodge, once the fire had died down, Snowflower and I were deprived of even our dumb-show hand signs and we could not read each other's face. Bitter charges could not be made and weaseling lawyerlike defense was impossible. All the hurtful words that might have been exchanged remained unspoken and unheard, because neither of us possessed enough words that the other understood. We were forced therefore to rely only on our bodies, our hands and lips and toes, soft murmurs and despairing sighs, seeking to repair and strengthen the bond between us. Some nights she would lie cold and rigid and remote beside me, no matter what I might try to do to restore her former warmth. Then she might suddenly catch afire, clasping me close and demanding all that my manhood could provide. Those months with the Snakes were shining times indeed, but our nights together at the end didn't always shine.

Still and all, we lived together happily enough. I hunted when I could and we always had meat for the cookfire and some to give away. My moccasins were always mended and from time to time she gifted me with fancy quilled shirts and leggin's, taking pride amongst the other womenfolk in showing off her well-turned-out white-eyes warrior man.

In her heart she must have known that I couldn't stay with her, that I could no more be a Snake than I could become a wapiti. I knew it, too, and there was little doubt in my mind that when the beaver thereabouts ran out at last, I would be leaving with my friends, seeking new and better beaver ponds.

Still and all, I knew it would not be an easy matter simply to pack up my possibles and plunder and ride off. Tender feelings for Snowflower ran deep within my spirit, impossibly tangled around my every impulse to bid farewell. I owed her my life, for she had surely saved me from death, but she never expected gratitude for that. Healing and comforting wounded critters came as naturally to her as breathing and loving her man. I counted myself fortunate and honored to be that man.

In those waning days with Snowflower, sitting silent and mostly content beside a flickering fire in her lodge, I thought long and hard about the men I had known, good ones and bad ones, who had fired and forged and hammered me into the man I had become — Pap and Uncle Ben, a remarkable contrast there — Powatawa and Fink, for another — Fink's bullies and Tom Fitzpatrick, Wah-shah-kee, Black Micah, and mean-spirited Luther Pike, Hamish and the Major, crafty Pretty-on-top and stern and steady Eddard Rose, who drew his strength and character from the best of many races, and reliable redheaded Paddy McBride, Old Foot and Little Mountain and all their resolute Delaware and Iroquois fellows, crabby Anse Tolliver and ambitious General Ashley, and, prized above all, Ned Godey, Brass Turtle, and Tuttle Thompson. What a rainbow of color there was amongst that lot, but color was not a key to their individual quality. Some were of the purest gold and others vile as rattler spit. Color matters not at all in the mountains — or anyplace else, as far as I can see.

The few women who had helped to shape my life were something of a rainbow, too — Ma and Sarah, Aunt Penny and Lucette, Night-eyes, Simone, and Snowflower — a power of differing color amongst them, to be sure, but each of them had honestly gifted me with the best they owned and, I reckon, made me a somewhat better man by virtue of their loving generosity.

The color of a fellow's hide matters not at all in the Rockies, no more than what he or his kinfolk might have been back in the Settlements. All that counts up there is, handsome is as handsome does and, hoss, what can you do? The Shining Mountains are truly a rainbow land and that is how I have come to think of it always — Rainbow Land.

ぞ ぞ ぞ

Wah-shah-kee and his headmen knew that we needed to be moving on when the beaver thereabouts were trapped out, and so it was that he called a council a few weeks into spring to tell us trappers of a place where beaver abounded, as he put it, like stars in the midsummer sky and hairs upon a dog. It was a river valley east and somewhat south of where we were and he offered two young men as pilots to guide us there.

He went on to tell us that not far to the west of that river valley was what the Snakes called the Backbone of the World, the mountain chains that divide the waters of all the rivers and streams of that vast land, causing some of them to flow east and the others to the west.

Naturally all of us flew at the chance to trap such a place as the valley Wah-shah-kee and his people described. We quickly busied ourselves gathering our plunder, baling our plews, and packing up for travel. Parting wasn't easy for many amongst us, nor for the women who had taken us to their hearts and beds. Several of them were with child and I reckon it was Snowflower's chief regret that she was not of their number. She told me as much and for a spell there I was halfway sorry that, for all our lovemaking, she remained childless. Children being half-white or half-Delaware or Iroquois would make no nevermind to the Snakes. They love kids, as all Indians do, and children mean survival of the People. They are more than somewhat tetchy about not breeding relatives into their blood — more so than a lot of whites I recalled from back home — and marriageable men amongst that band were in short supply, thanks to never-ending raids and warfare. Besides, they genuinely liked and admired us and, even if I say it myself, I reckon they thought our blood just might improve the breed.

Daybreak was no more than a rosy glow beyond the eastern mountains when we saddled up and lashed our plews and plunder onto the pack horses. I wore my finest garments, bright-colored quills woven onto a soft deerskin shirt and leggin's fringed with hair from the scalps I had taken. Naturally I was riding Patch to show my gratitude to Wah-shah-kee and to make Snowflower proud. Chiksika didn't like that much. He shrugged and shivered under his burden of plews, but I reckoned he would get over it.

Jake never fretted, accepting any chore I had a mind to put him to.Snowflower and I had made our farewells inside her lodge, embracing tightly and murmuring nothings that had no meaning for anyone but the two of us. Our final night together had been memorable for its warmth and Snowflower had striven mightily for motherhood, but when we stepped out into the lane and walked to where a herd boy held my horses, she was dry-eyed and her face betrayed no feelings, according to the etiquette of the People.

After we mounted up, Wah-shah-kee palavered for a spell, wishing us well and commending us for our bravery on behalf of his people, and old Black Otter flung water on us from his raven-wing fan, whilst we gazed a final time on that village where we had come so close to death and lived so fully because of it.

I looked for Snowflower, but she was nowheres to be seen. Eddard Rose called out, "Le's go!" and we reined our horses to the east, trailing behind the two young Snakes who would lead us to the new country. Indian-like, not one of us looked back or bade farewell, but I, for one, had trouble swallowing the lump in my throat. Nobody had much to say, not even Paddy McBride, who was more than likely thinking of a redheaded Indian child he would likely never see.

To keep from thinking of Snowflower, I strove to occupy my thoughts with imagined pictures of the beaver-rich valley and the mountains that lay to the west of it, the Backbone of the World. Then for a spell I indulged my fancy with self-flattering thoughts that my companions and I might be thought of, in a way, as another kind of backbone of the world, rough and ready and resolute as we had so far proved to be. Howsomever, I soon put such self-congratulating foolishness aside and gigged Patch to catch up with my all-too-human, very ordinary but serviceable comrades.

By time we halted to snug up girths, the village was out of sight, lost amongst the greening hills. That was just as well, for looking back makes neither meat nor beaver plews. All that was important now was the trail that lay ahead and the promise of new country to the west.

FINIS

Also by Edward Louis Henry
THE TEMPLE BUCK QUARTET
A Rocky Mountain Odyssey
1822-1837

Volume II: Free Men chronicles the exploits of Temple Buck and his rowdy trapper companions in the American Rocky Mountain fur trade from 1824-1826. In this, the second volume of the Temple Buck Quartet, they push ever farther west in their quest for beaver pelts, exploring new country and encountering fresh adventures, some of them welcome, others not at all. This well-researched tale, told in Temple's own words, blends historical and fictional characters against a colorful backdrop of actual events, pungently flavored with gory battles with hostile Indians, homespun humor, and earthy romance, culminating in Temple's disappointing return to his Ohio birthplace.

Volume III, Shinin' Times!, 1828-1833, describes Temple Buck's return to the Rockies, rejoining his trapping bunch and picking up the free, unfettered life of the American free trapper where he left off in 1826. He and the other members of his trapping bunch explore uncharted new country and gain new and different experience in a changing and expanding fur trade. Their personal lives change, as well, as they take on new responsibilities while continuing to enjoy the happy-go-lucky life of the Rocky Mountain free trapper, its rich flavor much improved now by their wider knowledge, deeper experience, and greater appreciation of everything that living in the American wilderness can provide for men who possess the the savvy and smarts and courage to survive on Nature's bosom.

Volume IV, Glory Days Gone Under, 1834-1837, is the fourth and final volume of the Temple Buck Quartet. All things, good and bad, come to an end. Fashions change and human greed injures even all-bountiful Nature. Faraway factors in Europe and the American East destroyed the market for beaver pelts, which occurred just when beaver were growing scarce in the mountains. Without a market, pelts were worthless. The mountaineer's income was wiped out. White settlers, following trails blazed by the early trappers, were moving west, bringing with them families, farming, civilized customs, laws, and missionaries, all of which the trappers despised, corrupting the Indians and crowding them off their ancestral lands, all in the name of a Manifest Destiny that mountaineers, tough, resourceful, and courageous as they were, were powerless to resist.

For more information on these and other great books, visit www.christophermatthewspub.com

CPSIA information can be obtained at www.ICGtesting.com
Printed in the USA
LVOW071612231011

251716LV00001B/83/P